GOLD MINE
AND
THE BURNING SHORE

Wilbur Smith was born in Central Africa in 1933. He was educated at Michaelhouse and Rhodes University.

He became a full-time writer in 1964 after the successful publication of *When the Lion Feeds*, and has since written twenty-five novels, all meticulously researched on his numerous expeditions worldwide. His books are now translated into fourteen languages.

He owns a farm and game reserve and has an abiding concern for the peoples and wildlife of his native continent, an interest strongly reflected in his novels.

WILBUR SMITH

GOLD MINE
AND
THE BURNING SHORE

PAN BOOKS

Gold Mine first published 1970 by William Heinemann Ltd.
First published in paperback by Pan Books 1972.
The Burning Shore first published 1985 by William Heinemann Ltd.
First published in paperback by Pan Books 1986

This omnibus edition published 2003 by Pan Books
an imprint of Pan Macmillan Ltd
Pan Macmillan, 20 New Wharf Road, London N1 9RR
Basingstoke and Oxford
Associated companies throughout the world
www.panmacmillan.com

ISBN 0 330 42101 8

A CIP catalogue record for this book is available from
the British Library.

Printed and bound in Great Britain by
Mackays of Chatham plc, Chatham, Kent

GOLD MINE

This book is for Danielle

It began in the time when the world was young, in the time before man, in the time before life itself had evolved upon this planet.

The crust of the earth was still thin and soft, distorted and riven by the enormous pressures from within.

What is now the flat, compacted shield of the African continent, stable and unchanging, was a series of alps. It was range upon range of mountains, thrown up and tumbled down by the movements of the magma at great depth. These were mountains such as man has never seen, so massive as to dwarf the Himalayas, mountains of steaming rock from whose clefts and gaping wounds the molten magma trickled.

It came up from the earth's centre along the fissures and weak places in the crust, bubbling and boiling, yet cooling steadily as it neared the surface so that the least volatile minerals were deposited deeper down, but those with a lower melting point were carried to the surface.

At one point in the measureless passage of time, another series of these fissures opened upon one of the nameless mountain ranges, but from them gushed rivers of molten gold. Some natural freak of temperature and chemical change had resulted in a crude but effective process of refinement during the journey to the earth's surface. The gold was in high concentration in the matrix, and it cooled and solidified at the surface.

If the mountains of that time were so massive as to challenge the imagination of man, then the storms of wind and rain that blew around them were of equal magnitude.

It was a hellish landscape in which the gold field was conceived, cruel mountains reaching stark and sheer in the clouds. Cloud banks dark with the sulphurous gases of the belching earth, so thick that the rays of the sun never penetrated them.

The atmosphere was laden with all the moisture that was to become the seas, so heavy with it that it rained in one perpetual wind-lashed storm upon the hot rock of the cooling earth, then the moisture rose in steam to condense and fall again.

As the years passed by their millions, so the wind and the rain whittled away at the nameless mountain range with its coating of gold-rich ore, grinding it loose and carrying it down in freshets and rivers and rushes of mud and rock into the valley between this range and the next.

Now as the country rock cooled, so the waters lay longer upon the earth before evaporating, and they accumulated in this valley to form a lake the size of an inland sea.

Into this lake poured the storm waters from the golden mountains, carrying with them tiny particles of the yellow metal which settled with other sand and quartz gravel upon the lake bed, to be compacted into a solid sheet.

In time all the gold was scoured from the mountains, transported and laid down upon the lake beds.

Then, as happened every ten million years or so, the earth entered another period of intense seismic activity. The earth shuddered and heaved as earthquake after mammoth earthquake convulsed it.

One fearsome paroxysm cracked the bed of the lake from end to end draining it and fracturing the sedimentary beds, scattering fragments haphazardly so that great sheets of rock many miles across tilted and reared on end.

Again and again the earthquakes gripped and shook the

earth. The mountains tottered and collapsed, filling the valley where the lake had stood, burying some of the sheets of gold-rich rock, pulverizing others.

That cycle of seismic activity passed, and the ages wheeled on in their majesty. The floods and the great droughts came and receded. The miraculous spark of life was struck and burned up brightly, through the time of the monstrous reptiles, on through countless twists and turns of evolution until near the middle of the Pleistocene age a man-ape – Australopithecus – picked up the thigh bone of a buffalo from beside an outcrop of rock to use it as a weapon, a tool.

Australopithecus stood at the centre of a flat, sun-seared plateau that reached five hundred miles in each direction to the sea, for the mountains and the lake beds had long ago been flattened and buried.

Eight hundred thousand years later, one of the Austral opithecus' distant but direct line stood at the same spot with a tool in his hand. The man's name was Harrison and the tool was more sophisticated than that of his ancestor, it was a prospector's pick of wood and metal.

Harrison stooped and chipped at the outcrop of rock that protruded from the dry brown African earth. He freed a piece of the stone and straightened with it in his hand.

He held it to catch the sun and grunted with disgust. It was a most uninteresting piece of stone, conglomerate, marbled black and grey. Without hope he held it to his mouth and licked it, wetting the surface before again holding it to the sun, an old prospectors' trick to highlight the metal in the ore.

His eyes narrowed in surprise as the tiny golden flecks in the rock sparkled back at him.

History remembers only his name, not his age nor his antecedents, not the colour of his eyes nor how he died, for within a month he had sold his claim for £10 and disappeared – in search, perhaps, of a really big strike.

He might have done better to retain his title to those claims.

In the eighty years since then an estimated five hundred million ounces of fine gold have been recovered from the fields of the Transvaal and Orange Free State. This is a fraction of that which remains, and which in time will be taken from the earth. For the men who mine the South African fields are the most patiently persistent, inventive and pig-headed of all Vulcan's brood.

This mass of precious metal is the foundation on which the prosperity of a vigorous young nation of eighteen million souls is based.

Yet the earth yields her treasure reluctantly – men must coax and wrest it from her.

– 2 –

Even with the electric fan blowing up a gale from the corner it was stinking hot in Rod Ironsides' office.

He reached for the silver Thermos of iced water at the edge of his desk, and arrested the movement as the jug began to dance before his finger tips touched it. The metal bottle skittered across the polished wooden surface; the desk itself shuddered, rustling the papers upon it. The walls of the room shook, so that the windows rattled in their frames. Four seconds the tremor lasted, and then it was still again.

'Christ!' said Rod, and snatched up one of the three telephones on his desk.

'This is the Underground Manager. Get me the rock mechanic's lab, honey, and snap it up, please.'

He drummed his fingers on the desk impatiently as he waited to be connected. The interleading door of his office opened and Dimitri put his head around the jamb.

'You feel that one, Rod? That was a bad one.'

'I felt it.' Then the telephone spoke into his ear.

'Dr Wessels here.'

'Peter, it's Rod. Did you read that one?'

'I haven't got a fix on it yet – can you hold on a minute?'

'I'll wait.' Rod curbed his impatience. He knew that Peter Wessels was the only person who could read the mass of complicated electronic equipment that filled the instrument room of the rock mechanic's laboratory. The laboratory was a joint research project by four of the major gold-mining companies; between them they had put up a quarter of a million Rand to finance an authoritative investigation of rock and seismic activity under stress. They had selected the Sonder Ditch Gold Mining Company's lease area as the site for the laboratory. Now Peter Wessels had his microphones sited thousands of feet down in the earth, and his tape recorders and stylus graphs ready to pinpoint any underground disturbance.

Another minute ticked by, and Rod swivelled his chair and stared out of the plate glass window at the monstrous head gear of No. 1 shaft, tall as a ten-storey building.

'Come on, Peter, come on, boy,' he muttered to himself. 'I've got twelve thousand of my boys down there.'

With the telephone still pressed to his ear, he glanced at his watch.

'Two-thirty,' he muttered. 'The worst possible time. They'll still be in the stopes.'

He heard the receiver picked up on the other end, and Peter Wessels' voice was almost apologetic.

'Rod?'

'Yes.'

'I'm sorry, Rod, you've had a force seven pressure burst at 9,500 feet in sector Sugar seven Charlie two.'

'Christ!' said Rod and slammed down the receiver. He was up from his desk in one movement, his face set and angry.

'Dimitri,' he snapped at his assistant still in the doorway.

'We won't wait for them to call us, it's a top sequence emergency. That was a force seven bump, with its source plumb in the middle of our eastern longwall at 95 level.'

'Sweet Mary Mother,' said Dimitri, and darted back into his own office. He bent his glossy black head of curls over the telephone and Rod heard him start his top sequence calls.

'Mine hospital ... emergency team ... Chief Ventilation Officer ... General Manager's office.'

Rod turned away, as the outer door of his office opened and Jimmy Paterson, his electrical engineer, came in.

'I felt it, Rod. How's it look?'

'Bad,' said Rod, then there were the other line managers crowding into his office talking quietly, lighting cigarettes, coughing and shuffling their feet, but all of them watching the white telephone on Rod's desk. The minutes crawled by like crippled insects.

'Dimitri,' Rod called out to break the tension. 'Have you got a cage held at the shaft head?'

'They're holding the Mary Anne for us.'

'I've got five men checking the high tension cable on 95 level,' said Jimmy Paterson, and they ignored him. They were watching the white phone.

'Have you located the boss yet, Dimitri?' Rod asked again; he was pacing in front of his desk. It was only when he stood close to other men that you saw how tall he was.

'He's underground, Rod. He went down at twelve-thirty.'

'Put in an all-stations call for him to contact me here.'

'I've done that already.'

The white phone rang.

Only once, a shrill note that ripped along Rod's nerve ends. Then he had the receiver up to his ear.

'Underground Manager,' he said. There was a long silence and he could hear the man breathing on the other end.

'Speak, man, what is it?'

'The whole bloody thing has come down,' said the voice. It was husky, rough with fear and dust.

'Where are you speaking from?' Rod asked.

'They're still in there,' said the voice. 'They're screaming in there. Under the rock. They're screaming.'

'What is your station?' Rod made his voice cold, hard, trying to reach the man through his shock.

'The whole stope fell in on them. The whole bloody thing.'

'God damn you! You stupid bastard!' Rod bellowed into the phone. 'Give me your station!'

There was stunned silence for a moment. Then the man's voice came back, steadier now, angry from the insult.

'95 level main haulage. Section 43. Eastern longwall.'

'We're coming.' Rod hung up, picked up his yellow fibreglass hard helmet and lamp from the desk.

'43 section. The hanging wall has come down,' he said to Dimitri.

'Fatals!' the little Greek asked.

'For sure. They've got squealers under the rock.'

Rod clapped on his hat.

'Take over on surface, Dimitri.'

– 3 –

Rod was still buttoning the front of his white overalls as he reached the shaft head. Automatically he read the sign above the entrance:

STAY ALERT.   STAY ALIVE.
WITH YOUR CO-OPERATION THIS MINE HAS WORKED
16 FATALITY-FREE DAYS.

'We'll have to change the number again,' Rod thought with grim humour.

7

The Mary Anne was waiting. Into its heavily wired confines were crowded the first aid team and emergency squad. The Mary Anne was the small cage used for lowering and hoisting personnel, there were two much larger cages that could carry one 120 men at one trip, while the Mary Anne could handle only forty. But that was sufficient for now.

'Let's go,' said Rod as he stepped into the cage, and the onsetter slammed the steel roller doors closed. The bell rang once, twice, and the floor dropped away from under him as the Mary Anne started down. Rod's belly came up to press against his ribs. They went down in one long continuous rush in the darkness. The cage jarring and racketing, the air changing in smell and taste, becoming chemical and processed, the heat building up rapidly.

Rod stood hunch-shouldered, leaning against the metal screen of the cage. The head room was a mere six foot three, and with his helmet on Rod stood taller than that. So today we get another butcher's bill, he thought angrily.

He was always angry when the earth took its payment in mangled flesh and snapping bones. All the ingenuity of man and the experience gained in sixty years of deep mining on the Witwatersrand were used in trying to keep the price in blood as low as possible. But when you go down into the ultra-deep levels below 8,000 feet and from those depths you remove a quarter of a million tons of rock each month, mining on an inclined sheet of reef that leaves a vast low-roofed chamber thousands of feet across, then you must pay, for the stress builds up in the rock as the focal points of pressure change until the moment when it reaches breaking point and she bumps. That is when men die.

Rod's knees flexed under him as the cage braked and then yoyoed to a halt at the brightly lit station on 66 level.

Here they must trans-ship to the sub-main shaft. The door rattled up and Rod left the cage, striding out down the main haulage the size of a railway tunnel; concreted and whitewashed, brightly lit by the bulbs that lined the roof, it curved gently away.

The emergency team followed Rod. Not running, but walking with the suppressed nervous energy of men going into danger. Rod led them towards the sub-main shaft.

There is a limit to the depth which you can sink a shaft into the earth and then equip it to carry men suspended on a steel cable in a tiny wire cage. The limit is about 7,000 feet.

At this depth you must start again, blast out a new headgear chamber from the living rock and below it sink your new shaft, the sub-main.

The sub-main Mary Anne was waiting for them, and Rod led them into it. They stood shoulder to shoulder, and the door rattled shut and again the stomach-swooping rush down into darkness.

Down, down, down.

Rod switched on his head lamp. Now there were tiny motes in the air – air that had been sterilely clean before.

Dust! One of the deadly enemies of the miner. Dust from the burst. As yet the ventilation system had been unable to clear it.

Endlessly they fell in darkness and now it was very hot, the humidity building up so the faces about him, both black and white, were shiny with sweat in the light of his head lamp.

The dust was thicker now, someone coughed. The brightly lit stations flashed past them – 76, 77, 78 – down, down. The dust was a fine mist now. 85, 86, 87. No one had spoken since entering the cage. 93, 94, 95. The deceleration and stop.

The door rattled up. They were 9,500 feet below the surface of the earth.

'Come on,' said Rod.

There were men cluttering the lobby of 95 station, a hundred and fifty, perhaps two hundred of them. Still filthy from their work in the stopes, clothing sodden with sweat, they were laughing and chattering with the abandon of men freshly released from frightful danger.

In a clear space in the centre of the lobby lay five stretchers, on two of them the bright red blankets were pulled up to cover the faces of the men upon them. The faces of the other three men looked as though they had been dusted with flour.

'Two' – grunted Rod – 'so far.'

The station was a shambles, with men milling aimlessly; each minute more of them came back down the haulages as they were pulled out of the undamaged stopes, which were now suspect.

Quickly Rod looked about him, recognizing the face of one of his mine captains.

'McGee,' he shouted. 'Take over here. Get them sitting down in lines ready to load. We'll start hauling the shift out immediately. Get onto the hoist room, tell them I want the stretcher cases out first.'

He paused long enough to watch McGee take control. He glanced at his watch. Two fifty-six. He realized with astonishment that only twenty-six minutes had passed since he felt the pressure burst in his office.

McGee had the station under a semblance of control. He was shouting into the hoist room telephone, on Rod's authority demanding priority to clear 95 station.

'Right,' said Rod. 'Come on.' And he led into the haulage.

The dust was thick. He coughed. The hanging wall was lower here. As he trudged on once more, Rod pondered the unfortunate choice of mining terminology that had named the roof of an excavation 'the hanging wall'. It made one think of a gallows, or at the best it emphasized the fact that there were millions of tons of rock *hanging* overhead.

The haulage branched, and unerringly Rod took the right fork. In his head he carried an accurate three-dimensional map of the entire 176 miles of tunnels that comprised the Sonder Ditch's workings. The haulage came to a T-junction and the arms were lower and narrower. Right to 42 section, left to 43 section. The dust was so thick that visibility was down to ten feet. The dust hung in the air, sinking almost imperceptibly.

'Ventilations knocked out here,' he called over his shoulder. 'Van den Bergh!'

'Yes, sir.' The leader of the emergency squad came up behind him.

'I want air in this drive. Get it on. Use canvas piping if you have to.'

'Right.'

'Then I want pressure on the water hoses to lay this dust.'

'Right.'

Rod turned into the drive. Here the foot wall – the floor – was rough and the going slower. They came upon a line of steel trolleys filled with gold reef abandoned in the centre of the drive.

'Get these the hell out of the way,' ordered Rod, and went on.

Fifty paces and he stopped abruptly. He felt the hair on his forearms stand on end. He could never accustom himself to the sound, no matter how often he heard it.

In the deliberately callous slang of the miner they called them 'squealers'. It was the sound of a grown man, with his legs crushed under hundreds of tons of rock, perhaps his spine broken, dust suffocating him, his mind unhinged by

11

the mortal horror of the situation in which he was trapped, calling for help, calling to his God, calling for his wife, his children, or his mother.

Rod started forward again, with the sound of it becoming louder, a terrifying sound, hardly human, sobbing and babbling into silence, only to start again with a blood-chilling scream.

Suddenly there were men ahead of Rod in the tunnel, dark shapes looming in the dust mist, their head lamps throwing shafts of yellow light, grotesque, distorted.

'Who is that?' Rod called, and they recognized his voice.

'Thank God. Thank God you've come, Mr Ironsides.'

'Who is that?'

'Barnard.' The 43 section shift boss.

'What's the damage?'

'The whole hanging wall of the stope came down.'

'How many men in the stope?'

'Forty-two.'

'How many still in?'

'So far we've got out sixteen unhurt, twelve slightly hurt, three stretcher cases and two dead 'uns.'

The squealer started again, but his voice was much weaker.

'Him?' asked Rod.

'He's got twenty ton of rock lying across his pelvis. I've hit him with two shots of morphine, but it won't stop him.'

'Can you get into the stope?'

'Yes, there is a crawling hole.' Barnard flashed his lamp over the pile of fractured blue quartzite that jammed the drive like a collapsed garden wall. On it was an aperture big enough for a fox terrier to run through. Reflected light showed from the hole, and faintly from within came the grating sounds of movement over loose rock and the muffled voices of men.

'How many men have you got working in there, Barnard?'

'I – ' Barnard hesitated, 'I think about ten or twelve.'

And Rod grabbed a handful of his overall front and jerked him almost off his feet.

'You think!' In the head lamps Rod's face was white with fury. 'You've put men in there without recording their numbers? You've put twelve of my boys against the wall to try and save nine?' With a heave Rod lifted the shift boss off his feet and swung him against the side wall of the drive, pinning him there.

'You bastard, you know that most of those nine are chopped already. You know that stope is a bloody killing ground, and you send in *twelve* more to get the chop *and* you don't record their numbers. How the hell would we ever know who to look for if the hanging fell again?' He let the shift boss free, and stood back. 'Get them out of here, clear that stope.'

'But, Mr Ironsides, the General Manager is in there, Mr Lemmer is in there. He was doing an inspection in the stope.'

For a moment Rod was taken aback, then he snarled. 'I don't give a good damn if the State President is in there, clear the stope. We'll start again and this time we'll do it properly.'

Within minutes the rescuers had been recalled, they came squirming out of the aperture, white with dust like maggots wriggling from rotten cheese.

'Right,' said Rod, 'I'll risk four men at a time.'

Quickly he picked four of the floury figures, among them an enormous man on whose right shoulder was the brass badge of a boss boy.

'Big King – you here?' Rod spoke in Fanikalo, the lingua franca of the mines which enabled men from a dozen ethnic groups to communicate.

'I am here,' answered Big King.

'You looking for more awards?' A month before, Big King had been lowered on a rope 200 feet down a vertical orepass to retrieve the body of a white miner. The bravery award by the company had been 100 rand.

'Who speaks of awards when the earth has eaten the flesh of men?' Big King rebuked Rod softly. 'But today is children's play only. Is the Nkosi coming into the stope?' It was a challenge.

Rod's place was not in the stope. He was the organizer, the co-ordinator. Yet, he could not ignore the challenge, no Bantu would believe that he had not stood back in fear and sent other men in to die.

'Yes,' said Rod, 'I'm coming into the stope.'

He led them in. The hole was only just big enough to admit the bulk of Rod's body. He found himself in a chamber the size of an average room, but the roof was only three and a half feet high. He played his lamp quickly across the hanging wall, and it was wicked. The rock was cracked and ugly, 'a bunch of grapes' was the term.

'Very pretty,' he said, and dropped the beam of his lamp.

The squealer was within an arm's length of Rod. His body from the waist up protruded from under a piece of rock the size of a Cadillac. Someone had wrapped a red blanket around his upper body. He was quiet now, lying still. But as the beam of Rod's lamp fell upon him, he lifted his head. His eyes were crazed, unseeing, his face running with the sweat of terror and insanity. His mouth snapped open, wide and pink in the shiny blackness of his face. He began to scream, but suddenly the sound was drowned by a great red-black gout of blood that came gushing up his throat, and spurted from his mouth.

As Rod watched in horror, the Bantu posed like that, his head thrown back, his mouth gaping as though he were a gargoyle, the life blood pouring from him. Then slowly the head sagged forward, and flopped face downwards. Rod crawled to him, lifted his head and pillowed it on the red blanket.

There was blood on his hands and he wiped it on the front of his overalls.

'Three,' he said, 'so far.' And leaving the dying man he crawled on towards the broken face of the fall.

Big King crawled up beside him with two pinch bars. He handed one to Rod.

Within an hour it had become a contest, a trial of strength between two men. Behind them the other three men were shoring up and passing back the rock that Rod and Big King loosened from the face. Rod knew he was being childish, he should have been back in the main haulage, not only directing the rescue, but also making all the other decisions and alternative arrangements that were needed now. The company paid him for his brains and his experience, not for his muscle.

'The hell with it,' he thought. 'Even if we miss the blast this evening, I'm staying here.' He glanced at Big King, and reached forward to get his hands onto a bigger piece of rock in the jam. He strained, using his arms first, then bringing the power of his whole body into it – the rock was solid. Big King placed huge black hands on the rock, and they pulled together. In a rush of smaller rock it came away, and they shoved it back between them, grinning at each other.

At seven o'clock Rod and Big King withdrew from the stope to rest and eat sandwiches, and drink Thermos coffee while Rod spoke to Dimitri over the field telephone that had been laid up to the face.

'We've pulled shift on both shafts, Rod, the workings are clear to blast. Except for your lot, there are fifty-eight men in your 43 section.' Dimitri's voice was reedy over the field telephone.

'Hold on.' Rod revolved the situation in his mind. He worked it out slower than usual, for he was tired, emotionally and physically drained. If he stopped the blast on both shafts for fear of bringing down more rock in 43 section, it would cost the Company a day's production, 10,000 tons of gold reef worth sixteen rand a ton, the formidable sum of R160,000 or £80,000 or $200,000 whichever way you looked at it.

It was highly probable that every man in the stope was already dead, and the original pressure burst had de-stressed the rock above and around the 95 level, so there was little danger of further bumps.

And yet there might be someone alive in there, someone lying pinned in the womb-warm darkness of the stope with a bunch of loose grapes hanging over his unprotected body. When they hit all the blast buttons on the Sonder Ditch Mine, they fired eighteen tons of Dynagel. The kick was considerable, it would bring down those grapes.

'Dimitri,' Rod made his decision, 'burn all longwalls on No. 2 shaft at seven-thirty exactly.' No. 2 shaft was three miles away. That would save the Company R80,000. 'Then at precisely five-minute intervals burn south, north and west longwalls here on No. 1 shaft.' Spreading the blast would reduce the disturbance, and that put another R60,000 in the shareholders' pockets. The total monetary loss inflicted by the disaster was around R20,000. Not too bad really, Rod thought sardonically, blood was cheap. You could buy it at three rand a pint from the Central Blood Transfusion Service.

'All right,' he stood up, and flexed his aching shoulders. 'I'm pulling everybody back into the safety of the shaft pillar while we blast.'

After the successive earth tremors of the blast, Rod put them back into the stope, and at nine o'clock they uncovered the bodies of two machine boys crushed against the metal of their own rock drill. Ten feet further on they found the white miner; his body was unmarked, but his head was flattened.

At eleven o'clock they found two more machine boys. Rod was in the haulage when they dragged them out through the small opening. Neither of them were recognizable as human, they looked more like lumps of raw meat that had been rubbed in dirt.

A little after midnight Rod and Big King went into the stope again to take over from the team at the face, and twenty minutes later they holed through the wall of loose rock into another chamber that had been miraculously left standing.

The air in here was steamy with heat. Rod recoiled instinctively from the filthy moist gush of it against his face. Then he forced himself to crawl forward and peer into the opening.

Ten feet away lay Frank Lemmer, the General Manager of the Sonder Ditch Mine. He lay on his back. His helmet had been knocked from his head, and a deep gash split the skin above his eye. Blood from the gash had run back into his silver hair and clotted black. He opened his eyes and blinked owlishly in the dazzle of Rod's lamp. Quickly Rod averted the beam.

'Mr Lemmer,' he said.

'What the bloody hell are you doing with the rescue team?' growled Frank Lemmer. 'It's not your job. Haven't you learned a single goddamned thing in twenty years of mining?'

'Are you all right, sir?'

'Get a doctor in here,' replied Frank Lemmer. 'You're going to have to cut me loose from this lot.'

Rod wriggled up to where he lay, and then he saw what Frank Lemmer meant. From the elbow his arm was pinned under a solid slab of rock. Rod ran his hands over the slab, feeling it. Only explosive would shift the rock. As always Frank Lemmer was right.

Rod wriggled out of the opening and called over his shoulder.

'Get the telephone up here.'

After a few minutes delay he had the receiver, and was through to the station at 95 level which had been set up as an advance aid post and rest station for the rescuers.

'This is Ironsides, get me Doctor Stander.'

'Hold on.'

Then moments later, 'Hello, Rod, it's Dan.'

'Dan, we've found the old man.'

'How is he, conscious?'

'Yes, but he's pinned – you'll have to cut.'

'Are you sure?' Dan Stander asked.

'Of course I'm bloody well sure,' snapped Rod.

'Whoa, boy!' admonished Dan.

'Sorry.'

'Okay, where's he caught?'

'Arm. You'll have to cut above the elbow.'

'Charming!' said Dan.

'I'll wait here for you.'

'Right. I'll be up in five minutes.'

'It's funny, you see them chopped time and again, but you know it will never happen to you.' Frank Lemmer's voice was steady and even. The arm must be numb, Rod thought as he lay beside him in the stope.

Frank Lemmer rolled his head towards Rod. 'Why don't you go farming, boy?'

'You know why,' said Rod.

'Yes.' Lemmer smiled a little, just a twitching of the lips. With his free hand he wiped his mouth. 'You know, I had just three months more before I went on pension. I nearly made it. You'll end like this, boy, in the dirt with your bones crunched up.'

'It's not the end,' said Rod.

'Isn't it?' asked Frank Lemmer, and this time he chuckled. 'Isn't it?'

'What's the joke?' asked Dan Stander, poking his head into the tiny chamber.

'Christ, it took you long enough to get here,' growled Frank Lemmer.

'Give me a hand, Rod.' Dan passed his bag through, then as he crawled forward he spoke to Frank Lemmer.

'Union Steel closed at 98 cents tonight. I told you to buy.'

'Over-priced, over-capitalized,' snorted Frank Lemmer. Dan lay on his side in the dirt and laid out his instruments, and they argued stocks and shares. When Dan had the syringe full of pentathol and was swabbing Frank Lemmer's stringy old arm, Lemmer rolled his head towards Rod again.

'We made a good dig here, Rodney, you and I. I wish they'd give it to you now, but they won't. You're still too young. But whoever they put in my place, you keep an eye on him, you know the ground – don't let him balls it up.'

And the needle went in.

Dan cut through the arm in four and a half minutes, and twenty-seven minutes later Frank Lemmer died of shock and exposure in the Mary Anne on his way to the surface.

– 7 –

O nce he had paid Patti's alimony there was not too much of Rod's salary left for extravagances, but one of these was the big cream Maserati. Although it was a 1967 model, and had done nearly 30,000 miles when he bought it, yet the instalments still took a healthy bite out of his monthly pay cheque.

On mornings like this he reckoned the expense worthwhile. He came twisting down from the Kraalkop ridge, and when the national road flattened and straightened for the final run into Johannesburg he let the Maserati go. The car seemed to flatten against the ground like a running lion, and the exhaust note changed subtly, becoming deeper, more urgent.

Ordinarily, it was an hour's run from the Sonder Ditch Mine into the city of Johannesburg, but Rod could clip twenty minutes off that time.

It was Saturday morning, and Rod's mood was light and expectant.

Since the divorce Rod had lived a Jekyll and Hyde existence. Five days of the week he was the company man in top-line management, but on the last two days of the week he went into Johannesburg with his golf clubs in the boot of the Maserati, the keys to his luxury Hillbrow apartment in his pocket, and a chuckle on his lips.

Today the anticipation was keener than ever for, in addition to the twenty-two-year-old blonde model who was prepared to devote her evening to entertaining Rodney Ironsides, there was the mysterious summons from Dr Manfred Steyner to answer.

The summons had been delivered by a nameless female caller describing herself as 'Dr Steyner's Secretary'. It had come the day after Frank Lemmer's funeral, and was for Saturday at 11 a.m.

Rod had never met Manfred Steyner, but he had, of course, heard of him. Anyone who worked for any of the fifty or sixty companies that comprised the Central Rand Consolidated Group must have heard of Manfred Steyner, and the Sonder Ditch Gold Company was just one of the Group.

Manfred Steyner had a bachelor's degree in Economics from Berlin University, and a Doctor's degree in Business Administration from Cornell. He had joined CRC a mere twelve years previously at the age of thirty, and now he was the front runner. Hurry Hirschfeld could not live for ever, although he gave indications of doing so, and when he went down to make a takeover bid on Hades, the word was that Manfred Steyner would succeed him as Chairman of CRC.

Chairmanship of CRC was an enviable position, the incumbent automatically became one of the five most powerful men in Africa, and that included heads of state.

The betting favoured Dr Steyner for a number of good reasons. He had a brain that had earned him the nickname of 'The Computer'; no one had yet been able to detect in him the slightest evidence of a human weakness, and more than this he had taken the trouble ten years previously to catch Hurry Hirschfeld's only granddaughter as she emerged from Cape Town University and marry her.

Dr Steyner was in a strong position, and Rod was intrigued with the prospect of meeting him.

The Maserati was registering 125 miles an hour as he went under the over-pass of the Kloof Gold Mining Company property.

'Johannesburg, here I come!' Rod laughed aloud.

It was ten minutes before eleven o'clock when Rod

found the brass plaque reading 'Dr M. K. Steyner' in a secluded lane of the lush Johannesburg suburb of Sandown. The house was not visible from the road, and Rod let the Maserati roll gently in through the tall white gates, with their imitation Cape Dutch gables.

The gates, he decided, were a display of shocking taste but the gardens beyond them were paradise. Rod knew rock, but flowers were his weak suit. He recognized the massed banks of red and yellow against the green lawns as cannas, but after that he had no names for the blazing beauty spread about him.

'Wow!' he muttered in awe. 'Someone has done a hell of a lot of work around here.'

Around a curve in the macadamized drive lay the house. It also was Cape Dutch and Rod forgave Dr Steyner his gates.

'Wow!' he said again, and involuntarily braked the Maserati to a standstill.

Cape Dutch is one of the most difficult styles to copy effectively, where one line in a hundred out of place could spoil the effect; this particular example worked perfectly. It gave the feel of timelessness, of solidarity, and mixed it subtly with a grace and finesse of line. He guessed that the shutters and beams were genuine yellow wood and the windows hand-leaded.

Rod looked at it, and felt envy prickle and burn within him. He loved fine things, like his Maserati, but this was another concept in material possessions. He was jealous of the man that owned it, knowing that his own entire year's income would not be sufficient for a down payment on the land alone.

'So I've got my flat,' he grinned ruefully, and coasted down to park in front of the line of garages.

It was not clear which was the correct entrance to use, and he chose at random from a number of paved paths that all led in the general direction of the house.

Around a bend in this path he came on another spectacle. Though smaller it had, if anything, a more profound effect on Rod than the house had. It was a feminine posterior of equal grace and finesse of line, clad in Helanka stretch ski-pants, and protruding from a large and exotic bush.

Rod was captivated. He stood and watched as the bush shook and rustled, and the bottom wriggled and heaved.

Suddenly, in ladylike tones there issued from the bush a most unladylike oath and the bottom shot backwards and its owner straightened up with her forefinger in her mouth, sucking noisily.

'It bit me!' she mumbled around the finger. 'Damned stinkbug bit me!'

'Well, you shouldn't tease them,' said Rod.

And she spun round to face him. The first thing Rod noticed were her eyes, they were enormous, completely out of proportion to the rest of her face.

'I wasn't—' she started, and then stopped. The finger came out of her mouth. Instinctively one hand went to her hair, and the other began straightening her blouse and brushing off bits of vegetation that were clinging to her.

'Who are you?' she asked, and those huge eyes swept over him. This was fairly standard reaction for any woman between the ages of sixteen and sixty viewing Rodney Ironsides for the first time, and Rodney accepted it gracefully.

'My name is Rodney Ironsides. I've an appointment to see Dr Steyner.'

'Oh.' She was hurriedly tucking her shirt-tails into her slacks. 'My husband will be in his study.'

He had known who she was. He had seen her photographs fifty times in the Group newspaper; but in them she was usually in full-length evening dress and diamonds, not in a blouse with a tear in one sleeve nor pig-tails that were coming down. In the pictures her make-up was immaculate, now she had none at all and her face was flushed and dewed with perspiration.

'I must look a mess. I've been gardening,' said Theresa Steyner unnecessarily.

'Did you do this garden yourself?'

'Only a very little of the muscle work, but I planned it,' she answered. She decided he was big and ugly – no, not really ugly, but battered-looking.

'It's beautiful,' said Rod.

'Thank you.' No, not battered-looking, she changed her mind, tough-looking, and the chest hair curled out of the V of his open neck shirt.

'This is a protea, isn't it?' He indicated the bush from which she had recently emerged. He was guessing.

'Nutans,' she said; he must be in his late thirties, there was greying at his temples.

'Oh, I thought it was a protea.'

'It is. "Nutans" is its proper name. There are over two hundred different varieties of proteas,' she answered seriously. His voice didn't fit his appearance at all, she decided. He looked like a prize fighter but spoke like a lawyer, probably was one. It was usually lawyers or business consultants who came calling on Manfred.

'Is that so? It's very pretty.' Rod touched one of the blooms.

'Yes, isn't it? I've got over fifty varieties growing here.'

And suddenly they were smiling at each other. 'I'll take you up to the house,' said Theresa Steyner.

'**M**r Ironsides is here, Manfred.'
'Thank you.' He sat at the stinkwood desk in a room that smelled of wax polish. He made no effort to rise from his seat.

'Would you like a cup of coffee?' Theresa asked from the doorway. 'Or tea?'

'No, thank you,' answered Manfred Steyner without consulting Rod who stood beside her.

'I'll leave you to it, then,' she said.

'Thank you, Theresa.' And she turned away. Rod went on standing where he was, he was studying this man of whom he had heard so much.

Manfred Steyner appeared younger than his forty-two years. His hair was light brown, almost blond, and brushed straight back. He wore spectacles with heavy black frames, and his face was smooth and silky-looking, soft as a girl's with no beard shadow on his chin. His hands that lay on the polished desk top were hairless, smooth, so that Rod wondered if he had used a depilatory on them.

'Come in,' he said, and Rod moved to the desk. Steyner wore a white silk shirt in which the ironing creases still showed, the cloth was snowy white and over it he wore a Royal Johannesburg Golf Club tie, with onyx cuff links. Suddenly Rod realized that neither shirt nor tie had ever been worn before; that much was true of what he had heard then. Steyner ordered his shirts hand-made by the gross and wore each once only.

'Sit down, Ironsides.' Steyner slurred his vowels slightly, just a trace of a Teutonic accent.

'Dr Steyner,' said Rod softly, 'you have a choice. You may call me Rodney or Mr Ironsides.'

There was no change in Steyner's voice nor expression.

'I would like to go over your background, please, Mr

Ironsides, as a preliminary to our discussion. You have no objection?'

'No, Dr Steyner.'

'You were born October 16th, 1931, at Butterworth in the Transkei. Your father was a native trader, your mother died January 1939. Your father was commissioned Captain in the Durban Light Infantry and died of wounds on the Po River in Italy during the winter of 1944. You were raised by your maternal uncle in East London. Matriculating from Queen's College, Grahamstown, in 1947, you were unsuccessful in obtaining a Chamber of Mines scholarship to Witwatersrand University for a B.Sc. (Mining Engineering) degree. You enrolled in the GMTS (Government Mining Training School) and obtained your blasting ticket during 1949. At which time you joined the Blyvooruitzicht Gold Mining Company Ltd as a learner miner.'

Dr Steyner stood up from his desk and crossing to the panelled wall he pressed a concealed switch and a portion of the panelling slid back to reveal a wash basin and towel rack. As he went on talking he began very meticulously to soap and wash his hands.

'In the same year you were promoted to miner and in 1952 to shift boss, 1954 to mine captain. You successfully completed the examination for the Mine Manager's ticket in 1959, and in 1962 you came to us as an Assistant Underground Manager, and in 1968 you achieved your present position as Underground Manager.'

Dr Steyner began drying his hands on a snowy white towel.

'You've memorized my company record pretty thoroughly,' Rod admitted.

Dr Steyner crumpled the towel and dropped it into a bin below the wash basin. He pressed the button and the panelling slid closed, then he came back to the desk stepping precisely over the glossy polished wooden floor, and Rod realized that he was a small man, not more than five and a half feet tall, about the same height as his wife.

'This is something of an achievement,' Steyner went on. 'The next youngest Underground Manager in the entire Group is forty-six years of age, whereas you are not yet thirty-nine.'

Rod inclined his head in acknowledgement.

'Now,' said Dr Steyner as he reseated himself and laid his freshly washed hands on the desk top. 'I would like briefly to touch on your private life – you have no objections?'

Again Rod inclined his head.

'The reason that your application for the Chamber of Mines scholarship was refused, despite your straight A matriculation, was the recommendation of your headmaster to the selection board in effect that you were of unstable and violent disposition.'

'How the hell did you know that?' ejaculated Rod.

'I have access to the board's records. It seems that once you had received your matric you immediately assaulted your former headmaster.'

'I beat the hell out of the bastard,' Rod agreed happily.

'An expensive indulgence, Mr Ironsides. It cost you a university degree.'

And Rod was silent.

'To continue: In 1959 you married Patricia Anne Harvey. Of the union was born a girl child in the same year, to be precise, seven and a half months after the wedding.'

Rod squirmed slightly in his chair, and Dr Steyner went on quietly.

'This marriage terminated in divorce in 1964. Your wife is suing you on the grounds of adultery, and receiving custody of the child, alimony and maintenance in the sum of R450.000 monthly.'

'What's all this about?' demanded Rod.

'I am attempting to establish an accurate picture of your present circumstances. It is necessary, I assure you.' Dr Steyner removed his spectacles and began polishing the lens on a clean white handkerchief. There were the marks of the frames on the bridge of his nose.

'Go on, then.' Despite himself, Rod was fascinated to learn just how much Steyner knew about him.

'In 1968 there was a paternity suit brought against you by a Miss Diane Johnson and judgement for R150.00 per month.'

Rod blinked and was silent.

'I should mention two further actions against you for assault, both unsuccessful on the grounds of justification or self-defence.'

'Is that all?' asked Rod sarcastically.

'Almost,' admitted Dr Steyner. 'It is only necessary to note further recurrent expenditure in the form of a monthly payment of R150.00 on a continental sports car, and a further R100.00 per month rental on the premises 596 Glen Alpine Heights, Corner Lane, Hillbrow.'

Rod was furious, he had believed that no one in CRC knew about the flat.

'Damn you! You've been prying into my affairs!'

'Yes,' agreed Dr Steyner levelly. 'I am guilty, but in good cause. If you bear with me, you'll see why.'

Suddenly Dr Steyner stood up from the desk, crossed the room to the concealed wash basin, and again began to wash his hands. As he dried them, he spoke again.

'Your monthly commitments are R850. Your salary, after deduction of tax, is less than one thousand Rand. You have no mining degree, and the chances of your taking the next step upwards to General Manager without it are remote. You are at your ceiling, Mr Ironsides. On your own ability you can go no further. In thirty years' time you will not be the youngest Underground Manager in the CRC Group, but the oldest.' Dr Steyner paused. 'That is, provided that your rather expensive tastes have not landed you in a debtors' prison, and that neither the quickness and heat of your temper, nor the matching speed and temperature of your genitalia have gotten you into really serious trouble.'

Steyner dropped the towel in the bin and returned to his seat. They sat in absolute silence, regarding each other for a full minute.

'You got me all the way up here to tell me this?' asked Rod, his whole body tense, his voice slightly husky. It needed only an ounce more of provocation to launch him across the desk at Steyner's throat.

'No.' Steyner shook his head. 'I got you up here to tell you that I will use all my influence, which I flatter myself is considerable, to secure your appointment – and I mean immediate appointment – to the position of General Manager of the Sonder Ditch Gold Mining Company Ltd.'

Rod recoiled in his chair as though Steyner had spat in his face. He stared at him aghast.

'Why?' he asked at last. 'What do you want in exchange?'

'Neither your friendship, nor your gratitude,' Dr Steyner told him. 'But your unquestioning obedience to my instructions. You will be my man – completely.'

Rod went on staring at him while his mind raced. Without Steyner's intervention he would wait at the very least ten years for this promotion, if it ever came. He wanted it, my God, how he wanted it. The achievement, the increase in income, the power that went with the job. His own mine! His own mine at the age of thirty-eight – and an additional 10,000 rand per annum.

Yet Rod was not gullible enough to believe that Manfred Steyner's price would be cheap. When the instruction came that he was to follow with unquestioning obedience, he knew it would stink like a ten-day corpse. But once he had the job he could refuse the instruction. Get the job first, then decide once he received the instruction whether to follow it or not.

'I accept,' he said.

Manfred Steyner stood up from the desk.

'You will hear from me,' he said. 'Now you may go.'

– 9 –

Rod crossed the wide-flagged stoep without seeing or hearing; vaguely he wandered down across the lawns towards his car. His mind was harrying the recent conversation, tearing it to pieces like a pack of wild dogs on a carcass. He almost bumped into Theresa Steyner before he saw her, and abruptly his mind dropped the subject of the General Managership.

Theresa had changed her clothing, made up her face and eyes, and the pig-tails were concealed under a lime-coloured silk scarf, all this in the half hour since their last meeting. She was hovering over a flower bed with a flower basket on one arm, as bright and pleasing as a hummingbird.

Rod was amused and flattered, vain enough to realize that the change was in his honour, and connoisseur enough to appreciate the improvement.

'Hello.' She looked up, contriving successfully to look both surprised and artless. Her eyes were really enormous, and the make-up was designed to enhance their size.

'You are a busy little bee.' Rod ran a knowledgeable appraisal over the floral slack suit she wore, and saw the colour start in her cheeks as she felt his eyes.

'Did you have a successful meeting?'

'Very.'

'Are you a lawyer?'

'No. I work for your grandfather.'

'Doing what?'

'Mining his gold.'

'Which mine?'

'Sonder Ditch.'

'What's your position?'

'Well, if your husband is as good as his word, I'm the new General Manager.'

'You're too young,' she said.

'That's what I thought.'

'Pops will have something to say on the subject.'

'Pops?' he asked.

'My grandfather.' And Rod laughed before he could stop himself.

'What's so funny?'

'The Chairman of CRC being called "Pops".'

'I'm the only one who calls him that.'

'I bet you are.' Rod laughed again. 'In fact I'd bet you'd get away with a lot of things no one else would dare.'

Suddenly the underlying sexuality of his last remark occurred to them both and they fell silent. Theresa looked down and carefully snipped the head off a flower.

'I didn't mean it that way,' apologized Rod.

'What way, Mr Ironsides?' She looked up and enquired with mischievous innocence, and they laughed together with the awkwardness gone again.

She walked beside him to the car, making it seem a completely natural thing to do, and as he slipped behind the steering-wheel she remarked:

'Manfred and I will be coming out to the Sonder Ditch next week. Manfred is to present long service and bravery awards to some of your men.' She had already refused the invitation to accompany Manfred, she must now see to it that she was re-invited. 'I shall probably see you then.'

'I look forward to it,' said Rod, and let in the clutch.

Rod glanced in the rear view mirror. She was a remarkably provocative and attractive woman. A careless man could drown in those eyes.

'Dr Manfred Steyner has got himself a big fat problem there,' he decided. 'Our Manfred is probably so busy soaping and scrubbing his equipment, that he never gets round to using it.'

– 10 –

Through the leaded windows Dr Steyner caught a glimpse of the Maserati as it disappeared around the curve in the driveway, and he listened as the throb of the engine dwindled into silence.

He lifted the receiver of the telephone and wiped it with the white handkerchief before putting it to his ear. He dialled and while it rang he inspected the nails of his free hand minutely.

'Steyner,' he said into the mouthpiece. 'Yes – yes.' He listened.

'Yes . . . He has just left . . . Yes, it is arranged . . . No, there will be no difficulty there, I am sure.' As he spoke he was looking at the palm of his hand, he saw the tiny beads of perspiration appear on his skin and an expression of disgust tightened his lips.

'I am fully aware of the consequences. I tell you, I know.'

He closed his eyes and listened for another minute without moving as the receiver squawked and clacked, then he opened his eyes.

'It will be done in good time, I assure you. Goodbye.'

He hung up and went to wash his hands. Now, he thought, as he worked up lather, to get it past the old man.

11

He was old now, seventy-eight long hard years old. His hair and his eyebrows were creamy white. His skin was folded and creased, freckled and spotted, hanging in unexpected little pouches under his chin and eyes.

His body had dried out, so he stood gaunt and stooped like a tree that has taken a set before the prevailing winds; but there was still the underlying urgency in the way he held himself, the same urgency that had earned him the name of 'Hurry' Hirschfeld when first he bustled into the gold fields sixty years ago.

On this Monday morning he was standing before the full length windows of his penthouse office, looking down on the city of Johannesburg. Reef House stood shoulder to massive shoulder with the Schlesinger Building on the Braamfontein ridge above the city proper. From this height it seemed that Johannesburg cowered at Hurry Hirschfeld's feet, as well it should.

Long ago, even before the great depression of the 'thirties, he had ceased to measure his wealth in terms of money. He owned outright a little over a quarter of the issued share capital of Central Rand Consolidated. At the present market price of R120 per share, this was a staggering sum. In addition, through a complicated arrangement of trusts, proxy rights and interlocking directorates, he had control of a further massive block of twenty per cent of the company's voting rights.

The overhead intercom pinged softly into this room of soft fabrics and muted colours, and Hurry started slightly.

'Yes,' he said, without turning away from the window.

'Dr Steyner is here, Mr Hirschfeld,' his secretary's voice whispered, ghostly and disembodied into the luscious room.

'Send him in,' snapped Hurry. That goddamned intercom

always gave him the creeps. The whole goddamned room gave him the creeps. It was, as Hurry had said often and loudly, like a fairy brothel.

For fifty-five years he had worked in a bleak uncarpeted office with a few yellowing photographs of men and machinery on its walls. Then they had moved him in here – he glanced around the room with the distaste that five years had not lulled. What did they think he was, a bloody ladies' hairdresser?

The panelling door slid noiselessly aside and Dr Manfred Steyner stepped neatly into the room.

'Good morning, Grandfather,' he said. For ten years, even since Terry had been bird-brained enough to marry him, Manfred Steyner had called Hurry Hirschfeld that, and Hurry hated it. He remembered now that Manfred Steyner was also responsible for the design and decor of Reef House, and therefore the author of his recent irritation.

'Whatever it is you want – No!' he said, and he moved across to the air-conditioning controls. The thermostat was already set at 'high', now Hurry turned it to 'highest'. Within minutes the room would be at the correct temperature for growing orchids.

'How are you this morning, Grandfather?' Manfred seemed not to have heard, his expression was bland and neutral as he moved to the desk and laid out his papers.

'Bloody awful,' said Hurry. It was impossible to disconcert the little prig, he thought, you might as well shout insults at an efficiently functioning piece of machinery.

'I am sorry to hear that.' Manfred took out his handkerchief and touched his chin and forehead. 'I have the weekly reports.'

Hurry capitulated and went across to the desk. This was business. He sat down and read quickly. His questions were abrupt, cutting and instantly answered, but Manfred's handkerchief was busy now, swabbing and dabbing. Twice he removed his spectacles and wiped steam from the lenses.

'Can I turn the air-conditioning down a little, Grandfather?'

'You touch it and I'll kick your arse,' said Hurry without looking up.

Another five minutes and Manfred Steyner stood up suddenly.

'Excuse me, Grandfather.' And he shot across the office and disappeared into the adjoining bathroom suite. Hurry cocked his head to listen, and when he heard the taps hiss he grinned happily. The air-conditioning was the only method he had discovered of disconcerting Manfred Steyner, and for ten years he had been experimenting with various techniques.

'Don't use all the soap,' he shouted gleefully. 'You are the one always on about office expenses!'

It did not seem ludicrous to Hurry that one of the richest and most influential men in Africa should devote so much time and energy to baiting his personal assistant.

At eleven o'clock Manfred Steyner gathered his papers and began packing them carefully in his monogrammed pigskin briefcase.

'About the appointment of a new General Manager for the Sonder Ditch to replace Mr Lemmer. You will recall my memo regarding the appointment of younger men to key positions—'

'Never read the bloody thing,' lied Hurry Hirschfeld. They both knew he read everything, and remembered it.

'Well—' Manfred went on to enlarge his thesis for a minute, then ended, 'In view of this, my department, myself concurring entirely, urges the appointment of Rodney Barry Ironsides, the present Underground Manager, to the position. I hoped that you would initial the recommendation and we can put it through at Friday's meeting.'

Dexterously Manfred slid the yellow memo in front of Hurry Hirschfeld, unscrewed the cap of his pen and offered it to him. Hurry picked the memo up between thumb and forefinger as though it were someone's dirty handkerchief and dropped it into the waste-paper bin.

'Do you wish me to tell you in detail what you and your planning department can do?' he asked.

'Grandfather,' Manfred admonished him mildly, 'you cannot run the company as though you were a robber baron. You cannot ignore the team of highly trained men who are your advisers.'

'I've run it that way for fifty years. You show me who's going to change that.' Hurry leaned back in his chair with vast satisfaction and fished a powerful-looking cigar out of his inner pocket.

'Grandfather, that cigar! The doctor said—'

'And I said Fred Plummer gets the job as Manager of the Sonder Ditch.'

'He goes on pension next year,' protested Manfred Steyner.

'Yes,' Hurry nodded. 'But how does that alter the position?'

'He's an old dodderer,' Manfred tried again, there was a desperate edge to his voice. He had not anticipated one of the old man's whims cutting across his plans.

'He's twelve years younger than I am,' growled Hurry ominously. 'How's that make him an old dodderer?'

12

Now that the weekend was over, Rod found the apartment oppressive, and he longed to get out of it.

He shaved, standing naked before the mirror, and he caught a whiff of the reeking ashtrays and half-empty glasses in the lounge. The char would have her customary Monday-morning greeting when she came in later today. From Louis Botha Avenue the traffic noise was starting to build up and he glanced at his watch – six o'clock in the morning. A good time to examine your soul, he decided, and leaned forward to watch his own eyes in the mirror.

'You're too old for this type of living,' he told himself seriously. 'You've had four years of it now, four years since the divorce, and that's about enough. It would be nice now to go to bed with the same woman on two consecutive nights.'

He rinsed his razor, and turned on the taps in the shower cabinet.

'Might even be able to afford it, if our boy Manfred delivers the goods.' Rod had not allowed himself to believe too implicitly in Manfred Steyner's promise; but during the whole of these last two days the excitement had been there beneath the cynicism.

He stepped into the shower and soaped himself, then turned the cold tap full on. Gasping he shut it off and reached for his towel. Still drying himself, he went through and stood at the foot of the bed; as he towelled himself he examined the girl who lay among the tousled sheets.

She was tanned dark toffee brown so she appeared to be dressed in white transparent bra and panties where the skin was untouched by the sun. Her hair was a blonde-gold flurry across her face and the pillow, at odds with the jet black triangle of body hair. Her lips in sleep were fixed in a soft pink pout, and she looked disquietingly young. Rod had to make a conscious effort to remember her name, she was not the companion with whom he had begun the weekend.

'Lucille,' he said, sitting down beside her. 'Wake up. Time to roll.'

She opened her eyes.

'Good morning,' he said and kissed her gently.

'Mmm.' She blinked. 'What time is it? I don't want to get fired.'

'Six,' he told her.

'Oh, good. Plenty of time.' And she rolled over and snuggled down into the sheets.

'Like hell.' He slapped her bottom lightly. 'Move, girl, can you cook?'

'No—' She lifted her head. 'What's your name again?' she asked.

'Rod,' he told her.

'That's right – Piston Rod,' she giggled. 'What a way to die! Are you sure you aren't powered by steam?'

'How old are you?' he asked.

'Nineteen. How old are you?'

'Thirty-eight.'

'Daddy, you're vintage!' she told him vehemently.

'Yes, sometimes I feel that way.' He stood up. 'Let's go.'

'You go. I'll lock up when I leave.'

'No sale,' he said, the last one he had left in the flat had cleaned it out – groceries, liquor, glasses, towels, even the ashtrays. 'Five minutes to dress.'

Fortunately she lived on his way. She directed him to a run-down block of flats under the mine dumps at Booysens.

'I'm putting three blind sisters through school. You want to help?' she asked as he parked the Maserati.

'Sure.' He eased a five-rand note out of his wallet and handed it to her.

'Ta muchly.' And she slipped out of the red leather seat, closed the door and walked away. She did not look back before she disappeared into the block, and Rod felt an unaccountable wave of loneliness wash over him. It was so intense that he sat quiescent for a full minute before he could throw it off, then he hit the gears and screeched away from the kerb.

'My little five-rand friend,' he said. 'She really cares!'

He drove fast, so that as he topped the Kraalkop ridge the shadows were still long, and the dew lay silver on the grass. He pulled the Maserati into a layby and climbed out. Leaning against the bonnet he lit a cigarette, grimacing at the taste, and looked down at the valley.

There was no natural surface indication of the immense treasure house that lay below. It was like any of the other countless grassy plains of the Transvaal. In the centre stood the town of Kitchenerville, which for half a century had rejoiced in the fact that Lord Kitchener had camped one night here in pursuit of the wily Boer: a collection of three dozen buildings which had expanded miraculously into three thousand, around a magnificent town hall and shopping complex. Dressed in public lawns and gardens, wide streets and bright new houses, all of it paid for by the mining houses whose lease areas converged on the town.

Out of the bleak veld surrounding the town their headgears stood like colossal monuments to the gold hunger of man. Around the headgears clustered the plants and workshops. There were fourteen headgears in the valley. The field was divided into five lease areas, following the original farm titles, and was mined by five separate companies. Thornfontein Gold Mining, Blaauberg Gold Mining, West Tweefontein Mining, Deep Gold Levels, and the Sonder Ditch Gold Mining Company.

It was to this last that Rod naturally directed his attention.

'You beauty,' he whispered, for in his eyes the mountainous dumps of blue rock beside the shafts were truly beautiful. The complex but carefully thought out pattern of the works buildings, even the sulphur-yellow acres of the slimes dam, had a functional beauty.

'Get it for me, Manfred,' he spoke aloud. 'I want it. I want it badly.'

On the twenty-eight square miles of the Sonder Ditch's property lived 14,000 human beings, 12,000 of them were Bantu who had been recruited from all over Southern Africa. They lived in the multi-storied hostels near the shaft heads, and each day they went down through two small holes in the ground to depths that were scarcely credible, and came up again out of those same two holes. 12,000 men down, 12,000 up. That was not all: out of those two same holes came 10,000 tons of rock daily, and down them went timber and tools and piping and explosive, ton upon ton of material and equipment. It was an undertaking that must evoke pride in the men who accomplished it.

Rod glanced at his watch, 7.35 a.m. They were down already, all 12,000 of them. They had started going down at three-thirty that morning and now it was accomplished. The shift was in. The Sonder Ditch was breaking rock, and bringing the stuff out.

Rod grinned happily. His loneliness and depression of an hour ago were gone, swallowed up in the immensity of his involvement. He watched the massive wheels of the headgears spinning, stopping briefly, and then spinning again.

Each of those shafts had cost fifty million rand, the surface plant and works another fifty million. The Sonder Ditch represented an investment of 150 million rand, 220 million dollars. It was big, and it would be his.

Rod flicked away the butt of his cigarette. As he drove down the ridge, his eyes moved eastward down the valley. All mining activity ceased abruptly along an imaginary north-south line, drawn arbitrarily across the open grassland.

There was no surface indication why this should be so, but the reason was deep down.

On that line ran a geological freak, a dyke, a wall of hard serpentine rock that had been named 'the Big Dipper'. It cut through the field like an axe stroke, and beyond it was bad ground. The gold reef existed in the bad ground, they knew this; but not one of the five companies had gone after it. They had prospected it tentatively and then shied away from it, for the boreholes that they sank were frightening in their inconsistency.

A big percentage of the Sonder Ditch lease area lay on the far side of the Dipper, and there was a diamond-drilling team working there now. They had already completed five holes.

Rod could remember accurately the results:-

Borehole SD No. 1.	Abandoned in water at 4,000 ft.
SD No. 2.	Abandoned in dry hole at 5,250 ft.
SD No. 3.	Intersected carbon leader reef at 6,600 ft.
Assay valve	27,323-inch penny-weights.
First deflection	6,212-inch penny-weights.
Second deflection	2,114-inch penny-weights.
SD No. 4.	Abandoned in artesian water at 3,500 ft.
SD No. 5.	Intersected carbon leader at 8,116 ft.
Assay valve	562-inch penny-weights.

And they were drilling the deflections on that one now.

The problem was to build up a picture from results like that. It looked like a mess of faulted and waterlogged ground with the gold reef fragmented and fluky, showing unbelievably high values at one spot, and then more than likely pinching out fifty feet away.

They may mine it one day, thought Rod, but I hope to hell I'm on pension by the time they do.

In the distance beyond the slimes dam he could just make out the spidery triangle of the drilling rig against the grown grass.

'Go to it, boys,' he muttered. 'Whatever you find there won't make much difference to me.'

And he went in through the imposing gates at the entrance to the mine property, halting carefully at the stop sign where the railway line crossed the road and he forked two fingers at the traffic policeman lurking behind the gates.

The traffic cop grinned and waved; he had caught Rod the previous week, so he was still one up.

Rod drove down to his office.

– 13 –

That Monday morning Allen 'Popeye' Worth was preparing to drill his first deflection on the SD No. 5. borehole. Allen was a Texan – not a typical Texan. He stood five feet four inches tall, but was as tough as the steel drill with which he worked. Thirty years before he had started learning his trade on the oilfields around Odessa and he had learned it well.

Now he could start at the surface and drill a four-inch hole down 13,000 feet through the earth's crust, keeping the hole straight all the way, an almost impossible task if you took into account the whippiness and torque in a jointed rod of steel that long.

If, as happened occasionally, the steel snapped and broke off thousands of feet down, Allen could fit a fishing tool on the end of his rig, and patiently grope for the stump, find it, grapple it and pull it out of the borehole. When he hit the reef down there, he could purposely kick his drill off the line and pierce the reef again and again to sample it over an area of hundreds of feet. This was what was meant by deflecting.

Allen was one of the best. He could command his own salary and behave like a prima donna, and his bosses would still fawn on him, for the things he could do with a diamond drill were almost magical.

Now he was assessing the angle of his first deflection. The previous day he had lowered a long brass bottle to the end of his borehole and left it overnight. The bottle was half filled with concentrated sulphuric acid, and it had etched the brass of the bottle. By measuring the angle of the etching he knew just how his drill was branching off from his original hole.

In the tiny wood and iron building beside the drilling rig he finished his measurements and stood back from the work bench, grunting with satisfaction.

From his hip pocket he drew a corncob pipe and pouch. Once he had stuffed tobacco into the pipe and lit it, it became very clear as to why his nickname was 'Popeye'. He was a dead ringer for the cartoon character, aggressive jaw, button eyes, battered maritime cap and all.

He puffed contentedly, watching through the single window of the shack as his gang went about the tedious business of lowering the drilling bit down into the earth. Then he took the pipe from his mouth and spat accurately through the window, replaced the pipe and stooped to minutely check his measurements.

His foreman driller interrupted him from the doorway.

'On bottom, and ready to turn, boss.'

'Huh!' Popeye checked his watch. 'Two hours forty to get down, you don't reckon to rupture a gut do you?'

'That's not bad,' protested the foreman.

'And it sure as hell isn't good either! Okay, okay, cut the cackle and let's get her turning.' He bounced out of the

43

shed and set off for the rig, darting quick beady little glances about him. The rig was a fifty-foot-high tower of steel girders and within it the drill rod hung down until it disappeared into the collar. The twin 200-horsepower diesel engines throbbed expectantly, waiting to provide the power, their exhausts smoking blue in the early morning sunlight. Beside the rig lay a mountainous heap of drilling rods, beyond them the 10,000-gallon puddling reservoir to provide water for the hole. Water was pumped into the hole continuously to cool and lubricate the tool as it cut into the rock.

'Stand by to turn her,' Popeye called to his gang, and they moved to their stations. Dressed in blue overalls, coloured fibreglass helmets, and leather gloves, they stood ready and tensed. This was an anxious moment for the whole team: power had to be applied with a lover's touch to the mile and a half length of rod, or it would buckle and snap.

Popeye climbed nimbly up onto the collar, and glanced about him to make sure all was in readiness. The foreman driller was at the controls, watching Popeye with complete absorption, his hands resting on the levers.

'Power up!' shouted Popeye and made the circular motion with his right hand. The diesels bellowed harshly, and Popeye reached out to lay his left hand on the drilling rod. This was how he did it, feeling the rod with his bare hand as he brought in the power, judging the tension by ear and eye and touch.

His right hand gestured and the foreman delicately let in the clutch, the rod moved under Popeye's hand, he gestured again and it revolved slowly. He could feel it was near breaking point and he cut down the power instantly, then let it in again. His right hand moved eloquently, expressively as an orchestral conductor, and the foreman followed it, the junior member of a highly skilled team.

Slowly the tension of the gang relaxed as the revolutions

of the drill built up steadily, until Popeye gave the clenched fist 'okay' and jumped down from the collar. They scattered casually to their other duties, while Popeye and the foreman strolled back to the shed, leaving the drill to grind away at a steady four hundred revolutions a minute.

'Got something for you,' said the foreman, as they entered the shed.

'What?' demanded Popeye.

'The latest *Playboy*.'

'You're kidding!' Popeye accused him delightedly, but the foreman fished the rolled magazine out of his lunch box.

'Hey, there!' Popeye snatched it from him and turned immediately to the coloured foldout.

'Isn't that something!' He whistled. 'This dolly could get a job in a stockyard beating the oxen to death with her boo-boos!'

The foreman joined the discussion of the young lady's anatomy, and so neither of them noticed the change in the sound of the drill until two minutes had passed. Then Popeye heard it through an erotic haze. He flung the magazine from him, and went through the door of the shed white-faced.

It was fifty yards from the shed to the rig, but even at that distance Popeye could see the vibration in the drilling rod. He could hear the labouring note of the diesels as they carried increased load, and he ran like a fox terrier, trying to reach the controls and shut off the engines before it happened.

He knew what it was. His drill had cut into one of the many fissures with which this badly faulted ground was criss-crossed. The puddling water from his borehole had drained away leaving the bit to run dry against dry rock. The friction head had built up, the dust from the cut was not being washed away – and in consequence the rod had jammed. It was being held tightly at one end while at the other the two big diesels were straining to turn it. The whole rig was seconds away from a twist-off.

There should have been an operator at the controls to meet just such an emergency, but he was a hundred yards away, just emerging from the wood and iron latrine beyond the puddling dam. He was desperately trying to hoist his pants, clinch the buckle of his belt and run all at the same time.

'You whore's chamberpot!' roared Popeye, as he ran. 'What the hell you goofing off—'

The words choked off in his throat, for as he reached the door of the engine room there was a report like a cannon shot as the rod snapped, and immediately the diesels screamed into over-rev as they were relieved of the load. Just too late, Popeye punched the earth buttons on the magnetos, and the engines spluttered into silence.

In that silence Popeye was sobbing with exertion and frustration and anger.

'A twist-off,' he sobbed. 'A deep one. Oh no! God, no!' It might take two weeks to fish out the broken rod, pump cement into the fissure to seal it, and then start again.

He removed the cap from his head, and with all his strength hurled it on the engine room floor. He then proceeded to jump on it with both feet. This was standard procedure. Popeye jumped on his cap at least once a week, and the foreman knew that when he had finished doing that he would then assault anybody within range.

Quietly the foreman slipped behind the wheel of the Ford truck, and the rest of the gang scrambled aboard. They all bumped away down the rutted track. There was a roadhouse on the main road where they went for coffee at times like this. When the mists of rage had dispersed sufficiently from his mind for Popeye to start seeking a human sacrifice, he looked about to find the drilling area strangely still and deserted.

'Stupid bunch of yellow-bellied baboons!' he bellowed in

46

frustration after the retreating truck, and, as the next best thing, went into the shed to phone his Managing Director.

This gentleman sitting in the air-conditioned offices of 'Hart Drilling and Cementation' high above Rissik Street in Johannesburg was a little taken aback to learn from Popeye Worth that he, the Managing Director, was directly responsible for the twist-off of an expensive diamond drill at the Sonder Ditch No. 5 hole.

'If you used that sack of custard that passes for a brain, you'd fight shy of trying to sink holes into this bunch of knitting,' Popeye yelled into the mouthpiece. 'I'd prefer to stick my old man into a meat grinder than put a drill into this ground. It stinks, I tell you! It's ugly down there. God help the poor son of a bitch who tries to mine it!'

He slammed down the phone and stuffed his pipe with trembling fingers. Ten minutes later his breathing had returned to normal and his hands were steady. He picked up the phone again and dialled the number of the road-house. The proprietor answered.

'José, tell my boys it's okay, they can come home now,' said Popeye.

– 14 –

For Rod Ironsides there was more excitement than usual in meeting and solving the dozen paper problems that lay on his desk to welcome him back to the office. As he worked he kept remembering that Manfred Steyner might be able to do it, might just be able to do it.

The Sonder Ditch might really belong to him soon. He dispatched the last problem and lay back in his swivel chair. His mind was clear of the last cobwebs of dissipation and, as always, he felt purged and cleansed.

If I get her, I'll make her the star performer in the whole field, he thought greedily, they'll talk about the Sonder

Ditch from Wall Street to the Bourse, and about the man who is running her. I know how to do it too. I'll cut the costs to the bone, I'll tighten her up solid. Frank Lemmer was a good man, he could get the stuff out of the ground, but he let it creep up on him. It cost him almost nine rand a ton to mill it.

Well, I'll get it out as well as he did *and* I'll get it out cheaper. An operation takes its temperament from the man at the head. Frank Lemmer would talk about costs every now and then, but he didn't mean it and we knew he didn't mean it. We have become a wasteful operation because we are on a rich reef, we have become big spenders. Well, I'm going to talk costs, and I'll skin the arse of anybody who thinks I'm joking.

Last year Hamilton at Western Holdings kept his working costs per ton milled down to just a touch over six rand. I could do the same here! I could jump our profits twelve million Rand in one year, if only they give me the job I'll shout the Sonder Ditch's name across the financial markets of the world.

The problem that Rod was pondering was the nightmare of the gold mining industry. Since the 1930s the price of gold had been fixed at $35 a fine ounce. Each year since then the cost of mining had crept up steadily. In those days they reckoned four penny-weights of gold in a ton of ore was payable value. Now around eight penny-weights was the marginal value.

So in the interim all those millions of tons of ore whose values fell between four and eight penny-weights had been placed beyond the reach of man until such time as they increased the price of gold.

There were many mines with vast reserves of goldbearing ore, millions in bullion, whose values lay just below the magical number eight. Those mines stood deserted and forlorn, rust reddening their headgears, and the corrugated iron roofs of the buildings collapsing wearily. Rising costs had shot the guts out of them, they were condemned by the single word 'UNPAY'.

The Sonder Ditch was running twenty to twenty-five penny-weights per ton. She was fat, but she could be fatter, Rod decided.

There was a knock at the door.

'Come in!' called Rod, and looked at his watch. It was nine o'clock already. Time for the Monday meeting of his mine captains.

They came in singly and in pairs, twelve of them. These were Rod's front-line men, his combat officers. They went down there each day, each to his own section, and directed the actual assault on the rock.

While they chatted idly, waiting for the meeting to begin, Rod looked them over surreptitiously and was reminded of a remark that Herman Koch of Anglo American had made to him once.

'Mining is a hard game, and it attracts a hard breed of men.'

These were men of the hard breed, physically and mentally tough, and Rod realized with a start that he was one of them. No, more than one of them. He was their leader, and with a fierce affection and pride he opened the meeting.

'Right, let's hear your gripes. Who is going to be first to break my heart?'

There are some men with a talent for controlling, and getting the very best results out of other men. Rod was one of them. It was more than his physical size, his compelling voice and hearty chuckle. It was a special magnetism, a personal charm and unerring sense of timing. Under his chairmanship the meeting would erupt, voices crackle and snap, then subside into chuckles and nods as Rod spoke.

They knew he was as tough as they were, and they respected that. They knew that when he spoke it made sense, so they listened. They knew that when he promised, he delivered, so they were placated. And they knew that when he made a decision or judgement, he acted upon it, so every man knew exactly where he stood.

If asked, any one of these mine captains would have admitted grudgingly that 'there was no bulldust in Ironsides'. This was the equivalent of a presidential citation.

'Very well then.' Rod terminated the meeting. 'You have spent a good two hours of the company's time beating your gums. Now, will you kindly haul arse, go down there and start sending the stuff out.'

– 15 –

As these men planned the week's operation, so their men were at work in the earth below them.

On 87 level, Kowalski moved like a great bear down the dimly-lit drive. He had switched off the lamp on his helmet, and he moved without sound, lightly for a man of such bulk. He heard their voices ahead of him in the dimly-lit tunnel, and he paused, listening intently. There was no sound of shovel crunching into loose rock, and Kowalski's Neanderthal features convulsed into a fearsome scowl.

'Bastards!' he muttered softly. 'They think I am in stopes, hey? They think it all right if they sit on fat black bum, no move da bloody rock, hey?'

He started forward again, a bear on cat's feet.

'They find plenty different from what they bloody think, soon!' he threatened.

He stepped round the angle of the drive and flashed his lamp. There were three men Kowalski had put on lashing, shovelling the loose stuff from the footwall into waiting cocopans. Two of them sat against the cocopan, smoking contentedly while the third regaled them with an account of a beer drink he had attended the previous Christmas.

Their shovels and sledge hammers leaned unemployed against the side wall of the drive.

All three of them froze into rigidity as the beam of Kowalski's lamp played over them.

'So!' The word burst explosively from Kowalski, and he snatched up a fourteen-pound hammer in one massive fist, reversed it and struck the butt of the handle against the foot wall. The steel head of the hammer fell off and Kowalski was left with a four-foot length of selected hickory in his hand.

'You, boss boy!' he bellowed, and his free hand shot out and fastened on the throat of the nearest Bantu. With one heave he jerked him off his feet onto his knees and began dragging him away up the drive. Even in his rage, Kowalski was making sure there were no witnesses. The other two men sat where they were, too horrified to move, while their companion's wails and cries receded into the darkness.

Then the first blow reverberated in the confined space of the drive, followed immediately by a shriek of pain.

The next blow, and another shriek.

The crack, thud, crack, thud, went on repeatedly, but the accompanying shrieks dwindled into moans and soft whimperings, then into complete silence.

Kowalski came back down the drive alone, he was sweating heavily in the lamp light, and the handle of the hammer in his hand was black and glistening with wet blood.

He threw it at their feet.

'Work!' he growled, and was gone, big and bearlike, into the shadows.

16

On 100 level, Joseph M'Kati was hosing down and sweeping the spillings from under the giant conveyor belt. Joseph had been on this job for five years, and he was a contented and happy man.

Joseph was a Shangaan approaching sixty years of age; the first frost was touching his hair. There were laughter lines around his eyes and at the corner of his mouth. He wore his helmet pushed to the back of his head, his overalls were hand-embroidered and ornamentally patched in blue and red, and he moved with a jaunty bounce and strut.

The conveyor was many hundreds of yards long. From all the levels above the shattered gold reef was scraped from the stopes and trammed back down the haulages in the cocopans. Then from the cocopans it was tipped into the mouths of the ore-passes. These were vertical shafts that dropped down to 100 level, hundreds of feet through living rock to spew the reef out onto the conveyor belt. A system of steel doors regulated the flow of rock onto the conveyor, and the moving belt carried it down to the shaft and dumped it into enormous storage bins. From there it was fed automatically into the ore cage in fifteen-ton loads and carried at four-minute intervals to the surface.

Joseph worked on happily beneath the whining conveyor. The spillings were small, but important. Gold is strange in its behaviour, it moves downwards. Carried by its own high specific gravity it works its way down through almost any other material. It would find any crack or irregularity in the floor and work its way into it. It would disappear into the solid earth itself if left long enough.

It was this behaviour of gold that accounted in some measure for Joseph M'Kati's contentment. He had worked his way to the end of the conveyor, washing and sweeping, and now he straightened, laid his bast broom aside and rubbed his kidneys with both hands, looking quickly around to make certain that there was no one else in the conveyor tunnel. Beside him was the ore storage bin into which the conveyor was emptying its load. The bin could hold many thousands of tons.

Satisfied that he was alone, Joseph dropped onto his hands and knees and crawled under the storage bin, ignoring the continuous roar of rock into the bin above him, working his way in until he reached the holes.

It had taken Joseph many months to chisel the heads off four of the rivets that held the seam in the bottom of the bin, but once he had done it, he had succeeded in constructing a simple but highly effective heavy media separator.

Free gold in the ore that was dumped into the storage bin immediately and rapidly worked its way down through the underlying rock, its journey accelerated by the vibration of the conveyor and bin as more reef was dropped. When the gold reached the floor of the bin, it sought an avenue through which to continue its downward journey, and it found Joseph's four rivet holes, beneath which he had spread a square of polythene sheet.

The gold-rich fines made four conical piles on the sheet of polythene, looking exactly like powdered black soot.

Crouched beneath the bin, Joseph carefully transferred the black powder to his tobacco pouch, replaced the polythene to catch the next filtering, stuffed the pouch into his hip pocket, and scrambled out from under the bin. Whistling a tribal planting tune Joseph picked up his broom and returned to the endless job of sweeping and hosing.

17

Johnny Delange was marking his shot holes. Lying on his side in the low stope of 27 section he was calculating by eye the angle and depth of a side cutter blast to straighten a slight bulge in his longwall.

In the Sonder Ditch they were on single blast. One daily, centrally fired, blast. Johnny was paid on *fathomage*, the cubic measure of rock broken and taken out of his stope. He must, therefore, position his shot holes to achieve the maximum disruption and blow-out from the face.

'So,' he grunted, and marked the position of the hole in red paint. 'And so.' With one bold stroke of the paint brush he set the angle on which his machine boy was to drill.

'Shaya, madoda!' Johnny clapped the shoulder of the black man beside him. 'Hit it, man.'

Machine boys were selected for stamina and physique; this one was a Greek sculpture in glistening ebony.

'Nkosi!' The machine boy grinned an acknowledgement, and with his assistant lugged his rock drill into position. The drill looked like a gargantuan version of a heavy-calibre machine gun.

The noise as the big Bantu opened the drill was shattering in the low-roofed, constricted space of the stope. The compressed air roared and fluttered into the drill, buffeting the eardrums. Johnny made the clenched-fist gesture of approval, and for a second they smiled at each other in the companionship of shared labour. Then Johnny crawled on up the stope to mark the next shot hole.

Johnny Delange was twenty-seven years old, and he was top rock breaker on the Sonder Ditch. His gang of forty-eight men were a tightly-knit team of specialists. Men fought each other for a place on 27 section, for that's where the money was. Johnny could pick and choose, so each month when the surveyors came in and measured up, Johnny Delange was way out ahead in fathomage.

Here was the remarkable position where the man at the lowest point of authority earned more than the man at the top. Johnny Delange earned more than the General Manager of the Sonder Ditch. Last year he had paid super-tax on an income of R22,000. Even a miner like Kowalski, who brutalized and bullied his gang until he was left with the dregs of the mine, would earn eight or nine thousand rand a year, about the same salary as an official of Rod Ironsides' rank.

Johnny reached the top of his longwall and painted in the last shot holes. Down the inclined floor of the stope below him all his drills were roaring, his machine boys lying or crouching behind them. He lay there on one elbow, removed his helmet and wiped his face, resting a moment.

Johnny was an extraordinary-looking young man. His long jet black hair was swept back and tied with a leather thong at the back of his head in a curlicue. His features were those of an American Indian, gaunt and bony. He had cut the sleeves out of his overalls to expose his arms – arms as muscular and sinuous as pythons, tattooed below the elbows, immensely powerful but supple. His body was the same, long and sinewy and powerful.

On his right hand he wore eight rings, two on each finger, and it was clear from the design of the rings that they were not merely ornamental. They were heavy gold rings with skull and cross-bones, wolves' heads and other irregularities worked into them, a mass of metal that formed a permanent knuckleduster. Of the big eyes in the one skull's head Rod Ironsides had once asked: 'Are those real rubies, Johnny?' And Johnny had replied seriously:

'If they aren't, then I've sure as hell been gypped out of three rand fifty, Mr Ironsides.'

Johnny Delange had been a really wild youngster, until

eight months ago. It was then he had met and married Hettie. Courtship and marriage occupying the space of one week. Now he was settling down very well. It was all of ten days since he had last fought anybody.

Lying in the stope he allowed himself five minutes to think about Hettie. She was almost as tall as he was, with a wondrously buxom body and chestnut red hair. Johnny adored her. He was not the best speech-maker in Kitchenerville when it came to expressing his affection, so he bought her things.

He bought her dresses and jewellery, he bought her a deep-freezer *and* a fifteen cubic foot Frigidaire, he bought her a Chrysler Monaco with leopard-skin upholstery and a Kenwood Chef. In fact, it was becoming difficult to enter the Delange household without tripping over at least one of Johnny's gifts to Hettie. The congestion was made more acute by the fact that living with them was Johnny's brother, Davy.

'Hell, man!' Happily Johnny shook his head. 'She's a bit of all-right, hey!'

There was an eye-level oven he had spotted in a furniture store in Kitchenerville the previous Saturday.

'She'll love that, man,' he muttered, 'and it's only four hundred rand. I'll get it for her on pay day.'

The decision made, he clapped his helmet onto his head and began crawling out of the stope. It was time now to go up to the station and collect the explosives for the day's blast.

His boss boy should have been waiting for him in the drive, and Johnny was furious to find no sign of him nor the piccaninny who was his assistant.

'Bastard!' he grunted, playing the beam of his lamp up and down the drive. 'He's been acting up like hell.'

The boss boy was a pock-marked Swazi, not a big man, but powerful for his size and highly intelligent. He was also a man of mean disposition; Johnny had never seen him smile, and for an extrovert like Johnny it was galling to work with someone so sullen and taciturn. He tolerated the Swazi because of his drive and reliability, but he was the only man in the gang that Johnny disliked.

'Bastard!' The drive was deserted, the roar of the rock drills was muted.

'Where the hell is he?' Johnny scowled impatiently. 'I'll skin him when I find him.'

Then he remembered the latrine.

'That's where he is!' Johnny set off down the drive. The latrine was a rock chamber cut into the side of the drive. A flap of canvas served as a door; beyond was a regular four-holer over sanitary buckets.

Johnny pulled the canvas aside and stepped into the cubicle. The boss boy and his assistant were there. Johnny stared in surprise, for a moment not understanding what they were doing. They were so absorbed they were unaware of Johnny's presence.

Suddenly realization dawned, and Johnny's face tightened with revulsion and disgust.

'You filthy—' Johnny snarled, and catching the boss boy by the shoulders pulled him backwards and pinned him against the wall. He lifted his heavily metalled fist and drew it back ready to hurl it into the boss boy's face.

'Strike me and you know what happens,' said the boss boy softly, his expression flat and neutral, looking steadily into Johnny's eyes. Johnny hesitated. He knew the Company rules, he knew the Government labour officers' attitude, he knew what the police would do. If he hit him, they would crucify him.

'You are a pig!' Johnny hissed at him.

'You have a wife,' said the boss boy. 'My wife is in Swaziland. Two years I have not seen her.'

Johnny lowered his fist. Twelve thousand men, and no women. It was a fact. The actuality sickened him, but he understood why it happened.

'Get dressed.' He stepped back, releasing the boss boy. 'Get dressed both of you. Come to the station. I will meet you there.'

– 18 –

For a week now, since the fall of hanging in 43 section, Big King had been out of the stopes.

Rod had ordered it that way. The excuse was that Big King's white miner had been killed in the fall and now he must await an allocation to another section. In reality Rod wanted to rest him. He had seen the strain both physical and emotional that Big King had undergone during the rescue. When together they had unearthed the miner's corpse, the man with whom Big King had worked and laughed, Rod had seen the tears roll unashamedly down Big King's cheeks as he picked up the body and held it easily against his chest.

'Hamba gahle, madoda,' Big King had muttered. 'Go in peace, man.'

Big King was a legend on the Sonder Ditch. They boasted about him; how much Bantu beer he could drink in a sitting, how much rock he could lash single-handed in a shift, how he could dance any other man off his feet. He had been awarded a total of over a thousand rand in bravery awards. Big King set the pace, others tried to equal him.

Rod had put him in charge of a transport team. For the first few days Big King had enjoyed the opportunity of showing off his strength and socializing, for the transport team moved about the workings allowing Big King to visit most of his numerous friends during a shift. But now Big King was becoming bored. He wanted to get back into the stopes.

'This,' he told his transport team contemptuously, 'is

work for old men and young women.' And with one snatch and lift he picked up a forty-four-gallon drum of dieseline and unaided placed it on the platform of the loco.

A forty-four-gallon drum of dieseline weighs a little over 800 lbs avoirdupois.

– 19 –

All this fuss for that. Davy Delange paused in his labour of tamping the Dynagel into the shot holes. He leaned forward to inspect the reef. In the face of the stope it was a black line, drawn against the blue quartz rock.

The carbon leader reef, it was called. A thin layer of carbon never more than a few inches thick, more often half an inch. Black soot, that's what it was. Davy shook his head thoughtfully. You could not even see the gold in it.

Davy was two years older than his brother Johnny, and there was no physical or mental resemblance between the two of them. Davy's sandy hair was cropped into a conventional 'short back and sides'. He wore no personal jewellery, and his manner was quiet and reserved.

Johnny was tall and lean, Davy squat and muscular. Johnny was extravagant, Davy careful beyond the point of meanness. Their only common trait was that they were both first-class miners. If Johnny broke more rock than Davy, it was only because Davy was more careful than Johnny; he did not take the same chances, he observed all the safety procedures which Johnny frequently flouted.

Davy earned less money than Johnny, but saved every penny he could. It was for his farm. Davy was going to buy a farm one day. Already he had saved a little over R49,000 towards it. In five more years he would have enough. Then he could get himself a farm and a wife to help run it. Johnny, on the other hand, spent every penny he earned. He was usually in debt to Davy by the end of each month.

'Lend us a hundred till pay day, Davy.' Disapprovingly, Davy lent him the money. Davy disapproved of Johnny, his appearance, attire and habits.

Abandoning his microscopic inspection of the carbon leader reef, Davy resumed tamping in the explosive, working carefully and precisely on this highly dangerous procedure. The sticks of explosive were charged with detonators and ready to burn. By law, nobody but the miner-in-charge could perform this operation, but Davy did it automatically while he thought about Johnny's latest trespass. He had raised Davy's rent.

'A hundred rand a month!' Davy protested aloud. 'I've got a good mind to move out and find my own digs.'

But he knew he would do no such thing. Hettie's cooking was too good, and her presence too feminine and alluring. Davy would stay on with them.

– 20 –

'Rod.' Dan Stander's voice was serious and low. 'I've got a nasty one for you.'

'Thanks for nothing.' Rod made his own voice weary and resigned as he spoke into the telephone. 'I'm just going on my underground tour. Can't it wait?'

'No,' Dan assured him. 'Anyway, it's on your way. I'm speaking from the first-aid station at the shaft head. Come across.'

'What is it?'

'Assault. White on Bantu.'

'Christ.' Rod jerked upright in his chair. 'Bad?'

'Ugly. Worked him over with the handle of a fourteen-pound hammer. I've put in forty-seven stitches, but I am worried about a fracture of the skull.'

'Who did it?'

'Miner by the name of Kowalski.'

'Him!' Rod was breathing heavily. 'All right, Dan. Can he make a statement?'

'No. Not for a day or two.'

'I'll be there in a few minutes.'

Rod hung up the phone and crossed the office.

'Dimitri.'

'Boss?'

'Pull Kowalski out of the stopes. I want him in my office soonest. Put someone in to finish his shift.'

'Okay, Rod, what's the trouble?'

'He beat up one of his boys.'

Dimitri whistled softly, and Rod went on.

'Call personnel, get them onto the police.'

'Okay, Rod.'

'Have Kowalski here when I get back from my tour.'

Dan was waiting for him in the first-aid room.

'Take a look.' He indicated the figure on the stretcher. Rod knelt beside him, his mouth tightening into a thin pale line.

The catgut stitches lay neatly across the dark swollen gashes in the man's flesh. One ear had been torn off, and Dan had sewn it back on. There was a black gap where teeth had been behind the swollen purple lips.

'You will be all right now.' Rod spoke gently, and the Bantu's eyes swivelled towards him. 'The man who did this will be punished.'

Rod stood up. 'Let me have a written report on his injuries, Dan.'

'I'll fix it. See you for a drink at the Club after work?'

'Sure,' said Rod, but underneath he was seething with anger, and it stayed with him during the whole of his underground tour.

21

R od dropped straight down to 100 level. His first duty was to get the stuff out, and he wanted to check the reserve in the ore storage bins. He came into the long brightly-lit tunnel beneath the ore passes, and paused. The loaded conveyor belt whined monotonously, speeding the broken reef towards the bins.

The tunnel was deserted, except for the lonely figure of the sweeper at the far end. It was one of the phenomena of a well-run gold mine that in a tour through the workings you encountered so few human beings. Mile after mile of haulage and drive were silent and devoid of life, and yet there were 12,000 men down here.

Rod set off towards the bins at the shaft end of the tunnel.

'Joseph,' he greeted the old sweeper with a smile.

'Nkosi.' Joseph ducked and bobbed with shy pleasure.

'All is well?' Rod asked. Joseph was one of Rod's favourites, he was always so cheerful, so uncomplaining, so patently honest and without guile. Rod always made a point of stopping to chat to him.

'It is well with me, Nkosi. Is it well with you?'

Rod's smile died suddenly, he had noticed the fine white powdering of dust on Joseph's upper lip.

'You old rogue!' he scolded him. 'How often must I tell you to hose down before you sweep? Water! You must use water!'

This was part of the ceaseless battle of the miner to keep down the dust.

'The dust will eat your lungs!'

Phthisis, the dread incurable occupational disease of the miner, caused by silica particles being drawn into the lungs and there solidifying.

Joseph grinned shamefaced, shifting from one foot to the

other. He was always embarrassed by Rod's childish obsession with dust. In Joseph's opinion this was one of the few flaws in Rod Ironsides' character. Apart from this weird delusion that dust could hurt a man, he was a good boss.

'It is much harder to sweep wet dirt than dry dirt,' Joseph explained patiently. Rod never seemed to understand this self-evident fact, Joseph had to point it out to him every time they had this particular discussion.

'Listen to me, old man, without water the dust will enter your body.' Rod was exasperated. 'The dust will kill you!'

Joseph bobbed again, grinning at Rod to placate him.

'Very well, I will use plenty water.'

To prove it he picked up the hose and began spraying the floor with enthusiasm.

'That is good!' Rod encouraged him. 'Use plenty of water.' And Rod went on down to the storage bins.

When Rod was out of sight, Joseph turned off the hose and leaned on his broom.

'The dust will kill you!' he mimicked Rod, and chuckled merrily, shaking his head in wonder at the childishness of it.

'The dust will kill you!' he repeated, and burst into delighted laughter, slapping his thigh.

He did a few shuffling dance steps, it was so funny.

The dance steps were awkward, for under his trousers, strapped to the calves of both legs, were heavy polythene bags filled with gold fines from under the bins.

22

Rod stepped out of the Mary Anne at 85 level, and paused to watch Big King loading a baulk of timber onto the loco while his transport team stood back respectfully and watched him. Turning from his task Big King saw Rod standing on the station landing and marched up to him.

'I see you,' he greeted Rod. Big King was not one to make hasty judgements, it was only after the rescue operations in 43 section that he had decided Rod was a man. He was now ready to accept him as an equal.

'I see you also, King Nkulu.' Rod returned the greeting.

'Find me work with men. I sicken of this.'

'You will be back in the stopes before the week is ended,' Rod promised.

'You are my father,' Big King thanked him and went back to the transport team.

23

Johnny Delange saw the Underground Manager coming up the haulage towards him. There was no mistaking that tall wide-shouldered silhouette, nor the man's free swinging stride.

'Whee!' Johnny whistled with relief, grateful for the premonition that had warned him to pack the fifty-pound cardboard cartons of Dynagel into the explosives locker of the railway truck, rather than, as he usually did, pile them haphazard onto the platform in defiance of safety standards.

'Stop!' Johnny commanded the boss boy and his assistant who were pushing the truck, and it trundled to a halt beside Rod.

'Morning, Johnny.'

'Hello, Mr Ironsides.'

'How's it going?'

Johnny hesitated before replying, and immediately Rod was aware of the tension between the three men. He glanced at the two Swazis, they were sullen and apprehensive.

'There's been trouble,' he thought. 'Not like Johnny, he's too clever to let tension cut down his fathomage.'

'Well—' Johnny paused again. 'Look, Mr Ironsides, get rid of this bastard for me.' He jerked his thumb at the boss boy. 'Give me someone else.'

'What's the trouble?'

'No trouble, I just can't work with him.'

Rod raised an eyebrow in disbelief, but turned to the boss boy.

'Are you happy in this section, or do you want transfer?'

'I want transfer!' growled the boss boy.

'Right.' Rod was relieved, sometimes in a case like this the Swazi would refuse transfer. 'Tomorrow you will be told your new section.'

'Nkosi!' The boss boy glanced sideways at his assistant. 'It is the wish of my friend that he transfers with me.'

So that's it, Rod thought, the ever-present spectre which we must ignore because we can find no way to lay it. Johnny had probably caught them at it.

'Your friend shall go with you,' Rod nodded, telling himself that this was not condonation, but merely practical politics. If he separated them, the boss boy would pick on someone else who might not be receptive. Then there would be more trouble, stabbings, faction fighting.

'I'll get you a replacement,' he told Johnny, and then suddenly a thought occurred to him. My God, yes! What a team they would make!

'Johnny, how would you like Big King?'

'Big King!' Johnny's gaunt bony features split into a wide smile. 'Now you're talking, boss!'

24

At three o'clock Rod had finished his tour and was in the cage on the way to the surface. The cage was crowded, men pressed shoulder to shoulder, the stench of sweat almost overpowering. They were hauling shift now, the day's work was over, the stopes were scraped and washed down, the shot holes drilled and charged, the fuses connected into the electrical circuit.

The men were out of the stopes now, falling back in orderly companies and battalions along the haulages to the stations. There to wait patiently for their turn to enter the cages and be whisked to the surface.

Rod was mulling over the myriad problems he had encountered during the day, and the solutions he had dreamed up. He had opened a new section in the back pages of his notebook and headed it simply 'COSTS'.

Already there were two entries there. Let them give me the job, he thought fervently, just let me have it one month and I'll move the world.

'Mr Ironsides.' The man beside him spoke. Rod glanced down at him recognizing him.

'Hello, Davy.' It was remarkable how dissimilar the two brothers were.

'Mr Ironsides, my boss boy has worked his ticket. He's going home at the end of the month. Can you see that I get a good man to replace him?'

'Your brother's boss boy has asked for transfer. Will you take him?'

'Ja!' Davy Delange nodded. 'I know him, he's a good boy.'

And that takes care of one more detail, thought Rod, as he stepped out of the cage into a bright summer's afternoon and tasted the fresh sweet air with pleasure. Now there are only the butt ends of the day's work to tidy up. Then I can go and fetch the drink that Dan promised me.

Dimitri met him in the passage outside the office.

'I've got Kowalski in my office.'

'Good,' said Rod grimly. He went into his own office and sat on the edge of his desk.

'Send him in,' he called through to Dimitri.

Kowalski came through the door and stopped. He stood very still, his long arms hanging slackly at his side, his belly bulging out over his belt.

'You call me,' he muttered thickly, his English hardly intelligible. It was a peasant's face, coarse-featured, dull-eyed. He had not shaved, dirt from the stopes clung in the thick black stubble of beard.

'You beat a man today?' Rod asked softly.

'He no work,' Kowalski nodded. 'I beat him. Maybe next time his brothers they work. No bloody nonsense!'

'You're fired,' said Rod. 'Pull your time and get the hell off this property.'

'You fire?' Kowalski blinked in surprise.

'There will be criminal charges pressed against you by the Company.' Rod went on. 'But in the meantime I want you off the property.'

'Police?' Kowalski growled. There was expression on his face now.

'Yes,' said Rod, 'police.'

The spade-sized hands at the end of Kowalski's arms balled slowly into massive fists.

'You call da bloody police!' He took a step towards the desk, big, menacing.

'Dimitri,' Rod called sharply, 'close the door.'

Dimitri had been listening intently, now he jumped up from his desk and closed the interleading door. He stood with his ear pressed to the panelling. For thirty seconds more there was the growl and mutter of voices, then suddenly a thud, a bellow, another thud and a shattering crash.

Dimitri winced theatrically.

'Dimitri!' Rod's voice, and he pushed the door open.

Rod sat on the edge of his desk, swinging one leg casually, he was sucking the knuckle of his right hand.

'Dimitri, tell them not to put so much polish on the floor. Our friend slipped and hit his jaw on the desk.'

Dimitri clucked sympathetically as he stood over the reclining hulk of the big Pole. Kowalski was snoring loudly through his mouth.

'Gave himself a nasty bump,' said Dimitri. 'Shame!'

– 25 –

Dr Steyner worked on quietly for the remainder of Monday morning. He favoured the use of a tape recorder, for this cut out human contact which Manfred found vaguely repellent. He disliked having to speak his thoughts to a female who sat opposite him with skirts up around her thighs, squirming her bottom and touching her hair. However, what he really could not abide was the odour. Manfred was very sensitive to smells, even his own body smell of perspiration disgusted him. Women, he found, had a peculiar cloying odour that he could detect beneath their perfume and cosmetics. It nauseated him. This was why he had insisted on separate bedrooms for Theresa and himself. Naturally he had not told her the reason, but had insisted instead that he was such a light sleeper that he could not share a room with another person.

His office was in white and ice-blue, the air clean and cold from the air-conditioning unit, his voice was crisp and impersonal, the whirr of the recorder subdued, and with the conscious portion of his mind Manfred was happily absorbed in his conjuring tricks with figures and money, past performance and future estimates, a three-dimensional structure of variables and contingencies which only a super-normal brain could visualize. But beneath it was a sense of disquiet; he was waiting, hanging in time, and the outward sign of his agitation was the way the fingers of his right hand ran up and down his thigh as he worked, a caressing narcissistic gesture.

A few minutes before noon the unlisted direct telephone on his desk rang, and the movement of his hand stilled. Only one caller could reach him here, only one caller had that number. For a few seconds he sat unmoving, delaying the moment, then deliberately he switched off the recorder and lifted the telephone.

'Dr Manfred Steyner.' He identified himself.

'You have got our man in?' the voice enquired.

'Not yet, Andrew.'

There was silence from the other end, a dangerous crackling silence.

'But there is no cause for alarm. It is nothing. A delay merely, not a setback.'

'How long?'

'Two days – at the latest by the end of the week.'

'You will be in Paris next week?'

'Yes.' Manfred was an adviser to the Government team which was to meet the French for gold price talks.

'He will meet you there. It would be best for you that your side of the bargain were completed by then. You understand?'

'I understand, Andrew.'

The discussion was ended, but Manfred interjected to prevent the caller from hanging up.

'Andrew!'

'Yes.'

'Will you ask him if—' Manfred's tone had changed almost imperceptibly, there was an obsequious edge in it. 'Ask him if I may play tonight, please, Andrew.'

'Wait.'

The minutes drifted by, and then the voice came back on the line.

'Yes, you may play. Simon will inform you of your limits.'

'Thank you. Tell him, thank you.'

Manfred made no effort to conceal his relief as he cradled the receiver. He sat beaming at the ice-blue paper on the far wall of his office, even his spectacles seemed to sparkle.

– 26 –

There were five men in the opulently furnished room. One of the men was subservient to the others, he was younger than they, attentive to their moods and wishes. Clearly he was a servant. Of the remaining four, one was just as obviously the host. He was seated at the focus of all their attention. He was fat, but not excessively so, the fat of good living not of gluttony. He was speaking, addressing himself to his three guests.

'You have expressed doubts as to the reliability of the tool I intend using in the coming venture. I have arranged a demonstration which I hope will convince you that your concern is groundless. That is the reason for the invitation that Andrew here conveyed to you this afternoon.'

The host turned to the younger man. 'Andrew, would you be good enough to go through and wait for Dr Steyner to arrive; as soon as that happens, please let Simon seat him while you come through and inform us.' He gave his orders with dignity and courtesy, a man accustomed to command.

'Now, gentlemen, while we wait may I offer you a drink?'

The conversation that sprang up between the four of them as they sipped their drinks was knowledgeable, and extraordinarily well informed. At its root was one subject:

wealth. Mineral wealth, industrial wealth, the harvest of the land and the sea. Oil, steel, coal, fish, wheat and – gold.

There were clues to the stature of these men in the cut and quality of the cloth they wore, the sparkle of a stone on a finger, the tone of authority in a voice, the casual unaffected use of a high name.

'He is here, sir,' Andrew interrupted them from the doorway.

'Oh! Thank you, my boy.' The host stood up. 'Would you mind stepping this way, please, gentlemen.'

He crossed the room and drew aside one of the gold and maroon drapes. Behind it was a window.

The four men clustered about the window and looked through into the room beyond. It was a gaming room of an expensive gambling establishment. There were men and women sitting about a baccarat table, and none of them so much as glanced up at the window overlooking them.

'This is a one-way glass, gentlemen,' the host explained. 'So you need not worry about being seen in such a den of iniquity.'

They chuckled politely.

'What kind of profit does this place show you?' one of them asked.

'My dear Robert!' The host feigned shock. 'You don't for a moment believe that I would be in any way associated with an illegal undertaking?'

This time they chuckled with genuine amusement.

'Ha!' exclaimed the host. 'Here he is.'

Across the gaming room Dr Manfred Steyner was being ushered to a seat at the table by a tall sallow-faced young man, who in his evening dress looked like an undertaker.

'I have asked Simon to place him so that you may watch his face as he plays.'

They were intent now, leaning forward slightly, scrutinizing the man as he arranged the plaques that Simon had stacked at his elbow.

Dr Manfred Steyner began to play. His face was completely devoid of expression, but the pallor was startling. Every few seconds the pink tip of his tongue slipped out between his lips, then disappeared again. In the intervals between each coup, there was a reptilian stillness about him, the stillness of a lizard or an iguana. Only a pulse beat steadily in his throat and his spectacles glittered like a snake's eyes.

'May I direct your attention to his right hand during the play of this coup,' the host murmured, and all their eyes flicked downwards.

Manfred's right hand lay open beside the pile of his chips, but as his card was laid before him so his fingers closed.

'*Carte.*' Soundlessly he mouthed the word, and now his hand was a fist, the knuckles whitened, the tension was so fierce that his fist trembled. Yet, still his face was neutral.

The banker flipped his card.

'*Sept!*' The croupier's mouth formed the number. He faced Manfred's card, then he swept Manfred's stake away. Manfred's hand flopped open and lay soft and hairless as a dead fish on the green baize.

'Let us leave him to his pleasures,' suggested the host and drew the curtains across the window. They returned to their chairs, and they were strangely subdued.

'Jesus,' muttered one of the guests. 'That was ugly. I felt like a peeping Tom, like watching someone, you know, pulling his pudding.'

The host glanced at him quickly, surprised at his perception.

'In effect, that is exactly what you were watching,' he told him. 'You will excuse me playing the role of lecturer, but I know a little about this man. It cost me nearly four hundred rand for an analytic report on him by one of our leading psychiatrists.'

The host paused, assuring himself of their complete attention.

'The reasons are obscure, probably arising from an event or series of events during the period in which Dr Steyner was an orphan wandering through the smoking ruins of war-torn Europe.' The host coughed, deprecating his own flight of oratory. 'Be that as it may. The results are there for all to see. Dr Manfred Kurt Steyner's intelligence quotient is a genius rating of 158. He neither smokes nor drinks. He has no hobbies, plays no sport, has never made so much as an improper remark to any woman other than his wife, and there is some doubt as to just how often or to what extent she is favoured by his attentions.' The host sipped his drink conscious of their intense interest. 'Mechanically, if that is the correct term, Dr Steyner is neither impotent nor deficient in his manhood. However, he finds all bodily contact, and especially the secretions that may arise from such contact, to be utterly loathsome. For arousal he relies on the baccarat cards, for release he might endure a brief contact with a member of the opposite sex, but more likely he would – oh, what was the expression you used, Robert?'

They absorbed this in silence.

'He is, to be precise, a compulsive gambler. He is also a compulsive loser.'

They stirred with disbelief.

'You mean he tries to lose?' demanded Robert incredulously.

'No.' The host shook his head. 'Not on the conscious level. He believes he is trying to win, but he lays bets against odds that, with his magnificent brain, he must realize are suicidal. It is a deep-seated subconscious need to lose, to be humiliated. A form of masochism.'

The host opened a black leather notebook and checked its contents.

'During the period from 1958 to 1963 Dr Steyner lost

73

the total sum of R227,000 at this table. In 1964 he was able to arrive at an arrangement with his sole creditor to discharge the debt plus the accumulated interest.'

You could see the faces change as they rapidly searched their memories for a set of circumstances which would fit the dates and principals. Robert reached the correct deduction first. In 1964 their host had sold his majority holdings in the North Maun Copper Co. to CRC at a price that could only be considered advantageous. Just prior to this Dr Steyner had been made head of finance and planning at CRC.

'North Maun Copper,' said Robert with admiration. That is how he had done it, the cunning old fox! He had forced Steyner to buy well above market value.

The host smiled softly, deferentially, neither confirming nor denying.

'Since 1964 to the present Dr Steyner has continued to patronize this establishment. His gambling losses for this further period amount to—' He consulted his notebook again, pretending surprise at the figure, 'to a touch over R300,000.'

They sighed and moved restlessly. Even to these men it was a very large sum of money.

'I think we can rely on him.' The host closed his notebook with a snap, and smiled around at them.

– 27 –

Theresa lay in the dark. The night was warm, the stillness spoiled only by the klonking of a frog down at the fishpond. The moonlight came in through the window, playing shadow pictures through the branches of the Pride of India tree onto the wall of her bedroom.

She threw back the single sheet, and swung her legs off the bed. She could not sleep, it was too warm, her nightdress kept binding under her armpits. She stood up and on a sudden reckless impulse she drew the nightdress off over her head and tossed it through the open door of her dressing-room, then, naked, she walked out onto the wide veranda. Into the moonlight, with the cool stone flags under her bare feet, and the warm night air moving like the touch of fairy hands on her skin.

She felt suddenly devilish and daring, she wanted to run down across the lawns and to have someone catch her doing it. She giggled, uncertain of this mood. It was so far removed from Manfred's conception of a good German Hausfrau's behaviour.

'He'd be furious,' she whispered with wicked delight, and then she heard the motor of the car.

She froze with horror, the headlights flicked through the trees as the car came up the driveway and she darted back into her room; in panic she dropped to her knees and searched for her nightgown, found it and ran to the bed as she dragged it on over her head.

She lay in the darkness and listened to the car door slam. There was silence until she heard him pass her door. His heels clacked on the yellow wood floor, he was almost running. Theresa knew the symptoms, the late night return, the suppressed urgency, and she lay rigid in her bed, waiting.

The minutes passed slowly, and then the interleading door from Manfred's suite swung open silently.

'Manfred, is that you?' She sat up and reached for the switch of the bedside lamp.

'Don't put the light on.' His voice was breathless, slurred as though he had been drinking but there was no trace of liquor on his breath as he stooped over her and kissed her. His lips were dry and tightly closed, as he slipped off his dressing-gown.

Two and a half minutes later he stood up from the bed, turning his back to Theresa as he quickly shrugged into the silk dressing-gown.

'Excuse me a minute, Theresa.' The breathlessness was gone from his voice. He went through the door of his own suite, and seconds later she heard the hiss of the shower and the tinkling splash of water.

She lay on her back and her fingernails cut into the palms of her hands. Her body was trembling with a mixture of revulsion and desire, it had been so fleeting a contact – enough to stir her, but so swift as to leave her with a feeling of having been used and sullied. She knew that the rest of the night would pass infinitely slowly, with restless burning tension, remorse and self-pity alternating with wild elation and half-crazed erotic fantasy.

'Damn him,' she screamed silently within her skull. 'Damn him! Damn him!'

She heard the shower stop, and then Manfred returned to her room. He smelt of 4711 Eau de Cologne, and he sat down carefully on the end of the bed.

'You may turn on the light, Theresa.'

It required a conscious effort for her to unclench her hand and reach out for the lamp switch. Manfred blinked behind his spectacles at the flood of light. His hair was damp and freshly combed, his cheeks shone like ripe apples.

'I hope you had an enjoyable day?' he asked, and listened seriously to her reply. Despite her tension, Theresa found herself falling under the almost hypnotic influence he wielded over her. His voice precise, almost monotonous. The glitter of his spectacles, the reptilian stillness of his body and features.

As she had so many times before, she thought of herself as a warm fluffy rabbit sitting tense and fascinated before the cobra.

'It is late,' he said at last and he stood up.

Looking down at her as she lay cuddled into the white silk sheets, he asked with as little emphasis as if he were requesting her to pass the sugar: 'Theresa, could you raise three hundred thousand rand without your grandfather knowing?'

'Three hundred thousand!' She sat up startled.

'Yes. Could you?'

'Good Lord, Manfred, that's a small fortune.' She truly saw nothing unusual in her choice of adjective. 'You know it's all in the Trust Fund, well, most of it. There is the farm and the – no, I couldn't find half of that without Pops knowing.'

'Pity,' murmured Manfred.

'Manfred, you aren't in – difficulties?'

'No. Good Lord, no. It was just a thought. Forget that I asked. Good night, Theresa, I hope you sleep well.'

Involuntarily she lifted her hands towards him in invitation.

'Good night, Manfred.'

He turned and left the room, she let her hands fall to her sides. For Theresa Steyner the long night had begun.

– 28 –

'Ladies and Gentlemen, it is customary for the General Manager to introduce the distinguished guest who presents our special service awards. Last week, in tragic circumstances, our General Manager, Mr Frank Lemmer, was killed in the Company's service, a loss which we all bitterly regret, and I am sure you all join me in sincere condolence to Mrs Eileen Lemmer.' Rod paused for the acknowledging murmur from his audience. There were 200 of them packed into the Mine Club hall. 'It falls upon me, therefore, as Acting General Manager, to introduce to you Dr Manfred Steyner who is a senior Director of Central Rand Consolidated, our parent company. He is also head of the Departments of Finance and Planning.'

Sitting beside her husband, Theresa Steyner had noticed

Manfred's irritation at Rod's mention of Frank Lemmer. It was company policy not to draw public attention to accidental death or injury inflicted on employees by the Company's operation. She liked Rod the better for his small tribute to Frank Lemmer.

Theresa was wearing sunglasses, for her eyes were swollen and red. In the dawning, after a sleepless night, she had succumbed suddenly to a fit of bitter weeping. The tears were without cause, or reason, and had left her feeling strangely lightheaded and with a brittle sense of well-being. However, her enormous eyes always showed up badly for hours after she had wept.

She sat with her legs demurely crossed, immaculate in a suit of cream shantung, a black silk scarf catching her hair and then letting it fall in a dark glossy brown cascade onto her shoulders. She leaned forward in polite attention to the speaker, one elbow on her knee, her chin cupped in her palm, one long tapered finger against her cheek. A lady with diamonds on her fingers and pearls at her throat, smiling an acknowledgement at Rod's reference to 'the lovely granddaughter of our Chairman'.

Except for the slight incongruity of the sunglasses, she was the perfect image of the young matron. Polished, poised, cosseted, secure in her unassailable virtue and duty.

However, the thoughts that were running through Theresa Steyner's head, and the flutterings and sensations that were prickling and tickling her, had they been known, would have broken up the assembly in disorder. All the formless fantasy and emotional disturbance of the previous night were now directed at one target – Rodney Ironsides. Suddenly, with a start of amusement and alarm, she was aware of a phenomenon that she had last experienced many years ago. She moved quickly, shifting her seat, for the cream shantung marked so easily with any moisture.

'Terry Steyner!' she thought, deliciously shocked at

herself, and found with relief that Rod had finished speaking and Manfred was standing up to reply. She joined in the applause enthusiastically to distract her errant fancy.

Manfred briefly mentioned the six gentlemen sitting in the front row of seats whose courage and devotion to duty they had come to honour, he then went on into an exploration of the prospects of an increase in the price of gold. In measured, carefully considered terms, he set out the advantages and benefits that would accrue to the industry, the nation and the world at large. It was an erudite and convincing dissertation, and there was a large contingent of newspaper men to record it. The press had been alerted by the public relations department of CRC to the text of Dr Steyner's speech and all the leading dailies, weeklies, financial gazettes and journals were represented.

At intervals a photographer would come to crouch below the platform and pop a flash bulb up at Dr Steyner. On the eve of the gold price talks with France this would make good copy, for Steyner was the boy genius in the South African team.

The six heroes sat uncomfortably, forlorn in their best suits, scrubbed like schoolboys at a prize-giving ceremony, staring up at the speaker, not understanding a single word of the foreign language, but maintaining expressions of grave dignity.

Rod caught Big King's eye and winked at him. Solemnly Big King's right eyelid drooped and rose in reply, and quickly Rod averted his gaze to prevent himself laughing out loud.

He looked straight into Theresa Steyner's face, taking her completely off her guard. Not even the dark glasses could conceal her thoughts, they were as clear as if she had spoken them aloud. Before she could drop her eyes to examine the hem of her skirt, Rod knew with a stomach swoop of excitement how it could be if he chose.

With a new awareness he examined her from the corner

of his eye, seeing her for the first time as an accessible woman, a highly desirable woman, but nevertheless still the granddaughter of Hurry Hirschfeld and the wife of Manfred Steyner. This made her as dangerous as a force ten pressure burst, he knew, but the desire and temptation were hard to deny, inflamed perhaps rather than dampened by the danger.

He saw that she was blushing now, her fingers picking nervously at the hem of her skirt. She was as agitated as a schoolgirl, she knew he was watching her. Rod Ironsides, who until five minutes before had been thinking of nothing but his speech, now found himself impelled into a completely new and exciting dimension.

After the awards had been made, tea had been drunk, biscuits consumed and the crowd had dispersed, Rod escorted the Steyners down across the vivid green lawns of Kikuyu grass to where the chauffeur was holding the Daimler.

'What a magnificent physique that Shangaan has, what was his name – King?' Terry was walking between the two men.

'King Nkulu. Big King, we call him.'

Rod found his speech unsteady, he had stuttered slightly. This thing between the two of them was suddenly overpowering, it hummed like a turbine, making the space between them crackle with tension. Unless he was deaf, Manfred Steyner must be aware of it.

'He is pretty special. There is nothing he can't do, and do it far and away better than his nearest rival. My God, you should see him dance.'

'Dance?' enquired Terry with interest.

'Tribal dancing, you know.'

'Of course.' Terry hoped the relief in her voice was not obvious; she had been racking her badly flustered brain for an excuse to visit the Sonder Ditch again or have Rod Ironsides come to Johannesburg. 'I have a friend who is absolutely mad keen on seeing the dances. She pesters me every time I see her.'

Quickly she selected a name from her list of friends, she must have one ready should Manfred ask.

'They dance every Saturday afternoon, bring her out any time.' Rod fielded the ball neatly.

'What about this Saturday?' Terry turned to her husband, 'Would that be all right, Manfred?'

'What's that?' Manfred looked at her vaguely, he had not been following the conversation. Manfred Steyner was a worried man, he was pondering his obligation to gain control of the management of the Sonder Ditch within two days.

'May we come out here on Saturday afternoon to watch the tribal dancing?' Terry repeated her question.

'Have you forgotten that I fly to Paris on Saturday morning, Theresa?'

'Oh, dear.' Terry bit her lip thoughtfully. 'It *had* slipped my mind. What a pity, I would have enjoyed it.'

Manfred frowned slightly, irritated.

'My dear Theresa, there is no reason why you shouldn't come out to the Sonder Ditch without me. I am sure you will be safe enough in Mr Ironsides' hands.'

His choice of words brought the colour to Terry's cheeks again.

– 29 –

After the award ceremony, Big King's first stop was the Recruiting Agency office at the entrance to the No.1 shaft hostel. There were men clustered about the counter, but they stood aside for Big King and he acknowledged the courtesy by slapping their backs indiscriminately and greeting them with:

'Kunjane, madoda. How is it, men?'

The clerk behind the counter hurried to serve him. Up at the Mine Club Big King might be a little out of his depth, but here he was treated like a reigning monarch.

In two neat bundles Big King placed the award money on the counter.

'Twenty-five rand you will send to my senior wife.' He instructed the clerk. 'And twenty-five rand you will put to my book.'

Big King was scrupulously fair. Half of all his earnings was remitted to the senior of his four wives, and half was added to the substantial sum already credited in his savings bank passbook.

The Agency was the procurer of labour for the insatiably man-hungry gold mines of the Witwatersrand and Orange Free State. Its representatives operated across the southern half of the continent. From the swamps and fever lagoons along the great Zambesi, from among the palm groves fringing the Indian Ocean, out of these simmering plains that the bushmen called 'the big dry', down from the mountains of Basutoland and the grass lands of Swaziland and Zululand they gathered the Bantu, the men themselves completing the first fifty or sixty miles of the journey on foot. Individuals meeting on a footpath to become pairs, arriving at a little general dealer's store in the bleak scrub desert to find three or four others already waiting, the arrival of the recruiting truck with a dozen men and their luggage aboard, the long bumping grinding progress through the bush. The stops at which more men scrambled aboard, until a full truck load of fifty or sixty disembarked at a railway siding in the wilderness.

Here the tiny trickle of humanity joined a stream, and at the first major centre they trans-shipped and became part of the great flood that washed towards 'Goldi'.

However, once they had reached Johannesburg and been allocated to one of the sixty major gold mines, the Agency's obligations towards its recruits were not yet discharged.

Between them the employing mine and the Agency must provide each man with employment, training, advice and comfort, maintain contact between him and his family, for very few of them could write, reassure him when he worried that his goats were sick or his wife unfaithful. They must provide a banking and savings service with a personal involvement unknown to any commercial banking institute. They had, in short, to make certain that a man taken from an environment that had not changed in a thousand years and deposited into the midst of a sophisticated and technological society would retain his health, happiness and sanity, so that at the end of his contract he would return to the place from which he had come and tell them all how wonderful it was at 'Goldi'. He would show them his hard helmet, and his new suitcase crammed with clothes, his transistor radio and the little blue book with its printed figures, inflaming them also with the desire to make the pilgrimage, and keep the flood washing towards 'Goldi'.

Big King completed his business transactions and went in through the gates of the hostel. He was going to take advantage of the fact that he had missed the shift and would be among the first at the ablutions and dining-hall.

He went down across the lawns to his block. Despite the size of an establishment that housed 6,000 men, the Company had tried to make it as attractive as possible. The result was an unusual design, halfway between a motel and an advanced penitentiary.

As a senior boss boy, Big King rated a room of his own. An ordinary labourer would share with five others.

Carefully Big King brushed down his suit and hung it in the built-in cupboard, wiped down his glossy shoes and racked them, then with a towel around his waist he set off for the ablution block and was irritated to find it already filled with new recruits up from the acclimatization centre.

Big King ran an appraising eye over their naked bodies and judged that this batch must be nearing the completion of their eight-day acclimatization. They were sleek and shiny, the muscle definition showing clearly through the skin.

You could not take a man straight out of his village, probably suffering from malnutrition, and put him down a gold mine to lash and bar and drill in a dry bulb heat of 91° Fahrenheit and 84% relative humidity, without running a serious risk of killing him with heat stroke or exhaustion.

Every recruit judged medically fit to work underground went into acclimatization. For eight days, eight hours a day, he and hundreds of others stood with only a loin cloth about his middle in a vast barn-like hall stepping up onto and down from a platform. The height of the platform was carefully matched to the man's height and body weight, the speed of his movements was regulated by a flashing panel of lights, the temperature and humidity were controlled at 91° and 84%, every ten minutes he was given water and his body temperature was registered by the half dozen trained medical assistants in charge of the room.

At the end of the eighth day he emerged as fit as an olympic athlete, and quite able to perform heavy physical labour in conditions of high temperature and humidity without discomfort or danger.

'Gwedeni!' growled Big King, and the nearest recruit, still white with soap suds, hurriedly vacated his shower with a respectful 'Keshle!' in deference to Big King's rank and standing. Big King removed his towel and stepped under the shower, revelling as always in the rush of hot water over his skin, flexing the great muscles of his arms and chest.

The messenger found him there.

'King Nkulu, I have word for thee.' The man used Shangaan, not the bastard Fanikalo.

'Speak,' Big King invited, soaping his belly and buttocks.

'The Induna bids you call at his house after you have eaten the evening meal.'

'Tell him I will attend his wishes,' said Big King and held his face up into the rush of steaming water.

Dressed in a white open-necked shirt and blue slacks, Big King sauntered down to the kitchens. Again the recruits were ahead of him, queueing with bowls in hand outside the serving hatches. Big King walked past them through the door marked 'No Admittance – Staff Only'.

The kitchens were cavernous, glistening with white porcelain tiles and stainless steel cookers and bins that could serve 18,000 hot meals a day.

When Big King entered a room, even one as large as this, no one was unaware of his presence. One of the assistant cooks snatched up a bowl not much smaller than a baby's bath, and hurried across to the nearest stainless steel bin. He opened the lid and looked expectantly at Big King. Big King nodded and the cook ladled about two litres of steaming sugar beans into the bowl, before passing on to the next bin where he again looked for and obtained Big King's approval. He added an equal quantity of mixed vegetables to the bowl, slammed down the lid and scampered across to where a second assistant waited with a spade beside yet another bin.

The spade was the same as those used for lashing gold reef underground, but the blade of this one had been polished to gleaming cleanliness. The second cook dug into the bin and came up with a spadeful of white maize porridge, cooked stiff as cake, the smell of it as saliva-making as the smell of new bread. This was the staple of Bantu diet. He deposited the spadeful in the bowl.

'I am hungry.' Big King spoke for the first time, and the second cook dug out another spadeful and added it to the bowl. They passed on to the end of the kitchens and at their approach another cook lifted the lid on a pressure cooker the size of a washing machine. From it arose a cloud of fragrant steam.

Apologetically the cook held out his hand and Big King produced his meat ticket. Meat was the only food that was rationed. Each man was limited to one pound of meat a day; the Company had long ago discovered to its astonishment and cost that a Bantu, offered unlimited supplies of fresh meat, was quite capable of eating his own weight of it monthly.

Having ascertained that Big King was entitled to his daily pound, the cook proceeded to ladle at least five pounds of it into the bowl.

'You are my brother,' Big King thanked him, and the little procession moved on to where yet another cook was filling a half-gallon jug of thick, gruel-like, mildly alcoholic Bantu beer from one of the multiple spiggots beneath the thousand-gallon tank.

The bowl and jug were ceremonially handed to Big King and he went out onto the covered terraces where benches and tables were set out for alfresco dining in mild weather.

While he ate, the terrace began to fill, for the shift was out of the mine now. Every man who passed his table greeted Big King, but only a few privileged persons took the liberty of seating themselves at the same table. One of them was Joseph M'Kati, the little old sweeper from 100 level.

'It has been a good week, King Nkulu.'

'You say so.' Big King was non-committal. 'I go now to a meeting with the Old One. Then we shall see.'

The Old One, the Shangaan Induna, lived in a Company house. A self-contained residence with lounge and dining-room, kitchen and bathroom. He was handsomely paid by the Company, provided with servants, food, furniture and all the other appurtenances of his rank and station.

He was the head of the Shangaan community on the Sonder Ditch. A chief of the blood, a greybeard and member of the tribal councils. In similar houses and with the same privileges and in equal style lived the Indunas of the other tribal groups that made up the labour force of the

Sonder Ditch. They were the paternal figureheads, the tribal jurists, ruling and judging within the framework of law and custom. The Company could not hope to maintain harmony and order without the assistance of these men.

'Baba!' Big King greeted his Induna from the doorway of his house, touching the forehead in respect not only for the man but also for what he represented.

'My son.' The Induna smiled his greeting. 'Come and sit by me.' He gestured for his servants to leave the room, and Big King went to squat at the feet of the old man. 'Is it true you go now to work with the mad one?' That was Johnny Delange's nickname.

They talked, the Induna questioning him on fifty matters that affected the welfare of his people. For Big King this was a comforting and nostalgic experience, for the Induna stood in the place of his father.

At last, satisfied, the Induna went on to other matters.

'There is a parcel ready tonight. Crooked Leg waits for you.'

'I shall go for it.'

'Go in peace then, my son.'

On his way through the gates of the hostel Big King stopped to chat with the guards. These men had the right to search over any person entering or leaving the hostel. Particularly they were concerned with preventing either women disguised as men or bottles of spirits entering the premises, both of which tended to have a disruptive effect on the community. As an afterthought they were also instructed to look out for stolen property entering or leaving. Big King had to ensure that none of them would ever, under any circumstances, take it into his head to search Big King.

While he stood at the gates, the last glow of the sunset faded and the lights began to come on across the valley. The clusters of red aerial warning lights atop the headgears, the massed yellow squares of the hotels, the strings of street lamps and the isolated pinpricks of the residential areas up on the ridge.

When it was truly dark, Big King left the guards and sauntered down the main road, until a bend in the road took him out of their sight. Then Big King left the road and started up the slope. He moved like a night animal, swiftly and with certainty of the path he followed.

He passed the ranch-type split-levels of the line management officials with their wide lawns and swimming-pools, pausing only once when a dog yapped nearby, then moving on again until he was into the broken rock and rank grass of the upper ridge; he crossed the skyline and started down the far side until he made out the grass-covered mound of rubble in the moonlight. He slowed and moved cautiously forward until he found the rusty barbed wire fence that guarded the entrance. He vaulted it easily and went on into the black mouth of the tunnel.

Fifty years before, a long-defunct mining company had suspected the existence of a gold reef in this area and had driven prospecting adits into the side of the ridge, exhausting its funds in the process, and finally abandoning the network of tunnels in despair.

Big King paused long enough to draw an electric torch from his pocket before going on into the tunnel, flashing the beam ahead of him. Soon the air stank of bats and their wings swished about his head. Unperturbed, Big King went on deeper and deeper into the side of the hill, taking a turning and fork in the tunnel without hesitation. At last there was a faint glow of yellow light ahead and Big King switched off his torch.

'Crooked Leg!' he called, his voice bounced and boomed along the tunnel. There was no reply.

'It is I, Big King!' he shouted again, and immediately a shadow detached itself from the sidewall and limped towards him, sheathing a wicked-looking knife as it came.

'All is ready.' The little cripple came to greet him. 'Come, I have it here.'

Crooked Leg had earned his limp and his nickname in a rockfall a dozen years ago. Now he owned and operated the concession photographic studio on the mine property, a flourishing enterprise, for dearly the Bantu love their own image on film. Not, however, as profitable as his nocturnal activities in the abandoned workings beyond the ridge.

He led Big King into a small rock chamber lit by a suspended hurricane lantern. Mingled with the bat stench was the acrid reek of sulphuric acid in high concentration.

On a wooden trestle table that occupied most of the chamber were earthenware jars, heavy glass bowls, polythene bags, and a variety of shoddy and very obviously second-hand laboratory equipment. In a clear space amongst all this clutter stood a large screw-topped bottle. The bottle was filled with a dirty yellow powder.

'Ha!' Big King exclaimed his pleasure. 'Plenty!'

'Yes. It has been a good week,' Crooked Leg agreed.

Big King picked up the bottle, marvelling once again at the unbelievable weight of it. This was not pure gold, for Crooked Leg's acid reduction methods were crude, but it was at least sixteen carats fine.

The bottle represented the week's collection of fines and concentrates by men like Joseph M'Kati from a dozen vulnerable points along the line of production; in some cases carried out from the company reduction works itself under the noses of the heavily armed guards.

All the men involved in this surreptitious milking off of the company's gold were Shangaans. There was only one man in whom was vested sufficient authority and prestige to prevent the greed and hostility which gold breeds from destroying the whole operation. That was the Shangaan Induna. There was only one man with the physical presence and necessary command of the Portuguese language to negotiate the disposal of the gold. That was Big King.

Big King placed the bottle in his pocket. The weight pulled his clothing out of shape.

'Run like a gazelle, Crooked Leg.' He turned back into the dark tunnel.

'Hunt like a leopard, King Nkulu,' chuckled the little cripple, as he disappeared into the moving shadows.

– 30 –

'A packet of Boxer tobacco,' said Big King. The eyes of José Almeida, the Portuguese owner of the mine concession store and the local roadhouse, narrowed slightly. He took down the yellow four-ounce packet from the shelves and handed it across the counter, accepted Big King's payment and counted the change into his palm.

He watched as the giant Bantu wandered down between the loaded shelves and racks of merchandise to disappear through the front door of the store into the night.

'Take charge,' he muttered in Portuguese to his plump little wife with her silky dark moustache, and she nodded in understanding, moving into José's place in front of the cash register. José went through into his storerooms and living quarters behind the store.

Big King was waiting in the shadows. When the back door opened he slipped through and José closed the door behind him. José led him through into a cubicle of an office, and from a cupboard he took down a jeweller's balance. Under Big King's watchful eye he began to weigh the gold.

José Almeida purchased the gold from the unofficial outlet of each of the five major mines on the Kitchenerville field, paying five Rands an ounce and selling again for sixteen. He justified the large profit margin he allowed himself by the fact that mere possession of unregistered gold was a criminal offence in South Africa, punishable by up to five years' imprisonment.

Almeida was a man in his middle thirties with lank black hair that he continually pushed back from his forehead, bright brown inquisitive eyes and dirty fingernails. Despite his grubby and well-worn clothing and unkempt hairstyle, he was a man of substance.

He had been able to pay in cash the 40,000 rand demanded by the Company for the monopoly concession to trade on the mine property. He had, therefore, an exclusive clientele of 12,000 well-paid Bantu, and had recovered his 40,000 during his first year of trading. He did not really need to run the risk of illicit gold buying, but gold is strange material. It infects most men who touch it with a reckless greed.

'Two hundred and sixteen ounces,' said José. His scale was set to record a twenty per cent error – in José's favour.

'One thousand and eighty rand,' agreed Big King in Portuguese, and José went to the big green safe in the corner.

– 31 –

Terry Steyner entered the 'Grape and Gable' bar of the President Hotel at 1.14 p.m. precisely, and as Hurry Hirschfeld stood to greet her he reflected that fourteen minutes was hardly late at all for a beautiful woman. Terry's grandmother would have considered herself to be early if she was only that late.

'You're late,' growled Hurry. No sense in letting her get away with it unscathed.

'And you are a big, cuddly, growly, lovable old bear,' said Terry and kissed him on the tip of his nose before he could duck. Hurry sat down quickly scowling thunderously with pleasure. He decided he didn't give a good damn if Marais and Hardy, who further down the bar were listening and trying to cover their grins, repeated the incident to the entire membership of the Rand Club.

'Good day, Mrs Steyner.' The scarlet-jacketed barman smiled his greeting. 'Can I mix you a Manhattan?'

'Don't tempt me, Thomas. I'm on a diet. I'll just have a glass of soda water.'

'Diet,' snorted Hurry. 'You're skinny enough as it is. Give her a Manhattan, Thomas, and put a cherry in it. Never was a Hirschfeld woman that looked like a boy, and you'll not be the first of them.' As an afterthought, he added: 'I've ordered your lunch also, you'll not starve yourself in my company.'

'You are a shocker, Pops,' said Terry fondly.

'Now, young lady, let's hear what you've been up to since I last saw you.'

They talked together as friends, very dear and trusted friends. The affection they felt for each other went beyond the natural duty of their blood tie. There was a kinship of the spirit as well as the flesh. They sat close, heads together, watching each other's face as they talked, completely lost in the pleasure of each other's company, the murmur of their voices interrupted by a tinkling burst of laughter or a deep chuckle.

They were so absorbed that Peter, the headwaiter, came through from the Transvaal Room to find them.

'Mr Hirschfeld, the chef is in tears.'

'Good Lord.' Hurry looked at the antique clock above the bar. 'It's almost two o'clock. Why didn't someone tell me?'

The oysters had been flown up from Mossel Bay that morning, and Terry sighed with pleasure after each of them.

'I was out at the Sonder Ditch with Manfred on Wednesday.'

'Yes, I saw the photograph in the paper.' Hurry engulfed his twelfth and final oyster.

'I must say I like your new General Manager.'

Hurry laid down his fork and a little flush of anger started in his withered old cheeks.

'You mean Fred Plummer?'

'Don't be silly, Pops, I mean Rodney Ironsides.'

'Has that cold fish of yours been briefing you?' Hurry demanded.

'Manfred?' She was genuinely puzzled by the question, Hurry could see that. 'What's he got to do with it?'

'All right, forget it.' Hurry dismissed Manfred with a shake of his head. 'Why do you like Ironsides?'

'Have you heard him speak?'

'No.'

'He's very good. I'm sure he must be a first-class mining man.'

'He is.' Hurry nodded, watchful and non-committal.

Peter whisked Terry's plate away, giving her the respite she needed to gather her resources. In the previous few seconds she had realized that Rodney Ironsides was not, as she had believed, a certainty for the job. In fact, Pops had already chosen old plum-faced Plummer for the General Managership. It took another moment for her to decide that she would use even the dirtiest in-fighting to see that Rod was not overlooked.

Peter laid plates of cold rock lobster in front of them, and when he had withdrawn Terry looked up at Hurry. She had perfected the trick of enlarging her already enormous eyes. By holding them open like this she could flood them with tears. The effect was devastating.

'Do you know, Pops, he reminds me so much of the photographs of Daddy.'

Colonel Bernard Hirschfeld, Terry's father, had burned to death in his tank at Sidi Rezegh. She saw Hurry

Hirschfeld's expression crack with pain, and Terry felt a sick little flutter of guilt. Had it been necessary to use such a vicious weapon to achieve her ends?

Hurry pushed at the rock lobster with his fork, his head was bowed so she could not see his face. She reached out to touch his hand.

'Pops—' she whispered, and he looked up. There was a restrained excitement in Hurry's manner.

'You know, you're bloody well right! He does look a bit like Bernie. Did I ever tell you about the time when your father and I—'

Terry felt dizzy with relief. I didn't hurt him, she told herself, he likes the idea, he really does. With a woman's instinct she had chosen the only form of persuasion that could have moved Hurry Hirschfeld from his decision.

– 32 –

Manfred Steyner fastened his safety belt and lay back in the seat of the Boeing 707, feeling slightly nauseated with relief.

Ironsides was in, and he was safe. Hurry Hirschfeld had sent for him two hours before to wish him farewell and good luck with the talks. Manfred had stood before him, trying desperately to think of some way in which he could bring up the subject naturally. Hurry saved him the trouble.

'By the way, I'm giving Ironsides the Sonder Ditch. Reckon it's about time we had some young blood in top management.'

It was as easy as that. Manfred had difficulty in persuading himself that those threats which had kept him lying awake during the past four nights were no longer of consequence. Ironsides was in. He could go to Paris and tell them. *Ironsides is in. We are ready to go.*

The note of the jets changed, and the Boeing began to roll forward. Manfred twisted his head against the neck rest and peered through the Perspex porthole. He could not distinguish Terry's figure amongst the crowd on the observation balcony of Jan Smuts Airport. They taxied past a Pan Am Boeing which cut off his view and Manfred looked straight ahead. Instantly his nostrils flared, he looked around quickly.

The passenger in the seat beside him had stripped to his shirtsleeves. He was a big beefy individual who very obviously did not use deodorant. Almost in desperation Manfred looked about. The aircraft was full, there would be little chance of changing seats and beside him the beefy individual produced a pack of cigarettes.

'You can't smoke,' cried Manfred. 'The light's on.' The combination of body odour and cigarette smoke would be unbearable.

'I'm not smoking,' said the man, 'yet.' And placed a cigarette between his lips, his lighter ready in the other hand.

Nearly two thousand miles to Nairobi, thought Manfred, with his stomach starting to heave.

– 33 –

'Terry darling, why on earth should I go all the way out to Kitchenerville to watch a lot of savages prancing around?'

'As a favour to me, Joy,' Terry pleaded into the telephone.

'It means mucking up my whole weekend. I've got rid of the kids to their grandmother, I've got a copy of A Small Town in Germany and I was going to have a lovely time reading and—'

'Please, Joy, you're my last hope.'

'What time will we be home?' Joy was weakening. Terry sensed her advantage and pressed forward ruthlessly.

'You might meet a lovely man out at the mine, and he'll sweep you—'

'No, thanks.' Joy had been divorced a little over a year ago, some people took longer than others to recover. 'I've had lovely men in big fat chunks.'

'Oh, Joy, you can't sit around moping for ever. Come on, I'll pick you up in half an hour.'

Joy sighed with resignation. 'Damn you, Terry Steyner.'

'Half an hour,' said Terry and hung up before she could change her mind.

'I'm playing golf. It's Saturday, and I'm playing golf,' said Doctor Daniel Stander stubbornly.

'You remember when I drove all the way to Bloemfontein to—' Rod began, and Dan interrupted quickly.

'All right, all right, I remember. You don't have to bring that up again.'

'You owe me plenty, Stander,' Rod reminded him. 'All I am asking is one of your lousy Saturday afternoons. Is that so much?'

'I can't let the boys down. It's a long-standing date.' Dan wriggled to escape.

'I've already phoned Ben. It will be a pleasure for him to take your place.'

There was a long gloomy silence, then Dan asked, 'What's this bird like?'

'She's a beautiful, rich nymphomaniac, and she owns a brewery.'

'Yeah! Yeah!' said Dan sarcastically. 'All right, I'll do it. But I hereby declare all obligations and debts to you fully discharged.'

'I'll give you a written receipt,' Rod agreed.

Dan was still sulking when the Daimler came up the drive and parked in the front of the Mine Club. He and Rod were standing at the Ladies' Bar, watching for the arrival of their guests.

Dan had just ordered his third beer.

'Here they come,' said Rod.

'Is that them?' Dan's depression lifted magically as he peered through the coloured-glass windows. The chauffeur was letting the two ladies out of the Daimler. They were both in floral slack suits and dark glasses.

'That's them.'

'Jesus!' said Dan with rare approval. 'Which one is mine?'

'The blonde.'

'Ha!' Dan grinned for the first time since their meeting. 'Why the hell are we standing here?'

'Why indeed?' asked Rod, his stomach was tied up in knots that twisted tighter as he went down the front steps toward Terry.

'Mrs Steyner. I'm so glad you could come.' With a wild lift of elation he saw it was still there, he had not imagined it, it was there in her eyes and her smile.

'Thank you, Mr Ironsides.' She was like a schoolgirl again, uncertain of herself, flustered.

'I'd like you to meet Mrs Albright. Joy, this is Rodney Ironsides.'

'Hello.' He smiled at her as he clasped her hand. 'It's gin time, I think.'

Dan was waiting at the bar for them, and Rod made the introductions.

'Joy is so excited at the chance of watching the dancing,' said Terry as they sat down on the bar stools. 'She's been looking forward to it for days.' And for an instant Joy looked stunned.

'You'll love it,' agreed Dan, moving in to take up a position at Joy's elbow. 'I wouldn't miss it for anything.'

Joy was a tall slim girl with long straight golden hair that hung to her shoulders, her eyes were cool green but her mouth when she smiled was soft and warm. She smiled now full into Dan's eyes.

'Nor would I,' she said, and with relief Rod knew he could devote all his attention to Terry Steyner. Joy Albright would be more than adequately looked after. He ordered drinks, and all four of them promptly lost further interest in tribal dancing.

At one stage Rod told Terry Steyner, 'I am going up to Johannesburg this evening. There is no point in your unfortunate chauffeur sitting around all afternoon. Let him go, and I'll take you home.'

'Good,' Terry agreed immediately. 'Would you tell him, please?'

The next time Rod looked at his watch it was half past three.

'Good Lord!' he exclaimed. 'If we don't hurry, it will be all over.' Reluctantly Joy and Dan, who had their heads close together, drew apart.

The overflow from the amphitheatre pressed about them, a merry jostling throng, all inhibitions long since evaporated in the primeval excitement of the dance, much like the crowd at a bull ring.

Rod and Dan ran interference for the girls, ploughing a path through the main gateway and down to their reserved seats in the front row. All four of them were laughing and flushed by the time they were seated, the excitement about them was infectious and the liquor had heightened their sensibilities.

An expectant hum of voices.

'The Shangaans!' And the audience craned towards the entrance from which pranced a dozen drummers, their long wooden drums hung on rawhide straps about their necks, they took up stations around the circular earthen stage.

Tap, tap. Tap, tap – from one of the drummers, and silence gripped the amphitheatre.

Tap, tap. Tap, tap. Naked, except for their brief loin cloths, stooped over the drums that they clasped between their knees, they began to lay down the rhythm of the dance. It was a broken, disturbing beat, that jerked and twitched like a severed nerve. A compelling, demanding sound, the pulse of a continent and a people.

Then came the dancers, shuffling, row upon row, head-dresses dipping and rustling, the animal tail kilts swirling, war rattles at the wrists and ankles, black muscles already oiled with the sweat of excitement, coming in slowly rank upon majestic rank, moving as though the drums were pumping life into them.

A shrill blast on a duiker horn and the ranks whirled like dry leaves in a wind, they fell again into a new pattern, and through the opening in their midst came a single gigantic figure.

'Big King!' The name blew like a sigh through the audience, and immediately the drums changed their rhythm. Faster, demanding, and the dancers hissed in their throats a sound like storm surf rushing up a stony beach.

Big King flung his arms wide, braced on legs like black marble columns, his head thrown back. He sang a single word of command, shrilling it, and in instantaneous response every right knee was brought up to the level of the chest. Half a second's pause and then 200 horny bare feet stamped down simultaneously with a crash that shook the amphitheatre to its foundations. The Shangaans began to dance, and reality was gone in the moving, charging, swirling, retreating ranks.

Once Rod tore his eyes from the spectacle. Terry Steyner was sitting forward on the bench, eyes sparkling, lips slightly parted, completely lost in the erotic turmoil and barbaric splendour of it.

Joy and Dan had a firm hold on each others' hands, their shoulders and the outside of their thighs were pressed tightly together, and Rod was stabbed by a painful thrust of envy.

Afterwards, back in the Ladies' Bar of the Club, there was very little conversation but they were all of them tensed up, restless, moved by strange undercurrents and interplays of primitive desires and social restraints.

'Well,' said Rod at last, 'if I am to get you two ladies back to Johannesburg at a decent hour—'

Dan and Joy spoke together.

'Don't worry, Rod, I'll—'

'Dan says he will—' Then they stopped and grinned at each other sheepishly.

'I take it that Dan has suddenly remembered that he has to go to Johannesburg this evening also, and he has offered to give you a lift?' asked Rod dryly, and they laughed in confirmation.

'It looks as though we are on our own, Mrs Steyner.' Rod turned to Terry.

'I'll trust you,' said Terry.

'If you do that, you're crazy,' said Dan.

Outside the Maserati, darkness was falling swiftly. The horizon blending into the black sky, isolated lights winking at them out of the surrounding veld.

Rod switched on the headlights, and the instrument panel glowed softly, turning the interior into a warm secluded place, isolating them from the world. The wind whispered, and the tyres and the engine hummed a gentle intimate refrain.

Terry Steyner sat with her legs curled up under her, cuddled into the soft maroon leather of the bucket seat.

She was staring ahead down the path of the headlights, and she seemed withdrawn and yet very close. Every few minutes Rod would take his eyes from the road and study her profile briefly. He did so again, and this time she met his gaze frankly.

'You realize what is happening?' she asked.

'Yes,' he answered as frankly.

'You know how dangerous it could be for you?'

'And you.'

'No, not me. I am invulnerable. I am a Hirschfeld – but you, it could destroy you.'

Rod shrugged.

'If we counted the consequences before every action, nobody would do anything.'

'Have you thought that I might be a spoiled little rich girl amusing myself? I might do this all the time.'

'You might,' Rod agreed. They were silent for a long while, then Terry spoke again.

'Rod?' She used his given name for the first time.

'Yes?'

'I don't, you know, I really don't.'

'I guessed that.'

'Thank you.' She opened her bag. 'I need a cigarette. I feel as though I'm standing poised on the edge of a cliff and I've got this terrible compulsion to hurl myself over the edge.'

'Light me one, Terry.'

'You need one also?'

'Badly.'

They smoked in silence again, both of them staring ahead, then Terry rolled down the window and flicked the cigarette butt away.

'You've got the job, you know.' All day she had wanted to tell him, it had been bubbling inside her. Watching his face, she saw his lips stiffen, his eyes crease into slits.

'Did you hear me?' she asked at last, and he braked the

Maserati, swinging it off onto the shoulder of the road. He pulled on the hand brake and turned to face her.

'Terry, what did you say?'

'I said, you've got the job.'

'What job?' he demanded harshly.

'Pops signed the instruction this morning. You'll receive it on Monday. You're the new General Manager of the Sonder Ditch.' She wanted to go on and say – *and I got it for you. I made Pops give it to you.*

I never will, she promised, I will never spoil it for him. He must believe he won it fairly, not as my gift.

– 34 –

It was Saturday night, the big night in Dump City.

The Blaauberg Mine was the oldest producer on the Kitchenerville field. There were sections of its property which had been worked out completely, and the old waste dumps were now abandoned and overgrown. Among the scrub and head-high weed in the valleys between these man-made hills had grown up a shanty town. Dump City, the inhabitants had named it. The buildings were made of discarded galvanized iron sheets and flattened oil drums, there was no sanitation or running water.

Remote from the main roads, the residential communities of the neighbouring mines or the town of Kitchenerville, hidden among the dumps, accessible only to a man on foot, never visited by members of the South African Constabulary, it was ideally suited to the purposes for which its 300 permanent inhabitants had chosen it.

Every one of the shacks was a shebeen, a clip joint where watered liquor was sold at inflated prices, where dagga*

* Marijuana.

was freely obtainable and where men from the surrounding mines gathered to carouse.

They came not so much for the liquor. Each of the mine hostels had a bar where a full range of liquor was on sale at club prices. Very few of them came for the dagga. There was little addiction amongst these well-fed, hard-worked and contented men. What they came for were the women.

Five mines in the area, each employing ten or twelve thousand men. Here at Dump City were 200 women, the only available women within twenty miles. It was not necessary for the young ladies of Dump City to solicit custom, even the fat, the withered, the toothless, could behave like queens.

Big King came down the path that skirted the mine dump. With him were two dozen of his fellow tribesmen, big Shangaans wearing their regalia, carrying their fighting sticks and still tensed up from the dancing. They came at a trot, Big King leading them. They were singing, not the gentle planting or courting melodies, not the work chant nor the song of welcome.

They were singing the fighting songs, those their fore-fathers had sung when they carried the spear in search of cattle and slaves. The driving inflammatory rhythm, the fiercely patriotic words wrought so mightily on the delicate susceptibilities of the average Shangaan that the Company had found it necessary to ban the singing of these songs.

Like a Scot hearing the pipes, when a Shangaan began singing these warlike chants, he was ready for violence.

The song ended as Big King led them down to the nearest shanty, and pushed aside the sacking that acted as a door. He stooped through the opening, and his comrades crowded in behind him.

A brittle electric silence fell on the large room. The air was so thick with smoke, and the light from the suspended hurricane lamps so feeble, that it was impossible to see the far wall. The room was filled with men, forty or fifty of them, the smell of humanity and bad liquor was solid. Among this press of men were half a dozen bright spots of the girls' dresses, but with their curiosity aroused by the singing more girls were coming through from the interleading doorways at the back, some of them had men with them and were still shrugging into their clothing. When they saw Big King and his warriors in full war kit, they fell silent and watchful.

At Big King's shoulder one of his Shangaans whispered:

'Basutos! They are all Basutos!' He was right, Big King saw that they were all men of that mountainous little independent state.

Big King started forward, swaggering just enough to make his leopard tail kilt swing and swirl and the heron feathers of his head-dress rustle. He reached the primitive bar counter.

'Flying Bird,' he told the crone who owned the house, and she placed a bottle of Eagle Brandy on the counter.

Big King half filled a tumbler, conscious that every eye was on him, and drained it.

Slowly he turned and surveyed the room.

'What is it,' he asked in a voice that carried to every corner, 'that sits on top of a mountain and scratches its fleas. Is it a baboon, or a Basuto?'

A roar of delight went up from his Shangaans.

'A Basuto!' they shouted, crowding forward to the bar, while a growl and a mutter went up from the rest of the room.

'What is it,' shouted a Basuto jumping to his feet, 'that has feathers on its head and crows from a dungheap? Is it a rooster, or a Shangaan?'

Without seeming to move, Big King picked up the bottle of Eagle Brandy and hurled it. With a crack it burst against the Basuto's forehead and he went over backwards taking two of his companions with him.

The old crone snatched up her cash register and ran as the room exploded into violent movement.

There was not enough space in which to use the fighting sticks, Big King realized, so he lifted a section of the bar counter off its trestles and, holding it in front of him like the blade of a bulldozer, he charged across the room, flattening all and everything before him.

The crash of breaking furniture and the yelp and squeal of men being struck down drove Big King beyond the frontiers of sanity into the red atavistic fury of the berserker.

Basuto is also one of the fighting tribes of the N'guni group. These wiry mountaineers rushed into the conflict with the same savage joy as the Shangaans, a conflict that raged and roared out of the single room to engulf the entire population of Dump City.

One of the girls, her dress ripped from her back so she was left with only a tattered pair of bloomers, had climbed on top of the remains of the bar counter from where, with her big melon breasts swinging in the lamp light, she shrilled that peculiar ululation that Bantu women used to goad their menfolk into battle frenzy. A dozen of the other girls joined in, trilling, squealing, and the sound was too much for Big King.

With the bar top held ahead of him he charged straight through the flimsy wall of the shack, bursting it open like a paper bag. The roof sagged down wearily, and Big King raged on unchecked down the narrow dirt street, striking down any man who crossed his path, scattering chickens and yelping dogs, roaring like a bull gorilla.

He turned at the end of the encampment and came back, his frustration mounting as he found the street deserted except for a few prostrate bodies; through the gaping hole in the wall he entered the shebeen once more to find that here also the fighting had died down. A few of the participants were crawling, or moaning as they lay on the carpet of broken glass.

Big King glared about him, seeking a further outlet for his wrath.

'King Nkulu!' The girl was still on the trestle table, her eyes bright with excitement, her legs trembling with it.

Big King let out another roar, and hurled the bar top from him. It clattered against the far wall and Big King started towards her.

'You are a lion!' She shrieked encouragement at him, and she took one of her big black velvety breasts in each hand and pointed them at him, squeezing them together, shaking with excitement.

'Eat me!' she screamed, as Big King swept her off the table and, lifting her high, ran with her out into the night. Carrying her into the scrub below the mine dumps, holding her easily with one arm, ripping the leopard-tail kilt from his own waist as he ran.

– 35 –

It was Saturday night in Paris also, but there were men who were still working, for there were lights burning in the upstairs rooms of one of the big embassies in the rue Royale.

The fat man who had been the host in the gambling establishment in Johannesburg was now the guest. He sat at ease in a leather club easy chair, his corpulence and the steel-grey hair at his temples giving him dignity. His face heavy, tanned, intelligent. His eyes glittery and hard as the diamond on his finger.

He was listening intently to a man of about the same age as himself who stood before a projected image on a screen that covered one wall of the room. There was that in the man's bearing and manner that marked him as a scholar, he was speaking now, addressing himself directly to the listener in the easy chair, pointing with a marker to the screen beside him.

'You see here a plan of the working of the five producing gold mines of the Kitchenerville fields in relation to each other.' He touched the screen with the marker. 'Thornfontein, Blaauberg, Tweefontein, Deep Gold Levels and Sonder Ditch.'

The man in the chair nodded. 'I have seen and studied this diagram before.'

'Good, then you will know that the Sonder Ditch property sits in the centre of the field. It has common boundaries with the other four mines and here,' he tapped the screen again, 'it is intersected by the massive serpentine dyke which they call the Big Dipper.'

Again the fat man nodded.

'It is for these reasons we have selected the Sonder Ditch as the trigger point.' The lecturer touched a button on the wall panel and the image on the screen changed.

'Now, here is something you have not seen before.'

The man in the chair crouched forward.

'What is it?'

'It is an underground map based on the borehole results of the five companies who have been exploring the ground to the east of the Big Dipper. These results have been pooled and interpreted by some of the finest brains in the fields of geology and hydrophysics. You have here a carefully considered representation of exactly what lies on the far side of the Big Dipper fault.'

The big man moved uncomfortably in his chair.

'It's a monster!'

'Yes, a monster. Lying just beyond the fault is an underground lake, no, that is not the correct word. Let us call it an underground sea, the size of, say, Lake Eyrie. The water is held in a vast sponge of porous dolomite rock.'

'My God.' For the first time the fat man had lost his

poise. 'If this is right, why don't the mining companies arrive at the same conclusion and keep well away from it?'

'Because,' the lecturer switched off the image and the overhead lights came on, 'because of their highly competitive attitude none of them has access to the findings of the others. It is only when all the results are studied that the picture becomes clear.'

'How did your government come to be in possession of *all* the results?' demanded the fat man.

'That is not important.' The lecturer was brusque, impatient of the interruption. 'We are also in possession of the findings of a certain Dr Peter Wessels who is at present head of a research team in Rock Mechanics based on the Sonder Ditch mine property. It is Company classified information and consists of a paper that Dr Peter Wessels has written on the shatter patterns and stresses of rock. His researches are directly related to the Ventersdorp quartzites which comprise the country rock of the Sonder Ditch workings.'

The lecturer picked up a pamphlet from his desk.

'I will not weary you by asking you to wade through its highly technical findings. Instead I will give it to you in capsule form. Dr Wessels arrives at the conclusion that a column of Ventersdorp quartzite 120 feet thick would shatter under a side pressure of 4,000 pounds per square inch.'

The lecturer dropped the pamphlet back on the desk.

'As you know, by law, the gold mining companies are bound to leave a barrier of solid rock 120 feet thick along their boundaries. That is all that separates one mine's working from another, just that wall of rock. You understand?'

'Of course. It is very simple.'

'Simple? Yes, it is simple! This Dr Steyner, over whom you have control, will instruct the new General Manager of the Sonder Ditch to drive a tunnel through the Big Dipper dyke. The drive will puncture the vast underground reservoir and the water will run back and flood the entire Sonder Ditch workings. Once they are flooded, the pressure delivered by a 6,000-foot head of water at the lower levels will be in excess of 4,000 pounds per square inch. That is sufficient to burst the rock walls, and flood the Thornfontein, the Blaauberg, Deep Gold Levels and Tweefontein gold mines.'

'The entire Kitchenerville gold fields would be effectively and permanently put out of production. The consequences for the economy of the Republic of South Africa would be catastrophic.'

The fat man was visibly shaken.

'Why do you want to do it?' he asked, shaking his head in awe.

'My colleague here,' the lecturer indicated a man who was sitting quietly in one corner, 'will explain that to you presently.'

'But – people!' the fat man protested. 'There will be people down there when it bursts, thousands of them.'

The lecturer smiled, raising one eyebrow. 'If I were to tell you that six thousand men would drown, would you refuse to proceed, and forfeit the million-dollar payment my government has offered you?'

The fat man looked down, embarrassed, and muttered barely audibly, 'No.'

The lecturer chuckled. 'Good! Good! However, you may salve you aching conscience by assuring yourself that we do not expect more than forty or fifty fatalities from the flooding. Naturally, those men actually working on the face will be killed. But that tremendous volume of water under immense pressure should make it a merciful death. For the rest of them, the mine can be evacuated swiftly enough to allow them excellent chances of survival. The surrounding mines will have days to evacuate before the water pressure builds up sufficiently to burst through the boundary walls.'

There was silence then in the room for nearly a minute.

'Have you any questions?'

The fat man shook his head.

'Very well, in that case I will leave it to my colleague to complete the briefing. He will explain the necessity for this operation, will arrange the terms of payment and conditions upon which you will proceed.' The lecturer gathered up the pamphlet and other papers from the desk. 'It remains only for me to wish you good luck.' He chuckled again and left the room quickly.

The little man, who up until them had remained silent, suddenly bounced out of his chair and began pacing up and down the wall-to-wall carpeting. He spoke rapidly, shooting occasional sideways glances at his audience, his bald head shining in the fluorescent lighting, wriggling his moustache like rabbit whiskers, puffing nervously at his cigarette.

'Reasons first. I'll make it short and sweet, right? The South Africans and the Frogs have got together. They're here in Paris now cooking up mischief. We know what they're up to, they're going to launch an all-out attack on my government's currency. Gold price increase, you know. Very complicated and very nasty for us, right? They might just be able to do it, South Africa is the world's biggest gold producer. With the Frogs helping her, they might just be able to force an increase.'

He stopped in front of the fat man and thrust out an accusing finger.

'Are we going to sit back and let them have a free run? No, sir! We are going to throw down our own curve ball! In three months time the Syndicate will be ready to attack. At that precise moment we will kick the chair out from under the South Africans by cutting their gold production in half. We will flood the Kitchenerville goldfields and the attack will fizzle out like a damp squib, right?'

'As simple as that?' asked the fat man.

'As simple as that!' The bald head nodded vigorously.

'Now, my next duty is to make clear to you that the agreed million dollars is *all* the reward you receive. Neither you nor your agents may indulge in any financial transactions that might, in retrospect, show that this was a planned operation, right?'

'Right.' The fat man nodded.

'You give your assurance that you will not deal in any of the shares of the companies involved?'

'You have my solemn word.' The fat man told him earnestly, and not for the first time in his life reflected how easily and painlessly a promise could be given.

With the assistance of the three men who had watched Manfred Steyner that night at the gambling club in Johannesburg, he intended launching a bear offensive on the stock exchanges of the world.

On the day that they drilled into the Big Dipper dyke he and his partners would sell millions of the shares of the five mining companies for one of the biggest financial killings in the history of money.

'We are agreed then.' The bald head bobbed. 'Now, as for this Dr Steyner, we have had a screening and personality analysis and we believe that, despite the secure hold you have on his loyalties, he would jib at giving the order to drive on the Big Dipper if he were aware of the consequences. Therefore we have prepared a second geological report,' he produced from his brief case a thick manila folder, 'incorporating those figures which he will recognize. In other words the drilling results of the CRC exploration teams, but the other figures are fictitious. This report purports to prove the existence of a fabulously rich gold reef beyond the fault.' He crossed to the fat man and handed him the folder. 'Take it. It will help you convince Dr Steyner, and he in turn to convince the new General Manager of the Sonder Ditch gold mine.'

111

'You have been thorough,' said the fat man.

'We try to give a satisfactory service to our customers,' said the bald man.

– 36 –

The game was five-card stud poker, and there were two big winners at the table, Manfred Steyner and the Algerian.

Manfred had timed his arrival in Paris to ensure himself an uninterrupted weekend before the rest of the delegates came in on the Monday morning flight.

He had checked in at the Hotel George Cinq on Saturday afternoon, bathed and rested for three hours until eight in the evening, then he had set out for the Club Chat Noir by taxi.

He had been playing now for five hours, and a steady succession of strong cards had pushed his winnings up to a formidable sum. It lay piled in front of him, a fruit salad of garish French bank notes. Across the table sat the Algerian, a slim dark-skinned Arab with toffee eyes and a silky black moustache. His teeth were very white against the creamy brown skin. He wore a turtle-neck shirt in pink silk, and a linen jacket of baby blue. With long brown fingers he kept smoothing and stacking his own pile of bank notes.

A girl sat on the arm of his chair, an Arab girl in a skin-tight gold trouser suit. Her hair was shiny black and hung onto her shoulders, her eyes were disconcertingly level as she watched Manfred.

'Ten thousand.' Manfred's voice was explosive, like that of a teutonic drillmaster. He was betting on his fourth card which had just been dealt to him. He and the Algerian were the remaining players in the game. The others had folded their hands and were sitting back watching with the casual interest of men no longer involved.

The Algerian's eyes narrowed slightly and the girl leaned down to whisper softly in his ear. He shook his head, annoyed, and drew on his cigarette. He had a pair of queens and a six showing and he leaned forward to study Manfred's cards.

The dealer's voice prodded. 'The bet is ten thousand francs, from four, five, seven of clubs. Possible straight flush.'

'Bet or drop,' said one of the uncommitted players. 'You're wasting time.'

The Algerian flashed him a venomous glance.

'Bet,' he said, and counted out ten thousand-franc notes into the pool.

'*Carte.*' The dealer slid a card face down in front of each of them. Quickly the Algerian lifted one corner of his card with his thumb, glanced at it and then closed the face.

Manfred sat very still, the card lying inches from his right hand. His face was pale, calm, but he was seething internally. Far from a possible straight flush, Manfred was holding four, five, seven of clubs and the eight of hearts. A six was the only card that could improve his hand and one six was already showing among the Algerian's cards. His chances were remote.

His lower belly and loins were tight and hot with excitement, his chest constricted. He drew out the sensation, wanting it to last for ever.

'Pair of queens still to bet,' murmured the dealer.

'Ten thousand.' The Algerian pushed the notes forward.

He has found another queen, thought Manfred, but he is uncertain of my flush or straight.

Manfred placed his smooth white hand over his fifth card, cupping it. He lifted it.

'Table,' said Manfred calmly, and there was a gasp and rustle from the watchers. The girl's hand tightened on the Algerian's sleeve, she stared with hatred into Manfred's face.

'The gentleman has made a table bet,' intoned the croupier. 'House rules. Any player may bet the entire stake he has upon the table.' He reached across and began to count the notes in front of Manfred.

Minutes later he announced the total. 'Two hundred and twelve thousand francs.' He looked across at the Algerian. 'It is now up to you to bet against the possible straight flush.'

The girl whispered urgently into the Arab's ear, but he snapped a single word at her and she recoiled. He looked about the room, as if seeking guidance, then he lifted and examined his hole cards again.

Suddenly his face hardened, and he looked steadily across at Manfred.

'Call!' he blurted, and Manfred's clenched right hand fell open upon the table.

The Arab faced his hand. Three queens. The whole room looked expectantly at Manfred.

He flicked over his last card. Two of diamonds. His hand was worthless.

With a birdlike cry of triumph the Algerian leaped from his seat and reaching across the table began raking Manfred's stake with both arms towards him.

Manfred stood up from the table, and the Arab girl grinned maliciously at him, taunting him in Arabic. He turned quickly away and almost ran down the steps that led to the cloakrooms. Twenty minutes later, feeling weak and slightly dizzy, Manfred slipped into the back seat of a Citroën taxi cab.

'George Cinq,' he told the driver. As he entered the lobby of the hotel he saw a tall figure rise from one of the leather armchairs and follow him across to the lifts. Shoulder to shoulder they stepped into the lift and as the doors slid closed the tall man spoke.

'Welcome to Paris, Dr Steyner.'

114

'Thank you, Andrew. I presume you have come to give me my instructions?'

'That is correct. He wishes to see you tomorrow at ten o'clock. I will call for you.'

It was Saturday night in Kitchenerville and in the men's bar of the Lord Kitchener Hotel the daily-paid men from the five gold mines were bellying up to the counter three deep.

The public dance had been in progress for three hours. At tables along the veranda the women-folk sat primly sipping their port and lemonade. Although they all were admirably ignoring the absence of the men, yet a constant and merciless vigil was kept on the door to the men's bar. Most of the wives already had the automobile keys safely in their handbags.

In the dining-hall, cleared of its furniture and sprinkled liberally with French chalk, the local four-piece band who played under the unlikely name of the 'Wind Dogs' launched without preliminaries into a lively rendition of 'Die Ou Kraal Liedjie', and from the men's bar, in various stages of inebriation, answering the call to arms came the troops.

Many of them had shed their jackets, the knots of their ties had slipped, their voices were boisterous and legs were a little unsteady as they led their women onto the dance floor and immediately showed to which school of the dance they belonged.

There was the cavalry squadron which tucked partner under one arm, very much like a lance, and charged. At the other end of the scale were those who plodded grimly around the perimeter, looking neither left nor right, speaking to no one, not even their partners. Then there were the sociables who reeled about the floor, red in the face, their movements completely unrelated to the music, shouting to their friends and attempting to pinch any feminine posterior that came within range. Their unpredictable progress interfered with the revolutions of the dedicated.

The dedicated took up their positions in the centre of the floor and twisted. A half dozen years previously the twist had swept like an Asian 'flu epidemic through the world and then faded out. Gone, forgotten, except in places like Kitchenerville. Here it had been taken and firmly entrenched into the social culture of the community.

Even in this stronghold of the twist, there was one master. 'Johnny Delange? Gott man, but he can twist, hey!' they murmured with awe.

With the sinuous erotic movements of an erect cobra, Johnny was twisting with Hettie. His shiny rayon suit caught the light and the lace ruffles of his shirt fluttered at his throat. There was a fierce grin of pleasure on his hawk features, and the jewelled buckles of his pointed Italian shoes twinkled as he danced.

A big girl with copper hair and creamy skin, Hettie was light on her feet. She had a tiny waist and a swelling regal bottom under the emerald-green skirt. She laughed as she danced, a full healthy laugh to match her body.

The two of them moved with the expertise of a couple who have danced together often. Hettie anticipated each of Johnny's movements, and he grinned his approval at her.

From the veranda Davy Delange watched them. He stood in the shadows, clutching a tankard of beer, a squat, lonely figure. When another dancing couple cut off his view of Hettie's luscious revolving buttocks he would exclaim with irritation and move restlessly.

The music ended and the dancers spilled out onto the veranda, laughing and breathless, mopping streaming faces;

girls squealing and giggling as the men led them to their seats, deposited them and then headed for the bar.

'See you.' Johnny left Hettie reluctantly, he would have liked to stay with her, but he was sensitive about what the boys would say if he spent the whole evening with his wife.

He was absorbed into the masculine crowd, to join their banter and loud laughter. He was deeply involved in a discussion of the merits of the new Ford Mustang, which he was considering buying, when Davy nudged him.

'It's Constantine!' he whispered, and Johnny looked up quickly. Constantine was a Greek immigrant, a stoper on the Blaauberg Mine. He was a big strong black-haired individual with a broken nose. Johnny had broken his nose for him about ten months previously. As a bachelor Johnny would fight him on the average of once a month, nothing serious, just a semi-friendly punch-up.

However, Constantine could not understand that nowadays Johnny was forbidden by his brand new wife from indulging in casual exchanges of fisticuffs. He had developed the erroneous theory that Johnny Delange was afraid of him.

He was coming down the bar room now, holding his glass in his massive hairy right hand with the little finger extended genteely. On his hip rested his other hand and he minced along with a simpering smile on his blue-jowled granite-textured features. Stopping in front of the mirror to pat his hair into place, he winked at his cronies and then came on down to where Johnny stood. He paused and ogled Johnny heavily, fluttering his eyelids and wriggling his hips. His colleagues from the Blaauberg Mine were weak with laughter, gurgling merrily, hanging onto each other's shoulders.

Then with a bump and grind that raised another howl of laughter Constantine disappeared into the lavatories, to emerge minutes later and blow Johnny a kiss as he went back to join his friends. They plied liquor on the Greek in appreciation of his act. Johnny's smile was a little strained as he resumed the discussion on the Mustang's virtues.

Twenty minutes and half a dozen brandies later, Constantine repeated his little act again on the way to the latrine. His repertoire was limited.

'Hold it, Johnny,' whispered Davy. 'Let's go and sit on the veranda.'

'He's asking for it. I'm telling you!' Johnny's smile had disappeared.

'Come on, Johnny, man.'

'No, hell, they'll think I'm running. I can't go now.'

'You know what Hettie will say,' Davy warned him. For a moment longer Johnny hesitated.

'The hell with what Hettie says.' Johnny bunched his right fist with its array of gold rings as he moved down to Constantine and leaned beside him on the counter.

'Herby,' he called the barman, and when he had his attention he indicated the Greek. 'Please give the lady a port and lemonade.'

And the bystanders scattered for cover. Davy shot out of the door onto the veranda to report to Hettie.

'Johnny!' he gasped. 'He's fighting again.'

'Is he!' Hettie came to her feet like a red-headed Valkyrie. But her progress to the men's bar was delayed by the crowd of spectators that jammed the doorway and all the windows. The crowd was tiptoeing and climbing onto the chairs and tables for a better view, every thud or crash of breaking furniture was greeted with a roar of delight.

Hettie had her handbag clutched in her right hand, and like a jungle explorer hacking his way through the undergrowth with a machete, she opened a path for herself to the bar room door.

At the door she paused. The conflict had reached a critical stage. Among a litter of broken glass and shattered stools, Johnny and the Greek were circling each other warily, waving and feinting, all their wits concentrated upon each other. Both of them were marked. The Greek was bleeding from his lip, a thin red ribbon of blood down his chin that dripped onto his shirt. Johnny had a shiny red swelling closing one eye. The crowd was silent, waiting.

'Johnny Delange!' Hettie's voice cracked like a Mauser rifle fired from ambush. Johnny started guiltily, dropping his hands, half turning towards her as the Greek's fist crashed into the side of his head. Johnny spun from the blow, hit the wall and slid down quietly.

With a roar of triumph Constantine rushed forward to put the boot into Johnny's prostrate form, but he pitched forward to sprawl unconscious beside Johnny. Hettie had hit him with the water bottle snatched up from one of the table tops.

'Please help me get my husband to the car,' she appealed to the men around her, suddenly helpless and little-girlish.

She sat beside Davy in the front of the Monaco, fuming with anger.

Johnny lay at ease upon the back seat. He was snoring softly.

'Don't be angry, Hettie.' Davy was driving sedately.

'I've told him, not once, a hundred times.' Hettie's voice crackled like static. 'I told him I wouldn't put up with it.'

'It wasn't his fault. The Greek started it,' Davy explained softly and placed his hand on her leg.

'You stick up for him, just because he is your brother.'

'That's not true,' Davy soothed her, stroking her leg. 'You know how I feel about you, Hettie.'

'I don't believe you.' His hand was moving higher. 'You men are all the same. You all stick together.'

Her anger was fast solidifying into a burning resentment of Johnny Delange, one in which she was willing to take a calculated revenge. She knew that Davy's hand was no longer trying to comfort her and quench her anger. Before she married Johnny Delange, Hettie had had every opportunity to learn about men, and she had been an enthusiastic and receptive pupil. She placed no special importance on an act of the flesh, dispensing her favours as casually as someone might offer a cigarette-case around.

'Why not?' she thought. 'That will fix Mr Johnny Delange! Not all the way, of course, but just enough to get my own back on him.'

'No, Hettie. It's true – I tell you.' Davy's voice was husky, as he felt her knees fall apart under his hand. He touched the silky-smooth skin above her stocking top.

The Monaco slowed to almost walking pace, and it was ten minutes more before they reached the company-owned house on the outskirts of Kitchenerville.

In the back seat Johnny groaned. Immediately Davy's hand jerked back to the steering-wheel, and Hettie sat up in the seat, straightening her skirt.

'Help me get him inside,' she said, and her voice was shaky and her cheeks flushed. She was no longer angry.

– 38 –

They were both a little tipsy. They had stopped to celebrate Rod's promotion at the Sunnyside Hotel. They had sat side by side in one of the booths, drinking quickly, excitedly, laughing together, sitting close but not touching.

Terry Steyner could not remember when she had last behaved this way. It must have been all of ten years ago, her last term at Cape Town varsity, swigging draught beer in the Pig and Whistle at Randall's Hotel and talking the most inane rubbish. All the matronly dignity that Manfred insisted she maintain was gone, she felt like a freshette on a first date with the captain of the rugby team.

'Let's get out of here,' Rod said suddenly, and she stood

up unquestioningly. He took her arm down the stairs, and the light touch of his fingers tingled on her bare skin.

In the Maserati again she experienced the feeling of isolation from reality.

'How often do you see your daughter, Rod?' she asked as he settled into the seat beside her, and he glanced at her, surprised.

'Every Sunday.'

'Tomorrow?'

'Yes.'

'How old is she?'

'Nine next birthday.'

'What do you do with her?'

Rod pressed the starter.

'How do you mean?'

'Where do you take her, what do you do together?'

'We go rowing on Zoo Lake, or eat ice cream sundaes. If it's cold or raining we sit in the apartment and we play mah-jong.' He let in the clutch, and as they pulled away he added, 'She cheats.'

'The apartment?'

'I keep a hideaway in town.'

'Where?'

'I'll show you,' said Rod quietly.

She sat on the studio couch and looked about her with interest. She had not expected the obvious care that he had taken in furnishing the apartment. It was in wheatfield gold, chocolate brown and copper. There was a glorious glowing autumn landscape on the far wall that she recognized as a Dino Paravano.

She noticed a little ruefully how Rod stage-managed the lighting for full romantic effect, and then moved automatically to the liquor cabinet.

'Where is the bathroom?' Terry asked.

'Second left, down the passage.'

She lingered in the bathroom, opening the medicine cabinet like a thief. There were three toothbrushes hanging in the slots, and below them an aerosol can of Bidex. Quickly she shut the cabinet. Feeling disturbed, not sure if it was jealousy or guilt at her own prying.

The bedroom door was open and so she could not help seeing the double bed as she went back to the lounge. She stood in front of the painting.

'I love his work,' she said.

'Not too photographic for your taste?'

'No. I love it.'

He gave her the drink and stood beside her, studying the painting. She tinkled the ice in her glass, and he turned towards her. The feeling of unreality was still holding Terry as she felt him take the glass from her hand.

She was conscious of his hands only, they were strong and very practised. They touched her shoulders, and then moved onto her back calmly. She felt a voluptuous shudder shake her whole body, and then his mouth came down over hers and the sense of unreality was complete. It was all warm and misty, and she let him take control.

She never knew how long afterwards she jerked back to complete, chilling reality. They were on the couch. She lay in his arms. The front of her slack suit was open to the waist and her bra was unhooked. His head was bowed over her and with a handful of thick springy hair she was directing his lips in their quest. His mouth was warm and sucky on her breast.

'I must be mad!' she gasped, and struggled violently from his arms. She was trembling with fright, horrified with herself. Nothing like this had ever happened to her before.

'This is madness!' Her eyes were great dark pools in her pale face, and her fingers were frantic as she buttoned her blouse. As the last button slipped into its hole, anger replaced her fright.

'How many women have you seduced on that couch, Rodney Ironsides?'

Rod stood up, reaching out a hand to reassure her.

'Don't touch me!' She stepped back. 'I want to go home!'

'I'll take you home, Terry. Just calm down. Nothing happened.'

'That's not your fault,' she blazed.

'No, it's not,' he agreed.

'If you had your way, you'd have—' she bit it off.

'Yes, I would have.' Rod nodded. 'But only if you wanted the same thing.'

She stared at him, starting to recover her temper and her control.

'I shouldn't have come up here, I know. It was asking for trouble, but please take me home now.'

– 39 –

The telephone woke Rod. He checked his wrist watch as he tottered naked and half asleep through to the lounge. Eight o'clock.

'Ironsides!' He yawned into the mouthpiece, and then came fully awake as he recognized her voice.

'Good morning, Rodney. How's your hangover?'

He had not expected to hear from her again.

'Just bearable.'

'I called to thank you for an amusing and – instructive evening.'

'Hark at the girl!' He grinned and scratched his chest. 'She changes with the wind. Last night I expected a bullet between the eyes.'

'Last night I got one big fright,' she admitted. 'It comes

as a bit of a shock to discover suddenly that you are quite capable of acting the wanton. Not all the names I called you were meant.'

'I am sorry for my contribution to your distress,' Rod said.

'Don't be, you were very impressive.' Then quickly, changing the subject, 'You are picking up your daughter today?'

'Yes.'

'I'd like to meet her.'

'That could be arranged.' Rod was cautious.

'Does she like horses?'

'She's crazy about them.'

'Would you like to take her and me out to my stud farm on the Vaal river?'

Rod hesitated. 'Is it safe? I mean, being seen together?'

'It's my reputation, I'll look after it.'

'Fine!' Rod agreed. 'We'd love to visit your farm.'

'I'll meet you at your apartment. When?'

'Half past nine!'

Patti was still in her dressing-gown and she offered Rod her cheek casually to be pecked. There were curlers in her hair and from her eyes he could tell she'd had a late night.

'Hello, you're getting thin. Melly is dressing. Do you want some coffee? Your maintenance cheque was late again this month.' And she took a swipe at the spaniel pup as it squatted on the carpet. 'Damn dog pees all over the place. *Melanie*.' She raised her voice. 'Hurry up! Your Papa is here.'

'Hello, Daddy!' Melanie's voice shrieked delightedly from the interior of the apartment.

'Hello, baby.'

'You can't come in, Daddy, I haven't got any clothes on.'

'Well hurry up! I've come a million miles to see you.'

'Not a *million*!' You couldn't fool Melanie Ironsides.

'Did you say you wanted coffee? It's no trouble, it's made already.' Pattie led him through into the sitting-room.

'Thanks.'

'How are things?' she asked as she filled a cup and gave it to him.

'They've made me General Manager of the Sonder Ditch.' He could not prevent himself, it was too good. He had to boast.

Patti looked at him, startled.

'You're joking!' she accused, and then he saw her mind beginning to work like a cash register.

He almost laughed out loud. 'No. It's true.'

'God!' She sat down limply. 'It will nearly *double* your salary.'

He looked at her dispassionately, and not for the first time felt a great wash of relief as he realized he was no longer shackled to her.

'It's usual to offer congratulations,' he prompted her.

'You don't deserve it.' She was angry now. 'You are a selfish, philandering bastard, Rodney Ironsides, you don't deserve the good things that keep happening to you.' He had cheated her. She could have been the General Manager's wife, first lady of the goldfields. Now she was a divorcée, stuck with a miserable four fifty a month. It had seemed good before, but not now.

'I hope you will have enough conscience to make a suitable adjustment for Melanie and me. We are entitled to a share.'

The door burst open and Melanie Ironsides arrived at a gallop to wrap herself around Rod's neck. She had long blonde hair and green eyes.

'I got nine out of ten for spelling!'

'You're not clever, you're a genius. Also you're beautiful.'

'Will you carry me down to the car, Daddy?'

'What's wrong? Your legs in plaster?'

'Please, please, pretty please times three.'

Patti interrupted the love feast. 'Have you got your jersey, young lady?'

And Melanie flew.

'I'll have her back before seven,' said Rod.

'You haven't answered my question.' Patti was surly. 'Do we get a share?'

'Yes, of course,' said Rod. 'The same big juicy four fifty you've had all along.'

They had been in Rod's apartment ten minutes when the doorbell announced Terry's arrival. She was in jeans and a checked shirt with her hair in a plait, and she greeted Rod self-consciously. When he introduced her to Melanie, she did not look much older than his daughter.

The two girls summed each other up solemnly. Melanie was suddenly very demure and refined, and Rod was relieved to see that Terry had the good sense not to gush over the child.

They were in the Maserati and half way to the village of Parys on the Vaal River before Melanie had completed her microscopic scrutiny of Terry.

'Can I come up front and sit on your lap?' she asked at last.

'Yes, of course.' Terry was hard put to conceal her relief and pleasure. Melanie scrambled over the seat and settled on Terry's lap.

'You are pretty,' Melanie gave her considered opinion.

'Thank you. So are you.'

'Are you Daddy's girlfriend?' Melanie demanded. Terry glanced across at Rod, then burst out laughing.

'Almost,' she gurgled, and then all three of them were laughing.

They laughed often that day. It was a day of sunshine and laughter.

Terry and Rod walked together with fingers almost touching through the green paddocks along the willow-lined bank of the Vaal. Melanie ran ahead of them shrieking with glee at the antics of the foals.

They went up to the stables where Melanie fed sugar lumps to a winner of the Cape Metropolitan Handicap and then kissed his velvety muzzle.

They swam in the pool beside the elegant whitewashed homestead, laughter mingling with the splashes, and when they drove back to Johannesburg in the evening Melanie curled in exhausted slumber on Terry's lap, her head cushioned on Terry's bosom.

Terry waited in the Maserati while Rod carried the sleeping child up to her mother, and when he returned and slipped into the driver's seat, Terry murmured, 'My car is at your apartment. You'll have to take me with you.'

Neither of them spoke until they were back in Rod's sitting-room. Then he said, 'Thank you for a wonderful day.' And he took her to his chest and kissed her.

In the darkness she lay pressed to his sleeping body, clinging to him, as though he might be taken from her. She had never felt such intensity of emotion before, it was a compound of awed wonder and gratitude. She had just been admitted to a new level of human experience she had never suspected existed.

The sheets were still damp. She felt bruised internally, aching, a slow voluptuous pulse of pain that she cherished.

Lightly she touched his body, not wanting to wake him, running her fingertips through the coarse curls that covered his chest, marvelling still at the infinity that separated this from what she had known before.

She shuddered with almost unbearable pleasure as she remembered his voice describing her body to her, making her proud of it for the first time in her life. She remembered the words he had used to tell her exactly what they were doing together, and the feel of his hands, so gentle, sure, so lovingly possessive upon her.

He was so unashamed, taking such obvious joy in her, that the reserves which the barren years of her marriage had placed in her mind were swept away and she was able to go with Rodney Ironsides beyond the storm into that tranquil state where mind and body are completely at peace.

She became aware of him awakening beside her, and she touched his face, his lips and his eyes with her fingertips.

'Thank you,' she whispered, and he seemed to understand, for he took her head and drew it gently down into the hollow of his shoulder.

'Sleep now,' he told her softly, and she closed her eyes and lay very still and quiet beside him, but she did not sleep. She would not miss one moment of this experience.

– 40 –

Rod's letter of appointment lay on his desk when he arrived at his office at seven-thirty on the Monday morning.

He sat down and lit a cigarette. Then he began to read it slowly, savouring each word.

'Duly instructed by the Board of Directors,' it began, and ended, 'it remains only to tender the congratulations of the Board, and to voice their confidence in your ability.'

Dimitri came through from his office, distracted.

'Hey! Rod! Christ what a start to the week! We've got a fault in the main high voltage cable on 90 level, and—'

'Don't come squealing to me,' Rod cut him short. 'I'm not the Underground Manager.'

Dimitri gaped at him, taken by surprise.

'What the hell, have they fired you?'

'Next best thing,' said Rod and flipped the letter across the desk. 'Look what the bastards have done to me.'

Dimitri read and then whooped, 'My God, Rod! My God!' He shot down the passage to carry the news to the other line managers. Then they were all in his office, shaking his hand. He judged most of their reactions as favourable, though occasionally he detected a false note. A twinge of envy here, one there who had recently had his ears burned by the Ironsides tongue, and an incompetent who knew his job was now in danger. The phone rang. Rod answered it, his expression changed and he cleared his office with a peremptory wave.

'Hirschfeld here.'

'Morning, Mr Hirschfeld.'

'Well, you've got your chance, Ironsides.'

'I'm grateful for it.'

'I want to see you. I'll give you today to sort yourself out. Tomorrow morning at nine o'clock, my office at Reef Buildings.'

'I'll be there.'

'Good.'

Rod hung up, and the day dissolved into a welter of activity and reorganization, constantly interrupted by a stream of well-wishers. He was still running the Underground Manager's job in addition to the General Manager's. It would be some considerable time before a new Underground Manager was transferred in from one of the other group mines. He was trying to arrange his move to the big office in the main Administrative Block up on the ridge, when he had another visitor, Frank Lemmer's secretary, Miss Lily Jordan, looking like a wardress from Ravensbruck in a severe grey flannel suit.

'Mr Ironsides, you and I have not seen eye to eye in the past.'

This was the understatement of the year. 'It is unlikely that we will in the future. Therefore, I have come to tender my resignation. I have made arrangements.'

The phone rang. Dan Stander's voice, breezy and carefree.

'Rod, I'm in love.'

'Oh Christ, no!' Rod groaned. 'Not this morning.'

'I've got to thank you for introducing me to her. She's the most wonderful—'

'Yeah, yeah!' Rod cut him short. 'Look, Dan, I'm rather busy. Some other time, all right?'

'Oh yes, I forgot. You are the new General Manager they tell me. Congratulations. You can buy me a drink at the Club. Six o'clock.'

'Right. By then I'll need one.' Rod hung up, and faced the hanging-judge expression of Miss Lily Jordan.

'Miss Jordan, in the past our interests have conflicted. In the future they will not. You are the best private secretary within a hundred miles of the Sonder Ditch. I need you, the Company needs you.'

That was the magic word. Miss Jordan had twenty-five years' service with the Company. She wavered visibly.

'Please, Miss Jordan, give me a chance.' Shamelessly Rod switched on his most engaging smile. Miss Jordan's femininity was not so completely atrophied that she could resist that smile.

'Very well, then, Mr Ironsides. I'll stay on initially until the end of the month. We'll see after that.' She stood up. 'Now, I'll get your things moved up to the new office.'

'Thank you, Miss Jordan.' With relief he let her take over, and tackled the problems that were piling up on his desk. One man, two jobs. Now he was responsible for surface operation as well as underground. The phone rang, men queued up in the passage, memos kept coming through from Dimitri's office. There was no lunch hour, and by the time she rang he was exhausted.

'Hello,' she said. 'Do I see you tonight?' Her voice was as refreshing as a wet cloth on the brow of a prizefighter between rounds.

'Terry.' He simply spoke her name in reply.

'Yes or no. If it's *no*, I intend jumping off the top of Reef Building.'

'Yes,' he said. 'Pops has summoned me to a meeting at nine tomorrow morning, so I'll be staying overnight at the apartment. I'll call you as soon as I get in.'

'Goody! Goody!' said she.

At five-thirty Dimitri stuck his head around the door.

'I'm going down to No. 1 shaft to supervise the shoot, Rod.'

'My God, what time is it?' Rod checked his watch. 'So late already.'

'It gets late early around here,' Dimitri agreed. 'I'm off.'

'Wait!' Rod stopped him. 'I'll shoot her.'

'No trouble.' Dimitri demurred. Company standard procedure laid down that each day's blast must be supervised by either the Underground Manager or his assistant.

'I'll do it,' Rod repeated. Dimitri opened his mouth to protest further, then he saw that expression on Rod's face and changed his mind quickly.

'Okay then. See you tomorrow.' And he was gone.

Rod grinned at his own sentimentality. The Sonder Ditch was his now and, by God, he was going to shoot his own first blast on her.

They were waiting for him at the steel door of the blast control room at the shaft head. It was a small concrete room like a wartime pillbox, and there were only two keys to the door. Dimitri had one, Rod the other.

The duty mine captain and the foreman electrician added their congratulations to the hundreds he had received during the day, and Rod opened the door and they went into the tiny room.

'Check her out,' Rod instructed, and the mine captain began his calls to the shaft overseers at both No. 1 and No. 2 for their confirmation that the workings of the Sonder Ditch were deserted, that every human being who had gone down that morning had come out again this evening.

Meanwhile, the foreman electrician was busy at the electrical control board. He looked up at Rod.

'Ready to close the circuits, Mr Ironsides.'

'Go ahead,' Rod nodded and the man touched a switch. A green light showed up on the board.

'No. 1 north longwall closed and green.'

'Lock her in,' Rod instructed and the electrician touched another switch.

'No. 1 east longwall closed and green.'

'Lock her in.'

The green light showed that the firing circuit was intact. A red light would indicate a fault and the faulty circuit would not be locked into the blast pattern.

Circuit after circuit was readied until finally the foreman stood back from the control board.

'All green and locked in.'

Rod glanced at the mine captain.

'All levels clear, Mr Ironsides. She's ready to burn.'

'Cheesa!' said Rod, the traditional command that had come down from the days when each fuse had been individually lit by a hand-held igniter stick.

'Cheesa' was the Bantu word for 'burn'.

The mine captain crossed to the control board and opened the cage that guarded a large red button.

'Cheesa!' echoed the mine captain and hit the button with the heel of his hand.

Immediately the row of green lights on the control board was extinguished, and in its place showed a row of red lights. Every circuit had been broken by the explosions.

The ground under their feet began to tremble. Throughout the workings the shots were firing. In the stopes the head charges fired at the top of the inclines, then in succession the other shots went off behind them. Each charge taking a ten-ton bite of rock and reef out of the face.

At the end of the development drives, a more complicated pattern was shooting. First a row of *cutters* went off down the middle of the oval face. Then the *shoulder charges* at the top corners, followed by the *knee charges* at the bottom corners. A moment's respite with the dust and nitrous fumes swirling back down the drive, then a roar as the *easers* on each side shaped the hole. Another respite and then the *lifters* along the bottom picked up the heap of broken rock and threw it back from the face.

Rod could imagine it clearly. Though no human eye had ever witnessed the blast, he knew exactly what was taking place down there.

The last tremor died away.

'That's it. A full blast,' said the mine captain.

'Thank you.' Rod felt tired suddenly. He wanted that drink, even though their brief exchange that morning had warned him that Dan would probably be insufferable. He could guess the conversation would revolve around Dan's new-found love.

Then he smiled as he thought about what waited for him in Johannesburg later that night, and suddenly he wasn't all that tired.

They sat facing each other.

'Only three things worry me,' Terry told Rod.

'What are they?' Rod rubbed soap into the face flannel.

'Firstly, your legs are too long for this bath.'

Rod rearranged his limbs, and Terry shot half out of the water with a squeak.

'Rodney Ironsides, would you be good enough to take a bit more care where you put your toes!'

'Forgive me.' He leaned forward to kiss her. 'Tell me what else worries you.'

'Well, the second thing that worries me is that I'm not worried.'

'What part of Ireland did you say you were from?' Rod asked. 'County Cork?'

'I mean, it's terrible but I'm not even a little conscience-stricken. Once I believed that if it ever happened to me I would never be able to look another human being in the eyes, I'd be so ashamed.' She took the flannel from his hands and began soaping his chest and shoulders. 'But, far from being ashamed, I'd like to stand in the middle of Eloff Street at rush hour and shout "Rodney Ironsides is my lover".'

'Let's drink to that.' Rodney rinsed the soap from his hands and reached over the side of the bath to pick up the two wine glasses from the floor. He gave one to Terry and they clinked them together, the sparkling Cape burgundy glowed ruby red.

'Rodney Ironsides is my lover!' she toasted him.

'Rodney Ironsides is your lover,' he agreed and they drank.

'Now, I give *you* a toast,' he said.

'What is it?' She held her glass ready, and Rod leaned

forward and poured the red wine from the crystal glass between her breasts. It ran like blood down her white skin and he intoned solemnly:

'Bless this ship and all who sail in her!'

Terry gurgled with delight.

'To her captain. May he keep a firm hand on the rudder!'

'May her bottom never hit the reef!'

'May she be torpedoed regularly!'

'Terry Steyner, you are terrible.'

'Yes, aren't I?' And they drained their glasses.

'Now,' Rod asked, 'what is your third worry?'

'Manfred will be home on Saturday.'

They stopped laughing, Rod reached down for the burgundy bottle and refilled the glasses.

'We still have five days,' he said.

– 42 –

It had been a week of personal triumph for Manfred Steyner. His address to the conference had been the foundation of the entire talks, all discussion had revolved upon it. He had been called upon to speak at the closing banquet which General de Gaulle had attended in person, and afterwards the General had asked Manfred to take coffee and brandy with him in one of the ante-rooms. The General had been gracious, had asked questions and listened attentively to the answers. Twice he had called his finance minister's attention to Manfred's replies.

Their farewells had been cordial, with a hint of state recognition for Manfred, a decoration. In common with most Germans, Manfred had a weakness for uniforms and decorations. He imagined how a star and ribbon might look on the snowy front of his dress shirt.

There had been a wonderful press both in France and at

home. Even a bad-tempered quarter column in *Time* magazine, with a picture, de Gaulle stooping over the diminutive Manfred solicitously, one hand on his shoulder. The caption read: 'The huntsman and the hawk. To catch a dollar?'

Now standing in the tiny cloakroom in the tail of the South African Airways Boeing, Manfred was whistling softly as he stripped his shirt and vest, crumpled them into a ball and dropped them into the waste bin.

Naked to the waist, he wiped his upper body with a wet cloth and then rubbed 4711 Eau de Cologne into his skin. From the briefcase he took an electric razor. The whistling stopped as he contorted his face for the razor.

Through his mind ran page after page of the report that Andrew had delivered that morning to his hotel room. Manfred had total recall when it came to written material. Although the report was in the briefcase beside him, in his mind's eye he could review it word for word, figure for figure.

It was a stupendous piece of work. How the authors had gained access to the drilling and exploration reports of the five Kitchenerville field companies he could not even guess, for the gold mining companies' security was as tight as that of any national intelligence agency. But the figures were genuine. He had checked those purporting to be from CRC carefully. They were correct. So therefore the other four must also be genuine.

The names of the authors of the report were legend. They were the top men in the field. Their opinions were the best in Harley Street. The conclusion that they reached was completely convincing. In effect it was this:

If a haulage was driven from 66 level of the Sonder Ditch No. 1 shaft through the Big Dipper dyke, it would pass *under* the limestone water-bearing foundations, and just beyond the fault it would intersect a reef of almost unbelievable value.

It had not needed the lecture that Manfred had received

from his corpulent creditor to show him the possibilities. The man who gave the order to drive through the Big Dipper would receive the credit. He would certainly be elected to the chairmanship of the Group when that office fell vacant.

There was another possibility. A person who purchased a big packet of Sonder Ditch shares immediately before the reef was intersected would be a very rich man when he came to sell those shares later. He would be so rich that he would no longer be dependent on his wife for the means to live the kind of life he wanted, and indulge his own special tastes.

Manfred blew the hairs from his razor and returned it to his brief case. Then as he took out a fresh shirt and vest, he began to sing the words to the tune:

> 'Heute ist der schönste Tag
> In meinem Leben.'

He would telephone Ironsides from Jan Smuts Airport as soon as he had passed through customs. Ironsides would come up to the house on Sunday morning and receive his orders.

As he knotted the silk of his tie Manfred knew that he stood at the threshold of a whole new world, the events of the next few months would lift him high above the level of ordinary men.

It was the chance for which he had worked and waited all these years.

Circumstances had changed completely since his last visit, Rod reflected, as he took the Maserati up the drive towards the Dutch gabled house.

He parked the car and switched off the ignition, sitting a while, reluctant to face the man who had sponsored his career and whom Rod in return had presented with a fine pair of horns.

'Courage, Ironsides!' he muttered and climbed out of the Maserati and went up the path across the lawns.

Terry was on the veranda in a gay print dress, with her hair loose, sprawled in a canvas chair with the Sunday papers scattered about her.

'Good morning, Mr Ironsides,' she greeted him as he came up the steps. 'My husband is in his study. You know the way, don't you?'

'Thank you, Mrs Steyner.' Rod kept his voice friendly but disinterested, then as he passed her chair he growled softly, 'I could eat you without salt.'

'Don't waste it, you gorgeous beast,' Terry murmured and ran the tip of her tongue over her lips.

Fifteen minutes later, Rod sat stony-faced and internally chilled before Manfred Steyner's desk. When at last he forced himself to speak, it felt as though the skin on his lips would tear with the effort.

'You want me to drive through the Big Dipper,' he croaked.

'More than that, Mr Ironsides. I want you to complete the drive within three months, and I want a complete security blanket on the development,' Manfred told him primly. Despite the fact that it was Sunday he was formally dressed, white shirt and dark suit. 'You will commence the drive from No. 1 shaft 66 level and make an intersect on reef at 6,600 feet with the SD No. 3 borehole 250 feet beyond the calculated extremity of the serpentine intrusion of the Big Dipper.'

'No,' Rod shook his head. 'You can't go through that. No one can take the chance. God alone knows what is on the other side, we only know that is bad ground. Stinking rotten ground.'

'How do you know that?' Manfred asked softly.

'Everybody on the Kitchenerville field knows it.'

'How?'

'Little things.' Rod found it hard to put into words. 'You get a feeling, the signs are there and when you've been in the game long enough you have a sixth sense that warns you when—'

'Nonsense,' Manfred interrupted brusquely. 'We no longer live in the days of witchcraft.'

'Not witchcraft, experience,' Rod snapped angrily. 'You've seen the drilling results from the other side of the fault?'

'Of course,' Manfred nodded. 'SD No. 3 found values of thousands of penny-weights.'

'And the other holes went dry and twisted off, or had water squirting out of them like a pissing horse!'

Manfred flushed fiercely. 'You will be good enough not to employ bar-room terminology in this house.'

Rod was taken off balance, and before he could answer Manfred went on.

'Would you put the considered opinions of,' Manfred named three men, 'before your own vague intuitions?'

'They are the best in the business,' Rod conceded reluctantly.

'Read that,' snapped Manfred. He tossed a manila folder onto the desk top, then stood up and went to wash his hands at the concealed basin.

Rod picked up the folder, opened it and was immediately engrossed. Ten minutes later, without looking up from the report, he fumbled a pack of cigarettes from his pocket.

'Please do not smoke!' Manfred stopped him sharply.

Three-quarters of an hour later, Rod closed the folder. During that time Manfred Steyner had sat with reptilian stillness behind his desk, with the glitter of his eyes the only signs of life.

'How the hell did you get hold of those figures and reports?' Rod asked with wonder.

'That does not concern you.' Manfred retrieved the folder from him, his first movement in forty-five minutes.

'So that's it!' muttered Rod. 'The water is in the limestone near the surface. We go in under it!' He stood up from the chair abruptly and began to pace up and down in front of Manfred's desk.

'Are you convinced?' Manfred asked, and Rod did not answer.

'I have promoted you above older and more experienced men,' said Manfred softly. 'If I tear you down again, and tell the world you were not man enough for the job, then, Rodney Ironsides, you are finished. No one else would take a chance on you again, ever!'

It was true. Rod knew it.

'However, if you were to follow my instructions and we intersected this highly enriched reef, then part of the glory would rub off on you.'

That was also true. Rod stopped pacing, he stood with shoulders hunched, in an agony of indecision. Could he trust that report beyond his own deep intuition? When he thought about that ground beyond the dyke, his skin tickled with gooseflesh. He almost had the stink of it in his nostrils. Yet he could be wrong, and the weight of the opposition was heavy. The eminent names on the report, the threats which he knew Manfred would not hesitate to put into effect.

'Will you give me a written instruction?' Rod demanded harshly.

'What effect would that have?' Manfred asked mildly.

'As General Manager, the decision to work certain ground or not to work it is technically yours. In the very unlikely event that you encountered trouble beyond the fault, it would be no defence to produce a written instruction from me. Just as if you murdered my wife you could not defend yourself by producing a written instruction from me to do so.'

This again was true. Rod knew he was trapped. He could refuse, and wreck his career. Or he could comply and take the consequences whatever they may be.

'No,' said Manfred, 'I will not give you a written instruction.'

'You bastard,' Rod said softly.

Manfred answered as gently. 'I warned you that you would not be able to refuse to obey me.'

And the last twinge of remorse that Rod felt for his association with Terry Steyner faded and was gone.

'You've given me three months to hit the Big Dipper. All right, Steyner. You've got it!'

Rod turned on his heel and walked out of the room.

Terry was waiting for him among the protea plants on the bottom lawn. She saw his face and dropped all pretence. She went to meet him.

'Rod, what is it?' Her hand on his arm, looking up into his eyes.

'Careful!' he warned her, and she dropped her hand and stood back.

'What is it?'

'That bloody Gestapo bastard,' Rod snarled, and then, 'I'm sorry, Terry, he's your husband.'

'What has he done?'

'I can't tell you here. When can I see you?'

'I'll find an excuse to get away later today. Wait for me at your apartment.'

141

Later she sat on the couch below the Paravano painting and listened while he told her about it. All of it, the report, the threat and the order to pierce the Big Dipper.

She listened but expressed neither approval nor disapproval of his decision.

Manfred turned away from the window and went back to his desk. Even at that distance there had been no doubt about his wife's gesture. The hand outstretched, the face turned up, the lips parted in anxious enquiry, and then the guilty start and withdrawal.

He sat down at his desk, and laid his hands neatly in front of him. For the first time he was thinking of Rodney Ironsides as a man and not a tool.

He thought how big he was, tall and as wide across the shoulders as a gallows. Any reprisal on Ironsides could not be physical, and it could not be immediate. It must be after the drive to the Big Dipper.

I can wait, he thought coldly, there is time for everything in this life.

– 44 –

Johnny and Davy Delange sat in the two chairs before Rod's desk. They were both awkward and uncomfortable up here in the big office with picture windows looking out over the Kitchenerville valley.

I don't blame them, Rod thought, even I am not accustomed to it yet. Wall-to-wall carpeting, air-conditioning, original paintings on the wood-panelled walls.

'I have sent for you because you two are the best rock breakers on the Sonder Ditch,' Rod began.

'Tin Ribs wants something,' thought Davy, with all the suspicion of the union man for management.

'We will now have a few words from our sponsor,' Johnny grinned to himself. 'Before we start the programme.'

Rod looked at their faces and knew exactly what they were thinking. He had been on daily pay himself once. Cut out the compliments, Ironsides – he advised himself – these are two tough cookies and they are not impressed.

'I am pulling you out of the stopes and putting you onto a special development end. You will take it in turns to work day and night shift. You will be directly responsible to me and there will be a security blanket on your activity.'

They watched him without reaction, their expressions guarded. Johnny broke the short silence.

'One end, one blast a day?' He was thinking of his pay. Calculated on the amount of rock broken, he would earn little more than basic salary with a blast on one small face daily.

'No.' Rod shook his head. 'Ultra-fast, multi-blast, and shaft sinkers' rates.'

And both the Delange brothers sat forward in their chairs.

'Multi-blast?' Davy asked. That meant that they could shoot just as soon as they were ready. A good team could blast three – maybe four times a shift.

'Ultra-fast?' Johnny demanded. That was language Johnny understood. It was a term employed only in emergency, as when driving in to rescue trapped men after a fall. It was tacit approval from management to waive standard safety procedure in favour of speed. Christ, Johnny exulted, I can shoot her four – maybe five times a shift.

'Shaft sinkers' rates?' they asked together. That was a 20 per cent bonus on stopers' rates. It was a fortune they were being offered.

Rod nodded affirmative to their questions, and waited for the reaction which he knew would follow. It came immediately.

The Delange brothers now began to look for the catch.

They sat stolidly turning the deal over in their minds, like two cautious housewives examining a tomato for blemishes because the price was too cheap.

'How long is this drive?' Johnny asked. If the drive was short, a few hundred feet, then it was worth nothing. They would hardly get into their stride before it was completed.

'Close on six thousand feet,' Rod assured him. They looked relieved.

'Where is it headed?' Davy discovered the rub.

'We are going to drive through the Big Dipper to intersect on reef at 6,000 feet.'

'Jesus!' said Johnny. 'The Big Dipper!' He was awed but unafraid. It excited him, the danger, the challenge. Had he been born earlier, Johnny Delange would have made a fine Spitfire pilot.

'The Big Dipper,' Davy murmured, his mind was racing. Nothing in this world or beyond would entice Davy Delange to drive through the Big Dipper. He had an almost religious fear of it. The name alone conjured up all sorts of hidden menace and unspeakable horror. Water. Gas. Friable ground, faults. Mud-rushes. All a miner's nightmare.

There was no question of him doing it, yet the money was too good to pass up. He could net ten or eleven thousand rand on those terms.

'All right, Mr Ironsides,' he said. 'I'll take the first night shifts. Johnny can start the day shifts.'

Davy Delange had made his decision. He would work until his drills hit the greenish-black serpentine rock of the dyke. He would then walk out of the drive and quit. He would go up to, but not beyond the dyke.

Afterwards, any of the other mines would snap him up, he had an impeccable record and he would force Johnny to follow him.

'Hey, Davy!' Johnny was delighted, he had expected Davy to turn the deal down flat.

Now he would be able to buy the Mustang for certain –

and perhaps an MGB GT for Hettie – and take a holiday to Durban over Christmas, and . . .

Rod was puzzled by Davy's easy agreement. He studied him a moment and decided that he had ferrety eyes. He's a sneaky little bastard, Rod decided, I'll have to watch him.

– 45 –

It took one shift only to prepare for the development. Rod selected the starting point. The main haulage curved away from the shaft on 66 level. 1,000 feet along this tunnel there was a chamber that had been cut out as a loco repair station but which was now out of use. Two large batwing ventilation doors were fitted to the opening of the chamber to provide privacy and behind them the chief underground surveyor set up his instruments and marked out the head of the tunnel that would fly arrow straight a mile and more through the living rock to strike through the Big Dipper into the unknown.

The area surrounding the head chamber was roped off band sign-posted with warnings.

DANGER
INDEPENDENT BLASTING

The mine captains were instructed to keep their men well away, and all loco traffic was rerouted through a secondary haulage.

On the doors of the chamber another notice was fixed.

FIERY MINE PROCEDURE IN FORCE
NO NAKED LIGHTS BEYOND THIS POINT

Owing to small deposits of coal and other organic substance in the upper stratas of rock, the Sonder Ditch was classed as a fiery mine and subject to the government legislation covering this subject. No matches, lighters or other spark-generating devices were allowed into a new development end, because the presence of methane gas was always suspected.

Colourless, odourless, tasteless, detectable only by test with a safety lamp, it was a real and terrifying danger. A nine per cent concentration in air was highly explosive. Stringent precautions were taken against accidental triggering of methane that may have oozed out of a fissure or cavity in the rock.

From the main compressed air-pipes running down the corners of the shaft were taken leads to air tanks in the haulage, ensuring that sixty pounds per square inch of pressure was available for the rock drills. Then drills, pinchbars, hammers, shovels, and the other tools were unloaded from the cage at 66 level and stored at the shaft head.

Lastly, explosive was placed in the red lockers at the head of the development, and on the evening of October 23rd 1968, thirty minutes after the main blast, Davy Delange and his gang disembarked from the cage and went to the disused loco shop.

Davy, with the surly little Swazi boss boy beside him, stood before the rock wall on which the surveyor had marked the outline of the tunnel. Behind him his gang had fallen unbidden to their labour, each man knowing exactly what was expected of him.

Already the machine boys and their assistants were lugging their ungainly tools forward.

'You! You! You! You!' Davy indicated to each of them the hole on which he was to begin and then stepped back.

'Shaya!' he commanded. 'Hit it!' And with a fluttering bellow that buffeted the eardrums the drive began.

The drilling ceased and Davy charged the holes. The

fuses hung like the tails of white mice from their holes. Each length carefully cut to ensure correct firing sequence.

'Clear the drive!' The boss boy's whistle shrilled, the tramp of heavy boots receded until silence hung heavy in the chemically cleaned air.

'Cheesa!' Davy and the boss boy, with the igniters burning like children's fireworks in their right hands, touched them to the hanging tails until the chamber was lit by the fierce blue light of the burning fuses. The shadows of the two men flickered gigantic and distorted upon the walls.

'All burning. Let's go!' And the two men walked quickly back to where the gang waited along the haulage.

The detonations sucked at their ears, and thrust against their lungs, so that afterwards the silence was stunning.

Davy checked his wristwatch. By law there was a mandatory thirty minutes' wait before anyone could go back to the face. There may be a hang-fire waiting to blow the eyes out of someone's head. Even if there were not, there was still the cloud of poisonous nitrous fumes that would destroy the hair follicles in a man's nostrils and render him still more vulnerable to the fine particles of rock dust that would seek to enter his lungs.

Davy waited those thirty minutes, by which time the ventilation had sucked away the fumes and dust.

Then, alone, he went up the haulage. With him he carried his safety lamp, its tiny blue flame burning behind the screen of fine brass wire mesh. That mesh was flash proof and insulated the flame from any methane in the air.

Standing before the raw circular wound in the rock wall, Davy tested for methane gas. Watching the blue flame for the tell-tale cap. There was no sign of it, and satisfied he extinguished the lamp.

'Boss boy!' he yelled, and the Swazi came up uncoiling the hose behind him.

'Water down!'

Only when the rock face and all the loose rubble below it were glistening and dripping with water was Davy satisfied that the dust was laid sufficiently to bring up his gang.

'Bar boys!' he yelled, and they came up, carrying the twelve-foot-long pinchbars, a tool like a giant crowbar.

'Bar down. Make safe!' And the bar boys attacked the bunches of loose rock that were flaking and crumbling from the hanging wall. Two of them manipulating one bar between them, with the steel point striking sparks from the rock. The dislodged fragments rained down, heavily at first and then less and less until the rock above their heads was solid and clean.

Only then did Davy scramble over the pile of rubble to reach the face and begin marking in the shot holes.

Behind him his gang were lashing the stuff into the waiting cocopans, and his machine boys were dragging the drills up to the face.

Davy's gang made three blasts that first night. As he rode up in the cage into a pink, sweet-smelling dawn, Davy was satisfied.

'Perhaps tonight we will get in four blasts,' he thought.

In the Company change house he showered, running the water steaming hot so his skin turned dull angry red, and he worked up a fat white lather of soap suds over his head and at his armpits and crotch.

He rubbed down with a rough thick towel and dressed quickly. Crossing the parking lot to his battered old Ford Anglia he felt happy and good-tired; hungry and ready for bed.

He drove into Kitchenerville at a steady forty miles an hour, and by this time the sun was just showing over the Kraalkop ridge. The dawn was misty rose, with long shadows against the earth, and he thought that this was how it would be in the early mornings on the farm.

On the outskirts of the town Johnny's Monaco roared past him going in the opposite direction. Johnny waved and blew the horn, shouting something that was lost in the howl of wind and motor.

'They'll catch him yet.' Davy shook his head in disapproval. 'The speed limit is forty-five along here.'

He parked the Anglia in the garage and let himself in through the kitchen door. The Bantu maid was busy over the stove.

'Three eggs,' he told her and went through to his bedroom. He shrugged off his jacket and threw it on the bed. Then he returned to the door and glanced quickly up and down the passage. It was deserted, and there was no sound besides the clatter of the maid in the kitchen.

Davy sidled into the passage. The door to Johnny's bedroom was ajar, and Davy moved quietly down to it. His heart was pounding in his throat, his breathing was stifled by his guilt and excitement.

He peered around the edge of the door and gasped aloud. This morning it was better than usual.

Hettie was a sound sleeper. Johnny always maintained it would take a shot of Dynagel to wake her. She never wore night clothes and she never rose before ten-thirty in the morning. She lay on her stomach, hugging a pillow to her chest, her hair a joyous tangle of flaming red against the green sheets. The morning was warm and her blankets had been kicked aside.

Davy stood in the passage. A nerve in his eyelid began to twitch, and under his shirt a drop of perspiration slid from his armpit down along his flank. On the bed Hettie mumbled unintelligibly in her sleep, drew her knees up and rolled slowly onto her back. One arm came up and flopped limply over her face, her eyes were covered by the crook of her elbow.

She sighed deeply. The twin mounds of her bosom were pulled out of shape by their own weight and the angle of her arm. The hair in her armpit and at the base of her belly was bright shiny red-gold. She was long and smooth and silky white, crowned and tipped with flame.

She moved her body languorously, voluptuously, and then settled once more into slumber.

'Breakfast ready, master,' the maid called from the kitchen. Davy started guiltily, then retreated down the passage.

He found with surprise that he was panting, as though he had run a long way.

– 46 –

Johnny Delange leaned against the sidewall of the haulage, his hard helmet tilted at a jaunty angle and a cigarette dangling from his lips.

Down at the face the shots began to fire. Johnny recognized each detonation, and when the last dull jar disrupted the air about them, he pushed himself away from the wall with his shoulder.

'That was the *lifters*,' he announced. 'Come on Big King!'

Not for Johnny Delange a thirty-minute waste of time. As he and Big King set off down the haulage together they were binding scarves over their noses and mouths. Ahead of them a bluey-white fog of dust and fumes filled the tunnel, and Big King had the hose going, using a fine mist spray to absorb the fumes and particles.

They pushed on up to the face, Johnny stooping over the safety lamp. Even he had a healthy respect for methane gas.

'Bar boys!' he bellowed, not waiting for Big King to finish watering down. They came up like ghosts in the fog. Hard behind them the machine boys hovered with their drills.

Taking calculated risks Johnny had his drills roaring

forty-five minutes sooner than Davy Delange would have in the same circumstances.

When he came back to the face from cutting fuses and priming his explosives, he found his lashing gang struggling with a massive slab of rock that had been blown intact from the face. Five of them were beating on it with fourteen-pound hammers in an attempt to crack it into manageable pieces. As Johnny reached them, Big King was berating them mercilessly.

'You look like a bunch of virgins grinding millet.'

The hammers clanged and struck sparks from the slab. Sweat oozed from every pore of the hammer boys' skin, greasing their bodies, flying from their heads in sparkling droplets with each blow.

'Shaya!' Big King goaded them on. 'Between you all you wouldn't crack the shell of an egg. Hit it, man! Hit it!'

One by one the men fell back exhausted, their chests heaving, gulping air through gaping mouths, blinded by their own sweat.

'All right,' Johnny intervened. The rock was holding up the whole blast. It warranted drastic measures to break it up.

'I'll pop her,' he said, and any government inspector or mine safety officer would have paled at those words.

'Stand far back and turn your faces away,' Big King instructed his gang. From the forehead of one of his men he took a pair of wire mesh goggles, designed to shield the eyes from flying splinters and rock fragments. He handed them to Johnny who placed them over his eyes.

From the canvas carrying bag he took out a stick of Dynagel. It looked like a candle wrapped in yellow greased paper.

'Give me your knife.' Big King opened a large clasp knife and handed it to Johnny.

Carefully Johnny cut a coin-shaped sliver of explosive from one end of the stick, a piece twice as thick as a penny.

He returned the remains of the stick to the bag and handed it to Big King.

'Get back,' he said and Big King moved away.

Johnny eyed the slab of rock thoughtfully and then placed the fragment of Dynagel in the centre of it. He adjusted the goggles over his eyes, and picked up one of the fourteen-pound hammers.

'Turn your eyes away,' he warned and took deliberate aim. Then with a smooth overhead two-handed swing he brought the hammer down on the Dynagel.

The explosion was painful in the confined space of the drive, and afterwards Johnny's ears hummed with it. A tiny drop of blood ran down his cheek from the scratch inflicted by a flying splinter. His wrists ached from the jolt of the hammer in his hands.

'Gwenyama!' grunted Big King in admiration. 'The man is a lion.'

The explosion had cracked the slab into three wedge-shaped segments. Johnny pushed the goggles onto his forehead and wiped the blood from his cheek with the back of his hand.

'Get it the hell out of here,' he grinned, then he turned to Big King.

'Come.' He jerked his head towards the end of the tunnel. 'Help me charge the holes.'

The two of them worked quickly, sliding the sticks of Dynagel into the shot holes and tamping them home with the charging sticks.

For anyone who was not in possession of a blasting licence, to charge up was an offence punishable by a fine of one hundred rand or two months' imprisonment, or both. Big King had no licence, but his assistance saved fifteen minutes on the operation.

Johnny and his gang blew the face five times that day, but as they rode up in the cage into the cool evening air he was not satisfied.

'Tomorrow we'll shoot her six times,' he told Big King.

'Maybe seven,' said Big King.

Hettie was waiting for him in the lounge when he got home. She flew to him and threw her arms about his neck.

'Did you bring me a present?' she asked with her lips against his ear, and Johnny laughed tantalizingly. It was very seldom that he did not have a gift for her.

'You did!' she exclaimed, and began to run her hands over his pockets.

'There!' She thrust her hand into the inside pocket of his jacket, and brought out the little white jeweller's box.

'Oh!' She opened it, and then her expression changed slightly.

'You don't like them?' Johnny asked anxiously.

'How much did they cost?' she enquired as she examined the porcelain and lacquer earrings, representing two vividly coloured parrots.

'Well,' Johnny looked shamefaced, 'you see, Hettie, it's the end of the month, you see, and well, like I'm a bit short till pay day, you see, so I couldn't—'

'How much?'

'Well, you see,' he took a breath, 'two rand fifty.'

'Oh,' said Hettie, 'they're nice.' And she promptly lost interest in them. She tossed the box carelessly onto the crowded mantelpiece and set off for the kitchen.

'Hey, Hettie,' Johnny called after her. 'How about we go across to Fochville? There's a dance there tonight. We go and twist, hey?'

Hettie turned back, her expression alive again.

'Gee, yes, man!' she enthused. 'Let's do that. I'll go and change, hey!' And she ran up the passage.

Davy came out of his bedroom, on his way to work.

'Hey, Davy.' Johnny stopped him. 'You got any money on you?'

'Are you broke again?'

'Just till pay day.'

'Hell, man, Johnny, you got a cheque for eleven hundred the beginning of the month. You spent it all?'

'Next month,' Johnny winked, 'I'm going to get a cheque for two or three thousand. Then watch me go! Come, Davy, lend me fifty. I'm taking Hettie dancing.'

– 47 –

For Rod the days flicked past like telegraph poles viewed from a speeding automobile. Each day he gained confidence in his own ability. He had never doubted that he could handle the underground operation and now he found that he had a firm grasp on the surface as well. He knew that his campaign to reduce working costs was having effect, but its full harvest would only be apparent when the quarterly reports were drafted.

Yet he lay awake in the big Manager's residence on the ridge in which he and his few sticks of furniture seemed lost and lonely, and he worried. There were always myriad nagging little problems, but there were others more serious.

This morning Lily Jordan had come through into his office.

'Mr Innes is coming up to see you at nine.'

'What's he want?' Herbert Innes was the Manager of the Sonder Ditch Reduction works.

'He wouldn't tell me,' Lily answered. The end of the month had come and gone and Lily was still with him. Rod presumed that he had been approved.

Herby Innes, burly and red-faced, sat down and drank the cup of tea that Lily provided, while he regaled Rod with a stroke by stroke account of his Sunday afternoon golf round. Rod interrupted him after he had hit a nine-iron short at the third and shanked his chip.

'Okay, Herby. What's the problem?'

'We've got a leak, Rod.'

'Bad?'

'Bad enough,' Herby grunted. To him the loss of a single ounce of gold during the process of recovery and refinement was catastrophic.

'What do you reckon?'

'Between the wash and the pour we are losing a couple hundred ounces a week.'

'Yes,' Rod agreed. 'That is bad enough.'

20,000 rand a month, 120,000 a year.

'Have you any ideas?'

'It's been going on for some time, even in Frank Lemmer's day. We have tried everything.'

Rod was a little hazy about the workings of the reduction plant, not that he would admit that, but he was. He knew that the ore was weighed and sampled when it reached the surface, from this a fairly accurate estimate of gold content was made and compared with actual recovery. Any discrepancy had to be investigated and traced.

'What is your recovery rate for the last quarter?'

'Ninety-six point seven-three.'

'That's pretty good,' Rod admitted. It was impossible to recover all the gold in the ore that was surfaced but Herby was getting most of it out. 96.73 per cent of it, to be precise. Which meant that very little of the missing 200 ounces was being lost into the dumps and the slimes dam.

'I tell you what, Herby,' Rod decided. 'I'll come down to the plant this afternoon. We'll go over it together, perhaps a fresh eye may be able to spot the trouble.'

'May do.' Herby was sceptical. 'We've tried everything else. We are pouring this afternoon. What time shall I expect you?'

'Two o'clock.'

They started at the shaft head, where the ore cage, the copie, arrived at the surface every four minutes with its cargo of rock which it dumped into a concrete shute. Each load was classified as either 'reef' or 'waste'.

The reef was dropped into the massive storage bins, while the waste was carried off on a conveyor to the wash house to be sluiced down before going to the dump. Tiny particles of gold sticking to the waste rock were gathered in this way.

Herby put his lips close to Rod's ear to make himself heard above the rumbling roar of rock rolling down the chute.

'I'm not worried about this end. It's all bulk here and very little shine.' Herby used the reduction plant slang for gold. 'The closer we get to the end, the more dangerous it is.'

Rod nodded and followed Herby down the steel ladder until they reached a door below the storage bins. They went through into a long underground tunnel very similar to the ore tunnel on 100 level.

Again there was a massive conveyor belt moving steadily along the tunnel while ore from the bins above was fed onto it. Rod and Herby walked along beside the belt until it passed under a massive electromagnet. Here they paused for a while. The magnet was extracting from the ore all those pieces of metal which had found their way into the ore passes and bins.

'How much you picking up?' Rod asked.

'Last week fourteen tons,' Herby answered, and taking Rod's arm led him through the door beside them. They were in an open yard that looked like a scrap-metal merchant's premises. A mountain of pinchbars, jumper bits, shovels, steel wire rope, snatch blocks, chains, spanners, fourteen-pound hammers, and other twisted and unrecognizable pieces of metal filled the yard. All of it was rusted, much of it unusable. It had been separated from the ore by the magnet.

Rod's mouth tightened. Here he was presented with indisputable evidence of the carelessness and it-belongs-to-the-company attitude of his men. This pile of scrap represented a waste that would total hundreds of thousands of rand annually.

'We will see about that!' he muttered.

'If one of those hammers got into my jaw mills it would smash it to pieces,' Herby told him dolefully and led him back into the conveyor tunnel.

The belt angled upwards sharply and they followed the catwalk beside it. They climbed steadily for five minutes and Herby was puffing like a steam engine. Through the holes in the honeycomb steel plate under his feet, Rod could see that they were now a few hundred feet above ground level.

The conveyor reached the head of a tall tower and dumped its load of ore into the gaping mouths of the screeners. As the rock fell down the tower to ground level again it was sorted for size, and the larger pieces diverted to the jaw crushers which chewed it into fistsize bites.

'See anything?' Herby asked, barely concealing the sarcasm.

Rod grinned at him.

They climbed down the steel ladders that seemed endless. The screeners rattling and the crushers hammering, until Rod's eardrums pleaded for mercy.

At last they reached ground level and went through into the mill room. This was a cavernous galvanized-iron shed the size of a large aircraft hangar. At least one hundred yards long and fifty feet high, it was filled with long rows of the cylindrical tube mills.

Forty of them in all, they were as thick as the boiler of a steam locomotive and about twice as long. Into one end of them was fed the ore which had been reduced in size by the jaw crushers. The tube mills revolved and the loose steel balls within them pounded the rock to powder.

157

If the noise before had been bad, it was hideous in the mill room. Rod and Herby made no effort to speak to each other until they had walked through into the comparative quiet of the first heavy-media separator room.

'Now,' Herby explained. 'This is where we start worrying.' He indicated the rows of pale blue six-inch piping that came through the wall from the mill room.

'In there is the powdered rock mixed with water to a smooth flowing paste. About forty per cent of the gold is free.'

'No one can get into those pipes and you've checked for any possible leak?' Rod asked. Herby nodded.

'But,' he said, 'have a look here!'

Along the far wall was a series of cages. They were made of heavy steel mesh, the perforations would not allow a man's finger through. The heavy steel doors were barred and locked. Outside each battery of cages stood a Bantu attendant in clean white overalls. They were all concentrating on the manipulation of the turncock that obviously regulated the flow of the powdered ore through the pipes.

Herby stopped at one of the cages.

'Shine!' He pointed. Beyond the heavy guard screen the grey paste of rock powder was flowing from a series of nozzles over an inclined black rubber sheet. The surface of the rubber sheet was deeply corrugated, and in each corrugation the free gold was collecting, held there by its own weight. The gold was thick as butter in a Dagwood sandwich, greasy yellow-looking in the folds of rubber.

Rod laid hold of the steel screen and shook it.

'No,' Herby laughed. 'No one will get in that way.'

'How do you clean the gold off that sheet? Does someone have access to the separator?' Rod asked.

'The separator cleans itself automatically,' Herby answered. 'Look!'

Rod noticed for the first time that the rubber sheet was moving very slowly, it was also an endless belt running round two rollers. As the belt inverted, so fine jets of water washed the gold from the corrugations into a collection tank.

'I'm the only one who has access. We change the collection tanks daily,' said Herby.

It looked foolproof, Rod had to admit.

Rod turned and glanced down the row of four Bantu attendants. They were all intent on their duties, and Rod knew that each of them had a high security rating. They had been carefully selected and screened before being allowed into the reduction works.

'Satisfied?' Herby asked.

'Okay,' Rod nodded, and the two of them went out through the door in the far wall. Locking it behind them.

Immediately they had gone the four Bantu attendants reacted. They straightened up, the scowls of concentration smoothed out to be replaced by grins of relief. One made a remark and they all laughed, and opened the waist bands of their tunics. From inside each trouser leg they drew a length of quarter-inch copper wire and began probing them through the steel screen.

It had taken Crooked Leg, the photographer, almost a year to work out a means of milking gold from the heavily screened and guarded separators. The method which he had discovered was, like all workable plans, extremely simple.

Mercury, quicksilver, absorbs gold the way blotting paper sucks up moisture. It will suck in any speck of gold that comes in contact with it. Mercury has a further property, it can be made to spread on copper like butter on bread. This layer of mercury on copper retains its powers of absorbing gold.

Crooked Leg had devised the idea of coating lengths of copper wire with mercury. The wire could be inserted through the apertures in the steel mesh and the wire laid across the corrugated rubber sheet, where it set about mopping up every speck of gold that flowed over it. The lengths of wire could be quickly slipped down the trouser leg at the approach of an official, and they could be smuggled in and out of the reduction works the same way.

Every evening Crooked Leg retrieved the gold-thickened wire, and issued his four accomplices with newly coated lengths. Every night in the abandoned workings beyond the ridge he boiled the mercury to make it release its gold.

'Now,' Herby could speak normally in the blessed quiet of the cyanide plant, 'we have skimmed off the free gold – and we are left with the sulphide gold.' He offered Rod a cigarette as they made their way between the massive steel tanks that spread over many acres. 'We pump this into the tanks and add cyanide. The cyanide dissolves the gold and takes it into solution. We tap it off and run it through zinc powder. The gold is deposited on the zinc, we burn away the zinc and we are left with the gold.'

Rod lit his cigarette. He knew all this but Herby was giving him a Cooks' tour for visiting VIPs. He flicked his lighter for Herby. 'There is no way anyone could swipe it when it's in solution.'

Herby shook his head, exhaling smoke. 'Apart from anything else, cyanide is a deadly poison.' He glanced at his watch. 'Three-twenty, they'll be pouring now. Shall we go across to the smelt house?'

The smelt house was the only brick building among all the galvanized iron. It stood a little isolated. Its windows were high up and heavily barred.

At the steel door Herby buzzed, and a peephole opened in the door. He and Rod were immediately recognized and the door swung open. They were in a cage of bars which could only be opened once the door was closed behind them.

'Afternoon, Mr Ironsides, Mr Innes.' The guard was apologetic. 'Would you sign, please?' He was a retired policeman with a paunch and a holstered revolver on his hip.

They signed and the guard signalled to his mate on the steel catwalk high above the smelt room floor. This guard tucked his pump action shotgun under one arm, and threw the switch on the walk beside him.

The cage door opened and they went through.

Along the far wall the electric furnaces were set into the brickwork. They resembled the doors of the bread ovens in a bakery.

The concrete floor of the room was uncluttered, except for the mechanical loader that carried the gold crucible in its steel arms, and the moulds before it. The half dozen personnel of the smelt house barely looked up as Rod and Herby approached.

The pour was well advanced, the arms of the loader tilted and a thin stream of molten gold issued from the spout of the crucible, and fell into the mould. The gold hissed and smoked and crackled, and tiny red and blue sparks twinkled on its surface as it cooled.

Already forty or fifty bars were laid out on the rubber-wheeled trolley beside the mould. Each bar was a little smaller than a cigar box. It had the knobby bumpy look of roughly cast metal.

Rod stopped and touched one of the bars. It was still hot and it had the slightly greasy feeling that new gold always has.

'How much?' he asked Herby, and Herby shrugged.

'About a million rand's worth, perhaps a little more.'

So that's what a million rand looks like, Rod mused, it's not very impressive.

'What's the procedure now?' Rod asked.

'We weigh it, and stamp the weight and batch number into each bar.' He pointed to a massive circular safe deposit door in the near wall. 'It's stored there overnight, and tomorrow a refinery armoured car will come out from Johannesburg and pick it up.' Herby led the way out of the smelt house. 'Anyway, that's not the trouble. Our leak is sucking off the shine before it ever reaches the smelt house.'

'Let me think about it for a few days,' Rod said. 'Then we'll get together again, try and find the solution.'

He was still thinking about it now. Lying in the darkness and smoking cigarette after cigarette.

There seemed to be only one solution. They would have to plant Bantu police in the reduction works.

It was an endless game involving all the mining companies and their reduction plant personnel. An inventive mind would devise a new system of sucking off the shine. The Company would become aware of the activity by comparison of estimated and actual recovery and they would work on the leak for a week, a month, sometimes a year. Then they would break the system. There would be prosecutions, stiff gaol sentences, and the Company would circularize its neighbours, and they would all settle back and wait for the next customer to appear.

Gold has many remarkable properties, its weight, its non-corruptibility and, not least, the greed and lust it conjures up in the hearts of men.

Rod stubbed his cigarette, rolled onto his side and pulled the bedclothes up over his shoulders. His last thought before sleep was for the major problem that, these days, was never very far from the surface of his mind.

The Delange brothers had driven almost 1,500 feet in two weeks. At this rate they would hit the Big Dipper seven weeks from now, then even the theft of gold would pale into insignificance.

At the time that Rod Ironsides was composing himself for sleep, Big King was taking a little wine with his business associate and tribal brother Philemon N'gabai, alias Crooked Leg.

They sat facing each other in a pair of dilapidated cane chairs with a lantern and a gallon jug of Jeripigo set between them. The bat stench of the abandoned workings did little to bring out the bouquet of the wine, which was of small concern to either man, for they were drinking not for taste but for effect.

Crooked Leg refilled the cheap glass tumbler that Big King proferred, and as the wine glug-glugged from the jar he continued his attack on the character and moral fibre of José Almeida, the Portuguese.

'For many months now I have had it in my heart to speak to you of these matters,' he told Big King, 'but I have waited until I could set a deadfall for the man. He is like a lion that preys upon our herds, we hear him roar in the night and in the dawn we see his spoor in the earth about the carcasses of our animals, but we cannot meet him face to face.'

Big King enjoyed listening to the oratory of Crooked Leg and while he listened he drank the Jeripigo as though it were water, and Crooked Leg kept refilling the tumbler for him.

'In counsel with myself I spoke thus: "Philemon N'gabai, it is not enough that thou should suspect this white man. It is necessary also that you see with your own eyes that he is eating your substance".'

'How, Crooked Leg?' Big King's voice was thickening, the level of the jug had fallen steadily and now showed less than half. 'Tell me how we shall take this man.' Big King showed a fist the size of a bunch of bananas. 'I will . . .'

'No, Big King.' Crooked Leg was scandalized. 'You must not hurt the man. How then would we sell our gold? We must prove he is cheating us and show him we know it. Then we will proceed as ever, but he will give us full measure in the future.'

Big King thought about that for some time, then at last he sighed regretfully. 'You are right, Crooked Leg. Still, I would have liked to . . .' He showed that fist again, and Crooked Leg went on hurriedly.

'Therefore, I have sent to my brother who drives a delivery van for SA Scale Company in Johannesburg, and he has taken from his Company a carefully measured weight of eight ounces.' Crooked Leg produced the cylindrical metal weight from his pocket and handed it to Big King who examined it with interest. 'Tonight, after the Portuguese has weighed the gold you take to him, you will say, "Now, my friend, please weigh this for me on your scale," and you will watch to see that his scale reads the correct number. Each time in the future he will weigh this on his scale before we sell our gold.'

'Hau!' Big King chuckled. 'You are a crafty one, Crooked Leg.'

Big King's eyes were smoky and blood-shot. The Jeripigo was a raw rough fortified wine, and he had drunk very nearly a gallon of it. He sat opposite the Portuguese store-keeper in the back room behind the concession store, and watched while he poured the gold dust into the pan of the jeweller's scale. It made a yellow pyramid that shone dully in the light from the single bare bulb above their heads.

'One hundred and twenty-three ounces.' Almeida looked up at Big King for confirmation, a strand of greasy black hair hung onto his forehead. His face was pale from lack of sun so that the blue stubble of beard was in heavy contrast.

'That is right,' Big King nodded. He could taste the

liquor fumes in the back of his throat, and they were as strong as his distaste for the man who sat opposite him. He belched.

Almeida removed the pan from the scale and carefully poured the dust back into the screw-top bottle.

'I will get the money.' He half rose from his chair.

'Wait!' said Big King, and the Portuguese looked at him in mild surprise.

Big King took the weight from the pocket of his jacket. He placed it on the desk.

'Weigh that on your scale,' he said in Portuguese.

Almeida's eyes flicked down to the weight, and then back to Big King's face. He sank back into his seat, and pushed the strand of hair off his forehead. He began to speak, but his voice cracked and he cleared his throat.

'Why? Is there something wrong?' Suddenly he was aware of the size of the man opposite him. He could smell the liquor on his breath.

'Weigh it!' Big King's voice was flat, without rancour. His face was expressionless, but the smoky red glare of his eyes was murderous.

Suddenly Almeida was afraid, deadly, coldly afraid. He could guess what would happen once the error in his balance was disclosed.

'Very well,' he said, and his voice was forced and off key. The pistol was in the drawer beside his right knee. It was loaded, with a cartridge under the hammer. The safety-catch was on, but that would only delay him an instant. He knew it would not be necessary to fire, once he had the weapon in his hand he would have control of the situation again.

If he did have to fire, the calibre was .45 and the heavy slug would stop even a giant like this Bantu. *Self-defence*, he was working it out feverishly. A *burglar*, I surprised him and he attacked. *Self-defence*. It would work. They'd believe it.

But how to get the pistol? Try and sneak it out of the drawer, or make a grab for it?

There was a desk between them, it would take a few seconds for the Bantu to realize what he was doing, a few more for him to get around the desk. He would have plenty of time.

He snatched the handle of the drawer, and it flew open. His fingernails scrabbled against the woodwork as he clawed for the big black U.S. Navy automatic, and with a surge of triumph his hand closed over the butt.

Big King came over the top of the desk like a black avalanche. The scale and the jar of gold dust were swept aside to clatter and shatter against the floor.

Still seated in his chair, with the pistol in his hand, Almeida was borne over backwards with Big King on top of him. Many years before, Big King had worked with a safari outfit in Portuguese East Africa, and he had seen the effect of gunshot wounds in the flesh of dead animals.

In the instant that he had recognized the weapon in Almeida's hand, he had been as afraid as the Portuguese. Fear had triggered the speed of his reaction, it was responsible for the savagery of his attack as he lay over the struggling body of the Portuguese.

He had Almeida's pistol hand held by the wrist and he was shaking it to force him to drop the firearm. With his right hand he had the Portuguese by the throat, and instinctively he was applying the full strength of his arms to both grips. He felt something break under his right hand, cracking like the kernel of a nut, and his fingers were suddenly without strength, and the gun skittered across the floor to come up against the far wall with a thump.

Only then did Big King begin to regain the sanity that fear had scattered. Suddenly he realized that the Portuguese was lying quietly under him. He released his grip and scrambled to his knees. The Portuguese was dead. His neck was twisted away from his shoulders at an impossible angle. His eyes were wide and surprised, and a smear of blood issued from one nostril over his upper lip.

Big King backed away towards the door, his gaze fixed in horror on the sprawling corpse. When he reached the door, he hesitated, fighting down the urge to run. He subdued it, and went back to kneel beside the desk. First he picked up the controversial cylindrical weight and placed it in his pocket, then he began sweeping up the scattered gold dust and the shattered fragments of the screw-topped container. He placed them into separate envelopes that he found among the papers on the desk. Ten minutes later he slipped out through the back door of the concession store, into the night.

– 49 –

At the time Big King was hurrying back towards the mine hostel, Rod Ironsides thrashed restlessly in a bed in which the sheets were already bunched and damp with sweat. He was imprisoned in his own fantasy, locked in a nightmare from which he could not break away. The nightmare was infinite and green, quivering, unearthly, translucent. He knew it was held back only by a transparent barrier of glass. He cowered before it, and he knew it was icy cold, he could see light shining through it, and he was deadly afraid.

Suddenly there was a crack in the glass wall, a hairline crack, and through it oozed a single drop. A large, pear-shaped drop, as perfect as though it had been painted by Tretchikoff. It glittered like a gemstone.

It was the most terrifying thing that Rod had ever seen in his life. He cried out in his sleep, trying to warn them, but the crack starred further, and the drop slid down the glass, to be followed by another and another. Suddenly a jagged slab of glass exploded out of the wall, and Rod screamed as the water burst through, in a frothing jet.

With a roar the entire glass wall collapsed, and a mountain high wave of green water hissed down upon him, carrying a white plume of spray at its crest.

He awoke sitting upright in his bed, a cry of horror on his lips and his body bathed in sweat. It took minutes for him to steady the wild racing of his heart. Then he went through to the bathroom. He ran a glass of water and held it up to the light. 'Water. It's there!' he muttered. 'I know it's there!' He drank from the tumbler.

Standing naked, with his sweat drying cold on his body, the tumbler held to his lips, the idea came to him. He had never heard of anyone trying it before, but then nobody he knew would be crazy enough to drive into a death trap like the Big Dipper.

'I'll drill and charge a matt of explosive into the hanging wall of the drive. I'll get the Delange boys on to it right away. Then at any time I choose I can blast the whole bloody roof in and seal off the tunnel.'

Rod was surprised at the strength of the relief that flooded over him. He knew then how it had been worrying him. He went back to the bedroom and straightened out his bedclothes. However, sleep would not come easily to him. His imagination was overheated, and a series of events and ideas kept playing through his mind, until abruptly he was presented with the image of Terry Steyner.

He had not seen her for almost two weeks, not since their meeting just after Manfred Steyner's return from Europe. He had spoken to her twice on the telephone, hasty, confused conversations that left him feeling dissatisfied. He was increasingly aware that he was missing her. His one attempt to find solace elsewhere had been a miserable failure. He had lost interest halfway through the approach manoeuvres and had returned the young lady to the bosom of her family at the unheard-of hour of eleven o'clock on a Saturday night.

Only the unremitting demands of his new job had prevented him from slipping away to Johannesburg and taking a risk.

'You know, Ironsides, you'd better start bracing up a little, don't lose your head over this woman. Remember our vow – *Never Again!*'

He punched the pillow into shape and settled into it.

Terry lay quietly, waiting for it. It was after one o'clock in the morning. It was one of those nights. He would come soon now. As never before she was filled with dread. A cold slimy feeling in the pit of her stomach. Yet she had been fortunate. He had not been near her since his return from Paris. Over two weeks, but it could not last. Tonight.

She heard the sound of the car coming up the drive and she felt physically ill. I can't do it, she decided, not any more, not ever again. It wasn't meant to be like this, I know that now. It's not dirty and furtive and horrible, it's like . . . like . . . it's the way Rod makes it.

She heard him in his bedroom, suddenly she sat up in bed. She felt desperate, hunted.

The door of her room opened softly.

'Manfred?' she asked sharply.

'It's me. Don't worry.' He came briskly towards her bed, a dark impersonal shape and he was undoing the cord of his dressing-gown.

'Manfred,' Terry blurted. 'I'm early this month, I'm sorry.'

He stopped. She saw his hands fall back to his sides, and he stood completely still.

'Oh!' he said at last, and she heard him shuffle his feet into the thick pile of the carpet. 'I just came to tell you,' he hesitated, seeking an excuse for his visit, 'that . . . that I'll be going away for five days. Leaving on Friday. I have to go to Durban and Cape Town.'

'I'll pack for you,' she said.

'What? Oh, yes – thank you.' He shuffled his feet again. 'Well, then.' He hesitated, then stooped quickly and brushed her cheek with his lips. 'Good night, Theresa.'

'Good night, Manfred.'

Five days. She lay alone in the darkness and gloated. *Five whole days alone with Rod.*

– 50 –

D etective Inspector Hannes Grobbelaar of the South African Criminal Investigation Department sat on the edge of the office chair with his hat tipped onto the back of his head and spoke into the telephone, which he held in a handkerchief-covered hand. He was a tall man with a long sad face and a mournful-looking moustache that was streaked with grey.

'Gold buying,' he said into the receiver, and then in reply to the obvious question, 'There's gold dust spilled all over the place and a jeweller's scale, and a .45 automatic with a full magazine and the safety-catch still on, dead man's prints on it.' He listened. 'Ja. Ja. All right, ja. Broken neck, looks like.' Inspector Grobbelaar swivelled his chair and looked down at the corpse that lay on the floor beside him. 'Bit of blood on his lip, but nothing else.'

One of the finger-print men came to the desk and Grobbelaar stood up to give him room to work, the receiver still held to his ear.

'Prints?' he asked in disgust. 'There are finger prints on everything, we have isolated at least forty separate sets so far.' He listened a few seconds. 'No, we will get him, all right. It must be a Bantu mine worker and we have got all the finger prints of the men from outside the Republic. It's just a matter of checking them all out and then questioning. Ja, we'll have him within a month, that's for sure! I'll be back at John Vorster Square about five o'clock, just as soon as we finish up here.' He hung up the receiver, and stood looking down at the murdered man.

'Ugly bastard,' said Sergeant Hugo beside him. 'Asked for it, buying gold. It's as bad as diamonds.' He drew attention to the large envelope he carried in his hand. 'I've got a whole lot of glass fragments. Looks like the container the gold was in. The murderer tried to clean up, but he didn't make a very good job. These were under the desk.'

'Prints?'

'Only one piece big enough. It's got a smeary print on it. Might be of use.'

'Good,' Grobbelaar nodded. 'Get cracking on that, then.'

There was a feminine wail from somewhere in the interior of the building, and Hugo grimaced.

'There she starts again. Hell, I thought she'd exhausted herself. Bloody Portuguese women are the end.'

'You should hear them having a baby,' grunted Grobbelaar.

'Where did you hear one?'

'There was one in the ward next door to my old girl at the maternity home. She nearly brought the bloody roof down.'

Grobbelaar's moustache took on a more melancholy droop as he thought about the work that lay ahead. Hours, days, weeks of questioning and checking and cross-checking, with a succession of sullen and uncooperative suspects.

He sighed and jerked a thumb at the corpse. 'All right, we've finished with him. Tell the butcher boys to come and fetch him.'

I t had taken Rod almost two days to design his dropblast matt. The angle and depth of the shot holes were carefully placed to achieve maximum disruption of the hanging wall. In addition he had decided to drill and charge the side walls of the drive with charges timed to explode *after* the hanging wall had collapsed. This would kick in on the rubble filling the tunnel and jam it solid.

Rod was fully aware of the power of water under pressures of 2,000 pounds per square inch and more and he had decided it was necessary to block at least 300 feet of the tunnel. His matt blast was designed to do so, and yet he knew that this would not seal off the water completely. It would, however, reduce the flow sufficiently to allow cementation crews to get in and plug the drive solid.

The Delange brothers did not share Rod's enthusiasm for the project.

'Hey man, that's going to take three or four days to drill and charge,' Johnny protested when Rod showed him his carefully drawn plan.

'Like hell it will,' Rod growled at him. 'I want it done properly. It will take at least a week.'

'You said ultra-fast. You didn't say nothing about drilling the hanging wall with more holes than a cheese!'

'Well, I'm saying it now,' Rod told him grimly. 'And I'm also saying that you will drill, but you won't charge the holes until I come down and make sure that you've gone in as deep as I want them.'

He didn't trust either Johnny or Davy to spend time drilling in twenty feet, when he could go in six feet, charge up and nobody would know the difference. Not until it was too late.

Davy Delange spoke for the first time.

'Will you credit us bonus fathomage while we fiddle around with this?' he asked.

'Four fathoms a shift.' Rod agreed to pay them for the removal of fictitious rock.

'Eight?' said Davy.

'Hell, no!' Rod exclaimed. That was robbery.

'I don't know,' Davy murmured, watching Rod with sly ferrety little eyes. 'Maybe I should talk to Brother Duivenhage, you know, ask his advice.'

Duivenhage was No. 1 shaft shop steward for the Mine Workers' Union. He had driven Frank Lemmer to the edge of a nervous breakdown and was now starting on Rodney Ironsides. Rod was pleading with Head Office to offer Duivenhage a fat job in management to get him out of the way. The last thing in the world that Rod wanted was Brother Duivenhage snooping around his drive on the Big Dipper.

'Six,' he said.

'Well . . .' Davy hesitated.

'Six is fair, Davy,' Johnny interrupted, and Davy glared at him. Johnny had snatched complete victory from his grasp.

'Good, that's agreed.' Quickly Rod closed the negotiations. 'You'll start drilling the matt right away.'

Rod's design demanded nearly 1,200 shot holes to be filled with two and a half tons of explosive. It was 1,000 feet down the drive from the main haulage on 66 level to where the matt began.

The drive now was a spacious, well lit and freshly ventilated tunnel, with the vent piping, the compressed air pipe, and the electrical cable bolted into the hanging wall, and a set of steel railway tracks laid along the floor.

All work on the face ceased while the Delange brothers set about drilling the matt. It was light work that demanded little from the men. As each hole was drilled, Davy would insert his charging rod to check the depth and then plug the entrance with a wad of paper. There was much time for drinking Thermos coffee and for thinking.

There were three subjects that endlessly occupied Davy's mind as he sat at ease, waiting for the completion of the next shot hole. Sometimes for half an hour at a time Davy would hold the image of that 50,000 rand in his mind. It was his, tax paid, painstakingly accumulated over the years and lovingly deposited with the local branch of the Johannesburg Building Society. He imagined it bundled and stacked in neat green piles in the Society's vault. Each bundle was labelled 'David Delange'.

Then his imagination would pass automatically on to the farm that the money would buy. He saw how it would be in the evenings when he sat on the wide stoep, with the setting sun striking the peaks of the Swart Berg across the valley, and the cattle coming in from the paddocks towards the homestead.

Always there was a woman sitting beside him on the stoep. The woman had red hair.

On the fifth morning Davy drove home in the dawn, he was not tired. The night's labours had been easy and unexacting.

The door of Johnny and Hettie's bedroom was closed. Davy read the newspapers with his breakfast; as always the cartoon strip adventures of Modesty Blaise and Willie Garvin intrigued him completely. This morning Modesty was depicted in a bikini and Davy studied her comparing her to the big healthy body of his brother's wife. The thought of her stayed with him as he rolled onto his bed, and he lay unsleeping, daydreaming an adventure in which

Modesty Blaise had become Hettie, and Willie Garvin was Davy.

An hour later he was still awake. He sat up and reached for the towel which lay across the foot of his bed. He wrapped the towel around his waist as he went down the passage to the bathroom. As he reached for the handle of the bathroom door, it opened under his hand and he was face to face with Hettie Delange.

She wore a white lace dressing-gown with ostrich-feather mules on her feet. Her face was innocent of make-up and she had brushed her hair and tied it with a ribbon.

'Oh!' she gasped with surprise. 'You gave me a fright, man.'

'I'm sorry, hey.' Davy grinned at her, holding the towel with one hand. Hettie let her eyes run quickly over his naked upper body.

Davy was muscled like a prizefighter. His chest hair was crisp and curly. On both arms the tattoos drew attention to the thickness and weight of muscle.

'Gee, you *are* built,' Hettie murmured in admiration, and Davy sucked in his belly reflexively.

'You think so?' His grin was self-conscious now.

'Yes.' Hettie leaned forward and touched his arm. 'It's hard too!'

The movement had allowed the front of her dressing-gown to gape open. Davy's face flushed as he looked down into the opening. He started to say something, but his voice had dried up on him. Hettie's fingers stroked down his arm, and she was watching the direction of his eyes. Slowly she moved closer to him.

'Do you like me, Davy?' she asked, her voice throaty and low, and with an animal cry Davy attacked her.

His hands ripping at the opening of her gown, pinning her to the wall of the bathroom with his mouth frantically hunting hers. His body pressing hard and urgent, his eyes wild, his breathing ragged.

175

Hettie was laughing, a breathless gasping laugh.

This was what she loved. When they lost their heads, when they went mad for her.

'Davy,' she said, jerking loose his towel. 'Davy.'

She kept wriggling away from his thrusting hips, knowing that it would inflame him further. His hands were tearing at her body, his eyes were maniacal.

'Yes!' she hissed into his mouth. He threw her off balance and she slid down the wall onto the floor.

'Wait,' she panted. 'Not here – the bedroom.'

But it was too late.

Davy had spent the afternoon locked in his bedroom, lying on his bed in an agony of black all-pervading remorse and guilt.

'My brother,' he kept repeating. 'Johnny is my brother.'

Once he wept, each sob tearing something in his chest. The tears squeezed out between burning eyelids, leaving him feeling exhausted and weak.

'My *own* brother,' he shook his head slowly in horrified disbelief. 'I cannot stay here,' he decided miserably. 'I'll have to go.'

He went to the washbasin and washed his eyes. Stooping over the basin, water still dripping from his face, he decided.

'I will have to tell him.' The burden of guilt was too heavy. 'I'll write to Johnny. I'll write it all, and then I'll go away.'

Frantically he searched for pen and paper, it was almost as though he could wipe away the deed by writing it down. He sat at the table by the window and wrote slowly and laboriously. When he had finished it was three o'clock. He felt better.

He sealed the four closely written pages into an envelope and slipped it into the inside pocket of his jacket. He dressed quickly, and crept out of the house, fearful of meeting Hettie, but she was nowhere about. Her big white Monaco was not in the garage, and with relief he turned out of the driveway and took the road out to the Sonder Ditch. He wanted to reach the mine before Johnny came off shift.

Davy listened to his brother's voice, as he kidded and laughed with the other off-duty miners in the company change house. He had locked himself in one of the lavatory closets to avoid meeting his brother, and he sat disconsolately on the toilet seat. The sound of Johnny's voice brought his guilt flooding back in its full strength. His letter of confession was buttoned into the top pocket of his overalls, and he took it out, broke open the flap and reread the contents.

'So long, then.' Johnny's voice sang out gaily from the change room. 'See you bastards tomorrow.'

There was an answering chorus from the other miners, then the door slammed.

Davy went on sitting alone for another twenty minutes in the stench of stale bodies and urine, dirty socks and rank disinfections from the foot baths. At last he tucked the letter away in his pocket and opened the closet door.

Davy's gang were at their waiting place at the head of the drive. They were sitting along the bench laughing and chatting. There was a holiday spirit amongst them for they knew it would be another shift of easy going.

They greeted Davy cheerfully, as he came down the haulage. Both the Delange brothers were popular with their gangs and it was unusual that Davy did not reply to the chorused greeting. He did not even smile.

The Swazi boss boy handed him the safety lamp, and Davy grunted an acknowledgement. He set off alone down the tunnel, trudging heavily, not conscious of his surroundings, his mind encased in a padding of guilt and self-pity.

A thousand feet along the drive he reached the day's work area. Johnny's shift had left the rock drills in place, still connected to the compressed air system, ready for use. Davy came to a halt in the centre of the work area, and without a conscious command from his brain his hands began the routine process of striking the wick of the safety lamp.

The little blue flame came alight behind the protective screen of wire mesh, and Davy held the lamp at eye level before him and walked slowly along the drive. His eyes were watching the flame without seeing it.

The air in the tunnel was cool and refrigerated, scrubbed and filtered, there was no odour nor taste to it. Davy walked on somnambulantly. He was wallowing in self-pity now. He saw himself in a semi-heroic role, one of the great lovers of history caught up in tragic circumstances. His brain was fully occupied with the picture. His eyes were unseeing. Blindly he performed the ritual that a thousand times before had begun the day's shift.

Slowly in its wire mesh cage the blue flame of the safety lamp changed shape. Its crest flattened, and there formed above it a ghostly pale line. Davy's eyes saw it, but his brain refused to accept the message. He walked on in a stupor of guilt and self-pity.

That line above the flame was called 'the cap', it signified that there was at least a five per cent concentration of methane gas in the air. The last shot hole that Johnny Delange's gang had drilled before going off shift had bored into a methane-filled fissure. For the previous three hours, gas had been blowing out of that hole. The ventilation system was unable to wash the air fast enough and now the gas had spread slowly down the drive. The air surrounding Davy's body was heavy with gas, he had breathed it into his lungs. It needed just one spark to ignite it.

Davy reached the end of the drive and snapped the snuffer over the wick, extinguishing the flame in the lamp.

'All safe,' he muttered, not realizing that he had spoken. He went back to his waiting men.

'All safe,' he repeated, and with the Swazi boss boy leading them the forty men of Davy Delange's gang trooped gaily into the mouth of the drive.

Moodily Davy followed them. As he walked he reached into his hip pocket and took out a pack of Lexington filter tips. He put one between his lips, returned the pack and began patting his pockets to locate his lighter.

Davy went from team to team of his machine boys, directing them in the line and spot to be drilled. Every time he spoke, the unlit cigarette waggled between his lips. He gesticulated with the hand that held his cigarette-lighter.

It took twenty minutes for him to set all his drills to work. And he stood and looked back along the tunnel. Each machine boy and his assistant formed a separate sculpture. Most of them were stripped to the waist. Their bodes appeared to be carved and polished in oiled ebony, as they braced themselves behind the massive rock drills.

Davy lifted his cupped hands, holding the cigarette-lighter near his face, and he flicked the cog wheel.

The air in the tunnel turned to flame. In a flash explosion, the flame reached the temperature of a welding torch. It seared the skin from the faces and exposed bodies of the machine boys, it burned the hair from their scalps. It turned their arms to charred stumps. It roasted their eyeballs in their sockets. It scorched their clothing, so as they fell the cloth smouldered and burned against their flesh.

In that instant, as the skin was licked from his face and hands, Davy Delange opened his mouth in a great gasp of agony. The flame shot down his throat into his gas-drenched lungs. Within the confines of his body the gas exploded and his chest popped like a paper bag, his ribs fanning outward about the massive wound like the petals of a sunflower.

Forty-one men died at the same moment. In the silence

179

after that whooshing, sucking detonation, they lay like scorched insects along the floor of the drive. One or two of them were moving still, an arched spine relaxing, a leg straightening, charred fingers unclenching, but within a minute all was absolutely still.

Half an hour later Doctor Dan Stander and Rodney Ironsides were the first men into the drive. The smell of burned flesh was overpowering. Both of them had to swallow down their nausea as they went forward.

– 52 –

Dan Stander sat at his desk and looked out over the car park in front of the mine hospital. He appeared to have aged ten years since the previous evening. Dan envied his colleagues the detachment they could bring to their work. He had never been able to perfect the trick. He had just completed forty-one examinations for issue of death certificates.

For fifteen years he had been a mine doctor, so he was accustomed to dealing with death in its more hideous forms. This, however, was the worst he had ever encountered. Forty-one of them, all victims of severe burning and massive explosion trauma.

He felt washed out, exhausted with ugliness. He massaged his temples as he examined the tray of pathetic possessions that lay on the desk before him. This was the contents of the pockets of the man Delange. Extracting them from the scorched clothing had been a filthy business in itself. Cloth had burned into the flesh, the man had been wearing a cheap nylon shirt under his overalls. The fabric had melted in the heat and had become part of his blistered skin.

There was a bunch of keys on a brass ring, a Joseph Rogers pen-knife with a bone handle, a Ronson cigarette-lighter which had been clutched in the man's clawed and charred right hand, a springbok skin wallet, and a loose envelope with one corner burned away.

Dan had already passed on the effects of the Bantu victims to the agent of the Bantu Recruiting Agency, who would send them on to the men's families. Now he sighed with distaste and picked up the wallet. He opened it.

In one compartment there were half a dozen postage stamps, and five rands in notes. The other flap bulged with paper. Dan glanced through salesmen's cards, dry-cleaning receipts, newspaper cuttings offering farms for sale, a folded page from the *Farmer's Weekly* on the planning of a dairy herd, a JBS savings book.

Dan opened the savings book and whistled when he saw the total. He fanned the remaining pages.

There was a much-fingered envelope, unsealed and tucked behind the cardboard cover of the savings book. Dan opened it, and pulled a face. It contained a selection of photographs of the type which one found offered for sale in the dock area of the Mozambique port of Lourenço Marques. It was for this type of material that Dan was searching.

When the man's possessions were returned to his grieving relatives, Dan wanted to spare them this evidence of human frailty. He burned the photographs and the envelope in his ashtray and then crushed the blackened sheets to powder before spilling it into his waste-paper bin.

He went across to the window and opened it to let the smell of smoke escape. He stood at the window and searched the car park for Joy's Alfa Romeo. She had not arrived as yet and Dan returned to his desk.

The remaining envelope caught his eye and he picked it up. There was a smear of blood upon it, and the corner was burned away. Dan removed the four sheets of paper and spread them on the desk:

Dear Johnny,

When Pa died you were still little – and I always reckoned you were more like my son, you know, than my brother.

Well, Johnny, I reckon now I've got to tell you something . . .

Dan read slowly, and he did not hear Joy come into the room. She stood at the door watching him. Her expression fond, a small smile on her lips, shiny blonde hair hanging straight to her shoulders. Then she moved up quietly behind his chair and kissed his ear. Dan started and turned to face her.

'Darling,' Joy said and kissed him on the mouth. 'What is so interesting that you ignore my arrival?'

Dan hesitated a moment before telling her.

'There was a man killed last night in a ghastly accident. This was in his pocket.'

He handed her the letter and she read it slowly.

'He was going to send this to his brother?' she asked, and Dan nodded.

'The bitch,' Joy whispered, and Dan looked surprised.

'Who?'

'The girl – it's her fault, you know.' Joy opened her purse and took out a tissue to dab her eyes. 'Damn it, now I'm messing my make-up.' She sniffed, and then went on. 'It would serve her right if you gave that letter to her husband.'

'You mean I shouldn't give it to him?' Dan asked. 'We have no right to play God.'

'Haven't we?' asked Joy, and Dan watched quietly as she tore the letter to tiny shreds, screwed them into a ball, then dropped them into the waste bin.

'You are wonderful,' he said. 'Will you marry me?'

'I've already answered that question, Dr Stander.' And she kissed him again.

53

Hettie Delange was in a turmoil.

It had started with the phone call that had roused Johnny from their bed. He had said something about trouble at the shaft as he pulled on his clothes, but she had come only briefly awake and then drifted off again as Johnny hurried out into the night.

He had come in hours later and sat on the edge of the bed, his hands clasped between his knees and his head bowed.

'What's wrong, man,' she had snapped at him. 'Come to bed. Don't just sit there.'

'Davy's dead.' His voice had been listless.

There was a moment's shock that had convulsed the muscles of her belly, and brought her fully awake. Then, immediately, she had felt a swift cleansing rush of relief.

He was dead. It was as easy as that! All day she had worried. She had been stupid to let it happen. Just that moment of weakness, that self-indulgent slip and she had been dreading the consequences all that day. She had imagined Davy trailing after her with puppy eyes, trying to touch her, making it so obvious that even Johnny would see it. She had enjoyed it but just the once was enough. She wanted no repeat performance and certainly no complications to follow the original deed.

Now it was all taken care of. He was dead.

'Are you sure?' she had asked anxiously, and Johnny heard the tone as concern.

'I saw him!' Johnny had shuddered, and wiped the back of his hand across his mouth.

'Gee, that's terrible.' Hettie had remembered her role, and sat up and put her arms about Johnny. 'That's terrible for you.'

She had not slept again that night. Somehow the

thought of Davy going directly from her to his violent death was exciting. It was like in the movies, or a book, or something. Like he was an airman and he had been shot down, and she was his girl. Perhaps she was pregnant and all alone in the world, and she would have to go to Buckingham Palace and get his medal for him. And the Queen would say . . .

The fantasies had played out in her mind until the dawn, with Johnny tossing and muttering beside her.

She woke him when it was first light in the room.

'How was he?' she asked softly. 'What did he look like, Johnny?'

Johnny shuddered again, and then he started to tell her. His voice was husky, and the sentences broken and disconnected. When he stumbled into silence, Hettie found herself trembling with excitement.

'How terrible,' she kept repeating. 'Oh, how awful!' And she pressed against him. After a while Johnny made love to her, and for Hettie it was better than she had ever known it to be.

All that morning there were phone calls, and four of her friends came over to drink coffee with her. A reporter and photographer from the *Johannesburg Star* called and asked questions. Hettie was the centre of attraction, and again and again she repeated the story with all its grisly details.

After lunch Johnny came home with a little dark-haired man in a charcoal suit and black Italian shoes, with a matching black briefcase.

'Hettie, this is Mr Boart. He was Davy's lawyer. He's got something to tell you.'

'Mrs Delange. May I convey to you my sincere condolences in the tragic bereavement you and your husband have suffered.'

'Yes, it's terrible, isn't it?' Hettie was apprehensive. Had Davy told this lawyer about them? Had this man come to make trouble?

'Your brother-in-law made a will of which I am the executor. Your brother-in-law was a wealthy man. His estate is in excess of fifty thousand rand.' Boart paused portentously. 'And you and your husband are the sole beneficiaries.'

Hettie looked dubiously from Boart to Johnny.

'I don't – what's that mean? Beneficiary?'

'It means that you and your husband share the estate between you.'

'I get half of fifty thousand rand?' Hettie asked in delighted disbelief.

'That's right.'

'Gee,' exulted Hettie. 'That's fabulous!' She could hardly wait for Johnny and the lawyer to go before she phoned her friends again. All four of them returned to drink more coffee, to thrill again and to envy Hettie the glamour and excitement of it.

'Twenty-five thousand,' they kept repeating the sum with relish.

'Hell, man, he must really have liked you a lot, Hettie,' one of the girls commented with heavy emphasis, and Hettie lowered her eyes and contrived to look bereft and mysterious.

Johnny came home after six, unsteady on his feet and reeking of liquor. Reluctantly Hettie's four friends left to rejoin their waiting families, and almost immediately after that a big white sports car pulled up in the driveway and Hettie's day of triumph was complete. Not one of her friends had ever had the General Manager of the Sonder Ditch Gold Mining Company call at their home.

She had the front door open the instant the doorbell rang. Her greeting had been shamelessly plagiarized from a period movie that had recently played at the local cinema.

'Mr Ironsides, how good of you to come.'

When she led Rod through into the over-furnished lounge, Johnny looked up but did not get to his feet.

'Hello, Johnny', said Rod. 'I have come to tell you that I'm sorry about Davy, and to . . .'

'Don't give me that bull dust, Tin Ribs,' said Johnny Delange.

'Johnny,' gasped Hettie, 'you can't talk to Mr Ironsides like that.' And she turned to Rod, laying a hand on his sleeve. 'He doesn't mean it, Mr Ironsides. He has been drinking.'

'Get out of here,' said Johnny. 'Get into the bloody kitchen where you belong.'

'Johnny!'

'Get out!' roared Johnny, rising from his chair, and Hettie fled from the room.

Johnny lurched across to the chrome and glass liquor cabinet that filled one corner. He sloshed whisky into two glasses and handed one to Rod.

'God speed to my brother,' he said.

'To Davy Delange, one of the best rock hounds on the Kitchenerville field,' said Rod, and tossed the drink back in one gulp.

'The best!' Johnny corrected him, and emptied his own glass. He gasped at the sting of the whisky, then leaned forward to speak into Rod's face.

'You've come to find out if I'm game to finish your bloody drive for you, or if I'm going to quit. Davy didn't mean nothing to you and I don't mean nothing to you. Only one thing worrying you – you want to know about your bloody drive.' Johnny refilled his glass. 'Well, hear this, friend, and hear it well. Johnny Delange don't quit. That drive ate my brother but I'll beat the bastard, so you got nothing to worry about. You go home and get a good night's sleep, 'cos Johnny Delange will be on shift and breaking rock tomorrow morning first thing.'

54

A Silver Cloud Rolls-Royce was parked amongst the trees in the misty morning. Ahead was the practice track with the white-painted railings curving away towards the willow-lined river. The mist was heavier along the river and the grass was very green against it.

The uniformed chauffeur stood away from the Rolls, leaving its two occupants in privacy. They sat on the back seat with an angora wool travelling rug spread over their knees. On the folding table in front of them was a silver Thermos of coffee, shell-thin porcelain cups, and a plate of ham sandwiches.

The fat man was eating steadily, washing each mouthful down with coffee. The little bald-headed man was not eating, instead he puffed quickly and nervously at his cigarette and looked out of the window at the horses. The grooms were walking the horses in circles, nostrils streaming in the morning chill, blankets flapping. The jockeys stood looking up at the trainer. They wore hard caps and polo-necked jerseys. All of them carried whips. The trainer was speaking urgently, his hands thrust deep into the pockets of his overcoat.

'It's a very fine service,' said the little man. 'I particularly enjoyed the stop in Rio. My first visit there.'

The fat man grunted. He was annoyed. They shouldn't have sent this agent out. It was a mark of suspicion, distrust, and it would seriously hamper his market operation.

The conference between trainer and jockeys had ended. The diminutive riders scattered to their mounts, and the trainer came towards the Rolls.

'Good morning, sir.' He spoke through the open window, and the fat man grunted again.

'I'm giving him a full run,' the trainer went on. 'Emerald Isle will make pace for him to the five, Pater Noster will take over and push him to the mile, I've Tiger Shark to pace him for the run in.'

'Very well.'

'Perhaps you'd like to keep time, sir.' The trainer proffered a stop-watch, and the fat man seemed to recover his urbanity and charm.

'Thank you, Henry.' He smiled. 'He looks good, I'll say that.'

The trainer was pleased by the condescension.

'Oh! He's red-hot! By Saturday I'll have him sharpened down to razor edge.' He stood back from the window. 'I'll get them off, then.' He walked away.

'You have a message for me?' asked the fat man.

'Of course.' The other wriggled his moustache like a rabbit's whiskers. It was an annoying habit. 'I didn't fly all this way out here to watch a couple of mokes trotting around a race-track.'

'Would you like to give me the message?' The fat man hid his affront. What the agent had called a moke was some of the finest horseflesh in Africa.

'They want to know about this gas explosion.'

'Nothing.' The fat man dismissed the question with a wave of his hand. 'A flash explosion. Killed a few men. No damage to the workings. Negligence on the part of the miner in charge.'

'Will it affect our plans?'

'Not one iota.'

The two horses had jumped away from the start, shoulder to shoulder, with the wreaths of mist swirling in their wake. The glossy bay horse on the rails ran with an easy floating action while the grey plunged along beside it.

'My principals are very concerned.'

'Well, they have no need to be,' snapped the fat man. 'I tell you it makes no difference.'

'Was the explosion due to an error of judgement on the part of this man Ironsides?'

188

'No.' The fat man shook his head. 'It was negligence of the miner in charge. He should have detected the gas.'

'Pity.' The bald man shook his head regretfully. 'We had hoped it was a flaw in the Ironsides character.'

The grey horse was tiring, while the bay ran on smoothly, drawing away from him. From the side rail a third horse came in to replace the grey, and ran shoulder to shoulder with the bay.

'Why should the character of Ironsides concern you?'

'We have heard disturbing reports. This is no pawn to be moved at will. He is taking the job of General Manager by the throat. Already our sources indicate that he has reduced running costs on the Sonder Ditch by a scarcely believable two per cent. He seems to be tireless, inventive – a man, in short, to reckon with.'

'Well and good,' the fat man conceded. 'But I still fail to see why your – ah, principals – are alarmed. Do they expect that this man will hold back the flood waters by the sheer force of his personality?'

The second pacemaker was faltering, but still the big bay ran on alone. A far figure in the mist, passing the mile post, joined at last by the third pacemaker.

'I know nothing about horses,' said the bald man watching the two flying forms. 'But I've just seen that one,' he pointed with his cigarette at the far-off bay. 'I've just seen him run the guts out of the other two. One after the other he has broken their hearts and left them staggering along behind him. We would call him an imponderable, one who cannot be judged by normal standards.' He puffed at his cigarette before going on. 'There are men like that also, imponderable. It seems to us that Ironsides is one of them, and we don't like it. We don't like them on the opposing team. It is just possible that he could upset the entire operation, not, as you put it, by sheer force of personality, but by suddenly doing the unexpected, by behaving in a manner for which we have not allowed.'

Both men fell silent watching the galloping horses come round the last bend and hit the straight.

'Watch this.' The fat man spoke softly, and as though in response to his words the big bay lengthened his stride, reaching out, driving strongly away from the other horse. His head was going like a hammer, twin jets of steam shot from wide flaring nostrils, and thrown turf and dirt flew from his hooves. Five lengths clear of the following horse he went slashing past the finish line and the fat man clicked his stop watch.

He scrutinized the dial of the watch anxiously and then chuckled like a healthy baby.

'And he wasn't really being extended!'

He rapped on the window beside him, and immediately the uniformed chauffeur opened the driving door and slid in behind the wheel.

'To my office,' instructed the fat man, 'and close the partition.'

When the sound-proof glass panel had slid closed between driver and passengers, the fat man turned to his guest.

'And so, my friend, you consider Ironsides to be an imponderable. What do you want me to do about him?'

'Get rid of him.'

'Do you mean what I think you mean?' The fat man lifted an eyebrow.

'No. Nothing that drastic.' The bald head bobbed agitatedly. 'You have been reading too much James Bond. Simply arrange it that Ironsides is far away and well occupied when the drive holes through the Big Dipper Dyke, otherwise there is an excellent chance that he will do something to frustrate our good intentions.'

'I think we can arrange that,' said the fat man and helped himself to another ham sandwich.

55

As he had promised, Manfred caught the Friday evening flight for Cape Town. On the Saturday night Rod and Terry took a wild chance on not being recognized and spent the evening at the Kyalami Ranch Hotel. They danced and dined in the Africa Room, but were on their way back to the apartment before midnight.

In the dawn a playful slap with the rolled-up Sunday papers which Rod delivered to Terry's naked posterior as she slept triggered off a noisy brawl in which a picture was knocked off the wall by a flying pillow, a coffee table overturned and the shrieking and laughter reached such a pitch that it called down a storm of indignant thumping from the apartment above them.

Terry made a defiant gesture at the ceiling, but they both subsided gasping with laughter back onto the bed to indulge in activity every bit as strenuous if not nearly so noisy.

Later, much later, they collected Melanie and once again spent the Sunday at the stud farm on the Vaal. Melanie actually *rode* a horse, a traumatic experience which bade fair to alter her whole existence. After lunch they launched the speedboat from the boat house on the bank of the river and water-skied down as far as the barrage, Terry and Rod taking turns at the wheel and on the skis. It occurred to Rod that Terry Steyner looked good in a white bikini. It was dark before Rod delivered his sleeping daughter to her mother.

'Who is this *Terry* that Melanie talks about all the time?' demanded Patti; she was still sulking about Rod's promotion. Patti had a memory like a tax collector.

'Terry?' Rod feigned surprise. 'I thought you knew.' And he left Patti glaring after him as he went back down the stairs.

Terry was curled up in the leather bucket seat of the Maserati, just the tip of her nose protruding from the voluminous fur coat she wore.

'I love your daughter, Mr Ironsides,' she murmured.

'It would appear that the feeling is reciprocated.'

Rod drove slowly towards the Hillbrow ridge, and Terry's hand came out of the wide fur sleeve and lay on his knee.

'Wouldn't it be nice if we had a daughter of our own one day?'

'Wouldn't it,' Rod agreed dutifully, and then found to his intense amazement that he really meant it.

He was still investigating this remarkable phenomenon as he parked the Maserati in the basement garage of his apartment and went round to open Terry's door.

Manfred Steyner watched Terry climb out of the Maserati and lift her face towards Rodney Ironsides. Ironsides stooped over her and kissed her, then he slammed and locked the door of the Maserati, and arm in arm the two of them crossed to the elevator.

'Peterson Investigations always delivers the goods,' said the man at the wheel of the black Ford parked in the shadows of the garage. 'We will give them half an hour to get settled in comfortably, then we will go up and knock on the door of his apartment.'

Manfred Steyner sat very still and unblinking on the seat beside the private detective. He had arrived back in Johannesburg three hours previously in answer to the summons from the investigation bureau.

'You will leave me here. Drive the Ford out and park at the corner of Clarendon Circle. Wait for me there,' said Manfred.

'Hey? Aren't you going to . . . ?' The detective was taken aback.

'Do as I tell you.' Manfred's voice stung like thrown vitriol, but the detective persisted.

'You will need evidence for the court, you need me as a witness . . .'

'Get out,' Manfred snapped, and opening the door of the Ford he climbed out and closed the door behind him. The detective hesitated a moment longer, then started the engine and drove out of the garage leaving Manfred alone.

Manfred moved slowly towards the big shiny sports car. From his pocket he took a gold-plated pen-knife and opened the large blade.

He had recognized that the car was of special significance to the man. It was the only form of retaliation he could make at the moment. Until Rodney Ironsides completed the drive on the Big Dipper Dyke, he could not confront him nor Theresa Steyner. He could not let them know he even suspected them.

Such human emotions as love and hate and jealousy Manfred Steyner seldom experienced, except in their mildest manifestations. Theresa Hirschfeld he had never loved, as he had never loved any woman. He had married her for her wealth and station in life. The emotion that gripped him was neither hatred nor jealousy. It was affront. He was affronted that these two insignificant persons should conspire to cheat him.

He would not rush in blindly now with threats of physical violence and divorce. No, he would administer an anonymous punishment that would hurt the man deeply. This would be part payment. Later, when he had served his purpose, Manfred would crush him as coldly as though he were stepping on an ant.

As for the woman, he was aware of a mild relief. Her irresponsible behaviour had placed her completely at his mercy, both legally and morally. As soon as the strike beyond the Big Dipper had made him financially secure and independent, he could throw her aside. She would have served her purpose admirably.

The journey which he had interrupted by this hurried return to Johannesburg was connected with the purchase of Sonder Ditch shares. He was touring the major centres arranging with various firms of stock brokers that on a given date they would commence to purchase every available scrap of Sonder Ditch script.

As soon as he had completed this business he would tell the private detective to drive him out to Jan Smuts Airport where he had a reservation on the night plane to Durban where he would continue his preparations.

It had all worked out very well, he thought, as he slipped the knife blade through the rubber buffer of the triangular side window of the Maserati. With a quick twist he lifted the window catch, and pushed the window open. He reached through and turned the door handle. The door clicked open and Manfred climbed into the driver's seat.

The blade of the pen-knife was razor sharp. He started on the passenger seat and then the driver's seat, ripping the leather upholstery to shreds before moving to the back seat and repeating the process there. He slid the panel that concealed the tray of tools each in their separate foam rubber padded compartment, and selected a tyre lever.

With this he smashed all the dials on the dashboard, broken glass tinkling and falling to the carpeted floor. With the point of the tyre lever he dug into the rosewood panelling and tore out a section, splintering and cracking the woodwork into complete ruin.

He climbed out of the Maserati and struck the windshield with the tyre lever. The glass starred. He rained blows on it, unable to shatter it but reducing it to a sagging opaque sheet.

Then he dropped the tyre lever and groped for his pen-knife again. On his knees he slashed at the front offside tyre. The rubber was tougher than he had allowed. Annoyed, he slashed again. The knife turned in his hand, the blade folding against the blow. It sliced the ball of his thumb, a deep stinging cut. Manfred came to his feet with a cry, clutching his injured thumb. Blood spurted from the wound.

'Mein Gott! Mein Gott!' Manfred gasped, horrified by his own blood. As he staggered wildly from the basement garage, he was wrapping a handkerchief around his thumb.

He reached the waiting Ford, hauled the door open and fell into the front seat beside the detective.

'A doctor! For God's sake, get me to a doctor. I'm badly hurt. Quickly! Drive quickly!'

– 56 –

Terry's husband is due back in town today, Rod thought, as he sat down at his desk. It was not a thought that gave him strength to work through a day he knew would be filled with hectic activity.

The quarterly reports were due at Head Office tomorrow morning. In consequence the entire administration was in its usual last-minute panic. Already there was a mob in the waiting-room outside his office that Lily Jordan would soon need a stock whip to control. At three o'clock he was due at a consultants' meeting at Head Office, but before that he wanted to go underground to check the drop-blast matt that Johnny Delange had now completed and charged up.

The phone went as Lily led in his first visitor, a tall, thin, sorrowful-looking man with a droopy moustache.

'Mr Ironsides?' said the voice on the phone.

'Yes.'

'Porters Motors here. I've got an estimate on the repairs to your Maserati.'

'How much?' Rod crossed his fingers.

'Twelve hundred rand.'

'Wow!' Rod gasped.

'Do you want us to go ahead?'

'No, I'll have to contact my insurance company first. I'll call you.' He hung up. That act of unaccountable vandalism still irked him terribly. He realized that he would be reduced to the Company Volkswagen for a further indefinite period.

He turned his attention to his visitor.

'Detective Inspector Grobbelaar,' the tall man introduced himself. 'I am investigating officer in the murder of José Almeida, the concession store proprietor on this mine.'

They shook hands.

'Have you any ideas on who did it?' Rod asked.

'We have always got ideas,' said the Inspector, so sadly that for a moment Rod had the impression that his name was on the list of suspects. 'We believe that the murderer is employed by one of the mines in the district, probably the Sonder Ditch. I have called on you to ask for your co-operation in the investigation.'

'Of course.'

'I will be conducting a great number of interrogations amongst your Bantu employees. I hoped you might find a room for me to use on the premises.'

Rod lifted his phone and while he dialled he told Grobbelaar, 'I'm calling our Compound Manager.' Then he transferred his attention to the mouthpiece. 'Ironsides here. I am sending an Inspector Grobbelaar down to see you. Please see that an office is placed at his disposal and that he receives full co-operation.'

Grobbelaar stood up and extended his hand.

'I won't take up more of your time. Thank you, Mr Ironsides.'

His next visitor was Van der Bergh, his Personnel Officer, brandishing his departmental reports as though they were a winning lottery ticket.

'All finished,' he announced triumphantly. 'All we need is your signature.'

As Rod uncapped his pen, the telephone squealed again.

'My God,' he muttered with pen in one hand and telephone in the other. 'Is it worth it?'

It was well after one o'clock when Rod fled his office, leaving Lily Jordan to hold back the tide. He went directly to No. 1 shaft where he was welcomed like the prodigal son by Dimitri and his old Line Managers. They were all anxious to know who would be replacing him as Underground Manager. Rod promised to find out that afternoon when he visited Head Office, and changed into his overalls and helmet.

At the spot where Davy Delange had died, Rod found a gang fixing a screen of wire mesh over the hanging wall to protect the fuses of his drop-blast. The electric cable that carried the blasting circuit to the surface was covered with a distinctive green plastic coating and securely pegged to the roof of the drive.

In the concrete blast room at the shaft head, his electrician had already set up a separate control for this circuit. It would be in readiness at all times. He could fire it within minutes. Rod felt as though a great weight had been lifted from his shoulders as he passed through the swinging ventilation doors and tramped on up the drive to speak to Johnny Delange.

Halfway to the face he met the gigantic figure of Big King coming back towards him with a small gang of lashing boys under his command. Rod greeted him, and Big King stopped and let his gang go on out of earshot before he spoke.

'I wish to speak.'

'Speak then.' Rod noticed suddenly that Big King's face was gaunt, his eyes appeared sunken and his skin had the dusty greyish look of sickness so evident in an ailing Bantu.

'I wish to return to my wives in Portuguese Mozambique,' said Big King.

'Why?' Rod was dismayed at the prospect of losing such a valuable boss boy.

'My blood is thin.' This was as non-committal an answer as any man has ever received. In essence it meant, 'My reasons are my own, and I have no intention of disclosing them.'

'When your blood is thick again, will you return to work here?' Rod asked.

'That is with the gods.' An answer signifying no more than the one preceding it.

'I cannot stop you if you wish to go, Big King, you know that,' Rod told him. 'Report to the Compound Manager and he will mark your notice.'

'I have told the Compound Manager. He wants me to work out my ticket, thirty-three more days.'

'Of course,' Rod nodded. 'You know that it is a contract. You must work it out.'

'I wish to leave at once,' Big King replied stubbornly.

'Then you must give me your reason. I cannot let you break contract except if there is some good reason.' Rod knew better than to set a dangerous precedent like that.

'There is no reason.' Big King admitted defeat. 'I will work out the ticket.'

He left Rod and followed his gang down the drive. Since the night he killed the Portuguese, Big King had slept little and eaten less. Worry had kept his stomach in a turmoil of dysentery, he had neither danced nor sung. Nothing that Crooked Leg nor the Shangaan Induna could say comforted him. He waited for the police to come. As the days passed, so the flesh melted from his body, he knew that they could come before the thirty-three days of his contract expired.

His approach to Rod had been a last despairing effort. Now he was resigned. He knew that the police were inexorable. One day soon they would come. They would lock the silver chains on his wrists and lead him to the closed van. He had seen many men led away like that and he had heard what happened to them after that. The white man's law was the same as the tribal law of the Shangaans. The taking of life must be paid for with life.

They would break his neck with the rope. His ancestors would have crushed his skull with a war club, it was the same in the end.

Rod found Johnny Delange drinking cold tea from his canteen while his gang barred down the face.

'How's it going?' he asked.

'Now we have finished messing about, it has started moving again.' Johnny wiped cold tea from his lips and recorked the canteen. 'We have broken almost fifteen hundred feet since Davy died.'

'That's good going.' Rod ignored the reference to the methane explosion and the drop-blast matt.

'Would have been better if Davy were still alive.' Johnny disliked Campbell, the miner who had replaced Davy on the night shift. 'The night shift aren't breaking their fair ground.'

'I'll chase them up,' Rod promised.

'You do that.' Johnny turned away to shout an order at his gang.

Rod stood and stared at the end of the drive. Less than a thousand feet ahead lay the dark hard rock of the Big Dipper – and beyond it . . . ? Rod felt his skin creep as he remembered his nightmare. That cold green translucent thing waiting for them beyond the dyke.

'All right, Johnny, you are getting close now.' Rod tore his imagination away from that green horror. 'As soon as you hit the serpentine rock you are to stop work immediately and report to me. Is that understood?'

'You'd better tell that to Campbell also,' said Johnny. 'The night shift may hit the Big Dipper.'

'I'll tell him,' Rod agreed. 'But you make sure you

remember. I want to be down here when we hole through the dyke.'

Rod glanced at his watch. It was almost two o'clock. He had an hour to get to the consultant's meeting at Head Office.

'You are late, Mr Ironsides.' Dr Manfred Steyner looked up from the head of the boardroom table.

'My apologies, gentlemen.' Rod took his seat at the long oak table. 'Just one of those days.'

The men about the table murmured sympathetic acknowledgement, and Dr Steyner studied him for a moment without expression before remarking, 'I would be obliged for a few minutes of your time after this meeting, Mr Ironsides.'

'Of course, Dr Steyner.'

'Good.' Manfred nodded. 'Now that Mr Ironsides has graced the table with his presence, the meeting can come to order.' It was the closest any of them had ever heard Dr Steyner come to making a joke.

It was dark outside when the meeting ended. The participants shrugged on their coats, made their farewells and left Manfred and Rod sitting at the table with its overflowing ashtrays and littered pencils and note pads.

Manfred Steyner waited for fully three minutes after the door had closed on the last person to leave. Rod was accustomed to these long intent silences, yet he was uneasy. He sensed a new hostility in the man's attitude. He covered his awkwardness by lighting another cigarette and blowing a series of smoke rings at the portrait of Norman Hradsky, the original chairman of the Company. Flanking Hradsky's portrait were two others. One of a slim blond man, with ravaged good looks and laughing blue eyes. The caption read: 'Dufford Charleywood. Director of CRC from 1867–1872.' The other portrait in its heavy gilt frame depicted an impressively built man with mutton-chop whiskers and black Irish features. 'Sean Courtney' said the caption, and the dates were the same as Charleywood's.

These three had founded the Company, and Rod knew a little of their story. They had been as pretty a bunch of rogues as would be found in any convict settlement. Hradsky had ruined the other two in an ingenious bear raid on the stock exchange, and had virtually stolen their shares in the Company.*

We have become a lot more sophisticated since then, thought Rod. He looked instinctively towards the head of the long table and met Dr Steyner's level, unblinking stare. *Or have we?* he wondered. Just what devilment has our friend in mind?

Manfred Steyner was examining Rod with detached curiosity. So remote from any emotional rancour was Manfred, that he intended using the relationship that had developed between this man and his wife to further the instructions he had received that morning.

'How far is the end of the drive from the dyke?' he asked suddenly.

'Less than a thousand feet.'

'How much longer before you reach it?'

'Ten days. No more, possibly less.'

'As soon as the dyke is reached, all work on it must cease immediately. The timing of this is important, do you understand?'

'I have already instructed my miners not to hole through without my specific orders.'

'Good.' Manfred lapsed into silence for another full minute. Andrew had called him that morning with instructions from the man. Ironsides was to be well away from the Sonder Ditch when they pierced the dyke. It was left to Manfred to engineer his absence.

---

* Read *When the Lion Feeds*.

'I must inform you, Mr Ironsides, that it will be at least three weeks before I give the order to drill through. When you reach the dyke, it will be necessary for me to proceed to Europe to make certain arrangements there. I will be away for at least ten days during which time no work of any type must be allowed in the drive to the Big Dipper.'

'You will be away over Christmas?' Rod asked with surprise.

'Yes,' Manfred nodded, and could read Rod's mind.

Terry will be alone, Rod thought quickly, she will be alone over Christmas. The Sonder Ditch goes onto *essential services only* for a full seven days over Christmas. Just a skeleton crew to keep her going. I could get away for a week, a whole week away together.

Manfred waited until he knew that Rod had reached the decision to which he had been steered, then he asked: 'You understand? You will await my order to hole through. You need not expect that order until the middle of January.'

'I understand.'

'You may go.' Manfred dismissed him.

'Thanks,' Rod acknowledged drily.

There was a coffee bar in the ground-floor shopping centre of Reef Building. Rod beat a bearded hippie to the tele-phone booth, and dialled the Sandown number. It was safe enough, he had just left Manfred upstairs.

'Theresa Steyner,' she answered his call.

'We've got a week to ourselves,' he told her. 'One whole glorious week.'

'When?' she demanded joyously.

And he told her.

'Where shall we go?' she asked.

'We'll think of somewhere.'

At 11.26 a.m. on December 16th, Johnny Delange blasted the face of the drive, and went forward in the fumes and dust.

In the beam of his lantern, the new rock blown from the face was completely different from the blueish Ventersdorp quartzite. It was a glassy, blackish green, veined with tiny white lines, more like marble than country rock.

'We are on the dyke.' He spoke to Big King, and stooped to pick up a lump of the serpentine rock. He weighed it in his hand.

'We've done it, we've beaten the bastard!'

Big King stood silently beside him. He did not share Johnny's elation.

'Right!' Johnny tossed the lump of rock back onto the pile. 'Bar down, and make safe. Then pull them out of the drive. We are finished here until further orders.'

'Well done, Johnny,' applauded Rod. 'Clean her up and pull out of the drive. I don't know how much longer it will be till we get the order to hole through the dyke. But take a holiday in the meantime. I'll pay you four fathoms of bonus a day while you are waiting.' He broke the connection with his finger, keeping the receiver to his ear. He dialled and spoke to the switch-board girl at Head Office. 'Get me Dr Steyner, please. This is Rodney Ironsides.' He waited a few seconds and then Manfred came on the line.

'We've hit the Big Dipper,' Rod told him.

'I will leave for Europe on tomorrow morning's Boeing,' said Manfred. 'You are to do nothing until I return.' Manfred cradled the receiver and depressed the button on his intercom.

'Cancel all my appointments,' he told his secretary. 'I am unavailable.'

'Very well, Dr Steyner.'

Manfred picked up the receiver of his unlisted, direct-line telephone. He dialled.

'Hello, Andrew. Will you tell him that I am ready to discharge my obligations. We have intersected the Big Dipper.' He listened for a few seconds, then spoke again. 'Very well, I will wait for your reply.'

Andrew replaced the telephone and went out through the sliding glass doors onto the terrace. It was a lazy summer's day, hushed with heat, and the sun sparkled on the crystal clear waters of the swimming-pool. Insects murmured languidly in the massed banks of blooms that surrounded the terrace.

The fat man stood before an artist's easel. He wore a blue beret and a white smock that hung like a maternity dress over his jutting stomach.

His model lay face down on an air mattress by the edge of the pool. She was a dainty, dark-haired girl with a pixy face and a doll-like body. Her discarded bikini lay in a damp bundle on the flags of the terrace. Drops of water caught the sun and bejewelled her creamy buttocks, giving her a paradoxical air of innocence and oriental eroticism.

'That was Steyner,' said Andrew. 'He reports that they have hit the Big Dipper.'

The fat man did not look up. He went on laying paint upon the canvas with complete concentration.

'Please lift your right shoulder, my dear, you are covering that utterly delightful bosom of yours,' he instructed, and the girl obeyed him immediately.

Finally he stepped back and regarded his own work critically.

'You may have a break now.' He wiped his brushes while the naked girl stood up, stretched like a cat and then dived into the pool. She surfaced with the water slicking her short dark hair against her head like the pelt of an otter, and swam slowly to the far end of the pool.

'Cable New York, Paris, London, Tokyo and Berlin the code word "Gothic",' he instructed Andrew. This was the word which would unleash the bear offensive on the financial markets of the world. On receipt of those cables, agents in the major cities would begin to sell the shares of the companies mining the Kitchenerville field, sell them by the millions.

'Then instruct Steyner to get Ironsides out of the way, and hole through the dyke.'

Manfred answered Andrew's return call on the unlisted line. He listened to, and acknowledged, his instructions. Afterwards he sat still as a lizard, running over his preparations. Reviewing them minutely, examining them for flaws. There were none.

It was time to begin the purchase of Sonder Ditch shares. He called his secretary on the intercom and instructed her to place calls to numbers in Cape Town, Durban and Johannesburg itself. He wanted the purchase orders to come through a number of different brokers, so that it would not be obvious that there was only one buyer in the market. There was also the question of credit; he was not covering the purchase orders with banker's guarantees. The stock brokers were buying for him simply on his name and reputation and position with CRC Manfred could not place too large a buying order with any one firm lest they ask him to provide surety. Dr Manfred Steyner had no surety to offer.

So, instead, he placed moderate orders with dozens of different firms. By three o'clock that afternoon Manfred had ordered the purchase of three quarters of a million rand's worth of shares. He had no means of paying for those shares but he knew he would never be called upon to do so. When he sold them again in a few weeks' time they would have doubled in value.

A few minutes after his final conversation with the firm of Swerling and Wright in Cape Town, his secretary came through on the intercom.

'SAA have confirmed your reservation on the Boeing to Salisbury. Flight 126 at nine a.m. tomorrow. You are booked to return to Johannesburg on the Rhodesian Airways Viking at 6 p.m. tomorrow evening.'

'Thank you.' Manfred grudged this wasted day but it was imperative that Theresa believed he had left for Europe. She must see him depart on the SAA flight. 'Please get my wife on the phone for me.'

'Theresa,' he told her, 'something important has come up. I have to fly to London tomorrow morning. I am afraid I will be away over Christmas.'

Her display of surprise and regret was unconvincing. She and Ironsides had made their own arrangements for the time he was away, Manfred was convinced of this.

It was all working out very well, he thought as he cradled the receiver, very well indeed.

– 58 –

The Daimler drew up under the portico of Jan Smuts Airport and the chauffeur opened the door for Terry and then for Manfred.

While the porter removed his luggage from the boot of the Daimler, Manfred swept the car park with a quick scrutiny. So early in the morning it was less than half filled. There was a cream Volkswagen with a Kitchenerville number plate parked near the far end. All the line and senior members of the Sonder Ditch had cream Volks-wagens as their official vehicles.

'The bee has come to the honeypot,' thought Manfred, and smiled bleakly. He took Terry's elbow into the main concourse of the airport.

Terry waited while Manfred went through his ticket and immigration formalities. On the outside she was a demure and dutiful wife, but she also had seen the Volkswagen and inside she was itching and bubbling with excitement. Darting surreptitious glances from behind her sunglasses, looking for that tall broad-shouldered figure among the crowds.

It seemed a lifetime until she stood alone on the observation balcony with the wind whipping her piebald calfskin coat around her legs, and blowing her hair into a snapping, dancing tangle. The long shark-like shape of the Boeing jet crouched at the far end of the runway and as it started forward Terry turned from the balcony rail and ran back into the main building.

Rod was waiting for her just inside the doors, and he swung her off her feet.

'Gottcha!'

With her feet dangling, she put her arms around his neck and kissed him.

The watchers paused and then smiled, and there was a minor traffic jam at the head of the stairs.

'Come on,' she entreated, 'let's not waste a minute of it.'

He put her on her feet, and they ran down the staircase hand in hand. Terry paused only to dismiss the chauffeur, and then they ran through the car park like children let out of school, and clambered into the Volkswagen. Their luggage was on the back seat.

'Go,' she said, 'go as fast as you can!'

Twenty minutes later Rod pulled the Volkswagen to a tyre-squealing halt in front of the hangars at the private airfield.

The twin-engined Cessna stood on the tarmac. Both engines were ticking over in readiness, and the mechanic climbed down from the cockpit when he recognized Terry.

'Hello, Terry, right on time,' he greeted her.

'Hello, Hank. You've got her warmed up already. You are a sweety!'

'Filed your flight plan also. Nothing too good for my most favourite customer.' The mechanic was a chunky grizzled little man, and he looked at Rod curiously.

'Give you a hand with the bags,' he said.

By the time they had the luggage stowed away in its compartment, Terry was in the cockpit speaking to the control tower.

Rod climbed up into the passenger seat beside her.

Terry switched off her radio and leaned over Rod's lap to speak to Hank.

'Thanks, Hank.' She paused delicately, and then went on with a rush. 'Hank, if anyone asks you, I was on my own today, okay?'

'Okay.' Hank grinned at her. 'Happy landings.' And he closed the cockpit door, and Terry taxied out onto the runway.

'Is this yours? Rod asked. It was a 100,000 rand's worth of aircraft.

'Pops gave it to me for my birthday,' Terry replied. 'Do you like it?'

'Not bad,' Rod admitted.

Terry turned upwind and applied the wheel brakes while she ran the engines up to peak revs, testing their response.

Suddenly Rod realized that he was in the hands of a woman pilot. He fell silent and his nerves began to tighten up.

'Let's go,' said Terry and kicked off the brakes. The Cessna surged forward, and Rod gripped the arm rests and froze with his gaze fixed dead ahead.

'Relax, Ironsides,' Terry advised him without taking her eyes off the runway, 'I've been flying since I was sixteen.'

At 3,000 feet she levelled out and banked gently onto an easterly heading.

'Now that didn't hurt too much did it?' She smiled sideways at him.

'You are quite a girl,' he told her. 'You can do all sorts of tricks.'

'You just wait,' she warned him. 'You ain't seen nothing yet!'

They flew in silence until the Highveld had fallen away behind them, and they were over the dense green mattress of the Bushveld.

'I'm going to divorce him.' She broke the silence, and Rod was not surprised that they were experiencing the mental telepathy of closely attuned minds. He had been thinking about her husband also.

'Good,' he said.

'You think I'd have a chance with you if I did?'

'If you played your cards right, you might get that lucky.'

'Conceited swine,' she said. 'I don't know why I love you.'

'Do you?' he asked.

'Yes.'

'And I you.'

They relapsed into a contented silence, until Terry put the Cessna in a shallow dive.

'What's wrong?' Rod asked with alarm.

'Going down to have a look for game.'

They flew low over thick olive-green bush broken by veils of golden brown grass.

'There,' said Rod, pointing ahead. A line of fat black bugs moving across one of the open places. 'Buffalo!'

'And over there.' Terry pointed left.

'Zebra and wildebeeste,' Rod identified them. 'And there

is a giraffe.' Its long stalk of a neck stuck up like a periscope. It broke into an awkward stiff-legged run as the aircraft roared overhead.

'We have arrived.' Terry indicated a pair of round granite koppies on the horizon ahead. They were as symmetrical as a young girl's breasts, and as they drew nearer Rod made out the thatched roof of a large building standing in the hollow between the koppies. Beyond it a long straight landing-strip had been cut from the trees, and the fat white sausage of a wind sock flew from its pole.

Terry throttled back and circled the homestead. On the lawns half a dozen tiny figures waved up at the Cessna, and as they watched, two of the figures climbed into a toy Land Rover and set off for the landing-strip. A ribbon of white dust blew out from behind it.

'That's Hans,' Terry explained. 'We can go down now.'

She lined the Cessna up for its approach, and then let it sink down with the motors bumbling softly. The ground came up and jarred the undercarriage, then they were taxiing to meet the racing Land Rover.

The man who piled out of the Land Rover was white-haired, and sunburned like old leather.

'Mrs Steyner!' He was making no attempt to conceal his pleasure. 'It's been much too long. Where have you been?'

'I've been busy, Hans.'

'New York? What the hell for?' said Hans surprisingly.

'This is Mr Ironsides.' Terry introduced them. 'Rod, this is Hans Kruger.'

'Van Breda?' asked Hans as they shook hands. 'You related to the van Bredas from Caledon?'

'I don't think so,' Rod muttered weakly and looked at Terry appealingly.

'He is stone deaf,' Terry explained. 'Both his ear drums blown out by a hangfire in the 1930s. He won't admit it though.'

'I'm glad to hear it,' Hans nodded, happily. 'You always

were a healthy girl. I remember when you were a little piccaninny.'

'He is an absolute darling though, so is his wife. They look after the shooting lodge for Pops,' Terry told Rod.

'Good idea!' Hans agreed heartily. 'Let's get your bags in the Land Rover and go up to the house. I bet Mr van Breda could use a drink also.' And he winked at Rod.

The lodge had thatch and rough-hewn timber roofing, stone-flagged floors covered with cured animal skins and Kelim rugs. There was a walk-in fireplace flanked by gun racks on which were displayed fifty fine examples of the gunsmith's art. The furniture was massive and masculine, leather-cushioned and low. The Spanish plaster walls were hung with trophies, horned heads and native weapons.

A vast wooden staircase led up to the bedrooms that opened off the gallery above the main room. The bedrooms were air-conditioned, and after they had got rid of Hans and his fat wife, Rod and Terry tested the bed to see if it was suitable.

An hour and a half later the bed had been judged eminently satisfactory, and as they went down to pass further judgement on the gargantuan lunch that fat Mrs Hans had spread for them, Terry remarked, 'Has it ever occurred to you, Mr Ironsides, that there are parts of your anatomy other than your flanks which are ferrous in character?' Then she giggled and added softly, 'And thank the Lord for that!'

Lunch was an exhausting experience and Terry pointed out that there was little sense in going out before four o'clock as the game would still be in thick cover avoiding the midday heat, so they went back upstairs.

After four o'clock Rod selected a .375 magnum Holland and Holland rifle from the rack, filled a cartridge belt with ammunition from one of the drawers, and they went out to the Land Rover.

'How big is this place?' Rod asked as he turned the Land

Rover away from the gardens and took the track out into the virgin bush.

'You can drive for twenty miles in any direction and it's all ours. Over there our boundary runs against the Kruger National Park,' Terry answered.

They drove along the banks of the river, skirting sandbanks on which grew fluffy-headed reeds. The water ran fast between glistening black rocks, then spread into slow lazy pools.

They saw a dozen varieties of big game, stopping every few hundred yards to watch some lovely animal.

'Pops obviously doesn't allow shooting here,' Rod remarked, as a kudu bull with long spiral horns and trumpet-shaped ears studied them with big wet eyes from a range of thirty feet. 'The game is as tame as domestic cattle.'

'Only family are allowed to shoot,' Terry agreed. 'You qualify as family, however.'

Rod shook his head. 'It would be murder.' Rod indicated the kudu. 'That old fellow would eat out of your hand.'

'I'm glad you feel like that,' Terry said, and they drove on slowly.

The evening was not cool enough to warrant a log fire in the cavernous fireplace of the lodge. They lit one anyway because Rod decided it would be pleasant to sit in front of a big, leaping fire, drink whisky and hold the girl you love.

– 59 –

When Inspector Grobbelaar lowered his teacup, there was a white scum of cream on the tips of his moustache. He licked it off carefully, and looked across at Sergeant Hugo.

'Who have we got next?' he asked.

Hugo consulted his notebook.

'Philemon N'gabai.' He read out the name, and Grobbelaar sighed.

'Number forty-eight, only sixteen more.' The single smeary fingerprint on the fragment of glass from the gold container had been examined by the fingerprint department. They had provided a list of sixty-four names any one of which might be the owner of that print. Each of them had to be interrogated, it was a lengthy and so far unrewarding labour.

'What do we know about friend Philemon?' Grobbelaar asked.

'He is approximately forty years old. A Shangaan from Mozambique. Height 5' 7½", weight 146 lb. Crippled right leg. Two previous convictions. 1956: 60 days for bicycle theft. 1962: 90 days for stealing a camera from a parked car,' Hugo read from the file.

'At one hundred and forty-six pounds I don't see him breaking many necks. But send him in, let's talk to him,' Grobbelaar suggested and dunked his moustache in the tea cup again. Hugo nodded to the African Sergeant and he opened the door to admit Crooked Leg and his escort of an African constable.

They advanced to the desk at which the two detectives sat in their shirt sleeves. No one spoke. The two interrogators subjected him to a calculated and silent scrutiny to set him at as great a disadvantage as possible.

Grobbelaar prided himself on being able to sniff out a guilty conscience at fifty paces, and Philemon N'gabai reeked of guilt. He could not stand still, he was sweating heavily, and his eyes darted from floor to ceiling. He was guilty as hell, but not necessarily of murder. Grobbelaar did not feel the slightest confidence as he shook his head sorrowfully and asked, 'Why did you do it, Philemon? We have found the marks of your hand on the gold bottle.'

The effect on Crooked Leg was instantaneous and

dramatic. His lips parted and began to tremble, saliva dripped onto his chin. His eyes for the first time fixed on Grobbelaar's face, wide and staring.

'Hello! Hello!' Grobbelaar thought, straightening in his chair, coming completely alert. He sensed Hugo's quickening interest beside him.

'You know what they do to people who kill, Philemon? They take them away to . . .' Grobbelaar did not have an opportunity to finish.

With a howl Crooked Leg darted for the door. His crippled gait was deceptive, he was fast as a ferret. He had the door open before the Bantu Sergeant collared him and dragged him gibbering and struggling back into the room.

'The gold, but not the man! I did not kill the Portuguese,' he babbled, and Grobbelaar and Hugo exchanged glances.

'Pay dirt!' Hugo exclaimed with deep satisfaction.

'Bull's eye!' agreed Grobbelaar, and smiled, a rare and fleeting occurrence.

– 60 –

'You see it has a little light that comes on to show you where the keyhole is,' said the salesman pointing to the ignition switch on the dashboard.

'Ooh! Johnny, see that!' Hettie gushed, but Johnny Delange had his head under the bonnet of the big glossy Ford Mustang.

'Why don't you sit in her?' the salesman suggested. He was very cute really, Hattie decided, with dreamy eyes and the most *fabulous* sideburns.

'Ooh! Yes, I'd love to.' She manoeuvred her bottom into the leather bucket seat of the sports car. Her skirt pulled up, and the salesman's dreamy eyes followed the hem all the way.

'Can you adjust the seat?' Hettie asked, innocently looking up at him.

'Here, I'll show you.' He leaned into the interior of the Mustang and reached across Hettie's lap. His hand brushed over her thigh, and Hettie pretended not to notice his touch. He smelled of Old Spice after-shave lotion.

'That's better!' Hettie murmured, and wriggled into a more comfortable position, contriving to make the movement provocative and revealing.

The salesman was encouraged, he lingered with his wrist just touching a sleek thigh.

'What's the compression ratio on this model?' Johnny Delange demanded as he emerged from the engine, and the salesman straightened up quickly and hurried to join him.

An hour later Johnny signed the purchase contract, and both he and Hettie shook the salesman's hand.

'Let me give you my card,' the salesman insisted, but Johnny had returned to his new toy, and Hettie took the cardboard business card.

'Call me if you need anything, anything at all,' said the salesman with heavy significance.

'Dennis Langley. Sales Manager,' Hettie read out aloud. 'My! You're very young to be Sales Manager.'

'Not all that young!'

'I'll bet,' Hettie murmured, and her eyes were suddenly bold. She ran the tip of a pink tongue over her lips. 'I won't lose it,' she promised, and placing the card in her handbag, walked to the Mustang, leaving him with a tantalizing promise and a memory of swaying hips and clicking heels.

They raced the new Mustang as far as Potchefstroom; Hettie encouraging Johnny to overtake slower vehicles with inches to spare for oncoming traffic. With horn blaring he tore over blind rises, forking ringed fingers at the protesting toots of other drivers. They had the speedometer registering

120 mph on the return run, and it was dark as they pulled into the driveway and Johnny hit the brakes hard to avoid running into the back of a big black Daimler that was parked outside their front door.

'Jesus,' gasped Johnny. 'That's Dr Steyner's bus!'

'Who is Dr Steyner?' Hettie demanded.

'Hell, he's one of the big shots from Head Office.'

'You're kidding!' Hettie challenged him.

'Truth!' Johnny affirmed. 'One of the real big shots.'

'Bigger than Mr Ironsides?' The General Manager of the Sonder Ditch was as high up the social ladder as Hettie had ever looked.

'Tin Ribs is chicken feed compared to this joker. Just look at his bus, it's five times better than Tin Ribs's clapped-out old Maserati.'

'Gee!' Hettie could follow the logic of this line of argument. 'What's he want with us?'

'I don't know,' Johnny admitted with a twinge of anxiety. 'Let's go and find out.'

The lounge of the Delange home was not the setting which showed Dr Manfred Steyner to best advantage.

He sat on the edge of a scarlet and gold plastic-covered armchair as stiff and awkward as the packs of china dogs that stood on every table and shelf of the show cabinet, or the porcelain wild ducks which flew in diminishing perspective along the pale pink painted wall. In contrast to the tinsel Christmas decorations that festooned the ceiling and the gay greeting cards that Hettie had pinned to strips of green ribbon, Manfred's black homburg and astrakhan-collared overcoat were unnecessarily severe.

'You will forgive my presumption,' he greeted them without rising. 'You were not at home and your maid let me in.'

'You're welcome, I'm sure,' Hettie simpered.

'Of course you are, Dr Steyner,' Johnny supported her.

'Ah! So you know who I am?' Manfred asked with satisfaction. This would make his task so much easier.

'Of course we do.' Hettie went to him and offered her hand. 'I am Hettie Delange, how do you do?'

With horror Manfred saw that her armpit was unshaven, filled with damp ginger curls. Hettie had not bathed since the previous evening. Manfred's nostrils twitched and he fought down a queasy wave of nausea.

'Delange, I want to speak to you alone.' He cowered away from Hettie's overwhelming physical presence.

'Sure.' Johnny was eager to please. 'How about you making us some coffee, honey,' he asked Hettie.

Ten minutes later Manfred sank with relief into the lush upholstery of the Daimler's rear seat. He ignored the two Delanges waving their farewells, and closed his eyes. It was done. Tomorrow morning Johnny Delange would be on shift and drilling into the glassy green rock of the Big Dipper.

By noon Manfred would own quarter of a million shares in the Sonder Ditch.

In a week he would be a rich man.

In a month he would be divorced from Theresa Steyner. He would sue with all possible notoriety on the grounds of adultery. He no longer needed her.

The chauffeur drove him back to Johannesburg.

It began on the floor of the Johannesburg Stock Exchange.

For some months nearly all the activity had been in the industrial counters, centring about the Alex Sagov group of companies and their merger negotiations.

The only spark of life in the mining and mining financials had been Anglo American Corporation and De Beers Deferred rights issues, but this was now old news and the prices had settled at their new levels. So it was that nobody was expecting fireworks when the call over of the gold mining counters began. The brokers' clerks crowding the floor were quietly spoken and behaved, when the first squib popped.

'Buy Sonder Ditch,' from one end of the hall.

'Buy Sonder Ditch,' a voice raised.

'Buy!' The throng stirred, heads turned.

'Buy.' The brokers suddenly agitated swirled in little knots, broke and reformed as transactions were completed. The price jumped fifty cents, and a broker ran from the floor to confer with his principal.

Here a broker thumped another on the back to gain his attention, and his urgency was infectious.

'Buy! Buy!'

'What the hell's happening?'

'Where is the buying coming from?'

'It's local!'

The price hit ten rand a share, and then the panic began in earnest.

'It's overseas buying.'

'Eleven rand!'

Brokers rushed to telephone warnings to favoured clients that a bull run was developing.

'Twelve fifty. It's only local buying.'

218

'Buy at best. Buy five thousand.'

Clerks raced back onto the floor carrying the hastily telephoned instructions, and plunged into the hysterical trading.

'Jesus Christ! Thirteen rand, sell now. Take your profit! It can't go much higher.'

'Thirteen seventy-five, it's overseas buying. Buy at best.'

In fifty brokers' offices around the country, the professionals who spent their lives hovering over the tickers regained their balance and, cursing themselves for having been taken unawares, they scrambled onto the bull wagon. Others, the more canny ones, recognized the makings of a sick run and off-loaded their holdings, selling industrial shares as well as mining shares. Prices ran amok.

At ten-fifteen there was a priority call from the offices of the Minister of Finance in Pretoria to the office of the President of the Johannesburg Stock Exchange.

'What are you going to do?'

'We haven't decided. We won't close the floor if we can possibly help it.'

'Don't let it go too far. Keep me informed.'

Sixteen rand and still spiralling when at eleven o'clock South African time, the London Stock Exchange came in. For the first fifteen wild minutes the price of Sonder Ditch gold mining rocketed in sympathy with the Johannesburg market.

Then suddenly and unexpectedly the Sonder Ditch shares ran head-on into massive selling pressure. Not only the Sonder Ditch, but all the Kitchenerville gold mining companies staggered as the pressure increased. The prices wavered, rallied a few shillings and then fell back, wavered again, and then crashed downwards, plummeting far below their opening prices.

'Sell!' was the cry. 'Sell at best!' Within minutes freshly-made paper fortunes were wiped away.

When the price of the Sonder Ditch gold mining shares

fell to five rand seventy-five cents, the committee of the Johannesburg Stock Exchange closed the door in the interests of the national welfare, preventing further trading.

But in New York, Paris and London the investing public continued to beat South African gold mining shares to death.

In the air-conditioned office of a skyscraper building, the little bald-headed man was smashing his balled fist onto the desk top of his superior officer.

'I told you not to trust him,' he was almost sobbing with anger. 'The fat greedy slug. One million dollars wasn't enough for him! No, he had to blow the whole deal!'

'Please, Colonel,' his chief intervened. 'Control yourself. Let us make a fair and objective appraisal of this financial activity.'

The bald-headed man sank back into his chair, and tried to light a cigarette with hands that trembled so violently as to extinguish the flame of his lighter.

'It sticks out a mile.' He flicked the lighter again, and puffed quickly. 'The first activity on the Johannesburg Exchange was Dr Steyner being clever. Buying up shares on the strength of our dummy report. That was quite natural and we expected it, in fact we wanted that to happen. It took suspicion away from us.' His cigarette had gone out, the tip was wet with spit. He threw it away and lit another.

'Fine! Everything was fine up to then. Dr Steyner had committed financial suicide, and we were on the pig's back.' He sucked at his new cigarette. 'Then! Then our fat friend pulls the big double-cross and starts selling the Kitchener-ville shares short. He must have gone into the market for millions.'

'Can we abort the operation at this late date?' his chief asked.

'Not a chance.' The bald head shook vigorously. 'I have

sent a cable to our fat friend ordering him to freeze the work on the tunnel, but can you imagine him obeying that order? He is financially committed for millions of dollars and he will protect that investment with every means at his disposal.'

'Could we not warn the management of the Sonder Ditch company?'

'That would put the finger squarely on us, would it not?'

'Hmm!' the chief nodded. 'We could send them an anonymous warning.'

'Who would put any credence on that?'

'You're right,' the chief sighed. 'We will just have to batten down our hatches and ride out the storm. Sit tight and deny everything.'

'That is all we can do.' The cigarette had gone out again, and there were bits of tobacco in his moustache. The little man flicked his lighter.

'The bastard, the fat, greedy bastard!' he muttered.

– 62 –

Johnny and Big King rode up shoulder to shoulder in the cage. It had been a good shift. Despite the hardness of the serpentine rock that cut down the drilling rate by fifty per cent, they had been able to get in five blasts that day. Johnny reckoned they had driven more than half-way through the Big Dipper. There was no night shift working now. Campbell had gone back to the stopes, so the honour of holing through would be Johnny's. He was excited at the prospect. Tomorrow he would be through into the unknown.

'Until tomorrow, Big King,' he said as they reached the surface and stepped out of the cage.

They separated, Big King heading for the Bantu hostel, Johnny to the glistening new Mustang in the car park.

Big King went straight to the Shangaan Induna's cottage without changing from his working clothes. He stood in the doorway and the Induna looked up from the letter he was writing.

'What news, my father?' Big King asked.

'The worst,' the Induna told him softly. 'The police have taken Crooked Leg.'

'Crooked Leg would not betray me,' Big King declared, but without conviction.

'Would you expect him to die in your place?' asked the Induna. 'He must protect himself.'

'I did not mean to kill him,' Big King explained miserably. 'I did not mean to kill the Portuguese, it was the gun.'

'I know, my son.' The Induna's voice was husky with helpless pity.

Big King turned from the doorway and walked down across the lawns to the ablution block. The spring and swagger had gone from his step. He walked listlessly, slouching, dragging his feet.

– 63 –

Manfred Steyner sat at his desk. His hands lay on the blotter before him, one thumb wearing a turban of crisp white bandage. His only movement was the steady beat of a pulse in his throat and a nerve that fluttered in one eyelid. He was deathly pale, and a light sheen of perspiration gave his features the look of having been sculptured from washed marble.

The volume of the radio was turned high, so the voice of the announcer boomed and reverberated from the panelled walls.

'The climax of the drama was reached at eleven forty-five South African time when the President of the Johannesburg Stock Exchange declared the floor closed and all further trading suspended.

'Latest reports from the Tokyo Stock Exchange are that Sonder Ditch gold mining shares were being traded at the equivalent of four rand forty cents. This compares with the morning's opening price of the same share on the Johannesburg Stock Exchange of nine rand forty-five cents.

'A spokesman for the South African Government stated that although no reason for these extraordinary price fluctuations was apparent, the Minister of Mines, Doctor Carel De Wet, had ordered a full-scale commission of inquiry.'

Manfred Steyner stood up from his desk and went through into the bathroom. With his flair for figures he did not need pen and paper to compute that the shares he had purchased that morning had depreciated in value by well over one million rand at the close of business that evening.

He knelt on the tiled floor in front of the toilet bowl and vomited.

– 64 –

The sky was darkening rapidly, for the sun had long ago sunk below a blazing horizon.

Rod heard the whisper of wings, and strained his eyes upwards into the gloom. They came in fast, in V-formation, slanting down towards the pool of the river. He stood up from the blind and swung the shotgun on them, leading well ahead of the line of flight.

He squeezed off both barrels. Wham! Wham! And the duck broke formation and rocketed upwards, whirring aloft on noisy wings.

'Damn it!' said Rod.

'What's wrong, dead-eye Dick, did you miss?' asked Terry.

'The light's too bad.'

'Excuses! Excuses!' Terry stood up beside him, and Rod pushed a balled fist lightly against her cheek.

'That's enough from you, woman. Let's go home.'

Carrying the shotguns and bunches of dead duck, they trudged along the bank in the dusk to the waiting Land Rover.

It was completely dark as they drove back to the lodge.

'What a wonderful day it's been,' Terry murmured dreamily. 'If for nothing else, I will always be grateful to you for teaching me how to enjoy my life.'

Back at the lodge, they bathed and changed into fresh clothes. For dinner they had wild duck and pineapple, with salads from Mrs Fat Hans' vegetable garden. Afterwards, they sprawled on the leopard-skin rugs in front of the fireplace and watched the log fire without talking, relaxed and happy and tired.

'My God, it's almost nine o'clock.' Terry checked her wristwatch. 'I fancy a bit of bed myself, how about you, Mr Ironsides?'

'Let's hear the nine o'clock news first.'

'Oh, Rod! Nobody ever listens to the news here. This is fairyland!'

Rod switched on the radio and the first words froze them both. They were 'Sonder Ditch'.

In horrified silence they listened to the report. Rod's expression was granite-hard, his mouth a tight grim line. When the news report ended, Rod switched off the radio set and lit a cigarette.

'There is trouble,' he said. 'Big trouble. I'm sorry, Terry, we must go back. As soon as possible. I have to get back to the mine.'

'I know,' Terry agreed immediately. 'But Rod, I can't take off from this landing-strip in the dark. There is no flare path.'

'We'll leave at first light.'

Rod slept very little that night. Whenever she woke, Terry sensed him lying unsleeping, worrying. Twice she heard him get up and go to the bathroom.

In the very early hours of the morning she woke from her own troubled sleep and saw him silhouetted against the starlit window. He was smoking a cigarette and staring out into the darkness. It was the first night they had spent together without making love. In the dawn Rod was haggard and puffy-eyed.

They were airborne at eight o'clock and they landed in Johannesburg a little after ten.

Rod went straight to the telephone in Hank's office and Lily Jordan answered his call.

'Miss Jordan, what the hell is happening? Is everything all right?'

'Is that you, Mr Ironsides. Oh! Thank God! Thank God you've come, something terrible has happened!'

– 65 –

Johnny Delange blew the face of the drive twice before nine o'clock, cutting thirty feet further into the glassy green dyke.

He had found that by drilling his cutter blast holes an additional three feet deeper, he could achieve a shatter effect on the serpentine rock which more than compensated for the additional drilling time. This next blast he was going to flout standard regulations and experiment with double-charging his cutter holes. He would need additional explosives.

'Big King,' he shouted to make himself heard above the roar of drills. 'Take a gang back to the shaft station. Pick up six cases of Dynagel.'

He watched Big King and his gang retreat back down the drive, and then he lit a cigarette and turned his attention to his machine boys. They were poised before the rock face, sweating behind their drills. The dark rock of the dyke absorbed the light from the overhead electric bulbs. It made the end of the drive a gloomy place, filled with a sense of foreboding.

Johnny began to think about Davy. He was aware suddenly of a sense of disquiet, and he moved restlessly. He felt the hair on his forearms come slowly erect, each on a separate goose pimple. *Davy is here*. He knew it suddenly, and surely. His flesh crawled and he went cold with dread. He turned quickly and looked over his shoulder. The tunnel behind him was deserted, and Johnny gave a sickly grin.

'Shaya, madoda,' he called loudly and unnecessarily to his gang. They could not hear him above the roar of the drills, but the sound of his own voice helped reassure him.

Yet the creepy sensation was still with him. He felt that Davy was still there, trying to tell him something.

Johnny fought the sensation. He walked quickly forward, standing close to his machine boys, as though to draw comfort from their physical presence. It did not help. His nerves were shrieking now, and he felt himself beginning to sweat.

Suddenly the machine boy who was drilling the cutter hole in the centre of the face staggered backwards.

'Hey!' Johnny shouted at him, then he saw that water was spurting in fine needle jets from around the drill steel. Something was squeezing the drill steel out of its hole, like toothpaste out of a tube. It was pushing the machine boy backwards.

'Hey!' Johnny started forward and at that instant the heavy metal drill was fired out of the rock with the force of a cannon ball. It decapitated the machine boy, tearing his head from his body with such savagery that his carcass was thrown far back down the drive, his blood spraying the dark rock walls.

From the drill hole shot a solid jet of water. It came out under such pressure that when it caught the machine boy's assistant in the chest it stove in his ribs as though he had been hit by a speeding automobile.

'Out!' yelled Johnny. 'Get out!' And the rock face exploded. It blew outwards with greater force than if it had been blasted with Dynagel. It killed Johnny Delange instantly. He was smashed to a bloody pulp by the flying rock. It killed every man in his gang with him, and immediately afterwards the monstrous burst of water that poured from the face picked up their mutilated remains and swept them down the drive.

Big King was at the shaft station when they heard the water coming. It sounded like an express train in a tunnel, a dull bellow of irresistible power. The water was pushing the air from the drive ahead of it, so that a hurricane of wind came roaring from the mouth of the drive, blowing out a cloud of dust and loose rubbish.

Big King and his gang stood and stared in uncomprehending terror until the head of the column of water shot from the drive, frothing solid, carrying with it a plug of debris and human remains.

Bursting into the T-junction of the main 66 level haulage, the strength of the flood was reduced, yet still it swept down towards the lift station in a waist-deep wall.

'This way!' Big King was the first to move. He leapt for the steel emergency ladder that led up to the level above. The rest of his gang were not fast enough, the water picked them up and crushed them against the steel-mesh barrier that guarded the shaft. The crest of the wave burst around Big King's legs, sucking at him, but he tore himself from its grip and climbed to safety.

Beneath him the water poured into the shaft like bath

water into a plug hole, forming a spinning whirlpool about the collar as it roared down to flood the workings below 66 level.

– 66 –

Leaving Terry at the airfield to solicit transport from Hank, the mechanic, Rod drove directly to the head of No. 1 shaft of the Sonder Ditch. He jumped from the Volkswagen into the clamouring crowd clustered above the shaft head.

Dimitri was wide-eyed and distracted, beside him Big King towered like a black colossus.

'What happened?' Rod demanded.

'Tell him,' Dimitri instructed Big King.

'I was at the shaft with my gang. A river leaped from the mouth of the drive, a great river of water running faster than the Zambesi in flood; roaring like a lion the water ate all the men with me. I alone climbed above it.'

'We've hit a big one, Rod,' Dimitri interrupted. 'It's pouring in fast. We calculate it will flood the entire workings up to 66 level in four hours from now.'

'Have you cleared the mine?' Rod demanded.

'All the men are out except Delange and his gang. They were in the drive. They've been chopped, I'm afraid,' Dimitri answered.

'Have you warned the other mines we could have a burst through into their workings?'

'Yes, they are pulling all their shifts out.'

'Right.' Rod set off for the blast control room with Dimitri trotting to keep up with him. 'Give me your keys, and find the foreman electrician.'

Within minutes the three of them were crowded into the tiny concrete control room.

'Check in the special circuit,' Rod instructed. 'I'm going to shoot the drop-blast matt and seal off the drive.'

The foreman electrician worked quickly at the control panel. He looked up at Rod.

'Ready!' he said.

'Check her in,' Rod nodded.

The foreman threw the switch. The three of them caught their breath together.

Dimitri said it for them: 'Red!'

On the control panel of the special circuit the red bulb glared balefully at them, the Cyclops eye of the god of despair.

'Christ!' swore the foreman. 'The circuit is shot. The water must have torn the wires out.'

'It may be a fault in the board.'

'No.' The foreman shook his head with certainty.

'We've had it,' whispered Dimitri. 'Goodbye the Sonder Ditch!'

Rod burst out of the control room into the expectant crowd outside.

'Johnson!' He singled out one of his mine captains. 'Go down to the Yacht Club at the dam, get me the rubber rescue dinghy. Quick as you can, man.'

The man scurried away, and Rod turned on the electrician foreman as he emerged from the control room.

'Get me a battery hand-operated blaster, a reel of wire, pliers, two coils of nylon rope. Hurry!'

The foreman went.

'Rod.' Dimitri caught his arm. 'What are you going to do?'

'I'm going down there. I'm going to find the break in the circuit and I'm going to blast her by hand.'

'Jesus!' Dimitri gasped. 'You are crazy, Rod. You'll kill yourself for sure!'

Rod completely ignored his protest.

'I want one man with me. A strong man. The strongest there is, we will have to drag the dinghy against the flood.' Rod looked about him. Big King was standing by the banksman's office. The two of them were tall enough to face each other over the heads of the men between them.

'Will you come with me, Big King?' Rod asked.

'Yes,' said Big King.

– 67 –

In less than twenty minutes they were ready. Rod and Big King were stripped down to singlets and bathing-trunks. They wore canvas tennis shoes to protect their feet, and the hard helmets on their heads were incongruous against the rest of their attire.

The rubber dinghy was ex-naval disposal. A nine-foot air-filled mattress, so light that a man could lift it with one hand. Into it was packed the equipment they would need for the task ahead. A water-proof bag contained the battery blaster, the reel of insulated wire, the pliers and a spare lantern. Lashed to the eyelets along the sides of the dinghy were two coils of light nylon rope, a small crowbar, an axe and a razor-sharp machete in a leather sheath. To the bows of the dinghy were fastened a pair of looped nylon towing lines.

'What else will you need, Rod?' Dimitri asked.

Rod shook his head thoughtfully. 'That's it, Dimitri. That should do it.'

'Right!' Dimitri beckoned and four men came forward and carried the dinghy into the waiting cage.

'Let's go,' said Dimitri and followed the dinghy into the cage. Big King went next and Rod paused a second to look up at the sky. It was very blue and bright.

Before the onsetter could close the shutter door, a Silver Cloud Rolls-Royce came gliding onto the bank. From the rear door emerged first Hurry Hirschfeld and then Terry Steyner.

'Ironsides!' roared Hurry. 'What the hell is going on?'

'We've hit water,' Rod answered him from the cage.

'Water? Where did it come from?'

'Beyond the Big Dipper.'

'You drove through the Big Dipper?'

'Yes.'

'You bastard, you've drowned the Sonder Ditch,' roared Hurry, advancing on the cage.

'Not yet, I haven't,' Rod contradicted.

'Rod.' Terry was white-faced beside her grandfather. 'You can't go down there.' She started forward.

Rod pushed the onsetter aside and pulled down the steel shutter door of the cage. Terry threw herself against the steel mesh of the guard barrier, but the cage was gone into the earth.

'Rod,' she whispered, and Hurry Hirschfeld put his arm around her shoulders and led her to the Rolls-Royce.

From the back seat of the Rolls, Hurry Hirschfeld was conducting a Kangaroo Court Trial of Rodney Ironsides. One by one he called for the line managers of the Sonder Ditch and questioned them. Even those who were loyal to Rod could say little in his defence, and there were others who took the opportunity to level old scores with Rodney Ironsides.

Sitting beside her grandfather, Terry heard such a condemnation of the man she loved as to chill her to the depths of her soul. There was no doubt that Rodney Ironsides, without Head Office sanction, had instituted a new development so risky and contrary to company policy as to be criminal in concept.

'Why did he do it?' muttered Hurry Hirschfeld. He seemed bewildered. 'What could he possibly achieve by driving through the Big Dipper? It looks like a deliberate attempt to sabotage the Sonder Ditch.' Hurry's anger began to seethe within him. 'The bastard! He has drowned the Sonder Ditch and killed dozens of men.' He punched his fist into the palm of his hand. 'I'll make him pay for this. I'll break him, so help me God, I'll smash him! I'll bring criminal charges against him. Malicious damage to property. Manslaughter. Culpable homicide! By Jesus, I'll have his guts for this!'

Listening to Hurry ranting and threatening, Terry could keep silent no longer.

'It wasn't his fault, Pops. Truly it wasn't. He was forced to do it.'

'Ha!' snorted Hurry. 'I heard you at the pithead a few minutes ago. Just what is this man to you, Missy, that you spring to his defence so nobly?'

'Pops, please believe me.' Her eyes were enormous in her pale face.

'Why should I believe you? The two of you are obviously up to mischief together. Naturally you will try and protect him.'

'Listen to me at least,' she pleaded, and Hurry checked the run of his tongue and breathing heavily he turned to face her.

'This better be good, young lady,' he warned her.

In her agitation she told it badly, and halfway through she realized that she wasn't even convincing herself. Hurry's expression became more and more bleak, until he interrupted her impatiently.

'Good God, Theresa, this isn't like you. To try and put the blame for this onto your own husband! That's despicable! To try and switch the blame for this . . .'

'It's true! As God is my witness.' Terry was almost in tears, she was tugging at Hurry's sleeve in her agitation. 'Rod was forced to do it. He had no option.'

'You have proof of this?' Hurry asked drily, and Terry fell silent, staring at him dumbly. What proof was there?

– 68 –

The cage checked and slowed as it approached 65 level. The lights were still burning, but the workings were deserted. They lugged the dinghy out onto the station.

They could hear the dull waterfall roar of the flood on the level below them. The displacement of huge volumes of water disturbed the air so that a strong cool breeze was blowing up the shaft.

'Big King and I will go down the emergency ladder. You will lower the dinghy to us afterwards,' Rod told Dimitri. 'Make sure all the equipment is tied into it.'

'Right.' Dimitri nodded.

All was in readiness. The men who had come down with them in the cage were waiting expectantly. Rod could find no reason for further delay. He felt something cold and heavy settle in his guts.

'Come on, Big King.' And he went to the steel ladder.

'Good luck, Rod.' Dimitri's voice floated down to him, but Rod saved his breath for that cold dark climb downwards.

All the lights had fused on 66 level, and in the beam of his lamp the water below him was black and agitated. It poured into the mouth of the shaft, bending the mesh barrier inwards. The mesh acted as a gigantic sieve, straining the floating rubbish from the flood. Amongst the timber and planking, the sodden sacking and unrecognizable objects, Rod made out the water-logged corpses of the dead pressed against the wire.

He climbed down and gingerly lowered himself into the water. Instantly it dragged at his lower body, shocking in its

233

power. It was waist-deep here, but he found that by bracing his body against the steel ladder he could maintain his footing.

Big King climbed down beside him, and Rod had to raise his voice above the hissing thunder of water.

'All right?'

'Yes. Let them send down the boat.'

Rod flashed his lamp up the shaft, and within minutes the dinghy was swaying slowly down to them. They reached up and guided it right side up to the surface of the water, before untying the rope.

The dinghy was sucked firmly against the wire mesh, and Rod checked its contents quickly. All was secure.

'Right.' Rod tied a bight of the nylon rope around his waist, and climbed up the wire mesh barrier until he could reach the roof of the tunnel. Behind him Big King was paying out the nylon line.

Rod leaned out until he could get his hands on the compressed air pipes that ran along the roof of the tunnel. The pipes were as thick as a man's wrist, bolted securely into the hanging wall of the drive; they would support a man's weight with ease. Rod settled his grip firmly on the piping and then kicked his feet free from the barrier. He hung above the rushing waters, his feet just brushing the surface.

Hand over hand, swinging forward with feet dangling, he started up the tunnel. The nylon rope hung down behind him like a long white tail. It was 300 feet to where the water boiled from the drive into the main haulage, and Rod's shoulder muscles were shrieking in protest before he reached it. It seemed that his arms were being wrenched from their sockets, for the weight of the nylon rope that was dragging in the water was fast becoming intolerable.

There was a back eddy in the angle formed by the drive and the haulage. Here the flood swirled in a vortex, and

Rod lowered himself slowly into it. The water buffeted him, but again he was able to cower against the side wall of the haulage and hold his footing. Quickly he began tying the rope onto the rawlbolts that were driven into the sidewall to consolidate the rock. Within minutes he had established a secure base from which to operate, and when he flashed his lamp back down the haulage he saw Big King following him along the compressed air piping.

Big King dropped into the waist-deep water beside Rod, and they gripped the nylon rope and rested their burning arm muscles.

'Ready?' asked Rod at last, and Big King nodded.

They laid hold of the rope that led back to the dinghy and hauled upon it. For a moment nothing happened, the other end might just as well have been anchored to a mountain.

'Together!' grunted Rod, and they recovered a foot of rope.

'Again!' And they drew the dinghy inch by inch up the haulage against the rush of water.

Their hands were bleeding when they at last pulled the laden dinghy up to their own position and anchored it to the rawlbolts beside them. It bounced and bobbed with the water drumming against its underside.

Neither Rod nor Big King could talk. They hung exhausted on the body lines with the water ripping at their skin and gasped for breath.

At last Rod looked up at Big King, and in the lamp light he saw his own doubts reflected in Big King's eyes. The drop-blast matt was 1,000 feet up the drive. The strength and speed of the water in the drive was almost double what it was in the haulage. Could they ever fight their way against such primeval forces as these that were now unleashed about them?

'I will go next,' Big King said, and Rod nodded his agreement.

The huge Bantu drew himself up the rope until he could reach the compressed air pipe. His skin in the lamplight glistened like that of a porpoise. Hand over hand he disappeared into the gaping black maw of the drive. His lamp threw deformed and monstrous shadows upon the walls of rock.

When Big King's lamp flashed the signal to him, Rod climbed up to the pipe and followed him into the drive. Three hundred feet later he found Big King had established another base. But here they were exposed to the full force of the flood, and they were pulled so violently against the body lines that the harsh nylon smeared the skin from their bodies. Together they dragged the dinghy up to them and anchored it.

Rod was sobbing softly as he held his torn hands to his chest and wondered if he could do it again.

'Ready?' Big King asked beside him, and Rod nodded. He reached up and placed the raw flesh of his palms onto the metal piping, and felt the tears of pain flood his eyes. He blinked them back and dragged himself forward.

Vaguely he realized that should he fall, he was a dead man. The flood would sweep him away, dragging him along the jagged side walls of the drive, ripping his flesh from the bone, and finally hurling him against the mesh surrounding the shaft to crush the life from his body.

He went on until he knew he could go no farther. Then he selected a rawlbolt in the side wall and looped the rope through it. And they repeated the whole heart-breaking procedure. Twice as he strained against the dinghy rope Rod saw his vision explode into stars and pinwheels. Each time he dragged himself back from the brink of unconsciousness by sheer force of will.

The example that Big King was setting was the inspiration which kept Rod from failing. Big King worked without change of expression, but his eyes were bloodshot with exertion. Only once Rod heard him grunt like a gut-shot lion, and there was bright blood on the rope where he touched it.

Rod knew he could not give in while Big King held on.

Reality dissolved slowly into a dark roaring nightmare of pain, wherein muscles and bone were loaded beyond all endurance, and yet continued to function. It seemed that for all time Rod had hung on arms that were leadened and slow with exhaustion. He was inching his way along the compressed air pipe for yet another advance up the drive. Sweat running into his eyes was blurring his vision, so at first he did not credit what he saw ahead of him in the darkness.

He shook his head to clear his eyes, and then squinted along the beam of his lamp. A heavy timber structure was hanging drunkenly from the roof of the drive. The bolts that held it were resisting the efforts of the water to tear it loose.

Rod realized abruptly that this was what remained of the frame which had held the ventilation doors. The doors were gone, ripped away, but the frame was still in position. He knew that just beyond the ventilation doors the drop-blast matt began. They had reached it!

New strength flowed into his body and he swung forward along the pipe. The timber frame made a fine anchor point and Rod secured the rope to it, and flashed back the signal to Big King. He hung in the loop of rope and rested awhile, then he forced himself to take an interest in his surroundings. He played the beam over the distorted timber frame and saw instantly why the blasting circuit had been broken.

In the lamp light the distinctive green plastic-coated blasting cable hung in festoons from the roof of the drive; clearly it had become entangled in the ventilation doors and been severed when they were ripped away. The loose end of the cable dangled to the surface of the racing water.

Rod fastened his eyes on it, drawing comfort and strength from the knowledge that they would not have to continue their agonized journey down the drive.

When Big King came up out of the gloom, Rod indicated the dangling cable.

'There!' he gasped, and Big King narrowed his eyes in acknowledgement; he was unable to speak.

It was five minutes before they could commence the excruciating business of hauling the dinghy up and securing it to the door frame.

Again they rested. Their movements were slowing up drastically. Neither of them had much strength left to draw upon.

'Get hold of the end of the cable.' Rod instructed Big King, and he dragged himself over the side of the dinghy and lay sprawled full-length on the floor boards.

His weight forced the dinghy deeper, increasing its resistance to the racing water, and the rope strained against the wooden frame. Rod began clumsily to unpack the battery blaster. Big King stood waist-deep clinging with one arm to the wooden frame, reaching forward with the other towards the end of the green-coated cable. It danced just beyond his fingertips, and he edged forward against the current, steadying himself against the timber frame, placing a greater strain on the retaining bolts.

His fingers closed on the cable and with a grunt of satisfaction he passed it back to Rod.

Working with painstaking deliberation, Rod connected the crocodile clips from the reel of wire to the loose end of the green cable. Rod's plan was for both he and Big King to climb aboard the dinghy, and, paying out the nylon rope, let themselves be carried back down the drive. At the same time they would be letting the wire run from its reel. At a safe distance they would fire the drop-blast matt.

Rod's fingers were swollen and numbed. The minutes

passed as he completed his preparations and all that while the strain on the wooden frame was heavy and constant.

Rod looked up from his task, and crawled to his knees.

'All right, Big King,' he wheezed as he knelt in the bows of the dinghy and gripped the wooden frame to steady the dinghy. 'Come aboard. We are ready.'

Big King waded forward and at that instant the retaining bolts on one side of the heavy timber frame gave way. With a rending, tearing sound the frame slewed across the tunnel. The beams of timber crossed each other like the blades of a pair of gigantic scissors. Both Rod's arms were between the beams. The bones in his forearms snapped with the loud crackle of breaking sticks.

With a scream of pain Rod collapsed onto the floorboards of the dinghy, his arms useless, sticking out at absurd angles from their shattered bones. Three feet away Big King was still in the water. His mouth was wide open, but no sound issued from his throat. He stood still as a black statue and his eyes bulged from their sockets. Even through his own suffering Rod was horrified by the expression on Big King's contorted features.

Below the surface of the water the bottom timber beams had performed the same scissor movement, but this time they had caught Big King's lower body between them. They had closed across his pelvis and crushed it. Now they held him in a vicelike grip from which it was not possible to shake them.

The white face and the black face were but a few feet apart. The two stricken companions in disaster looked into each other's eyes and knew that there was no escape. They were doomed.

'My arms,' whispered Rod huskily. 'I cannot use them.' Big King's bulging eyes held Rod's gaze.

'Can you reach the blaster?' Rod whispered urgently. 'Take it and turn the handle. Burn it, Big King, burn it!'

Slow comprehension showed in Big King's pain-glazed eyes.

'We are finished, Big King. Let us go like men. Burn it, bring down the rock!'

Above them the rock was sown with explosive. The blaster was connected. In his agitation Rod tried to reach out for the blaster. His forearm swung loosely, the fingers hanging open like the petals of a dead flower, and the pain checked him.

'Get it, Big King,' Rod urged him, and Big King picked up the blaster and held it against his chest with one arm.

'The handle!' Rod encouraged him. 'Turn the handle!'

But instead Big King reached into the dinghy once more and drew the machete from its sheath.

'What are you doing?' Rod demanded, and in reply Big King swung the blade back over his shoulder and then brought it forward in a gleaming arc aimed at the nylon rope that held the dinghy anchored to the wooden frame. Clunk! The blade bit into the wood, severing the rope that was bound around it.

Freed by the stroke of the machete, the dinghy was whisked away by the current. Lying in the dancing rubber dinghy, Rod heard a bull voice bellow above the rush of the water.

'Go in peace, my friend.'

Then Rod was careening back along the drive, a hell ride during which the dinghy spun like a top and in the beam of his lamp the roof and walls melted into a dark racing blur as Rod lay maimed on the floor of the dinghy.

Then suddenly the air jarred against his ear drums, a long rolling concussion in the confines of the drive and he knew that Big King had fired the drop-blast matt. Rodney Ironsides slipped over the edge of consciousness into a soft warm dark place from which he hoped never to return.

Dimitri squatted on his haunches above the shaft at 65 level. He was smoking his tenth cigarette. The rest of the men waited as impatiently as he did; every few minutes Dimitri would cross to the shaft and flash his lamp down the hundred-foot hole to 66 level.

'How long have they been gone?' he asked, and they all glanced at their watches.

'An hour and ten minutes.'

'No, an hour and fourteen minutes.'

'Christ, call me a liar for four minutes!'

And they lapsed into silence once more. Suddenly the station telephone shrilled, and Dimitri jumped up and ran to it.

'No, Mr Hirschfeld, nothing yet!'

He listened a moment.

'All right, send him down then.'

He hung up the telephone, and his men looked at him enquiringly.

'They are sending down a policeman,' he explained.

'What the hell for?'

'They want Big King.'

'Why?'

'Warrant of arrest for murder.'

'Murder?'

'Ja, they reckon he murdered the Portuguese store-keeper.'

'Jeez!'

'Big King, is that so!' Delighted to have found something to pass the time, they fell into an animated debate.

The police inspector arrived in the cage at 65 level, but he was disappointing. He looked like a down-at-heel undertaker, and he replied to their eager questions with a sorrowful stare that left them stuttering.

For the fifteenth time Dimitri went to the shaft and peered down into it. The blast shook the earth around them, a long rumbling that persisted for many seconds.

'They've done it!' yelled Dimitri, and began to caper wildly. His men leapt to their feet and began beating each other on the back, shouting and laughing. The police inspector alone took no part in the celebrations.

'Wait,' yelled Dimitri at last. 'Shut up all of you! Shut up! Damn it! Listen!'

They fell silent.

'What is it?' someone asked. 'I can't hear anything.'

'That's just it!' exulted Dimitri. 'The water! It has stopped!'

Only then did they become aware that the dull roar of water to which their ears had become resigned was now ended. It was quiet; a cathedral hush lay upon the workings. They began to cheer, their voices thin in the silence, and Dimitri ran to the steel ladder and swarmed down it like a monkey.

From thirty feet up Dimitri saw the dinghy marooned amongst the filth and debris around the shaft. He recognized the crumpled figure lying in the bottom of it.

'Rod!' he was shouting before he reached the station at 66 level. 'Rod, are you all right?'

The floor of the haulage was wet, and here and there a trickle of water still snaked towards the shaft. Dimitri ran to the stranded dinghy and started to turn Rod onto his back. Then he saw his arms.

'Oh, Christ!' he gasped in horror, then he was yelling up the ladder. 'Get a stretcher down here.'

Rod regained consciousness to find himself covered with blankets and strapped securely into a mine stretcher. His arms were splinted and bandaged, and from the familiar rattle and rush of air he knew he was in the cage on the way to the surface.

He recognized Dimitri's voice raised argumentatively.

'Damn it! The man is unconscious and badly injured, can't you leave him alone?'

'I have my duty to perform,' a strange voice answered.

'What's he want, Dimitri?' Rod croaked.

'Rod, how are you?' At the sound of his voice Dimitri was kneeling beside the stretcher anxiously.

'Bloody awful,' Rod whispered. 'What does this joker want?'

'He's a police officer. He wants to arrest Big King for murder,' Dimitri explained.

'Well, he's a bit bloody late,' whispered Rod, and even through his pain this seemed to Rod to be terribly funny. He began to laugh. He sobbed with laughter, each convulsion sending bright bursts of pain along his arms. He was shaking uncontrollably with shock, sweat pouring from his face, and he was laughing wildly.

'He's a bit bloody late,' he repeated through his hysterical laughter as Dr Dan Stander pushed the hypodermic needle into his arm and shot him full of morphine.

– 70 –

Hurry Hirschfeld stood in the main haulage on 66 level. There was bustle all around him. Already the crews from the cementation company were manhandling their equipment up towards the blocked drive.

These were specialists from an independent contracting company. They were about to begin pumping thousands of tons of liquid cement into the rock jam that sealed the drive. They would pump it in at pressures in excess of 3,000 pounds per square inch, and when that concrete set it would form a plug that would effectively seal off the drive for all time. It would also form a burial vault for the body of Big King, thought Hurry, a fitting monument to the man who had saved the Sonder Ditch.

He would arrange to have a commemorative plaque placed on the outer wall of the cement plug with a suitable inscription describing the man and the deed.

The man's dependants must be properly taken care of; perhaps they could be flown down for the unveiling of the plaque. Anyway he could leave that to Public Relations and Personnel.

The haulage stank of wetness and mud. It was dank and clammy cool, and it would not improve his lumbago. Hurry had seen enough; he started back towards the shaft. Faintly he was aware of the muted clangour of the mighty pumps which in a few days would free the Sonder Ditch of the water that filled her lower levels.

The laden stretchers with their grisly blanket-covered burdens stood in a row under the hastily rigged electric lights along one wall of the tunnel. Hurry's expression hardened as he passed them.

'I'll have the guts of the man responsible for this,' he vowed silently as he waited for the cage.

Terry Steyner rode in the rear of the ambulance with Rod. She wiped the mud from his face.

'How bad is it, Dan?' she asked.

'Hell, Terry, he'll be up and about in a few days. The arms of course are not very pretty, that's why I'm taking him directly to Johannesburg. I want a specialist orthopaedic surgeon to set them. Apart from that he is suffering from shock pretty badly and his hands are superficially lacerated. But he will be fine.'

Dan watched curiously as Terry fussed ineffectually with the damp hair of the drugged man.

'You want a smoke?' he asked.

'Light me one, please Dan.'

He passed her the cigarette.

'I didn't know that you and Rod were so friendly,' he ventured.

Terry looked up at him quickly.

'How very delicate you are, Dr Stander,' she mocked him.

'None of my business, of course.' Hurriedly Dan withdrew.

'Don't be silly, Dan. You're a good friend of Rod's and Joy is mine. You two are entitled to know. I am desperately, crazily in love with this big hunk. I intend divorcing Manfred just as soon as possible.'

'Is Rod going to marry you?'

'He hasn't said anything about marriage but I'll sure as hell start working on him,' Terry grinned, and Dan laughed.

'Good luck to you both, then. I'm sure Rod will be able to get another job.'

'What do you mean?' Terry demanded.

'They say your grandfather is threatening to fire him so high he'll be the first man on the moon.'

Terry relapsed into silence. Proof was what Pops had asked for, but what proof was there?

'They'll be waiting on the X-ray reports.' Joy Albright gave her opinion. Since her engagement to Dan, Joy had suddenly become something of a medical expert. She had rushed down to the Johannesburg Central Hospital at Dan's hurried telephonic request. Dan wanted her to keep Terry company while she waited for Rod to come out of emergency. They sat together in the waiting-room.

'I expect so,' Terry agreed. Something Joy had just said had jolted in her mind, something she must remember.

'It takes them twenty minutes or so to expose the plates

and develop them. Then the radiologist has to examine the plates and make his report to the surgeon.'

There, Joy had said it again. Terry sat up straight and concentrated on what Joy had said. Which word had disturbed her?

Suddenly she had it.

'The report!' she exclaimed. 'That's it. The report, that's the proof.'

She leapt out of her chair.

'Joy! Give me the keys of your car,' she demanded.

'What on earth?' Joy looked startled.

'I can't explain now. I have to get home to Sandown urgently, give me your keys. I'll explain later.'

Joy fished in her handbag and produced a leather key folder. Terry snatched it from her.

'Where are you parked?' Terry demanded.

'In the car park, near the main gate.'

'Thanks, Joy.' Terry dashed from the waiting-room, her high heels clattered down the passage.

'Crazy woman.' Joy looked after her bewildered.

Ten minutes later Dan looked into the waiting-room.

'Rod's fine now. Where's Terry?'

'She went mad—' And Joy explained her abrupt departure. Dan looked grave.

'I think we'd better follow her, Joy.'

'I think you're right, darling.'

'I'll just grab my coat,' said Dan.

There was only one place where Manfred would keep the geological report on the Big Dipper that Rod had told her about. That was in the safe deposit behind the panelling in his study. Because her jewellery was kept in the same safe, Terry had a key and the combination to the lock.

Even in Joy's Alfa Romeo, taking liberties with the traffic regulations, it was a thirty-five-minute drive out to

Sandown. It was after five in the evening when Terry coasted down the long driveway and parked before the garages.

The extensive grounds were deserted, for the gardeners finished at five, and there was no sign of life from the house. This was as it should be, for she knew Manfred was still in Europe. He was not due back for at least another four days.

Leaving the ignition keys in the Alfa, Terry ran up the pathway and onto the stoep. She fumbled in her handbag and found the keys to the front door. She let herself in, and went directly to Manfred's study. She slid the concealing panel aside and set about the lengthy business of opening the steel safe. It required both key and combination to activate the mechanism, and Terry had never developed much expertise at tumbling the combination.

Finally, however, the door swung open and she was confronted by the voluminous contents. Terry began removing the various documents and files, examining each one and then stacking them neatly on the floor beside her.

She had no idea of the shape, size nor colour of the report for which she was searching, it was ten minutes before she selected an unmarked folder and flicked open the cover. 'Confidential Report on the geological formations of the Kitchenerville gold fields, with special reference to those areas lying to the east of the Big Dipper Dyke.'

Terry felt a wonderful lift of relief as she read the titling for she had begun doubting that the report was here. Quickly she thumbed through the pages and began reading at random. There was no doubt.

'This is it!' she exclaimed aloud.

'I'll take that, thank you.' The dreaded familiar voice cut into her preoccupation, and Terry spun around and came to her feet in one movement, clutching the file protectively to her breast. She backed away from the man who stood in the doorway.

She hardly recognized her own husband. She had never

seen him like this. Manfred was coatless, and his shirt was without collar or stud. He appeared to have slept in his trousers, for they were rumpled and baggy. There was a yellow stain down the front of his white shirt.

His scanty brown hair was dishevelled, hanging forward wispily onto his forehead. He had not shaved, and the skin around his eyes was discoloured and puffy.

'Give that to me.' He came towards her with hand outstretched.

'Manfred.' She kept moving away from him. 'What are you doing here? When did you get back?'

'Give it to me, you slut.'

'Why do you call me that?' she asked, trying for time.

'Slut!' he repeated, and lunged towards her. Terry whirled away from him lightly.

She ran for the study door, with Manfred close behind her. She beat him into the passage and raced for the front door. Her heel caught in one of the Persian carpets that covered the floor of the passage, and she staggered and fell against the wall.

'Whore!' He was on her instantly trying to wrestle the report out of her hands, but she clung to it with all her strength. Face to face they were almost of a height, and she saw the madness in his eyes.

Suddenly Manfred released her. He stepped back, bunched his fist and swung it round-armed into her cheek. Her head jerked back and cracked against the wall. He drew back his fist and hit her again. She felt the quick warm burst of blood spurt from her nose, and staggered through the door beside her into the dining-room. She was dizzy from the blows and she fell against the heavy stink-wood table.

Manfred was close behind her. He charged her, sending her sprawling backwards onto the table. He was on top of her, both his hands at her throat.

'I'm going to kill you, you whore,' he wheezed. His thumbs hooked and pressed deep into the flesh of her throat. With the frenzied strength of despair, Terry clawed at his eyes with both hands. Her nails scored his face, raking long red lines into his flesh. With a cry Manfred released her, and backed away holding both hands to his injured face, leaving Terry lying gasping across the table.

He stood for a moment, then uncovered his face and inspected the blood on his hands.

'I'll kill you for that!'

But as he advanced towards her, Terry rolled over the table.

'Whore! Slut! Bitch!' he screamed at her, following her around the table. Terry kept ahead of him.

There were a matched pair of heavy Stuart crystal decanters on the sideboard, one containing port, the other sherry. Terry snatched up one of them and turned to face Manfred. She hurled the decanter with all her remaining strength at his head.

Manfred did not have time to duck. The decanter cracked against his forehead, and he fell backwards, stunned. Terry snatched up the report and ran out of the dining-room, down the passage, out of the front door and into the garden. She was running weakly, following the driveway towards the main road.

Then behind her she heard the engine of an automobile roar into life. Panting wildly, holding the report, she stopped and looked back. Manfred had followed her out of the house. He was behind the steering wheel of Joy's Alfa Romeo. As she watched he threw the car into gear and howled towards her, blue smoke burning from the rear tyres with the speed of the acceleration. His face behind the windscreen was white and streaked with the marks of her nails, his eyes were staring, insane, and she knew he was going to ride her down.

She kicked off her shoes and ran off the driveway onto the lawns.

Crouched forward in the driver's seat of the Alfa, Manfred watched the fleeing figure ahead of him.

Terry ran with the full-hipped sway of the mature woman, her long legs were tanned and her hair flew out loosely behind her.

Manfred was not concerned with the return of the geological report, its existence was no longer of significance to him. What he wanted was to completely destroy this woman. In his crazed state, she had become the symbol and the figurehead of all his woes. His humiliation and fall were all linked to her, he could exact his vengeance by destroying her, crushing that revolting warm and clinging body, bruising it, ripping it with the steel of the Alfa Romeo's chassis.

He hit second gear and spun the steering-wheel. The Alfa swerved from the driveway, and as its rear wheels left the tarmac, they skidded on the thick grass. Deftly Manfred checked the skid and lined up on Terry's running back.

Already she was among the protea bushes on the lower terrace. The Alfa buck-jumped the slope, flying bird-free before crashing down heavily on its suspension. Wheels spun and bit, and the sleek vehicle shot forward again.

Terry looked back over her shoulder, her face was white and her eyes very big and fear-filled. Manfred giggled. He was aware of a sense of power, the ability to dispense life or death. He steered for her, reckless of all consequences, intent on destroying her.

There was a six-foot-tall protea bush ahead of him, and Manfred roared through it, bursting it asunder. Scattering branches and leaves, giggling again, he saw Terry directly ahead of him. She was still looking back at him, and at that moment she stumbled and fell onto her knees.

She was helpless. Her face streaked with tears and blood,

her hair falling forward in wild disorder, kneeling as though for the headsman's stroke. Manfred felt a flood of disappointment. He did not want it to end so soon, he wanted to savour this sadistic elation, this sense of power.

At the last possible moment he yanked the wheel over and the car slewed violently. It shot past Terry with six inches to spare, and its rear wheels pelted her with clods of turf and thrown dirt.

Laughing aloud, wild-eyed, Manfred held the wheel hard over, bringing the Alfa around in a tight skidding circle, crackling sideways through another protea bush.

Terry was up and running again. He saw immediately that she was heading for the changing rooms of the swimming-pool among the trees on the bottom lawn and she was far enough ahead to elude him, perhaps.

'Bitch!' he snarled, and crash-changed into third gear, with engine revs peaking. The Alfa howled in pursuit of the running girl.

Had Terry thrown the bulky report aside, she might have reached the brick change rooms ahead of the racing sports car, but the report hampered and slowed her. She still had twenty yards to cover, she was running along the paved edge of the swimming-pool, and she sensed that the car was right on top of her.

Terry dived sideways, hitting the water flat on her side, and the Alfa roared past. Manfred trod heavily on the brakes, the Michelin metallic tyres screeched against the paving stones, and Manfred leapt out of the driver's seat the moment the Alfa stopped.

He ran back to the pool side. Terry was floundering towards the far steps. She was exhausted, weak with exertion and terror. Her sodden hair streamed down over her face, and she was gasping open-mouthed for air.

Manfred laughed again, a high-pitched, almost girlish giggle, and he dived after her, landing squarely between

Terry's shoulder blades with his full weight. She went under, sucking water agonizingly into already aching lungs, and when she surfaced she was coughing and gagging, blinded with water and her own wet hair.

Almost immediately she felt herself seized from behind and forced face down into the water. For half a minute she struggled fiercely, then her movements slowed and became weaker.

Manfred stood over her, chest deep in the clear water, gripping her around the waist and by a handful of her sodden hair, forcing her face deep below the surface. He had lost his spectacles, and he blinked owlishly. The wet silk of his shirt clung to his upper body, and the water had slicked his hair down.

As he felt the life going out of her, and her movements becoming sluggish and slow, he began to laugh again. The broken, incoherent laughter of a madman.

'Dan!' Joy pointed off through the trees. 'That's my car down there, parked by the swimming-pool!'

'What the hell is it doing there?'

'There's something wrong, Terry wouldn't drive through her beloved garden, unless there was!'

Dan braked sharply and pulled his Jaguar to the side of the driveway.

'I'm going to take a look.' He slid out of the car and started off across the lawns. Joy opened her own door and trotted after him.

Dan saw the man in the water, fully dressed, intent on what he was doing. He recognized Manfred Steyner.

'What the hell is he up to?' Dan started running. He reached the edge of the pool, and suddenly he realized what was happening.

'Christ! He's drowning her,' he shouted aloud, and he sprang into the water.

He did not waste time struggling with Manfred. He hit him a great open-handed, round-armed blow, that cracked against the side of Manfred's head like a pistol shot and sent him lurching sideways, releasing his grip on Terry.

Ignoring Manfred, Dan picked Terry from the water like a drowned kitten and waded to the steps. He carried her out and laid her face down on the paving. He knelt over her and began applying artificial respiration. He felt Terry stir under his hands, then cough and retch weakly.

Joy came up at the run and dropped on her knees beside him.

'My God, Dan, what happened?'

'That little bastard was trying to drown her.'

Dan looked up from his labours without interrupting the rhythm of his movement over Terry. She spluttered and retched again.

On the far side of the pool Manfred Steyner had dragged himself from the pool. He was sitting on the edge with his feet still dangling into the water, his head was hanging and he was fingering the side of his face where Dan had hit him. On his lap he held a wet pulpy mess that had been the geological report.

'Joy, can you take over here? Terry's not too far gone, and I want to get my hands on that little Hun.'

Joy took Dan's place over Terry's prostrate form, and Dan stood up.

'What are you going to do to him?' Joy asked.

'I'm going to beat him to a pulp.'

'Good show!' Joy encouraged him. 'Give him one for me.'

Manfred had heard the exchange and as Dan ran around the edge of the pool he scrambled to his feet, and staggered to the parked Alfa. He slammed the door and whirred the engine to life. Dan was just too late to stop him. The car shot forward across the lawns, leaving Dan running, futile, behind it.

'Look after her, Joy!' Dan shouted back.

By the time Dan had run up the terrace to his Jaguar and reversed it to point in the opposite direction, the Alfa had disappeared through the white gates with a musical flutter of its exhaust.

'Come on, girlie,' Dan spoke to his Jaguar. 'Let's go get him.'

The rear wheels spun as he pulled away.

Without his spectacles Manfred Steyner's vision was blurred and milky. The outlines of all objects on which he looked were softened and indistinct.

He instinctively checked the Alfa at the stop street at the bottom of the lane. He sat undecided, water still streaming from his clothing, squelching in his shoes. Beside him on the passenger seat lay the sodden report, its pages beginning to disintegrate from its soaking and the rough handling it had received.

He had to get rid of it. It was the shred of incriminating evidence. That was the only clear thought Manfred had. For the first time in his life the crystalline clarity of his thought processes was interrupted. He was confused, his mind jerking abruptly from one subject to another, the intense pleasure of inflicting hurt on Terry mingled with the sting and smart of his own injuries. He could not concentrate on either sensation for overlying it all was a sense of fear, of uncertainty. He felt vulnerable, hunted, hurt and shaken. His brain flickered and wavered as though a computer had developed an electrical fault. The answers it produced were nonsensical.

He looked in the rear view mirror, saw the Jaguar glide out between the white gates and turn towards him.

'Christ!' he panicked. He rammed his foot down on the accelerator and engaged the clutch. The Alfa screeched out into the main highway, swerved into the path of a heavy truck, bounded over the far kerb and swung back into the road.

Dan watched it tear away towards Kyalami.

He let the truck pass and then swung into the traffic behind it. He had to wait until the road was clear ahead before he could overtake the truck, and by that time the Alfa was a dwindling cream speck ahead of him.

Dan settled back in the leather bucket seat, and gave the Jaguar its head. He was furious, outraged by the treatment he had seen Manfred meting out to Terry. Her swollen and bruised face had shocked him and his feet were firmly set upon the path of vengeance.

His hands gripped the steering-wheel fiercely, he was muttering threats of violence as the speedometer moved up over the hundred mile per hour mark and he began relentlessly overhauling the cream sports car.

Steadily he moved up behind the Alfa until he was driving almost on its rear bumper. The Alfa was held up by a green school bus. Dan could not pass, however, for there was a steady stream of traffic coming in the opposite direction.

He fastened his attention on the back of Manfred's head, still fuming with anger.

Dan dropped down a gear, ready to pull out and overtake the Alfa when the opportunity arose. At that moment Manfred looked up into his rear view mirror. Dan saw the reflection of his white face with disordered damp hair hanging onto the forehead, saw his expression change immediately he recognized Dan and the Alfa shot out into the face of the approaching traffic.

There was a howl and blare of horns, vehicles swerved to make way for Manfred's wild rush. Dan glimpsed frightened faces flicking past, but the Alfa had squeezed around the green bus and was speeding away.

Dan dropped back, then sent the Jaguar like a thrown javelin through the gap between bus and kerb, overtaking on the wrong side and ignoring the bus driver's yell of protest.

The Jaguar had a higher top speed, and on the long straight Pretoria highway Dan crept up steadily on the cream Alfa.

He could see Manfred glancing repeatedly into his driving-mirror, and he grinned mirthlessly.

Ahead of them the highway rose and then dipped over a low rounded ridge. A double avenue of tall blue gum trees flanked each side of the road.

Travelling in the same direction as the two high performance sports cars was a Mini of a good vintage year. Its elderly driver was triumphantly about to overtake an overloaded vegetable truck. Neck and neck they approached the blind rise at twenty-five miles per hour, between them they effectively blocked half the road.

The horn of the Alfa wailed a high-pitched warning, and Manfred pulled out to overtake both slower vehicles. He was level with them, well out over the white dividing line, when a cement truck popped up over the blind rise.

Dan stood on his brake pedal with all the strength of his right leg, and watched it happen.

The cement truck and the Alfa came head on towards each other at a combined speed of well over a hundred miles per hour. At the last moment the Alfa began to turn away but it was too late by many seconds.

It caught the heavy cement truck a glancing blow and was hurled across the path of the two slower vehicles, miraculously touching neither of them; it skidded sideways leaving reeking black smears of rubber on the tarmac, and hurdled the low bank. It struck one of the blue gums full on, with a force that shivered the giant tree trunk and brought down a rain of leaves.

Dan pulled the Jaguar into the side of the road, parked it, and walked back.

He knew there was no hurry. The drivers of the Mini

and the vegetable truck were there before him. They were attempting to talk each other down, both of them excited and relieved by their own escapes.

'I'm a doctor,' said Dan, and they fell back respectfully.

'He doesn't need a doctor,' said one of them. 'He needs an undertaker.'

One look was sufficient. Dr Manfred Steyner was as dead as Dan had ever seen anybody. His crushed head was thrust through the windscreen. Dan picked up the sodden bundle of paper from the seat beside the huddled body. He was aware that some particular importance was attached to it.

Dan's anger had evaporated entirely, and he felt a twinge of pity as he looked into the wreckage at the corpse. It appeared so frail and small – of such little consequence.

– 71 –

The sunlight was sparkling bright, broken into a myriad eyestinging fragments by the rippling surface of the bay.

The breeze was strong enough for the Arrow class yachts to fly their spinnakers as they came down on the wind. The sails bulged out blue and yellow and bright scarlet against the sombre green of the great whale-back bluff above Durban Bay.

Under the awning on the afterdeck of the motor yacht it was cool, but the fat man wore only a pair of white linen slacks with his feet thrust into dark blue cloth espadrilles.

Sprawled in a deck-chair, his belly bulged smooth and hard over the waistband of his slacks; he was tanned a dark mahogany colour and his body-hair grew thick and curly from chest to navel.

'Thank you, Andrew.' He extended his empty glass, and the younger man carried it to the open-air bar. The fat man watched him as he mixed another Pimms No. 1 cup.

A white-clad crew member clambered down the companion way from the bridge. He touched his cap respectfully to the fat man.

'Captain's respects, sir, and we are ready to sail when you give the order.'

'Thank you. Please tell the captain we will sail as soon as Miss du Maine comes aboard.' And the crew man ran back to the bridge.

'Ah!' The fat man sighed happily as Andrew placed the Pimms in his outstretched hand. 'I have really earned this break. The last few weeks have been nerve-racking, to say the least.'

'Yes, sir,' Andrew agreed dutifully. 'But, as usual, you snatched victory from the ashes.'

'It was close,' the fat man agreed. 'Young Ironsides gave us all a nasty fright with his drop-blast matt. I was only just able to make good my personal commitments before the price shot up again. The profit was not as high as I had anticipated, but then I have never made a habit of peering into the mouths of gift-horses.'

'It was a pity that our associates lost all that money,' Andrew ventured.

'Yes, yes. A great pity. But rather them than us, Andrew.'

'Indeed, sir.'

'In a way I am glad it worked out as it did. I am a patriotic man, at heart. I am relieved that it was not necessary to disrupt the economy of the country to make our little profit.'

He stood up suddenly, his interest quickening as a taxi cab came down onto the Yacht Club jetty. The cabby opened a rear door and from it emerged a very beautiful young lady.

'Ah, Andrew! Our guest has arrived. You may warn the captain that we will be sailing within minutes; and send a man to fetch her luggage.'

He went to the entry port to welcome the young lady.

72

I n mid-summer in the Zambesi Valley the heat is a solid white shimmering thing. In the noonday nothing moves in the merciless sunlight.

At the centre of the native village grew a baobab tree. A monstrous bloated trunk with malformed branches like the limbs of a polio victim. The carrion crows sat in it, black and shiny as cockroaches. A score of grass huts ringed the tree, and beyond them lay the tilled fields. The millet stood tall and green in the sun.

Along the rude track towards the village came a Land Rover. It came slowly, lurching and jolting over the rough ground, its motor growling in low gear. Printed in black on its sides were the letters ARC, African Recruiting Corporation.

The children heard it first, and crawled from the grass huts. Naked black bodies, and shrill excited voices in the sunlight.

They ran to meet the Land Rover and danced beside it, shrieking and laughing. The Land Rover came to a halt in the meagre shade under the baobab tree. An elderly white man climbed from the cab. He wore khaki safari clothes and a wide-brimmed hat. Complete silence fell, and one of the oldest boys fetched a carved stool and placed it in the shade.

The white man sat on the stool. A girl came forward, knelt before him and offered a gourd of millet beer. The white man drank from the gourd. No one spoke, none would disturb an honoured guest until he had taken refreshment, but from the grass huts the adult members of the village came. Blinking into the sunlight, winding their loin clothes about their waists. They came and squatted in a semi-circle before the white man on his stool.

He lowered the gourd and set it aside. He looked at them.

'I see you, my friends,' he greeted them, and the response was warm.

'We see you, old one,' they chorused, but the expression of their visitor remained grave.

'Let the wives of King Nkulu come forward,' he called. 'Let them bring each their first-born son with them.'

Four women and four adolescent boys left the crowd and came shyly into the open. For a moment the white man studied them compassionately, then he stood and stepped forward. He placed a hand on the shoulder of each of the two eldest lads.

'Your father has gone to *his* fathers,' he told them. There was a stirring, an intake of breath, a startled cry, and then, as was proper, the eldest wife let out the first sobbing wail of mourning.

One by one each wife sank down onto the dry musty earth and covered her head with her shawl.

'He is dead,' the white man repeated against the background of their keening lament. 'But he died in such honour as to let his name live on forever. So great was his dying that for all their lives money will each month be paid to his wives, and for each of his sons there is already set aside a place at the University that each may grow as strong in learning as his father was in body. Of Big King there will be raised up an image in stone.

'The wives of Big King and his sons will travel in a flying machine to I'Goldi, that their eyes also may look upon the stone image of the man who was their husband and their father.' The white man paused for breath, it was a lengthy speech in the midday heat of the valley. He wiped his face and then tucked the handkerchief into his pocket.

'He was a lion!'

'Ngwenyama!' whispered the sturdy twelve-year-old boy standing beside the white man. The tears started from his

260

when he caught Terry's scandalized glare. Silently her lips formed the words: 'Your doctor!'

Guiltily Hurry Hirschfeld stuffed the cigar back into his pocket.

eyes and greased down his cheeks. He turned away and ran alone into the millet fields.

73

Dennis Langley, the Sales Manager of Kitchenerville Motors who were the local Ford agents, stretched his arms over his head luxuriously. He sighed with deep contentment. What a lovely way to spend a working-day morning.

'Happy?' asked Hettie Delange beside him in the double bed. In reply Dennis grinned and sighed again.

Hettie sat up and let the sheet fall to her waist. Her breasts were big and white, and damp with perspiration. She looked down on his naked chest and arm muscles approvingly.

'Gee, you're built nicely.'

'So are you,' Dennis smiled up at her.

'You're different from the other chaps I've gone out with,' Hettie told him. 'You speak so nicely – like a gentleman, you know.'

Before Dennis Langley could decide on a suitable reply, the front door bell shrilled, the sound of it echoing through the house. Dennis shot into an upright position with a fearful expression on his face.

'Who's that?' he demanded.

'It's probably the butcher delivering the meat.'

'It may be my wife!' Dennis cautioned her. 'Don't answer it.'

'Of course I've got to answer it, silly.' Hettie threw back the sheet, and rose in her white and golden glory to find her dressing-gown. The sight was enough to momentarily quiet Dennis Langley's misgivings, but as she belted her gown and hid it from view he urged her again.

'Be careful! Make sure it's not her before you open the door.'

Hettie opened the front door, and immediately drew her gown more closely around her with one hand, while the other she tried to pat her hair into a semblance of order.

'Hello,' she breathed.

The tall young man in the doorway was really rather dreamy. He wore a dark business suit and carried an expensive leather briefcase.

'Mrs Delange?' he enquired. He had a nice soft dreamy voice.

'Yes, I'm Mrs Delange.' Hettie fluttered her eyelashes. 'Won't you come in?'

She led him through to the lounge, and she was pleasantly aware of his eyes on the opening of her gown.

'What can I do for you?' she asked archly.

'I am your local representative of the Sanlam Insurance Company, Mrs Delange. I have come to express my company's condolences on your recent sad bereavement. I would have called sooner, but I did not wish to intrude on your sorrow.'

'Oh!' Hettie dropped her eyes, immediately adopting the role of the widow.

'However, we hope we can bring a little light to disperse the darkness that surrounds you. You may know that your husband was a policy-holder with our Company?'

Hettie shook her head, but watched with interest while the visitor opened his briefcase.

'Yes, he was. Two months ago he took out a straight life policy with double indemnity. The policy was ceded to you.' The insurance man extracted a sheaf of papers from his case. 'I have here my company's cheque in full settlement of all claims under the policy. If you will just sign for it, please.'

'How much?' Hettie abandoned the role of the bereaved.

'With the double indemnity, the cheque is for forty-eight thousand rand.'

Hettie's eyes flew wide with delight.

'Gee!' she gasped. 'That's *fabulous*!'

– 74 –

Hurry's original intentions had expanded considerably. Instead of a plaque on the cement plug at 66 level, the monument to Big King had become a life-sized statue in bronze. He sited it on the lawns in front of the Adminstrative offices of the Sonder Ditch on a base of black marble.

It was effective. The artist had captured a sense of urgency, of vibrant power. The inscription was simple, just the name of the man – 'King Nkulu' – and the date of his death.

Hurry attended the unveiling in person, even though he hated ceremonies and avoided them whenever possible. In the front row of guests facing him his granddaughter sat beside Doctor Stander and his very new blonde wife. She winked at him and Hurry frowned lovingly back at her.

From the seat beside Hurry, young Ironsides stood up to introduce the Chairman. Hurry noted the expression on his granddaughter's face as she transferred all her attention to the tall young man with both his arms encased in plaster of Paris and supported by slings.

'Perhaps I should have fired him, after all,' thought Hurry. 'He is going to cut one out of my herd.'

Hurry glanced sideways at his General Manager, and decided with resignation, 'Too late'. Then he went on to cheer himself. 'Anyway he looks like good breeding stock.'

His line of thought switched again. 'Better start making arrangements to transfer him up to Head Office. He will need a lot of grooming and polishing.'

Without thinking he fished a powerful-looking cigar from his breast pocket. He had it halfway to his mouth

THE BURNING SHORE

This book is for Danielle Antoinette
with all my love always

So have I heard on Afric's burning shore,
A hungry lion give a grievous roar.

William Barnes Rhodes, *Bombastes Furioso*, sc. IV

Michael awoke to the mindless fury of the guns.

It was an obscene ritual celebrated in the darkness before each dawn in which the massed banks of artillery batteries on both sides of the ridges made their savage sacrifice to the gods of war.

Michael lay in the darkness under the weight of six woollen blankets and watched the gunfire flicker through the canvas of the tent like some dreadful aurora borealis. The blankets felt cold and clammy as a dead man's skin, and light rain spattered the canvas above his head. The cold struck through his bedclothes and yet he felt a glow of hope. In this weather they could not fly.

False hope withered swiftly, for when Michael listened again to the guns, this time more intently, he could judge the direction of the wind by the sound of the barrage. The wind had gone back into the south-west, muting the cacophony, and he shivered and pulled the blankets up under his chin. As if to confirm his estimate, the light breeze dropped suddenly. The patter of rain on canvas eased and then ceased. Outside he could hear the trees of the apple orchard dripping in the silence – and then there was an abrupt gust so that the branches shook themselves like a spaniel coming out of the water and released a heavy fall of drops on to the roof of the tent.

He decided that he would not reach across to his gold half-hunter on the inverted packing-case which acted as a bedside table. It would be time all too soon. So he snuggled down in the blankets and thought about his fear. All of them suffered under the affliction of fear, and yet the rigid conventions under which they lived and flew and died forbade them to speak of it – forbade them to refer to it in even the most oblique terms.

Would it have been a comfort, Michael wondered, if last night he had been able to say to Andrew as they sat with the bottle of whisky between them, discussing this morning's mission, 'Andrew, I'm frightened gutless by what we are going to do'?

He grinned in the darkness as he imagined Andrew's embarrassment, yet he knew that Andrew shared it with him. It was in his eyes, and in the way the little nerve twitched and jumped in his cheek so that he had constantly to touch it with a fingertip to still it. All the old hands had their little idiosyncracies; Andrew had the nerve in his cheek and the empty cigarette-holder which he sucked like an infant's comforter. Michael ground his teeth in his sleep so loudly that he woke himself; he bit the nail of his left thumb down into the quick and every few minutes he blew on the fingers of his right hand as though he had just touched a hot coal.

The fear drove them all a little mad, and forced them to drink far too much – enough to destroy the reflexes of normal men. But they were not normal men and the alcohol did not seem to affect them, it did not dull their eyesight nor slow their feet on the rudder bars. Normal men died in the first three weeks, they went down flaming like fir trees in a forest fire, or they smashed into the doughy, shell-ploughed earth with a force that shattered their bones and drove the splinters out through their flesh.

Andrew had survived fourteen months, and Michael eleven, many times the life-span that the gods of war had allotted to the men who flew these frail contraptions of wire and wood and canvas. So they twitched and fidgeted, and blinked their eyes, and drank whisky with everything, and laughed in a quick loud bray and then shuffled their feet with embarrassment, and lay in their cots at dawn, stiff with terror, and listened for footsteps.

Michael heard the footsteps now, it must be later than he had realized. Outside the tent Biggs muttered a curse as he splashed into a puddle, and his boots made obscene little sucking noises in the mud. His bull's-eye lantern glowed through the canvas as he fumbled with the flap and then he stooped into the tent.

'Top of the morning, sir—' his tone was cheerful, but he kept it low, out of courtesy to the officers in the neighbouring tents who were not flying this morning ' – wind has gone sou'-sou'-west, sir, and she's clearing something lovely, she is. Stars shining out over Cambrai—' Biggs set the tray he carried on the packing-case and bustled about the tent, picking up the clothing that Michael had dropped on the duckboards the night before.

'What time is it?' Michael went through the pantomime of awaking from deep sleep, stretching and yawning so that Biggs would not know about the hour of terror, so that the legend would not be tarnished.

'Half past five, sir.' Biggs finished folding the clothes away, then came back to hand him the thick china mug of cocoa. 'And Lord Killigerran is up and in the mess already.'

'Bloody man is made of iron,' Michael groaned, and Biggs picked the empty whisky bottle off the floor beneath the cot and placed it on the tray.

Michael drained the cocoa while Biggs worked up a lather in the shaving mug and then held the polished steel mirror and the lantern while Michael shaved with the straight razor, sitting up in his cot with the blankets over his shoulders.

'What's the book?' Michael demanded, his voice nasal as he pinched his own nostrils and lifted the tip of his nose to shave his upper lip.

'They are giving three to one that you and the major take them both with no butcher's bill.'

Michael wiped the razor while he considered the odds. The sergeant rigger who ran the betting had operated his own book at Ascot and Aintree before the war. He had decided that there was one chance in three that either Andrew or Michael, or both of them, would be dead by noon – no butcher's bill, no casualties.

'Bit steep, don't you think, Biggs?' Michael asked. 'I mean, both of them, damn it?'

'I've put half a crack on you, sir,' Biggs demurred.

'Good on you, Biggs, put on a fiver for me.' He pointed to the sovereign case that lay beside his watch, and Biggs pressed out five gold coins and pocketed them. Michael always bet on himself. It was a racing certainty: if he lost the bet, it wasn't going to hurt much, anyway.

Biggs warmed Michael's breeches over the chimney of the lamp and then held them while Michael dived out from under the blankets into them. He stuffed his night-shirt into the breeches while Biggs went on with the complicated procedure of dressing his man against the killing cold of flight in an open cockpit. There followed a silk vest over the nightshirt, two cable-stitched woollen fisherman's jerseys, then a leather gilet, and finally an army officer's greatcoat with the skirts cut off so that they would not tangle with the controls of the aircraft.

By this time Michael was so heavily padded that he could not bend to pull on his own footwear. Biggs knelt in front of him and snugged silk undersocks over his bare feet, then two pairs of woollen hunting socks, and finally eased on the tall boots of tanned kudu skin that Michael had had made in Africa. Through their soft, pliable soles, Michael had touch and feel on the rudder bars. When he stood up, his lean muscular body was dumpy and shapeless under the burden of clothing, and his arms stuck out like the wings of a penguin. Biggs held the flap of the tent open, and then lit his way along the duckboards through the orchard towards the mess.

As they passed the other darkened tents beneath the apple trees Michael heard little coughs and stirrings from

4

each. They were all awake, listening to his footsteps pass, fearing for him, perhaps some of them cherishing their relief that it was not they who were going out against the balloons this dawn.

Michael paused for a moment as they left the orchard and looked up at the sky. The dark clouds were rolling back into the north and the stars were pricking through, but already paling out before the threat of dawn. These stars were still strange to Michael; though he could at last recognize their constellations, they were not like his beloved southern stars – the Great Cross, Achernar, Argus and the others – so he lowered his gaze and clumped after Biggs and the bobbing lantern.

The squadron mess was a ruined labourers' *chaumière* which they had commandeered and repainted, covering the tattered thatch with tarpaulin so that it was snug and warm.

Biggs stood aside at the doorway. 'I'll 'ave your fifteen quid winnings for you when you get back, sir,' he murmured. He would never wish Michael good luck, for that was the worst of all possible luck.

There was a roaring log fire on the hearth and Major Lord Andrew Killigerran was seated before it, his booted feet crossed on the lip of the hearth, while a mess servant cleared the dirty plates.

'Porridge, my boy,' he removed the amber cigarette holder from between his even white teeth as he greeted Michael, 'with melted butter and golden syrup. Kippers poached in milk—'

Michael shuddered. 'I'll eat when we get back.' His stomach, already knotted with tension, quailed at the rich smell of kippers. With the co-operation of an uncle on the general staff who arranged priority transport, Andrew kept the squadron supplied with the finest fare that his family estates in the highlands could provide – Scotch beef, grouse and salmon and venison in season, eggs and cheeses and

5

jams, preserved fruits – and a rare and wonderful single malt whisky with an unpronounceable name that came from the family-owned distillery.

'Coffee for Captain Courtney,' Andrew called to the mess corporal, and when it came he reached into the deep pocket of his fleece-lined flying jacket and brought out a silver flask with a big yellow cairngorm set in the stopper and poured a liberal dram into the steaming mug.

Michael held the first sip in his mouth, swirling it around, letting the fragrant spirit sting and prickle his tongue, then he swallowed and the heat hit his empty stomach and almost instantly he felt the charge of alcohol through his bloodstream.

He smiled at Andrew across the table. 'Magic,' he whispered huskily, and blew on his fingertips.

'Water of life, my boy.'

Michael loved this dapper little man as he had never loved another man – more than his own father, more even than his Uncle Sean who had previously been the pillar of his existence.

It had not been that way from the beginning. At first meeting, Michael had been suspicious of Andrew's extravagant, almost effeminate good looks, his long, curved eyelashes, soft, full lips, his neat, small body, dainty hands and feet, and his lofty bearing.

One evening soon after his arrival on the squadron, Michael was teaching the other new chums how to play the game of Bok-Bok. Under his direction one team formed a human pyramid against a wall of the mess, while the other team attempted to collapse them by taking a full run and then hurling themselves on top of the structure. Andrew had waited for the game to end in noisy chaos and had then taken Michael aside and told him, 'We do understand that you hail from somewhere down there below the equator, and we do try to make allowances for you colonials. However—'

6

Their relationship had thenceforth been cool and distant, while they had watched each other shoot and fly.

As a boy, Andrew had learned to take the deflection of a red grouse, hurtling wind-driven only inches above the tops of the heather. Michael had learned the same skills on rocketing Ethiopian snipe and sand-grouse slanting on rapid wingbeat down the African sky. Both of them had been able to adapt their skills to the problem of firing a Vickers machine-gun from the unstable platform of a Sopwith Pup roaring through the three dimensions of space.

Then they watched each other fly. Flying was a gift. Those who did not have it died during the first three weeks; those who did, lasted a little longer. After a month Michael was still alive, and Andrew spoke to him again for the first time since the evening of the game of Bok-Bok in the mess.

'Courtney, you will fly on my wing today,' was all he said.

It was to have been a routine sweep down the line. They were going to 'blood' two new chums who had joined the squadron the day before, fresh from England with the grand total of fourteen flying hours as their combined experience. Andrew referred to them as 'Fokker fodder', and they were both eighteen years of age, rosy-faced and eager.

'Did you learn aerobatics?' Andrew demanded of them.

'Yes, sir.' In unison. 'We have both looped the loop.'

'How many times?'

Shamefaced they lowered their shining gaze. 'Once,' they admitted.

'God!' muttered Andrew and sucked loudly on his cigarette-holder. 'Stalls?'

They both looked bemused, and Andrew clutched his brow and groaned.

'Stalls?' Michael interposed in a kindly tone. 'You know,

7

when you let your airspeed drop and the kite suddenly falls out of the sky.'

They shook their heads, again in unison. 'No, sir, nobody showed us that.'

'The Huns are going to love you two,' Andrew murmured, and then he went on briskly, 'Number one, forget all about aerobatics, forget about looping the loop and all that rot, or while you are hanging there upside down the Hun is going to shoot your anus out through your nostrils, understand?'

They nodded vigorously.

'Number two, follow me, do what I do, watch for my hand signals and obey them instantly, understand?' Andrew jammed his tam-o'-shanter down on his head and bound it in place with the green scarf that was his trademark. 'Come along, children.'

With the two novices tucked up between them they barrelled down past Arras at 10,000 feet, the Le Rhône engines of their Sopwith Pups bellowing with all their eighty horsepower, princes of the heavens, the most perfect flying fighting machines man had ever devised, the machines that had shot Max Immelmann and his vaunted Fokker Eindekkers out of the skies.

It was a glorious day, with just a little fairweather cumulus too high up there to hide a boche Jagdstaffel, and the air so clear and bright that Michael spotted the old Rumpler reconnaissance biplane from a distance of ten miles. It was circling low over the French lines, directing the fire of the German batteries on to the rear areas.

Andrew picked out the Rumpler an instant after Michael, and he flashed a laconic hand signal. He was going to let the new chums take a shot at her. Michael knew of no other squadron commander who would stand aside from an easy victory when a big score was the high road to promotion and the coveted decorations. However, he nodded agreement and they shepherded the two young pilots down, patiently pointing out the lumbering German two-seater below them, but with their untrained eyes neither of them could pick it out. They kept shooting puzzled glances across at the two senior pilots.

The Germans were so intent on the bursting high explosive beneath them that they were oblivious of the deadly formation closing swiftly from above. Suddenly the young pilot nearest Michael grinned with delight and relief and pointed ahead. He had seen the Rumpler at last.

Andrew pumped his fist over his head in the old cavalry command, 'Charge!' and the youngster put his nose down without closing the throttle. The Sopwith went into a howling dive so abrupt that Michael winced as he saw the double wings bend back under the strain and the fabric wrinkle at the wing roots. The second novice followed him just as precipitously. They reminded Michael of two half-grown lion cubs he had once watched trying to bring down a scarred old zebra stallion, falling over themselves in comical confusion as the stallion avoided them with disdain.

Both the novice pilots opened fire at a range of a thousand yards, and the German pilot looked up at this timely warning; then, judging his moment, he banked under the noses of the diving scoutplanes, forcing them into a blundering overshoot that carried them, still firing wildly, half a mile beyond their intended victim. Michael could see their heads screwing around desperately in the open cockpits as they tried to find the Rumpler again.

Andrew shook his head sadly and led Michael down. They dropped neatly under the Rumpler's tailplane, and the German pilot banked steeply to port in a climbing turn to give his rear gunner a shot at them. Together Andrew and Michael turned out in the opposite direction to frustrate him, but as soon as the German pilot realized the manoeuvre had failed and corrected his bank, they whipped the Sopwiths hard over and crossed his stern.

9

Andrew was leading. He fired one short burst with the Vickers at a hundred feet and the German rear gunner bucked and flung his arms open, letting the Spandau machine-gun swivel aimlessly on its mounting as the 303 bullets cut him to pieces. The German pilot tried to dive away, and Andrew's Sopwith almost collided with his top wing as he passed over him.

Then Michael came in. He judged the deflection of the diving Rumpler, touched his port rudder bar so that his machine yawed fractionally just as though he were swinging a shotgun on a rocketing snipe, and he hooked the forefinger of his right hand under the safety bar of the Vickers and fired a short burst — a flurry of .303 ball. He saw the fabric of the Rumpler's fuselage ripped to tatters just below the rim of the pilot's cockpit, in line with where his upper body must be.

The German was twisted around staring at Michael from a distance of a mere fifty feet. Michael could see that his eyes behind the lens of his goggles were a startled blue, and that he had not shaved that morning, for his chin was covered with a short golden stubble. He opened his mouth as the shots hit, and the blood from his shattered lungs blew out between his lips and turned to pink smoke in the Rumpler's slipstream, and then Michael was past and climbing away. The Rumpler rolled sluggishly on to its back and with the dead men lolling in their straps, fell away towards the earth. It struck in the centre of an open field and collapsed in a pathetic welter of fabric and shattered struts.

As Michael settled his Sopwith back into position on Andrew's wingtip, Andrew looked across at him, nodded matter-of-factly, and then signalled him to help round up the two new chums who were still searching in frantic circles for the vanished Rumpler. This took longer than either of them anticipated, and by the time they had them

10

safely under their protection again, the whole formation had drifted further west than either Andrew or Michael had ever flown before. On the horizon Michael could make out the fat shiny serpent of the Somme river winding across the green littoral on its way down to the sea.

They turned away from it and headed back east towards Arras, climbing steadily to reduce the chances of an attack from above by a Fokker Jagdstaffel.

As they gained height, so the vast panorama of northern France and southern Belgium opened beneath them, the fields a patchwork of a dozen shades of green interspersed with the dark brown of ploughed lands. The actual battle lines were hard to distinguish; from so high, the narrow ribbon of shell-churned earth appeared insignificant, and the misery and the mud and the death down there seemed illusory.

The two veteran pilots never ceased for an instant their search of the sky and the spaces beneath them. Their heads turned to a set rhythm in their scan, their eyes never still, never allowed to focus short or become mesmerized by the fan of the spinning propeller in front of them. In contrast, the two novices were carefree and self-congratulatory. Every time Michael glanced across in their direction they grinned and waved cheerfully. In the end he gave up trying to urge them to search the skies around them, they did not understand his signals.

They levelled out at 15,000 feet, the effective ceiling of the Sopwiths, and the sense of unease that had haunted Michael while he had been flying at low altitude over unfamiliar territory passed as he saw the town of Arras abeam of them. He knew that no Fokker could be lurking above them in that pretty bank of cumulus, they simply did not have the ability of fly that high.

He swept another searching glance along the lines. There were two German observation balloons just south of

Mons, while below them a friendly flight of DH2 single-seaters was heading back towards Amiens, which meant they were from No. 24 Squadron.

In ten minutes they would be landing – Michael never finished the thought, for suddenly and miraculously the sky all around him was filled with gaudily painted aircraft and the chatter of Spandau machine-guns.

Even in his utter bewilderment Michael reacted reflexively. As he pulled the Sopwith into a maximum-rate turn, a shark-shaped machine checkered red and black with a grinning white skull superimposed on its black Maltese cross insignia flashed across his nose. A hundredth of a second later and its Spandaus would have savaged Michael. They had come from above, Michael realized; even though he could not believe it, they had been above the Sopwiths, they had come out of the cloud bank.

One of them, painted red as blood, settled on Andrew's tail, its Spandaus already shredding and clawing away the trailing edge of the lower wing, and swinging inexorably towards where Andrew crouched in the open cockpit, his face a white blob beneath the tam-o'-shanter and the green scarf. Instinctively, Michael drove at him, and the German, rather than risk collision, swung away.

'Ngi dla!' Michael shouted the Zulu warcry as he came on to the killing quarter on the tail of the red machine, and then in disbelief watched it power away before he could bring the Vickers to bear. The Sopwith juddered brutally to the strike of shot and a rigging wire above his head parted with a twang like a released bow string as another one of these terrible machines attacked across his stern.

He broke away, and Andrew was below him, trying to climb away from yet another German machine which was swiftly overhauling him, coming up within an ace of the killing line. Michael went at the German head-on and the red and black wings flickered past his head – but instantly

12

there was another German to replace him, and this time Michael could not shake him off, the bright machine was too fast, too powerful, and Michael knew he was a dead man.

Abruptly the stream of Spandau fire ceased, and Andrew plunged past Michael's wingtip, driving the German off him. Desperately Michael followed Andrew around, and they went into the defensive circle, each of them covering the other's belly and tail while the cloud of German aircraft milled around them in murderous frustration.

Only part of Michael's mind recorded the fact that both the new chums were dead. They had died in the first seconds of the assault; one was in a vertical dive under full power, the maimed Sopwith's wings buckling under the strain and at last tearing away completely, while the other was a burning torch, smearing a thick pall of black smoke down the sky as it fell.

As miraculously as they had come, the Germans were gone – untouched and invulnerable, they disappeared back towards their own lines, leaving the pair of battered, shot-torn Sopwiths to limp homewards.

Andrew landed ahead of Michael and they parked wingtip to wingtip at the edge of the orchard. Each of them clambered down and walked slowly round his own machine, inspecting the damage. Then at last they stood in front of each other, stony-faced with shock.

Andrew reached into his pocket and brought out the silver flask. He unscrewed the cairngorm and wiped the mouth of the flask with the tail of the green scarf, then handed the flask to Michael.

'Here, my boy,' he said carefully, 'have a dram. I think you earned it – I really do.'

So on the day that Allied superiority was wiped from the skies above France by the shark-nosed Albatros D type scoutplanes of the German Jagdstaffels, they had become comrades of desperate necessity, flying at each other's wingtips, forming the defensive, mutually protective circle whenever the gaily painted minions of death fell upon them. At first they were content merely to defend themselves, then between them they tested the capability of this new and deadly foe, poring together at night over the intelligence reports that belatedly came in to them – learning that the Albatros was driven by a 160 horse-power Mercedes engine, twice as powerful as the Sopwith's Le Rhône, and that it had twin Spandau 7.92 mm machine-guns with interrupter gear firing forward through the arc of the propeller, against the Sopwith's single Vickers .303. They were outgunned and outpowered. The Albatros was 700 pounds heavier than the Pup and could take tremendous weight of shot before it fell out of the sky.

'So, old boy, what we'll do is learn to fly the arses off them,' Andrew commented, and they went out against the massed formations of the Jastas and they found their weaknesses. There were only two. The Sopwiths could turn inside them, and the Albatros radiator was situated in the upper wing directly above the cockpit. A shot through the tank would send a stream of boiling coolant hissing over the pilot, scalding him to a hideous death.

Using this knowledge, they made their first kills, and found that in testing the Albatros they had tested each other and found no fault there. Comradeship became friendship, which deepened into a love and respect greater than that between brothers of the blood. So now they could sit quietly together in the dawn, drinking coffee laced with whisky, waiting to go out against the balloons, and take comfort and strength from each other.

'Spin for it?' Michael broke the silence, it was almost time to go.

Andrew flicked a sovereign into the air and slapped it on to the table-top, covering it with his hand.

'Heads,' said Michael and Andrew lifted his hand.

'Luck of a pox-doctor!' he grunted, as they both looked down on the stern, bearded profile of George V.

'I'll take number-two slot,' said Michael, and Andrew opened his mouth to protest.

'I won, I call the shot.' Michael stood up to end the argument before it began.

Going against the balloons was like walking on to a sleeping puff-adder, that gross and sluggish serpent of the African veld; the first man woke it so that it could arch its neck into the 'S' of the strike, the second man had the long recurved fangs plunged into the flesh of his calf. With the balloons they had to attack in line astern, the first man alerted the ground defences and the second man received their full fury. Michael had deliberately chosen the number-two slot. If he had won, Andrew would have done the same.

They paused shoulder to shoulder in the door of the mess, pulling on their gauntlets, buttoning their coats and looking up at the sky, listening to the rolling fury of the guns and judging the breeze.

'The mist will hang in the valleys,' Michael murmured. 'The wind won't move it, not yet.'

'Pray for it, my boy,' Andrew answered, and, hampered by their clothing, they waddled down the duckboards, to where the Sopwiths stood at the edge of the trees.

How noble they had once appeared in Michael's eyes, but how ugly now when the huge rotary engine, vomiting forward vision, was compared to the Albatros' sleek shark-like snout, with its in-line Mercedes engine. How frail when considered against the Germans' robust airframe.

'God, when are they going to give us real aeroplanes to fly!' he grunted, and Andrew did not reply. Too often they had lamented the endless wait for the new SE5a that they had been promised – the Scout Experimental No. 5a that would perhaps allow them to meet the Jastas on equal terms at last.

Andrew's Sopwith was painted bright green, to match his scarf, and the fuselage behind the cockpit was ringed by fourteen white circles, one for each of his confirmed victories, like notches on a sniper's rifle. The aircraft's name was painted on the engine housing: 'The Flying Haggis'.

Michael had chosen bright yellow, and there was a winged tortoise with a worried frown painted below his cockpit and the appeal, 'Don't ask me – I just work here.' His fuselage was ringed by six white circles.

Assisted by their ground crews, they clambered up on to the lower wing, and then eased themselves into the narrow cockpits. Michael settled his feet on to the rudder bars and pumped them left and right, peering back over his shoulder to watch the response of the rudder as he did so. Satisfied, he held up a thumb at his mechanic who had worked most of the night to replace one of the cables shot away on the last sortie. The mechanic grinned and ran to the front of the machine.

'Switches off?' he called.

'Switches off!' Michael confirmed, leaning out of the cockpit to peer around the monstrous engine.

'Suck in!'

'Suck in!' Michael repeated, and worked at the handle of the hand fuel pump. When the mechanic swung the propeller, he heard the suck of fuel into the carburettor under the cowling as the engine primed.

'Switches on! Contact!'

'Switches on!'

At the next swing of the propeller the engine fired and blathered. Blue smoke blew out of the exhaust ports, and there was the stink of burning castor oil. The engine surged, and missed, caught again and settled down to its steady idling beat.

As Michael completed his pre-flight checks, his stomach rumbled and spasmed with colic. Castor oil lubricated the precision engines, and the fumes they breathed from the exhausts gave them all a perpetual low-grade diarrhoea. The old hands soon learned to control it; whisky had a marvellously binding effect if taken in sufficient quantity. However, the new chums were often affectionately referred to as 'treacle bottoms' or 'slippery breeks' when they returned red-faced and odorous from a sortie.

Michael settled his goggles and glanced across at Andrew. They nodded at each other, and Andrew opened his throttle and rolled out on to the soggy turf. Michael followed him, his mechanic trotting at his starboard wing-tip to help him swing and line up on the narrow muddy strip between the apple trees.

Ahead of him Andrew was airborne and Michael opened his throttle wide. Almost immediately the Sopwith threw her tail up, clearing his forward vision, and Michael felt a prick of conscience at his earlier disloyalty. She was a lovely plane and a joy to fly. Despite the sticky mud of the strip, she broke swiftly free of the earth, and at 100 feet Michael levelled out behind Andrew's green machine. The light was just good enough by now for him to make out to his right the green copper-clad spire of the church of the little village of Mort Homme; ahead of him lay the T-shaped grove of oak and beech trees, the long leg of the T perfectly aligned with the squadron's landing strip, a most convenient navigational aid when coming in during bad weather. Beyond the trees stood the pink-roofed château set in the midst of its lawns and formal gardens, and behind the château the low knoll.

Andrew banked fractionally to the right, to pass the knoll. Michael conformed, peering ahead over the edge of his cockpit. Would she be there? It was too early – the knoll was bare. He felt the slide of disappointment and dread. Then he saw her – she was galloping up the pathway towards the crest. The big white stallion lunging powerfully under her slim girlish body.

17

The girl on the white horse was their good-luck talisman. If she was there waiting on the knoll to wave them away, all would be well. Today, when they were going against the balloons, they needed her – how desperately they needed her benediction.

She reached the crest of the knoll and reined the stallion down. Just a few seconds before they drew level she whipped the hat off her head and the thick dark bush of her hair burst from under it. She waved the hat, and Andrew waggled his wings as he roared past.

Michael edged in closer to the crest. The white stallion backed up and nodded nervously as the yellow machine came bellowing at him, but the girl sat him easily, waving gaily. Michael wanted to see her face. He was almost at the same height as the top of the hillock and very close to where she sat. For an instant he looked into her eyes. They were huge and dark, and he felt his heart trip. He touched his helmet in salute, and he knew now, deep down, that it would go well this day – then he put the memory of those eyes from his mind and looked ahead.

Ten miles ahead, where the low chalk ridges ran across their front, he saw with relief that he had been right, the breeze had not yet dispersed the morning mist that hung in the valleys. The chalk ridges were horribly chewed by shellfire, no vegetation remained upon them, the stumps of the shattered oak trees were nowhere as tall as a man's shoulder, and the shell craters overlapped each other, brimming with stagnant water. The ridges had been fought over, month after month, but at the moment they were in Allied hands, taken at the beginning of the preceding winter at a cost in human lives that challenged belief. The leprous and pockmarked earth seemed deserted, but it was peopled by the legions of the living and the dead rotting together in the waterlogged earth. The smell of death borne on the breeze reached even to the men in the low flying machines, an obscenity that coated the back of their throats and made them gag.

Behind the ridges the Allied troops, South Africans and New Zealanders of the Third Army, were preparing reserve positions as a contingency measure, for should the Allied offensive which was being prepared upon the Somme river further to the west fail, then all the fury of the German counter-attack would be unleashed upon them.

The preparation of the new line of defences was being seriously hampered by the massed German artillery to the north of the ridges, which deluged the area with an almost continuous barrage of high explosive. As they roared towards the front, Michael could see the yellow haze from the bursting howitzer shells hanging in a poison bank below the ridges, and he could imagine the anguish of the men toiling in the mud, harassed by the unremitting fall of explosives.

As Michael raced towards the ridges, the sound of the barrage rose above even the thunder of the big rotary Le Rhône engine and the buffeting rush of the slipstream. The barrage was like the sound of storm surf on a rocky shore, like the beat of a demented drummer, like the fevered pulse of this sick, mad world, and Michael's fierce resentment at the men who had ordered them to go against the balloons abated as the roar of the barrage mounted. It was work that must be done – he realized it when he saw this dreadful suffering.

Yet the balloons were the most feared and hated targets that any man could fly against – that was why Andrew Killigerran would send nobody else. Michael saw them now, like fat silver slugs hanging in the dawn sky high above the ridges. One was directly ahead, the other a few miles further east. At this range the cables that tethered them to earth were invisible, and the wicker basket from which the observers obtained a grandstand view over the

Allied rear areas were merely dark specks suspended beneath the shining spheres of hydrogen-filled silk.

At that moment there was a shocking disruption of air that hit the Sopwiths and rocked their wings, and immediately ahead of them a fountain of smoke and flame shot into the sky, rolling upon itself, black and bright orange, rising anvil-headed, high above the low-flying Sopwiths, forcing them to bank away steeply to avoid its fiery pillar. A German shell directed from one of the balloons had hit a forward Allied ammunition dump, and Michael felt his fear and resentment shrivel, to be replaced by a burning hatred of the gunners and of the men hanging in the sky, with eyes like vultures, calling down death with cold dispassion.

Andrew turned back towards the ridges, leaving the tall column of smoke on their right wingtips, and he dropped lower and still lower, until his undercarriage was skimming the tops of the sandbagged parapets and they could see the South African troops moving in file along the communication trenches, dun-coloured beasts of burden, not really human, toiling under the weight of their packs and equipment. Very few of them bothered to look up as the gaily painted machines thundered overhead. Those that did had grey, mud-streaked faces, the expression dulled and the eyes blank.

Ahead of them opened the mouth of one of the low passes that bisected the chalk ridges. The pass was filled with the morning mist. With the thrust of the dawn breeze agitating it, the mist bank undulated softly as though the earth was making love beneath a silver eiderdown.

There was the rattle of a Vickers machine-gun close ahead. Andrew was testfiring his weapon. Michael turned slightly out of line to clear his front and fired a short burst. The phosphorus-tipped incendiary bullets spun pretty white trails in the clear air.

Michael turned back into line behind Andrew and they hurtled into the mist, entering a new dimension of light and muted sound. The diffused light spun rainbow-coloured haloes around both aircraft and the moisture condensed on Michael's goggles. He lifted them on to his forehead and peered ahead.

The previous afternoon, Andrew and Michael had carefully reconnoitred this narrow pass between the ridges, reassuring themselves that there were no obstacles or obstructions, and memorizing the way it twisted and turned through the higher ground – and yet it was still a perilous passage, with visibility down to 600 feet or less and the chalky slopes rising steeply at each wingtip.

Michael closed up on the green tailplane and flew on that alone, trusting Andrew to take him through, while the icy cold of the mist ate corrosively through his clothing and numbed his fingertips through the leather gauntlets.

Ahead of him Andrew banked steeply, and as Michael followed him round, he caught a glimpse of the barbed wire, brown with rust and tangled like bracken beneath his wheels.

'No man's land,' he muttered, and then the German front lines flashed beneath them, a mere glimpse of parapets beneath which crouched men in field-grey uniforms and those ugly coal-scuttle helmets.

Seconds later they burst out of the mist bank into a world lit by the first low rays of the sun, into a sky that dazzled them with its brilliance – and Michael realized that they had achieved total surprise. The mist bank had hidden them from the observers in the balloon and it had deadened the beat of their engines.

Directly ahead, the first balloon hung suspended in the sky, 1,500 feet above them. Its steel anchor-cable, fine as a spider's strand of gossamer, led down to the ugly black steam winch half-buried in its emplacement of sandbags. It

21

looked utterly vulnerable, until Michael's eye dropped to the peaceful-seeming fields beneath the balloon, and there were the guns.

The machine-gun nests resembled ant-lion burrows in the African soil, tiny dimples in the earth, lined with sandbags. He could not count them in the brief seconds left to him, there were so many. Instead, he picked out the anti-aircraft guns, standing tall and ungainly as giraffes on their circular baseplates, the long barrels already pointed skywards, ready to hurl their air-burst shrapnel as high as 20,000 feet into the sky.

They were waiting. They knew that sooner or later the planes would come, and they were ready. Michael realized that the mist had won them only seconds, for he could see the gunners running to man their weapons. One of the long anti-aircraft barrels began to move, depressing and swinging towards them. Then, as Michael pushed the throttle lever hard open against its stop and the Sopwith surged forward, he saw a cloud of white steam spurt from the massive winch as the ground crew began desperately to haul the balloon down into the protective fire of the banks of guns. The shimmering sphere of silk sank swiftly towards the earth, and Andrew lifted the nose of his machine and roared upwards.

With the throttle wide open and the big rotary engine howling in full power, Michael followed him up, aiming his climb at the cable halfway between the earth and the balloon, at the spot where the balloon would be when he reached it, and that was a mere 500 feet above the heads of the gunners.

Andrew was four hundred yards ahead of Michael, and still the guns had not opened up. Now he was on line with the balloon and engaging it. Michael clearly heard the clatter of his Vickers and saw the streaking phosphorus trails of the incendiary bullets, lacing through the icy dawn air, joining the balloon and the racing green aircraft for fleeting seconds. Then Andrew banked away, his wingtip brushed the billowing silk, and it rocked sedately in his slipstream.

Now it was Michael's turn, and as he picked up the balloon in his gunsight, the gunners below him opened up. He heard the rip-crash of shrapnel bursts, and the Sopwith rocked dangerously in the tornado of passing shot, but the shells were all fused too long. They burst in bright silver balls of smoke three or four hundred feet above him.

The machine-gunners were more accurate, for they were at almost point-blank range. Michael felt the solid crash of shot into his plane, and tracer flew thick and white as hail about him. He hit the rudder bar and at the same time threw on opposite stick, crossing controls to induce a gut-wrenching side-slip, throwing off the sheets of fire for a moment while he lined up for the balloon.

It seemed to rush towards him; the silk had the repulsively soft sheen of a maggot coated in silver mucus. He saw the two German observers dangling in their open wicker basket, both of them bundled in clothing against the cold. One stared at him woodenly, the other's face was contorted with terror and fury as he screamed a curse or a challenge that was lost in the blare of engines and the rattling clatter of machine-gun fire.

It was barely necessary to aim the Vickers, for the balloon filled all his vision. Michael opened the safety lock and pressed down on the firing lever; the gun hammered, shaking the entire aircraft, and the smoke of burning phosphorus from the incendiary bullet blew back into his face, choking him.

Now that he was flying straight and level, the ground gunners found him again, shooting the Sopwith to tatters – but Michael held on, pressing on alternate rudders to wing his nose slightly from side to side, directing his incendiaries into the balloon as though he was wielding a garden hose.

'Burn!' he screamed. 'Burn! Damn you, burn!'

Pure hydrogen gas is not inflammable, it has to mix with oxygen in proportions of 1:2 before it becomes violently explosive. The balloon absorbed his fire without visible effect.

'Burn!' he screamed at it, his clawed hand locked on the firing handle, the Vickers hammering, and the spent brass shells spewing from the breech. Hydrogen must be pouring from the hundreds of bullet holes that both he and Andrew had shot in the silk; the gas must be mingling with the air.

'Why won't you burn?' He heard the anguish and despair in his own wild cry. He was on the balloon – he must break away now, he must turn to avoid collision, it had all been in vain. Then, in that instant of failure, he knew that he would never give up. He knew he was going to fly into the balloon if he had to.

As he thought it, the balloon exploded in his face. It seemed to swell to a hundred times its size, to fill the sky and at the same time turn to flame. A stunning dragon's breath licked over Michael and the Sopwith, scorching the exposed skin of his cheeks, blinding him, flinging both man and machine aloft like a green leaf from a garden bonfire. Michael fought for control as the Sopwith tried to turn on her back, then tumbled down the sky. He caught her before she smashed into the earth and as he climbed away he looked back.

The hydrogen gas had burned away in that single demoniac gust, and now the empty, fiercely burning silk shroud collapsed, spreading like a fiery umbrella over the basket and its human cargo.

One of the German observers jumped clear and fell 300 feet, his greatcoat fluttering about him, his legs kicking convulsively, disappearing abruptly, without sound or trace, into the short green grass of the field. The second observer stayed with the basket and was enveloped by the billows of burning silk.

On the ground the crew were scrambling from the winch emplacement, like insects from a disturbed nest, but the burning silk fell too swiftly, trapping them in its fiery folds. Michael felt no pity for any of them, but was overcome instead by a savage triumph, a primeval reaction from his own terror. He opened his mouth to shout his warcry, and at that moment a shrapnel shell, fired from one of the guns near the north edge of the field, burst beneath the Sopwith.

Again it was tossed upwards, and humming, hissing shards of steel tore up through the belly of the fuselage. As Michael struggled to control this second wild surge and drop, the floor of the cockpit was ripped open so that he could see the ground below him and arctic winds howled up under his greatcoat, making the folds billow.

He held her on an even keel, but she was hard-hit. Something was loose below the fuselage, it banged and whipped in the wind and she was flying one wing heavy, so he had to hold her up by brute force — but at least he was out of range of the guns at last.

Then Andrew appeared on his wingtip, craning across at him anxiously, and Michael grinned and whooped with triumph. Andrew was signalling for his attention, and stabbing his thumb in the signal, 'Return to base!'

Michael glanced around him. While he had been fighting for control, they had been roaring northwards, deeper and still deeper into German territory. They flashed over a crossroads jammed with animal-drawn and motorized transport; startled field-grey figures scattered for cover in the ditches. Michael ignored them and swivelled in the cockpit; three miles away across the flat and featureless green fields the second balloon still sailed serenely above the ridges.

25

Michael gave Andrew the cut-out negative and pointed at the remaining balloon. 'No – continue the attack.'

Andrew's signal was urgent. 'Return to base!' and he pointed at Michael's machine, and gave him the cut-throat signal. 'Danger!'

Michael looked down through the hole between his feet where the belly had been shot out of her. That banging was probably one of his landing wheels dangling on the bracing wires. Bullet holes had peppered the wings and body of the aircraft, and loose ribbons of torn fabric fluttered like Buddhist prayer flags as the slipstream plucked at them, but the Le Rhône engine roared angrily, still under full throttle, without check or stutter in its warlike beat.

Andrew was signalling again, urging him to turn back, but Michael gave him a curt flick of the hand – 'Follow me!' – and threw the Sopwith up on one wingtip, bringing her round in a steep turn that strained her damaged bodywork.

Michael was lost in the raptures of fighting madness, the berserker's wild passion, in which the threat of death or fearful injury was of no consequence. His vision was heightened to unnatural clarity, and he flew the damaged Sopwith as though it were an extension of his own body, as though he were part-swallow skimming the water to drink in flight, so lightly did he brush the hedgerows and touch the stubble in the fields with his single remaining landing wheel, and part-falcon, so cruel was his unblinking gaze as he bated at the ponderously descending balloon.

Of course, they had seen the fiery destruction of the first balloon, and they were winching in. They would be down before Michael reached the site. The gunners would be fully alerted, waiting with finger on the trigger. It would be a ground-level attack, into the prepared positions – but even in his suicidal rage, Michael had lost none of the hunter's cunning. He was using every stick of available cover for his approach run.

A narrow country lane angled across the front; the row of slim, straight poplars that flanked it was the only feature on this dreary plain below the ridge. Michael used the line of trees, banking steeply to run parallel with them, keeping them between him and the balloon site, and he glanced up at the mirror fixed to the wing section above his head. Andrew's green Sopwith was so close behind him that the spinning propeller almost touched his rudder. Michael grinned like a shark and gathered the Sopwith in his hands and lifted it over the palisade of poplar trees the way a hunter takes a fence at full gallop.

The balloon site was three hundred yards ahead. The balloon itself had just reached ground level. The ground crew were helping the observers out of the basket and then running in a group for the cover of the nearest trench. The machine-gunners, their aim frustrated up to that moment by the row of poplar trees, had a fair target at last, and they opened together.

Michael flew into a torrent of fire. It filled the air about him, and the shrapnel shells sucked at the air as they passed, so that his eardrums clicked and ached with the pressure drops. In the emplacements he saw the faces of the gunners turned up towards him; they were pale blobs behind the foreshortened barrels that swung to follow him and the muzzle flashes were bright and pretty as fairy lights. However, the Sopwith was roaring in at well over 100 miles an hour and he had barely 300 yards to cover. Even the solid crunch of bullets into the heavy engine block could not distract Michael as he lined up his sights with delicate touches on the rudder bars.

The group of running men escaping from the balloon was directly ahead of him, racing back towards the trench. In their midst the two observers were slow and clumsy, still

27

stiff with the cold of the upper air, burdened by their heavy clothing. Michael hated them as he might hate a venomous snake; he dropped the Sopwith's nose fractionally and touched the firing lever. The group of men blew away, like grey smoke, and disappeared into the low stubble. Instantly Michael lifted the aim of the Vickers.

The balloon was tethered to earth, looking like a circus tent. He fired into it, bullets streaming on silvery trails of phosphorus smoke into the soft silken mass without effect.

In the berserker's rage, Michael's brain was clear, his thought so swift, that time seemed to run slower and still slower. The micro-seconds as he closed with the stranded silken monster seemed to last an eternity, so that he could follow the flight of each individual bullet from the muzzle of his Vickers.

'Why won't she burn?' he screamed the question again, and the answer came to him.

The hydrogen atom is the lightest of all in weight. The escaping gas was rising to mingle with oxygen above the balloon. It was so obvious then, that he was shooting too low. Why hadn't he realized it before?

He hauled the Sopwith up on her tail, streaming his fire upwards across the swelling side of the balloon, still up until he was shooting into empty air, over the top of the balloon – and the air turned to sudden flame. As the great exhalation of fire rolled towards him, Michael kept the Sopwith climbing into the vertical and jerked the throttle closed. Without power she hung for an instant on her nose and then stalled and dropped. Michael kicked hard at the rudder bar, spinning her into the classic stall turn, and as he opened the throttle again he was headed back, directly away from the immense funeral pyre that he had created. Beneath him he caught a green flash as Andrew banked on to his wingtip in a maximum-rate turn, breaking out left, almost colliding with Michael's undercarriage, and then hurtling away at right angles to his track.

There was no more ground fire; the sudden acrobatics of the two attackers and the roaring pillar of burning gas entirely distracted the gunners, and Michael dropped back behind the cover of the poplar trees. Now that it was all over, his rage abated almost as swiftly as it had arisen, and he swept the skies above him, realizing that the columns of smoke would be a beacon for the Albatros Jagdstaffels. Apart from the smoke, the skies were clear, and he felt a lift of relief and looked for Andrew as he banked low over the hedgerows. There he was, a little higher than Michael, already heading back towards the ridges, but angling in to intercept him.

They came together. Strange what comfort there was in having Andrew on his wingtip, grinning at him and shaking his head in mock disapproval of the disobeyed order to return to base and the berserker fit which had seized Michael.

Side by side they roared low across the German front lines again, contemptuous of the splattering of fire they drew, and then as they began to climb to cross the ridge, Michael's engine spluttered and lost power.

He dropped towards the chalky earth, and then the engine fired again, bellowed and surged, lifting him just clear of the crest, before missing and banging unevenly once more. Andrew was still beside him, mouthing encouragement – and the engine roared again, and then missed and popped.

Michael nursed it, pumping the throttle, fiddling with the ignition setting, and whispering to the wounded Sopwith. 'Come on, my darling. Stick it out, old girl. Nearly home, there's my sweetheart.'

Then he felt something break in her body, one of the main frames shot through, and the controls went soft in his hands, and she sagged, sick unto death. 'Hold on,' Michael exhorted her – but suddenly there was the pungent stink of petrol in his nostrils, and he saw a thin transparent trickle of it ooze from under the engine cowling and turn to white vapour in the slipstream as it blew back past his head.

'Fire.' It was the airman's nightmare, but the vestiges of rage were still with Michael and he murmured stubbornly, 'We're going home, old girl. Just a little longer.'

They had crossed the ridges, there was flat terrain ahead, and he could already make out the dark T-shaped wood which marked the approach to the airstrip. 'Come on, my sweetheart.'

Beneath him there were men, out of the trenches, lining the parapets, waving and cheering as the damaged Sopwith clattered and popped close above their heads, one of its landing wheels shot away, the other dangling and slamming against its belly.

Their faces were upturned, and he saw their open mouths as they called to him. They had heard the storm of fire that heralded the attack, and seen the great balls of burning hydrogen shoot into the sky beyond the ridges, and they knew that for a little while the torment of the guns would ease, and they cheered the returning pilots, shouting themselves hoarse.

Michael left them behind, but their gratitude was uplifting and ahead lay all the familiar landmarks – the spire of the church, the pink roof of the château, the little knoll.

'We are going to make it, my sweetheart,' he called to the Sopwith, but under the engine cowling a dangling wire touched the metal of the engine block and a tiny blue spark arced across the gap. There was the whoosh of explosive combustion, and the white trail of vapour turned to flame. Heat washed over the open cockpit like the pressure flame from a blow lamp, and Michael instinctively flung the Sopwith into another side-flip so that the flames were pushed out obliquely away from his face and he could see ahead.

Now he had to get her down, anywhere, anyhow, but fast, very fast, before he was cooked and charred in the burning carcass of the Sopwith. He dipped towards the field that opened ahead of him, and now his greatcoat was burning, the sleeve of his right arm smouldered and burst into flame.

He brought the Sopwith down, holding the nose up to bleed off speed, but she hit the ground with a force that cracked his teeth together in his jaw, and instantly she pivoted on her one remaining wheel and then cartwheeled, tearing off one wing and crashing into the hedgerow that bordered the field.

Michael's head slammed against the edge of the cockpit, stunning him, but there were flames crackling and leaping up all around him now and he clawed himself out of the cockpit, fell on to the crumpled wing and rolled on to the muddy earth. On his hands and knees he crawled desperately away from the flaming wreckage. The burning wool of the greatcoat flared and the heat spurred him to his feet with a scream. He ripped at the buttons, trying to rid himself of the agony, running and flapping his arms, wildly, fanning the flames and making them fiercer and hotter.

In the crackling roar of the burning wreckage, he did not even hear the galloping horse.

The girl put the big white stallion to the hedge and they flew over it. Horse and rider landed in balance and immediately plunged forward again after the burning, screaming figure in the centre of the field. The girl unhooked her leg from the pommel of the side-saddle, and as they came up behind Michael she pulled the stallion down to a sliding halt and at the same time launched herself from his back.

She landed with her full weight between Michael's shoulder-blades, and both arms locked around his neck, so that he was knocked sprawling flat on his face with the girl on his back. She rolled to her feet and, whipping the thick

31

gaberdine skirt of the riding-habit from around her waist, spread it over the burning figure at her feet. Then she dropped to her knees beside him and wrapped the voluminous skirt tightly around him, beating with her bare hands at the little tendrils of flame that escaped from around it.

As soon as the flames were snuffed out, she pulled off her skirt and heaved Michael into a sitting position on the muddy ground. With quick fingers, she unbuttoned the smoking greatcoat and stripped it off his shoulders and flung it aside. She pulled away the smouldering jerseys – there was only one place where the flames had reached his flesh. They had burned through across his shoulder and down his arm. He cried out with the pain when she tried to pull the nightshirt away. 'For the love of Christ!' The cotton shirt had stuck to the burns.

The girl leaned over him, took the cloth in her teeth and worried it until it tore. Once she had started it, she ripped it open with her hands and her expression changed. 'Mon Dieu!' she said, and jumped up. She stamped on the smoking greatcoat to extinguish the last of the smouldering wool.

Michael stared at her, the agony of his burned arm receding. With her long skirt removed, her riding jacket reached only to the top of her thighs. On her feet she wore black patent-leather riding boots fastened up the sides with hooks and eyes. Her knees were bare, and the skin at the back of them was smooth and flawless as the inner lining of a nautilus shell, but her knee-caps were smudged with mud where she had knelt to help him. Above the knees she wore a pair of cami-knickers of a sheer material through which he could distinctly make out the sheen of her skin. The legs of the knickers were fastened above the knee with pink ribbons, and they clung to her thighs and lower body as though she were naked – no, the semi-veiled lines were even more riveting than naked flesh would have been.

Michael felt his throat swell, so that he could not

breathe, as she stooped to pick up his charred coat, and he was allowed a brief vision of her small, firm buttocks, round as a pair of ostrich eggs, gleaming palely in the early-morning light. He stared so hard, he felt his eyes begin to water and as she turned back to him, he saw in the fork framed by her hard young thighs a dark triangular shadow through the thin silk. She stood with that mesmeric shadow six inches from his nose while she spread the coat gently over his burned shoulder, murmuring to him in the tone a mother uses to a hurt child.

Michael caught only the words 'froid' and 'brûlé'. She was so close that he could smell her; the natural musk of a healthy young woman sweating with the exertion of hard riding was mingling with a perfume that smelled like dried rose petals. Michael tried to speak, to thank her, but he was shaking with shock and pain. His lips wobbled and he made a little slurring sound.

'Mon pauvre,' she cooed to him, and stepped back. Her voice was husky with concern and exertion, and she had the face of a pixie with huge dark Celtic eyes. He wondered if her ears were pointed, but they were hidden by the dark bush of her hair. It was windblown and kinked into dense springy curls. Her skin was tinted by her Celtic blood to the colour of old ivory and her eyebrows were thick and dark as her hair.

She began to speak again, but he could not help himself, and he glanced down again to that intriguing little shadow under the silk. She saw the movement of his eyes and her cheeks glowed with a dusky rose colour as she snatched up her muddy skirts and whipped them around her waist – and Michael ached more with embarrassment at his gaffe than he did from his burns.

The overhead roar of Andrew's Sopwith gave them both respite and they looked up gratefully as Andrew circled the field. Painfully and unsteadily Michael clambered to his feet, as the girl settled her skirts, and he waved up at

Andrew. He saw Andrew lift his hand and give him a relieved salute, then the green Sopwith circled out and came in on a straight run not higher than fifty feet above their heads – and the green scarf, with something knotted in one end, fluttered down and plunked into the mud a few yards away.

The girl ran to it and brought it back to Michael. He unknotted the tail of the scarf and grinned lopsidedly as he brought out the silver flask. He unscrewed the stopper and lifted the flask to the sky. He saw the flash of Andrew's white teeth in the open cockpit and the raised gauntleted hand – and then Andrew turned away towards the airfield.

Michael lifted the flask to his lips, and swallowed twice. His eyes clouded with tears and he gasped as the heavenly liquid flowed scalding down his throat. When he lowered the flask, she was watching him, and he offered it to her.

She shook her head, and asked seriously, '*Anglais?*'

'*Oui – non – Sud Africain.*' His voice shook.

'*Ah, vous parlez français!*' She smiled for the first time, and it was a phenomenon almost as stunning as her pearly little bottom.

'*A peine* – hardly.' He denied it swiftly, staving off the flood of voluble French that he knew from experience an affirmative would have brought down on his head.

'You have blood.' Her English was appalling; only when she pointed to his head did he understand what she had said. He lifted his free hand and touched the trickle of blood which had escaped from under his helmet. He inspected his smeared fingertips.

'Yes,' he admitted. 'Buckets of it, I'm afraid.'

The helmet had saved him from serious injury when his head had struck the side of the cockpit.

'*Pardon?*' She looked confused.

'*J'en ai beaucoup,*' he translated.

'Ah, you *do* talk French.' She clapped her hands in an

endearing, childlike gesture of delight and took his arm in a proprietorial gesture.

'Come,' she ordered, and snapped her fingers for the stallion. He was cropping the grass, and pretended not to hear her.

'*Viens ici tout de suite, Nuage!*' She stamped her foot. 'Come here, this instant, Cloud!'

The stallion took another mouthful of grass to demonstrate his independence and then sidled across in leisurely fashion.

'Please,' she asked, and Michael made a stirrup of his cupped hands and boosted her up into the saddle. She was very light and agile.

'Come up.' She helped him, and he settled behind her on the stallion's broad rump. She took one of Michael's hands and placed it on her waist. Her flesh under his fingers was firm and he could feel the heat of it through the cloth.

'*Tenez*, hold on!' she instructed, and the stallion cantered towards the gate at the end of the field nearest the château.

Michael looked back at the smoking wreckage of his Sopwith. Only the engine block remained, the wood and canvas had burned away. He felt a shadow of deep regret at her destruction – they had come a long way together.

'How do you call yourself?' the girl asked over her shoulder, and he turned back to her.

'Michael – Michael Courtney.'

'Michel Courtney,' she repeated experimentally, and then, 'I am Mademoiselle Centaine de Thiry.'

'*Enchanté*, mademoiselle.' Michael paused to compose his next conversational gem in his laboured schoolboy French. 'Centaine is a strange name,' he said, and she stiffened under his hand. He had used the word '*drôle*', or comical. Quickly he corrected himself, 'An exceptional name.'

35

Suddenly he regretted that he had not applied himself more vigorously to his French studies; shaken and shocked as he still was, he had to concentrate hard to follow her rapid explanation.

'I was born one minute after midnight on the first day of the year 1900.' So she was seventeen years and three months old, teetering on the very brink of womanhood. Then he remembered that his own mother had been barely seventeen when he was born. The thought cheered him so much that he took another quick nip from Andrew's flask.

'You are my saviour!' He meant it light-heartedly, but it sounded so crass that he expected her to burst into mocking laughter. Instead, she nodded seriously. The sentiment was in accord with Centaine's own swiftly developing emotions.

Her favourite animal, apart from Nuage the stallion, had once been a skinny mongrel puppy which she had found in the ditch, blood-smeared and shivering. She had nursed it and cherished it, and loved it until a month previously when it had died under the wheels of one of the army trucks trundling up to the front. Its death had left an aching gap in her existence. Michael was thin, almost starved-looking under all those charred and muddy clothes; apart, then, from his physical injuries, she sensed the abuse to which he had been subjected. His eyes were a marvellous clear blue, but she read in them a terrible suffering, and he shivered and trembled just as her little mongrel had.

'Yes,' she said firmly. 'I will look after you.'

The château was larger than it had seemed from the air, and much less beautiful. Most of the windows had been broken and boarded up. The walls were pocked with shell splinters, but the shell craters on the lawns had grassed over – the fighting last autumn had come within extreme artillery range of the estate, before the final push by the Allies had driven the Germans back behind the ridges again.

The great house had a sad and neglected air, and Centaine apologized. 'Our workmen have been taken by the army, and most of the women and all the children have fled to Paris or Amiens. We are three only.' She raised herself in the saddle and called out sharply in a different language, 'Anna! Come and see what I have found.'

The woman who emerged from the vegetable gardens behind the kitchens was squat and broad with a backside like a percheron mare and huge shapeless breasts beneath the mud-stained blouse. Her thick dark hair, streaked with grey, was pulled back into a bun on top of her head, and her face was red and round as a radish; her arms, bare to the elbows, were thick and muscular as a man's and caked with mud. She held a bunch of turnips in one large, calloused hand.

'What is it, *Kleinjie* – little one?'

'I have saved a gallant English airman, but he is terribly wounded—'

'He looks very well to me.'

'Anna, don't be such an old grouse! Come and help me. We must get him into the kitchen.'

The two of them were gabbling at each other, and to Michael's astonishment, he could understand every word of it.

'I will not allow a soldier in the house, you know that, *Kleinjie!* I won't have a tomcat in the same basket with my little kitten—'

'He's not a soldier, Anna, he's an airman.'

'And probably as randy as any tomcat—'

She used the word 'fris', and Centaine flashed at her, 'You are a disgusting old woman – now come and help me.'

Anna looked Michael over very carefully, and then conceded reluctantly, 'He has nice eyes, but I still don't trust him – oh, all right, but if he so much as—'

'Mevrou,' Michael spoke for the first time, 'your virtue is safe with me, I give you my solemn word. Ravishing as you are, I will control myself.'

Centaine swivelled in the saddle to stare at him, and Anna reeled back with shock and then guffawed with delight.

'He speaks Flemish!'

'You speak Flemish!' Centaine echoed the accusation.

'It's not Flemish,' Michael denied. 'It's Afrikaans, South African Dutch.'

'It's Flemish,' Anna told him as she came forward. 'And anybody who speaks Flemish is welcome in this house.' She reached up to Michael.

'Be careful,' Centaine told her anxiously. 'His shoulder—' She slipped to the ground and between the two of them they helped Michael down and led him to the door of the kitchen.

A dozen chefs could have prepared a banquet for five hundred guests in this kitchen, but there was only a tiny wood fire burning in one of the ranges and they seated Michael on a stool in front of it.

'Get some of your famous ointment,' Centaine ordered, and Anna hurried away.

'You are Flemish?' Michael asked. He was delighted that the language barrier had evaporated.

'No, no.' Centaine was busy with an enormous pair of shears, snipping away the charred remnants of the shirt from his burns. 'Anna is from the north – she was my nurse when my mother died, and now she thinks she is my mother and not just a servant. She taught me the language in the cradle. But you, where did you learn it?'

'Where I come from, everybody speaks it.'

'I'm glad,' she said, and he was not sure what she meant, for her eyes were lowered to her task.

'I look for you every morning,' he said softly. 'We all do, when we fly.'

She said nothing, but he saw her cheeks turn that lovely dusky pink colour again.

'We call you our good luck angel, *l'ange du bonheur*,' and she laughed.

'I call you *le petit jaune*, the little yellow one,' she answered. The yellow Sopwith – Michael felt a surge of elation. She knew him as an individual, and she went on, 'All of you, I wait for you to come back, counting my chickens, but so often they do not come back, the new ones especially. Then I cry for them and pray. But you and the green one always come home, then I rejoice for you.'

'You are kind,' he started, but Anna bustled back from the pantry carrying a stone jar that smelled of turpentine and the mood was spoiled.

'Where is Papa?' Centaine demanded.

'In the basement, seeing to the animals.'

'We have to keep the livestock in the cellars,' Centaine explained as she went to the head of the stone stairs, 'otherwise the soldiers steal the chickens and geese and even the milch cows. I had to fight to keep Nuage, even.'

She yelled down the stairs, 'Papa! Where are you?'

There was a muffled response from below and Centaine called again, 'We need a bottle of cognac.' And then her tone became admonitive. 'Unopened, Papa. It is not a social need, but a medicinal one. Not for you but for a patient – here.'

Centaine tossed a bunch of keys down the stairs and minutes later there was a heavy tread and a large shaggy man with a full belly shambled into the kitchen with a cognac bottle held like an infant to his chest.

He had the same dense bush of kinky hair as Centaine, but it was woven with grey strands and hung forward on to his forehead. His moustaches were wide and beeswaxed into impressive spikes, and he peered at Michael through a single dark glittering eye. The other eye was covered by a piratical black cloth patch.

'Who is this?' he demanded.

'An English airman.'

The scowl abated. 'A fellow warrior,' he said. 'A comrade-in-arms – another destroyer of the cursed boche!'

'You have not destroyed a boche for over forty years,' Anna reminded him without looking up from Michael's burns, but he ignored her and advanced on Michael, opening his arms like a bear to envelop him.

'Papa, be careful. He is wounded.'

'Wounded!' cried Papa. 'Cognac!' as though the two words were linked, and he found two heavy glass tumblers and placed them on the kitchen table, breathed on them with a decidedly garlicky breath, wiped them on his coat-tails, and cracked the red wax from the neck of the bottle.

'Papa, you are not wounded,' Centaine told him severely as he filled both tumblers up to the brim.

'I would not insult a man of such obvious valour by asking him to drink alone.' He brought one tumbler to Michael.

'Comte Louis de Thiry, at your service, monsieur.'

'Captain Michael Courtney. Royal Flying Corps.'

'A *vôtre santé*, Capitaine!'

'A *la vôtre*, Monsieur le Comte!'

The comte drank with undisguised relish, then sighed and wiped his magnificent dark moustaches on the back of his hand and spoke to Anna.

'Proceed with the treatment, woman.'

'This will sting,' Anna warned, and for a moment Michael thought she meant the cognac, but she took a handful of the ointment from the stone jar and slapped it on to the open burns.

Michael let out an anguished whinny and tried to rise, but Anna held him down with one huge, red, work-chafed hand.

'Bind it up,' she ordered Centaine, and as the girl wound

40

on the bandages, the agony faded and became a comforting warmth.

'It feels better,' Michael admitted.

'Of course it does,' Anna told him comfortably. 'My ointment is famous for everything from smallpox to piles.'

'So is my cognac,' murmured the comte, and recharged both tumblers.

Centaine went to the wash basket on the kitchen table and returned with one of the comte's freshly ironed shirts, and despite her father's protests, she helped Michael into it. Then as she was fashioning a sling for his injured arm, there was a buzzing clatter of an engine outside the kitchen windows and Michael caught a glimpse of a familiar figure on an equally familiar motor-cycle skidding to a halt in a spray of gravel.

The engine spluttered and hiccoughed into silence and a voice called agitatedly, 'Michael, my boy, where are you?'

The door burst open and admitted Lord Andrew Killigerran in tam-o'-shanter, followed closely by a young officer in the uniform of the Royal Medical Corps. 'Thank God, there you are. Panic not, I've brought you a sawbones—' Andrew pulled the doctor to Michael's stool and then, with relief and a shade of pique in his voice, 'You seem to be doing damn well without us, I'll say that for you. I raided the local field hospital. Kidnapped this medico at the point of a pistol – been eating my heart out about you, and here you are with a glass in your hand, and—'

Andrew broke off and looked at Centaine for the first time, and forgot all about Michael's condition. He swept the tam-o'-shanter from his head. 'It's true!' he declaimed in perfect sonorous French, rolling his Rs in true Gallic fashion. 'Angels do indeed walk the earth.'

'Go to your room immediately, child,' Anna snapped, and her face screwed up like one of those fearsome carved dragons that guard the entrance to Chinese temples.

'I am not a child,' Centaine gave her an equally ferocious glare, then recomposed her features as she turned to Michael. 'Why does he call you his boy? You are much older than he is!'

'He's Scots,' Michael explained, already ridden by jealousy, 'and the Scots are all mad – also, he has a wife and four children.'

'That's a filthy lie,' Andrew protested. 'The children, yes, I admit to them, poor wee bairns! But no wife, definitely no wife.'

'*Ecossais*,' murmured the comte, 'great warriors and great drinkers.' Then, in reasonable English, 'May I offer you a little cognac, monsieur?' They were descending into a babble of languages, crossing from one to the other in midsentence.

'Will somebody kindly introduce me to this paragon among men, that I may accept his fulsome offer?'

'Le Comte de Thiry, I have the honour to present Lord Andrew Killigerran.' Michael waved them together and they shook hands.

'*Tiens!* A genuine English milord.'

'Scots, my dear fellow – big difference.' He saluted the comte with the tumbler. 'Enchanted, I'm sure. And this beautiful young lady is your daughter – the resemblance – beautiful—'

'Centaine,' Anna interposed, 'take your horse to the stable and groom him.'

Centaine ignored her and smiled at Andrew. The smile stopped even his banter; he stared at her, for the smile transformed her. It seemed to glow through her skin like a lamp through alabaster, and it lit her teeth and sparkled in her eyes like sunlight in a crystal jar of dark honey.

'I think I should have a look at our patient.' The young army doctor broke the spell and stepped forward to unwrap Michael's bandages. Anna understood the gesture, if not the words, and she interposed her bulk between them.

42

'Tell him, if he touches my work, I will break his arm.'

'Your services are not required, I'm afraid,' Michael translated for the doctor.

'Have a cognac,' Andrew consoled him. 'It's not bad stuff – not bad at all.'

'You are a landowner, milord?' the comte asked Andrew with subtlety. 'Of course?'

'*Bien sûr*—' Andrew made an expansive gesture which portrayed thousands of acres and at the same time brought his glass within range of where the comte was filling the doctor's glass. The comte topped him up and Andrew repeated, 'Of course, the family estates – you understand?'

'Ah.' The comte's single eye glittered as he glanced across at his daughter. 'Your deceased wife has left you with four children?' He had not followed the earlier exchange all that clearly.

'No children, no wife – my humorous friend,' Andrew indicated Michael, 'he likes to make jokes. Very bad English jokes.'

'Ha! English jokes.' The comte roared with laughter and would have clapped Michael on his shoulder had not Centaine rushed forward to protect him from the blow.

'Papa, be careful. He is wounded.'

'You will stay for lunch – all of you,' the comte declared. 'You will see, milord, my daughter is one of the finest cooks in the province.'

'With a little help,' Anna muttered disgustedly.

'I say, I rather think I should be getting back,' the young doctor murmured diffidently. 'I feel rather superfluous.'

'We are invited to lunch,' Andrew told him. 'Have a cognac.'

'Don't mind if I do.' The doctor succumbed without a struggle.

The comte announced, 'It is necessary to descend to the cellars.'

'Papa—' Centaine began ominously.

'We have guests!' The comte showed her the empty cognac bottle and she shrugged helplessly.

'Milord, you will assist me in the selection of suitable refreshments?'

'Honoured, Monsieur le Comte.'

As Centaine watched the pair, arms linked, descend the stone staircase, there was a thoughtful look in her eyes.

'He is a *drôle* one, your friend – and very loyal. See how he rushed here to your aid. See how he places a charm on my Papa.'

Michael was surprised by the strength of his dislike for Andrew at that moment. 'He smelled the cognac,' he muttered. 'That's the only reason he came.'

'But what of the four children?' Anna demanded. 'And their mother?' She was having as much difficulty as the comte in following the conversation.

'Four mothers,' Michael explained. 'Four children, four different mothers.'

'He is a polygamist!' Anna swelled with shock and affront, and her face went a shade redder.

'No, no,' Michael assured her. 'You heard him deny it. He is a man of honour, he would not do such a thing. He is married to none of them.' Michael felt not a qualm, he had to have an ally somewhere in the family, but at that moment the happy pair returned from the cellars laden with black bottles.

'Aladdin's cave,' Andrew rejoiced. 'The comte has got it filled with good stuff!' He placed half a dozen bottles on the kitchen table in front of Michael. 'Look at this! Thirty years old, if it's a day!' Then he peered closely at Michael. 'You look awful, old boy. Death warmed up.'

'Thanks,' Michael grinned at him thinly. 'You are so kind.'

'Natural brotherly concern—' Andrew struggled to draw the cork from one of the bottles, and dropped his voice to a conspiratorial whisper. 'By God, isn't she a corker!' He

44

glanced across the kitchen to where the women were at work over the big copper pot. 'I'd rather feel her than feel sick, what?' Michael's dislike for Andrew turned to active hatred.

'I find that remark utterly revolting,' he said. 'To talk like that about a young girl, so innocent, so fine, so – so—' Michael stuttered into silence, and Andrew held his head on one side and peered at him wonderingly.

'Michael, my boy, this is worse than just a few burns and bruises, I'm afraid. It's going to need intensive treatment.' He filled a glass. 'To start with, I prescribe a liberal dose of this excellent claret!'

At the head of the table the comte had the cork out of another of the bottles, and refilled the doctor's glass.

'A toast!' he cried. 'Confusion to the damned boche!'

'A *bas les boches!*' they all cried, and as soon as the toast was drunk the comte placed his hand over the black patch which covered the socket of his missing eye.

'They did this to me at Sedan in '70. They took my eye, but they paid dearly for it, the devils – *Sacré bleu*, how we fought! Tigers! We were tigers—'

'Tabby cats!' Anna called across the kitchen.

'You know nothing of battle and war – these brave young men, they know, they understand! I drink to them!' He did so copiously and then demanded, 'Now, where is the food?'

It was a savoury ragoût of ham and sausage and marrow bones. Anna brought bowls of it steaming from the stove and Centaine piled small loaves of crisp new bread on the bare table.

'Now tell us, how goes the battle?' the comte demanded as he broke bread and dipped it into his bowl. 'When will this war end?'

'Let us not spoil good food.' Andrew waved the question away, but with crumbs and gravy on his moustache the comte insisted.

45

'What of a new Allied offensive?'

'It will be in the west, on the Somme river again. It is there that we have to break through the German lines.' It was Michael who answered; he spoke with quiet authority, so that almost immediately he had all their attention. Even the two women came from the stove and Centaine slipped on to the bench beside Michael, turning serious eyes up to him as she struggled to understand the English conversation.

'How do you know all this?' the comte interrupted.

'His uncle is a general,' Andrew explained.

'A general!' The comte looked at Michael with new interest. 'Centaine, do you not see that our guest is in difficulty?' And while Anna gruffed and scowled, Centaine leaned over Michael's bowl and cut the meat into manageable portions so that he could eat with one hand.

'Go on! Continue!' the comte urged Michael. 'What then?'

'General Haig will pivot right. This time he will succeed in cutting across the German rear, and roll up their line.'

'Ha! So we are secure here.' The comte reached for the claret bottle, but Michael shook his head.

'I am afraid not, not entirely anyway. This section of the line is being stripped of reserves, regimental fronts of the line are being reduced to battalion strength – everything that can be spared is being moved to take part in a new push across the Somme.'

The comte looked alarmed. 'That is criminal folly – surely the Germans will counter-attack here to try and reduce pressure on their front at the Somme?'

'The line here, it will not hold?' Centaine asked anxiously and involuntarily glanced up at the kitchen windows. From where they sat, they could see the ridges on the horizon.

Michael hesitated. 'Oh, I am sure that we will be able

to hold them long enough – especially if the fighting round the Somme goes as well and as quickly as we expect. Then the pressure here will swiftly be relieved as the Allied advance swings across the German rear.'

'But if the battle bogs down and is stalemated once again?' Centaine asked softly in Flemish.

For a girl, and one with little English, she had a firm grasp on the essentials. Michael treated her question with respect, answering, in Afrikaans, as though he was speaking to another man.

'Then we will be hard-pressed, especially as the Huns have aerial superiority. We may lose the ridges again.' He paused and frowned. 'They will have to rush in reserves. We may even be forced to pull back as far as Arras—'

'Arras!' Centaine gasped. 'That means—' She did not finish, but looked around at her home as though already taking farewell of it. Arras was far to the rear.

Michael nodded. 'Once the attack begins, you will be in extreme danger here. You will be well advised to evacuate the château and go back south to Arras or even Paris.'

'Never!' cried the comte switching back into French. 'A de Thiry never retreats.'

'Except at Sedan,' Anna muttered, but the comte did not deign to hear such levity.

'I will stand here, on my own land.' He pointed at the ancient *chassepot* rifle that hung on the kitchen wall. 'That is the weapon I carried at Sedan. The boche learned to fear it there. They will relearn that lesson. Louis de Thiry will teach it to them!'

'Courage!' cried Andrew. 'I give you a toast. French valour and the triumph of French arms!'

Naturally the comte had to reply with a toast to 'General Haig and our gallant British Allies!'

'Captain Courtney is a South African,' Andrew pointed out. 'We should drink to them.'

47

'Ah!' the comte responded enthusiastically in English. 'To General – what is your uncle, the general, called? To General Sean Courtney and his brave South Africans.'

'This gentleman,' Andrew indicated the slightly owl-eyed doctor swaying gently on the bench beside him, 'is an officer in the Royal Medical Corps. A fine service, and worthy of our toast!'

'To the Royal Medical Corps!' The comte accepted the challenge, but as he reached for his glass again, it trembled before he touched it, and the surface of the red wine was agitated into little circular ripples which lapped against the crystal bowl. The comte froze and all their heads lifted.

The glass of the kitchen window-panes rattled in their frames and then the rumble of the guns rolled down from the north. Once again the German guns were hunting along the ridges, clamouring and barking like wild dogs, and as they listened in silence, they could imagine the misery and agony of the men in the muddy trenches only a few miles from where they sat in the warm kitchen with their bellies filled with food and fine wine.

Andrew lifted his glass and said softly, 'I give you those poor blighters out there in the mud. May they endure.' And this time even Centaine sipped from Michael's glass and her eyes swam with dark tears as she drank the toast.

'I hate to be a killjoy,' the young doctor stood up unsteadily, 'but that artillery barrage is the work-whistle for me, I'm afraid, the butchers' vans will be on their way back already.'

Michael tried to rise with him, but clutched quickly at the edge of the table for support. 'I wish to thank you, Monsieur le Comte,' he began formally, 'for your gentility—' The word tripped on his tongue and he repeated it, but his tongue blurred and lost track of his speech. 'I salute your daughter, Mademoiselle de Thiry, *l'ange du bonheur*—' His legs folded up under him, and he collapsed gently.

'He is wounded!' Centaine cried as she leaped forward

48

and caught him before he hit the floor, supporting him with one slim shoulder under his armpit. 'Help me,' she pleaded. Andrew reeled forward to her assistance, and between them they half-carried, half-dragged Michael through the kitchen door.

'Careful, his poor arm,' Centaine gasped under the weight, as they lifted Michael into the side-car of the motor-cycle. 'Do not hurt him!' He lolled in the padded seat with a beatific grin on his pale features.

'Mademoiselle, rest assured he is beyond all pain, the lucky devil.' Andrew tottered around the machine to take the controls.

'Wait for me!' cried the doctor as he and the comte, giving each other mutual support, bounced off the door jamb and came crabbing down the steps in an unintended sideways charge.

'Climb aboard,' Andrew invited, and at the third attempt kick-started the Ariel in a roar of blue smoke. The doctor clambered on to the pillion behind him, and the comte thrust one of the two bottles of claret that he carried into Andrew's side pocket.

'Against the cold,' he explained.

'You are a prince among men.' Andrew let out the clutch and the Ariel screeched into a tight turn.

'Look after Michael!' cried Centaine.

'My cabbages!' screamed Anna, as Andrew took a short cut through the vegetable garden.

'*A bas les boches!*' howled the comte and took a last surreptitious pull at the other claret bottle, before Centaine could confiscate it from him and relieve him of the cellar keys once more.

At the end of the long drive that led down from the château Andrew braked the motor-cycle and then at a more sedate pace joined the pathetic little procession that was trickling back from the ridges along the muddy, rutted main road.

The butchers' vans, as the field ambulances were irreverently known, were heavily loaded with the fruits of the renewed German bombardment. They chugged through the muddy puddles, with the racks of canvas stretchers in the open backs swaying and lurching to each bump. The blood from the wounded men in the upper tiers soaked through the canvas and dripped on to those below.

On the verges of the lane little groups of walking wounded straggled back, their rifles discarded, leaning on each other for support, lumpy field dressings strapped over their injuries, all their faces blank with suffering, their eyes dead of expression, their uniforms caked with mud and their movements mechanical, beyond caring.

Beginning to sober rapidly, the doctor climbed down off the pillion and selected the more seriously hurt men from the stream. They loaded two of them on to the pillion, one astride the petrol tank in front of Andrew and three more into the side-car with Michael. The doctor ran behind the overloaded Ariel, pushing it through the mud holes, and he was completely sober when a mile up the road they reached the VAD hospital in a row of cottages at the entrance to the village of Mort Homme. He helped his newly acquired patients out of the side-car and then turned back to Andrew.

'Thanks. I needed that break.' He glanced down at Michael, still passed out in the side-car. 'Look at him. We can't go on like this for ever.'

'Michael is just slightly pissed, that is all.'

But the doctor shook his head. 'Battle fatigue,' he said. 'Shell shock. We don't understand it properly yet, but it seems there is just a limit to how much these poor bastards

50

can stand. How long has he been flying without a break – three months?'

'He will be all right,' Andrew's voice was fierce, 'he's going to get through.' He placed a protective hand on Michael's injured shoulder, remembering that it was six months since his last leave.

'Look at him, all the signs. Thin as a starvation victim,' the doctor went on, 'twitching and trembling. Those eyes – I'll bet he is showing unbalanced illogical behaviour, sullen dark moods alternating with mad wild moods? Am I correct?'

Andrew nodded reluctantly. 'One minute he calls the enemy loathsome vermin and machine-guns the survivors of crashed German aircraft, and the next they are gallant and worthy foes – he punched a newly arrived pilot last week for calling them Huns.'

'Reckless bravery?'

Andrew remembered the balloons that morning, but he did not answer the question.

'What can we do?' he asked helplessly.

The doctor sighed and shrugged, and offered his hand. 'Goodbye and good luck, major.' And as he turned away, he was already stripping off his jacket and rolling up his sleeves.

At the entrance to the orchard, just before they reached the squadron's bivouac, Michael suddenly heaved himself upright in the side-car and with all the solemnity of a judge pronouncing the death sentence, said, 'I am about to be sick.'

Andrew braked the motor-cycle off the road and held his head for him.

'All that excellent claret,' he lamented. 'To say nothing of the Napoleon cognac – if there was only some way to save it!'

Having noisily unburdened himself, Michael slumped down again and said, just as solemnly, 'I want you to know

51

that I am in love,' and his head flopped back as he passed out cold once more.

Andrew sat on the Ariel and drew the cork from the claret bottle with his teeth. 'That definitely calls for a toast. Let's drink to your true love.' He offered the bottle to the unconscious form beside him. 'Not interested?'

He drank from it himself, and when he lowered the bottle, he began unaccountably and uncontrollably to sob. He tried to choke back the tears, he had not wept since he was six years old, and then he remembered the young doctor's words, 'unbalanced and illogical behaviour', and the tears overwhelmed him. They poured down his cheeks, and he did not even attempt to wipe them away. He sat on the driver's seat of the motor-cycle, shaking with silent grief.

'Michael, my boy,' he whispered. 'What is to become of us? We are doomed, there is no hope for us. Michael, no hope at all for any of us,' and he covered his face with both hands and wept as though his heart was breaking.

Michael awoke to the clatter of the tin tray as Biggs placed it beside his field cot.

He groaned as he tried to sit up, but his injuries pulled him down again. 'What time is it, Biggs?'

''Alf past seven, sir, and a lovely spring morning.'

'Biggs – for God's sake – why didn't you wake me? I've missed the dawn patrol—'

'No, we 'aven't, sir,' Biggs murmured comfortably, 'we've been grounded.'

'Grounded?'

'Lord Killigerran's orders, grounded until further orders, sir.' Biggs ladled sugar into the cocoa mug and stirred it. ''Igh time too, if I may be allowed to say so. We've flown thirty-seven days straight.'

'Biggs, why do I feel so bloody?'

'According to Lord Killigerran – we were severely attacked by a bottle of cognac, sir.'

'Before that, I smashed up the old flying tortoise—' Michael began to remember.

'Spread her all over France, sir, like butter on toast,' Biggs nodded.

'But we got them, Biggs!'

'Both of the blighters, sir.'

'The book paid out, I trust, Biggs? You didn't lose your money?'

'We made a nice packet, thanking you, Mr Michael,' and Biggs touched the other items on the cocoa tray. ''Ere's your loot—' There was a neat sheaf of twenty one-pound notes. 'Three to one, sir, plus your original stake.'

'You are entitled to ten per cent commission, Biggs.'

'Bless you, sir.' Two notes disappeared magically into Biggs' pocket.

'Now, Biggs. What else have we here?'

'Four aspirins, compliments of Lord Killigerran.'

'He is flying, Biggs, of course?' Gratefully Michael swallowed the pills.

'Of course, sir. They took off at dawn.'

'Who is his wingman?'

'Mr Banner, sir.'

'A new chum,' Michael brooded unhappily.

'Lord Andrew will be all right, don't you worry, sir.'

'Yes, of course, he will – and what is this?' Michael roused himself.

'Keys to Lord Killigerran's motor-cycle, sir. He says as you are to give the count his salaams – whatever those may be, sir – and his tender admiration to the young lady—'

'Biggs—' the aspirins had worked a miracle – Michael felt suddenly light and carefree and gay. His wounds no longer pulled and his head no longer ached. 'Biggs,' he repeated, 'do you think you could lay out my number ones and give the brass buckles a lick and the boots a bit of a shine?'

Biggs grinned at him fondly. 'Going calling, are we, sir?'

'That we are, Biggs, that we are.'

Centaine woke in darkness and listened to the guns. They terrified her. She knew she would never become accustomed to that bestial, insensate storm that so impersonally dealt death and unspeakable injury, and she remembered the months of late summer the previous year when, for a brief period, the German batteries had been within range of the château. That was when they had abandoned the upper levels of the great house and moved below stairs. By then the servants had long since fled – all except Anna, of course – and the tiny cell that Centaine now occupied had belonged to one of the maids.

Their whole way of life had changed dramatically since the stormwaves of war had swept over them. Though they had never kept the same grand style as some of the other leading families of the province, there had always been dinners and house-parties and twenty servants to sustain them, but now their existence was almost as simple as had been that of their servants before the war.

Centaine threw off her forebodings with her bedclothes, and ran down the narrow stoneflagged corridor on bare feet. In the kitchen Anna was at the stove, already feeding it with split oak.

'I was on my way to you with a jug of cold water,' she said gruffly, and Centaine hugged her and kissed her until she smiled, and then went to warm herself in front of the stove.

Anna poured boiling water into the copper basin on the floor and then added cold. 'Come along, mademoiselle,' she ordered.

'Oh, Anna, do I have to?'

'Move!'

Reluctantly Centaine lifted the nightdress over her head, and shivered as the cold raised a fine rash of goosepimples on her forearms and over her small rounded buttocks.

'Hurry.' She stepped into the basin and Anna knelt beside her and dunked a flannel. Her movements were methodical and businesslike as she soaped down Centaine's body, starting at the shoulders and working to the fingertips of each arm, but she could not conceal the love and pride that softened her ugly red face.

The child was delightfully formed, though perhaps her breasts and bottom were a little too small – Anna hoped to plump them out with a good starchy diet, once that was freely obtainable again. Her skin was a smooth, buttery colour, where the sun had not touched it, though where it had been exposed, it tended to take on a dark bronze sheen that Anna found most unsightly.

'You must wear your gloves and long sleeves this summer,' she scolded. 'Brown is so ugly.'

'Do hurry up, Anna.' Centaine hugged her soapy breasts and shivered, and Anna lifted her arms one at a time and scrubbed the dense bushes of dark curly hair under them. The suds ran in long lacy lines down her lean flanks where the rack of her ribs showed through.

'Don't be so rough,' Centaine wailed. And Anna examined her limbs critically: they were straight and long, though much too strong for a lady – all that riding and running and walking. Anna shook her head.

'Oh, what now?' Centaine demanded.

'You are as hard as a boy, your belly is too muscular for having babies.' Anna ran the flannel down her body.

'Ouch!'

'Stay still – you don't want to smell like a goat, do you?'

55

'Anna, don't you just love blue eyes?' Anna grunted, knowing instinctively where the discussion was headed.

'What colour eyes would a baby have, if its mother's eyes were brown and its father's a lovely shimmering blue?'

Anna slapped her bottom with the flannel. 'That is enough of that. Your father will not like that kind of talk.'

Centaine did not take the threat seriously, she went on dreamily. 'Airmen are so brave, don't you think, Anna? They must be the bravest men in the world.' She became brisk. 'Hurry, Anna, I'll be late to count my chickens.'

She sprang from the basin, scattering water drops on the flagged floor, while Anna wrapped her in a towel that she had heated in front of the stove.

'Anna, it's almost light outside.'

'You come back here immediately after,' Anna ordered. 'We have a lot of work to do today. Your father has reduced us to starvation level with his misplaced generosity.'

'We had to offer a meal to those gallant young airmen.'

Centaine pulled on her clothes and sat on the stool to hook up her riding boots.

'Don't go mooning off into the woods—'

'Oh, hush, Anna.' Centaine jumped up and went clattering down the stairs.

'You come straight back!' Anna yelled after her.

Nuage heard her coming and whickered softly. Centaine flung both arms around his neck and kissed his velvety grey muzzle.

'*Bonjour* my darling.' She had stolen two cubes of sugar from under Anna's nose and now Nuage salivated over her hand as she fed them to him. She wiped her palm on his neck and then when she turned to lift down the saddle from its rack, he bumped her in the small of the back, demanding more.

Outside it was dark and cold, and she urged the stallion into a canter, revelling in the icy flow of air across her face, her nose and ears turning bright pink and her eyes beginning to stream tears. At the crest of the hillock, she reined Nuage to a standstill and looked into the soft gunmetal sheen of dawn, watching the sky above the long horizon turn to the colour of ripe oranges. Behind her the false dawn caused by the harsh, intermittent glow of the artillery barrage flickered against the heavens, but steadfastly she turned her back to it and waited for the planes to come.

She heard the distant beat of their engines, even over the sound of the guns, and then they came snarling into the yellow dawn, as fierce and swift and beautiful as falcons, so that, as always, she felt her pulse race, and she rose high in the saddle to greet them.

The lead machine was the green one with its tiger stripes of victory, the mad Scotsman. She lifted both hands high above her head.

'Go with God – and come back safely!' she shouted her blessing, and saw the flash of white teeth under the ridiculous tartan tam-o'-shanter, and the green machine waggled its wings and then it was past, climbing away into the sinister sombre clouds that hung above the German lines.

She watched them go, the other aircraft closing up around the green leader into their fighting formation, and she was overwhelmed with a vast sadness, a terrible sense of inadequacy.

'Why couldn't I be a man!' she cried aloud. 'Oh, why couldn't I be going with you!' But already they were out of sight, and she turned Nuage down the hill.

'They will all die,' she thought. 'All the young and strong and beautiful young men – and we will be left only with the old and maimed and ugly.' And the sound of the distant guns counterpointed her fears. 'I wish, oh, how I wish—' she said aloud, and the stallion flicked his ears back to listen to her, but she did not go on, for she did not know what it was she wished for. She knew only that there was a void within her that ached to be filled, a vast wanting for she did not know what, and a terrible sorrow for all the world. She turned Nuage loose to graze in the small field behind the château and carried his saddle back on her shoulder.

Her father was sitting at the kitchen table and she kissed him casually. His eyepatch gave him a rakish air despite that fact that his other eye was bloodshot; his face was as baggy and wrinkled as a bloodhound's and he smelled of garlic and stale red wine.

As usual, he and Anna were bickering in a companionable fashion, and as Centaine sat opposite him cupping the big round coffee bowl in her hands, she wondered suddenly if Anna and her father mated together, and immediately after she wondered why the notion had never occurred to her before.

As a country girl, the processes of procreation were no mystery to her. Despite Anna's original protests, she was always there to assist when mares from the surrounding district were brought to visit Nuage. She was the only one who could manage the big white stallion once he smelt the mare, and calm him sufficiently to enable him to perform his business without injuring himself or the object of his affections.

By a process of logic, she had reached the conclusion that man and woman must work on similar principles. When she had questioned Anna, she had at first threatened to report Centaine to her papa and wash her mouth out with lye soap. Patiently Centaine had persisted until at last Anna had in a hoarse whisper confirmed her suspicions, and glanced across the kitchen at the comte with a look on her face that Centaine had never seen before, and at the time could not fathom, but which now made logical sense.

Watching them argue and laugh together, it all fell into place – the occasions when after a nightmare she had gone to Anna's room for comfort and found her bed empty, the puzzling presence of one of Anna's petticoats under her father's bed when she was sweeping out his bedroom. Only last week Anna had come out of the cellar after helping the comte clean out the improvised animal stalls with straw sticking both to the back of her skirts and to the bun of greying hair on the top of her head.

The discovery seemed somehow to increase Centaine's desolation and her feeling of emptiness. She felt truly alone now, isolated and without purpose, empty and aching.

'I'm going out.' She sprang up from the kitchen table.

'Oh no.' Anna barred her way. 'We have got to get some food into this house, since your father has given away all we possess, and, m'demoiselle, you are going to help me!'

Centaine had to escape from them, to be alone, to come to terms with this terrible new desolation of her spirit. Nimbly she ducked under Anna's outstretched arm and flung open the kitchen door.

On the threshold stood the most beautiful person she had ever seen in all her life.

He was dressed in glossy boots and immaculate riding breeches of a lighter tan colour than his khaki uniform jacket. His narrow waist was belted in lustrous leather and burnished brass, his Sam Browne crossed his chest and emphasized his wide shoulders. On his left breast were the RFC wings and a row of coloured ribbons, on his epaulettes sparkled the badges of his rank, and his cap had been carefully crushed in the manner affected by veteran fighter pilots and set at a jaunty angle over his impossibly blue eyes.

Centaine fell back a pace and stared up at him, for he towered over her like a young god, and she became aware of a sensation that was entirely new to her. Her stomach seemed to turn to jelly, hot jelly, heavy as molten lead that spread downwards through her lower body until it seemed that her legs could no longer support the weight of it. At the same time she had great difficulty breathing.

'Mademoiselle de Thiry.' This vision of martial splendour spoke and touched the peak of his cap in salute. The voice was familiar, and she recognized the eyes, those cerulean blue eyes, and the man's left arm was supported by a narrow leather strap –

'Michel—' her voice was unsteady and she corrected herself. 'Captain Courtney,' and then she changed languages, 'Mijnheer Courtney?'

The young god smiled at her, and it did not seem possible that this was the same man, tousled, bloodied and muddied, swaddled in ill-fitting charred rags, trembling and shaking and pathetic, that she had helped load in a stupor of pain and weakness and inebriation into the side-car of the motor-cycle the previous afternoon.

When he smiled at her, Centaine felt the world lurch beneath her feet. When it steadied, she realized that it had altered its orbit and was on a new track amongst the stars. Nothing would ever be the same again.

'Entrez, monsieur.' She fell back, and as he stepped over the threshold, the comte rose from the table and hurried to meet him.

'How goes it with you, captain?' He took Michael's hand. 'Your wounds?'

'They are much better.'

'A little cognac would help them,' the comte suggested and looked at his daughter slyly. Michael's stomach quailed at the suggestion and he shook his head vehemently.

'No,' said Centaine firmly, and turned to Anna. 'We must see to the captain's dressing.'

Protesting only mildly, Michael was led to the stool in front of the stove and Anna unbuckled his belt, while Centaine stood behind him and eased his jacket off his shoulders.

Anna unwrapped the dressings and grunted with approval.

'Hot water, child,' she ordered.

Carefully they washed and dried his burns, and then smeared them with fresh ointment and rebandaged them with clean linen strips.

'They are healing beautifully,' Anna nodded, while Centaine helped him into his shirt.

She had not realized how smooth a man's skin could be, there down his flanks and across his back. His dark hair curled on to the nape of his neck, and he was so thin that each knuckle of his spine stood out as cleanly as beads on a rosary, with two ridges of lean muscle running down each side of it.

She came round to button the front of his shirt.

'You are very gentle,' he said softly, and she dared not look into his eyes, lest she betray herself in front of Anna.

His chest hair was thick and crisp and springy as she brushed it almost unintentionally with her fingertips, and the nipples of his flat hard chest were dusky-pink and tiny, yet they hardened and thrust out under her gaze, a phenomenon which both amazed and enchanted her. She had never dreamed that happened to men also.

'Come, Centaine,' Anna chided her, and she started as she realized that she had been staring at his body.

'I came to thank you,' Michael said. 'I didn't mean to make work for you.'

'It is no trouble.' Centaine still dared not look into his eyes.

'Without your help I might have burned to death.'

'No!' Centaine said with unnecessary emphasis. The idea of death and this marvellous creature was totally unacceptable to her.

Now she looked at his face again at last, and it seemed

61

that the summer sky showed through chinks in his skull – so blue were his eyes.

'Centaine, there is much work to do.' Anna's tone was sharper still.

'Let me help you,' Michael cut in eagerly. 'I have been grounded – I am not allowed to fly.' Anna looked dubious, but the comte shrugged.

'Another pair of hands, we could use.'

'A small repayment,' Michael insisted.

'Your fine uniform.' Anna was looking for excuses, and she glanced down at his glossy boots.

'We have rubber boots and overalls,' Centaine cut in swiftly, and Anna threw up her hands in capitulation.

Centaine thought that even the blue *serge de Nim*, or denim as it was colloquially known, and black rubber boots looked elegant on Michael's tall lean body as he descended to help the comte muck out the animal stalls in the cellars.

Centaine and Anna spent the rest of the morning in the vegetable gardens, preparing the soil for the spring sowing.

Every time Centaine went down to the cellars on the flimsiest of excuses, she paused beside wherever Michael was working under the comte's direction, and the two of them made halting and self-conscious conversation until Anna came down the staircase.

'Where is that child now! Centaine! What on earth are you doing?' As if she did not know.

All four of them ate lunch in the kitchen – omelettes flavoured with onions and truffles, cheese and brown bread, and a bottle of red wine over which Centaine relented, but not enough to hand over the cellar keys to her father. She fetched it herself.

The wine softened the mood, even Anna took a glass of it and allowed Centaine to do the same, and the talk became easy and unrestrained, punctuated with bursts of laughter.

'Now, captain—' the comte turned to Michael at last with a calculating glitter in his single eye ' – you and your family, what do you do in Africa?'

'Farmers,' Michael replied.

'Tenant farmers?' the comte probed cautiously.

'No, no—' Michael laughed. 'We farm our own lands.'

'Landowners?' The comte's tone changed, for, as all the world knew, land was the only true form of wealth. 'What size are your family estates?'

'Well—' Michael looked embarrassed ' – quite large. You see, it is mostly held in a family company – my father and my uncle—'

'Your uncle, the general?' the comte prompted.

'Yes, my Uncle Sean—'

'A hundred hectares?' the comte insisted.

'A little more.' Michael squirmed on the bench and fiddled with his bread roll.

'Two hundred?' The comte looked so expectant that Michael could not evade him longer.

'Altogether, if you take the plantations and the cattle ranches, and some land we own in the north, it's about forty thousand hectares.'

'Forty thousand?' The comte stared at him, and then repeated the question in English so there could be no musunderstanding. 'Forty thousand?'

Michael nodded uncomfortably. It was only recently that he had begun to feel a little self-conscious about the extent of his family's worldly possessions.

'Forty thousand hectares!' The comte breathed reverently, and then, 'And, of course, you have many brothers?'

Michael shook his head. 'No, unfortunately I am an only son.'

'Ha!' said the comte with transparent relief. 'Do not feel too badly about that!' And patted his arm in a paternal gesture.

The comte shot a glance at his daughter, and for the

first time recognized the expression on her face as she looked at the airman.

'Quite right too,' he thought comfortably. 'Forty thousand hectares, and an only son!' His daughter was a Frenchwoman, and knew the value of a sou and a franc, *sacré bleu*, she knew it better than he did himself. He smiled lovingly across the table at her. A child in many ways, but a shrewd young Frenchwoman in others. Since the comte's factor had fled to Paris, leaving the accounts and books of the estate in chaos, it had been Centaine who had taken over the purse-strings. The comte had never bothered much with money anyway, for him land would always remain the only true wealth, but his daughter was the clever one. She even counted the bottles in the cellar and the hams on the smoke-rack. He took a mouthful of red wine and mused happily to himself. There would be so few eligible young men left after this slaughter, this charnel-house . . . and forty thousand hectares!

'*Chérie*,' he said. 'If the captain were to take the shotgun and get us a few fat pigeon, and you were to fill a basket with truffles – you might still find some – what a dinner we could have this evening!' Centaine clapped her hands with delight, but Anna glared at him in red-faced indignation across the table.

'Anna will go with you as chaperone,' he said hastily. 'We don't want any unseeming scandal, now, do we?' Might as well sow a seed, he thought, if it wasn't already ripely germinating. Forty thousand hectares, *merde*!

The pig was named Kaiser Wilhelm, or Klein Willie, for short. He was a piebald boar, so gross that as he waddled into the oak forest, he reminded Michael of a bull hippopotamus. His pointed ears drooped forward over his eyes and his tail curled like a roll of barbed wire up over his back, exposing ample evidence of his gender, contained in a bright pink sac that looked as though it had been boiled in oil.

'Vas-Y, Willie! Cherche!' cried Centaine and Anna in unison; at the same time it required both of them on the leash to restrain the enormous beast. 'Cherche! Seek up!' And the boar snuffled eagerly at the damp, chocolate-brown earth under the oak trees, dragging the two women behind him. Michael followed them, a spade over his good shoulder, laughing delightedly at the novelty of the hunt, and trotting to keep up with it.

Deeper into the forest they came across a narrow stream, running strongly with discoloured water from the recent rains, and they followed the bank, with snorts and cries of encouragement. Suddenly the pig let out a gleeful squeal and began rooting in the soft earth with his flat wet snout.

'He's found one!' Centaine shrieked with excitement and she and Anna hauled unavailingly on the leash.

'Michel!' she panted over her shoulder. 'When we get him away, you must be very quick with the spade. Are you ready?'

'Ready!'

From the pocket of her skirt Centaine pulled a wizened nub of a truffle that was mildewed with age. She pared off a sliver with a clasp knife, and held it as close to the boar's snout as she could reach. For a few moments the pig ignored her, and then it got the fresher scent of the cut truffle and grunted gluttonously, tried to take her hand in his streaming jaws. Centaine jerked away and backed off with the boar following her.

'Quickly, Michel!' she cried, and he went at the earth

with the spade. In half a dozen strokes he had exposed the buried fungus and Anna dropped to her kness and freed it from the earth with her bare hands. She lifted it out, crusty with chocolate soil, a dark knobbly lump almost the size of her fist.

'Look, what a beauty!'

At last Centaine allowed the pig to take the sliver of fungus from her fingers, and when he had gulped it, she let him return to the empty hole and snuffle around in the loose earth to satisfy himself that the truffle had disappeared, then *'Cherche!'* she shouted at him, and the hunt was on again. Within an hour the small basket was filled with the unappetizing-looking lumpy fungi, and Anna called a halt.

'More than this will merely spoil. Now for some pigeons. Let's see if our captain from Africa can shoot!'

They hurried after the boar, laughing and panting back through the open fields to the château, where Centaine locked the truffles in the pantry and Anna returned the boar to his stall in the cellars and then lifted the shotgun down from its rack on the kitchen wall. She handed the weapon to Michael and watched as he opened the breech and checked the barrels, then snapped them closed and put the gun to his shoulder and tried the balance. Despite the burns that hampered his swing a little, Anna could tell a good workman by the way he handled his tools, and her expression softened with approval.

For Michael's part he was surprised and then delighted to discover that the weapon was a venerable Holland and Holland – only the English gunsmiths could fashion a barrel that would throw a perfectly even pattern of shot no matter how fast the gun was traversed.

He nodded at Anna. 'Excellent!' And she handed him the canvas bag of cartridges.

'I will show you a good place.' Centaine took his hand to lead him and then saw Anna's expression and dropped it hurriedly. 'In the afternoon the pigeons come back to the woods,' she explained.

They skirted the edge of the forest, Centaine leading and lifting her skirts over the mud puddles so that Michael had an occasional flash of her smooth white calves, and his pulse accelerated beyond the exertion of keeping up with her. On her short, stubby legs, Anna fell far behind and they ignored her calls to 'Wait, wait for me.'

At the corner of the forest, in the angle of the T that the pilots used as the landmark for the return to the airfield, there was a sunken lane with high hedges on each side.

'The pigeons come in from there,' Centaine pointed across the open fields and vineyards, all of them overgrown and neglected. 'We should wait here.'

The hedgerow afforded excellent cover, and when Anna came up they all three hid themselves and began to search the sky. Heavy low cloud had begun to roll in again from the north, threatening rain, and forming a perfect backdrop against which the tiny specks of a pigeon flock showed clearly to Michael's trained eye.

'There,' he said, 'coming straight in.'

'I don't see them.' Centaine searched agitatedly. 'Where – oh yes, now I see them.'

Although they were quick on the wing, they were flying straight and descending only gently towards the forest. For a marksman of Michael's calibre, it was simple shooting. He waited until two birds overlapped each other, and took them both with his first shot. They crumpled in mid-air and as the rest of the flock flared up and scattered, he knocked down a third pigeon in a burst of feathers with his second barrel.

The two women raced out into the open field to bring in the birds.

'Three with two shots.' Centaine came back and stood close beside him, stroking the soft warm body of the dead pigeon and looking up at Michael.

'It was a fluke,' said Anna gruffly. 'Nobody shoots two pigeons by intention – not if they are flying.'

The next flock was a larger one, and the birds were bunched. Michael took three of them with his first barrel and a fourth bird with his second, and Centaine turned triumphantly to Anna.

'Another fluke,' she gloated. 'What luck the captain is having today.'

Two more flocks came within range in the next half hour, and Centaine asked seriously, 'Do you never miss, Mijnheer?'

'Up there,' Michael looked into the sky, 'if you miss, you are dead. So far I have never missed.'

Centaine shivered. Death – that word again. Death was all around them, on the ridges over there where for the moment the sound of the guns was just a low rumble, death in the sky above them. She looked at Michael and thought, 'I don't want him to die – never! Never!'

Then she shook herself, driving away the gloom, and she smiled and said, 'Teach me to shoot.' The request was inspired. It allowed Michael to touch her, even under Anna's jealous gaze. He stood her in front of him, and coached her into the classic stance, with her left foot leading.

'This shoulder a little lower.' They were both electrically aware of each contact. 'Just turn your hips this way slightly.' He placed his hands upon them and Michael's voice sounded as though he were choking as she pushed back with her buttocks against him, an untutored but devastating pressure.

Centaine's first shot drove her back against his chest, and he clasped her protectively while the pigeons headed untouched for the horizon.

'You are looking at the muzzle of the gun, not the bird,' Michael explained, still holding her. 'Look at the bird, and the gun will follow on its own.'

68

At her next shot a fat pigeon tumbled out of the sky, amid shrieks of excitement from both women, but when Anna ran out to pick it up, the rain that had been holding off until that moment fell upon them in a silver curtain.

'The barn!' cried Centaine, and led them scampering down the lane. The rain slashed the tree-tops and exploded in miniature shell bursts on their skin so that they gasped at its icy sting. Centaine reached the barn first, and her blouse was sticking to her skin, so that Michael could see the exact shape of her breasts. Strands of her dark hair were plastered against her forehead, and she shook the drops off her skirts and laughed at him, making no attempt to avoid his gaze.

The barn fronted on to the lane. It was built of squared yellow stone blocks and the thatched roof was tattered and worn as an old carpet. It was half-filled with bales of straw that rose in tiers to the roof.

'This will set in,' Anna groused darkly, staring out at the streaming rain and shaking the rain off herself like a water buffalo emerging from the swamp. 'We will be stuck here.'

'Come, Anna, let's clean the birds.'

They found comfortable perches on the straw bales, Centaine and Michael with their shoulders almost touching, and while they plucked the pigeons they chatted.

'Tell me about Africa,' Centaine demanded. 'Is it really so dark?'

'It's the sunniest land in the world – too much sun, even,' Michael told her.

'I love the sun,' Centaine shook her head. 'I hate the cold and the wet. There could never be too much sun for me.'

He told her about the deserts where it never rained. 'Not as much in a year as it does here in a single day.'

'I thought there were only black savages in Africa.'

'No,' he laughed. 'There are plenty of white savages too

– and black gentlemen,' and he told her about the tiny yellow pygmies of the Ituri forests, tall as a man's waist, and the giant Watusi who considered any man under two metres tall to be a pygmy, and those noble warriors of Zulu who called themselves children of heaven.

'You talk as though you love them,' she accused.

'The Zulu?' he asked, and then nodded. 'Yes, I suppose I do. Some of them, anyway. Mbejane—'

'Mbejane?' She did not pronounce the name right.

'A Zulu – he has been with my Uncle Sean since they were lads together.' He used the Zulu word 'Umfaan' and had to translate for her.

'Tell me about the animals.' Centaine did not want him to stop talking. She could listen to his voice and his stories for ever. 'Tell me about the lions and the tigers.'

'No tigers,' he smiled at her, 'but plenty of lions.' And even Anna's hands, busy with plucking the birds, stilled as she listened while Michael described a camp on the hunting veld where he and his Uncle Sean had been besieged by a pride of lions, and had had to stand by the horses' heads all night, protecting and soothing them, while the great pale cats prowled back and forth at the edge of the firelight, roaring and grunting, trying to drive the horses into the darkness where they would have been easy prey.

'Tell us about the elephants.' And he told her about those sagacious beasts. He described how they moved with that slow somnambulistic gait, huge ears flapping to cool their blood, picking up dirt to dash it over their heads for a dust bath.

He told them about the intricate social structures of the elephant herds, how the old bulls avoided the uproar of breeding herds. 'Just like your father,' said Anna. And how the barren old queens took upon themselves the duties of nanny and midwife: how the great grey beasts formed relationships with each other, almost like human friendships, that lasted their lifetimes; and about their strange preoccupation with death, how if they killed a hunter who had plagued and wounded them they would often cover his body with green leaves, almost as though they were trying to make atonement. He explained how when one of the members of the herd was stricken, the others would try to succour it, holding it on its feet with their trunks, supporting it from each side with their bulks, and when it fell at last – if it was a cow, the herd bull would mount her, as though trying to frustrate death with the act of generation.

This last tale roused Anna from her listening trance and reminded her of her role of chaperone; she glanced sharply at Centaine.

'It has stopped raining,' she announced primly, and she began to gather up the naked carcasses of the pigeons.

Centaine still watched Michael with huge shining dark eyes.

'One day I will go to Africa,' she said softly, and he returned her gaze steadily and nodded.

'Yes,' he said. 'One day.'

It was as though they had exchanged a vow. It was a thing between them, firm and understood. In that moment she became his woman and he her man.

'Come,' Anna insisted at the door of the barn. 'Come on, before it rains again,' and it took a vast effort from both of them to rise and follow her out into the wet and dripping world.

They dragged on leaden feet up the lane towards the château, side by side, not touching but so acutely aware of each other that they might as well have been locked in each other's arms.

Then the planes came out of the dusk, low and swift, the thunder of their engines rising to a crescendo as they passed overhead. In the lead was the green Sopwith. From this angle they could not see Andrew's head, but they could see daylight through the rents in the fabric of his wings, through the lines of bullet holes which the Spandaus had torn. The five aircraft that followed Andrew had all been shot up as well. There were tears and neatly punched holes in their wings and fuselages.

'It's been a hard day,' Michael murmured, with his head thrown back.

Another Sopwith trailed the others, its engine popping and missing, vapour trailing back in a stream behind it, one wing skewed out of line where the struts had been shot through. Centaine, watching them, shuddered, and crept closer to Michael.

'Some of them died out there today,' she whispered, and he did not have to reply.

'Tomorrow you will be with them again.'

'Not tomorrow.'

'Then the next day – or the next.'

Once more it was not necessary to reply.

'Michel, oh Michel!' There was physical agony in her voice. 'I must see you alone. We might never – we might never have another chance. From now on we must live each precious minute of our lives as though it is the last.'

The shock of her words was like a blow to his body. He could not speak, and her own voice dropped.

'The barn,' she whispered.

'When?' He found his voice, and it croaked in his own ears.

'Tonight, before midnight – I will come as soon as I am able to. It will be cold.' She looked directly into his face – social conventions had been burned away in the furnace of war. 'You must bring a blanket.'

She whirled then and ran to catch up with Anna, leaving Michael staring after her in a daze of disbelief and uncertain ecstasy.

Michael washed at the pump outside the kitchen and changed back into his uniform. When he entered the kitchen again, the pigeon pie was rich and redolent of fresh truffles under its crumbly brown crust, and Centaine was filling and refilling her father's glass without a protest from him. She did the same for Anna, but with a lighter more cunning hand, so that Anna did not seem to notice, though her face became redder and her laughter more raucous.

Centaine placed Michael in charge of the His Master's Voice gramophone, her most prized possession, and made it his duty to keep it fully wound up and change each of the wax discs as they ended. From the huge brass trumpet of the machine blared the recording of Toscanini conducting the La Scala orchestra in Verdi's *Aïda*, filling the kitchen with glorious sound. When Centaine brought his plate laden with pigeon pie to where he sat opposite the comte, she touched the nape of Michael's neck – those dark silky curls – and she purred in his ear as she leaned over him, 'I love *Aïda*, don't you, Captain?'

When the comte questioned him closely on the production of his family estates, Michael found it difficult to concentrate on his replies.

'We were growing a great deal of black wattle, but my father and uncle are convinced that after the war the motor-car will completely supersede the horse, and therefore there will be a drastic reduction in the need for leather harness, and consequently the demand for wattle tanning—'

'What a great shame that the horse should have to give way to those noisy, stinking contraptions of the devil,' the comte sighed, 'but they are right, of course. The petrol engine is the future.'

'We are replanting with pines and Australian blue gums. Pit props for the gold mines and raw material for paper.'

'Quite right.'

'Then, of course, we have the sugar plantations and the cattle ranches. My uncle believes that soon there will be ships fitted with cold rooms that will carry our beef to the world—'

The more the comte listened, the more pleased he became.

'Drink up, my boy,' he urged Michael, as an earnest of his approval. 'You have had hardly a drop. Is it not to your taste?'

'Excellent, truly, however, *le foie* – my liver.' Michael clasped himself under the ribs and the comte made sounds of sympathy and concern. As a Frenchman he understood that most of the ills and woes of the world could be attributed to the malfunctions of that organ.

'Not serious. But please don't let my little indisposition prevent you.' Michael made a self-deprecating gesture, and obediently the comte recharged his own glass.

Having served the men, the two women brought their own plates to the table to join them. Centaine sat beside her father, and spoke little. Her head turned between the two men as though in dutiful attention, until Michael felt a light pressure on his ankle and with a leap of his nerves realized that she had reached out with her foot beneath the table. He shifted guiltily under the comte's scrutiny, not daring to look across at Centaine. Instead, he made that nervous gesture of blowing on his fingertips as though he had burned them on the stove, and he blinked his eyes rapidly.

Centaine's foot withdrew as secretly as it had advanced, and Michael waited two or three minutes before reaching out his own. Then he found her foot and took it between both of his; from the corner of his eye he saw her start and a flush of dark blood spread up her throat to her cheeks and ears. He turned to stare at her, so enchanted that he could not pull his eyes away from her face, until the comte raised his voice.

'How many?' the comte repeated with mild asperity, and guiltily Michael jerked his foot back.

'I am sorry. I did not hear—'

'The captain is not well,' Centaine cut in quickly and a little breathlessly. 'His burns are not healed, and he has worked too hard today.'

'We should not keep him unnecessarily,' Anna agreed with alacrity, 'if he has finished his dinner.'

'Yes. Yes.' Centaine stood up. 'We must let him go home to rest.'

The comte looked truly distressed to be deprived of a drinking companion, until Centaine reassured him. 'Don't disturb yourself, Papa, you sit here and finish up your wine.'

Anna accompanied the couple out into the darkness of the kitchen yard and stood close by, eagle-eyed and arms akimbo, while they said their shy goodbyes. She had taken just enough of the claret to dull the razor-edge of her instincts, or she might have wondered why Centaine was so eager to see Michael on to his motor-cycle.

'May I call upon you again, Mademoiselle de Thiry?'

'If you wish, Captain.'

Anna's heart, softened by wine, went out to them. It took an effort to harden her resolve.

'Goodbye, Mijnheer,' she said firmly. 'This child will catch a chill. Come inside now, Centaine.'

The comte had found it imperative to wash down the claret with a *fine de champagne* or two. It cut the acidity of the wine, he explained seriously to Centaine. It was, therefore, necessary for the two women to help him to bed. He made this rather perilous ascent singing the march from *Aïda* with more gusto than talent. When he reached his bed, he went down like a felled oak, flat upon his back. Centaine took each of his legs in turn, straddled it and pulled off the boot with her knees.

'Bless you, my little one, your Papa loves you.'

Between them they sat him up and dropped his night-shirt over his head, then let him collapse back on to the bolster. His decency preserved by the nightshirt, they removed his breeches and rolled him into the bed.

'May angels guard your sleep, my pretty,' the comte mumbled, as they spread an eiderdown over him and Anna blew out the candle.

Under cover of darkness, Anna reached out and caressed the tousled wiry brush of the comte's head. She was rewarded by a reverberating snore and followed Centaine from the room, softly closing the door behind her.

C entaine lay and listened to the old house groan and creak around her in the night.

Wisely, she had resisted the temptation to climb fully clothed beneath her bedclothes, for Anna made one of her unannounced visits just as Centaine was about to extinguish her candle. She sat on the edge of the bed, garrulous with wine, but not so befuddled that she would not have known if Centaine had not been in her night-clothes. By yawning and sighing Centaine tried telepathically to make her feel sleepy, but when that didn't work, and she heard the distant chimes of the church clock at Mort Homme strike ten o'clock, she herself feigned sleep. It was agony to lie still and regulate her breathing, for she burned and itched with excitement.

At last Anna realized that she was talking to herself, and she moved around the tiny chamber, picking up and folding Centaine's discarded clothing, and finally stooping over her to kiss her cheek and then pinch out the wick of the lamp.

As soon as she was alone, Centaine sat up and hugged herself in a ferment of anticipation and trepidation. Although it was very clear in her mind what the final outcome of this meeting with Michael must be, the precise mechanics were at this stage still tantalizingly obscure. A process of logic had suggested to her that the broad concept could not differ too widely from what she had witnessed countless times in field and barnyard.

She had received confirmation of this one drowsy summer afternoon, when a mild commotion in one of the disused stables had attracted her attention. She had climbed into the loft and through a chink watched Elsa, the kitchenmaid, and Jacques the undergroom with amazement, until gradually it had dawned upon her that they were playing rooster and hen, stallion and mare. She had thought about it for days afterwards, and then eavesdropped with more attention upon the gossip of the female servants. Finally, she had taken her courage in both hands and gone to Anna with her questions.

All these researches had left her confused and puzzled by the contradictions. According to Anna, the procedure was extremely painful, accompanied by profuse bleeding and dire danger of pregnancy and disease. This conflicted with the unrestrained glee with which the other female servants discussed the subject, and with the giggles and muffled cries of delight that she had heard coming from Elsa as she lay beneath Jacques on the straw of the stable floor.

Centaine knew that she had a high threshold of pain; even the good doctor Le Brun had remarked upon it after he had reset her broken forearm without benefit of chloroform. 'Not a cheep out of her,' he had marvelled. No, Centaine knew she could bear pain as well as any of the peasant girls on the estate, and apart from her monthly courses she had bled before. Often, when she was certain that she was unobserved, she would take the cumbersome

77

side-saddle from Nuage's back, tuck up her skirts and ride him astride. The previous spring, riding bareback, she had put the stallion to the stone wall that bordered North Field, jumping him from the low side and dropping down seven feet to the deep side of the wall. As they landed, she had come down hard on Nuage's withers, and a pain like a knife blade had shot up through her body. She had bled so that Nuage's white shoulders were stained pink and she was so ashamed that despite the pain she had washed him off in the pond at the end of the field before limping home, leading Nuage behind her.

No, neither pain nor blood frightened her. Her trepidation had another source. She was deadly afraid that Michael might find her disappointing – Anna had also warned her of that.

'Afterwards men always lose interest in a woman, *les cochons*.'

'If Michael loses interest in me, I think I will die,' she thought, and for a moment she hesitated. 'I will not go – I will not take that chance.

'Oh, but how can I *not* go?' she whispered aloud, and felt her chest swelling with the strength of her love and her wanting. 'I must. I simply must.'

In an agony of impatience she listened to the sounds of Anna preparing for bed in the chamber next door. Even after there was silence, she waited on, heard the church clock strike the quarter and then the half-hour before she slipped from under the eiderdown.

She found her petticoats and cami-knickers where Anna had folded them away, and then paused with one foot in the leg of the knickers.

'What for?' she asked herself and smothered a giggle with her hand as she kicked them off again.

She buttoned on the thick woollen riding skirts and jacket, then spread a dark shawl over her head and shoulders. Carrying her boots in her hand, she slipped into the passage and listened outside Anna's door.

Anna's snores were low and regular and Centaine crept down into the kitchen. Sitting on the stool before the fire she buckled on her boots and then lit the bull's-eye lantern with a taper from the stove. She unlocked the kitchen door and let herself out. The moon was in its last quarter, sailing sharp-prowed through wisps of flying cloud.

Centaine kept to the grassy verge, so that the gravel would not crunch under her boots, and she did not open the shutter of the lantern, but hurried down the lane by the moon's faint silvery light. In the north, up on the ridges, there was a sudden brilliance, a dawn of orange light, that subsided slowly, and then came the rumble of the explosion muted by the wind.

'A mine!' Centaine paused for a moment, wondering how many had died in that monstrous upheaval of earth and fire. The thought spurred her resolve. There was so much death and hatred, and so little love. She had to grasp at every last grain of it.

She saw the barn ahead of her at last, and started to run. There was no light showing within, no sign of the motor-cycle.

'He has not come.' The thought left her desperate with desire. She wanted to scream his name. She tripped at the threshold of the barn, and almost fell.

'Michel!' She could restrain herself no longer, she heard the panic in her own voice as she called again, 'Michel!' and opened the shutter of the lantern.

He was coming towards her, out of the gloom of the barn. Tall and broad-shouldered, his pale face beautiful in the lantern light.

'Oh, I thought you were not coming.'

He stopped in front of her. 'Nothing,' he said softly, 'nothing in this world could have kept me away.'

They stood facing each other, Centaine with her chin lifted to look up at him, staring at each other hungrily and yet neither of them knowing what to do next, how to bridge those few inches between them that seemed like the void of all eternity.

'Nobody saw you?' he blurted.

'No, no, I don't think so.'

'Good.'

'Michel?'

'Yes, Centaine.'

'Perhaps I should not have come – perhaps I should go back?'

It was exactly the right thing to say, for the implied threat galvanized Michael and he reached out and seized her, almost roughly.

'No, never – I don't want you to go, ever.'

She laughed, a husky breathless sound, and he pulled her to him and tried to kiss her, but it was a clumsy attempt. They bumped noses and then their teeth clashed together in their haste, before they found each other's lips. However, once he found them, Centaine's lips were hot and soft, and the inside of her mouth was silky and tasted like ripe apples. Then her shawl slipped forward over her head, half smothering them both and they had to break apart, breathless and laughing with excitement.

'Buttons,' she whispered, 'your buttons hurt, and I am cold.' She shivered theatrically.

'I'm sorry.' He took the lantern from her and led her to the back of the barn. He handed her up over the bales of straw, and in the lamplight she saw that he had made a nest of soft straw between the bales and lined it with grey army blankets.

'I went back to my tent to get them,' he explained, as he set the lamp down carefully, and then turned to her again, eagerly.

'*Attends!*' She used the familiar form of address to

restrain him, and then unbuckled his Sam Browne belt. 'I will be covered in bruises.'

Michael tossed the belt aside and seized her again. This time they found each other's mouths and clung together. Great waves of feeling washed over Centaine, so powerful that she felt giddy and weak. Her legs sagged but Michael held her up and she tried to match the flood of kisses that he rained on her mouth and her eyes and her throat – but she wanted him to go down on to the blankets with her. Deliberately she let her legs go and pulled him off balance, so that he fell on top of her as she tumbled into the blanket-lined nest in the straw.

'I'm sorry.' He tried to disentangle himself, but she locked one arm around his neck and held his face to hers. Over his shoulder she reached out and pulled the blankets to cover them both. She heard herself making little mewing sounds like a kitten denied the teat, and she ran her hands over his face and into his hair as she kissed him. His body weight on top of her felt so good that when he tried to roll off her, she hooked her ankle into the back of his knee to prevent him.

'The light,' he croaked, and groped for the lantern to close the shutter.

'No. I want to see your face.' She caught his wrist and pulled his hand back, holding it to her bosom as she looked up into his eyes. They were so beautiful in the lamplight that she thought that her heart might break – and then she felt his hand on one of her breasts, and she held it there while her nipples ached with the need for his touch.

It all became a delirium of delight and wanting, becoming more and more powerful until at last it was unbearable, something had to happen before she fainted away with the strength of it – but it did not happen, and she felt herself coming back off the heights and it made her impatient and almost angry with disappointment.

Her critical faculties that had been dulled by desire

returned to her, and she sensed that Michael was floundering in indecision, and she became truly angry. He should have been masterful, taking her up there where she longed to go. She took his wrist again and she drew his hand downwards, at the same time she moved beneath him so that her thick woollen skirts rode up and bunched about her waist.

'Centaine,' he whispered. 'I don't want to do anything that you don't want.'

'*Tais-toi!*' she almost hissed at him. 'Be quiet!' – and she knew that she would have to lead him all the way, she would have to lead him always, for there was a difference in him that she had not been aware of before, but she did not resent it. Somehow it made her feel very strong and sure of herself.

They both gasped as he touched her. After a minute, she let go his wrist and searched for him and when she found him she cried out again, he was so big and hard that she felt daunted. For a moment, she wondered if she was capable of the task she had taken upon herself – then she rallied. He was awkward above her, and she had to wriggle a little and fumble. Then abruptly, when she was not expecting it, it happened – and she gasped with the shock.

But Anna had been wrong, there was no pain, there was only a breathtaking stretching and filling sensation and after the shock abated, a sense of great power over him.

'Yes, Michel, yes, my darling.' She encouraged him as he butted and moaned and thrashed in the enfolding crucifix of her limbs, and she rode his assault easily, knowing that in these moments he belonged to her completely, and revelling in that knowledge.

When the final convulsion gripped him, she watched his face, and saw how the colour of his eyes changed to indigo in the lamplight. Yet although she loved him then with a strength that was physically painful, still there was a tiny suspicion in the depths of her consciousness that she had missed something. She had not felt the need to scream as Elsa had screamed beneath Jacques in the straw, and immediately after that thought she was afraid.

'Michel,' she whispered urgently, 'do you still love me? Tell me you love me.'

'I love you more than my own life.' His voice was broken and gusty, she could not for an instant doubt his sincerity.

She smiled in the darkness with relief and held him close, and when she felt him going small and soft within her, she was overcome with a wave of melting compassion.

'My darling,' she whispered, 'there, my darling, there,' and she stroked his thick springing curls at the back of his head.

It was a little time before her emotions had calmed enough for her to realize that something had changed irrevocably within her during the few brief minutes of that simple act they had performed together. The man in her arms was physically stronger than she was but he felt like a child, a sleepy child, as he cuddled against her. While she felt wiser and vital, as though her life up until that moment had been becalmed, drifting without direction, but now she had found her trade winds and like a tall ship she was at last bearing away purposefully before them.

'Wake up, Michel.' She shook him gently and he mumbled and stirred. 'You cannot sleep now – talk to me.'

'What about?'

'Anything. Tell me about Africa. Tell me how we will go to Africa together.'

'I've told you that already.'

'Tell me again. I want to hear it all again.'

And she lay against him and listened avidly, asking questions whenever he faltered.

'Tell me about your father. You haven't told me what he looks like.'

So they talked the night away cuddled in their cocoon of grey blankets.

Then, too soon for both of them, the guns began their murderous chorus along the ridges, and Centaine held him to her with desperate longing. 'Oh, Michel, I don't want to go!' then she drew away from him, sat up and began to pull on her clothes and refasten the buttons.

'That was the most wonderful thing that has ever happened to me,' Michael whispered as he watched her, and in the light of the lantern and the flickering glow of the guns, her eyes were huge and soft as she turned to him again.

'We will go to Africa, won't we, Michel?'

'I promise you we will.'

'And I will have your son in the sunshine, and we will live happily ever after just like in the fairy stories, won't we, Michel?'

They went up the lane clinging together under Centaine's shawl, and at the corner of the stables they kissed with quiet intensity until Centaine broke out of his grip and fled across the paved yard.

She did not look back when she reached the kitchen door, but disappeared into the huge dark house, leaving Michael alone and unaccountably sad when he should have been joyous.

B iggs stood over the cot and looked down fondly at Michael as he slept. Biggs's eldest son, who had died in the trenches at Ypres a year ago, would have been the same age. Michael looked so worn and pale and exhausted that Biggs had to force himself to touch his shoulder and wake him.

'What time is it, Biggs?' Michael sat up groggily.

'It's late, sir, and the sun's shining – but we aren't flying, we are still grounded, sir.'

Then a strange thing happened. Michael grinned at

him, a sort of inane idiotic grin that Biggs had never seen before. It alarmed him.

'God, Biggs, I feel good.'

'I'm glad, sir.' Biggs wondered with a pang if it might be fever. 'How's our arm, sir?'

'Our arm is marvellous, bloody marvellous, thank you, Biggs.'

'I would have let you sleep, but the major is asking for you, sir. There is something important that he wants to show you.'

'What is it?'

'I'm not allowed to say, Mr Michael, Lord Killigerran's strict instructions.'

'Good man, Biggs!' Michael cried without apparent reason, and bounded from his cot. 'Never do to keep Lord Killigerran waiting.'

Michael burst into the mess and was disappointed to find it empty. He wanted to share his good spirits with somebody. Andrew for preference, but even the mess corporal had deserted his post. The breakfast dishes still cluttered the dining-table, and magazines and newspapers lay on the floor where they had obviously been dropped in haste. The adjutant's pipe, with malodorous wisps of smoke still rising from it, lay in one of the ashtrays, proof of how precipitously the mess had been abandoned.

Then Michael heard the sound of voices, distant but excited, coming through the open window that overlooked the orchard. He hurried out and into the trees.

Their full squadron strength was twenty-four pilots, but after the recent attrition they were down to sixteen, including Andrew and Michael. All of them were assembled at the edge of the orchard, and with them were the mechanics and ground staff, the crews from the anti-aircraft batteries that guarded the field, the mess servants and batmen – every living soul was on the field, and it seemed that all of them were talking at once.

They were gathered round an aircraft parked in the No. 1 position at the head of the orchard. Michael could see only the upper wings of the machine and the cowling of the motor over the heads of the crowd, but he felt a sudden thrill in his blood. He had never seen anything like it before.

The nose of the machine was long, giving the impression of great power, and the wings were beautifully raked yet with the deep dihedral which promised speed, and the control surfaces were full, which implied stability and easy handling.

Andrew pushed his way out of the excited throng around the aircraft and hurried to meet Michael with the amber cigarette-holder sticking out of the corner of his mouth at a jaunty angle.

'Hail, the sleeping beauty arises like Venus from the waves.'

'Andrew, it's the SE5a at last, isn't it?' Michael shouted above the uproar, and Andrew seized his arm and dragged him towards it.

The crowd opened before them and Michael came up short and stared at it with awe. At a glance he could see it was heavier and more robust than even the German Albatros DIIIs – and that engine! It was enormous! Gargantuan!

'Two hundred gee-gees!' Andrew patted the engine cowling lovingly.

'Two hundred horsepower,' Michael repeated. 'Bigger than the German Mercedes.' He went forward and stroked the beautifully laminated wood of the propeller as he looked up over the nose at the guns.

There was a .303 Lewis gun on a Foster mount set on the top wing, a light, reliable and effective weapon firing over the arc of the propeller, and below it mounted on the fuselage ahead of the cockpit was the heavier Vickers with interrupter gear to fire through the propeller. Two guns, at last they had two guns and an engine powerful enough to carry them into battle.

Michael let out the highland yell that Andrew had taught him, and Andrew unscrewed the cairngorm and sprinkled a few drops of whisky on the engine housing.

'Bless this kite and all who fly in her,' he intoned, and then took a swig from the flask before handing it to Michael.

'Have you flown her?' Michael demanded, his voice hoarse from the burn of whisky, and he tossed the flask to the nearest of his brother officers.

'Who the devil do you think brought her up from Arras?' Andrew demanded.

'How does she handle?'

'Just like a young lady I know in Aberdeen – quick up, quick down and soft and loving in between.'

There was a chorus of cat-calls and whistles from the assembled pilots, and somebody yelled, 'When do we get the chance to fly her, sir?'

'Order of seniority,' Andrew told them, and gave Michael a wicked grin. 'If only Captain Courtney were fit to fly!' He shook his head in mock sympathy.

'Biggs!' shouted Michael. 'Where is my flying jacket, man?'

'Thought you might want it, sir.' Biggs stepped out of the crowd behind him and opened the jacket for Michael to slide his arms into the sleeves.

The mighty Wolseley Viper engine hurled the SE5a down the narrow muddy runway, and as the tail lifted Michael had a sweeping view forward over the engine cowling. It was like sitting in a grandstand.

'I'll get Mac to strip off this piddling little windshield,' he decided, 'and I'll be able to spot any Hun within a hundred miles.'

He lifted the big machine into the air and grinned as he felt her begin to climb.

'Quick up,' Andrew had said, and he felt himself pressed down firmly into the seat, as he lifted the nose through the horizon and they went up like a vulture in a thermal.

'There's no Albatros been built that is going to climb away from us now,' he exalted, and at five thousand feet he levelled out and swept her into a right-hand turn, pulling the turn tighter and tighter still, hauling back hard on the stick to keep the nose up, his starboard wing pointing vertically down at the earth and the blood draining from his brain by the centrifugal force so that his vision turned grey and colourless, then he whipped her hard over the opposite way and yelled with elation in the buffet of wind and the roar of the huge engine.

'Come on, you bastards!' He twisted to look back at the German lines. 'Come and see what we have got for you now!'

When he landed, the other pilots surrounded the machine in a clamorous pack.

'What's she like, Mike?'

'How does she climb?'

'Can she turn?'

And standing on the lower wing above them, Michael bunched all his fingers together and then kissed them away towards the sky.

That afternoon Andrew led the squadron in tight formation, still in their shot-riddled, battered and patched old Sopwith Pups, down to the main airfield at Bertangles and they waited outside No. 3 hangar in an impatiently excited group as the big SE5a's were trundled out by the ground crews and parked in a long line abreast on the apron.

Through his uncle at divisional headquarters, Andrew had arranged for a photographer to be in attendance. With the new fighters as a backdrop, the squadron pilots formed up around Andrew like a football team. Every one of them was differently dressed, not a single regulation RFC uniform amongst them. On their heads they wore forage caps and peaks and leather helmets, while as always Andrew sported his tam-o'-shanter. Their jackets were naval monkey jackets, or cavalry tunics, or cross-over leather flying coats; but every one of them wore the embroidered RFC wings on his breast.

The photographer set up his heavy wooden tripod and disappeared under the black cloth while his assistant stood by with the plates. Only one of the pilots was not included in the group. Hank Johnson was a tough little Texan, not yet twenty years old, the only American on the squadron, who had been a horse tamer – or, as he put it, a bronco buster – before the war. He had paid his own passage over the Atlantic to join the Lafayette Squadron, and from there had found his way into Andrew's mixed bunch of Scots and Irish and colonials and other strays that made up No. 21 Squadron RFC.

Hank stood behind the tripod with a thick black Dutch cigar in his mouth giving bad advice to the harassed photographer.

'Come on, Hank,' Michael called to him. 'We need your lovely mug to give the picture some class.'

Hank rubbed his twisted nose, kicked into that shape by one of his broncos, and shook his head.

'None of you old boys ever hear that it's bad luck to have your picture took?'

They booed him, and he waved his cigar at them affably. 'Go ahead,' he invited, 'but my daddy got himself bit by a rattle snake the same day he had his picture took for the first time.'

'There aren't any rattle snakes up there in the blue,' one of them taunted.

'No,' Hank agreed. 'But what there is, is a whole lot worse than a nest of rattle snakes.' The derisive cries lost their force. They glanced at each other and one of them made as if to leave the group.

'Smile, please, gentlemen.' The photographer emerged from beneath his black cloth, freezing them, but their smiles were just a shade fixed and sickly as the shutter opened and their images were burned into silver nitrate for posterity.

Quickly Andrew acted to change the sombre mood that held them as they broke up. 'Michael, pick five,' he ordered. 'The rest of us will give you ten minutes' start, and you're to try and head us off, and make a good interception before we reach Mort Homme.'

Michael led his formation of five into the classic ambush position, up sun and screened by wisps of cloud, blocking the return route to Mort Homme. Still, Andrew almost gave them the slip; he had taken his group well south and was sneaking in right down on the ground. It would have worked with duller eyes than Michael's, but he picked up the flash of the low sun off the glass of a windshield from six miles and fired the red Very flare to signal 'Enemy in Sight' to his group. Andrew, realizing that they had been spotted, climbed up to meet them, and the two formations came together in a whirl of turning, diving, twisting machines.

Michael picked Andrew's SE5a out of the pack and went for him, and the two of them locked into an intricate aerial duet, pushing the big powerful machines harder and still harder, seeking their outer limits of speed and endurance; but evenly matched in skill and aircraft, neither was able to wrest the final advantage, until quite by chance as Andrew came up on his tail, almost into the killing line, Michael kicked on full rudder without bank and the SE5a tail skidded, turning flat, whipping him around with a force that almost dislocated his neck, and he found himself roaring back head-on to Andrew's attack.

They flashed past each other, only the lightning reflexes of veteran fighter pilots saving them from collision, and instantly Michael repeated the flat skid turn and was flung violently against the side of the cockpit, striking his partially healed shoulder on the rim so that his vision starred with the pain – but he was round in a flash and he fastened on to Andrew's tail. Andrew twisted desperately, but Michael matched every evasive twist and held him in the ring sight of the Vickers, pressing closer until the spinning boss of his propeller almost touched Andrew's rudder.

'*Ngi dla!*' Michael howled triumphantly. 'I have eaten!' – the ancient Zulu warcry that King Chaka's warriors had screamed as they put the long silver blade of the assegai into living flesh.

He saw Andrew's face reflected in the rear-view mirror on the cross struts of the wing above his head, and his eyes were wide with dismay and disbelief at that incredible manoeuvre.

Andrew fired a green Very flare to signal the recall to the squadron and to concede victory to Michael. The squadron was scattered across the sky, but at the recall they re-formed on Andrew and he led them back to Mort Homme.

The moment they landed, Andrew sprang from his machine and rushed to Michael, seizing him by both shoulders and shaking him impatiently.

'How did you do that – how the hell did you do that?'

Quickly Michael explained.

'It's impossible.' Andrew shook his head. 'A flat turn – if I hadn't seen it—' He broke off. 'Come on. Let's go and try it again.'

Together the two big scout planes roared off the narrow strip, and only returned as the last light was fading. Michael and Andrew jumped down from their cockpits and fell on each other, slapping each other on the back and dancing in a circle, so padded by their flying clothes that they looked like a pair of performing bears. Their ground crews stood by with indulgent grins until they sobered a little and then Mac, the head mechanic, stepped forward and tipped his forage cap.

'Begging your pardon, sir, but that paint job is like my mother-in-law's Sunday-go-to-meeting dress, sir, dull and dirty and God-help-us.'

The SE5a's were in factory drab. A colour that was intended to make them inconspicuous to the enemy.

'Green,' said Andrew. A few of the pilots on both sides, German as well as British, desired the opposite effect. With them it was a matter of pride that their paintwork should be bright enough to advertise their presence to the enemy, a direct challenge. 'Green,' Andrew repeated. 'Bright green to match my scarf, and don't forget the flying haggis on the nose.'

'Yellow, please, Mac,' Michael decided.

'Now what made me think you would choose yellow, Mr Michael?' Mac grinned.

'Oh, Mac, while you are about it, take that awful little windshield off her and tighten up the rigging wires, won't you?'

The old hands all believed that by screwing up the rigging wires and increasing the dihedral angle of the wings, they could put a few knots on their speed.

'I'll see to it,' Mac promised.

'Trim her to fly hands off,' Michael added. The aces were all fusspots, everybody knew that. If the SE5a flew straight and level with hands off the controls, the pilot could use both hands for the guns.

'Hands off it is, sir!' Mac grinned indulgently.

'Oh, and Mac, train the guns for fifty yards—'

'Anything else, sir?'

'That will do for now, Mac,' Michael answered his grin, 'but I'll work on it.'

'I'm sure you will, sir.' Mac shook his head with resignation. 'She'll be ready by dawn.'

'There's a bottle of rum for you if she is,' Michael promised.

'And now, my boy,' Andrew threw his arm around Michael's shoulders,' how about a drink?'

'I thought you would never offer,' Michael said.

The mess was full of excited young men all eagerly and loudly discussing the new machines.

'Corporal!' Lord Killigerran called over their heads to the mess servant. 'All drinks tonight will be on my book, please,' and his pilots cheered him delightedly before turning back to the bar to make the most of the offer.

An hour later when all eyes were glittering feverishly and the laughter had reached that raucous pitch which Andrew judged to be appropriate, he hammered on the bar for their attention and announced solemnly, 'As Grand Bok-Bok Champion of Aberdeen and greater Scotland, not to mention the outer Hebrides, it behoves me to challenge all comers to a bout of that ancient and honourable sport.'

'Behoves, forsooth!' Michael cocked a mocking eye at him. 'Kindly pick your team, sir.'

Michael lost the toss and his team was required to form the rugger scrum against the far wall of the mess, while the mess servants swiftly stowed away all breakables. Then one at a time Andrew's lads took a run across the mess and landed with all possible force upon the scrum, endeavouring to collapse it for an outright win. If, however, any part of their anatomy touched the ground in the process, it would have meant an immediate disqualification of their team.

Michael's scrum withstood the weight and violence of the onslaught, and finally all eight of Andrew's men, making sure that not a toe or finger touched the ground, were perched like a troop of monkeys on top of Michael's pyramid.

From the top of the pile Andrew asked the crucial

question which would decide glorious victory or ignoble defeat.

'Bok-Bok, how many fingers do I hold up?'

His voice muffled by the weight of bodies above him, Michael guessed. 'Three.'

'Two!' Andrew claimed victory and with a dismal groan the scrum deliberately collapsed itself, and in the ensuing chaos Michael found Andrew's ear within inches of his mouth.

'I say, do you think I might borrow the motor-cycle tonight?' he asked.

Pinned as he was, Andrew could not move his head, but he rolled his eyes towards Michael.

'Going out for a breath of air, my boy, once again?' And then when Michael looked sheepish and could find no clever reply, he went on, 'All I have is yours, go with my blessing and give the lucky lady my deepest respects, won't you?'

Michael parked the motor-cycle in the woods behind the barn, and carrying the bundle of army blankets sloshed through the mud to the entrance. As he stepped in there was a flash of light as Centaine lifted the shutter of the lantern and shone it in his face.

'Bonsoir, monsieur.'

She was sitting up on top of the bales of straw with her legs tucked under her and she grinned impishly down at him. 'What a surprise to meet you here.'

He scrambled up to her and seized her.

'You are early,' he accused.

'Papa went to bed early—' she got no further, for his mouth covered hers.

'I saw the new airplanes,' she gasped when they broke

apart to breathe, 'but I didn't know which was you. They are all the same. It troubled me not to know which was you.'

'Tomorrow mine will be yellow again. Mac is re-doping it for me.'

'We must arrange signals,' she told him, as she took the blankets from him and began to build their nest in between the bales of straw.

'If I lift my hand over my head like this, that will mean that I will meet you in the barn tonight,' he suggested.

'That is the signal I will look for hardest.' She smiled up at him and then patted the blankets. 'Come here,' she ordered, and her voice had gone husky and purring.

A long time later as she lay with her ear against his naked chest and listened to his heart pumping, he stirred slightly and then whispered, 'Centaine, it's no good! You cannot travel to Africa with me.'

She sat up quickly and stared at him, her mouth hardening, and her eyes, dark as gunmetal, gleamed dangerously.

'I mean, what would people say? Think of my reputation, travelling with a woman who was not my wife.'

She went on staring at him, but her mouth softened into the beginning of a smile.

'There must be a solution, though.' He pretended to puzzle over it. 'I have it!' He snapped his fingers. 'What if I were to marry you!'

She put her cheek back against his chest. 'Only to save your reputation,' she whispered.

'You have not yet said "yes".'

'Oh, yes. Yes! A million times yes!'

And then, characteristically, her next question was pragmatic.

'When, Michel?'

'Soon, as soon as possible. I have met your family, but tomorrow I will take you to meet mine.'

'Your family?' She held him at arm's length. 'Your family is in Africa.'

'Not all of it,' he assured her. 'Most of it is here. When I say most I don't mean numbers, I mean the most important single part of it.'

'I don't understand.'

'You will, *ma chérie*, you will!' he assured her.

Michael had explained to Andrew what he had in mind.

'If you get caught I will disclaim any knowledge of the whole nefarious scheme. I will, furthermore, preside with great enjoyment at your court martial, and will personally command the firing-squad,' Andrew warned him.

Michael had paced out the firm ground at the edge of North Field on the side of the de Thiry estate furthest from the squadron base. He had to slide-slip the bright yellow SE5a down behind the line of oaks that guarded the field, and then as he skimmed over the seven-foot stone wall, he shut the throttle and let her drop to the soft earth. He pulled up quickly, and left the engine idling as he clambered out on the wing.

Centaine was running out from the corner of the wall where she had been waiting. He saw she had followed his instructions and was warmly dressed: fur-lined boots under her yellow woollen skirt, and a yellow silk scarf at her throat. Over it all she wore a lustrous cape of silver fox fur, and the hood dangled down her back as she ran. She carried a soft leather bag on a strap over one shoulder.

Michael jumped down and swung her in his arms.

'Look! I am wearing yellow – your favourite.'

'Clever girl.' He sat her down. 'Here!' He pulled the borrowed flying helmet from the pocket of his greatcoat and showed her how to fit it over her thick dark curls and buckle the strap under the chin.

'Do I look gallant and romantic?' she asked, posing for him.

'You look marvellous.' And it was true. Her cheeks were rouged with excitement, and her eyes sparkled.

'Come on.' Michael climbed back on to the wing and then lowered himself into the tiny cockpit.

'It is so small.' Centaine hesitated on the wing.

'So are you, but I think you are also afraid, no?'

'Afraid, ha!' She flashed a look of utter scorn at him, and began to climb in on top of him.

This was a complicated business, which involved lifting her skirts above her knees and then balancing precariously over the open cockpit, like a beautiful bird settling on its clutch of eggs. Michael could not resist the temptation, and as she came down on top of him, he ran his hand up under the skirts, almost to the junction of her luscious silk-clad thighs. Centaine squealed with outrage. 'You are forward, monsieur!' and she plopped down on to his lap.

Michael fastened the safety-belt over both of them and then nuzzled her neck below the edge of the helmet. 'You are in my power now. You cannot escape.'

'I am not sure that I wish to,' she giggled.

It took some further minutes for them to arrange all Centaine's skirts and furs and petticoats, and to make sure that Michael could manipulate the controls with her strapped on to his lap.

'All set,' he told her, and taxied to the end of the field, giving himself every inch of runway that he could, for the earth was soft and the strip short. He had ordered Mac to remove the ammunition from both guns and drain the coolant from the Vickers, which saved almost sixty pounds in weight, but still they were overloaded for the length of runway available to them.

'Hold on,' he said in her ear, and opened the throttle and the big scoutplane bounded forward.

'Thank God for the south wind,' he murmured as he felt her unstick from the mud and strive mightily to lift them into the air.

As they scraped over the far wall, Michael banked slightly to lift his port wing over one of the oaks, and then they were climbing away. He felt how rigid Centaine was in his lap, and he thought she was really afraid. He was disappointed.

'We are safe now,' he shouted over the engine beat, and she turned her head, and he saw in her eyes not fear but ecstasy.

'It's beautiful,' she said, and kissed him. To know that she shared his passion for flight delighted him.

'We will go over the château,' he told her, and banked away steeply, dropping down again.

For Centaine it was the second most marvellous experience of her whole life, better than riding or music, almost as good as Michael's loving. She was a bird, an eagle, she wanted to shout her joy aloud, she wanted to hold the moment for ever. She wanted to always be on high with the wild wind howling around her and the strong arm of the man she loved holding her protectively.

Below her lay a new world, familiar places that she had known since her earliest childhood, now viewed from a different and enchanting dimension. 'This is the way the angels must see the world!' she cried, and he smiled at the fancy. The château loomed ahead of them, and she had not realized how big it was, or how pink and pretty was the roof of baked tiles. And there was Nuage in the field behind the stables, galloping ahead of them, racing the roaring yellow aircraft – and she laughed and shouted in the wind, 'Run, my darling!' and then they passed over him, and she saw Anna in the gardens, straightening up from her plants as she heard the engine, shading her eyes, peering up at them. She was so close that Centaine could see the frown on her red face, and she leaned far out from the cockpit. Her yellow scarf flowed behind her in the slipstream as she waved, and she saw the look of crumpled disbelief on Anna's face as they flashed by.

Centaine laughed in the wind and called to Michael, 'Go higher. Go up higher.'

He obeyed and she was never still for a moment, twisting and hopping about in his lap, leaning out of the cockpit first on one side, then on the other.

'Look! Look! There is the convent – if only the nuns could see me now. There, that is the canal – and there is the cathedral at Arras – oh, and there—' Her excitement and enthusiasm were infectious, and Michael laughed with her, and when she turned her head back to him, he kissed her, but she broke away.

'Oh, I don't want to miss a second!'

Michael picked out the main airforce base at Bertangles; the runways formed a cross of mown green turf through the dark forest, with the cluster of hangars and buildings nestling in the arms of the cross.

'Listen to me,' he shouted in her ear. 'You must keep your head down while we land.' She nodded. 'When I give you the word, jump down and run into the trees. You will find a stone wall on your right. Follow it for three hundred metres until you reach the road. Wait there.'

Michael joined the Bertangles circuit in textbook fashion, taking advantage of his sedate down-wind leg to scrutinize the base for any activity which might indicate the presence of high-ranking officers or other potential troublemakers. There were half a dozen aircraft parked in front of the hangars, and he saw one or two figures working on them or wandering about amongst the buildings.

'Looks as though it's clear,' he muttered, and turned crosswind and then on to final approach, with Centaine scrunched down on his lap, out of sight from the ground.

Michael came in high, like a novice; he was still at fifty feet when he passed the hangars, and he touched down deep at the far end of the runway and let his rollout carry them almost to the edge of the forest before he swung broadside and braked hard.

'Get out and run!' he told Centaine, and boosted her out of the cockpit. Hidden from the hangars and buildings by the fuselage of the SE5a, she hoisted up her skirts, tucked her leather bag under her arm, and scampered into the trees.

Michael taxied back to the hangars and left the SE5a on the apron.

'Better sign the book, sir,' a sergeant mechanic told him as he jumped down.

'Book?'

'New procedure, sir – all flights have to log in and out.'

'Damned red tape,' Michael groused. 'Can't do a thing without a piece of paper these days.' But he went off to find the duty officer.

'Oh yes, Courtney, there is a driver for you.'

The driver was waiting behind the wheel of a black Rolls-Royce parked at the back of No. 1 hangar, but as soon as he saw Michael he sprang out and stood to attention.

'Nkosana!' he grinned with huge delight, his teeth gleaming in his dark moon-shaped face, and he threw Michael a sweeping salute that quivered at the peak of his cap. He was a tall young Zulu, taller even than Michael, and he wore the khaki uniform and puttees of the African Service Corps.

'Sangane!' Michael returned the salute, grinning as widely, then impulsively hugged him.

'To see your face is like coming home again.' Michael spoke easy fluent Zulu.

The two of them had grown up together, roaming the grassy yellow hills of Zululand with their dogs and hunting-sticks. Naked they had swum together in the cool green pools of the Tugela river, and fished them for eels as long and thick as their arms. They had cooked their game on the same smoky fire, and lain beside it in the night, studying the stars and seriously discussing the occasions of small boys, deciding on the lives they would live and the world they would build when they were grown men.

'What news from home, Sangane?' Michael demanded as the Zulu opened the door of the Rolls. 'How is your father?'

Mbejane, Sangane's father, was the old servant companion and friend of Sean Courtney, a prince of the royal house of Zulu, who had followed his master to other wars, but was now too old and infirm, and was forced to send his son in his place.

They chatted animatedly, as Sangane drove the Rolls out of the base and turned on to the main road. On the back seat Michael stripped his flying gear to reveal his dress uniform, complete with wings and decorations, that he wore beneath.

'Stop over there, Sangane, at the edge of the trees.'

Michael jumped out and called anxiously, 'Centaine!'

She stepped out from behind one of the tree trunks and Michael gaped at her. She had used the time since he had left her to good effect, and he realized now why she brought the leather bag. Michael had never seen her wearing make-up before, but she had applied it so artfully that he could not at first fathom the transformation. It was simply that all her good points seemed enhanced, her eyes more luminous, her skin more glowing and pearly.

'You are beautiful,' he breathed. She was no longer a child-woman, she was possessed of a new poise and confidence, and he felt awed by her.

'Do you think your uncle will like me?' she asked.

'He will love you – any man would.'

The yellow suit was of a peculiar shade that seemed to

101

gild her skin and throw golden reflections into her dark eyes. The brim of the billycock hat was narrow on one side and full on the other, where it was pinned up to the crown with a spike of green and yellow feathers. Beneath the jacket she wore a blouse of fine creamy crêpe-de-chine, with a high lace collar, that emphasized the line of her throat and the dainty set of her small head above it. The boots had been replaced by elegant shoes.

He took both her hands and kissed them reverently, and then handed her into the back of the limousine.

'Sangane, this woman will be my wife one day soon.'

The Zulu nodded in approval, judging her as he would a horse or a young thoroughbred heifer.

'May she bear you many sons,' he said.

When Michael translated, Centaine blushed and laughed.

'Thank him, Michael, but tell him I would like at least one daughter.' She looked about the luxurious cab of the Rolls. 'Do all the English generals have such motor-cars?'

'My uncle brought it from Africa with him.' Michael ran his hand over the fine soft leather seat. 'It was a gift from my aunt.'

'Your uncle has style to go to war in such a chariot,' she nodded, 'and your aunt has good taste. One day I hope I will be able to give you such a gift, Michel.'

'I should like to kiss you,' he said.

'Never in public,' she told him primly, 'but as much as you want when we are alone. Now tell me, how far is it?'

'Five miles or so, but with this traffic on the road, God alone knows how long it will take us.'

They had turned into the main Arras–Amiens road, and it was clogged with military transport, guns and ambulances and heavy supply lorries, horse-drawn wagons and carts, the verges of the road crowded with marching men, hunch-backed beneath their heavy packs, with the steel helmets giving them a mushroom-headed uniformity.

Michael caught resentful and envious glances as San-gane threaded the big glistening Rolls through the slower traffic. The men trudging in the mud looked into the interior and saw an elegant officer with a pretty girl on the soft leather seat beside him. However, most of those sullen stares turned to grins when Centaine waved to them.

'Tell me about your uncle,' she demanded, turning back to Michael.

'Oh, he's a very ordinary chap, not much to tell actually. He was thrown out of school for beating up his headmaster, fought in the Zulu War and killed his first man before he was eighteen, made his first million pounds before he was twenty-five and lost it in a single day. Shot a few hundred elephant while he was a professional ivory hunter – killed a leopard with his bare hands. Then, during the Boer War, he captured Leroux, the Boer general, almost unaided, made another million pounds after the war, helped negoti-ate the charter of Union for South Africa. He was a cabinet minister in Louis Botha's government, but he resigned to come to this war. Now he commands the regiment. He stands a few inches over six feet and can lift a 200-lb sack of maize in each hand.'

'Michel, I am afraid to meet such a man,' she murmured seriously.

'Why on earth—'

'I am afraid I might fall in love with him.'

Michael laughed delightedly. 'I also am afraid. Afraid he will fall in love with you!'

Regimental Headquarters was temporarily located in a deserted monastery on the outskirts of Amiens. The monastery grounds were unkempt and overgrown, for they had been abandoned by the monks during the fighting of the previous autumn, and the rhododendron bushes had turned to jungle. The buildings were of red brick, moss-covered and with wistaria climbing to the grey roof. The bricks were pocked with old shell splinters.

A young second lieutenant met them at the front entrance.

'You must be Michael Courtney – I am John Pearce, the general's ADC.'

'Oh, hello.' Michael shook hands. 'What happened to Nick van der Heever?'

Nick had been at school with Michael, and he had been General Courtney's aide-de-camp ever since the regiment arrived in France.

'Oh, didn't you hear?' John Pearce looked grave, the familiar expression so often these days when someone asked after an acquaintance. 'Nick bought the farm, I'm afraid.'

'Oh God, no!'

'Afraid so. He was up at the front with your uncle. Sniper got him.' But the lieutenant's attention was wavering. He couldn't keep his eyes off Centaine. Obligingly, Michael introduced him and then cut short the lieutenant's pantomime of admiration.

'Where is my uncle?'

'He asked you to wait.' The young lieutenant led them through to a small enclosed garden which had probably belonged to the abbot. There were climbing roses on the stone walls and a sun-dial on a sculptured plinth in the centre of the small neat lawn.

A table had been laid for three in the corner where the sun penetrated. Uncle Sean was keeping his usual style – king's pattern silver and Stuart crystal, Michael noticed.

'The general will be with you as soon as he can, but he asked me to warn you that it will be a very short lunch. The spring offensive, you know—' The lieutenant made a gesture towards the decanter on the small serving table. 'In the meantime, may I offer you a sherry, or something with claws?'

Centaine shook her head, but Michael nodded. 'Claws, please,' he said. Although he loved his uncle as much as he did his own father, yet he always found his imminent presence after a long absence unnerving. He needed something to soothe those nerves.

The aide-de-camp poured Michael a whisky. 'Will you forgive me, but I do have a few things—' Michael waved him away and took Centaine's arm.

'Look, the buds are beginning to form on the roses – and the narcissus—' She leaned against him. 'Everything is coming to life again.'

'Not everything,' Michael contradicted softly. 'For the soldier, spring is the time of death.'

'Oh, Michel,' she began, and then broke off and looked towards the glass doors behind him with an expression that made Michael turn swiftly.

A man had stepped through them, a tall man, erect and broad-shouldered. He stopped when he saw Centaine and looked at her with penetrating appraisal. His eyes were blue and his beard was thick but neatly trimmed in the same style as the king's.

'Those are Michel's eyes!' Centaine thought, staring back into them, but so much fiercer, she realized.

'Uncle Sean!' Michael cried and released her arm. He stepped forward to shake hands, and those fierce eyes swivelled to him and softened.

'My boy.'

'He loves him—' Centaine understood. 'They love each other very deeply,' and she studied the general's face. His skin was sun-darkened and tanned like leather, with deep creases at the corners of his mouth and around those incredible eyes. His nose was large, like Michael's, and hooked, his forehead broad and deep, and above it was a dense dark cap of hair, shot through with silver threads, that glistened in the spring sunlight.

They were talking earnestly, still gripping each other's hands, exchanging the vital assurances, and as Centaine watched them, the full extent of their resemblance came through to her.

'They are the same,' she realized, 'differing only in age and in force. More like father and son, than—'

The fierce blue eyes came back to her. 'So this is the young lady.'

'May I present Mademoiselle de Thiry. Centaine, this is my uncle, General Sean Courtney.'

'Michel has told me much – a great deal—' Centaine stumbled over the English.

'Speak Flemish!' Michael cut in quickly.

'Michel has told me all about you,' she obeyed, and the general grinned delightedly.

'You speak Afrikaans!' he answered in that language. When he smiled, his whole person changed. That savage, almost cruel streak that she had sensed seemed illusory.

'It isn't Afrikaans,' she denied, and they fell into an animated discussion and argument, and within the first few minutes Centaine found that she liked him – liked him for his resemblances to Michael, and for the vast differences that she detected between them.

'Let's eat!' Sean Courtney exclaimed, and took her arm. 'We have so little time—' He seated her at the table.

'Michael over here – and we'll let him carve the chicken. I'll take care of the wine.'

Sean gave them the toast. 'To the next time the three of us meet again,' and they all drank it fervently, all too aware of what lay behind it, though here they were out of earshot of the guns.

They chatted easily, the general quickly and effortlessly smoothing over any uneasy silences, so that Centaine realized that for all his bluff exterior he was intuitively gracious, but always she was aware of the scrutiny of those eyes, the valuations and appraisals that were in progress behind them.

'Very well, *mon Général*,' she thought defiantly, 'look all you want, but I am me and Michel is mine.' And she lifted her chin and held his gaze, and answered him directly and without simperings or hesitations, until she saw him smile – and nod almost imperceptibly.

'So this is the one Michael has chosen,' Sean mused. 'I would have hoped for a girl of his own people, who spoke his own language and observed the same faith. I would have wanted to know a damned sight more about her before I gave my blessing. I would have made them take their time to consider each other and the consequences, but there is no time. Tomorrow or the next day, God knows what will happen. How can I spoil what might be their only moment of happiness ever?' For a moment longer he looked at her, searching for signs of spite or meanness, for weakness or vanity, and saw only the small determined jaw, the mouth that could smile easily but just as easily harden, and the dark intelligent eyes. 'She's tough and she's proud,' he decided, 'but I think she will be loyal, with strength to stay the full distance.' So he smiled and nodded and saw her relax, and he saw also true affection and liking dawn in her eyes before he turned to Michael.

'All right, my boy, you didn't come all this way to chew on this stringy little bird. Tell me why you came, and see if you can surprise me.'

'Uncle Sean, I have asked Centaine to be my wife.'

Sean wiped his moustaches carefully and then laid down his napkin.

'Do not spoil it for them,' he warned himself. 'Don't put the smallest cloud on their joy.'

107

He looked up at them and he began to smile.

'You don't surprise me, you stun me! I had given up expecting you to do something sensible.' He turned to Centaine. 'Of course, young lady, you had too much good sense to accept, didn't you?'

'General, I hang my head when I admit that I did not. I have accepted him.'

Sean looked fondly at Michael. 'Lucky blighter! She is too darned good for you, but don't let her get away.'

'Don't worry, sir.' Michael laughed with relief. He hadn't expected such instant acceptance. The old boy could still surprise him. He reached across the table to take Centaine's hand, and Centaine looked at Sean Courtney with puzzlement. 'Thank you, General, but you know nothing about me – or my family.' She remembered the catechism to which her own father had subjected Michael.

'I doubt that Michael is intending to marry your family,' Sean said drily. 'And about you, my dear. Well, I am one of the best judges of horseflesh in Africa, and that's not false modesty. I can judge a likely filly when I see one.'

'You are calling me a horse, General?' she bridled playfully.

'I'm calling you a thoroughbred, and I'll be surprised if you aren't a country girl and a horsewoman, and if you haven't got some pretty fancy bloodlines – tell me that I'm wrong,' he challenged.

'Her papa is a count, she rides like a centaur, and they have an estate that was mostly vineyards before the Huns shelled it.'

'Ha!' Sean looked triumphant, and Centaine made a gesture of resignation.

'He knows everything, your uncle.'

'Not everything—' Sean turned back to Michael. 'When do you plan to do it?'

'I would have liked my father—' Michael did not have to finish the thought, ' – but we have so little time.'

108

Sean, who knew truly how little time there was, nodded. 'Garry, your father, will understand.'

'We want to marry before the spring offensive begins,' Michael went on.

'Yes. I know.' Sean frowned and sighed. Some of his peers could send the young men out there with dispassion, but he was not a professional as they were. He knew he would never grow hardened to the pain and the guilt of it, sending men to die. He began to speak and stopped himself, sighed again and then went on.

'Michael, this is for you alone. Though you'll learn of it soon enough, anyway. A field order has been issued to all fighter squadrons. That order is to prevent all enemy aerial observation over our lines. We will be throwing in all our squadrons to keep the German spotters from following our preparations over the next weeks.'

Michael sat quietly, considering what his uncle had told him. It meant that as far ahead as he could anticipate, the future would be an incessant and ruthless battle with the German Jagdstaffels. He was being warned that few of the fighter pilots could expect to survive that battle.

'Thank you, sir,' he said softly. 'Centaine and I will marry soon – as soon as we can. May I hope that you will be there?'

'I can only promise you that I will do my level best to be there.' Sean looked up as John Pearce came back into the garden. 'What is it, John?'

'I'm sorry, sir. Urgent despatch from General Rawlinson.'

'I'm coming. Give me two minutes.' He turned to his young guests.

'Bloody awful lunch, I'm sorry.'

'The wine was excellent, and the company was even better,' Centaine demurred.

'Michael, go and find Sangane and the Rolls. I want a word with this young lady in private.'

He offered Centaine his arm, and they followed Michael out of the small garden and down the cloisters towards the stone portals of the monastery. Only when she stood at his side did Centaine realize how big he was, and that he had a slight limp, so that his footfalls on the stone paving were uneven. He spoke quietly but with force, leaning over her slightly to make each word tell.

'Michael is a fine young man – he is kind, he is thoughtful, he is sensitive. But he does not have the ruthlessness that a man needs in this world to get to the top of the mountain.' Sean paused, and she looked up at him attentively.

'I think you have that strength. You are still very young, but I believe that you will grow stronger. I want you to be strong for Michael.'

Centaine nodded, finding no words to reply.

'Be strong for my son,' Sean said softly, and she started.

'Your son?' and she saw the consternation in his eyes, which was swiftly masked, and he corrected himself.

'I'm sorry, his father is my twin – sometimes I think of him that way.'

'I understand,' she said, but somehow she sensed that it had not been a mistake. 'One day I will follow that until I find the truth,' she thought, and Sean repeated, 'Look after him well, Centaine, and I will be your friend to the gates of hell.'

'I promise you that I will.' She squeezed his arm, and they had reached the entrance where Sangane waited with the Rolls.

'*Au revoir, Général,*' Centaine said.

'Yes,' Sean nodded. 'Until we meet again,' and helped her into the back seat of the Rolls.

'I will let you know as soon as we decide the day, sir.' Michael shook his uncle's hand.

'Even if I can't be there, be happy, my boy,' said Sean

110

Courtney, and watched the Rolls purr sedately down the driveway, then with an impatient shrug, he turned and marched back down the cloisters with that long uneven stride.

With her hat and jewellery and shoes packed back into the soft leather bag, and with the fur-lined boots on her feet and the flying helmet on her head, Centaine crouched at the edge of the forest.

When Michael taxied the SE5a down to where she waited and swung it broadside to the distant airport buildings, she sprinted out from cover, tossed the bag up to him, and scrambled on to the wing. This time there was no hesitation and she clambered up into the cockpit like an old hand.

'Head down,' Michael ordered and swung the aircraft on to line for the take-off.

'All clear,' he told her once they were airborne and she popped her head up again, just as eager and excited as she had been on the first flight. They climbed higher and still higher.

'See how the clouds look like fields of snow – and the sunshine fills them with rainbows.'

She wriggled around in his lap, to look back over the tailplane, and then a quizzical look came into her eyes and she seemed to lose interest in the rainbows.

'Michel!' She moved again in his lap, but with deliberation.

'Michel!' No longer a query, and her tight round buttocks performed a cunning little oscillation that made him squirm.

'Forgive me!' He tried desperately to move out of

111

contact, but her posterior hunted after him, and she twisted her upper body around so that she could place both arms around his neck and she whispered to him.

'Not in broad daylight – not at five thousand feet!' He was shocked by her suggestion.

'Why not, *mon chéri?*' She kissed him lingeringly. 'Nobody will ever know,' and Michael realized that the SE5a had dropped a wing and was starting a shallow spiral dive. Hastily he corrected the machine, and she hugged him and began to move in a slow voluptuous rhythm in his lap.

'Don't you want to?' she asked.

'But, but – nobody has ever done it before, not in an SE5a. I don't know if it's possible.' His voice was becoming weaker, his flying more erratic.

'We will find out,' she said firmly. 'You fly the aeroplane and do not fret yourself,' and she hoisted herself slightly and began drawing up the back of her fur coat and the yellow skirt with it.

'Centaine,' he said uncertainly, and then a little later, 'Centaine!' more definitely, and a little later still, 'Oh my God, Centaine!'

'It is possible!' she cried triumphantly, and almost immediately she was aware of sensations which she had never suspected were harboured within her. She felt herself borne upwards and outwards as though she was departing her own body, and as though she were drawing Michael's soul out with her. At first she was terrified by the strength and strangeness of it, and then all other emotions were swept away.

She felt herself tumbling and swirling, upwards and upwards, with the wild wind roaring about her, and the rainbow-girded clouds undulating on every side – and then she heard herself screaming, and she thrust all her fingers into her mouth to still her own cries, but it was too strong to be contained, and she threw her head back and screamed

112

and sobbed and laughed with the wonder of it, as she went over the peak and fell down the other side into the gulf, spinning downwards, settling softly as a snowflake into her own body again, and feeling his arms around her, hearing him groaning and gasping in her ear, and she twisted and held him fiercely and cried, 'I love you, Michel, I will always love you!'

Mac hurried to meet Michael as soon as he cut the engine and climbed out of the cockpit.

'You're just in time, sir. There is a pilots' briefing in the mess. The major has been asking for you – best hurry, sir,' and then, as Michael started along the duckboards towards the mess, he called after him, 'How is she flying, sir?'

'Like a bird, Mac. Just reload the guns for me.'

First time ever that he hadn't fussed about his machine, Mac thought wonderingly, as he watched Michael walk away.

The mess was full of pilots, all the armchairs were taken and one or two new chums were standing against the wall at the back. Andrew sat on the bar counter swinging his legs and sucking on the amber cigarette-holder. He broke off as Michael appeared in the doorway.

'Gentlemen, we are being honoured. Captain Michael Courtney has graciously consented to join us. Despite other pressing and important business, he has been kind enough to devote an hour or two to help us settle our little difference with Kaiser Wilhelm II. I think we should show our appreciation.'

There were howls and cat-calls, and somebody blew a loud raspberry.

'Barbarians,' Michael told them haughtily, and dropped into the armchair hastily vacated by a new chum.

'Are you comfortable?' Andrew asked him solicitously. 'Do you mind if I carry on? Good! Well, as I was saying, the squadron has received an urgent despatch, delivered by motor-cycle less than half an hour ago, direct from divisional headquarters.'

He held it up and waved it at arm's length, pinching his nostrils with the other hand so that his voice was nasal as he went on.

'You will be able to smell the quality of the literary style and the contents from where you are sitting—'

There were a few polite guffaws, but the eyes that watched him were screwed up nervously, and here and there were little nervous movements, the shuffling of feet, one of the old hands cracking his knuckles, another nibbling on his thumbnail, Michael unconsciously blowing on his fingertips – for all of them knew that the scrap of coarse yellow paper that Andrew was waving at them might be their death warrant.

Andrew held it at arm's length and read from it.

From Divisional Headquarters, Arras.
To the Officer Commanding No. 21 Squadron RFC.
Near Mort Homme.
As of 2400 hrs 4th April 1917, you will at all costs
prevent any enemy aerial observation over your
designated sector until further orders to the contrary.

'That's all, gentlemen. Four lines, a mere bagatelle, but let me point out to you the succinct phrase "at all costs" without dwelling upon it.'

He paused and looked over the mess slowly, watching it register on each strained and gaunt face.

'My God, look how old they have grown,' he thought, irrelevantly. 'Hank looks fifty years old, and Michael—' he glanced up at the mirror over the mantelpiece, and when he saw his reflection, he brushed nervously at his own

114

forehead where in the last few weeks the sandy hair had receded in two deep bays, leaving pink skin like a beach at low tide. Then he dropped his hand selfconsciously and went on.

'Beginning at 0500 hours tomorrow morning, all pilots will fly four daily sorties until further notice,' he announced. 'There will be the usual dawn and dusk sweeps, but from now on they will be at full squadron strength.' He looked around for questions; there were none. 'Then each flight of aircraft will make an additional two sorties – one hour on, and two hours off – or as our friends in the Royal Navy are wont to say, "Standing watch and watch". That way we will maintain a perpetual presence over the squadron's designated area.'

They all stirred again and then heads turned towards Michael, for he was the eldest and their natural spokesman. Michael blew on his fingers and then studied them minutely.

'Do I have any questions?'

Hank cleared his throat.

'Yes?' Andrew turned to him expectantly, but Hank subsided back into his armchair.

'Just to get this straight,' Michael spoke at last. 'We will all fly the two hours' dawn and dusk patrols, that's four hours – and then an additional four hours during the day? Is my arithmetic correct, or does that make eight hours of combat a day?'

'Give Captain Courtney a coconut,' Andrew nodded.

'My trade union isn't going to like it,' and they laughed, a nervous braying chorus quickly cut off. Eight hours was too much, far too much, no man could exercise the vigilance and nervous response necessary to sustain that length of combat flight for a single day. They were being asked to do it day after day without promise of respite.

'Any other questions?'

'Service and maintenance of the aircraft?'

115

'Mac has promised me that he can do it,' Andrew replied to Hank. 'Anything else? No? All right, gentlemen, my book is open.'

But the pilgrimage to the bar to take advantage of Andrew's offer was subdued, and nobody discussed the new orders. They drank quietly but determinedly, avoiding each other's eyes. What was there to discuss?

The Comte de Thiry, with a vista of forty thousand hectares of lush farming land before his eyes, gave his rapturous approval to the wedding, and shook hands with Michael as though he were wringing an ostrich's neck.

Anna hugged Centaine to her bosom. 'My baby!' she wheezed, slow fat tears seeping out of the creases around her eyes and coursing down her face. 'You are going to leave Anna.'

'Don't be a goose, Anna, I will need you still. You can come with me to Africa,' and Anna sobbed aloud.

'Africa!' And then even more dolorously, 'What kind of wedding will it be? There are no guests to invite, Raoul the chef is in the trenches fighting the boche – oh, my baby, it will be a scandalous wedding!'

'The priest will come over, and the general, Michel's uncle, has promised – and the pilots from the squadron. It will be a wonderful wedding,' Centaine contradicted her.

'No choir,' sobbed Anna. 'No wedding feast, no wedding dress, no honeymoon.'

'Papa will sing, he has a wonderful voice, and you and I will bake the cake and kill one of the suckling pigs. We can alter Mama's dress, and Michel and I will have our honeymoon here, just the way Papa and Mama did.'

'Oh, my baby!' Once Anna's tears had started, they would not that readily be dried.

116

'When will it be?' The comte had not yet relinquished Michael's hand. 'Name the day.'

'Saturday – at eight in the evening.'

'So soon!' wailed Anna. 'Why so soon?'

The comte struck his thigh as inspiration came to him.

'We will open a bottle of the very best champagne – and perhaps even a bottle of the Napoleon cognac! Centaine, my little one, where are the keys?' And this time she could not refuse him.

In their nest of blankets and straw they lay in each other's embrace, and in halting sentences Michael tried to explain the new squadron orders to her. She could not fully comprehend their dreadful significance. She understood only that he was going into dire peril and she held him with all her strength.

'But you will be there on our wedding day? Whatever happens, you will come to me on our wedding day?'

'Yes, Centaine, I will be there.'

'Swear it to me, Michel.'

'I swear it.'

'No! No! Swear the most dreadful oath you can think of.'

'I swear it on my life and on my love for you.'

'Ah, Michel,' she sighed and pressed against him, satisfied at last. 'I will watch for you as you fly by each dawn and each dusk – and I will meet you here each night.'

They made love in a frenzy, a madness of the blood, as though they were trying to consume each other, and the fury of it left them exhausted so that they slept in each other's arms until Centaine woke, and it was late. The birds were calling in the forest and the first light filtered into the barn.

'Michel! Michel! It is almost half past four.' By the light

117

of the lantern she checked the gold watch pinned to her jacket.

'Oh, my God,' Michael began pulling on his clothes, still groggy with sleep, 'I'll miss the dawn patrol—'

'No. Not if you go directly.'

'I can't leave you.'

'Don't argue! Go, Michel! Go quickly.'

Centaine ran all the way, slipping and sliding in the mud of the lane, but determined to be on the hill for the squadron take-off, to wave them away.

At the stables she stopped, panting and clutching her chest to try and control her breathing. The château was in darkness, lying like a sleeping beast in the dawn, and she felt a rush of relief.

She crossed the yard slowly, giving herself time to catch her breath, and at the door she listened carefully before letting herself into the kitchen. She slipped off her muddy boots and placed them in the airing cupboard behind the stove, then she climbed the stairs, keeping close to the wall so that the tread would not squeak under her bare feet.

With another lift of relief she opened the door to her cell, crept in and then closed it behind her. She turned to face the bed, and then froze with surprise as a match flared and was touched to a lantern wick, and the room bloomed with yellow light.

Anna, who had just lit the lantern, was sitting on her bed, with a shawl around her shoulders and a lace nightcap on her head. Her red face was stony and forbidding.

'Anna!' Centaine whispered. 'I can explain – you haven't told Papa?'

Then the chair by the window creaked and she turned to find her father sitting in it and staring at her with his single malevolent eye.

She had never seen such an expression upon his face.

Anna spoke first. 'My little baby creeping out at night to go whoring after soldiers.'

'He is not a soldier,' Centaine protested. 'He is an airman.'

'Harlotry,' said the comte. 'A daughter of the house of de Thiry behaving like a common harlot.'

'Papa, I am to be Michel's wife. We are as good as married to each other.'

'Not until Saturday night, you are not.' The comte rose to his feet. There was a dark smudge of sleeplessness under his one eye and his thick mane of hair stood on end.

'Until Saturday,' his voice rose to an angry bellow, 'you are confined to this room, child. You will remain here until one hour before the ceremony begins.'

'But, Papa, I have to go to the hill—'

'Anna, take the key. I place you in charge of her. She is not to leave the house.'

Centaine stood in the centre of the room looking around her, as though for escape, but Anna rose and took her wrist in a powerful calloused hand and Centaine's shoulders slumped as she was led to the bed.

T he pilots of the squadron were scattered in dark groups of threes and fours amongst the trees at the edge of the orchard, talking softly and smoking the last cigarettes before take-off, when Michael came clumping down the duckboards, still buttoning his greatcoat and pulling on his flying gauntlets. He had missed the pre-flight briefing.

Andrew nodded a greeting as he joined them, making no mention of Michael's late arrival or of the example to the new pilots, and Michael did not apologize. They were both acutely aware of the dereliction of his duty, and Andrew unscrewed his silver flask and drank without offering it to Michael; the rebuke was deliberate.

'Take-off in five minutes,' Andrew studied the sky, 'and

it looks like a good day to die.' It was his term for good flying weather, but today it jarred on Michael.

'I'm getting married on Saturday,' he said, as though the ideas were linked, and Andrew stopped with the flask halfway back to his lips and stared at him.

'The little French girl up at the château?' he asked, and Michael nodded.

'Centaine – Centaine de Thiry.'

'You crafty old dog!' Andrew began to grin, his disapproval forgotten. 'So that is what you've been up to. Well, you have my blessing, my boy.'

He made a benedictory gesture with the flask. 'I drink to your long life and joy together.'

He passed the flask to Michael, but Michael paused before drinking.

'I'd be honoured if you would agree to act as my best man.'

'Don't worry, my boy, I will be flying at your wingtip as you go into action, I give you my oath on it.' He punched Michael's arm and they grinned happily at each other and then marched side by side to the green and yellow machines standing at the head of the squadron line-up.

One after another the Wolseley Viper engines crackled and snarled and blue exhaust smoke misted the trees of the orchard. Then the SE5a's bumped and rocked over the uneven ground for the massed take-off.

Today, because it was a full squadron sweep, Michael would not be flying as Andrew's wingman, but as leader of 'B' flight. He had five other machines in his flight, and two of his pilots were new chums and would need protecting and shepherding. Hank Johnson was leading 'C' flight and he waved across as Michael taxied past him, and then gunned his machine into his slot behind him.

As soon as they were airborne, Michael signalled to his flight to close the formation into a tight V and he followed

Andrew, conforming to his slight left-hand turn that would carry them past the hillock beyond the château.

He lifted the goggles on to his forehead and slipped his scarf down off his nose and mouth so that Centaine would be able to see his face, and flying one-handed he prepared to make their private rendezvous signal to her as he passed. There was the knoll – he started smiling in anticipation, then the smile faded.

He could not see Nuage, the white stallion. He leaned far out of the cockpit, and ahead of him Andrew was doing the same, screwing his head around as he searched for the girl and the white horse.

They roared past and she was not there. The hillock was deserted. Michael peered back over his shoulder as it receded, making doubly sure. He felt the dull weight in his belly, the cold and heavy stone of forboding. She wasn't there, their talisman had forsaken them.

He lifted the scarf over his mouth and covered his eyes with the goggles, as the three flights of aircraft bore upwards, climbing for the vital advantage of height, aiming to cross the ridges at 12,000 feet before levelling out into the patrol pattern.

His mind kept going back to Centaine. Why wasn't she there? Was something wrong?

He found it hard to concentrate on the sky around him. 'She has taken our luck. She knows what it means to us and she has let us down.'

He shook his head. 'I mustn't think about it – watch the sky! Don't think about anything but the sky and the enemy.'

The light was strengthening, and the air was clear and icy cold. The land beneath them was patched with the geometrical patterns of fields and studded with the villages and towns of northern France, but directly ahead was that dung-brown strip of torn and savaged earth that marked the lines, and above it the scattered blobs of morning cloud, dull as bruises on one side and brilliant gold on the side struck by the rising sun.

To the west lay the wide basin of the Somme river where the beast of war crouched ready to spring, and in the east the sun hurled great burning lances of fire through the sky, so that when Michael looked away, his vision was starred with the memory of its brilliance.

'Never look at the sun,' he reminded himself testily. Because of his distraction, he was making the mistakes of a novice.

They crossed the ridges, looking down on the patterns of opposing trenches, like worm castings on a putting green.

'Don't fix!' Michael warned himself again. 'Never stare at any object.' He resumed the veteran fighter pilot's scan, the quick flitting search that covered the sky about him, sweeping back and forth, and down and over.

Despite all his efforts to prevent it, the thought of Centaine and her absence from the knoll crept insidiously back into his mind again, so that suddenly he realized that he had been staring at one whale-shaped cloud for five or six seconds. He was fixing again.

'God, man, pull yourself together!' he snarled aloud.

Andrew, in the leading flight, was signalling, and Michael swivelled to pick out his sighting.

It was a flight of three aircraft, four miles south-west of their position, and 2,000 feet below them.

'Friendlies.' He recognized them as De Havilland two-seaters. Why hadn't he seen them first? He had the best eyes in the squadron.

'Concentrate.' He scanned the line of woods south of Douai, the German-held town just east of Lens, and he picked out the freshly dug gun emplacements at the edge of the trees.

'About six new batteries,' he estimated, and made a note

for his flight log without interrupting the pattern of his scan again.

They reached the western limit of their designated patrol area, and each flight turned in succession. They started back down the line, but with the sun directly into their eyes now, and that line of dirty grey-blue cloud on their left hand.

'Cold front building,' Michael thought, and then suddenly he was thinking of Centaine again, as though she had slipped in through the back door of his mind.

'Why wasn't she there? She could be sick. Out at night in the rain and cold – pneumonia is a killer.' The idea shocked him. He imagined her wasting away, drowning in her own fluids.

A red Very pistol flare arched across the nose of his machine, and he started guiltily. Andrew had fired the 'Enemy in Sight' signal while he was dreaming.

Michael searched frantically. 'Ah!' with relief. 'There it is!' Below and to the left.

It was a German two-seater, a solitary artillery spotter, just east of the ridges, bustling down in the direction of Arras, a slow and outdated type, easy prey for the swift and deadly SE5a's. Andrew was signalling again, looking back at Michael, the green scarf aflutter, and that devil-may-care grin on his lips.

'I am attacking! Give me top cover.'

Both Michael and Hank acknowledged the hand signals and stayed on high as Andrew banked away into a shallow diving interception, with the other five aircraft of his flight streaming down behind in attacking line astern.

'What a grand sight!' Michael watched them go. Thrilling to the chase, that wild charge down the sky, cavalry of the heavens in full flight, swiftly overhauling their slow and cumbersome prey.

Michael led the rest of the squadron into a series of slow shallow S-turns, holding them in position to cover the attack, and he was leaning from the cockpit waiting for the kill when abruptly he felt a slide of unease, that cold weight of premonition in his guts again, the instinct of impending disaster, and he swept the sky above and around him.

It was clear and peacefully empty, then his gaze switched towards the blinding glare of the sun and he held up his hand to cover it, and with one eye only looked past his fingers – and there they were.

They were boiling out of the cloud line like a swarm of gaudy glittering poisonous insects. It was the classic ambush. The decoy sent in low and slow to draw the enemy, and then the swift and deadly onslaught from out of the sun and the clouds.

'Oh, sweet Mother of God,' Michael breathed, as he snatched the Very pistol out of its holster beside his seat.

How many? It was impossible to count that vicious host. Sixty, perhaps more – three full Jagdstaffels of Albatros DIIIs in their rainbow colours dropping falcon-swift upon Andrew's puny flight of SE5a's.

Michael fired the red Very flare to warn his pilots and then winged over into a dive, aiming to intercept the enemy squadron before it could reach Andrew. Swiftly he estimated the triangle of speeds and distances and realized that they were too late, four or five seconds too late to save Andrew's flight.

Those four or five seconds which he had squandered in dreaming and fruitlessly watching the attack on the German decoy plane, those crucial seconds in which he had neglected his duty, weighed on him like leaden bars as he pushed the throttle of the SE5a to its stop. The engine whined, that peculiar wailing protest of overdriven machinery as the tip of the spinning propeller accelerated through the speed of sound, and he could feel the wings flexing and bending under the strain as the speed and pressure built up in that suicidal dive.

'Andrew!' he shouted. 'Look behind you, man!' and his voice was lost in the howl of wind and the scream of the overdriven engine.

All Andrew's attention was fixed on his quarry, for the German decoy pilot had seen them and was also diving away towards the earth, drawing the SE5a's after him and transforming the hunters into unwitting prey.

The massed German Jagdstaffel held their diving attack, though they must have been fully aware of Michael's desperate attempt to head them off. They would know as well as Michael did that his attempt was futile, that he had left it too late. The Albatroses would be able to make an attacking run over Andrew's flight, and with complete surprise aiding them must destroy most of the SE5a's in that single stroke before turning back to face Michael's avenging counter-stroke.

Michael felt the adrenalin surge burning in his blood like the clean bright flame of a spirit lamp. Time seemed to slow down into those eternal micro-seconds of combat, so that he floated sedately downwards, and the horde of enemy aircraft appeared to hang suspended on their multi-coloured wings, as though they were set like gems in the heavens.

The colours and patterns of the Albatroses were fantastic, with scarlet and black the dominant colours, but some were chequered like harlequins, and others had the silhouettes of bat wings or birds outlined on their wings and fuselage.

At last he could see the faces of the German airmen, turning towards him and then back towards their primary quarry.

'Andrew! Andrew!' Michael lamented in agony as each second made it clearer just how late he would be to prevent the ambush succeeding.

His fingers numb with cold and dread, Michael reloaded the Very pistol and fired another flare forward over his own nose, trying to attract Andrew's attention, but the red ball of flame fell away towards the earth, fizzling and spinning a pathetic thread of smoke, while half a mile further on Andrew lined up on the hapless German spotter plane, and Michael heard the tut-tut-tuttering of his Vickers as he attacked from astern.

In the same instant the wave of Albatroses broke over Andrew's flight, from above.

Michael saw two of the SE5a's mortally struck in the first seconds, and spin away with smoke and pieces of fuselage flying from them; the rest of them scattered widely, each with two or three Albatroses racing after them, almost jostling each other for a chance to take the killing line.

Only Andrew survived. His response to the first crackle of the Spandau machine-gun was instantaneous. He kicked the big green machine into that flat skidding turn that he and Michael had practised so often. He went tearing back straight into the heart of the pack, forcing the Albatroses to swerve wildly away from his head-on charge, firing furiously into their faces, emerging from behind them seemingly unscathed.

'Good on you!' Michael rejoiced aloud, and then he saw the rest of Andrew's flight shot out of the sky, burning and twisting downwards, and his guilt turned to anger.

The German machines, having wrought quick destruction, were wheeling now to face the charge of Michael's and Hank's flights. They came together and the entire pattern of aircraft disintegrated into a milling cloud, turning like dust and debris in a whirlwind.

Michael came out on the quarter of a solid black Albatros with scarlet wings on which the black Maltese crosses stood out like gravestones. As he crossed, he laid off his aim for the deflection of their combined tracks and speeds, and fired for the radiator in the junction of the scarlet wings above the German pilot's head, attempting to cook him alive in boiling coolant liquid.

He saw his bullets hitting exactly where he had aimed, and at the same time noticed the small modification in the Albatros's wing structure. The Germans had altered the Albatros. They had been forcibly shown the lethal design fault, and they had relocated the radiator. The German ducked from Michael's field of fire, and Michael pulled up the nose of his machine.

An Albatros had picked on one of Michael's new chums, sticking on his tail like a vampire, within an ace of the killing line. Michael came out under the Albatros's belly and reached up to swivel the Lewis gun on its Foster mounting, aiming upwards, so close that the muzzle of the Lewis gun almost touched the bright pink belly of the Albatros.

He fired the full drum of ammunition into the German's guts, waggling his wings slightly to spray his fire from side to side, and the Albatros reared up on its tail like a harpooned shark, and then fell over its wing and dropped away in its death plunge.

The new chum waved his thanks to Michael – they were almost touching wingtips, and Michael signalled imperiously, 'Return to base!' and then gave him the clenched fist. 'Imperative!'

'Get out of here, you bloody fool!' he shouted uselessly, but his contorted face emphasized the hand signal, and the novice broke off and fled.

Another Albatros came at Michael and he turned out hard, climbing and twisting, firing at fleeting targets, turning – turning for very life. They were outnumbered six or seven to one, and the enemy were all veterans, it showed in the way they flew, quick and agile, and unafraid. To stay and fight was folly. Michael managed to reload the Very pistol, and he fired the green flare of the recall. In these circumstances it was the order to the squadron to break off and run for home with all possible speed.

He came round hard, fired at a pink and blue Albatros,

and saw his bullets cut through the cowling of the engine a few inches too low to hit the German's fuel tank.

'Damn! Damn it to hell!' he swore, and he and the Albatros turned out in opposite directions and Michael had a clear run for home. He saw his remaining pilots already tearing away, and he put the yellow machine's nose down and went after them, heading for the ridges and Mort Homme.

He swivelled his head just ônce more, to make sure that his tail was clear – and at that moment he saw Andrew.

Andrew was a thousand metres out on Michael's starboard side. He had been separated from the main dogfight, engaged with three of the attacking Albatroses, fighting them single-handed, but he had given them the slip and now he too was running for home like the rest of the British squadron.

Then Michael looked above Andrew and he realized that not all the German Albatroses had come down in that first attacking wave. Six of them had remained up there under the clouds, led by the only Albatros that was painted pure scarlet from tail to nose, and from wingtip to wingtip. They had waited for the dogfight to develop and for stragglers to emerge. They were the second set of jaws to the trap – and Michael knew who piloted the all-red Albatros. The man was a living legend on both sides of the lines, for he had already killed over thirty Allied aircraft. It was the man they called the Red Baron of Germany.

The Allies were countering the legend, trying to smear the invincible image that Baron Manfred Von Richthofen was building, by calling him a coward and a hyena who had built up his score of kills by avoiding combat on equal terms and by singling out novices and stragglers and damaged aircraft before attacking.

Perhaps there was truth to that claim, for there he was, hovering above the battlefield like a scarlet vulture, and there was Andrew, isolated and vulnerable below him, his

128

nearest ally, Michael, 1,000 metres away – and Andrew seemed unaware of this new menace. The scarlet machine dropped from above, the shark-like nose aimed directly at Andrew. The five other hand-picked veteran German fighter pilots followed him down.

Without thought, Michael began the turn that would carry him to Andrew's assistance, and then his hands and feet, acting without conscious volition, countered the turn and kept the yellow SE5a roaring on its shallow dive for the safety of the British lines.

Michael stared over his shoulder and superimposed on the pattern of swirling aircraft was Centaine's beloved face, the great dark eyes dark with tears, and her words whispered in his head louder than guns and screaming engines, 'Swear to me you will be there, Michael!'

With Centaine's words still ringing in his ears, Michael saw the German attack sweep over Andrew's solitary aircraft, and once again miraculously Andrew survived that first deadly wave and whirled to face and fight them.

Michael tried to force himself to turn the yellow SE5a, but his hands would not obey, and his feet were paralysed upon the rudder bars. He watched while the German pilots worked the solitary green aircraft the way a pack of sheepdogs might round up a stray ewe, driving Andrew relentlessly into each other's crossfire.

He saw Andrew fighting them off with a magnificent display of courage and flying skill, turning into each new attack, and facing it head-on, forcing each antagonist to break away, but always there were others crossing his flanks and quarters, raking him with Spandau fire.

Then Michael saw that Andrew's guns were silenced. The drum of his Lewis gun was empty, and he knew that it was a lengthy process to reload it. Clearly the Vickers machine-gun on the cowling had overheated and jammed. Andrew was standing in the cockpit, hammering at the breech of the weapon with both fists, trying to clear it, and

Von Richthofen's red Albatros dropped into the killing line behind Andrew.

'Oh God, no!' Michael heard himself whimpering, still running for safety, stricken as much by his own cowardice as by Andrew's peril.

Then another miracle happened, for without opening fire the red Albatros turned away slightly, and for an instant flew level with the green SE5a.

Von Richthofen must have seen that Andrew was unarmed, and he had declined to kill a helpless man. As he passed only feet from the cockpit in which Andrew was struggling with the blocked Vickers, he lifted one hand in a laconic salute – homage to a courageous enemy – and then turned away in pursuit of the rest of the fleeing British SE5a's.

'Thank you, God,' Michael croaked.

Von Richthofen's fight followed him into the turn. No, not all of them followed him. There was a single Albatros that had not broken off the engagement with Andrew. It was a sky-blue machine with its top wing chequered black and white, like a chessboard. It fell into the killing line behind Andrew that Von Richthofen had vacated, and Michael heard the stuttering rush of its Spandau.

Flame burst into full bloom around the silhouette of Andrew's head and shoulders as his fuel tank exploded. Fire, the airman's ultimate dread, enveloped him and Michael saw Andrew lift himself out of the flames like a blackened and scorched insect and throw himself over the side of the cockpit, choosing the swift death of the fall to that of the flames.

The green scarf around Andrew's throat was on fire, so that he wore a garland of flame until his body accelerated and the flames were snuffed out by the wind. His body turned with his arms and legs spread out in the form of a crucifix, and dwindled swiftly away. Michael lost sight of him before he struck the earth 10,000 feet below.

'In the name of all that is holy, couldn't anyone have let us know that Von Richthofen had moved back into the sector?' Michael shouted at the squadron adjutant. 'Isn't there any bloody intelligence in this army? Those desk wallahs at Division are responsible for the murder of Andrew and six other men we lost today!'

'That is really unfair, old man,' the adjutant murmured, as he puffed on his pipe. 'You know how this fellow Von Richthofen works. Will-o'-the-wisp, and all that stuff.'

Von Richthofen had devised the strategy of loading his aircraft on to open goods trucks and shuttling the entire Jagdstaffel up and down the line. Appearing abruptly, with his sixty crack pilots, wherever he was least expected, wreaking dreadful execution amongst the unprepared Allied airmen for a few days or a week, and then moving on again.

'I telephoned Division as soon as the first of our planes landed, and they had only just received the intelligence themselves. They think Von Richthofen and his circus have taken up temporary residence at the old airstrip just south of Douai—'

'A lot of good that does us now, with Andrew dead.' As he said it, the enormity of it at last hit Michael, and his hands began to shake. He felt a nerve jumping in his cheek. He had to turn away to the small window of the cottage that the adjutant used as the squadron office. Behind him the adjutant remained silent, giving Michael time to collect himself.

'The old airstrip at Douai—' Michael thrust his hands into his pockets to keep them still, and he drove his mind from the memory of Andrew to consider instead the technical aspects ' – those new gun emplacements, they must have moved up to guard Von Richthofen's Jagdstaffel.'

'Michael, you are commanding the squadron – at least temporarily, until Division confirms or appoints another commander.'

131

Michael turned back, hands still in pockets, and nodded, not yet trusting his voice.

'You will have to draw up a new duty roster,' the adjutant prompted him gently, and Michael shook his head slightly as though to clear it.

'We can't send out less than full squadron strength,' he said, 'not with the circus out there. Which means that we can't maintain full-time daylight cover over the designated squadron sector.'

The adjutant nodded in agreement. It was obvious that to send out single flights was suicidal.

'What is our operational strength?' Michael demanded.

'At the moment, eight – four machines were badly shot up. If it goes on like this, it's going to be a bloody April, I am afraid.'

'All right,' Michael nodded. 'We will scrub the old roster. We can only fly two more sorties today. All eight aircraft. Noon and dusk. Keep the new chums out of it as much as possible.'

The adjutant was making notes, and as Michael concentrated on his new duties, his hands stopped shaking and that corpse-grey pallor of his face improved. 'Telephone Division and warn them that we will not be able to cover the sector adequately. Ask them when we can expect to be reinforced. Tell them that an estimated six new batteries have been moved up to—' Michael read the map references off his note-pad ' – and tell them also that I noticed a design modification on the Albatroses of the circus.' He explained the relocation of the engine radiator. 'Tell them I estimate the boche have sixty of these new Albatros in Von Richthofen's Jagdstaffel. When you have done all that call me, and we will work out a new roster, but warn the lads there will be a squadron sweep at noon. Now I need a shave and a bath.'

Mercifully, there was no time during the rest of that day for Michael to dwell on Andrew's death. He flew both sorties with the depleted squadron, and although the knowledge that the German circus was in the sector worked on all their nerves, the patrols were completely uneventful. They saw not a single enemy machine.

When they landed for the last time in the dusk, Michael took a bottle of rum down to where Mac and his team of mechanics were working by lantern light on the damaged SE5a's and spent an hour with them, giving them encouragement, for they were all anxious and depressed by the day's losses – particularly the death of Andrew, whom they had all adored and hero-worshipped.

'He was a good 'un.' Mac, with black grease to the elbows, looked up from the engine he was working on, and accepted the tin mug of rum that Michael handed him. 'He was a real good 'un, the major was.' He said it for all of them. 'Don't often find one like him, you don't.'

Michael trudged back through the orchard; looking up at the sky through the trees, he could see the stars. It would be flying weather again tomorrow – and he was deadly afraid.

'I've lost it,' he whispered. 'My nerve has gone. I am a coward, and my cowardice killed Andrew.' That knowledge had been at the back of his mind all that day, but he had suppressed it. Now, when he faced it squarely, it was like a hunter following a wounded leopard into cover. He knew it was there, but the actual sight of it as they came face to face turned a man's belly to water.

'A coward,' he said aloud, lashing himself with the word, and he remembered Andrew's smile and the tam-o'-shanter set jauntily on his head.

'What cheer, my boy?' He could almost hear Andrew's voice, and then he saw him falling down the sky with the burning green scarf around his throat, and Michael's hands began to shake again.

'A coward,' he repeated, and the pain was too much to bear alone and he hurried to the mess, blinded by his guilt

133

so that he missed his footing and stumbled more than once.

The adjutant and the other pilots, some of them still in flying rig, were waiting for Michael. It was the senior officer's duty to begin the wake, that was squadron ritual. On a table in the centre of the mess were seven bottles of Black Label Johnny Walker whisky, one for each of the missing airmen.

When Michael entered the room, everybody stood – not for him, but as a last respect to the missing men.

'All right, gentlemen,' Michael said. 'Let us send them on their way.'

The most junior officer, briefed by the others in his duties, opened a bottle of whisky. The black labels gave the correct funereal touch. He came to Michael and filled his glass, then moved on to the others, in order of seniority. They held the brimming glasses and waited while the adjutant, his briar still clamped in his teeth, seated himself at the ancient piano in the corner of the mess and began to bang out the opening chords of Chopin's Funeral March. The officers of No. 21 Squadron stood to attention and tapped their glasses on table-tops and the bar counter, keeping time with the piano, and one or two of them hummed quietly.

On the bar counter were laid out the personal possessions of the missing pilots. After dinner these would be auctioned off, and the squadron pilots would pay extravagant prices so that a few guineas could be sent to a new widow or a bereaved mother. There were Andrew's golf clubs, which Michael had never seen him use, and the Hardy trout rod, and his grief came back fresh and strong so that he thumped his glass on the counter with such force that whisky slopped over the rim, and the fumes prickled his eyes. Michael wiped them on his sleeve.

The adjutant crashed through the last bar and then stood up and took his glass. Nobody said a word, but they all lifted their own glasses, thought their own thoughts for a second, and then drained them. Immediately the junior officer refilled each tumbler. All seven bottles must be finished, that was part of the tradition. Michael ate no supper, but stood by the bar and helped consume the seven bottles. He was still sober, the liquor seemed to have no effect on him.

'I must be an alcoholic at last,' he thought. 'Andrew always said I had great potential.' And the liquor did not even deaden the pain that Andrew's name inflicted.

He bid five guineas each for Andrew's golf clubs and the Hardy split-cane rod. By that time the seven bottles were all empty. He ordered another bottle for himself and went alone to his tent. He sat on the cot with the rod in his lap. Andrew had boasted that he had landed a fifty-pound salmon with that stick, and Michael had called him a liar.

'Oh ye of little faith,' Andrew had chided him sorrowfully.

'I believed you all along.' Michael caressed the old rod and drank straight from the bottle.

A little later, Biggs looked in. 'Congratulations on your victory, sir.' Three other pilots had confirmed Michael's shooting down of the pink Albatros.

'Biggs, will you do me a favour?'

'Of course, sir.'

'Bugger off – there's a good fellow.'

There was three-quarters of the bottle of whisky left when Michael, still in his flying clothes, stumbled out to where Andrew's motor-cycle was parked. The ride in the cold night air cleared his head, but left him feeling brittle and fragile as old glass. He parked the motorcycle behind the barn, and went to wait among the bales of straw.

135

The hours, marked by the church clock, passed slowly, and with each of them his need for Centaine grew until it was almost too intense to bear. Every half-hour he would go to the door of the barn and peer up the dark lane, before returning to the bottle and the nest of blankets.

He sipped the whisky, and in his head those few seconds of battle in which Andrew had died played over and over, like a gramophone record that had been scratched. He tried to shut out the images, but he could not. He was forced to relive, time and again, Andrew's last agony.

'Where are you, Centaine? I need you so much now.' He longed for her, but she did not come, and again he saw the sky-blue Albatros with the black and white chequered wings bank steeply on to the killing line behind Andrew's green aircraft, and yet again he glimpsed Andrew's pale face as he looked back over his shoulder and saw the Spandaus open fire. Michael covered his eyes and pressed his fingers into the sockets until the pain drove out the images.

'Centaine,' he whispered. 'Please come to me.'

The church clock struck three o'clock and the whisky bottle was empty.

'She isn't coming.' He faced it at last, and as he staggered to the door of the barn and looked up at the night sky, he knew what he had to do to expiate his guilt and grief and shame.

The depleted squadron took off for the dawn patrol in the grey half-light. Hank Johnson was now second-in-command, and he flew on the other wing.

Michael turned out slightly, as soon as they were above the trees, and headed for the knoll beyond the château. Somehow he knew that she would not be there this morning, yet he pushed up his goggles and searched for her.

The hilltop was deserted, and he did not even look back.

'It's my wedding day,' he thought, searching the sky above the ridges, 'and my best man is dead, and my bride—' He did not finish the thought.

The cloud had built up again during the night. There was a solid ceiling at 12,000 feet, dark and forbidding, stretching unbroken to every reach of the horizon. Below that it was clear to 5,000 feet where straggly grey cloud formed a layer that varied in thickness between 500 and 1,000 feet.

Michael led the squadron up through one of the holes in this intermittent layer, and then levelled out just below the top bank of cloud. The sky below them was empty of aircraft. To a novice it would seem impossible that two large formations of fighter planes could patrol the same area, each searching for the other, and still fail to make contact. However, the sky was so deep and wide that the chances were much against a meeting, unless the one knew precisely where the other would be at a given time.

While his eyes raked back and forth, Michael reached with his free hand into the pocket of his greatcoat and assured himself that the package he had prepared just before take-off was still there.

'God, I could use a drink,' he thought. His mouth was parched and there was a dull ache in his skull. His eyes burned, but his vision was still clear. He licked his dry lips.

'Andrew always used to say that only a confirmed drunkard can drink on top of a hangover. I just wish I'd had the courage and common sense to bring a bottle.'

Through the holes in the cloud beneath him he kept a running check on the squadron's position. He knew every inch of the squadron's designated area the way a farmer knows his lands.

They reached the outward limit and Michael made the turn, with the squadron coming round behind him, and he checked his watch. Eleven minutes later he picked out the bend in the river, and a peculiarly shaped copse of beech trees that gave him an exact positional fix.

He eased the throttle a fraction and his yellow machine drifted back a few yards until he was flying on Hank Johnson's wingtip. He glanced across at the Texan and nodded. He had discussed his intentions with Hank before take-off and Hank had tried to dissuade him. Across the gap Hank screwed up his mouth as though he had sucked a green persimmon, to show his disapproval, then raised a war-weary eyebrow and waved Michael away.

Michael backed the throttle a little further and dropped below the squadron. Hank kept leading them eastwards, but Michael made an easy turn into the north and began to descend.

Within a few minutes the squadron had disappeared into the limitless sky, and Michael was alone. He went down until he reached the lower layer of broken cloud and then used it as cover. Dodging in and out of the cold damp banks and the intervening open patches, he crossed the front lines a few miles south of Douai, and then picked out the new German gun emplacements at the edge of the woods.

The old airstrip was marked on his field map. He was able to pick it out from a distance of four miles or more, for the wheels of the German Albatroses on landing and take-off had traced muddy ruts in the turf. Two miles out, he could see the German machines parked along the edge of the forest, and in the trees beyond he made out the rows of tents and portable sheds which housed the German crews.

Suddenly there was a woof and a crack of bursting explosive, and an anti-aircraft shell burst above and slightly ahead of him. It looked like a ripe cotton pod, popping open and spilling fluffy white smoke, deceptively pretty in the muted light below the clouds.

'Good morning, Archie,' Michael greeted it grimly.

It was a ranging burst from one of the guns, and was followed immediately by the thud and crack of a full salvo. The air all around him was studded with shrapnel bursts.

Michael pushed his nose down and let the speed build up, and the needle of the rev counter in front of him began to wind upwards into the red sector. He fumbled in his pocket, pulled out the cloth package and placed in on his lap.

The earth and forest came up swiftly towards him, and he dragged a long smear of bursting shrapnel behind him. Two hundred feet above the tree-tops he levelled out, and the airfield was directly ahead of him. He could see the multicoloured biplanes standing in a long row, their shark-like snouts pointed up towards him. He looked for the sky-blue machine with the chequered wings but could not pick it out.

There was agitated movement all along the edge of the field. German ground crews, anticipating a torrent of Vickers machine-gun fire, were running into the forest, while off-duty pilots, trying to struggle into their flying jackets, were racing towards the parked aircraft. They must know it was useless to take off and try to intercept the British machine, but they were making the attempt nonetheless.

Michael reached for the firing-handle. The aircraft were parked in a neat line, the pilots crowding towards them – and he smiled without humour and depressed his nose, picking them up in the ring sight of the Vickers.

At one hundred feet he levelled again, dropped his right hand from the firing handle and picked up the cloth package from his lap. As he passed over the centre of the German line, he leaned from the cockpit and tossed the package overboard. The ribbon he had attached to it unrolled in the slipstream of the SE5a and fluttered down to the edge of the field.

As Michael opened the throttle and climbed away again towards the cloud layer, he glanced up into the mirror above his head and saw one of the German pilots stoop over the package – and then the SE5a bounced and rocked as the German anti-aircraft guns opened up on him again, and a shell burst just below him. Within seconds he was into the haven of the cloud bank with his guns cold and unfired, and a few shrapnel tears in the belly and the underwings.

He turned on to a heading for Mort Homme. While he flew he thought about the package he had just dropped.

During the night he had torn a long ribbon from one of his old shirts to use as a marker and weighted the end of it with a handful of .303 cartridges. Then he had stitched his handwritten message into the other end of the ribbon.

He had at first considered attempting the message in German, and then admitted to himself that his German was hopelessly inadequate. Almost certainly there would be an officer on Von Richthofen's Jagdstaffel who could read English well enough to translate what he had written.

To the German pilot of the blue Albatros with black and white chequered wings.
Sir,
    The unarmed and helpless British airman whom you murdered yesterday was my friend.
    Between 1600 hrs and 1630 hrs today I will be patrolling over the villages of Cantin and Aubigny-au-Bac, at a height of 8,000 feet.
    I will be flying an SE5a scoutplane painted yellow.
    I hope to meet you.

140

The rest of the squadron had already landed when Michael returned to the base.

'Mac, I seem to have picked up some shrapnel.'

'I noticed, sir. Don't worry, fix it in a jiffy.'

'I haven't fired the guns, but check the sights again, will you.'

'Fifty yards?' Mac asked for the range at which he wanted fire from both Lewis and Vickers gun to converge.

'Make it thirty, Mac.'

'Working close, sir,' Mac whistled through his teeth.

'I hope so, Mac, and by the way, she is a touch tail-heavy. Trim her hands-off.'

'See to it myself, sir,' Mac promised.

'Thank you, Mac.'

'Give the bastards one for Mr Andrew, sir.'

The adjutant was waiting for him. 'We have all aircraft operational again, Michael. Twelve on the duty roster.'

'All right, Hank will take the noon patrol, and I will fly at 15.39 hrs alone.'

'Alone?' The adjutant took his pipe out of his mouth in surprise.

'Alone,' Michael confirmed. 'Then a full squadron sweep at dusk, as usual.'

The adjutant made a note. 'By the way, message from General Courtney. He will do his best to attend the ceremony this evening. He thinks he will almost certainly be there.'

Michael smiled for the first time that day. He had wanted very badly for Sean Courtney to be at his wedding.

'Hope you can make it also, Bob.'

'You can bet on it. Whole squadron will be there. Looking forward to it no end.'

Michael wanted a drink badly. He started towards the mess.

'God, it's eight o'clock in the morning,' he thought, and stopped. He felt brittle and dried-out; whisky would put warmth and juice into his body again, and he felt his hands begin to tremble with his deep need for it. It took all his resolve to turn away from the mess and go to his tent. He remembered then that he hadn't slept the previous night.

Biggs was sitting on a packing-case outside the tent, polishing Michael's boots, but he jumped to attention, his face expressionless.

'Enough of that!' Michael smiled at him. 'Sorry about last night, Biggs. Bloody rude of me. I didn't mean it.'

'I know, sir.' Biggs relaxed. 'I felt the same way about the major.'

'Biggs, wake me at three. I've got some sleep to catch up on.'

It was not Biggs who woke him but the shouts of the ground crews, the sound of running men, the deep bellowing tone of the anti-aircraft guns along the edge of the orchard, and the roaring overhead of a Mercedes aircraft engine.

Michael staggered out of his tent with tousled hair and bloodshot eyes, still half-asleep.

'What the hell is happening, Biggs?'

'A Hun, sir – cheeky blighter beating up the base.'

'He's pushed off again.' Other pilots and ground crew were shouting amongst the trees as they ran to the edge of the field.

'Didn't even fire a shot.'

'Did you see him?'

'An Albatros – blue with black and white wings. The devil almost took the roof of the mess.'

'He dropped something – Bob's picked it up.'

Michael ducked back into the tent and pulled on his jacket and a pair of tennis shoes. He heard two or three of the aircraft starting up as he ran out of the tent again. Some of his own pilots were setting off in pursuit of the German interloper.

'Stop those men from taking off!' Michael yelled, and

before he reached the adjutant's office he heard the engines switched off again in response to his order.

There was small crowd of curious pilots at the door, and Michael pushed through them just as the adjutant untied the drawstring that closed the mouth of the canvas bag that the German machine had dropped. The chorus of question and comment and speculation was silenced immediately as they all realized what the bag contained. The adjutant gently ran the strip of green silk through his fingers. There were black-rimmed holes burned through it and it was stained with dried black blood.

'Andrew's scarf,' he said unnecessarily, 'and his silver flask.' The silver was badly dented, but the cairngorm stopper gleamed yellow and gold as he turned it in his hands, and the contents gurgled softly. He set it aside and one by one drew the other items from the bag: Andrew's medal ribbons, the amber cigarette-holder, a spring-loaded sovereign case that still contained three coins, his pigskin wallet. The photograph of Andrew's parents standing in the grounds of the castle fell from the wallet as he turned it over.

'What's this?' The adjutant picked out a buff-coloured envelope of thick glossy paper sealed with a wax wafer. 'It's addressed – ' he read the face of the envelope ' – to the pilot of the yellow SE5a.' The adjutant looked up at Michael, startled.

'That's you, Michael – how the hell?'

Michael took the envelope from him and split the seal with his thumbnail.

There was a single sheet of the same first-quality paper. The letter was handwritten, and though the writing was obviously continental, for the capitals were formed in Gothic script, the text was in perfect English:

Sir,
    Your friend, Lord Andrew Killigerran, was buried

this morning in the cemetery of the Protestant church at Douai. This Jagdstaffel accorded him full military honours.

I have the honour to inform you, and at the same time also to warn you that no death in war is murder. The object of warfare is the destruction of the enemy by all means possible.

I look forward to meeting you.

OTTO VON GREIM.

Jasta II   Near Douai.

They were all looking expectantly at Michael as he folded the letter and thrust it into his pocket.

'They recovered Andrew's body,' he said quietly, 'and he was buried with full military honours at Douai this morning.'

'Bloody decent of them,' one of the pilots murmured.

'Yes, for Huns, that is,' said Michael, and turned towards the door.

'Michael,' the adjutant stopped him, 'I think Andrew would have wanted you to have this.'

He handed the silver hip flask to Michael. Michael turned it slowly in his hands. The dent in the metal had probably been caused by the impact, he thought, and he shivered.

'Yes,' he nodded. 'I'll look after it for him.' He turned back to the door and pushed his way through the group of silent officers.

B iggs helped him dress with even more than his usual attention to detail.

'I gave them a good rub of dubbin, sir,' he pointed out as he helped Michael into the soft kudu-skin boots.

Michael appeared not to have heard the remark. Although he had lain down again after the disturbance of the German aircraft's fly-over, he had not managed to sleep. Yet he felt calm, even placid. 'What's that, Biggs?' he asked vaguely.

'I said, I'll have your number ones laid out for you when you come back – and I've arranged with the cook for a good five gallons of hot water for your bath.'

'Thank you, Biggs.'

'Not every day it happens, Mr Michael.'

'That's true, Biggs, once in a lifetime is enough.'

'I'm sure you and the young lady are going to be very happy. Me and my missus been married twenty-two years come June, sir.'

'A long time, Biggs.'

'I hope you break my record, Mr Michael.'

'I'll try.'

'One other thing, sir.' Biggs was embarrassed, he did not look up from the lacings of the boots. 'We shouldn't ought to be flying alone, sir. Not safe at all, sir, we should take Mr Johnson with us at least, beg your pardon, sir – I know it's not my place to say so.'

Michael laid his hand on Biggs' shoulder for a moment. He had never done that before.

'Have that bath ready for me when I get home,' he said as he stood up.

Biggs watched him stoop out through the flap of the tent, without saying goodbye or wishing him luck, though it took an effort to restrain himself from doing so, then he picked up Michael's discarded jacket and folded it with exaggerated care.

When the Wolseley engine fired and caught, Michael advanced the ignition until she settled to a fine deep rumble. Then he listened to it critically for thirty seconds before he looked up at Mac who was standing on the wing beside the cockpit, his hair and overalls fluttering in the wash of the propeller.

'Lovely, Mac!' he shouted above the engine beat, and Mac grinned.

'Give them hell, sir,' and jumped down to pull the chocks from in front of the landing-wheels.

Instinctively Michael drew a deep breath, as though he were about to dive into one of those cool green pools of the Tugela river, and then eased the throttle open and the big machine rolled forward.

The knoll behind the château was deserted once again, but he had not expected anything else. He lifted the nose into the climb attitude and then changed his mind, let it drop again and brought her round in a tight turn, his wingtip almost brushing the tops of the oaks.

He came out of the turn with the château directly ahead, and he flew past it at the height of the pink-tiled roof. He saw no sign of life and as soon as he was past, he banked the SE5a into a figure-of-eight turn and came around again, still at roof level.

This time he saw movement. One of the windows at ground level, near the kitchens, was thrown open. Someone was waving a yellow cloth from it, but he could not make out who it was.

He came around again and this time dropped down until his landing-wheels almost touched the stone wall that enclosed Anna's vegetable garden. He saw Centaine in the window. He could not mistake that dark bush of hair and the huge eyes. She was leaning far out over the sill, shouting something and waving the yellow scarf that she had worn the day they flew together to meet Sean Courtney.

As Michael lifted the nose and opened the throttle to climb away, he felt rejuvenated. The placid and passive mood that had held him evaporated and he felt charged and vital again. He had seen her, and now it would be all right.

'It was Michel,' Centaine cried happily as she turned back from the window to where Anna sat on the bed, 'I saw him, Anna, it was surely him. Oh, he is so handsome – he came to find me, despite Papa!'

Anna's face crumpled and reddened with disapproval. 'It is bad luck for a groom to see his bride on the wedding day.'

'Oh nonsense, Anna, sometimes you talk such rubbish. Oh, Anna, he is so beautiful!'

'And you will not be if we do not finish before this evening.'

Centaine fluffed out her skirts and settled on to the bed beside Anna. She took the antique ivory-coloured lace of the wedding dress into her lap, and then held the needle up to the light and squinted as she threaded it.

'I have decided,' she told Anna as she recommenced work on the hem of the dress, 'I will have only sons, at least six sons, but no daughters. Being a girl is such a bore, I don't wish to inflict it on any of my children.'

She completed a dozen stitches and then stopped. 'I'm so happy, Anna, and so excited. Do you think the general will come? When do you think this silly war will end, so that Michel and I can go to Africa?'

Listening to her chatter Anna turned her head slightly to hide her doting smile.

The yellow SE5a bored up powerfully into the soft grey belly of the sky. Michael chose one of the gaps in the lower layer of cloud, roared swiftly through it and burst out into the open corridor. High above there was still the same high roof of solid cloud, but below it the air was limpid as crystal. When his altimeter registered 8,000 feet, Michael levelled out. He was in the clear, equidistant from the layers of cloud above and below him, but through the gaps he could pick up his landmarks.

The villages of Cantin and Aubigny-au-Bac were deserted, shell-shattered skeletons. Only a few stone chimney-pieces had survived the waves of war which had washed back and forth over them. These stuck up like funeral monuments from the muddy torn earth.

The two villages were four miles apart, the road that once joined them had been obliterated, and the front lines twisted like a pair of maimed adders through the brown fields between them. The shell holes, filled with stagnant water, blinked up at him like the eyes of the blind.

Michael glanced at his watch. It was four minutes to four o'clock, and his eyes immediately returned to their endless search of the empty sky. One at a time he lifted his hands from the controls and flexed his fingers, at the same time wriggling his toes in the kudu-skin boots – loosening up like a runner before the pistol. He reached up to the firing-handle with both hands, to test the trim of the machine, and she flew on straight and level. He fired both his guns, a short burst from each of them, and he nodded and blew on the gloved fingers of his right hand.

'I need a drink,' he told himself, and took Andrew's silver flask from his pocket. He took a mouthful and gargled it softly, and then swallowed. The fire of it bloomed in his bloodstream, but he resisted the temptation to drink again. He stoppered the flask and dropped it back into his pocket. He touched the left rudder to begin his turn into the square patrol pattern and at that moment he picked up the fleablack speck on the grey mattress of the clouds far ahead and he met the turn, holding her steady while he blinked his eyes rapidly and checked his sighting.

The other machine was at 8,000 feet, exactly his own height, and it was closing swiftly, coming in from the north, from the direction of Douai, and he felt the spurt of adrenalin mingle with the alcohol in his blood. His cheeks burned and his guts spasmed. He eased the throttle open and flew on to meet it.

The combined speeds of the two aircraft hurled them together, so that the other machine swelled miraculously in front of Michael's eyes. He saw the bright blue of the nose and propeller-boss hazed by the spinning blades, and the wide black hawk's wings outstretched. He saw the helmeted top of the pilot's head between the two black Spandau machine-guns mounted on the engine cowling, and the flash of his goggles as he leaned forward to peer into his sights.

Michael pushed the throttle fully open and the engine bellowed. His left hand held the joystick like an artist holding his brush with the lightest pressure of his fingertips, as he positioned the German exactly in the centre of the concentric rings of his own gun-sight, and his right hand reached up for the firing-handle.

His hatred and his anger grew as swiftly as the image of his enemy, and he held his fire. The battle clock in his head started to run so that the passage of time slowed. He saw the muzzles of the Spandau machine-guns begin to wink at him, bright sparks of fire, flickering red as the planet Mars on a moonless night. He aimed for the head of the other pilot, and he pressed down on the trigger and felt the aircraft pulse about him as his guns shook and rattled.

No thought of breaking out of that head-on charge even occurred to Michael. He was completely absorbed by his aim, trying to stream his bullets into the German's face, to rip out his eyes, and blow his brains out of the casket of his skull. He felt the Spandau bullets plucking and tugging at the fabric and frame of his machine, heard them passing his head with sharp flitting sounds like wild locusts, and he ignored them.

He saw his own bullets kicking white splinters off the German's spinning propeller, and in anger knew that they were being deflected from his true aim. The two aircraft were almost in collision, and Michael braced himself for the impact without lifting his hand from the firing-handle, without attempting to turn.

Then the Albatros winged up violently, at the very last instant avoiding the collision, flicking out to starboard as the German hurled her over. There was a jarring bang that shook the SE5a. The two wings had just brushed each other as they passed. Michael saw the torn strip of fabric trailing from his own wingtip. He kicked on full rudder, into that flat skidding turn that only the SE5a was capable of, and felt the wings flex at the strain, and then he was around. The Albatros was ahead of him, but still out of effective range.

Michael thrust with all his strength on the throttle handle, but it was already wide open, the engine straining at full power and still the Albatros was holding him off.

The German turned and went up left, and Michael followed him. They climbed more steeply, going up almost into the vertical, and the speed of both machines began to bleed off, but the SE5a more rapidly so that the German was pulling ahead.

'It's not the same Albatros.' Michael realized with a shock that the relocation of the radiator was not the only modification. He was fighting a new type of aircraft, an advanced type, faster and more powerful than even his own SE5a.

He saw the wide sweep of those black and white chequered wings, and the head of the German pilot craning to watch him in his mirror, and he tried to bring his guns to bear, swinging his right sight in a short arc as he wrenched his nose across.

The German flipped his Albatros into a stall-turn and came straight back at Michael, head-on again with the Spandaus flicking their little red eyes at him, and this time Michael was forced to break, for the German had height and speed.

For a crucial moment, Michael was hanging in his turn, his speed had dwindled and the German rounded on him, and dropped on to his tail. The German was good, Michael's guts tightened as he realized it. He pushed his nose down for speed, and at the same time flung the SE5a into a vertical turn. The Albatros followed him round, turning with him, so that they were revolving around each other like two planets caught in immutable orbits.

He looked across at the other pilot, lifting his chin to do so, for each of them was standing on one wingtip. The German stared back at him, the goggles making him appear monstrous and inhuman, and then for an instant Michael looked beyond the bright blue fuselage, up towards the high cloud ceiling, his hunter's eyes drawn by a tiny insect speckle of movement.

For an instant his heart ceased to pump and his blood seemed to thicken and slow in his veins – then with a leap like a startled animal, his heart raced away and his breathing hissed in his throat.

'I have the honour to inform you, and at the same time also to warn you,' the German had written, 'the object of warfare is the destruction of the enemy by all means possible.'

Michael had read the warning, but only now did he understand. They had turned his woolly-headed romantic notion of a single duel into a death-trap. Like a child, he had placed himself in their power. He had given them time and place, even the altitude. They had used the blue machine merely as a decoy. His own naivety amazed him

151

now, as he saw them come swarming down out of the high cloud.

'How many of them?' There was no time to count them, but it looked like a full Jasta of the new-type Albatroses, twenty of them at least, in that swift and silent flock, their brilliant colours sparkling jewel-like against the sombre backdrop of cloud.

'I'm not going to be able to keep my promise to Centaine,' he thought, and looked down. The low cloud was 2,000 feet below him, it was a remote haven, but there was no other. He could not hope to fight twenty of Germany's most skilled aces, he would not last for more than a few seconds when they reached him, and they were coming fast, while the blue machine pinned and held him for the killing stroke.

Suddenly, faced with the death which he had deliberately sought, Michael wanted to live. He had been dragging back on the joystick with all his weight, holding the SE5a into its turn. He flicked the stick forward and she was flung outwards, like a stone from a slingshot.

Michael was hurled up against his shoulder straps as the forces of gravity were inverted, but he collected the big machine and used its own impetus to push it into a steep dive, going down with a gut-swooping rush towards the low cloud bank. The manoeuvre caught his opponent off-balance, but he recovered instantly and the Albatros was after him in a blue flash of speed, while the swarming multicoloured pack was overhauling them both from above.

Michael watched them in the mirror above his head, realizing how much quicker this new type of Albatros was in the dive. He glanced ahead to the clouds. Their grey folds which had seemed so clammy and uninviting a few seconds before were his only hope of life and salvation, and now that he had started to flee his terror came back and settled upon him like a dark and terrible succubus, draining him of his courage and manhood.

He wasn't going to make it, they would catch him before he reached cover, and he clung to the joystick, frozen with his new and crippling terror.

The clatter of twin Spandaus roused him. In the mirror he saw the dancing red muzzle flashes, so close behind him, and something hit him a numbing blow low down in his back. The force of it drove the air from his lungs, and he knew he must turn out of the killing line of the blue Albatros's guns.

He hit the rudder bar with all his force, attempting the flat skidding turn that would bring him face to face with his tormentors, but his speed was too great, the angle of dive too steep – the SE5a would not respond. She lurched and yawed into a turn that brought him broadside on to the pursuing pack, and although the blue Albatros overshot, the others fell upon him one after the other, each successive attack a split second after the last. The sky was filled with flashing wings and bright-coloured fuselages. The crash of shot into his aircraft was continuous and unbearable; the SE5a dropped a wing and went into a spin.

Sky and cloud and patches of earth, interspersed with bright-coloured Albatroses with flickering, chattering guns, spun through Michael's field of vision in dizzying array. He felt another blow, this time in his leg, just below the fork of his crotch. He looked down and saw that a burst had come up through the floor, and a bullet, misshapen and deformed, had ripped through his thigh. Blood pumped from it in bright arterial jets. He had seen a Zulu gunbearer, savaged by a wounded buffalo, bleed this way from a ruptured femoral artery; he had died in three minutes.

Streams of machine-gun fire were still coming in at him from every angle, and he could not defend himself for his aircraft was out of control, flicking through the turns of the spin, throwing her nose up viciously, and then dropping it again in that savage rhythm.

Michael fought her, thrusting on opposite rudder to try to break the pattern of her rotation, and at the exertion the blood pumped more strongly from his torn thigh and he felt the first giddy weakness in his head. He dropped one hand from the joystick and thrust his thumb into his groin, seeking the pressure point, and the great pulsing red spurts shrivelled as he found it.

Again he coaxed the maimed aircraft, stick forward to stop that high-nose attitude, and a burst of throttle to power her out of the spin. She responded reluctantly, and he tried not to think about the machine-gun fire that tore at him from every side.

The clouds and earth stopped revolving about him, as her tight turns slowed and she dropped straight. Then with one hand only he pulled her nose up and felt the overstressing of her wings and the suck of gravity in his belly, but at last the world tilted before his eyes as she came back on to an even keel.

He glanced in the mirror and saw that the blue Albatros had found him again and was pressing in close on his tailplane for the *coup de grâce*.

Before that dreadful rattling chatter of the Spandau could begin again, Michael felt the cold damp rush across his face as grey streamers of cloud blew over the open cockpit, and then the light was blotted out and he was into a dim, blind world, a quiet, muted world where the Spandaus could no longer desecrate the silences of the sky. They could not find him in the clouds.

Automatically his eyes fastened on the tiny glycerine-filled glass tubes set on the dashboard in front of him, and with small controlled adjustments he aligned the bubbles in the tubes within their markers so that the SE5a was flying straight and level through the cloud. The he turned her gently on to a compass heading for Mort Homme.

He wanted to be sick – that was his first reaction from terror and the stress of combat. He swallowed and panted to control it, and then he felt the weakness come at him again. It was as though a bat was trapped in his skull. The dark soft wings beat behind his eyes and his vision faded in patches.

He blinked away the darkness and looked down. His thumb was still thrust into his own groin, but he had never seen so much blood. His hand was coated, his fingers sticky with it. The sleeve of his jacket was soaked to the elbow. Blood had turned his breeches into a sodden mass and it had run down into his boots. There were pools of blood on the floor of the cockpit, already congealing into lumps like blackcurrant jam, and snakes of it slithering back and forth with each movement of the machine.

He let go of the stick for a moment, leaned forward against his shoulder straps and groped behind his back. He found the other bullet wound, three inches to the side of his spine and just above the girdle of his pelvis. There was no exit wound. It was still in there and he was bleeding internally, he was certain of it. There was a swollen, stretched feeling in his belly as his stomach cavity filled with blood.

The machine dropped a wing, and he snatched for the joystick to level her, but it took him many seconds to make the simple adjustment. His fingers prickled with pins and needles, and he felt very cold. His reactions were slowing down, so that each movement, no matter how small, was becoming an effort.

However, there was no pain, just a numbness that spread down from the small of his back to his knees. He removed his thumb to test the wound in his thigh, and immediately there was a full spray of bright blood from it like a flamingo's feather, and hastily he stopped it again and concentrated on his flying instruments.

How long to reach Mort Homme? He tried to work it out, but his brain was slow and muzzy. Nine minutes from Cantin, he reckoned, how long had he been flying? He did

155

not know, and he rolled his wrist so that he could see his watch. He found he had to count the divisions on the dial like a child.

'Don't want to come out of the cloud too soon, they'll be waiting for me,' he thought heavily, and the dial of his wristwatch multiplied before his eyes.

'Double vision,' he realized.

Quickly he looked ahead, and the silver clouds billowed around him, and he had the sensation of falling. He almost lurched at the stick to counteract it, but his training restrained him and he checked the bubbles in his artificial horizon – they were still aligned. His senses were tricking him.

'Centaine,' he said suddenly, 'what time is it? I'm going to be late for the wedding.' He felt panic surface through the swamp of his weakness, and the wings of darkness beat more frantically behind his eyes.

'I promised her. I swore an oath!' He checked his watch.

'Six minutes past four – that's impossible,' he thought wildly. 'Bloody watch is wrong.' He was losing track of reality.

The SE5a burst out of the cloud into one of the holes in the layer.

Michael flung up his hand to protect his eyes from the brilliance of the light, and then looked around him.

He was on the correct heading for the airfield, he recognized the road and railway line and the star-shaped field between them. 'Another six minutes' flying,' he calculated. The sight of the earth had orientated him again. He took a grip on the real world and looked upwards. He saw them there, circling like vultures above the lion kill, waiting for him to emerge from the cloud. They had spotted him, he saw them turn towards him on their rainbow-coloured wings – but he plunged into the cloud on the far side of the opening, and the cold wet billows enfolded him, hid him from their cruel eyes.

'I've got to keep my promise,' he mumbled. The loss of contact with the earth confused him. He felt the waves of vertigo wash over him again. He let the SE5a sink slowly down through the layer of cloud, and once again came out into the light. There was all the familiar countryside below him, the ridges and the battle lines far behind him, the woods and the village and the church spire ahead, so peaceful and idyllic.

'Centaine, I'm coming home,' he thought, and a terrible weariness fell over him, its great weight seemed to smother him and crush him down in the cockpit.

He rolled his head and he saw the château. Its pink roof was a beacon, drawing him irresistibly, the nose of his aircraft turned towards it seemingly without his bidding.

'Centaine,' he whispered. 'I'm coming – wait for me, I'm coming.' And the darkness drew in upon him, so that it seemed that he was receding into a long tunnel.

There was a roaring in his ears, like the sound of surf heard in a seashell, and he concentrated with all his remaining strength, staring down the ever-narrowing tunnel through the darkness, looking for her face, and listening over the sea sounds in his ears for her voice.

'Centaine, where are you? Oh God, where are you, my love?'

Centaine stood before the heavy mirror in its walnut and gilt frame, and she looked at her reflection with dark and serious eyes.

'Tomorrow I will be Madame Michel Courtney,' she said solemnly, 'never again Centaine de Thiry. Isn't that a formidable thought, Anna?' She touched her own temples. 'Do you think I will feel different? Surely such a momentous event must alter me – I can never be the same person after that!'

'Wake up, child,' Anna prodded her. 'There is still so much to do. This is no time for dreaming.' She lifted the bulky skirt and dropped it over Centaine's head, then, standing behind her, she fastened the waistband.

'I wonder if Mama is watching, Anna. I wonder if she knows I am wearing her dress, and if she is happy for me?'

Anna grunted as she went down on her knees to check the hem. Centaine smoothed the delicate old lace over her hips and listened to the muffled sound of men's laughter from the *grand salon* on the floor below.

'I am so happy that the general could come. Isn't he a handsome man, Anna, just like Michel? Those eyes – did you notice them?'

Again Anna grunted, but with more emphasis; for a moment her hands faltered as she thought about the general.

'Now, that is a real man,' she had told herself, as she watched Sean Courtney step down from the Rolls and come up the front staircase of the château.

'He looks so grand in his uniform and medals,' Centaine went on. 'When Michel is older, I will insist that he grows a beard like that. So much presence—'

There was another burst of laughter from below. 'He and Papa like each other, don't you think, Anna? Listen to them!'

'I hope they leave some cognac for the other guests,' Anna grumped, and hoisted herself to her feet, then paused with one hand on the small of her back as a thought struck her.

'We should have laid out the blue Dresden service rather than the Sèvres. It would have looked better with the pink roses.'

'You should have thought of that yesterday,' Centaine cut in quickly. 'I'm not going to go over all that again.'

The two of them had worked all the previous day and most of the night to reopen the *grand salon* which had been closed ever since the servants left. The draperies had been floury with dust, and the high ceilings so laced with cobwebs that the scenes from mythology that decorated them were almost obscured.

They had finished the cleaning red-eyed and sneezing before beginning on the silver, which had been all tarnished and spotted. Then each piece of the red and gold Sèvres dinner service had to be washed and hand-dried. The comte, protesting volubly – 'A veteran of Sedan and the army of the Third Empire forced to labour like a common varlet' – had been dragooned in to assist.

Finally it had all been done. The *salon* once again splendid, the floor of intricately fitted and patterned wooden blocks glossy with wax, the nymphs and goddesses and fauns dancing and cavorting and chasing each other across the domed ceiling, the silver aglitter and the first of Anna's cherished roses from the greenhouse glowing like great gems in the candlelight.

'We should have made a few more pies,' Anna worried. 'Those soldiers have appetites like horses.'

'They are not soldiers, they are airmen,' Centaine corrected her, 'and we have enough to feed the entire Allied army, not merely a single squadron—' Centaine broke off. 'Listen, Anna!'

Anna waddled to the window and looked out. 'It is them!' she declared. 'So early!' The drab brown truck came puttering up the long gravel drive, looking prim and old-maidish on its high narrow wheels, the back crowded with all the off-duty officers from the squadron, the adjutant at the wheel with his pipe clamped in his jaws and a fixed and terrified expression on his face as he steered the vehicle on an uneven course from one verge of the wide driveway to the other, loudly encouraged by his passengers.

'Have you locked the pantry?' Anna demanded anxiously. 'If that tribe find the food before we are ready to serve—'

Anna had enlisted her cronies from the village, those who had not fled the war, and the pantry was an Aladdin's cave of cold pies and pâtés and the wonderful local terrines, of hams and apple tarts, of pigs' trotters with truffles in aspic, and a dozen other delights.

'It's not the food they have come for so early in the day.' Centaine joined her at the window. 'Papa has the keys to the cellar. They will be well taken care of.'

Her father was already halfway down the marble staircase to greet them, and the adjutant braked with such abruptness that two of his pilots landed in the front seat with him in a tangle of legs and arms.

'I say,' he cried in obvious relief at being once again at a standstill, 'you must be the jolly old count, what? We are the advance guard, how do you say it in French, *le d'avant garde*, don't you know?'

'Ah, to be sure!' The comte seized his hand. 'Our brave allies. You are welcome! Welcome! May I offer you a small glass of something?'

'You see, Anna,' Centaine smiled as she turned back from the window, 'there is no need to worry. They understand each other. Your food will be safe from them, for a while at least.'

She picked up the wedding veil from the bed and arranged it loosely over her head, and studied herself in the mirror.

'This must be the happiest day of my life,' she whispered. 'Nothing must happen to spoil it.'

'Nothing will, my child,' Anna came up behind her and arranged the filmy lace of the veil upon her shoulders. 'You will be the loveliest bride, what a pity that none of the gentry will be here to see you.'

'Enough, Anna,' Centaine told her gently. 'No regrets. Everything is perfect. I would not have it any other way.'

She cocked her head slightly. 'Anna!' Her expression became animated.

160

'What is it?'

'Do you hear?' Centaine spun away from the mirror. 'It's him. It's Michel. He is coming back to me.'

She ran to the window, and unable to contain herself, she hopped up and down, dancing like a little girl at the window of a toy shop.

'Listen! He is coming this way!' She could recognize the distinctive beat of the engine that she had so often listened for.

'I don't see him.' Anna was behind her, screwing up her eyes, looking upwards in the ragged clouds.

'He must be very low,' Centaine began. 'Yes! Yes! There he is, just above the forest.'

'I see him. Is he going to the airfield in the orchard?'

'No, not with this wind. I think he's coming this way.'

'Is it him? Are you sure?'

'Of course I'm sure – can't you see the colour? *Mon petit jaune!*'

Others had heard it also. There were voices below the window, and a dozen of the wedding guests trooped out through the french doors of the *salon* on to the terrace. They were led by Sean Courtney in the full dress uniform of a British general, and the comte even more resplendent in the blue and gold of a colonel of the infantry of Napoleon III. They all carried their glasses and their voices were raised in mounting spirits and cheerful camaraderie.

'That's Michael all right,' someone called. 'I'll bet he's going to give us a low-level beat-up. Take the roof off the château, you'll see!'

'It should be a victory roll, considering what he's got in store.'

Centaine found herself laughing with them, and she clapped her hands as she watched the yellow machine approaching – then her hands froze an instant before they came together.

'Anna,' she said, 'there is something wrong.'

The aircraft was close enough now for them to see how irregularly it was flying – one wing dropped and the machine yawed and dipped towards the tree-tops, then pulled up sharply, and its wings wobbled, and then it dropped on the opposite side.

'What's he up to?' The timbre of the voices from the terrace changed.

'By God, he's in trouble – I think—'

The SE5a began a meandering, purposeless turn to starboard, and they could see the side of the damaged fuselage and the torn wing surfaces as it banked. It looked like the carcass of a fish that had been attacked by a pack of sharks.

'He's been badly shot up!' one of the pilots yelled.

'Yes, he's hard hit.'

The SE5a turned back too steeply, the nose dropped and almost hit the trees.

'He's going to try for a forced landing!' Some of the pilots jumped over the wall of the terrace and ran out on to the lawns, frantically signalling to the crippled aircraft.

'This way, Michael!'

'Keep the nose up, man!'

'Too slow!' screamed anther. 'You'll stall her in! Open the throttle. Give her the gun!'

They shouted their futile advice, and the aircraft settled heavily towards the open lawns.

'Michel,' Centaine breathed, twisting the lace between her fingers and not even feeling it tear, 'come to me, Michel.'

There was one last row of trees, ancient copper beech, with the new leaf buds on their gnarled branches just beginning to pop open. They guarded the bottom of the lawns furthest from the château.

The yellow SE5a dropped behind them, the beat of her engine faltering.

'Get her up, Michael!'

'Pull her up! Damn it!'

They were shouting to him, and Centaine added her own entreaty.

'Please, Michel, fly over the trees. Come to me, my darling.'

The Viper engine roared again at full power, and they saw the machine rocket up like a great yellow pheasant rising from cover.

'He's going to make it.'

The nose was too high, they all saw it, she seemed to hover above the stark, leafless branches, and they reached up like the claws of a monster – then the yellow nose dropped.

'He's over!' one of the pilots exulted, but one of the landing-wheels caught on a heavy curved branch, and the SE5a somersaulted in mid-air, then fell out of the sky.

It hit the soft earth at the edge of the lawn, landing on its nose, the spinning propeller exploding in a blur of white splinters, and then with the wooden frames of the fuselage crackling, the entire machine collapsed, crushed like a butterfly, its bright yellow wings folding around the crumpled body – and Centaine saw Michael.

He was daubed with his own blood, it had streaked his face, his head was thrown back, and he was hanging halfway out of the open cockpit, dangling in his straps like a man on the gallows.

Michael's brother officers were streaming down the lawn. She saw the general throw his glass aside and hurl himself over the terrace wall. He ran with a desperate, uneven gait, the limp throwing him off balance, but he was gaining on the younger men.

The first of them had almost reached the wrecked aircraft when the flames engulfed it with miraculous suddenness. They shot upwards with a drumming, roaring sound, very pale-coloured but plumed with black smoke at their crests – and the running men stopped and hesitated

163

and then drew back, holding up their hands to protect their faces from the heat.

Sean Courtney charged through them, going straight into the flames, oblivious of the searing, dancing waves of heat, but four of the young officers leaped forward and seized his arms and his shoulders, and pulled him back.

Sean was struggling in their grip, so wildly that three others had to run up and help to restrain him. Sean was roaring, a deep, throaty, incoherent sound, like a bull buffalo in a trap, trying to reach out through the flames to the man trapped in the crumpled body of the yellow aircraft.

Then quite suddenly the sound ceased and he sagged. If the men had not been holding him, he would have fallen to his knees. His hands dropped to his sides, but he went on staring into the wall of flame.

Years before, on a visit to England, Centaine had watched with horrid fascination as the children of her host had burnt the effigy of an English assassin called Guy Fawkes on a pyre that they had built themselves in the garden. The effigy had been cleverly fashioned, and as the flames rose up over it, it had blackened and begun to twist and writhe in a most lifelike fashion. Centaine had woken in the sweat of nightmare for weeks afterwards. Now, as she watched from the upper window of the château, she heard somebody near her begin to scream. She thought that it might be Anna. They were cries of the utmost anguish, and she found herself shaking to them the way a sapling shakes to the high wind.

It was the same nightmare as before. She could not look away as the effigy turned black and began to shrivel, its limbs spasming and jack-knifing slowly in the heat, and the screams filled her head and deafened her. Only then did she realize that it was not Anna, but that the screams were her own. As these gusts of agonized sound came up from the depths of her chest, they seemed to be of some abrasive substance, like particles of crushed glass, that ripped at the lining of her throat.

She felt Anna's strong arms around her lifting her off her feet, carrying her away from the window. She fought with all her strength, but Anna was too powerful for her. She laid Centaine on the bed and held her face to her vast soft bosom, stifling those wild screams. When at last she was quiet, she stroked her hair and began to rock her gently, humming to her as she used to do when Centaine was an infant.

They buried Michael Courtney in the churchyard of Mort Homme, in the section reserved for the de Thiry family.

They buried him that night by lantern light. His brother officers dug his grave, and the padre who should have married them said the office for the burial of the dead over him.

'I am the resurrection and the life, saith the Lord—'

Centaine was on the arm of her father, with black lace covering her face. Anna took her other arm, holding her protectively.

Centaine did not weep. After those screams had silenced, there had been no tears. It was as though her soul had been scorched by the flames into a Saharan dryness.

'O remember not the sins and offences of my youth—'

The words were remote, as though spoken from the far side of a barrier.

'Michel had no sin,' she thought. 'He was without offence, but, yes, he was too young – oh Lord, too young. Why did he have to die?'

Sean Courtney stood opposite her across the hastily prepared grave, and a pace behind him was his Zulu driver and servant, Sangane. Centaine had never seen a black man weep before. His tears shone on his velvety skin like drops of dew running down the petals of a dark flower.

'Man that is born of a woman hath but a short time to live, and is full of misery—'

Centaine looked down into the deep muddy trench, at the pathetic box of raw deal, so swiftly knocked together in the squadron workshop, and she thought, 'That is not Michel. This is not real. It is still some awful nightmare. Soon I will wake and Michel will come flying back – and I will be waiting with Nuage on the hilltop to welcome him.'

A harsh, unpleasant sound roused her. The general had stepped forward, and one of the junior officers had handed him a spade. The clods rattled and thumped on the lid of the coffin and Centaine looked upwards, not wanting to watch.

'Not down there, Michel,' she whispered behind the dark veil. 'You don't belong down there. For me, you will always be a creature of the sky. For me, you will be always up there in the blue—' And then, 'Au revoir, Michel, till we meet again, my darling. Each time I look to the sky I will think of you.'

C entaine sat by the window. When she placed the lace wedding veil over her shoulders Anna started to object, and then stopped herself.

Anna sat on the bed near her, and neither of them spoke.

They could hear the men in the *salon* below. Someone had been playing the piano a short while before, playing it very badly, but Centaine had been able to recognize Chopin's Funeral March, and the others had been humming along and beating time to it.

Centaine had instinctively understood what was happening, that it was their special farewell to one of their own, but she had remained untouched by it. Then later she had heard their voices take on that rough raw quality. They were becoming very drunk, and she knew that this too was part of the ritual. Then there was laughter – drunken laughter but with a sorrowful underlying timbre to it – and then more singing, raucous and untuneful, and she had felt nothing. She had sat dry-eyed in the candlelight and watched the shell-fire flickering on the horizon and listened to the singing and the sounds of war.

'You must go to bed, child,' Anna had said once, gentle as a mother, but Centaine had shaken her head and Anna had not insisted. Instead, she had trimmed the wick, spread a quilt over Centaine's knees and gone down to fetch a plate of ham and cold pie and a glass of wine from the *salon*. The food and wine lay untouched on the table at Centaine's elbow now.

'You must eat, child,' Anna whispered, reluctant to intrude – and Centaine turned her head slowly to her.

'No, Anna,' she said. 'I am not a child any longer. That part of me died today – with Michel. You should never call me that again.'

'I promise you I will not,' and Centaine turned slowly back to the window.

The village clock struck two and a little later they heard the officers of the squadron leaving. Some of them were so drunk that they had to be carried by their companions and thrown into the back of the truck like sacks of corn, and then the truck puttered away into the night.

There was a soft tap on the door, and Anna rose from the bed and went to open it.

'Is she awake?'

'Yes,' Anna whispered back.

'May I speak to her?'

'Enter.'

Sean Courtney came in and stood near Centaine's chair. She could smell the whisky, but he was steady as a granite boulder on his feet and his voice was low and controlled: despite that, she sensed there was a wall within him, holding back his grief.

'I have to leave now, my dear,' he said in Afrikaans, and she rose from the chair, letting the quilt slip off her knees, and with the wedding veil over her shoulders went to stand before him, looking up into his eyes.

'You were his father,' she said, and his control shattered. He reeled and put his hand on the table for support, staring at her.

'How did you know that?' he whispered, and now she saw his grief come to the surface, and at last she allowed her own to rise and mingle with his. The tears started, and her shoulders shook silently. He opened his arms to her, and she went into them and he held her to his chest. Neither of them spoke again for a long time, until her sobs muted and at last ceased. Then Sean said, 'I will always think of you as Michael's wife, as my own daughter. If you need me, no matter where or when, you have only to send for me.'

She nodded rapidly, blinking her eyes, and then stepped back as he opened his embrace.

'You are brave and strong,' he said. 'I recognized that when first we met. You will endure.'

He turned and limped from the room, and minutes later she heard the crunch of wheels on the gravel of the drive as the Rolls with the big Zulu at the wheel pulled away.

A t sunrise Centaine was on the knoll behind the château, mounted on Nuage, and as the squadron took off on dawn patrol, she rose high in the saddle and waved them away.

The little American whom Michael had called Hank was flying in the lead, and he waggled his wings and waved to her, and she laughed and waved back, and the tears ran down her cheeks while she laughed and they felt like icicles on her skin in the cold morning wind.

She and Anna worked all morning to close the *salon* again, cover the furniture with dust sheets, and pack away the service and the silver. The three of them ate lunch in the kitchen, terrines and ham left over from the previous evening. Though Centaine was pale and her eyes were underscored with blue as dark as bruises, and though she barely tasted the food or sipped her wine, she spoke normally, discussing the chores and tasks that must be done that afternoon. The comte and Anna watched her anxiously but surreptitiously, uncertain how to take her unnatural calm, and at the end of the meal the comte could contain himself no longer.

'Are you all right, my little one?'

'The general said that I would endure,' she answered. 'I want to prove him to be right.' She stood up from the table. 'I will be back within the hour to help you, Anna.'

She took the armful of roses that they had salvaged from the *salon*, and went out to the stables. She rode Nuage down to the end of the lane, and the long columns of khaki-clad men, bowed under their weapons and packs, called to her as she passed, and she smiled and waved at them, and they looked back after her wistfully.

She hitched Nuage to the churchyard gate, and with her arms full of flowers, went around the side of the moss-covered stone church. A dark green yew tree spread its branches over the de Thiry plot, but the newly turned earth was trampled and muddy and the grave looked like one of Anna's vegetable beds, only not as neatly dressed and squared.

Centaine fetched a spade from the shed at the far end of the churchyard and set to work. When she had finished, she arranged the roses and stood back. Her skirts were muddy and there was dirt under her fingernails.

'There,' she said with satisfaction. 'That's much better. As soon as I can find a mason I will arrange the headstone, Michel, and I'll come again tomorrow with fresh flowers.'

That afternoon she worked with Anna, hardly looking up from her tasks or pausing for a moment, breaking off just before dusk to ride up to the knoll and watch the planes come back from the north. That evening, there were two more of them missing from the squadron, and the burden of mourning that she carried as she rode home was for them as well as for Michael.

After dinner she went to her bedchamber as soon as she and Anna had washed the dishes. She knew that she was exhausted and she longed for sleep, but instead the grief that she had held at bay all that day came at her out of the darkness and she pulled the bolster over her face to smother it.

Still Anna heard it, for she had been listening for it. She came through in her frilled bed-cap and nightdress, carrying a candle. She blew out the candle and slipped under the bedclothes and took Centaine in her arms, crooning to her and holding her until at last she slept.

At dawn Centaine was on the knoll again, and the days and weeks repeated themselves, so that she felt trapped and hopeless in the routine of despair. There were only small variations from this routine: a dozen new SE5as in the squadron flights, still painted in factory drab, and flown by pilots whose every manoeuvre proclaimed even to Centaine that they were new chums, while the numbers of the brightly painted machines that she knew dwindled at each return. The columns of men and equipment and guns moving up the main road below the château became denser each day, and there was a building current of anxiety and tension that infected even the three of them in the château.

'Any day now,' the comte kept repeating, 'it's going to begin. You see if I'm wrong.'

Then one morning the little American circled back

over where Centaine waited on the hillock and he leaned far out of the open cockpit and let something drop. It was a small package, with a long bright ribbon attached to it as a marker. It fell beyond the crest of the hillock and Centaine urged Nuage down the slope and found the ribbon dangling in the hedgerow at the bottom. She reached up and disentangled it from the thorns, and when Hank circled back again, she held it up to show him that she had retrieved it, and he saluted her and climbed away towards the ridges.

In the privacy of her room Centaine opened the package. It contained a pair of embroidered RFC wings and a medal in its red leather case. She stroked the lustrous silk from which the silver cross was suspended, and then turned it over to find the date and Michael's name and rank engraved upon it. The third item, in a buff envelope, was a photograph. It showed the squadron aircraft drawn up in a wide semi-circle, wingtip to wingtip, in front of the hangars at Bertangles, and in the foreground the pilots stood in a group and grinned self-consciously at the photographer. The mad Scotsman, Andrew, stood beside Michael, barely reaching to his shoulder, while Michael had his cap on the back of his head and his hands in his pockets. He looked so debonair and carefree that Centaine's heart squeezed until she felt she was suffocating.

She placed the photograph in the same silver frame as that of her mother, and kept it beside her bed. The medal and the RFC wings she placed in her jewelbox with her other treasures.

Then every afternoon Centaine spent an hour in the churchyard. She paved the raw grave with red bricks that she had found behind the toolshed.

'Only until we can find a mason, Michel,' she explained to him as she worked on her hands and knees, and she scoured the fields and the forest of wild flowers to bring to him.

171

In the evenings she played the *Aïda* recording and pored over that page of her atlas that depicted the horse-head-shaped continent of Africa, and the vast red expanses of empire that were its predominant coloration, or she read aloud from the English books, Kipling and Bernard Shaw, that she had retrieved from her mother's upstairs bedroom, while the comte listened attentively and corrected her pronunciation. None of them mentioned Michael, but they were all aware of him every minute; he seemed to be part of the atlas and the English books and the jubilant strains of *Aïda*.

When at last Centaine was certain she was utterly exhausted, she would kiss her father and go to her room. However, as soon as she blew out the candle, her grief would overwhelm her once again, and within minutes the door would open softly and Anna would come to take her in her arms, and the whole cycle would begin again.

The comte broke in. He hammered on Centaine's bedroom door, awakening them in those dark and early hours of the morning when all human energy is at its lowest ebb.

'What is it?' Anna called sleepily.

'Come!' the comte shouted back. 'Come and see.'

With gowns hastily thrown over their nightclothes, they followed him through the kitchens and out into the paved yard. There they stopped and stared up at the eastern sky in wonder, for although there was no moon, it glowed with a strange wavering orange light as though somewhere below the horizon Vulcan had thrown open the door to the furnace of the gods.

'Listen!' commanded the comte, and they heard the sussuration upon the light breeze, and it seemed that the earth beneath their feet trembled to the force of that distant conflagration.

'It has begun,' he said, and only then did they realize

that this was the opening barrage of the great new Allied offensive upon the Western Front.

T hey sat up the rest of that night in the kitchen, drinking pots of black coffee, and every little while trooping out again into the yard to watch the fiery display as though it were some astronomical phenomenon.

The comte was exultant as he described to them what was taking place. 'This is the saturation barrage which will flatten the barbed wire and destroy the enemy trenches. The boche will be annihilated,' he pointed to the fiery sky. 'Who could withstand that!'

The thousands of artillery batteries were each firing on a front of a hundred yards, and over the next seven days and nights they never ceased. The sheer weight of metal which they hurled on to the German lines obliterated the trench work and parapets, and ploughed and reploughed the earth.

The comte was aflame with warlike and patriotic ardour. 'You are living in history. You are witness to one of the great battles of the ages—' But for Centaine and Anna, seven days and seven nights was too long a time; the first amazement soon turned to apathy and disinterest. They went about the daily life of the château, no longer heeding the distant bombardment, and at night slept through the pyrotechnics and the comte's summonses to 'Come and watch!'

Then on the seventh morning, while they were at breakfast, even they were aware of the change in the sound and intensity of the guns.

The comte sprang up from the table and ran into the yard again, his mouth still full of bread and cheese, and the coffee bowl in his hand.

'Listen! Do you hear it? The rolling barrage has begun!'

The artillery batteries were rolling their fire forward, creating a moving barrier of high explosive through which no living things could advance or retreat.

'The brave Allies will be ready for the final assault now—'

In the forward British trenches they waited below the parapets. With each man in full battle-dress, his equipment burden was almost sixty pounds in weight.

The thunder of the bursting high-explosives rolled away from them, leaving them with dulled senses and singing eardrums. The whistles of the section leaders shrilled along the trenches, and they roused themselves and crowded to the feet of the assault ladders. Then, like an army of khaki lemmings, they swarmed out of their burrows into the open, and peered around them dazedly.

They were in a transformed and devastated land, so ravaged by the guns that no blade of grass nor twig of tree remained. Only the shattered tree stumps stuck up from the soft faecal-coloured porridge of mud before them. This dreadful landscape was shrouded in the yellowish fog of burned explosives.

'Forward!' the cry passed down the line, and again the whistles trilled and goaded them on.

The long Lee Enfield rifles held out before them, the fixed bayonets aglitter, sinking ankle and knee deep into the soft earth, slipping into the overlapping shell holes and dragging themselves out again, their line bulging and lagging, their horizon limited to a mere hundred paces by swirling nitrous fog, they trudged forward.

Of the enemy trenches they saw no sign, the parapets had been obliterated and flattened. Overhead passed the continuous roar of the barrage, while every few seconds a short shell from their own guns fell into their densely packed lines.

174

'Close up in the centre!' The gaps torn in their ranks by the guns were filled by other amorphous khaki bodies.

'Keep the line! Keep the line!' The orders were almost drowned by the tumult of the guns.

Then in the wilderness ahead of them they saw the glint of metal through the smoke. It was a low wall of metal, interlocking scales of grey steel like those on the back of a crocodile.

The German machine-gunners had had the benefit of seven days' forewarning, and as the British barrage rolled away behind them, they carried their weapons up the shafts from their dugouts to the surface and set them up on their tripods on the churned muddy lip of the ruined trenches. The Maxim machine-guns were each fitted with a steel shield to protect the crews from rifle-fire, and the guns were so closely aligned that the edges of the shields overlapped each other.

The British infantry was out in the open, walking down on a wall of machine-guns. The front ranks yelled when they saw the guns and started forward at a run, trying to reach them with the bayonet. Then they ran into the wire.

They had been assured that the barbed wire would be cut to pieces by the barrages. It was not. The high-explosive had made no impression upon it, except to tangle and twist it into an even more formidable barrier. While they floundered and struggled in the grip of the wire, the German Maxim machine-guns opened up on them.

The Maxim machine-gun has a cyclic rate of fire of 500 rounds per minute. It has the reputation of being the most reliable and rugged machine-gun ever built, and that day it added to that reputation the distinction of becoming the most lethal weapon that man had ever devised. As the plodding ranks of British infantry emerged from the fog of nitro-smoke, still attempting to maintain their rigid formation, shoulder to shoulder and four ranks deep, they made a perfect target for the Maxims. The solid sheets of fire swung back and forth, the scythe-blades of the harvesters, and the carnage surpassed anything seen before upon the battlefields of history.

The losses would certainly have been greater had not the troops, under the extreme duress of the Maxims, used their common sense and broken ranks. Instead of that ponderous, wooden-headed advance, they had tried to creep and crawl forward in small groups, but even these had finally been beaten back by the wall of machine-guns.

Then with another grand offensive on the Western Front decimated almost as it began, the German force holding the ridges opposite Mort Homme counter-attacked jubilantly.

Centaine became gradually aware of the cessation of that distant holocaust, and the strange stillness which followed it.

'What has happened, Papa?'

'The British troops have overrun the German artillery positions,' the comte explained excitedly. 'I have a mind to ride across and view the battlefield. I want to bear witness to this turning-point in history—'

'You will do no such idiotic thing,' Anna told him brusquely.

'You don't understand, woman, even as we stand here talking, our Allies are rolling forward, eating up the German lines—'

'What I understand is that the milch cow has to be fed, and the cellars have to be mucked out.'

'While history passes me by,' the comte capitulated ungraciously, and went muttering down to the cellar.

Then the guns began again, much closer, and the

windows rattled in their frames. The comte shot up the stairs and into the yard.

'What is happening now, Papa?'

'It is the death-throes of the German army,' the comte explained, 'the last thrashings of a dying giant. But do not worry, my little one, the British will soon invest their positions. We have nothing to fear.'

The thunder of the guns rose to a crescendo and was heightened by the din of the British counter-barrages as they sought to destroy the German counter-attack that was massing in the front-line trenches facing the ridges.

'It sounds just like last summer.' Centaine stared with foreboding at the stark outline of the chalk ridges upon the horizon. They were blurring slightly before her eyes, shrouding in the haze of shell-bursts.

'We must do what we can for them,' she told Anna.

'We have to think of ourselves,' Anna protested. 'We still have to go on living and we cannot—'

'Come, Anna, we are wasting time.'

Under Centaine's insistence they cooked up four of the huge copper kettles of soup, turnip and dried peas and potato, flavoured with ham bones. They used up their reserves of flour at a prodigious rate to bake ovenful after ovenful of bread loaves, and then they loaded the small hand-cart and trundled it down the lane to the main road.

Centaine remembered clearly the fighting of the previous summer, but what she witnessed now shocked her afresh.

The highway was choked, filled from hedgerow to hedgerow with the tides of war, flowing in both directions, piling up and intermingling and then separating again.

Down from the ridges came the human detritus of the battle, torn and bloody, mutilated and bleeding, crowded into the slowly moving ambulances, into horse-drawn carts and drays, or limping on improvised crutches, borne on the shoulders of their stronger fellows, or clinging to the sides of the over-crowded ambulances for support as they stumbled through the deep muddy ruts.

In the opposite direction marched the reserves and reinforcements moving up to help hold the ridges against the German assault. They were in long files, already worn down under the weight of equipment they carried, not even glancing at the torn remnants of the battle which they might soon be joining. They trudged forward, watching their feet, and stopped when the way ahead was blocked, standing with bovine patience, only moving forward again when the man ahead of them started.

After the initial shock, Centaine helped Anna push the hand-cart up on to the verge, and then while Anna ladled out the thick soup, she handed the mugs, each with a thick slice of newly baked bread, to the exhausted and injured soliders as they stumbled past.

There was not nearly enough, she could feed only one man in a hundred. Those whom she picked out as being in greatest need gulped down the soup and wolfed the bread.

'Bless yer, missus,' they mumbled, and then staggered on.

'Look at their eyes, Anna,' Centaine whispered as she held up the mugs to be refilled. 'They have already seen beyond the grave.'

'Enough of that fanciful nonsense,' Anna scolded her, 'you will give yourself nightmares again.'

'No nightmare can be worse than this,' Centaine answered quietly. 'Look at that one!'

His eyes had been torn out of his head by shrapnel and the empty sockets bound up with bloody rags. He followed another soldier, both of whose shattered arms were strapped across his chest. The blind man held on to his belt, and almost dragged him down when he tripped on the rough and slippery roadway.

Centaine drew them out of the stream, and she held the mug to the lips of the armless soldier.

'You are a good girl,' he whispered. 'Do you have a cigarette?'

'I'm sorry.' She shook her head and turned to rearrange the bandages over the other man's eyes. She had a glimpse of what lay beneath them, and she gagged and her hands faltered.

'You sound so young and pretty—' The blinded man was about the same age as Michael; he also had thick dark hair, but it was clotted with dried blood.

'Yes, Fred, she's a pretty girl.' His companion helped him to his feet again. 'We'd best be getting on again, miss.'

'What is happening up there?' Centaine asked them.

'All hell is what is happening.'

'Will the line hold?'

'Nobody knows that, miss,' and the two of them were washed away on the slowly moving river of misery.

The soup and bread were soon finished, and they wheeled the cart back to the château to prepare more. Remembering the wounded soldiers' pleas, Centaine raided the cupboard in the gunroom where the comte kept his hoard of tobacco, and when she and Anna returned to their post at the end of the lane, she was able for a short time to give that extra little comfort to some of them.

'There is so little we can do,' she lamented.

'We are doing all we can,' Anna pointed out. 'No sense in grieving for the impossible.'

They laboured on after dark, by the feeble yellow light of the storm lantern, and the stream of suffering never dried up, rather it seemed to grow ever denser, so that the pale ravaged faces in the lantern light blurred before Centaine's exhausted eyes and became indistinguishable one from the other, and the feeble words of cheer which she gave each of them were repetitive and meaningless in her own ears.

179

At last, well after midnight, Anna led her back to the château, and they slept in each other's arms, still in their muddy, bloodstained clothes, and woke in the dawn to boil up fresh kettles of soup and bake more bread.

Standing over the stove, Centaine cocked her head as she heard the distant roar of engines.

'The airplanes!' she cried. 'I forgot them! They will fly without me today – that is bad luck!'

'Today there will be many suffering from bad luck,' Anna grunted as she wrapped a blanket around one of the soup kettles to prevent it cooling too quickly, and then lugged it to the kitchen door.

Halfway down the lane Centaine straightened up from the handle of the cart.

'Look, Anna, over there on the edge of North Field!'

The fields were swarming with men. They had discarded their heavy back-packs and helmets and weapons, and they were labouring in the early summer sun, stripped to the waist or in grubby vests.

'What are they doing, Anna?'

There were thousands of them, working under the direction of their officers. They were armed with pointed shovels, tearing at the yellow earth, piling it up in long lines, sinking into it so swiftly that as they watched, many of them were already knee-deep, then waist-deep behind the rising earth parapets.

'Trenches.' Centaine found the answer to her own question. 'Trenches, Anna, they are digging new trenches.'

'Why, why are they doing that?'

'Because,' Centaine hesitated. She did not want to say it aloud. 'Because they are not going to be able to hold the ridges,' she said softly, and both of them looked up to the high ground where the shellfire sullied the bright morning with its sulphurous yellow mists.

When they reached the end of the lane, they found that

the roadway was clogged with traffic, the opposing streams of vehicles and men hopelessly interlocked, defying the efforts of the military police to disentangle them and get them moving again. One of the ambulances had slid off the road into the muddy ditch, adding to the confusion, and a doctor and the ambulance driver were struggling to unload the stretchers from the back of the stranded vehicle.

'Anna, we must help them.'

Anna was as strong as a man, and Centaine was as determined. Between them they seized the handles of one of the stretchers and dragged it up out of the ditch.

The doctor scrambled out of the mud.

'Well done,' he panted. He was bare-headed, but his tunic sported the serpent and staff insignia of the medical corps at the collar, and the white armbands with the scarlet crosses.

'Ah, Mademoiselle de Thiry!' He recognized Centaine over the wounded man on the stretcher between them. 'I should have known it was you.'

'Doctor, of course—' It was the same officer who had arrived on the motor-cycle with Lord Andrew, and who had helped the comte with the consumption of Napoleon cognac on the day that Michael crashed in North Field.

They set the stretcher down under the hedgerow and the young doctor knelt beside it, working over the still figure under the grey blanket.

'He might make it – if we can get help for him soon.' He jumped up. 'But there are others still in there. We must get them out.'

Between them they unloaded the other stretchers from the back of the ambulance and laid them in a row.

'This one is finished.' With his thumb and forefinger the doctor closed the lids of the staring eyes, and then covered the dead man's face with the flap of the blanket.

'The road is blocked – it's hopeless trying to get through,

181

and we are going to lose these others,' he indicated the row of stretchers, 'unless we can get them under cover, where we can work on them.'

He was looking directly at Centaine, and for a moment she did not understand his enquiring gaze.

'The cottages at Mort Homme are overfilled, and the road is blocked,' he repeated.

'Of course,' Centaine cut in quickly. 'You must bring them up to the château.'

The comte met them on the staircase of the château and when Centaine hastily explained their needs, he joined enthusiastically in transforming the *grand salon* into a hospital ward.

They pushed the furniture against the walls to clear the centre of the floor and then stripped the mattresses from the upstairs bedrooms and bundled them down the stairs. Assisted by the ambulance driver and three medical orderlies the young doctor had recruited, they laid the mattresses out on the fine woollen Aubusson carpet.

In the meantime the military police, under instructions from the doctor, were signalling the ambulances out of the stalled traffic on the main road and directing them up the lane to the château. The doctor rode on the running-board of the leading vehicle, and when he saw Centaine, he jumped down and seized her arm urgently.

'Mademoiselle! Is there another way to reach the field hospital at Mort Homme? I need supplies – chloroform, disinfectant, bandages – and another doctor to help me.'

His French was passable, but Centaine answered him in English.

'I can ride across the fields.'

'You're a champion. I'll give you a note.' He pulled the pad from his top pocket and scribbled a short message. 'Ask

182

for Major Sinclair,' he tore out the sheet of paper and folded it, 'the advance hospital is in the cottages.'

'Yes, I know it. Who are you? Who must I tell them sent me?' With recent practice, the English words came more readily to Centaine's lips.

'Forgive me, Mademoiselle, I haven't had a chance to introduce myself before. My name is Clarke, Captain Robert Clarke, but they call me Bobby.'

Nuage seemed to sense from her the urgency of their mission, and he flew furiously at the jumps and threw clods of mud from his hooves as he raced across the fields and down the rows of vineyards. The streets of the village were jammed with men and vehicles, and the advance hospital in the row of cottages was chaotic.

The officer she had been sent to find was a big man with arms like a bear, and thick greying curls that flopped forward on his forehead as he leaned over the soldier on whom he was operating.

'Where the hell is Bobby?' he demanded, without looking up at Centaine, concentrating on the neat stitches he was pulling into the deep gash across the soldier's back. As he pulled the thread tight and knotted it, the flesh rose in a peak and Centaine's gorge rose with it, but she explained quickly.

'All right, tell Bobby I'll send what I can, but we are running short of dressing ourselves.'

They lifted his patient off the table, and in his place laid a boy with his entrails hanging out of him in an untidy bunch.

'I can't spare anybody to help him either. Off you go, and tell him.'

The soldier writhed and shrieked as the doctor began to stuff his stomach back into him.

'If you give me the supplies, I will carry them back with me.' Centaine stood her ground, and he glanced up at her and gave her the ghost of a smile.

'You don't give up easily,' he grudged. 'All right, speak to him.' He pointed across the crowded room of the cottage with the scalpel in his right hand. 'Tell him I sent you, and good luck, young lady.'

'To you also, doctor.'

'God knows, we all need it,' he agreed, and stooped once more to his work.

Centaine pressed Nuage as hard as before on the ride back and let him in his stall. As she entered the courtyard, she saw that there were three more ambulances parked in the yard; the drivers unloading their cargoes of wounded and dying men. She hurried past them into the house carrying a heavy kitbag over her shoulder, and paused at the door of the *salon* in amazement.

All the mattresses were full, and other wounded men were lying on the bare floor, or propped against the panelled walls. Bobby Clarke had lit every branch of the silver candelabra in the centre of the massive ormolu dinner table and was operating by candlelight.

He looked up and saw Centaine. 'Did you bring the chloroform?' he called across to her.

For a moment she could not reply and she hesitated at the tall double doors, for the *salon* already stank. The cloying odour of blood mingled with the reek of the bodies and clothing of men who had come from the mud of the trenches, mud in which the dead had been buried and had decomposed to the same soupy consistency, men with the acrid sweat of fear and pain still upon them.

'Did you get it?' he repeated impatiently, and she forced herself to go forward.

'They do not have anyone to help you.'

'You'll have to do it. Here, stand on this side of me,' he ordered. 'Now hold this.'

For Centaine it all became a blur of horrors and blood and labour that exhausted her both physically and nervously. There was no time to rest, barely time to snatch a hasty mug of coffee and one of the sandwiches which Anna turned out in the kitchen. Just when she believed that she had seen and experienced so much that nothing else could shock her, then there would be something even more harrowing.

She stood beside Bobby Clarke as he cut down through the muscles of a man's thigh, tying off each blood vessel as he came to it. When he exposed the white bone of the femur and took up the gleaming silver bone-saw, she thought she would faint with the sound it made, like a carpenter sawing a hardwood plank.

'Take it away!' Bobby ordered, and she had to force herself to touch the disembodied limb. She exclaimed and jerked back when it twitched under her fingers.

'Don't waste time,' Bobby snapped, and she took it in her hands; it was still warm and surprisingly weighty.

'Now there is nothing that I will not dare to do,' she realized as she carried it away.

At last she reached the stage of exhaustion when even Bobby realized that she could not stay on her feet.

'Go and lie down somewhere,' he ordered, but instead she went to sit beside a young private on one of the mattresses. She held his hand, and he called her 'mother' and spoke disjointedly of a day at the seaside long ago. At the end she sat helplessly and listened to his breathing change, panting to stay alive, and his grip tightened as he felt the darkness coming on. The skin of his hand turned clammy with sweat and his eyes opened very wide and he called out, 'Oh Mother, save me!' and then relaxed, and she wanted to cry for him, but she did not have the tears. So she closed those staring eyes as she had seen Bobby Clarke do and stood up and went to the next man.

He was a sergeant, a heavily built fellow almost her

father's age, with a broad, pleasant face covered with grey stubble, and a hole in his chest through which each breath puffed in a froth of pink bubbles. She had to put her ear almost to his lips to hear his request, and then she looked round quickly and saw the silver Louis XV soup tureen on the sideboard. She brought it to him and unfastened his breeches and held the tureen for him, and he kept whispering, 'I'm sorry – please forgive me, a young lady like you. It isn't proper.'

So they worked on through the night, and when Centaine went down to find fresh candles to replace those that were guttering in the holders of the candelabra, she had just reached the kitchen floor when she was seized by sudden compelling nausea, and she stumbled to the servants' toilet and knelt over the noisome bucket. She finished, pale and trembling, and went to wash her face at the kitchen tap. Anna was waiting for her.

'You cannot go on like this,' she scolded. 'Just look at you, you are killing yourself—' she almost added 'child', but caught herself. 'You must rest. Have a bowl of soup and sit by me for a while.'

'It never ends, Anna – there are always more of them.'

By now the wounded had overflowed the *salon* and were lying on the landing of the staircase and down the passageways, so that the orderlies bringing out the dead on the canvas stretchers had to step over their recumbent bodies. They laid the dead on the cobbles at the side of the stables, each wrapped in a grey blanket, and the row grew longer every hour.

'Centaine!' Bobby Clarke shouted from the head of the stairs.

'He is familiar, he should call you Mademoiselle,' Anna huffed indignantly, but Centaine leapt up and ran up the stairs, dodging the bodies that sprawled upon them.

'Can you get through to the village again? We need more chloroform and iodine.' Bobby was haggard and unshaven, his eyes red-rimmed and bloodshot, and his bare arms caked with drying blood.

'It's almost light outside,' Centaine nodded.

'Go past the crossroads,' he said. 'Find out if the road is clearing, we have to begin moving some of these.'

Centaine had to turn Nuage back twice from the crowded roads and find a short cut across the fields, so by the time she reached the hospital at Mort Homme, it was almost full daylight.

She saw at once that they were evacuating the hospital. Equipment and patients were being loaded into a mongrel convoy of ambulances and animal-drawn vehicles, and those wounded who could walk were being assembled into groups and led out into the road to begin to trek southwards.

Major Sinclair was bellowing instructions to the ambulance-drivers. 'By God, man, be careful, that chap has a bullet through his lung—' but he looked up at Centaine as she rode up on the big stallion.

'You again! Damn it all, I'd forgotten about you. Where is Bobby Clarke?'

'Still at the château, he sent me to ask—'

'How many wounded has he got there?' the major interrupted.

'I do not know.'

'Dash it all, girl, is it fifty or a hundred, or more?'

'Perhaps fifty or a few more.'

'We have to get them out – the Germans have broken through at Haut Pommier.' He paused and examined her critically, noting the purple weals under her eyes and the almost translucent sheen of her skin. 'At the end of her tether,' he decided, and then saw that she still held her head up and that there was light in her eyes, and he changed his estimate. 'She's made of good stuff,' he thought. 'She can still go on.'

'When will the Germans get here?' Centaine asked.

He shook his head. 'I don't know, soon I think. We are digging in just beyond the village, but we may not even be able to hold them there. We have to get out – you, too, young lady. Tell Bobby Clarke I'll send him as many vehicles as I can. He must get back to Arras. You can ride with the ambulances.'

'Good.' She turned Nuage's head. 'I will wait for them at the crossroads and guide them to the château.'

'Good girl,' he called after her as she galloped out of the yard and swung the stallion into the vineyard on the eastern side of the village.

Beyond the wall of the vineyard she reached the path that led up to her knoll above the forest. Then she gave Nuage his head and they went flying up the slope and came out on the crest. It was her favourite lookout, and she had a fine view northward to the ridges and over the fields and woods surrounding the village. The early sun was shining, the air bright and clean.

Instinctively she looked first to the orchard at the base of the T-shaped forest, picking out the open strip of turf that served as the airstrip for Michael's squadron.

The tents were gone, the edge of the orchard where the brightly painted SE5a's were usually drawn up was now deserted, there was no sign of life; the squadron had moved out during the night, gone like gypsies, and Centaine's spirits lurched and sank. While they had been there it was as though something of Michael also remained, but now they had gone and they had left an empty hole in her existence.

She turned away, and looked to the ridges. At first glance the countryside seemed so peaceful and undisturbed. The early summer weather painted it a lovely green in the early sunlight, and near her in the brambles a lark was calling.

Then she stared harder and saw the tiny specks of many men in the fields, scurrying back from the ridges like

188

insects. They were so distant and insignificant that she had almost overlooked them, but now she realized how many there were, and she tried to work out what they were doing.

Abruptly she saw a tiny greyish-yellow puff of smoke spurt up in the midst of one of the groups of running men, and as it drifted aside, she saw four or five of the antlike figures lying in an untidy tangle, while the others ran on.

Then there were more of those smoke puffs, scattered haphazardly on the green carpet of the fields, and she heard the sound of it on the wind.

'Shellfire!' she whispered, and understood what was going on out there. These were troops that had been driven out of their trenches and earthworks by the German attack, and in the open ground they were being harassed by the artillery batteries which the Germans must have brought up behind their advancing infantry.

Now, when she looked down at the base of the hillock on which she stood, she could make out the line of hastily dug trenches that she and Anna had seen them preparing the previous morning. The trenches ran like a brown serpent along the edge of the oak forest, then under the lee of the stone wall on the top side of North Field, turning slightly to follow the bank of the stream and then losing themselves amongst the vineyards that belonged to the Concourt family.

She could see the helmets of the troops in the trenches, and make out the stubby swollen barrels of the machine-guns protruding over the earthern parapets as they were lifted into position. Some of the running figures began to reach the trench line, and fell out of sight into it.

She started at a crashing explosion close behind her, and when she looked around, she saw the thin grey feathers of smoke drifting from a British artillery battery at the foot of the hill. The guns were so cleverly concealed beneath their camouflage nets that she had not noticed them until they fired.

Then she saw other guns, concealed in forest and orchard, begin firing at the unseen enemy, and the answering German salvoes burst in random fury along the line of freshly dug fortifications. A raised voice roused her from her fearful fascination, and she looked around to see a platoon of infantry men doubling up the path to the crest of the hill. They were led by a subaltern who waved his arms wildly at her.

'Get out of here, you damned fool! Can't you see that you are in the middle of a battle?'

She swung Nuage's head around to the path and urged him into a gallop. She swept past the file of soldiers and when she looked back, they were already frantically digging into the stony earth at the crest of the hill.

Centaine checked her mount as they reached the crossroads. All the vehicles had passed, except those stuck in the ditches and abandoned. However, the roadway was crowded with a rabble of retreating infantry who staggered under their loads, carrying on their backs the dismembered machine-guns and boxes of ammunition, and the other equipment that they had managed to salvage. Amid the squeal of whistles and shouted orders their officers were rallying them and sending them off the roadway to the freshly dug trenches.

Suddenly over Centaine's head passed a mighty rushing sound, like a hurricane wind, and she ducked fearfully. A shell burst a hundred paces from where she sat, and Nuage reared on his hind legs. She caught her balance and gentled him with voice and touch.

Then she saw a lorry come towards the crossroads from the village, and when she stood in her stirrups she could make out the red cross in its white circle painted on the side. She galloped down to meet it, and seven more ambulances followed the first through the bend. She reined in beside the cab of the leading ambulance.

'Have you been sent to the château?'

'What's that, luv?'

The driver could not understand her heavily accented English, and she bounced on her saddle with frustration.

'Captain Clarke?' she tried again, and he understood. 'You seek Captain Clarke?'

'Yes, that's it. Captain Clarke! Where is he?'

'Come!' Centaine raised her voice as another shell burst beyond the stone wall beside them and there was the electric sound of shrapnel passing overhead. 'Come!' she gestured, and swung Nuage into the lane.

With the line of ambulances following her, she galloped up the driveway towards the château, and saw a shell burst just beyond the stables and another hit the greenhouse at the bottom of the vegetable gardens. The glass panels splintered into a diamond spray in the sunlight.

'The Château is a natural target,' she realized, and galloped Nuage into the yard.

Already they were bringing out the wounded, and as the first ambulance pulled up at the bottom of the stairs, the driver and his orderly sprang out to help load the stretchers into the back of the truck.

Centaine turned Nuage into the paddock beside the stables and ran back to the kitchen door. Behind her a howitzer shell hit the tiled roof of the long stable building, blowing a hole through it and knocking out part of the stone wall. However, the stables were empty, so Centaine darted into the kitchen.

'Where have you been?' Anna demanded. 'I have been so worried—'

Centaine pushed past her and ran through to her own room. She pulled the carpet bag from the top of her wardrobe and began to throw clothing into it.

There was a deafening crash from somewhere above, and the plaster ceiling cracked and chunks of it fell around her. Centaine swept the silver frame of photographs off the bedside table into the bag, then opened the drawer and

191

found her jewelbox and her travelling toilet set. The air was full of white plaster dust.

Another shell burst on the terrace outside her room, and the window over her bed exploded. Flying glass rattled against the walls and a shard grazed her forearm and left a bloody line on her skin. She licked the blood away and dropped on her knees, creeping half under the bed, and prised up the loose floorboard.

The leather purse with their hoard of cash lay in the recess beneath it. She weighed the purse in one hand – almost two hundred francs in gold *louis d'or* – then dropped it into the bag.

Lugging the carpet bag, she ran down the stairs into the kitchen.

'Where is Papa?' she shouted at Anna.

'He went up to the top floor.' Anna was stuffing strings of onions, hams and bread loaves into a grain sack. She pointed with her chin at the empty hooks on the wall. 'He has taken his gun and plenty of cognac.'

'I will fetch him,' Centaine panted. 'Take care of my bag.' She hitched up her skirts and raced back up the stairs.

The upper levels of the château were in confusion. The ambulance orderlies were trying to clear the *salon* and the main staircase.

'Centaine!' Bobby Clarke called across the stairwell at her. 'Are you ready to leave?'

He was manhandling one end of a stretcher, and he had to raise his voice above the shouts of the orderlies and the groans of the wounded.

Centaine fought her way up against the press of humanity descending the stairs, and Bobby caught her sleeve as she came level with him.

'Where are you going? We have to get out!'

'My father – I must find my father.' She shook off his hand and went on.

The topmost levels of the house were deserted and

Centaine ran through them, shouting shrilly, 'Papa! Papa! Where are you?'

She ran down the long gallery, and from the walls the portraits of her ancestors gazed down haughtily upon her. At the end of the gallery she threw her weight on to the double doors which led through into the suite of bedrooms that had been her mother's and which the comte had kept unchanged all these years.

He was in the dressing-room, slumped in the high-backed tapestry-covered chair in front of the portrait of Centaine's mother, and he looked up as Centaine burst into the room.

'Papa, we must leave immediately.'

He did not seem to recognize her. There were three unopened cognac bottles on the floor between his feet, and he held another by the neck. It was half-empty, and he lifted it and took a mouthful of the raw spirit, still gazing at the portrait.

'Please, Papa, we must go!'

His single eye did not even blink as another shell crashed into the château, somewhere in the east wing.

She seized his arm and tried to pull him to his feet, but he was a big man and heavy. Some of the brandy spilled down his shirt front.

'The Germans have broken through, Papa! Please come with me.'

'The Germans!' he roared suddenly, and pushed her away from him. 'I will fight them once again.'

He threw up the long-barrelled *chassepot* rifle that had lain across his lap and fired a shot into the painted ceiling. Plaster dust filtered down on his hair and moustache, ageing him dramatically.

'Let them come!' he roared. 'I, Louis de Thiry, say, let them all come! I am ready for them!'

He was mad with liquor and despair, but she tried to pull him to his feet.

'We must leave.'

'Never!' he bellowed, and threw her aside, more roughly than before. 'I will never leave. This is my land, my home – the home of my dear wife—' his eye glittered insanely ' – my dear wife.' He reached towards the portrait. 'I will stay here with her, I will fight them here on my own soil.'

Centaine caught the outstretched wrist and tugged at it, but with a heave he threw her back against the wall, and began to reload the ancient rifle on his lap.

Centaine whispered, 'I must fetch Anna to help me.'

She ran to the door and another shell ploughed into the north side of the château. The crash of bursting brickwork and splintering glass was followed immediately by the blast wave. It threw her to her knees, and some of the heavy portraits were torn from the gallery walls.

She pulled herself up and raced down the gallery. The nitro-acid stink of explosive was mingled with the biting odour of smoke and burning. The staircase was almost empty. The very last of the wounded were being carried out. As Centaine ran into the yard two of the ambulances, both of them overloaded, pulled out through the gateway and turned down the driveway.

'Anna!' Centaine screamed. She was strapping the carpet bag and bulging sack on to the roof of one of the ambulances, but she jumped down and ran to Centaine.

'You must help me,' Centaine gasped. 'It's Papa.'

Three shells hit the château in quick succession, and more burst in the stable field and in the gardens. The German observers must have noted the activity around the building. Their batteries were finding the range.

'Where is he?' Anna ignored the shellfire.

'Upstairs. Mama's dressing-room. He is mad, Anna. Mad drunk. I cannot move him.'

The moment they entered the house they smelt the smoke, and as they climbed the stairs the stench became stronger and dense wreaths of it eddied about them. By the time they reached the second level, they were both coughing and wheezing for breath.

The gallery was thick with smoke, so they could not see more than a dozen paces ahead, and through the smoke shone a wavering orange glow – the fire had taken hold in the front rooms and was burning through the doors.

'Go back,' Anna gasped, 'I will find him.'

Centaine shook her head stubbornly and started down the gallery. Another salvo of howitzer fire crashed into the château, and part of the gallery wall collapsed, partially blocking it, and swirling brick dust mingled with the dense smoke, blinding them so that they crouched at the head of the staircase.

It cleared slightly and again they ran forward, but the opening that had been torn in the wall acted as a flue for the flames. They roared up furiously and the heat came at them like a solid thing, barring their way.

'Papa!' screamed Centaine, as they cringed away from it. 'Papa! Where are you?'

The floor jumped under them as more shellfire hit the ancient building, and they were deafened by the thunder of collapsing walls and falling ceilings, and by the rising roar of the flames.

'Papa!' Centaine's voice was almost drowned, but Anna bellowed over her.

'Louis, *viens*, *chéri* – come to me, darling.'

Even in her distress, Centaine realized that she had never heard Anna use an endearment to her father. It seemed to summon him.

Through the smoke and the dust the comte loomed. Flames roared all around him, rising around his feet as the floorboards burned, licking at him from the panelled walls, and smoke covered him in a dark mantle, so that he seemed like a creature from hell itself.

His mouth was open and he was making a wild, anguished sound.

'He is singing,' whispered Anna. 'The *Marseillaise*.'

'To arms, Citizens! Form the ship of State.'

Only then did Centaine recognize the garbled chorus.

'Let an impure blood swirl in the gutters—'

The words became indistinguishable, and the comte's voice weakened as the heat enveloped him. The rifle he was carrying slipped from his hand, and he fell and dragged himself up and began to crawl towards them. Centaine tried to go to him again, but the heat stopped her dead and Anna pulled her back.

Dark brown blotches began to appear on her father's shirt, as the white linen scorched, but still that terrible sound came from his open mouth, and still he crawled along the burning floor of the gallery.

Suddenly the thick dark bush of his hair burst into flames, so that it seemed that he wore a golden crown. Centaine could not look away, could not speak again, but she clung helplessly to Anna and felt the sobs wracking the older woman's body, and the arm around Centaine's shoulder tightened so that the grip was crushingly painful.

Then the floor of the gallery gave way beneath her father's weight, and the burning floorboards opened like a dark mouth with fangs of fire and sucked him in.

'No!' Centaine shrieked, and Anna lifted her off her feet and ran with her to the head of the stairs. Anna was still sobbing and tears streamed down her fat red cheeks, but her strength was unimpaired.

Behind them part of the burning ceiling fell, taking the rest of the gallery floor with it, and Anna set Centaine on her feet and dragged her down the staircase. The smoke cleared as they went down, and at last they burst out into the yard again, and sucked in the sweet air.

The château was in flames from end to end, and shellfire still crashed into it or burst in tall columns of smoke and singing shrapnel upon the lawns and in the surrounding fields.

Bobby Clarke was supervising the loading of the last ambulances, but his face lit with relief as he saw Centaine, and he ran to her. The flames had frizzled the ends of her hair and scorched her eyelashes, soot streaked her cheeks.

'We have to get out of here – where is your father?' Bobby took her arm.

She could not answer him. She was shaking and the smoke had burned her throat and her eyes were red and streaming tears.

'Is he coming?'

She shook her head and saw the quick sympathy in his expression. He glanced up at the flaming building.

He took her other arm and led her towards the nearest ambulance.

'Nuage,' Centaine croaked. 'My horse.' Her voice was roughened by smoke and shock.

'No—' Bobby Clarke said sharply and tried to hold her, but she pulled out of his grip and ran towards the stable paddock.

'Nuage!' She tried to whistle, but no sound came through her parched lips, and Bobby Clarke caught up with her at the paddock gate.

'Don't go in there!' His voice was desperate, and he held her.

Confused and bewildered, she craned to look over the gate.

'No, Centaine!' He pulled her back, and she saw the horse and screamed.

'Nuage!' The rushing roar and thunder of another salvo drowned out her heart cry, but she fought in his grip.

'Nuage!' she screamed again, and the stallion lifted his head. He lay upon his side; one of the shell bursts had shattered both his back legs and ripped open his belly.

'Nuage!' He heard her voice and he tried to lift himself on to his forefeet, but the effort was too much and he fell

197

back. His head thudded on the earth and he blew a soft fluttering sound through his wide nostrils.

Anna ran to help Bobby and between them they dragged Centaine to the waiting ambulance.

'You can't leave him like that!' she pleaded, trying with all her might to resist them. 'Please, please, don't leave him to suffer.'

Another salvo of shells straddled the yard, driving in their eardrums and filling the air around them with hissing chips of stone and steel fragments. 'No time,' Bobby grunted, 'we must go.'

They forced Centaine into the rear of the vehicle, between the tiers of stretchers, and crowded in after her. Immediately the driver clashed the gears and pulled away, the ambulance swung in a tight circle, bouncing over the cobbles, and then accelerated through the gateway and out into the driveway.

Centaine dragged herself to the tailboard of the speeding vehicle and looked back at the château. The flames were rushing up through the shell holes in the pink tiles, and dark black smoke towered above it, rising straight up into the sunlit sky.

'Everything,' Centaine whispered. 'You've taken everything that I love. Why? Oh Lord, why have you done this to me?'

Ahead of them the other vehicles had pulled off the road at the edge of the forest, and parked under the trees to avoid the shellfire. Bobby Clarke jumped down and ran to each in turn, giving orders to the drivers and regrouping them into a convoy. Then, with his own vehicle in the lead, they sped down to the crossroads and turned into the main road.

Again shellfire fell close about them, for the German observers already had the crossroads well covered. Like a conga line the convoy wove from one side of the road to the other to avoid the shell holes and the litter of destroyed carts, dead draught-animals and abandoned equipment.

As soon as they were clear, they closed up and followed the curve of the road down towards the village. As they passed the churchyard, Centaine saw that there was already a shell hole through the green copper-clad spire. Although she glimpsed the upper branches of the yew tree that marked the family plot, Michael's grave was out of sight from the road.

'I wonder if we will ever come back, Anna?' Centaine whispered. 'I promised Michael—' her voice trailed off.

'Of course we will. Where else would we ever go?' Anna's voice was rough with her own grief and the jolting of the ambulance.

Both of them stared back at the shot-holed church spire and the ugly black column of smoke that poured up into the sky above the forest marking the pyre of their home.

The ambulance convoy caught up with the tail of the main British retreat on the outskirts of the village. Here the military police had set up a temporary roadblock. They were sending all able-bodied troops off the road to regroup and to set up a secondary line of defence, and they were searching all vehicles for deserters from the battlefield.

'Is the new line holding, sergeant?' Bobby Clarke asked the policeman who checked his papers. 'Can we halt in the village? Some of my patients—'

He was interrupted by a shellburst that hit one of the cottages beside the road. They were still within extreme range of the German guns.

'There is no telling, sir,' the sergeant handed Bobby

back his papers. 'If I were you I would pull back as far as the main base hospital at Arras. It's going to be a bit hairy around here.'

So the long, slow retreat began. They were a part of the solid stream of traffic that blocked the road for as far ahead as they could see, and reduced to the same excruciating pace.

The ambulances would start with a jolt, roll forward a few yards with noses to tails, and then pull up again for another interminable wait. As the day wore on so the heat built up, and the roads so recently running with winter mud turned to talcum dust. The flies came from the surrounding farmyards to the bloody bandages and crawled on the faces of the wounded men in the tiers of stretchers, and they moaned and cried out for water.

Anna and Centaine went to ask for water at one of the farmhouses alongside the road, and found it already deserted. They helped themselves to milk pails and filled them from the pump.

They moved down the convoy, giving out mugs of water, bathing the faces of those in fever from their wounds, helping the ambulance orderlies clean those who had not been able to contain their bodily functions, and all the time trying to appear cheerful and confident, giving what comfort they could, despite their own grief and bereavement.

By nightfall the convoy had covered less than five miles, and they could still hear the din of the battle raging behind them. Once more the convoy was stalled, waiting to move on.

'It looks like we have managed to hold them at Mort Homme,' Bobby Clarke paused beside Centaine. 'It should be safe to stop for the night.' He looked more closely at the face of the soldier whom Centaine was tending. 'God knows, these poor devils cannot take much more of this. They need food and rest. There is a farmyard with a large barn around the next bend. It hasn't been taken over by anyone else yet – we'll bag it.'

Anna produced a bunch of onions from her sack and used them to flavour the stew of canned bully beef that they boiled up over an open fire. They served the stew with dry army biscuit and mugs of black tea, all of it begged from the commissary trucks parked in the stalled column of traffic.

Centaine fed the men who were too weak to help themselves, and then worked with the orderlies changing the dressings. The heat and dust had done their worst, and many of the wounds were inflamed and swollen and beginning to ooze yellow pus.

After midnight Centaine slipped out of the barn and went to the water pump in the yard. She felt soiled and sweaty and longed to bathe her entire body and change into clean, freshly ironed clothes. There was no privacy for that, and the few clothes she had packed in the carpet bag she knew she must hoard. Instead she slipped off her petticoat and knickers from under her skirt and washed them out under the tap, then wrung them and hung them over the gate while she bathed her face and arms with cold water.

She let the night breeze dry her skin and slipped her underclothes on again, still damp. Then she combed out her hair and she felt a little better, although her eyes still felt raw and swollen from the smoke and there was the heavy weight of her grief like a stone in her chest, and an enormous physical fatigue dragged at her legs and arms. The images of her father in the smoke and the white stallion lying on the grass assailed her once again, but she shut her mind to them.

'Enough,' she said aloud as she leaned against the gate to the yard. 'Enough for today, I'll cry again tomorrow.'

'Tomorrow never comes.' A voice replied in broken French from the darkness, and she was startled.

'Bobby?'

She saw the glow of his cigarette then, and he came out of the shadows and leaned over the gate beside her.

'You are an amazing girl,' he went on in English, 'I have six sisters, but I've never known a girl like you. Matter of fact, I've known damned few chaps that could match you, either.'

She was silent, but when he drew on his cigarette, she studied his face in the glow. He was about Michael's age, and handsome. His mouth was full and sensitive-looking, and there was a gentleness about him that she had never had an opportunity to notice before.

'I say—' he was suddenly embarrassed by her silence ' – you don't mind me talking to you, do you? I'll leave you alone if you prefer.'

She shook her head. 'I don't mind.' And for a while they were silent, Bobby puffing on his cigarette and both of them listening to the distant sound of the battle and to the occasional soft groan from one of the wounded in the barn.

Then Centaine stirred and asked, 'Do you remember the young airman, the first day you came up to the château?'

'Yes. The one with the burned arm. What was his name again – Andrew?'

'No, that was his friend.'

'The wild Scot – yes, of course.'

'His name was Michel.'

'I remember both of them. What became of them?'

'Michel and I were to be married, but he is dead—' and her pent-up emotions came pouring out.

He was a stranger and gentle, and she found it so easy to talk to him in the darkness. She told him in her quaint English about Michel and how they had planned to live in Africa, then she told him about her father and how he had changed since her mother had died, and how she had tried to look after him and stop him drinking so much. Then

202

she described what had taken place that morning in the burning château.

'I think that was what he wanted. In his own way he was tired of living. I think he wanted to die and be with Mama again. But now both he and Michel are gone. I have nothing.'

When at last she finished she felt drained and tired, but quietly resigned.

'You have really been through the grinder.' Bobby reached out and squeezed her arm. 'I wish I could help you.'

'You have helped me. Thank you.'

'I could give you something – a little laudanum, it would help you sleep.'

Centaine felt a surge in her blood, a longing for the quick oblivion he offered her, it was so strong that it frightened her. 'No,' she refused with unnecessary emphasis. 'I will be all right.' She shivered. 'I'm cold and it's late now. Thank you again for listening to me.'

Anna had hung a blanket as a screen at one end of the barn and made a mattress of straw for them. Centaine dropped almost immediately into a deathlike sleep, and woke in the dawn in a sickly sweat with the urgent nausea on her again.

Still groggy with sleep, she stumbled out and managed to get behind the stone wall of the yard before heaving up a little bitter yellow bile. When she straightened up and wiped her mouth, clinging to the wall for support, she found that Bobby Clarke was beside her, his expression troubled as he took her wrist and checked her pulse rate.

'I think I had better have a look at you,' he said.

'No.' She felt vulnerable. This new sickness worried her for she had always been so healthy and strong. She was afraid he might discover some dreadful disease.

'I am all right, truly.' But he led her firmly by the hand

to the parked ambulance and drew down the canvas side screens to give them privacy.

'Lie there, please.' He ignored her protests and unfastened her blouse to sound her chest.

His manner was so clinical and professional that she no longer argued, and submitted meekly to his examination, sitting up and coughing and breathing at his instruction.

'Now I will examine you,' he said. 'Do you wish your maid to be present as a chaperone?'

She shook her head mutely and he said, 'Please remove your skirt and petticoat.'

When he had finished, he made a show of packing his instruments back in the roll and tying up the retaining ribbons, while she rearranged her clothing.

Then he looked up at her with such a peculiar expression that she was alarmed. 'Is it something serious?'

He shook his head. 'Centaine, your fiancé is dead. You told me that last night.'

She nodded.

'It is still very early to be certain, very early – but I believe that you will need a father for the child you are carrying.'

Her hands flew to her stomach, an involuntary protective gesture.

'I have really known you only a few days, but that is long enough for me to realize that I have fallen in love with you. I would be honoured—' his voice trailed off, for she was not listening to him.

'Michel,' she whispered. 'Michel's baby. I have not lost everything. I still have a part of him.'

Centaine ate the sandwich of ham and cheese that Anna brought her with such relish that Anna examined her suspiciously.

'I feel so much better now,' Centaine forestalled her inquiry.

They helped feed the wounded and ready them for the day's trek. Two of their critical cases had died during the night, and the orderlies buried them hastily in shallow graves at the edge of the field and then the ambulances started up and pulled out into the main stream of traffic.

The congestion of the previous day's route had abated as the army shook itself out of mindless confusion into a semblance of order. The traffic still rolled slowly, but with fewer halts and false starts, and alongside the road they passed the rudimentary supply dumps and advanced head-quarters echelons that had been set up during the night.

During one of their halts on the outskirts of a tiny village, half-concealed by trees and vineyards, Centaine made out the shapes of aircraft parked at the edge of the vineyard.

She climbed up on the running-board of the ambulance for a better view, and a flight of aircraft took off from the field and flew low over the road.

Her disappointment was intense as she realized that they were ungraceful two-seater De Havilland scouts, not the lovely SE5a's of Michael's squadron. She waved to them, and one of the pilots looked down at her and waved back.

It cheered her somehow and as she returned to her self-imposed duties, she felt strong and lighthearted, and she joked with the wounded men in her accented English, and they reacted with delight. One of them called her 'Sunshine' and the name passed quickly down the line of ambulances.

Bobby Clarke stopped her as she passed. 'Great stuff – but remember, don't overdo it.'

'I will be all right. Don't worry about me.'

'I can't help it.' He dropped his voice. 'Have you thought about my offer? When will you give me an answer?'

'Not now, Bobby.' She pronounced his name with equal emphasis on each syllable, 'Bob-bee', and every time she said it he lost his breath. 'We will talk later – but you are very *gentil*, very kind.'

Now the roadway was almost impassable once more, for the reserves were being hastened up to help hold the new line at Mort Homme. Endless columns of marching men slogged past them, and interspersed between the ranks of bobbing steel helmets were batteries of guns and lines of supply trucks loaded with all the accoutrements of war.

Their forward progress faltered, and for hours at a time the ambulances were signalled off the roadway into a field or a side lane while fresh hordes streamed past.

'I'll have to send the ambulances back soon,' Bobby told Centaine during one of their halts. 'They are needed back there. As soon as we can find a field hospital, I'll hand over these patients.'

Centaine nodded and made as if to go to the next vehicle where one of the men was calling weakly. 'Over here, Sunshine, can you give me a hand.'

Bobby caught her wrist. 'Centaine, when we reach the hospital there is bound to be a chaplain there. It would only take a few minutes—'

She gave him her new smile, and reached up to touch his unshaven cheek with her fingertips. 'You are a kind man, Bobby – but Michel is the father of my son. I have thought about it, and I do not need another father.'

'Centaine, you don't understand! What will people think? A child without a father, a young mother without a husband – what will they say?'

'As long as I have my baby, Bobby, I don't give a – how do you say in English – I don't give them a fig! They can say what they like. I am the widow of Michel Courtney.'

In the late afternoon they found the field hospital they were searching for. It was in a field outside Arras.

There were two cottage tents, emblazoned with the red crosses. These were serving as operating theatres. Rough shelters had also been hastily thrown up around them to accommodate the hundreds of wounded waiting their turns on the tables. They were built of tarpaulins over timber frames, or of corrugated iron scavenged from the surrounding farms.

Anna and Centaine helped unload their own wounded and carry them into one of the crowded shelters, then they retrieved their baggage from the roof of the leading ambulance. One of their patients noticed their preparations to leave.

'You aren't going, Sunshine, are you?' And hearing him, others pulled themselves up on an elbow to protest.

'What are we going to do without you, luv?'

She went to them for the last time, passing from one to the next with a smile and a joke, stooping to kiss their filthy, pain-contorted faces, and then at last, unable to bear it any more, hurrying back to where Anna waited for her.

They picked up the carpet bag and Anna's sack, and started along the convoy of ambulances which were being refuelled, ready to return to the battlefield.

Bobby Clarke had waited for them, and now he ran after Centaine.

'We are going back, orders from Major Sinclair.'

'Au revoir, Bobby.'

'I'll always remember you, Centaine.'

She went up on tiptoe to kiss his cheek.

'I hope it will be a boy,' he whispered.

'It will be,' she told him seriously. 'A boy, I am certain of it.'

The convoy of ambulances trundled away, back into the north, and Bobby Clarke waved and shouted something that she did not catch, as they were carried away on the river of marching men and lumbering equipment.

'What do we do now?' Anna asked.

'We go on,' Centaine told her. Somehow, subtly, she had taken charge, and Anna, increasingly indecisive with each mile between her and Mort Homme, plodded after her. They left the sprawling hospital area and turned southwards again into the crowded roadway.

Ahead of them over the trees Centaine could make out the roofs and spires of the town of Arras against the fading evening sky.

'Look, Anna!' she pointed. 'There is the evening star – we are allowed a wish. What is yours?'

Anna looked at her curiously. What had come over the child? She had seen her father burned to death and her favourite animal mutilated barely two days before, and yet there was a ferocious gaiety about her. It was unnatural.

'I wish for a bath and a hot meal.'

'Oh, Anna, you always ask for the impossible.' Centaine smiled at her over her shoulder, transferring the heavy carpet bag from one hand to the other.

'What is your wish, then?' Anna challenged.

'I wish that the star leads us to the general, like it led the three wise men—'

'Don't blaspheme, girl.' But Anna was too tired and uncertain for the rebuke to have real force behind it.

C entaine knew the town well, for it contained the convent where she had spent her schooldays. It was dark by the time they made their way through the town centre. The fighting of the early years of the war had left terrible scars on the lovely seventeenth-century Flemish architecture. The picturesque old town hall was pocked with shrapnel splinters and part of the roof destroyed. Many of the gabled brick houses surrounding the Grande Place were also roofless and deserted, although the windows of others were candlelit. The more stubborn of the population had moved back again immediately the tides of war had rolled by.

Centaine had not made a special note of the way to the monastery that General Courtney was using as his headquarters when she had last visited it with Michael, so she could not hope to find it in the dark. She and Anna camped in a deserted cottage, eating the last scraps of stale bread and dried-out cheese from Anna's sack, using the carpet bag for a pillow and each other for warmth as they lay on the bare floor.

The next morning Centaine dreaded finding the monastery deserted when she finally rediscovered the lane leading to it, but there was a guard on the main gate.

'Sorry, miss, Army property. Nobody goes in.'

She was still pleading with him when the black Rolls came racing down the lane behind her and braked as it reached the gates. It was coated with dried mud and dust, and there was a long ugly scratch down both the doors on the nearest side.

The guard recognized the pennant on the bonnet and waved the Zulu driver on, and the Rolls accelerated through the tall gates, but Centaine ran forward and shouted desperately after the car. In the back seat was the young officer she had met on her last visit.

'Lieutenant Pearce!' She remembered his name, and he glanced back, then looked startled as he recognized her. Quickly he leaned across to speak to the driver, and the Rolls pulled up sharply and then reversed.

'Mademoiselle de Thiry!' John Pearce jumped out and hurried to her. 'The last person I expected – what on earth are you doing here?'

'I must see Michel's uncle, General Courtney. It's important.'

'He is not here at the moment,' the young officer told her, 'but you can come with me. He should be back fairly soon, and in the meantime we'll find you a place to rest, and something to eat. It seems to me that you could use both.'

He took Centaine's carpet bag from her. 'Come along – is this woman with you?'

'Anna, my servant.'

'She can sit in front with Sangane.' He helped Centaine into the Rolls. 'The Germans have made it a pretty busy few days,' he settled beside her on the soft leather, 'and it looks as though you have been through it as well.'

Centaine looked down at herself: her clothes were dusty and bedraggled, her hands were dirty and her fingernails had black half-moons under them. She could guess what her hair looked like.

'I have just come back from the front. General Courtney went up to take a look for himself.' John Pearce politely looked away as she tried to put her hair into place again. 'He likes to be right up there – still thinks he's fighting the Boer War, the old devil. We got as far as Mort Homme—'

'That is my village.'

'Not any more,' he told her grimly. 'It's German now, or almost so. The new front line runs just north of it, and the village is under fire. Most of it shot away already – you wouldn't recognize it, I'm sure.'

Centaine nodded again. 'My home was shelled and burned down.'

'I'm sorry.' John Pearce went on quickly. 'Anyway, it looks as though we have stopped them. General Courtney is sure we can hold them at Mort Homme—'

'Where is the general?'

'Staff meeting at Divisional HQ. He should be back later this evening. Ah, here we are.'

John Pearce found a monk's cell for them, and had a servant bring them a meal and two buckets of hot water.

Once they had eaten, Anna stripped off Centaine's clothes, and then stood her over one of the buckets and sponged her down with hot water.

'Oh, that feels marvellous.'

'For once there are no squeals,' Anna muttered. She used her petticoat to dry Centaine, then slipped a clean shift from the carpet bag over her head and brushed out her hair. The thick dark curls were tangled.

'*Oh là*, Anna, that hurts!'

'It was too good to last,' Anna sighed.

When she had finished, she insisted that Centaine lie on the cot to rest, while she bathed herself and washed out their soiled clothes. However, Centaine could not lie still and she sat up and hugged her knees.

'Oh darling Anna, I have the most wonderful surprise for you—'

Anna twisted the thick grey horse-tail of her damp hair up on to her head and looked at Centaine quizzically.

'Darling Anna, is it? It must be good news indeed.'

'Oh it is, it is! I'm going to have Michel's baby.'

Anna froze. The blood drained from her ruddy features, leaving them grey with shock, and she stared at Centaine, unable to speak.

'It's going to be a boy, I'm sure of it. I can just feel it. He will be just like Michel!'

'How can you be sure?' Anna blurted.

'Oh, I am sure.' Centaine knelt quickly and pulled up the shift. 'Look at my tummy – can't you just see, Anna?'

Her pale smooth stomach was flat as ever, with the neat dimple of the navel its only blemish. Centaine pushed it out strenuously.

'Can't you see, Anna! It might even be twins, Michel's father and the general were twins. It may run in the family – think of it, Anna, two like Michel!'

'No,' Anna shook her head, aghast. 'This is one of your fairy stories. I won't believe that you and that soldier—'

'Michel isn't a soldier, he's a—' Centaine began, but Anna went on, 'I won't believe that a daughter of the house of de Thiry allowed a common soldier to use her like a kitchenmaid.'

'Allowed, Anna!' Centaine pulled down her shift angrily. 'I didn't allow it, I helped him do it. He didn't seem to know what to do, at first, so I helped him, and we worked it out beautifully.'

Anna clapped both hands over her ears. 'I don't believe it, I'm not going to listen. Not after I taught you to be a lady – I just won't listen.'

'Then what do you think we were doing at night when I went out to meet him – you know I went out, you and Papa caught me at it, didn't you?'

'My baby!' wailed Anna. 'He took advantage—'

'Nonsense, Anna, I loved it. I loved every little thing he did to me.'

'Oh no! I won't believe it. Besides, you couldn't possibly know, not so soon. You are teasing old Anna. You are being wicked and cruel.'

'You know how I've been sick in the morning.'

'That doesn't prove—'

'The doctor, Bobby Clarke, the army doctor. He examined me. He told me.'

Anna was struck dumb at last, there was no more protests. It was inescapable: the child had been out at night, she had been sick in the morning, and Anna believed implicitly in the infallibility of doctors. Then there was Centaine's strange and unnatural elation in the face of all her adversity, it was inescapable.

'It's true, then,' she capitulated. 'Oh, what are we going to do? Oh, the good Lord save us from scandal and disgrace – what are we going to do?'

'Do, Anna?' Centaine laughed at her theatrical lamentations. 'We are going to have the most beautiful baby boy, or if we are lucky, two of them, and I'm going to need you to help me care for them. You will help me, won't you, Anna? I know nothing about babies, and you know everything.'

Anna's first shock passed swiftly, and she began to consider not the disgrace and scandal, but the existence of a real live infant; it was over seventeen years since she had experienced that joy. Now, miraculously, she was being promised another infant. Centaine saw the change in her, the first stirrings of maternal passion.

'You are going to help me with our baby. You won't leave us, we need you, the baby and I! Anna, promise me, please promise me,' and Anna flew to the cot and swept Centaine into her arms and held her with all her strength, and Centaine laughed with joy in her crushing embrace.

I t was after dark when John Pearce knocked again at the door of the monk's cell.

'The general has returned, Mademoiselle de Thiry. I have told him you are here, and he wishes to speak to you as soon as possible.'

Centaine followed the aide-de-camp down the cloisters and into the large refectory which had been converted into the regimental operations room. Half a dozen officers were poring over the large-scale map that had been spread over one of the refectory tables. The map was porcupined with coloured pins, and the atmosphere in the room was tense and charged.

As Centaine entered, the officers glanced up at her, but even a young and pretty girl could not hold their attention for more than a few seconds and they returned to their tasks.

On the far side of the room, General Sean Courtney was standing with his back to her. His jacket, resplendent with red tabs and insignia and ribbons, hung over the chair on which he was resting one booted foot. He leaned his elbow on his knee and scowled furiously at the earpiece of a field telephone from which a faint distorted voice quacked at him.

Sean wore a woollen singlet with sweat-stained armpits and marvellously flamboyant embroidered braces, decorated with stags and running hounds, over his shoulders. He was chewing on an unlit Havana cigar, and suddenly he bellowed into the field telephone without removing the cigar from his mouth.

'That is utter horse-shit! I was there myself two hours ago. I know! I need at least four more batteries of 25-pounders in that gap, and I need them before dawn – don't give me excuses, just do it, and tell me when it's done!' He slammed down the hand-set, and saw Centaine.

'My dear,' his voice altered and he came to her quickly and took her hand. 'I was worried. The château has been completely destroyed. The new front line runs not a mile beyond it—' He paused, and studied her for a moment. What he saw reassured him and he asked, 'Your father?'

She shook her head. 'He was killed in the shelling.'

'I'm sorry,' Sean said simply, and turned to John Pearce. 'Take Miss de Thiry through to my quarters.' Then to her, 'I will follow you in five minutes.'

The general's room opened directly into the main refectory, so that with the door open Sean Courtney could lie on his cot and watch everything that went on in his operations room. It was sparsely furnished, just the cot and a desk with two chairs, and his locker at the foot of the cot.

'Won't you sit here, Mademoiselle?' John Pearce offered her one of the chairs, and while she waited, Centaine glanced round the small room.

The only item of interest was the desk. On it stood a hinged photograph frame, one leaf of which contained the picture of a magnificent mature woman, with dark Jewish beauty. It was inscribed across the bottom corner, 'Come home safely to your loving wife, Ruth.'

The second leaf of the frame held the picture of a girl of about Centaine's age. The resemblance to the older woman was apparent – they could only be mother and daughter – but the girl's beauty was marred by a petulant, spoiled expression; the pretty mouth had a hard, acquisitive quirk to it, and Centaine decided that she did not like her very much at all.

'My wife and daughter,' Sean Courtney said from the doorway. He had put on his jacket and was buttoning it as he came in.

'You have eaten?' he asked as he sank into the chair opposite Centaine.

'Yes, thank you.' Centaine stood up and picked up the silver box of Vestas from the desk, struck one and held it for him to light the Havana. He looked surprised, then leaned forward and sucked the flame into the tip of the cigar. When it was well lit, he leaned back in the chair and said, 'My daughter, Storm, does that for me.'

Centaine blew out the match, sat down again and waited quietly for him to enjoy the first few puffs of fragrant smoke. He had aged since their last meeting – or perhaps it was only that he was very tired, she thought.

'When did you last sleep?' she asked, and he grinned. Suddenly, he looked thirty years younger.

'You sound like my wife.'

'She is very beautiful.'

'Yes,' Sean nodded and glanced at the photograph, then back to Centaine. 'You have lost everything,' he said.

'The château, my home – and my father.' She tried to be calm, not let the terrible hurt show.

'You have other family, of course.'

'Of course,' she agreed. 'My uncle lives in Lyon, and I have two aunts in Paris.'

'I will arrange for you to travel to Lyon.'

'No.'

'Why not?' He looked piqued at her abrupt refusal.

'I don't want to go to Lyon, or Paris. I am going to Africa.'

'Africa?' Now he was taken aback. 'Africa? Good Lord, why Africa?'

'Because I promised Michel – we promised each other we would go to Africa.'

'But, my dear—' He dropped his eyes, and studied the ash of his cigar. She saw the pain that the mention of Michael's name inflicted, she shared it with him for a moment, and then said, 'You were going to say, "But Michel is dead."'

He nodded. 'Yes'. His voice was almost a whisper.

'I promised Michel something else, General. I told him that his son would be born in the sunshine of Africa.'

Slowly Sean lifted his head and stared at her.

'Michael's son?'

'His son.'

'You are bearing Michael's child?'

'Yes.'

All the stupid mundane questions rushed to his lips.

'Are you sure?'

'How can you be certain?'

'How do I know it's Michael's child?'

And he bit them back. He had to have time to think – to adjust to this incredible twist of fate.

'Excuse me.' He stood up and limped back into the operations room.

'Are we in contact with the third battalion yet?' he demanded of the group of officers.

'We had them for a minute, then lost them again. They are ready to counter-attack, sir, but they need artillery support.'

'Get on to those damned shell wallahs again, and keep

trying to get through to Caithness.' He turned to another of his staff. 'Roger, what is happening to the First?'

'No change, sir. They have broken two enemy attacks, but they are taking a beating from the German guns. Colonel Stevens thinks they can hold.'

'Good man!' Sean grunted. It was like trying to close the leaks in a dyke, holding back the ocean with handfuls of clay, but somehow they were doing it, and every hour they held on was blunting the cutting edge of the German attack.

'The guns are the key, if we can get them up soon enough. How is the traffic on the main road?'

'Clearing and moving faster, it seems, sir.'

If they could move the 25-pounders into the gap before morning, then they could make the enemy pay dearly for their gains. They would have them in a salient, they could hit them from three sides, pound them with artillery.

Sean felt his spirits droop again. This was a war of guns, it all came back in the end to the bloody attrition of the guns. At the front of his mind Sean made the calculations, assessed the risks and the costs and gave the orders, but behind that he was making other calculations. He was thinking of the girl and her claims upon him.

Firstly he had to control his natural reaction to what she had told him, for Sean was a son of Victoria, and he expected all people, but especially his own family, to live by the code that had been set in the previous century. Of course, young men were expected to sow their wild oats – by God, Sean himself had sown them by the barrow-load – and he grinned shamefacedly at the memory. But decent young men left decent young girls alone, until after they were married.

'I'm shocked,' he realized, and smiled again. The officers at the operations table saw the smile and looked puzzled and uneasy. 'What is the old devil up to now?' They exchanged nervous glances.

'Have you got hold of Colonel Caithness yet?' Sean covered the smile with a ferocious scowl, and they applied themselves diligently to their tasks once more.

'I'm shocked,' Sean told himself again, still amused at himself but this time keeping his face impassive. 'And yet Michael himself was your own love-baby, the fruit of one of your escapades. Your first-born—' The pain of Michael's death assailed him again, but he drove it back.

'Now, the girl.' He began to think it out. 'Is she really pregnant, or is this some elaborate form of blackmail?' It did not take him more than a few seconds to decide.

'I can't be that wrong in my estimate of her. She truly believes she is pregnant.' There were areas of the female anatomy and the feminine mind that were completely alien terrain to Sean. He had learned, however, that when a girl believed she was pregnant, she sure as all hell was. How she knew escaped him, but he was prepared to accept it. 'All right, she's pregnant, but is it Michael's child, and not some other young—'

Again his rejection of the idea was swift. 'She's a child of a decent family, carefully guarded by her father and that dragon of hers. How she and Michael managed it beats me—' He almost grinned again as he recalled how often and how adroitly he had managed it in his youth, against equally fearsome odds. 'The ingenuity of young love.' He shook his head. 'All right, I accept it. It's Michael's child. Michael's son!'

And only then did he allow the joy to rise in him. 'Michael's son! Something of Michael still lives on.' Then he cautioned himself quickly. 'Steady on now, don't let's go overboard. She wants to come out to Africa, but what the hell are we going to do with her? I can't take her in at Emoyeni.' For a moment the image appeared in his mind of the beautiful home on the hill, 'The place of the wind' in Zulu, which he had built for his wife. The longing to be back there with her came powerfully upon him. He had to fight it off and apply himself to the immediate problems again.

'Three of them – three pretty girls, all of them proud and strong-willed, living in the same house.' Instinctively he knew that this little French girl and his own beloved but lovingly indulged daughter would fight like two wild cats in a sack. He shook his head. 'By God, that would be the perfect recipe for disaster, and I wouldn't be there to turn them over my knee. I've got to come up with something better than that. What in the name of all that is holy do we do with this pregnant little filly?'

'Sir! Sir!' one of his officers called, and offered Sean the head-set of the field telephone. 'I've got through to Colonel Caithness at last.'

Sean snatched the set from him. 'Douglas!' He barked into it. The line was bad, the background hissed and rushed like the sea, so Douglas Caithness's voice seemed to come from across an ocean.

'Hello, sir, the guns have just come up—'

'Thank God,' Sean growled.

'I have deployed them —' Caithness gave the map reference. 'They are hammering away already and the Huns seem to have run out of steam. I am going to raid them at dawn.'

'Douglas, be careful, there are no reserves behind you, I won't be able to support you before noon.'

'All right, I understand, but we can't let them regroup unopposed.'

'Of course not,' Sean agreed. 'Keep me informed. In the meantime I'm moving up four more batteries, and elements of the Second Battalion, but they won't reach you before noon.'

'Thank you, sir, we can use them.'

'Go to it, man.' Sean handed the instrument back, and while he watched the coloured pins rearranged on the map, the solution to his personal problem came to him.

'Garry—' He thought of his twin brother, and felt the familiar twinge of guilt and compassion. Garrick Courtney, the brother whom Sean had crippled.

It had happened so many years ago and yet every instant of that dreadful day was still so clear in Sean's mind that it might have taken place that very morning. The two of them, teenage scamps, arguing over the shotgun that they had stolen out of their father's gunroom and loaded with buckshot, as they trotted through the golden grass of the Zululand hills.

'I saw the inkonka first,' Garry protested. They were going out to hunt an old bushbuck ram whose lair they had discovered the previous day.

'I thought of the shotgun,' Sean told him, tightening his grip on the weapon, 'so I do the shooting.' And, of course, Sean prevailed. It was always that way.

It was Garry who took Tinker, their mongrel hunting dog, and circled out along the edge of thick bush to drive the antelope back where Sean waited with the shotgun.

Sean heard again Garry's faint shouts at the bottom of the hill, and Tinker's frantic barks as he picked up the scent of the wary bushbuck. Then the rush in the grass, and the long yellow stems bursting open as the inkonka came out, heading straight up to where Sean lay on the crest of the hill.

He looked immense in the sunlight, for in alarm his shaggy mane was erected and his dark head with the heavy spiral horns was raised high on the thick powerful neck. He stood three foot high at the shoulder and weighed almost two hundred pounds, and his chest and flanks were barred and spotted with delicate patterns, pale as chalk on the dark rufous ground. He was a magnificent creature, quick and formidable, those horns were sharp as pikes and could rip the belly out of a man or slice through his femoral artery – and he came straight at Sean.

Sean fired the choke barrel, and he was so close that the

charge of buckshot struck in a solid blast, and tore through the animal's barrel chest into lung and heart. The bushbuck screamed and went down, kicking and bleating, its sharp black hooves clashing on the rocky ground as it slid back down the hill.

'I got him!' howled Sean, leaping from his hiding place. 'I got him first shot. Garry! I got him!'

From below Garry and the dog came pelting through the coarse golden grass. It was a race as to which of them could get to the dying animal first. Sean carried the shotgun, the second barrel still loaded, and the hammer at full cock, and as he ran a loose stone rolled under his foot and he fell. The gun flew from his grip. He hit the ground with his shoulder and the second barrel fired with a stunning thump of sound.

When Sean scrambled up again, Garry was sitting beside the dead bushbuck, whimpering. His leg had taken the full charge of buckshot at almost point blank range. It had hit him below the knee, and the flesh was wet red ribbons, the bone white chips and slivers and the blood a bright fountain in the sunlight.

'Poor Garry,' Sean thought, 'now a lonely one-legged old cripple.' The woman whom Sean had put with child, and whom Garry had married before she gave birth to Michael, had finally been driven insane by her own hatred and bitterness and died in the flames she herself had set. Now Michael, too, was gone, and Garry had nothing — nothing except his books and his scribblings.

'I'll send him this bright pert girl and her unborn infant.' The solution came to Sean with a flood of relief. 'At last I can make some retribution for all I have done to him. I will send him my own grandchild, the grandchild I should so dearly love to claim as my own, I'll send to him in part payment.'

He turned from the map and limped quickly back to where the girl waited.

She rose to meet him and stood quietly, her hands clasped demurely in front of her, and Sean saw the worry and fear of rejection in her dark eyes, and the way her lower lip trembled as she waited for his judgement.

He closed the door behind him, and he went to her and took her small neat hands in his great hairy paws and he stooped over her and kissed her gently. His beard scratched her soft cheek, but she sobbed with relief and flung both arms around him.

'I'm sorry, my dear,' he said. 'You took me by surprise. I just had to get used to the idea.' Sean hugged her – but very gently, for the mystery of pregnancy was one of the very few things that daunted and awed Sean Courtney. Then he settled her back in the chair.

'Can I go to Africa?' She was smiling, though the tears still trembled in the corners of her eyes.

'Yes, of course, that's your home now, for as far as I am concerned, you are Michael's wife. Africa is where you belong.'

'I'm so happy,' she told him softly, but it was more than mere happiness. It was a vast sense of security and protection, this man's aura of power and strength was now held over her like a shield.

'You are Michael's wife,' he had said. He had acknowledged that which she herself believed, somehow his endorsement made it a fact.

'This is what I am going to do. The German U-boats have been playing such havoc. A sailing for you on one of the Red Cross hospital ships that leave directly from the French Channel ports will be the safest way of getting you home.'

'Anna—' Centaine cut in quickly.

'Yes, of course, she must go with you. I'll fix that also. You will both volunteer for nursing duties, and I'm afraid you'll be expected to work your passage.'

Centaine nodded eagerly.

'Michael's father, my brother, Garrick Courtney—' Sean started.

'Yes, yes! Michel told me all about him. He is a great hero – he won the cross of the English Queen Victoria for his courage in a battle against the Zulus,' Centaine cut in excitedly, 'and he is a scholar who writes books of history.'

Sean blinked at the description of poor Garry, but of course it was factually correct and he nodded.

'He is also a kind and gentle person, a widower who has just lost his only son—' An almost telepathic understanding passed between them; although Centaine knew the truth, from now on Michael would always be referred to as Garrick Courtney's son. 'Michael was his whole life, and you and I know how he must feel at the loss, for we share it.'

Centaine's eyes sparkled with unshed tears and she bit down on her lower lip as she nodded vehemently.

'I will cable him. He will be at Cape Town to meet you when the ship docks. I will also give you a letter to take to him. You can be certain of his welcome and his protection, for both you and Michael's child.'

'Michel's son,' said Centaine firmly, and then hesistantly, 'but I will see you also, General, sometimes?'

'Often,' Sean assured her, leaning forward to pat her hand gently. 'Probably more often than you wish.'

After that it all happened very quickly; she would learn that with Sean Courtney, this was always the way.

She remained only five more days at the monastery, but in that time the German breakthrough at Mort Homme was contained by dour bloody fighting, and once the line was stabilized and reinforced, Sean Courtney had a few hours each day to spare for her.

They dined together every evening, and he answered her endless questions about Africa and its people and animals, about the Courtney family and its members, with good-natured patience. Mostly they spoke English, but when at a loss for a word, Centaine lapsed into Flemish again. Then at the end of the meal she would prepare his cigar and light it for him, pour his cognac and then perch beside him, talking still, until Anna came to fetch her or Sean was summoned to the operations room; then she would come to him and hold up her face for his kiss with such a childlike innocence, that Sean found himself dreading the approaching hour of her departure.

John Pearce brought their nursing uniforms to Centaine and Anna. The white veils and the white cross-straps of the apron were worn over a blue-grey dress and Centaine and Anna made the finer adjustments themselves, their needles giving a touch of French flair to the baggy shapeless outfits.

Then it was time to leave, and Sangane loaded their meagre baggage into the Rolls, and Sean Courtney came down the cloisters, gruff and stern with the pain of leave-taking.

'Look after her,' he ordered Anna, and Anna glowered at him in righteous indignation at this gratuitous advice.

'I will be at the docks to meet you when you come home,' Centaine promised him, and Sean scowled with embarrassment and pleasure when she went up on tiptoe to kiss him in front of his staff. He watched the Rolls pull away with the girl waving at him through the back window, then roused himself and rounded on his staff.

'Well, gentlemen, what are we all gawking at – we're fighting a war here, not conducting a bloody Sunday-school picnic.'

And he stomped back down the cloisters, angry at himself for already feeling the girl's absence so painfully.

The *Protea Castle* had been a mailship of the Union Castle Line. She was a fast three-funnel passenger liner which had operated on the Cape to Southampton run before being converted to a hospital ship and repainted pristine white with scarlet crosses on her sides and funnels.

She lay at the dock of the inner harbour of Calais, taking on her passengers for the southward voyage, and they were a far cry from the elegant affluent travellers who had filled her pre-war lists. Five railway coaches had been shunted on to the rail spur of the wharf, and from these the pathetic stream of humanity crossed to the liner and went up her fore and aft gangways.

These were the veritable sweepings of the battlefield. They had been rejected by the medical board as so incapacitated that they could not even be patched up sufficiently to feed the man-hungry Baal of the British Expeditionary Force.

There would be twelve hundred on board for the southbound voyage, and on the return northbound leg the *Protea Castle* would be repainted in the camouflage of an ordinary troopship and bring another load of young eager and healthy young men for a sojourn in the hell of the trenches of northern France.

Centaine stood beside the Rolls at the wharfside and stared with dismay at this ruined legion as they went aboard. There were the amputees, missing an arm or a leg, the lucky ones with the severance below knee or elbow. They swung across the wharf on their crutches, or with an empty sleeve of their tunic pinned up neatly.

Then there were the blind, led by their companions, and the spinal cases carted aboard on their stretchers, and the gas victims with the mucous membranes of their noses and throats burned away by the chlorine gas, and the shell-shocked who twitched and jerked and rolled their eyes uncontrollably, and the burn victims with monstrous pink shiny scar tissue that had contracted to trap their limbs into the bent position, or drawn down their ravaged heads on to their chests, so that they were as twisted and contorted as hunchbacks.

'You can give us a hand here, luv.' One of the orderlies had spotted her uniform, and Centaine roused herself. She turned quickly to the Zulu driver.

'I will find your father – Mbejane?—'

'Mbejane!' Sangane grinned happily that she had the name right.

'And I will give him your message.'

'Go in peace, little lady.' Centaine clasped his hand, then snatched her carpet bag from him and, followed by Anna, hurried to her new duties.

The loading went on through the night, and only when it was completed a little before dawn were they free to try and find the quarters that they had been allocated.

The senior medical officer was a grim-faced major, and it was apparent that word had been whispered to him from on high.

'Where have you been?' he demanded when Centaine reported to his cabin. 'I have been expecting you since noon yesterday. We sail in two hours.'

'I have been here since noon down on "C" Deck, helping Dr Solomon.'

'You should have reported to me,' he told her coldly. 'You can't just wander around the ship suiting yourself. I am responsible to General—' he cut himself off, and went off on a new tack. 'Besides, "C" Deck is other ranks.'

'*Pardon?*' Through practice, Centaine's English had improved immeasurably, but many terms still eluded her.

'Other ranks, not officers. From now on you will be working with officers only. The lower decks are out of bounds to you – out of bounds,' he repeated slowly, as though speaking to a backward child. 'Am I making myself clear to you?'

Centaine was tired, and not used to this type of treatment. 'Those men down there hurt just as much as the officers do,' she told him furiously. 'They bleed and die just like officers do.'

The major blinked and sat back in his chair. He had a daughter the same age as this French chippy, but she would never have dared answer him like that.

'I can see, young lady, that you are going to be a handful,' he said ominously. 'I did not like the idea of having you ladies on board – I knew it would lead to trouble. Now you listen to me. You are going to be quartered in the cabin right across from mine,' he pointed through the open door. 'You will report to Dr Stewart and work to his orders. You will eat in the officers' mess, and the lower decks are out of bounds to you. I expect you to conduct yourself with the utmost propriety at all times, and you can be certain that I will be keeping a very sharp eye on you.'

After such a bleak introduction, the quarters that she and Anna had been allocated came as a delightful surprise, and again she suspected that the hand of General Sean Courtney had moved. They had a suite that would have cost 200 guineas before the war, twin beds rather than bunks, a small drawing-room with sofa and armchairs and writing-desk, and their own shower and toilet, all tastefully furnished in autumn shades.

Centaine bounced on the bed and then fell back on the pillows and sighed blissfully.

'Anna, I am too tired to undress.'

'Into your nightdress,' Anna ordered. 'And don't forget to clean your teeth.'

They were wakened by the alarm gongs ringing, the blast of whistles in the companionway and a hammering on the cabin door. The ship was under way, vibrating to her engines and working to the scend of the sea.

After the first moments of panic, they learned from their

cabin steward that it was a boat drill. Dressing and strapping themselves hastily into their bulky lifejackets, they trooped on to the upper deck and found their lifeboat station.

The ship had just cleared the harbour breakwater and was standing out into the Channel. It was a grey misty morning and the wind whipped about their ears so that there was a general murmur of relief when the 'stand-down' was sounded and breakfast was served in the first-class dining-room, which had been converted into the officers' mess for the walking wounded.

Centaine's entrance caused a genteel pandemonium. Very few of the officers had realized that there was a pretty girl on board, and they found it difficult to conceal their delight. There was a great deal of jockeying for position, but very quickly the first officer, taking advantage of the fact that the captain was still on the bridge, exercised his rank, and Centaine found herself installed at his right hand surrounded by a dozen attentive and solicitous gentlemen, with Anna seated opposite, glowering like a guardian bull-dog.

The ship's officers were all British, but the patients were colonials, for the *Protea Castle* was going on eastwards after rounding the Cape of Good Hope. Seated around Centaine there were a captain of Australian Light Horse who had lost a hand, a pair of New Zealanders, one with a piratical black patch over his missing eye and the other with an equally piratical Long John Silver wooden stump, a young Rhodesian named Jonathan Ballantyne who had won an MC at the Somme but paid for it with a burst of machine-gun fire through the belly, and other eager young men who had all lost parts of their anatomy.

They plied her with food from the buffet. 'No, no, I cannot eat your great English breakfasts, you will make me fat and ugly like a pig.' And she glowed at their concerted denials. The war had been in progress since Centaine was a mere fourteen years old, and with all the young men gone, she had never known the pleasure of being surrounded by a horde of admirers.

She saw the senior medical officer scowling at her from the captain's table, and as much to spite him as for her own amusement, she set herself out to be pleasant to the young men surrounding her. Although she felt a stirring of guilt that she might be less than faithful to Michael's memory, she consoled herself.

'It is my duty, they are my patients. A nurse must be good to her patients.' And she smiled and laughed with them, and they were pathetically eager to catch her attention, render small services for her and answer her questions.

'Why are we not sailing in convoy?' she asked. 'Is it not dangerous to go down Channel *en plein soleil* – in broad daylight? I have heard about the *Rewa*.'

The *Rewa* was the British hospital ship, with 300 wounded on board, that had been torpedoed by a German U-boat in the Bristol Channel on January 4th that year. Fortunately, the ship had been abandoned with the loss of only three lives, but it had fuelled the anti-German propaganda. Displayed in most public places were the posters headed: 'What a *Red Rag* is to a bull, the *Red Cross* is to the Hun,' with a graphic account of the atrocity beneath.

Centaine's question precipitated a lively argument at the breakfast table.

'The *Rewa* was torpedoed at night,' Jonathan Ballantyne pointed out reasonably. 'The U-boat commander probably didn't see the red crosses.'

'Oh, come now! Those U-boat chaps are absolute butchers—'

'I don't agree. They are just ordinary fellows like you and me. The captain of this ship obviously believes that too – that's why we are covering the most dangerous down-channel leg in daylight, to let the U-boats get a good look at our Red Cross markings. I think they'll leave us alone, once they know what we are.'

'Nonsense, damned Huns would torpedo their own mothers-in-law—'

'So would I, mind you!'

'This ship is steaming at twenty-two knots,' the first officer reassured Centaine. 'The U-boat is capable of only seven knots when submerged. It would have to be lying directly in our track to have any chance of a shot at us. Odds of a million to one, miss, you don't have to worry at all. Just enjoy the voyage.'

A tall, round-shouldered young doctor with a mild scholarly air and steel-rimmed spectacles stood before Centaine as she rose from the breakfast table.

'I am Dr Archibald Stewart, Nurse de Thiry, and Major Wright has put you in my charge.'

Centaine liked the new form of address. 'Nurse de Thiry' had a nice professional ring to it. She was not so certain that she enjoyed being in anyone's charge, however.

'Do you have any medical or nursing training?' Dr Stewart went on, and Centaine's initial liking for him cooled. He had exposed her in the first few seconds, and in front of her new-found admirers. She shook her head, trying not to make the confession public, but he went on remorselessly.

'I thought not.' He eyed her dubiously, and then seemed to become aware of her embarrassment. 'Never mind, a nurse's most important duty is to cheer up her patients. From what little I've seen, you are very good at that. I think we'll make you chief cheerer-upper, but only on "A" Deck. Strict orders from Major Wright. "A" Deck only.'

Dr Archibald Stewart's appointment turned out to be inspired. From an early age, Centaine's organizational skills had been honed in the running of the château of Mort Homme, where she had been her father's hostess and assistant housekeeper. Effortlessly she manipulated the band of young men that had gathered about her into an entertainments team.

The *Protea Castle* had a library of many thousands of volumes, and she quickly instituted a distribution and collection scheme for the bedridden cases, and a roster of readers for the blind and illiterate amongst the men on the lower decks. She arranged smoking concerts and deck games and card tournaments – the comte had been a wicked bridge player and taught her his skills.

Her team of one-eyed, one-legged, maimed assistant alleviators of the boredom of the long voyage vied with each other to win her approval and render their services; and the patients in the tiers of bunks thought up a dozen tricks to delay her beside them when she made her unofficial rounds each morning.

Amongst the patients was a captain of the Natal Mounted Rifles who had been in the convoy of ambulances during the retreat from Mort Homme, and he greeted her ecstatically the first time she entered his ward with her armful of books.

'Sunshine! It's Sunshine herself!' and the nickname followed her about the ship.

'Nurse Sunshine.' When the usually surly chief medical officer, Major Wright, used the nickname for the first time, Centaine's adoption by the ship's company was unanimous.

In the circumstances there was little time for mourning, but every night just before composing herself for sleep, Centaine lay in the darkness and conjured up Michael's image in her mind's eye, and then clasped both hands over her lower stomach.

'Our son, Michel, our son!'

The brooding skies and brutal black seas of the Bay of Biscay were left behind on the long white wake, and ahead of the bows the flying fish spun like silver coins across the blue velvet surface of the ocean.

At latitude 30 degrees north, the debonair young Captain Jonathan Ballantyne, who was the reputed heir to the 100,000-acre cattle ranches of his father Sir Ralph Ballantyne, Prime Minister of Rhodesia, proposed marriage to Centaine.

'I can hear poor Papa,' Centaine mimicked the comte so accurately that it cast a shadow in Anna's eyes. '"A hundred thousand acres, you crazy wicked child. *Tiens alors!* How can you refuse a hundred thousand acres?"'

After that the marriage proposals became an epidemic – even Dr Archibald Stewart, her immediate superior, blinking through his steel-rimmed spectacles and sweating nervously, stammered through a carefully rehearsed speech, and looked more gratified than abashed when Centaine kissed both his cheeks in polite refusal.

At the equator Centaine prevailed on Major Wright to don the regalia of King Neptune, and the crossing ceremony was conducted amidst wild hilarity and widespread inebriation. Centaine herself turned out to be the main attraction, clad in a mermaid costume of her own design. Anna had protested strenuously at the *décolleté* all the while she helped to sew it, but the ship's company adored it. They whistled and clapped and stamped, and there was another rash of proposals immediately after the crossing.

Anna huffed and gruffed, but secretly was well content with the change she saw coming over her charge. Before her eyes Centaine was making that wonderful transformation from girl to young womanhood. Physically she was beginning to bloom with early pregnancy. Her fine skin took on a lustre like mother-of-pearl, she lost the last vestiges of adolescent gawkiness as her body filled without losing any of its grace.

However, more powerful were the other changes – the growing confidence and poise, the awareness of her own powers and gifts that she was only now beginning to exercise fully. Anna had known that Centaine was a natural mimic, could switch from the *midi* accent of Jacques, the groom, to the Walloon of the chambermaids and then to the Parisian intellectual of her music teacher, but now she realized that the child had a talent for languages which had never been tested. Centaine was already speaking such fluent English that she could differentiate between the Australian and South African and pure Oxford English accents, and take them off with startling accuracy. When she greeted her Aussies with a dinky 'Gid die!', they hooted with delight.

Anna had known also that Centaine had a way with figures and money. She had taken over the family accounts when the estate factor had fled to Paris in the first months of the war, and Anna had marvelled at her ability to cast a long column of figures simply by running her pen down it, without the laborious carrying over of digits, and without moving her lips, all of which Anna considered miraculous.

Now Centaine demonstrated the same acumen. She partnered Major Wright at the bridge table and they made a formidable pair, and her share of the winnings flabbergasted Anna who did not really approve of gambling. Centaine reinvested these. She organized a syndicate with Jonathan Ballantyne and Dr Stevens and they were big punters on the daily auction and sweepstake on the ship's run. By the time they crossed the equator, Centaine had added nearly two hundred sovereigns to the hoard of *louis d'or* they had salvaged from the château.

Anna had always known that Centaine read too much. 'It will damage your eyes,' she had warned her often enough, but she had never realized the depth of the knowledge that Centaine had gathered from her books, not until she heard it demonstrated in conversation and discussion. She held her own even against such formidable debaters as Dr Archibald Stewart, and yet Anna noticed that she was cunning enough not to antagonize her audience by ostentatiously flaunting her learning, and would usually end an argument on a conciliatory note that allowed her male victim to retreat with only slightly ruffled dignity.

'Yes,' Anna nodded comfortably to herself, as she watched the girl blooming and opening like some lovely flower in the tropical sunshine, 'she's a clever one, just like her Mama.'

It seemed that Centaine really had a physical need for warmth and sunlight. She would turn her face up to the sun every time she went on deck. 'Oh, Anna, I did so hate the cold and the rain. Doesn't this feel wonderful?

'You are turning ugly brown,' Anna warned her. 'It's so unladylike.'

And Centaine considered her own limbs thoughtfully. 'Not brown, Anna, gold!'

Centaine had read so much and queried so many people, that she seemed already to know the southern hemisphere into which their ship now thrust its bows. Centaine would wake Anna and take her on to the upper deck to act as chaperone while the officer of the watch showed her the southern stars. And despite the late hour, Anna was dazzled by the splendours of this sky that each evening revealed more of itself before their upturned eyes.

'Look, Anna, there is Achernar at last! It was Michel's own special star. We should all have a special star, he said, and he chose mine for me.'

'Which is it?' Anna asked. 'Which is your star?'

'Acrux. There! The brightest star in the Great Cross. There is nothing between it and Michel's star, except the pivot of the whole world, the celestial South Pole. He said between us we would hold the axis of the earth. Wasn't that romantic, Anna?'

'Romantic twaddle,' Anna sniffed, and secretly regretted that she had never had a man to say such things to her.

Then Anna came to recognize in her charge a talent that seemed to make all the others pale. It was the ability of making men listen to her. It was quite extraordinary to see men like Major Wright and the *Protea Castle*'s captain actually keep silent and attend, without that infuriatingly indulgent masculine smirk, when Centaine spoke seriously.

'She's only a child,' Anna marvelled, 'yet they treat her like a woman – no, no, more than that even, they are beginning to treat her like an equal.'

That was truly astonishing. Here were these men according to a young girl the respect that thousands of other women, Emmeline Pankhurst and Annie Kenney at their head, had been burning property, throwing themselves under racehorses, hunger-striking and enduring prison sentences to obtain – so far unsuccessfully.

Centaine made the men listen to her, and very often she made them do what she wanted, although she was not above using the sly sexual tricks to which women over the ages have been forced to resort; Centaine achieved her ends by adding logic, cogent argument and force of character. These, combined with an appealing smile and level look from dark, fathomless eyes, seemed irresistible. For instance, it took her a mere five days to get Major Wright to rescind his order confining her to 'A' Deck.

Although Centaine's days were filled to the last minute, she never for a moment lost sight of the ultimate destination. Each day her longing for first sight of the land where Michael had been born, and where his son would be born, became stronger.

However busy she was, she never missed the noonshot, and a few minutes before the hour she would race up the companionway to the bridge and arrive in a swirl of her uniform skirts, gabbling breathlessly, 'Permission to enter the bridge, sir?' And the officer of the watch, who had been waiting for her, would salute.

'Permission granted. You are only just in time, Sunshine.'

Then she would watch fascinated as the navigating officers stood on the wing of the bridge with the sextants raised and made the noonday shot of the sun, and then worked out the day's run and the ship's position and marked it on the chart.

'There you are, Sunshine, 17°23″ south. One hundred and sixty nautical miles north-west of the mouth of the Cunene river. Cape Town in four days' time, God and the weather permitting.'

Centaine studied the map eagerly. 'So we are already off the South African coast?'

'No, no! That is German West Africa; it was one of the Kaiser's colonies, until the South Africans captured it two years ago.'

'What is it like – jungles? Savannahs?'

'No such luck, Sunshine, it's one of the most Godforsaken deserts in the entire world.'

And Centaine left the chartroom and went out on to the wing of the bridge again and stared into the east, towards the great continent that still lay far below her watery horizon.

'Oh, I can barely wait to see it at last!'

Tis horse was an animal of the desert, its distant ancestors had carried kings and Bedouin chieftains over the burning wastes of Arabia. Its blood-lines had been taken north by the crusaders to the colder climes of Europe, and then hundreds of years later they had been brought out to Africa again by the colonial expedition of Germany and landed at the port of Lüderitzbucht with the cavalry squadrons of Bismarck. In Africa these horses had been crossed and recrossed with the shaggy hardy mounts of the Boers and the desert-forged animals of the Hottentots until this animal emerged, a creature well suited to this rugged environment and to the tasks to which it was committed.

It had the wide nostrils and fine head of its Arabian type, broad spatulate hooves to cover the soft desert earth, great lungs in its barrel chest, pale chestnut coloration to repel the worst of the sun's rays, a shaggy coat to insulate it from both the burning noon heat and the crackling cold of the desert nights, and the legs and heart to carry its rider to far milky horizons and beyond.

The man upon his back was also of mixed blood-lines and, like his mount, a creature of the desert and the boundless land.

His mother had come out from Berlin when her father had been appointed second-in-command of the military forces in German West Africa. She had met and, despite her family's opposition, married a young Boer from a family rich only in land and spirit. Lothar was the only child of that union, and at his mother's insistence had been sent back to Germany to complete his schooling. He had proved a good scholar, but the outbreak of the Boer War had interrupted his studies. The first his mother had known of his decision to join the Boer forces was when he arrived back in Windhoek unannounced. Hers was a warrior family, so her pride was fierce when Lothar had ridden away with a Hottentot servant and three spare horses to seek his father who was already in the field against the English.

Lothar had found his father at Magersfontein with his uncle Koos De La Rey, the legendary Boer commander, and had undergone his initiation to battle two days later when the British tried to force the passage through the Magersfontein hills and relieve the siege of Kimberley.

Lothar De La Rey was five days past his fourteenth birthday on the dawn of the battle, and he killed his first Englishman before six that morning. It had been a less difficult target than a hundred springbok and running kudu had offered him before.

Lothar, one of the five hundred picked marksmen, had

stood to the parapet of the trench that he had helped dig along the foot of the Magersfontein hills. The idea of digging a trench and using it as cover had at first repelled the Boers, who were essentially horsemen and loved to range fast and wide. Yet General De La Rey had persuaded them to try this new tactic, and the lines of advancing English infantry had walked unsuspectingly on to the trenches in the deceptive early light.

Leading the advance towards where Lothar lay was a powerful, thickset man with flaming red muttonchop whiskers. He strode a dozen paces ahead of the line, his kilts swinging jauntily, a tropical pith helmet set at a rakish angle over one eye and bared sword in his right hand.

At that moment the sun rose over the Magersfontein hills, and its ripe orange light flooded the open, featureless veld. It lit the ranks of advancing highlanders like a stage effect – perfect shooting light – and the Boers had paced out the ranges in front of their trenches and marked them with cairns of stones.

Lothar took his aim on the centre of the Englishman's forehead, but like the men beside him was held by a strange reluctance, for this seemed not much short of murder. Then, almost at its own volition, the Mauser jumped against his shoulder and the crack of the shot seemed to come from very far away. The British officer's helmet sprang from his head and spun end over end. He was driven back a pace and his arms flew open. The sound of the bullet striking the man's skull came back to Lothar, like a ripe watermelon dropped on to a stone floor. The sword flashed in the sunlight as it fell from the soldier's hand, then with a slow, almost elegant pirouette, he sank into the low coarse scrub.

Hundreds of highlanders had lain pinned in front of the trenches all that day. Not a man of them dared lift his head, for the waiting rifles in the trenches a hundred paces from where they lay were wielded by some of the finest marksmen in the world.

The African sun burned the backs of their knees below the kilts until they swelled, and the skin burst open like over-ripe fruit. The wounded highlanders cried for water and some of the Boers in the trenches threw their water-bottles towards them, but they fell short.

Though Lothar had killed fifty men since then, that was the day he would remember all his life. He always marked it as the day he had become a man.

Lothar was not among those who had thrown his water-bottle. Instead, he had shot dead two of the Englishmen as they wriggled forward on their bellies to try and reach the water-bottles. His hatred of the English, learned at the knees of both his mother and his father, had truly begun to flower that day and had come into full fruiting in the years that followed.

The English had hunted him and his father like wild animals across the veld. His beloved aunt and three female cousins had died of diphtheria, the white sore throat, in the English concentration camps, but Lothar had made himself believe the story that the English had put fish-hooks in the bread that they fed the Boer women to rip out their throats. It was an English thing, this war on the women and the young girls and the children.

He and his father and his uncles had fought on long after all hope of victory was gone, the Bitter Enders, they called themselves with pride. When the others, starved to walking skeletons, sick with dysentery and covered with the running ulcerations which they called veld sores, caused by exposure and malnutrition, dressed in their rags and sacking, with only three rounds a piece remaining in their bandoliers, had gone in to surrender to the English at Vereeniging, Petrus De La Rey and his son Lothar had not gone in with them.

'Witness my oath, oh Lord of my people.' Petrus had stood bareheaded in the veld, with his seventeen-year-old son Lothar beside him. 'The war against the English will never end. This I swear in your sight, oh Lord God of Israel.'

Then he had placed the black leather-covered Bible in Lothar's hands and made him swear the same oath.

'The war against the English will never end—' Lothar had stood beside his father as he cursed the traitors, the cowards who would no longer fight on, Louis Botha and Jannie Smuts, even his own brother Koos De La Rey. 'You, who would sell your people to the Philistine, may you live all your lives under the English yoke and all burn in hell for ten thousand years.'

Then the father and the boy had turned their backs and ridden away, towards the vast arid land that was the domain of Imperial Germany, and left the others to make peace with England.

Because both father and son were strong, hard workers, both of them endowed with natural shrewdness and courage, because Lothar's mother was a German of good family with excellent connections and some wealth, they had prospered in German South-West Africa.

Petrus De La Rey, Lothar's father, was a self-taught engineer of considerable skill and ingenuity. What he did not know he could improvise: the saying was, "*N Boer maak altyd 'n plan*' – a Boer will always make a plan. Through his wife's connections he obtained the contract to reconstruct the breakwater of Lüderitzbucht harbour, and when that was successfully completed, the contract to build the railway line northwards from the Orange river to Windhoek, the capital of German South-West. He taught Lothar his engineering skills. The boy learned swiftly, and by the age of twenty-one was a full partner in the construction and road-building company of De La Rey and Son.

His mother, Christina De La Rey, selected a pretty blonde German girl of good family and moved her diplomatically into her son's orbit, and they were married before Lothar's twenty-third birthday. She bore Lothar a beautiful blond son on whom he doted.

Then the English intruded upon their lives once more, threatening to plunge the entire world into war by opposing the legitimate ambitions of the German empire. Lothar and his father had gone to Governor Seitz with an offer to build up, at their own expense, supply dumps in the remote areas of the territory to be used by the German forces to resist the English invasion, which would surely come from the Union of South Africa, now governed by those traitors and turncoats Smuts and Louis Botha.

There had been a German naval captain in Windhoek at the time; he had quickly recognized the value of the De La Rey offer and prevailed on the governor to accept it. He had sailed with the father and son along that dreadful littoral that so well deserved the name Skeleton Coast, to select a site for a base from which German naval vessels could refuel and revictual, even after the ports of Lüderitzbucht and Walvis Bay were captured by the Union forces.

They discovered a remote and protected bay three hundred miles north of the tenuous settlements at Walvis Bay and Swakopmund, a site almost impossible to reach overland, for it was guarded by the fiery deserts. They loaded a small coastal steamer with the naval stores sent out to them secretly from Bremerhaven in a German cruise ship. There were 500 tons of fuel oil in 44-gallon drums, engine spares and canned foods, small arms and ammunition, nine-inch naval shells, and fourteen of the long Mark VII acoustic torpedoes, to re-arm the German U-boats if they should ever operate in these southern oceans. These supplies were ferried ashore and buried amongst the towering dunes. The lighters were painted with protective tar and buried with the stores.

This secret supply base was finally established only weeks before the Archduke Franz Ferdinand was assassinated at Sarajevo and the Kaiser was forced to move against the Serbian revolutionaries to protect the interests of the German empire. Immediately France and Britain had seized upon this as a pretext for precipitating the war after which they had been lusting.

Lothar and his father saddled their horses and called out their Hottentot servants, kissed their women and Lothar's son farewell, and rode out on commando against the English and their unionist minions once again. They were six hundred strong, riding under the Boer General Maritz, when they reached the Orange river and built their laager and waited for the moment to strike.

Each day armed men rode in to join them, tough, bearded men, proud, hard fighters with the Mausers slung on their shoulders and the bandoliers of ammunition criss-crossing their wide chests. After each joyous greeting, they gave their news, and it was all good.

The old comrades were flocking to the cry of 'Commando!' Everywhere Boers were repudiating the treacher-ous peace which Smuts and Botha had negotiated with the English. All the old Boer generals were taking to the field. De Wet was camped at Mushroom Valley, Kemp was at Treurfontein with eight hundred, Beyers and Fourie were all out and had declared for Germany against England.

Smuts and Botha seemed reluctant to precipitate a conflict between Boer and Boer, for the Union forces consisted of seventy per cent Dutch-born soldiers. They were begging, wheedling and pleading with the rebels, sending envoys to their camps, prostrating themselves in the attempt to avoid bloodshed, but each day the rebel forces grew stronger and more confident.

Then a message reached them, carried by a horseman riding in great haste across the desert from Windhoek. It was a message from the Kaiser himself, relayed to them by Governor Seitz.

Admiral Graf Von Spee with his squadron of battle-cruisers had won a devastating naval battle at Coronel on the Chilean coast. The Kaiser had ordered Von Spee to round the Horn and cross the southern Atlantic to blockade and bombard the South African ports in support of their rebellion against the English and the Unionists.

They stood under the fierce desert sun and cheered and sang, united and sure of their cause, and certain of their victory. They were waiting only for the last of the Boer generals to come in to join them before they marched on Pretoria.

Koos De La Rey, Lothar's uncle, grown old and feeble and indecisive, had still not come in. Lothar's father sent messages to him, urging him to do his duty, but he vacillated, swayed by the treacherous oratory of Jannie Smuts and his misguided love and loyalty for Louis Botha.

Koen Brits was the other Boer leader they were waiting for, that giant of granite, standing six foot six inches tall, who could drink a bottle of fiery Cape Smoke the way a lesser man might quaff a mug of ginger beer, who could lift a trek ox off its feet, spit a stream of tobacco juice a measured twenty paces and with his Mauser hit a running springbok at two hundred paces. They needed him, for a thousand fighting men would follow him when he decided which way to ride.

However, Jannie Smuts sent this remarkable man a message: 'Call out your commando, Oom Koen, and ride with me.' The reply was immediate. '*Ja*, my old friend, we are mounted and ready to ride – but who do we fight, Germany or England?' So they lost Brits to the Unionists.

Then Koos De La Rey, travelling to a final meeting with Jannie Smuts at which he would make his decision, ran into a police roadblock outside Pretoria and instructed his chauffeur to drive through it. The police marksmen shot him in the head. So they lost De La Rey.

Of course, Jannie Smuts, that cold, crafty devil, had an excuse. He said that the roadblock had been ordered to prevent the escape of the notorious band of bank robbers, the Foster gang, from the area, and that the police had opened fire on a mistaken identity. However, the rebels knew better. Lothar's father had wept openly when they received the news of his brother's murder, and they had known that there was no turning back, no further chance for parley, they would have to carry the land at rifle-point.

The plan was for all the rebel commandos to join up with Maritz on the Orange river, but they had underestimated the new mobility of the forces against them, afforded by the petrol-driven motor-car. They had forgotten also that Botha and Smuts had long ago proved themselves the most able of all the Boer generals. When at last they moved, these two moved with the deadly speed of angry mambas.

They caught De Wet at Mushroom Valley and smashed his commando with artillery and machine-guns. There were terrible casualties, and De Wet fled into the Kalahari, pursued by Koen Brits and a motorized column that captured him at Waterburg in the desert.

Then the Unionists swung back and engaged Beyers and his commando near Rustenberg. Once the battle was lost Beyers tried to escape by swimming the flooded Vaal river. His boot-laces became entangled and they found his body three days later on the bank downstream.

On the Orange river, Lothar and his father waited for the inevitable onslaught, but bad news reached them before the Unionists did.

The English Admiral, Sir Doveton Sturdee, had intercepted Von Spee at the Falkland Islands, and sunk his great cruisers *Scharnhorst* and *Gneisenau* and the rest of his squadron with only ten British seamen killed. The rebels' hope of succour had gone down with the German fleet.

Still they fought doggedly when the Unionists came, but it was in vain. Lothar's father took a bullet through the gut, and Lothar carried him off the field and tried to get him back across the desert to Windhoek where Christina could nurse him. It was five hundred miles of terrible going through the waterless wastes. The old man's pain was so fierce that Lothar wept for him, and the wound was contaminated by the contents of his perforated intestines and mortified so that the stench brought the hyenas howling around the camp at night.

But he was a tough old man and it took him many days to die.

'Promise me, my son,' he demanded with his last breath that stank of death, 'promise me that the war with the English will never end.'

'I promise you, Father.' Lothar leaned over him to kiss his cheek, and the old man smiled and closed his eyes.

Lothar buried him under a camelthorn tree in the wilderness; he buried him deeply so that the hyena would not smell him and dig him up. Then he rode on home to Windhoek.

Colonel Franke, the German commander, recognized Lothar's value, and asked him to raise a levy of scouts. Lothar assembled a small band of hardy Boers, German settlers, Bondelswart Hottentots and black tribesmen, and took them out into the desert to await the invasion of Unionist troops.

Smuts and Botha came with 45,000 men and landed at Swakopmund and Lüderitzbucht. From there they drove into the interior, employing their usual tactics, lightning forced marches, often without water for great distances, double-pronged attacks and encircling movements, using the new-fangled petrol-driven motor-cars the same way they had used horses during the Boer War. Against this multitude Franke had 8,000 German troops to defend a territory of over 300,000 square miles with a 1,000-mile coastline.

Lothar and his scouts fought the Unionists with their own tactics, poisoning the water-holes ahead of the Union troops, dynamiting the railway lines, hooking around them to attack their supply lines, setting ambushes and land-mines, raiding at night and at dawn, driving off the horses, pushing his scouts to even their far borders of endurance.

It was all unavailing. Botha and Smuts caught the tiny German army between them, and with a casualty list of only 530 dead and wounded exacted an unconditional surrender from Colonel Franke, but not from Lothar De La Rey. To honour the promise he had made to his father, he took what remained of his band of scouts northwards into the dreaded kakao veld to continue the struggle.

Lothar's mother, Christina, and his wife and child went into the internment camp for German nationals that was set up by the Unionists at Windhoek, and there all three of them died.

They died in a typhoid epidemic, but Lothar De La Rey knew who was ultimately to blame for their deaths, and in the desert he cherished and nourished his hatred, for it was all that he had left. His family was slain by the English and his estates seized and confiscated. Hatred was the fuel that drove him forward.

He was thinking of his murdered family now as he stood at his horse's head on the crest of one of the high dunes that overlooked the green Atlantic Ocean where the Benguela current steamed in the early sunlight.

His mother's face seemed to rise out of the twisting fog banks before him. She had been a beautiful woman. Tall and statuesque, with thick blonde hair that hung to her knees when she brushed it out, but which she wore twisted into thick plaited golden ropes on top of her head to enhance her height. Her eyes had been golden also, with the direct cold gaze of a leopardess.

She could sing like one of the Valkyries from Wagner, and she had passed on to Lothar her love of music and learning and art. She had passed on to him also her fine looks, classical Teutonic features, and the dense curls that now hung to his shoulders from under the wide terai hat with the waving bunch of ostrich feathers stuck jauntily in the puggaree. Like Christina's, his hair was the colour of newly minted bronze, but his eyebrows were thick and dark over the golden leopard eyes that were now probing the silver mists of the Benguela.

The beauty of the scene moved Lothar the way that music could; like the violins playing Mozart – it induced in him the same feeling of mystic melancholy at the centre of his soul. The sea was green and still, not a ripple spoiled its velvety sheen. The low and gentle sound of the ocean swelled and subsided like the breathing of all creation. Yet along the shoreline the dense growth of dark sea-kelp absorbed the sea's motion and there was no break of white water. The kelp beds danced a slow, graceful minuet, bowing and undulating to the rhythm of the ocean.

The horns of the bay were armed with rock, split into geometric shapes and streaked white with the droppings of the seabirds and seals that basked upon them. The coats of the seals glowed in the mist-filtered sunlight, and their weird honking cries carried on the windless air to where Lothar stood on the crest of the dune high above them.

In the throat of the bay the rock gave way to tawny, lion-coloured beach, and behind the first dune was trapped a wide lagoon hemmed in by nodding reedbeds, the only green in this landscape. In its shallow waters there waded troops of long-legged flamingo. The marvellous pink of their massed formations burned like unearthly fire, drawing Lothar's gaze away from his search of the sea.

The flamingo were not the only birds upon the lagoon.

There were troops of pelican and white egrets, solitary blue herons and a legion of smaller long-legged waders foraging the food-rich waters.

The dunes upon which Lothar waited rose like the crested back of a monstrous serpent, writhing and twisting along the shoreline, rising five hundred feet and more against the misty sky, their restless, every-changing bulk sculptured by the sea wind into soft plastic coils and knife-sharp peaks.

Suddenly, far out on the sea there was a dark boil of movement, and the silk green surface changed to the colour of gunmetal. Lothar felt the jump of his nerves and the race of anticipation through his veins as his gaze darted to it. Was this what he had waited and kept vigil for all these weary weeks? He lifted the binoculars that hung upon his chest, and felt the slide of disappointment.

What he had seen was merely a shoal of fish, but what a shoal! The tip-top of the living mass dimpled the surface, but as he watched, the rest of the shoal rose to feed on the rich green plankton and the commotion spread out until as far as he could see, to the edge of the fog banks three miles out; the ocean seethed and boiled with life. It was a shoal of pilchards five miles across, each individual only as long as a man's hand, but in their countless millions generating the power to move the ocean.

Over this mighty multitude, the yellow-headed gannets and hysterical gulls shrieked and wheeled and plunged, their bodies kicking up white puffs of spray as they hit the water. Squadrons of seals charged back and forth, like the cavalry of the sea, breaking the water white as they gorged on the silver masses, and through this gluttonous chaos, the triangular fins of the great sharks passed with the stately motion of tall sailing ships.

For an hour Lothar watched in wonder, and then abruptly, as though at a signal, the entire living mass sounded, and within minutes the stillness descended over the ocean again. The only movement was the gentle swell of waters and the soft advance and retreat of the silver fog banks under the watery sun.

Lothar hobbled his horse, took a book from his saddlebag and settled on the warm sand. Every few minutes he raised his eyes from the page, but the hours wore away and at last he stood and stretched and went to his horse, his fruitless vigil ended for another day. With one foot in the stirrup, he paused and made a last careful survey of the seascape smudged to bloody carnelian and dull brass by the sunset.

Then, even as he watched, the sea opened before his eyes, and out of it rose an enormous dark shape, in the image of Leviathan, but greater than any living denizen of the oceans. Shining with wetness, gleaming water streaming from its decks and steel sides, it wallowed upon the surface.

'At last!' Lothar shouted with excitement and relief. 'I thought they would never come.'

He stared avidly through his binoculars at the long sinister black vessel. He saw the encrustations of barnacle and weed that fouled the hull. She had been long at sea, and battered by the elements. On the tall conning tower her registration numerals were almost obliterated. 'U-32.' Lothar read them with difficulty, and then his attention was diverted by activity on the submarine's foredeck.

From one of the hatches a gun team swarmed out and ran forward to man the quick-firing cannon near the bows. They were taking no chances. Lothar saw the weapon traverse towards him, ready to reply to any hostile geture from the shore. On the conning tower human heads appeared, and he saw binoculars trained towards him.

Hastily Lothar found the signal rocket in his saddlebag. Its glowing red fireball arced out over the sea, and was answered immediately by a rocket from the submarine hurling skyward on a tail of smoke.

Lothar flung himself on to the back of his mount and pushed him over the edge of the dune. They went sliding down, the horse squatting on its haunches and bringing down a slipping, hissing cascade of sand around them.

At the bottom of the dune Lothar gathered his mount and they went flying across the hard damp beach, with Lothar waving his hat, standing in the stirrups and shouting with laughter. He rode into the camp at the edge of the lagoon and sprang from the saddle. He ran from one of the crude shelters of driftwood and canvas to the next, dragging out his men and kicking them from their blankets.

'They have come, you sleeping lizards. They have come, you pups of desert jackals. Come on! Get off your buttocks before they rot!'

They were an unlikely gang of cut-throats that Lothar had assembled: tall, muscled Hereros, yellow, mongol-faced Hottentots with slanted eyes, fierce Koranas and sly, handsome Ovambos, dressed in tribal finery and the lootings of the battlefields, in cloaks of softly tanned hide of kudu and zebra, in the feathers of ostrich and the tattered tunics and helmet of the Union soldiers they had killed. Armed with Mannlicher and Mauser and Martini Henry and Lee-Enfield .303s, with knife and spear, they were as bloodthirsty as hunting dogs, as wild and savage and unpredictable as the desert that had spawned them. They called only one man their master; if any other had lifted a hand to them or spurned them with his foot, they would have slit his throat or put a ball through the back of his skull, but Lothar De La Rey kicked them to their feet and drove the laggards before him with his fists.

'Move, you devourers of hyena dung, the English will be upon you before you have finished scratching your lice.'

The two lighters were hidden in the reeds. They had come up on the transport with the rest of the stores in those heady days just before the outbreak of war. In the weeks that they had waited for the U-boat, his men had recaulked the seams with oakum and tar, and fashioned rollers from the driftwood that littered the beaches.

Now at Lothar's urging they dragged the sturdy wooden boats from the reeds, twenty men straining at each side, for the boats were heavy. They had been built to carry forty tons of guano each and still stank of seabird droppings. They had wide beam and deep draught, and the wooden rollers laid across the beach sank into the tawny sand as the weight of the hulls passed over them.

They left the two boats at the edge of the water and then hurried back to where the drums of fuel oil were buried at the foot of the dune. They heaved them from the damp sand and rolled them down the beach. Already Lothar had rigged a tripod and tackle and the 44-gallon drums were hoisted and lowered into the lighters. As they worked, the light faded away into the desert night, and the submarine merged with the darkness of the ocean.

'Everybody to help launch!' Lothar bellowed, and his men swarmed out of the darkness and began the rhythmic work chant, each concerted heave moving the heavily laden lighter a few inches forward, until the water lifted her and she slid forward and floated free.

Lothar stood in the bows with a storm lantern held high, and his oarsmen drove the lighter, almost gunwale deep, through the cold black waters. In the blackness ahead, a signal lamp flashed to guide them, and then abruptly the high dark bulk of the U-boat loomed out of the night and the lighter bumped against its side. German seamen were ready with mooring lines and one of them gave Lothar an arm as he leaped the gap and scrambled up the steep steel side.

The U-boat captain was waiting for him on the bridge.

'Unterseeboot Kapitän Kurt Kohler.' He clicked his heels and saluted, then stepped forward to shake Lothar's hand.

'I am very happy to see you, Herr De La Rey, we have

only enough fuel oil left for two days' steaming.' In the glow of the bridge light the submariner was gaunt-faced. His skin had the waxy pallor of a creature that had lived away from the light for a long time. His eyes had sunk into dark cavities, and his mouth was like the scar from a sabre cut. Lothar could recognize that here was a man who had come intimately to understand death and fear down there in the dark and secret depths.

'You have had a successful cruise, Kapitän?'

'One hundred and twenty-six days at sea and twenty-six thousand tons of enemy shipping,' the submariner nodded.

'With God's help, another twenty-six thousand tons,' Lothar suggested.

'With God's help, and your fuel oil,' the captain agreed, and glanced down at the deck where the first drums were being swayed aboard. Then he looked back at Lothar. 'You have torpedoes?' he asked anxiously.

'Content yourself,' Lothar reassured him. 'The torpedoes are ready, but I thought it prudent to refuel before rearming.'

'Of course.' Neither of them had to mention the consequence of the U-boat, with her tanks empty, being caught against a hostile shore by an English warship.

'I still have a little schnapps,' the captain changed the subject, 'my officers and I would be honoured.'

As Lothar descended the steel ladder into the submarine's interior, he felt his gorge rise. The stench was a solid thing, so that he wondered that any man could endure it more than a few minutes. It was the smell of sixty men living in a confined space for months on end, living without sunlight or fresh air, without the means of washing their bodies or their clothing. It was the smell of pervading damp and of the fungus that turned their uniforms green and rotted the cloth off their bodies, the stench of hot fuel oil and bilges, of greasy food and the sickly sweat of fear, the

252

clinging odour of bedding that had been slept in for 126 days and nights, of socks and boots that were never changed and the reek of the sewage buckets which could only be emptied once every twenty-four hours.

Lothar hid his revulsion and clicked his heels and bowed when the captain introduced his junior officers. The overhead deck was so low that Lothar had to hunch his head down on his shoulders, and the space between the bulkheads was so narrow that two men were forced to turn sideways to pass each other. He tried to imagine living in these conditions and found his face beading with cold sweat.

'Do you have any intelligence of enemy shipping, Herr De La Rey?' The captain poured a tiny measure of schnapps into each of the crystal glasses and sighed when the last drop fell from the bottle.

'I regret that my intelligence is seven days old.' Lothar saluted the naval officers with a raised glass, and when they had all drunk went on, 'The troopship *Auckland* docked at Durban eight days ago for bunkers. She is carrying 2,000 New Zealand infantry, and was expected to sail again on the 15th—'

There were many sympathizers in the civil service of the Union of South Africa, men and women whose fathers and family had fought in the Boer War, and had ridden with Maritz and De Wet against the Union troops. Some of them had relatives who had been imprisoned and even executed for treason once Smuts and Botha had crushed the rebellion. Many of these were employed by the South African Railway and Harbours Authority, others had key positions in the Department of Post and Telegraphs. Thus vital information was gathered and swiftly encoded and disseminated to German agents and rebel activists over the Union government's own communications network.

Lothar reeled off the list of arrivals and sailings from South African ports, and again apologized. 'My information is received at the telegraph station at Okahandja, but it takes five to seven days for it to be carried across the desert by one of my men.'

'I understand,' the German captain nodded. 'Nevertheless, the information you have given me will be invaluable in helping me plan the next stage of my operations.' He looked up from the chart on which he had been marking the enemy dispositions which Lothar had given him, and for the first time noticed his guest's discomfort. He kept his expression attentive and courteous, but inwardly he gloated, 'You great hero, handsome as an opera star, so brave out there with the wind in your face and the sun shining over your head, I wish I could take you with me and teach you the true meaning of courage and sacrifice! How would you like to hear the English destroyers go drumming overhead as they hunt you, how would you like to hear the click of the primer as the death-charge sinks down towards you? Oh, I would enjoy watching your face when the blast beats against the pressure hull and water squirts in through the cracks and the lights go out. How would you like to smell yourself shit with fear in the dark and feel it running hot and liquid down your legs?' Instead he smiled and murmured, 'I wish I was able to offer you a little more schnapps—'

'No, no!' Lothar waved the offer aside. This corpse-faced creature and his stinking vessel disgusted and sickened him. 'You have been most gracious. I must go ashore and supervise the loading. These Schwarzes, you cannot trust them. Lazy dogs and born thieves, all of them. They understand only the whip and the goad.'

Lothar escaped thankfully up the ladder and in the conning tower sucked the sweet cool night air greedily into his lungs. The submarine captain followed him up.

'Herr De La Rey, it is essential that we complete bunkering and stores before dawn – you realize how vulnerable we are here, how helpless we would be, trapped against the shore, with our hatches open and our tanks empty?'

'If you could send some of your seamen ashore to assist with the loading—'

The captain hesitated. Placing his valuable crew on land would make him more vulnerable still. He weighed the odds swiftly. War was all a gambler's throw, risk against reward, for the stakes of death and glory.

'I will send twenty men to the beach with you.' He made the decision in seconds, and Lothar, who had understood his quandary, nodded with reluctant admiration.

They had to have light. Lothar built a bonfire of driftwood on the beach, but built a screen between it and the sea, trusting on this and the hovering fog banks to shield them from any searching English warships. By the diffused glow they loaded and reloaded the lighters and rowed them out to the submarine. As each drum of fuel oil was funnelled into the vessel's tanks, the empty canister was holed and thrown overboard to sink into the kelp beds, and gradually the long slim vessel sank lower in the water.

It was four in the morning before the fuel tanks were brimming, and the U-boat captain fretted and fumed on his bridge, glancing every few seconds towards the land where the false dawn was giving a hard knife-edge to the dark crests of the dunes – and then down again to the approaching lighter with the long glistening shape of a torpedo balanced delicately across the thwarts.

'Hurry.' He leaned over the gunwale of the conning tower to urge on his men, as they fitted the slings around the monstrous weapon, gingerly took the weight on the straining tackle and swung it on board. The second lighter was already alongside with its murderous burden, and the first lighter was thrashing back towards the beach, as the torpedo was eased gently into the forward hatch and slid into the empty tube below deck.

Swiftly the light strengthened and the efforts of the crew and the black guerrillas became frantic as they fought off their fatigue and struggled to complete the loading before full daylight exposed them to their enemies.

Lothar rode out with the last torpedo, sitting casually astride its shining back as though upon his Arab, and the captain watching him in the dawn found himself resenting him more fiercely, hating him for being tall and sungilded and handsome, hating him for his casual arrogance, and for the ostrich feathers in his hat and the golden curls that hung to his shoulders, but hating him most of all because he would ride away into the desert and leave the U-boat commander to go down again into the cold and deadly waters.

'Captain,' Lothar scrambled out of the lighter and climbed the ladder to the bridge of the conning tower. The captain realized that his handsome face was glowing with excitement.

'Captain, one of my men has just ridden into camp. He has been five days reaching me from Okahandja, and he has news. Splendid news.'

The captain tried not to let the excitement infect him, but his hands began to tremble as Lothar went on.

'The assistant harbour master at Cape Town is one of our men. They are expecting the English heavy battle cruiser *Inflexible* to reach Cape Town within eight days. She left Gibraltar on the 5th and is sailing direct.'

The captain dived back into the hatch, and Lothar suppressed his repugnance and followed him down the steel ladder. The captain was already bending eagerly over the chart-table with the dividers in his hands firing questions at his navigating officer.

'Give me the cruising speed of the enemy "I" class battle cruisers!'

The navigator thumbed swiftly through intelligence files. 'Estimated 22 knots at 260 revolutions, captain.'

'Ha!' The captain was chalking in the approximate course from Gibraltar down the western coastline of the African continent, around the great bulge and then on to the Cape of Good Hope.

'Ha!' Again, this time with delight and anticipation. 'We can be in patrol position by 1800 hours today, if we sail within the hour, and she cannot possibly have passed by then.'

He raised his head from the chart and looked at his officers crowded around him.

'An English battle cruiser, gentlemen, but not an ordinary one. The *Inflexible*, the same ship that sank the *Scharnhorst* at the Falkland Islands. A prize! What a prize for us to take to the Kaiser and *Das Vaterland*.'

E xcept for the two lookouts in the wings, Captain Kurt Kohler stood alone in the conning tower of U-32 and shivered in the cold sea mist despite the thick white rollneck sweater he wore under his blue peajacket. 'Start main engine secure to diving stations!' He bent to the voice tube, and immediately his lieutenant's confirmation echoed back to him.

'Start main engine. Secure to diving stations.'

The deck trembled under Kohler's feet and the diesel exhaust blurted above his head. The oily reek of burned fuel oil made his nostrils flare.

'Ship ready to dive!' the lieutenant's voice confirmed, and Kohler felt as though a crushing burden had been lifted from his back. How he had fretted through those helpless and vulnerable hours of refuelling and rearming. However, that was past – once again the ship was alive beneath his feet, ready to his hand, and relief buoyed him up above his fatigue.

'Revolutions for seven knots,' he ordered. 'New course

270 degrees.' As his order was repeated, he tipped his cap with its gold-braided peak on to the back of his head, and turned his binoculars towards land.

Already the heavy wooden lighters had been dragged away and hidden amongst the dunes; there remained only the drag marks of their keels in the sand. The beach was empty, except for a single mounted figure.

As Kohler watched him, Lothar De La Rey lifted the wide-brimmed hat from his brazen curls and the ostrich feathers fluttered as he waved. Kohler lifted his own right hand in salute and the horseman swung away, still brandishing his hat, and galloped into the screen of reeds that choked the valley between two soaring dunes. A cloud of water fowl, alarmed by the horseman, rose from the surface of the lagoon and milled in a gaudily-coloured cloud above the forbidding dunes, and the horse and rider disappeared.

Kohler turned his back upon the land, and the long pointed bows of the U-boat sliced into the standing curtains of silver fog. The hull was shaped like a sword, a broadsword 170 feet long, to be driven at the throat of the enemy by her great 600-horsepower diesel engine, and Kohler did not try to suppress the choking sense of pride that he always felt at the beginning of a cruise.

He was under no illusion but that the outcome of this global conflict rested upon him and his brother officers in the submarine service. It was in their power alone to break the terrible stalemate of the trenches where two vast armies faced each other like exhausted heavyweight boxers, neither having enough strength left to lift their arms to throw a decisive punch, slowly rotting in the mud and the decay of their own monstrous strivings.

It was these slim and secret and deadly craft that could still wrest victory out of despair and desperation before the breaking-point was reached. If only the Kaiser had decided to use his submarines to their full potential from the very beginning, Kurt Kohler brooded, how different the outcome might have been.

In September 1914, the very first year of the war, a single submarine, the U-9, had sunk three British cruisers in quick succession, but even with this conclusive demonstration, the German high command had hesitated to use the weapon that had been placed in their hands, fearful of the outrage and condemnation of the entire world, of the simplistic cry of 'the beastly underwater butchers'.

Of course, the American threats after the sinking of the *Lusitania* and *Arabic* with the loss of American lives had served also to constrain the use of the undersea weapon. The Kaiser had feared to arouse the sleeping American giant, and to have its mighty weight hurled against the German Empire.

Now, when it was almost too late, the German high command had at last let slip the U-boats, and the results were staggering, surpassing even their own expectations.

The last three months of 1916 saw more than 300,000 tons of Allied shipping go down before the torpedoes. That was only a beginning; in the first ten days of April 1917, alone, another incredible 250,000 tons was destroyed, 875,000 tons for the full month – the Allies were reeling under this fearful infliction.

Now that two million fresh and eager young American troops were ready to cross the Atlantic to join the conflict, it was the duty of every officer and seaman of the German submarine service to make whatever sacrifice was demanded of him. If the gods of war chose to place a British heavy battle cruiser of such illustrious lineage as the *Inflexible* on a converging course with his battered little vessel, Kurt Kohler would gladly give up his own life and the lives of his crew for an opportunity to empty his torpedo tubes at her.

'Revolutions for twelve knots,' Kurt spoke into the voice

tube. That was the U-32's top surface speed, he had to get into patrol position as swiftly as possible. His calculations indicated that the *Inflexible* must pass between 110 and 140 nautical miles offshore, but Kurt refused to calculate his chances of making a good interception, even if he reached the patrol area before the cruiser passed by.

The horizon from the U-32's lookout wings was a mere seven miles, the range of her torpedoes 2,500 yards, the quarry capable of a sustained speed of 22 knots or more. He had to manoeuvre his vessel within 2,500 yards of the speeding cruiser, but the chances were many thousands of times against him even sighting her. Even if he obtained a sighting, it would probably be only to watch the distinctive tripod-shaped superstructure of the cruiser pass hull down on his limited horizon.

He thrust his forebodings aside. 'Lieutenant Horsthauzen to the bridge.'

When his first officer clambered up to the bridge, Kurt gave him orders to drive out of the patrol area with all possible speed, with the ship secured to diving stations ready for instant action.

'Call me at 1830 hours if there is no change.'

Kurt's exhaustion was aggravated by the dull headache from the diesel fumes. He took one last look around the horizon before going below. The fog banks were being stripped away by the rising wind, the sea was darkening, its anger rising at the whip of the elements. The U-32 thrust her bows into the next swell, and white water broke over her foredeck. Spray splattered icily into Kurt's face.

'The glass is dropping swiftly, sir,' Horsthauzen told him quietly. 'I think we are in for a sharp blow.'

'Stay on the surface, maintain speed.' Kurt ignored the opinion. He didn't want to hear anything that might complicate the hunt. He slid down the ladder and went immediately to the ship's logbook on the chart-table.

He made his entry in his meticulous formal script. 'Course 270 degrees. Speed 12 knots. Wind north-west, 15 knots and freshening.' Then he signed it with his full signature and pressed his fingers into his temples to still the ache within his skull.

'My God, I am tired,' he thought, and then saw the navigation officer watching his reflection surreptitiously, in the polished brass of the main control panel. He dropped his hands to his sides, brushed aside the temptation to go to his bunk immediately and instead told his coxswain, 'I will inspect the ship.'

He made a point of stopping in the engine compartment to compliment the engineers on the swift and efficient refuelling procedure, and in the torpedo compartment in the bows he ordered the men to remain in their bunks when he stooped in through the narrow entrance.

The three torpedo tubes were loaded and under compression, and the spare torpedoes were stacked in the narrow space; their long shiny bulk almost filled the entire cabin and made any movement difficult. The torpedo men would be forced to spend much of their time crouched in their tiny bunks, like animals in a tier of cages.

Kurt patted one of the torpedoes. 'We'll make more room for you soon,' he promised them, 'just as soon as we mail these little parcels off to Tommy.'

It was an antique joke, but they responded dutifully and, noting the timbre of the laughter, Kurt realized how those few hours on the surface in the sweet desert air had refreshed and enlivened them all.

Back in the tiny curtained cubicle which was his cabin, he could let himself relax at last, and instantly his exhaustion overcame him. He had not slept for forty hours; every minute of that time he had been exposed to constant nervous strain. Still, before he crawled laboriously into his narrow, confined bunk, he took down the framed photograph from its niche above his desk and studied the image of the placid young woman and the small boy at her knee, dressed in Lederhosen.

'Goodnight, my darlings,' he whispered. 'Goodnight to you, also, my other son, whom I have never seen.'

The diving klaxon woke him, bellowing like a wounded beast, echoing painfully in the confines of the steel hull, so that he was torn from deep black sleep and cracked his head on the jamb of the bunk as he tried to struggle out of it.

He was aware instantly of the pitch and roll of the hull. The weather had deteriorated, and then he felt the deck cant under his feet as the bows dropped and the submarine plunged below the surface. He ripped open the curtains and burst fully dressed into the control centre, just as the two lookouts came tumbling down the ladder from the bridge. The dive had been so swift that seawater cascaded down on to their heads and shoulders before Horsthauzen could secure the main hatch in the tower.

Kurt glanced at the clock at the top of the brass control panel as he took control. '18.23 hrs.' He made the calculation and estimated that they must be 100 nautical miles offshore on the edge of their patrol area. Horsthauzen would probably have called him in another few minutes, if he had not been forced to make this emergency dive.

'Periscope depth,' he snapped at the senior helmsman seated before the control panel, and used the few moments of respite to rally his senses and orientate himself fully by studying the navigational plot.

'Depth nine metres, sir,' said the helmsman, spinning the wheel to check her wild plunge.

'Up periscope,' Kurt ordered, as Horsthauzen dropped

down the tower, jumped off the ladder and took up his action station at the attack table.

'The sighting is a large vessel showing green and red navigation lights, bearing 060 degrees,' he reported quietly to Kurt. 'I could make out no details.'

As the periscope rose up through the deck, the hydraulic rams hissing loudly, Kurt ducked down, unfolded the side handles and pressed his face into the rubber pads, peering into the Zeiss lens of the eyepiece and straightening his body to follow the telescope up, already swinging it on to the bearing marks 060 degrees.

The lens was obscured by water, and he waited for it to clear.

'Late twilight—' he judged the light up there on the surface, and then to Horsthauzen, 'range estimate?'

'Sighting is hull down.' That meant she was probably eight or nine miles, but red and green navigation lights indicated that she was headed almost directly towards the U-32. That she should be showing lights at all indicated the vessel's supreme confidence that she was alone on the ocean.

The lens cleared of water and Kurt traversed slowly.

There she was. He felt his pulse leap and his breathing check. It never failed – no matter how often he saw the enemy, the shock and the thrill was as intense as the very first time.

'Bearing mark!' he snapped at Horsthauzen, and the lieutenant entered the bearing on the attack table.

Kurt stared at the quarry, feeling the hunger in his guts, the almost sexual ache in his loins as though he were watching a beautiful naked and available woman; at the same time he was gently manipulating the knob of the rangefinder with his right hand.

In the lens of the periscope the double images of the target ship were brought together by the rangefinder.

'Range mark!' Kurt said clearly as the images coalesced into a single sharp silhouette.

'Bearing 075 degrees,' said Horsthauzen. 'Range 7,650 metres!' and entered the numerals into the attack table.

'Down periscope! New heading 340 degrees!' ordered Kurt, and the thick telescoping steel sections of the periscope hissed down into their well on the deck between his feet. Even at this range and in the bad light Kurt was taking no chances that a wary lookout might pick out the plume of spray thrown up by the tip of the periscope as it cut the surface, turning on to an interception course into the north.

Kurt was watching the second hand of the clock on the control panel. He must give Horsthauzen at least two minutes before he made his next sighting. He glanced across at his first officer and found him totally absorbed in his calculations, stopwatch in his right hand, left hand manipulating the tumblers of the attack table like a Chinaman with an abacus.

Kurt switched his attention to his own calculations concerning the light and the surface condition of the sea. The fading light favoured him. As always, the hunter needed stealth and secrecy, but the rising sea would hamper his approach; breaking over the lens of the periscope, it might even affect the running of his torpedoes.

'Up periscope!' he ordered. The two minutes had expired. He found the image almost instantly.

'Bearing mark! Range mark!'

Now Horsthauzen had his references, elapsed time between sights and the relative ranges and bearings of the submarine and its target, together with the U-32's own speed and course.

'Target is on a heading of 175 degrees. Speed 22 knots,' he read off the attack table.

Kurt did not look away from the eyepiece of the periscope, but felt the thrill of the chase in his blood like the flush of strong spirits. The other ship was coming straight down on them, and its speed was almost exactly that to be expected of a British battle cruiser making a long passage. He stared at the distance image, but the light was going even as he studied the shadowy superstructure just visible between the pinpricks of the navigational lights – and yet, and yet – he was not absolutely certain, perhaps he was seeing what he wished to see – but there was a vague triangular shape against the darkening sky, the sure tripod mark of the new 'I'-class battle cruiser.

'Down periscope.' He made his decision. 'New heading 355 degrees,' the head-on course to intercept the target, 'designate the target as the "chase".' That was the intimation to his officers that he was attacking, and he saw their expression turn wolfish in the subdued light and they exchanged eager gloating glances. 'The chase is an enemy cruiser. We will attack with our bow tubes. Report battle stations.'

In quick succession the reports came in assuring him of the instant readiness of the entire ship. Kurt nodded with satisfaction, standing facing the brass control panel, studying the dials over the heads of his seated helmsmen, his hands thrust deeply into the pockets of his pea-jacket so that their trembling did not betray his agitated excitement, but a nerve jumped in his lower eyelid, making him wink sardonically, and his thin pale lips trembled uncontrollably. Each second seemed an eternity, until he could ask, 'Estimated bearing?'

The seaman with the hydrophones over his ears looked up. He had been closely monitoring the distant sound of the chase's propellers.

'Bearing steady,' he replied, and Kurt glanced at Horsthauzen.

'Estimated range?' Horsthauzen kept all his attention on his attack table.

'Estimated range 4,000 metres.'

'Up periscope.'

She was still there, exactly where he had expected her – she had not turned away. Kurt felt almost nauseated with relief. At any time that she suspected his presence the chase could simply turn and run away from him, without even bothering to increase speed, and he would be helpless to stop her. But she was coming on unsuspectingly.

It was fully dark in the world above the surface, and the sea was breaking and tumbling with white caps. Kurt had to make the decision which he had postponed to the last possible moment. He made one last sweep of the entire horizon, swinging the handles of the periscope the full 360 degrees, shuffling around behind the eyepiece, satisfying himself that there was no other enemy creeping up behind his stern, no destroyers escorting the cruiser, and then he said, 'I will shoot from the bridge.'

Even Horsthauzen glanced up momentarily, and he heard the sharp intake of breath from his junior officers when they realized they were going to surface almost under the bows of an enemy battle cruiser.

'Down periscope!' Kurt ordered his senior helmsman. 'Reduce speed to five knots and come to tower depth.'

He saw the needles on the control dials tremble and then begin to move, the speed dropping back, the depth decreasing gently, and he moved across to the ladder.

'I am transferring to the bridge,' he told Horsthauzen, and stepped on to the ladder. He climbed nimbly and at the top spun the locking wheel of the main hatch.

As the submarine broke through the surface, the internal air pressure blew the hatch open and Kurt sprang through it.

The wind lashed him immediately, tugging at his clothing and blowing spray into his face. All about him the sea was breaking and boiling, and the ship rolled and wallowed. Kurt had relied on the turmoil of waters to disguise the disturbance that the U-32 would make as she surfaced.

With one glance, he satisfied himself that the enemy was almost dead ahead and coming on swiftly and unswervingly. He bowed to the aiming table at the forward end of the bridge, unstoppered the voice pipe and spoke into it.

'Prepare to attack! Stand by bow tubes.'

'Bow tubes closed up,' Horsthauzen answered him from below, and Kurt began to feed him the details of the range and bearing, while on the deck below, the lieutenant read off from the attack table the firing heading and passed it to the helmsman. The submarine's bows swung gradually as the helmsman kept her on the exact aiming mark.

'Range 2,500 metres,' Kurt intoned. She was at extreme range now, but closing swiftly.

There were lights burning on her upper decks but apart from that she was merely a huge dark shape. There was no longer any definite silhouette against the night sky, although Kurt could make out the shapeless loom of her triple funnels.

The lights troubled Kurt. No Royal Naval captain should be so negligent of the most elementary precautions. He felt a small chill wind of doubt cool his excitement and battle ardour. He stared at the enormous vessel through the spray and darkness and for the first time in a hundred such dangerous nerve-racking situations, he felt himself hesitant and uncertain.

The vessel before him was in the exact position and on the exact course where he had expected to find the *Inflexible*. It was the right size, it had three funnels and a tripod superstructure, it was steaming at 22 knots – and yet it was showing lights.

'Repeat range mark!' Horsthauzen spoke through the voice tube, gently prodding him, and Kurt started. He had been staring at the chase, neglecting the rangefinder. Quickly he gave the decreasing range and then realized that within thirty seconds he would have to make his final decision.

'I will shoot at 1,000 metres,' he said into the voice tube.

It was point-blank range; even in this confused sea there was no question of missing with one of the long sharklike missiles.

Kurt stared into the lens of the rangefinder, watching the numerals decreasing steadily as hunter and hunted came together. He drew a deep breath like a diver about to plunge into the cold black waters and then he raised his voice for the first time.

'Number one tube – *los!*'

Almost immediately Horsthauzen's voice came back to him, with that slight catchy stutter that always afflicted him when he was over-excited.

'Number one fired and running.'

There was no sound, nor recoil. No movement of the submarine's hull to signal the release of the first torpedo.

In the darkness and the breaking white waters, Kurt could not even distinguish the wake of the speeding torpedo.

'Number two tube – *los!*'

Kurt was firing a spread of torpedoes, each on a minutely diverging course – the first aimed forward, the second amidships, the third aft.

'Number three tube – *los!*'

'All three fired and running!'

Kurt raised his eyes from the aiming table and slitted them against the flying spray and the wind as he gazed down the track of his torpedoes. It was standard service procedure to crash dive immediately all torpedoes were fired and to await the explosions of the hits down in the safety of the depths, but this time Kurt felt compelled to remain on top and watch it happen.

'Running time?' he demanded of Horsthauzen, watching the tall bulk of his victim festooned with lights like a cruise ship, so that she paled out the fields of stars that sprinkled the black curtain of the sky behind her.

'Two minutes fifteen seconds to run,' Horsthauzen told him, and Kurt clicked down the button of his stopwatch.

Always in this time of waiting after his weapons were sped upon their way, the remorse assailed Kurt. Before the firing there was only the heat of the chase and the tingling excitement of the stalk, but now he thought of the brave men, brothers of the sea, whom he had consigned to the cold dark and merciless waters.

The seconds dragged, so that he had to check the luminous dial of his stopwatch to assure himself that his torpedoes had not sounded or swerved nor run past.

Then there was that vast blurt of sound which even when expected made him flinch, and he saw the pearly fountain of spray rise against the bulk of the battle cruiser, shining in the starlight and in the decklights with a beautiful iridescent radiance.

'Number one – hit.' Horsthauzen's shout of triumph came from the voice pipe, followed immediately by another thunderous roar as though a mountain had fallen into the sea.

'Number two – hit.'

And yet again, while the first two tall shining columns of spray still hovered, the third leapt high in the dark air beside them.

'Number three – hit.'

As Kurt still watched, the columns of spray mingled, subsided and blew away on the wind, and the great ship ran on, seemingly unscathed.

'Chase is losing speed,' Horsthauzen exalted. 'Altering course to starboard.'

The doomed ship began a wide aimless turn into the wind. It would not be necessary to fire their stern tubes.

'Lieutenant Horsthauzen to the bridge,' Kurt said into

the voice tube. It was a reward for a task perfectly performed. He knew how avidly the young lieutenant would relate every detail of the sinking to his brother officers later. The memory of this victory would sustain them all through the long days and nights of privation and hardship that lay ahead. Horsthauzen burst from the hatch and stood shoulder to shoulder with his captain, peering at their monstrous victim.

'She has stopped!' he cried. The British ship lay like a rock in the sea.

'We will move closer,' Kurt decided, and relayed the order to the helmsman.

The U-32 crept forward, butting into the creaming waves, only her conning tower above the surface, closing the range gradually and gingerly. The cruiser's guns might still be manned and only a single lucky shot was needed to hole the submarine's thin plating.

'Listen!' Kurt ordered abruptly, turning his head to catch the sounds that came to them faintly above the clamour of the wind.

'I hear nothing.'

'Stop engines!' Kurt ordered, and the vibration and hum of the diesels ceased. Now they could hear it more clearly.

'Voices!' Horsthauzen whispered. It was a pathetic chorus, borne to them on the wind. The shouts and cries of men in dire distress, rising and falling on the vagaries of the wind, punctuated by a wild scream as somebody fell or leapt from the high deck.

'She is listing heavily.' They were close enough to see her against the stars.

'She's sinking by the bows.'

The great stern was rearing out of the black.

'She's going quickly – very quickly.'

They could hear the crackle and rumble of her hull as the waters raced through her, and twisted and distorted her plating.

'Man the searchlight,' Kurt ordered, and Horsthauzen turned to stare at him.

'Did you hear my order?' Horsthauzen roused himself. It went against all a submariner's instincts to betray himself so blatantly to the eyes of the enemy, but he crossed to the searchlight in the wing of the deck.

'Switch on!' Kurt urged him when he hesitated still, and the long white beam leapt out across half a mile of tempestuous sea and darkness. It struck the hull of the ship and was reflected in a dazzle of purest white.

Kurt threw himself across the bridge and shouldered his lieutenant from the searchlight. He gripped the handles and swung the solid beam across and down, slitting his eyes against the dazzling reflection from the ship's paintwork; he searched frantically and then froze, with his fingers hooked like claws over the searchlight handles.

In the perfect round circle of the searchlight beam, the scarlet arms of the huge painted cross were outflung, like the limbs of a condemned man upon the crucifix.

'Mother of the Almighty God,' Kurt whispered, 'what have I done?'

With horrid fascination he moved the beam slowly from side to side. The decks of the white ship were canted steeply towards him, so he could see the clusters of human figures that scurried about them, trying to reach the lifeboats dangling from their davits. Some of them were dragging stretchers or leading stumbling figures dressed in long blue hospital robes, and their cries and supplications sounded like a colony of nesting birds at sunset.

As Kurt watched, the ship suddenly tipped towards him with a rush, and the men on the decks were sent sliding across them, piling up against the railings. Then singly and in clusters they began to fall overboard.

One of the lifeboats let go and dropped out of control to hit the water alongside the hull and immediately capsized. Still men were dropping from the high decks, and he could hear their faint shrieks above the wind, see the small spouts of white spray as they struck the water.

'What can we do?' Horsthauzen whispered beside Kurt, staring with him down the searchlight beam, his expression pale and appalled.

Kurt switched off the searchlight. After the intense light, the darkness was crushing.

'Nothing,' said Kurt in the darkness. 'There is nothing we can do.' And he turned and stumbled to the hatchway.

By the time he reached the bottom of the ladder, he had control of himself again, and his voice was flat and his expression stony as he gave his orders.

'Lookouts to the bridge. Revolutions for 12 knots, new course 150 degrees.'

He stood at ease as they turned away from the sinking ship, fighting the urge to lift his hands to cover his ears. He knew he could not shut out the cries and shrieks that still echoed in his skull. He knew he would never be able to shut them out, and that he would hear them again at the hour of his own death.

'Secure from action stations,' he said with dead eyes, his waxen features wet with spray and sweat. 'Resume patrol routine.'

C entaine was perched on the foot of the lowest bunk in her favourite ward on 'C' deck. She had the book open on her lap.

It was one of the large cabins, with eight bunks, and all the young men in the bunks were spinals. Not one of them would ever walk again, and almost in defiance of this fact they were the noisiest, gayest and most opinionated bunch on board the *Protea Castle*.

Every evening, during the hour before lights-out, Centaine read to them – or that was the intention. It usually only required a few minutes of the author's opinions to trigger a spirited debate which ran unchecked until the dinner gong finally intervened.

Centaine enjoyed these sessions as much as any of them, and she invariably chose a book on a subject about which she wanted to know more, always an African theme.

This evening she had selected volume II of Levaillant's *Voyage dans l'interieur de l'Afrique* in the original French. She translated directly from the page of Levaillant's description of a hippopotamus hunt which her audience followed avidly, until she reached the description: 'The female beast was flayed and cut up on the spot. I ordered a bowl to be brought me, which I filled with her milk. It appears to be much less disagreeable than that of the elephant and the next day had changed almost wholly to cream. It had an amphibious taste, and a filthy smell which gave disgust, but in coffee it was even pleasant.'

There were cries of revulsion from the bunks. 'My God!' somebody exclaimed. 'Those Frenchies! Anybody who will drink hippo milk and eat frogs—'

Instantly they all turned upon him. 'Sunshine is a Frenchy, you dog! Apologize immediately!' and a barrage of pillows was hurled across the cabin at the offender.

Laughing, Centaine jumped up to restore order, and as she did so the deck bucked under her feet and she was hurled backwards on to the bunk again, and the blast of a massive explosion ripped through the ship.

Centaine struggled up and was knocked down again by another explosion more violent than the first.

'What is happening?' she screamed, and a third explosion plunged them into darkness and threw her from the bunk on to the deck. In the utter darkness somebody tumbled on top of her, pinning her in a welter of bedclothes.

She felt herself suffocating and she screamed again. The ship rang to other cries and shouts.

273

'Get off me!' Centaine fought to free herself, crawled to the doorway and pulled herself upright. The pandemonium all around her, the rush of bodies in the dark, the shouts and senseless bawling of orders, the sudden terrifying tilt of the deck under Centaine's feet panicked her. She lashed out to protect herself as an unseen body crashed into her, and then groped her way down the long narrow corridor.

The alarm bells began to ring through the darkness, a shrill, nerve-ripping sound that added to the confusion, and a voice roared, 'The ship is sinking – they are abandoning ship. We'll be trapped down here.'

There was an immediate rush to the companionway, and Centaine found herself borne along helplessly, fighting to keep her balance, for she knew if she fell she would be trampled. Instinctively she tried to protect her belly, but she was sent reeling into the bulkhead with a force that clashed her teeth and she bit her own tongue. As she fell, her mouth filled with the slick metallic taste of blood; she flung out both hands and they closed on the guide rail of the companionway and she hung on with all her strength. She dragged herself up the staircase, sobbing with the effort to keep her feet in the crush of panic-stricken bodies.

'My baby!' She heard herself saying it aloud. 'You can't kill my baby.'

The ship lurched, and there was the crackle and shriek of metal on metal, the crash of breaking glass, and the renewed rush and trample of feet all around her.

'It's going down!' shrieked a voice beside her. 'We've got to get out! Let me out—'

The lights went on again, and she saw the companionway to the upper deck choked with struggling, cursing men. She felt bruised and crushed and helpless.

'My baby!' she sobbed, as she was pinned against the bulkhead. The lights seemed to sober the men around her, shaming them out of their blind terror.

'Here's Sunshine!' a voice bellowed. It was a big Afrikaner, one of her most fervent admirers, and he swung his crutch to forge an opening for her.

'Let her through – stand back, you bastards, let Sunshine through.'

Hands seized her, and she was lifted off her feet.

'Let Sunshine through!'

They passed her overhead, like a doll. She lost her veil and one of her shoes.

'Here's Sunshine, pass her up!' She found herself sobbing as she was jostled and hard fingers seized her and bit painfully into her flesh, but she was borne swiftly upwards.

At the top of the companionway, other hands grabbed her and hustled her out on to the open deck. It was dark out here and the wind snatched at her hair and wrapped her skirts constrictingly about her legs. The deck was listing heavily, but as she stepped upon it, it canted even more viciously and she was hurled against a stanchion with a force that made her cry out.

Suddenly she thought about the helplessly maimed young men that she had left down there on 'C' deck.

'I should have tried to help them,' she told herself, and then she thought of Anna. Hesitating and confused she looked back. Men still swarmed up and out of the companionways. It would be impossible to move against that throng, and she knew that she did not have the strength needed to assist a man who could not walk himself.

All around her the officers were trying to restore order, but most of these men who had stoically borne the hell of the trenches were terrified witless by the thought of being trapped in a sinking ship, and their faces were contorted and their eyes wild with unreasoning terror. However, there were others who were dragging out the cripples and the blind and leading them to the lifeboats along the rail.

Clinging to the stanchion, Centaine was torn with indecision and fear and horror for the hundreds of men below who she knew would never reach the deck. Then beneath her the ship rumbled and belched in its death throes, air rushed from the holes beneath her waterline with the roarings of a sea monster and the sound decided Centaine.

'My baby,' she thought. 'I have to save him, the others don't matter – only my baby!'

'Sunshine!' One of the officers had seen her and he slid down the steep deck to her and put an arm around her protectively.

'You've got to get to a lifeboat – the ship will go at any moment.'

With his free hand he ripped open the tapes that secured his bulky canvas lifejacket, and he pulled it off his shoulders and lifted it over Centaine's head.

'What happened?' Centaine gasped as the knotted the tapes of the lifejacket under her chin and down her chest.

'We've been torpedoed. Come on.'

He dragged her along with him, reaching for handholds, for it was impossible to stand unaided on the steep angle of the deck.

'That lifeboat! We've got to get you into it.'

Just ahead of them a crowded lifeboat was swinging wildly on its davits, an officer was bellowing orders as they tried to clear the jammed tackle.

Looking down the ship's side, Centaine saw the black sea boiling and foaming, and the wind blew her hair into her face and half-blinded her.

Then, from far out on the black waters, a solid white shaft of light burst over them, and they flung up their hands to protect their eyes from the cruel glare.

'Submarine!' shouted the officer who held Centaine in the crook of his arm. 'The swine has come to gloat on his butchery.'

The beam of light left them and swivelled away down the side of the hull.

'Come on, Sunshine.' He dragged her towards the ship's

rail, but at that moment the tackle of the lifeboat gave way at the bows, and spilled its frantic cargo screaming into the pounding waves far below.

With yet another vast exhalation of air from her underwater wounds the ship swung further outwards to an impossible angle, and Centaine and the officer slid irresistibly across the deck and hit the rail together.

The merciless beam of white light moved from one end of the ship to the other and when it passed over them, it left them blinded and it seemed the night was even blacker and more menacing than before.

'The swines! The bloody swines!' The officer's voice was rough and hoarse with rage.

'We must jump!' Centaine shouted back at him. 'We have to get off!'

W hen the first torpedo struck, Anna was seated at the dressing-table in the cabin. She also had spent the afternoon working with the men on 'C' deck and had left them only to help Centaine prepare for dinner. She had expected Centaine to be in the cabin waiting for her and was mildly irritated when she was not.

'That child has no idea of time,' she muttered, but laid out clean underwear for her charge before beginning her own toilet.

The first explosion threw Anna off the stool and she struck the back of her head on the corner of the bed. She lay there stunned while the successive blasts tore into the ship, and then darkness blinded her. She dragged herself on to her knees with the alarm bells deafening her, and forced herself to begin the drill that they had practised almost daily since leaving Calais.

'Lifejacket!' She groped under the bed and pulled the clumsy apparatus over her head and began to crawl towards the door. Suddenly the lights went on again and she dragged herself to her feet and leaned against the bulkhead and massaged the lump on the back of her head.

Her senses cleared and immediately she thought of Centaine.

'My baby!' She started towards the door and the ship lurched under her. She was thrown back against the dressing-table and at the same moment Centaine's jewel-box slid across the table-top and would have fallen, but instinctively Anna caught it and held it to her chest.

'Abandon ship!' a voice shrieked outside the cabin. 'The ship is sinking! Abandon ship!'

Anna had learned enough English to understand. Her practical phlegmatic sense reasserted itself.

The jewelbox contained all their money and documents. She opened the locker over her head and pulled out the carpet bag and dropped the box into it. Then she looked around her swiftly. She swept the silver frame with the photographs of Centaine, her mother and Michael's squadron into the bag, then she jerked open the drawer and stuffed warm clothing for Centaine and herself on top of the jewelbox and the picture frame. She fastened the bag as she glanced quickly about the cabin. That was all of value that they possessed, and she heaved open the door and stepped into the passageway beyond.

Immediately she was picked up in the relentless stream of men, most of them still struggling with their lifejackets. She tried to turn back – 'I must find Centaine, I must find my baby!' – but she was borne out on to the dark deck and hustled towards one of the lifeboats.

Two seamen grabbed her. 'Come on then, luv. Ups-a-daisy!' and though she aimed a blow at the head of one of them with the carpet bag, they boosted her over the side of the lifeboat and she landed in a tangle of skirts and limbs between the thwarts. She dragged herself up, still clutching the carpet bag, and tried to climb out of the boat again.

'Catch hold of that silly bitch, somebody!' a seaman shouted with exasperation, and rough hands seized her and pulled her down.

In minutes the lifeboat was so crowded that Anna was packed helplessly between bodies and could only rave and implore in Flemish and French and broken English.

'You must let me out. I have to find my little girl—'

Nobody took any notice of her, and her voice was drowned out by the shouting and scurrying, by the moaning of the wind and the crash of waves against the steel hull, and by the ship's own groans and squeals and dying roars.

'We can't take any more!' a commanding voice shouted. 'Swing her out and let go!'

There was a gut-swooping drop down through the darkness and the lifeboat struck the surface with such force that water was sprayed over them and Anna was once more thrown to the half-flooded deck with a huddle of bodies on top of her. She dragged herself up again, with the lifeboat tossing and leaping and thudding against the ship's side.

'Get those oars out!' The voice again, harsh with authority. 'Fend her off there, you men. That's right! All right, give way starboard. Pull, damn you, pull!'

They dragged themselves away from the ship's side and got their bows into the seas before they were swamped. Anna crouched in the bottom of the boat, clutching her bag to her chest, and looked up at the tall hull that rose above them like a cliff.

At that instant a great white shaft of light sprang out of the darkness behind them and struck the ship. It played slowly across the glistening white hull, like the spotlight of a theatre, picking out brief tragic vignettes before passing on – groups of men trapped at the rail, a twisting figure in an unattended stretcher sliding across the deck, a seaman caught in the tackle of a lifeboat and swinging like a figure on the gallows tree – and finally the beam rested for a few moments on the huge red crosses painted on the white hull.

'Yes, take a good look, you bloody swine!' one of the men near Anna in the lifeboat yelled, and immediately the cry was taken up.

'You murdering Hun—'

'You filthy butchers—'

All around Anna they were howling their anger and outrage.

Implacably the beam of searchlight travelled on, swinging down to the waterline of the hull. The surface of the sea was dotted with the heads of hundreds of swimmers. There were clusters of them, and individuals whose pale faces shone like mirrors in the intense white light, and still others were dropping and splashing into the water amongst them, while the sea surged and sucked them back and forth and threw them against the steel cliff of the hull.

The searchlight lifted up to the high decks again, and they were canted at an improbable angle while the ship's bows were already thrusting below the surface and the stern was rising swiftly against the star-riddled sky.

For an instant the searchlight settled on a tiny group of figures pinned against the ship's rail and Anna shrieked, 'Centaine!'

The girl was in the middle of the group, her face turned towards the sea, looking down at the dark drop beneath her, the wild bush of her dark hair whipping in the wind.

'Centaine!' Anna screamed again, and with a lithe movement the girl had leaped to the top of the brass rail. She had lifted the heavy woollen skirts to her waist and for an instant she balanced like an acrobat. Her bare legs were pale and slim and shapely, but she looked frail as a bird as she leaped away from the rail and with her skirts ballooning wildly about her, fell out of the beam of light into the blackness beneath.

'Cantaine!' Anna screamed one last time with despair in her voice and ice in her heart. She tried to rise, the better to watch the fall of that small body, but somebody pulled her down again, and then the searchlight beam was extinguished and Anna crouched in the lifeboat and listened to the cries of the drowning men.

'Pull, you men! We must get clear, or she will suck us down with her when she goes.'

They had oars out on both sides of the lifeboat and were striking out raggedly, inching away from the stricken liner.

'There she goes!' somebody yelled. 'Oh God, will you look at that!'

The stern of the huge ship swung up, higher and still higher into the night sky, and the rowers rested on their oars and stared up at her.

When she reached the vertical she hung for long seconds. They could see the silhouette of her propeller against the stars, and her lights were still burning in the rows of portholes.

Slowly she began to slide downwards, bows first, her lights still shining beneath the water like drowning moons. Faster and still faster she slid downwards, and her plates began to buckle and crackle with pressure, air burst out of her in a seething frothy turmoil, and then she was gone. Vast spoutings and eruptions of air and white foam still fountained up out of the black waters, but slowly these subsided and once again they could hear the lonely cries of the swimmers.

'Pull back! We must pick up as many as we can!'

All the rest of that night they worked under the direction of the ship's first officer who stood at the tiller in the stern of the lifeboat. They dragged the sodden shivering wretches from the sea, packing them in until the lifeboat wallowed dangerously and took water over her gunwales at every swell, and they had to bale continuously.

'No more!' the officer shouted. 'You men will have to tie yourselves on to the lifelines.'

The swimmers clustered around the overloaded vessel like drowning rats, and Anna was close enough to the stern to hear the first officer murmur, 'The poor devils won't last until morning – the cold will get them, even if the sharks don't.'

They could hear other lifeboats around them in the night, the splash of oars and voices on the wind.

'The current is running up into the north-north-east at four knots,' Anna overheard the first officer again, 'we will be scattered to the horizon by dawn. We must try to keep together.' He rose in the stern and hailed, 'Ahoy there! This is lifeboat sixteen.'

'Lifeboat five,' a faint voice hailed back.

'We will come to you!'

They rowed through the darkness, guided by cries from the other boat, and when they found each other they lashed the two hulls together. During the night they called two other lifeboats to them.

In the watery grey dawn they found another lifeboat half a mile away; the sea between them was strewn with wreckage and dotted with the heads of swimmers, but all of them were insignificant specks in the immense reaches of ocean and sky.

In the boats they huddled together like cattle in the abattoir truck, already slumping into bovine lethargy and indifference, while those in the water bobbed and nodded as they hung in their lifejackets, a macabre dance of death, for already the icy green water that tumbled over their heads had sucked the body warmth from many of them and they lolled pale and lifeless.

'Sit down, woman!' Anna's neighbours roused themselves as she tried to stand on the thwart.

'You'll have us all in the water, for God's sake!' But Anna ignored their protests.

'Centaine!' she called. 'Is Centaine anywhere?' And when they stared at her uncomprehendingly, she searched for the nickname and remembered it at last.

'Sunshine!' she cried. '*Het iemand Sunshine gesien?* Has anybody seen Sunshine?' and there was a stir of interest and concern.

'Sunshine? Is she with you?' The query was passed swiftly about the cluster of tossing lifeboats.

'I saw her on the deck, just before the ship went down.'

'She had a lifejacket.'

'She isn't here?'

'No, she isn't here.'

'I saw her jump, but I lost her after that.'

'She isn't here – not in any of the boats.'

Anna sagged down again. Her baby was gone. She felt despair overwhelm and begin to suffocate her. She looked over the side of the lifeboat at the dead men hanging in their lifejackets, and imagined Centaine killed by the green waters, dead of the cold and the infant in her womb dead also, and she groaned aloud.

'No,' she whispered, 'God cannot be that cruel. I don't believe it. I'll never believe it.' The denial gave her strength and the will to endure. 'There were other lifeboats, Centaine is alive somewhere out there,' she looked to the wind-smeared horizon, 'she's alive, and I will find her. If it takes my whole life, I will find her again.'

The small incident of the search for the missing girl had broken the torpor of cold and shock that had gripped them all during the night, and now the leaders emerged to rally them, to adjust the loading and the trim of the lifeboats, to count and take charge of the fresh-water containers and the emergency rations, to see to the injured, to cut loose the dead men and let them float away and to allocate duties to the rowers – and finally to set a course for the mainland a hundred miles and more out there in the east.

With teams of rowers alternating at the long oars, they began to inch across the wild sea, nearly every small gain wasted by the following wave that dashed into their bows and drove them back.

'That's it, lads,' the first officer exhorted from the stern. 'Keep it up—' any activity would stave off despondency, their ultimate enemy ' – let's sing, shall we? Who'll give us a tune? What about *Tipperary*? Come along, then.

'"It's a long way to Tipperary, It's a long way to go – "' But the wind and the sea grew stronger, and flung them about so that the oars would not bite, and one after the other the rowers gave up and slumped glumly, and the song died away and they sat and waited. After a while the sense of waiting for something to happen passed, and they merely sat. Long after midday, the sun broke through the low scudding cloud for a few minutes and they lifted their faces to it, but then the cloud obscured it again and their heads drooped like wild Namaqua daisies at sunset.

Then from the lifeboat alongside where Anna sat a voice spoke in a dull, almost disinterested tone.

'Look, isn't that a ship?'

For a while there was silence, as though it took time to understand such an unlikely proposition, and then another voice, sharper and more alive.

'It is – it's a ship!'

'Where? Where is it?'

A babble of excited voices now.

'There, just below that dark patch of cloud.'

'Low down, just the top—'

'It's a ship!'

'A ship!'

Men were trying to stand, some of them had stripped off

284

their jackets and were waving frantically and shouting as though their lungs might burst.

Anna blinked her eyes and stared in the direction they were all pointing in. After a moment she saw a tiny triangular shape, darker grey against the dreary grey of the horizon.

The first officer was busy in the stern, and abruptly there was a fierce whooshing sound and a trail of smoke shot up into the sky and burst in a cluster of bright red stars as he fired one of the signal rockets from the stern locker.

'She has seen us!'

'Look! Look, she's altering course!'

'It's a warship – three funnels.'

'Look at the tripod director tower – she's one of the "I" class cruisers—'

'By God, it's the *Inflexible*! I saw her at Scapa Flow last year—'

'God bless her, whoever she is. She's seen us! Oh, thank God, she's seen us!'

Anna found herself laughing and sobbing, and clutching the carpet bag that was her only link with Centaine.

'It will be all right now, my baby,' she promised. 'Anna will find you now. You don't have to worry any more, Anna is coming to get you.'

And the deadly grey shape of the warship raced down upon them, shouldering and breaking the waters aside with her tall, axe-sharp bows.

Anna stood at the rail of HMS *Inflexible* in a group of the survivors from the lifeboats and watched that immense flat-topped mountain rise out of the southern ocean.

From this distance the proportions of the mountain were so perfect, the tableland at its summit so precisely cut and the steep slopes so artfully fashioned that it might have been sculptured by a divine Michelangelo. The men around her were excited and voluble, hanging on the rail and pointing out the familiar features of the land as their swift approach made each apparent. This was a homecoming of which most of them had many times despaired, and their relief and joy were pathetically childlike.

Anna shared none of it with them. The sight of land induced in her only a corrosive impatience that she knew she could not long abide. The drive of the great ship under her was too puny, too snail-like for her anticipation – every minute spent out here upon the ocean was wasted, for it delayed the moment when she could set out on the quest which had in a few short days become the central driving force of her existence.

She fretted while the drama of sea and elements unfolded before her, while the wind which had crossed the wide sweep of the Atlantic free and unfettered, met the sudden constraint of the great mountain, and like a wild horse feeling the bit for the first time, reared and struggled in monstrous pique.

Before Anna's eyes a dense white cloud blossomed upon the broad flat summit of the mountain and began to boil over the sheer lip in a slow, gelatinous tide down the stark cliffs, and when the men around her exclaimed with wonder, she had only an insufferable desire to feel the land beneath her feet, and to turn those feet back into the north to begin the search.

Now the angry wind racing down the cliffs came again to the sea and ripped the placid sweet blue first to sombre gunmetal and then to foam-flecked fury. As the *Inflexible* came out of the lee of the mountain into the narrow roadway between Table Harbour and Robben Island, the south-easter struck her like a mallet, and even she was forced to make obeisance and heel to the power of the wind.

In the days of sail, many great ships had come this close to the mountain only to be blown out again with rigging in disarray, not to sight land again for days or even weeks, but *Inflexible*, once she had acknowledged its force, drove in through the concrete breakwater, and surrendered only to the attentions of the fussy little steam tugs which bustled out to meet her. Like a lover she kissed the wharf, and the crowd that lined it waved up at the decks, the women struggling with rebellious skirts and the men clutching their hats to their heads, the strains of the Marine band on the cruiser's foredeck rising and falling as the wind squalls gave 'Rule Britannia' an unusual cadence.

As soon as the gangways were lowered, a group of figures hurried up them, harbour officials and naval officers in tropical whites and gold braid, together with a few obviously important civilians.

Now, despite herself, Anna felt a slight prickle of interest as she studied the white buildings of the town that were scattered along the foot of the high grey cliffs.

'Africa,' she murmured. 'So what was all the fuss about? I wonder what Centaine—'

At the thought of the girl, all else was banished from her mind; although she still stared towards the shore, she saw nothing and heard nothing, until a light touch on her shoulder pulled her back to the present.

One of the ship's midshipmen, callow as a schoolboy even in his smart tropical whites, saluted her diffidently.

'There is a visitor for you in the wardroom, ma'am.'

When it was obvious that Anna did not understand, he beckoned her to follow him.

At the door of the wardroom, the midshipman stood aside and ushered her through. Anna stood in the entrance and glowered around her suspiciously, holding the carpet bag protectively in front of her hips. Visitors and officers were already doing full justice to the ship's store of gin and tonic, but the cruiser's flag lieutenant saw Anna.

'Ah, here we are. This is the woman,' and he drew one of the civilians from the group of men and led him to meet Anna.

Anna looked him over carefully. He was a slim, boyish figure dressed in a dove-grey three-piece suit of expensive material and superior cut.

'Mevrou Stok?' he asked, almost diffidently, and with surprise Anna realized that, far from being a boy, he was probably twenty years or so her senior.

'Anna Stok?' he repeated. His hair had receded in deep bays on each side of the smooth scholarly forehead, but had been allowed to grow feathery wisps down his neck and on to his shoulders.

'We should take the scissors to you,' she thought, and said '*Ja*, I am Anna Stok,' and he replied in Afrikaans that she understood readily.

'A pleasant meeting – *aangename kennis* – I am Colonel Garrick Courtney, but I am saddened, as you must be, by the terrible loss we have experienced.'

For a few moments Anna did not understand what he was talking about. Instead she studied him more closely, and now she saw that his unbarbered hair had sprinkled the shoulder of his expensive suit with flakes of white dandruff. There was a button missing from his waistcoat and the thread dangled loosely. There was a grease spot on his silk cravat and the toe of one of his boots was scuffed.

'A bachelor,' Anna decided. Despite his intelligent eyes and the sensitive gentle mouth, there was something childlike and vulnerable about him, and Anna felt her maternal instincts stir.

He stepped closer to her, and the clumsy movement reminded Anna of what General Courtney had told Centaine and her, that Garrick Courtney had lost one of his legs in a hunting accident when he was a boy.

'Coming on top of the death in action of my only son,' Garrick lowered his voice and the look in his eyes was enough to soften Anna's reserves, 'this new loss is almost too much to bear. I have not only lost my son, but my daughter and my grandson before even I had a chance to know them.'

Now at last Anna understood what he was talking about, and her face flushed with such fury that Garry recoiled instinctively.

'Never say that again!' She followed him as he retreated, thrusting her face so close to his that their noses almost touched. 'Don't you dare ever to say that again!'

'Madam,' Garry faltered, 'I am sorry, I don't understand – have I given you offence?'

'Centaine is not dead and don't you ever dare again to speak as though she is! Do you understand?'

'You mean Michael's wife is alive?'

'Yes, Centaine is alive. Of course, she is alive.'

'Where is she?' Slow delight dawned in Garry's faded blue eyes.

'That is what we have got to find out,' Anna told him firmly. 'We have got to find her again – you and I.'

G arry Courtney had a suite at the Mount Nelson Hotel above the centre of Cape Town.

There was, of course, no real alternative lodging for a gentleman traveller visiting the Cape of Good Hope. Its guest book read like a roll of honour: statesmen and explorers, diamond magnates and big game hunters, gallant soldiers and illustrious peers of the realm, princes and admirals had all made it their temporary home.

The Courtney brothers, Garry and Sean, always had the same suite on the corner of the top floor with a view on one side over the gardens laid out by the governors of the Dutch East India Company, across the waters of Table Bay to the smoky blue mountains on the far side; on the other side the grey rock ramparts of the mountain were so close that they blotted out half the sky.

These legendary views did not distract Anna for a moment. She glanced quickly around the sitting-room, then placed the carpet bag on the centre table and rummaged in it. She brought out the silver picture frame and showed it to Garry, who was hovering behind her indecisively.

'Good Lord – that's Michael—' He took the frame from her and stared hungrily at the photograph of No. 21 Squadron, taken only a few months previously. 'It's so hard to believe—' Garry broke off and gulped before going on. 'Could I please have a copy of this made for myself?'

Anna nodded, and Garry transferred his attention to the two photographs in the second leaf. 'This is Centaine?' He pronounced it in the English way.

'Her mother.' Anna touched the other. 'This is Centaine.' She corrected his pronunciation.

'They are so much alike,' Garry turned the photographs to catch the light. 'Yet the mother is prettier, but the daughter – Centaine – has more force of character.'

Anna nodded again. 'Now you know why she cannot be dead, she does not give up easily.' Her manner became brusque. 'But we are wasting time. We need a map.'

The hotel porter knocked on the door within minutes of Garry's call, and they spread the chart he brought between them.

'I do not understand these things,' Anna told him. 'Show me where the ship was torpedoed.'

Garry had the position from the *Inflexible*'s navigating officer, and he marked it for her.

'Do you see?' Anna was triumphant. 'It is only a few centimetres from the land.' She stroked the outline of Africa with her finger. 'So close, so very close—'

'It's a hundred miles – even further perhaps.'

'Are you always so miserable?' Anna snapped. 'They told

me that the tide runs towards the land, and the wind also was blowing so strongly towards the land – anyway, I know my little girl.'

'The current runs at four knots and the wind,' Garry made a quick calculation. 'It's possible. But it would have taken days.'

Already Garry was enjoying himself. He liked this woman's absolute assurance. All his life he had been a victim of his own doubts and indecision, he could not remember even once being as certain of a single thing as she seemed certain of everything.

'So, with the wind and water pushing her, where has she come ashore?' Anna demanded. 'Show me.'

Garry pencilled in his estimates. 'I would say – about here!'

'Ah!' Anna placed a thick powerful finger on the map and smiled. When she smiled, she looked less like Chaka, Garry's huge fierce mastiff, and Garry grinned with her. 'Ah, so! Do you know this place?'

'Well, I know a bit about it. I went with Botha and Smuts in 1914, as a special correspondent for *The Times*. We landed here, at Walvis Bay, the Bay of Whales.'

'Good! Good!' Anna cut him short. 'So there is no problem. We will go there and find Centaine, yes? When can we leave, tomorrow?'

'It isn't quite that easy.' Garry was taken aback. 'You see, that is one of the fiercest deserts in the world.'

Anna's smile disappeared. 'Always you find problems,' she told him ominously. 'Always you want to talk instead of doing things, and while you talk, what is happening to Centaine, hey? We must go quickly!'

Garry stared at her in awe. Already she seemed to know him intimately. She had recognized that he was a dreamer and a romantic, content to live in his imagination, to live through the characters of his writings rather than in the real harsh world which frightened him so.

'Now there is no more time for your talking. There are things to be done. First, we will make a list of these things – and then we will do them. Now begin. What is the first thing?'

Nobody had ever spoken to Garry like this, not at least since his childhood. With his military rank and his Victoria Cross, with his inherited wealth, his scholarly works of history and his reputation as a philosopher, the world treated him with the respect accorded to a sage. He knew he did not truly merit any of these considerations, so they terrified and confused Garry, and his defence was to withdraw further into this imaginary world.

'While you make the list, take off your waistcoat.'

'Madam?' Garry looked shocked.

'I am not madam, I am Anna. Now give me your waistcoat – there is a button missing.'

He obeyed quietly.

'The first thing,' Garry, in his shirtsleeves, wrote on a sheet of hotel notepaper, 'is to cable the military governor in Windhoek. We will need permits, this is all a closed military area. We will need his co-operation, he will be able to arrange provisions and water points.'

Now that Garry had been prodded into taking action, he was working quickly. Anna sat opposite him, stitching on the button with those strong, capable fingers.

'What provisions? You will need a second list for those.'

'Of course—' Garry pulled another sheet towards him.

'There!' Anna bit off the thread and handed him back his waistcoat. 'You can put it on now.'

'Yes, Mevrou,' said Garry meekly, but he could not remember when last he had felt so good.

It was after midnight when Garry went out on to the small balcony of his bedroom in his dressing-gown to take a last breath of night air, and while he reviewed the events of the day, the buoyant feeling of well-being remained with him.

Between them, he and Anna had performed prodigies of labour. They already had a reply from the military governor in Windhoek. As always, the Courtney name had opened the door to wholehearted co-operation. Their reservations had been made on the passenger train that would leave tomorrow afternoon, and take them over the Orange river and across the wastes of Namaqualand and Bushmanland, four days' travel to Windhoek.

They had even completed the major part of outfitting the expedition. Garry had spoken on the telephone, an instrument which he usually viewed with grave misgivings, to the owner of Stuttafords General Dealer Stores. The stores he required would be packed in wooden cases, the contents of each clearly labelled on it, and delivered to the railway station the following afternoon. Mr Stuttaford had given Garry his personal assurance that it would all be ready in time, and had sent one of his green motor vans up to the Mount Nelson Hotel with a selection of safari clothing for both Garry and Anna.

Anna had rejected most of Mr Stuttaford's offerings as being either too expensive or too frivolous – 'I am not a *poule*' – and she chose long thick calico skirts and heavy lace-up boots with hob-nailed soles, flannel underwear and only at Garry's insistence – 'the African sun is a killer' – a cork solar topee with a green neck-flap.

Garry had also arranged a transfer of £3,000 to the Standard Bank in Windhoek to cover the expedition's final outfitting. It had all been done swiftly, decisively and efficiently.

Garry took a long draw on his cigar and flicked the butt over the edge of the balcony, then turned back into his bedroom. He dropped his dressing-gown over the chair and climbed in between white sheets as crisp as lettuce leaves, and switched out the bedside light. Instantly all his old misgivings and self-doubts came crowding out of the darkness.

'It's madness,' he whispered, and in his mind's eye saw again those terrible deserts, shimmering endlessly in the blinding heat. A thousand miles of coastline, swept by a cruel current so cold that even a strong man could survive in those waters for only a few hours before hypothermia sucked the life out of him.

They were setting out to look for a young girl of delicate breeding, a pregnant girl, who had last been seen plunging from the high deck of a stricken liner into the icy dark sea a hundred miles from this savage coast. What were their chances of finding her? He flinched from even trying to estimate them.

'Madness,' he repeated miserably, and suddenly he wished that Anna was there to bolster him. He was still trying to find an excuse to summon her from her single bedroom at the end of the corridor when he fell asleep.

Centaine knew that she was drowning. She had been sucked so deeply beneath the surface that her lungs were crushing under the weight of the dark waters. Her head was full of the monstrous roaring of the sinking ship, and of the crackle and squeal of the pressure in her own eardrums.

She knew she was doomed, but she fought with all her strength and determination, kicking and clawing for life against the cold leaden drag of waters, fighting against the burning agony of her lungs and the need to breathe; the turbulence swirled her into vertigo so that she lost any sense of upward and downward movement, but still she fought on and she knew that she would die fighting for her baby's life.

Then suddenly she felt the cracking weight of water on her ribs releasing, felt her lungs swelling in her chest, and an updraught of air and bubbles from the ruptured hull picked her up like a spark from a campfire and hurled her towards the surface with the pressure pain burning in her eardrums, and the drag of the lifejacket cutting into her armpits.

She broke through the surface and was thrown high on the seething fountain of escaping air. She tried to breathe but took water into her straining lungs and coughed and wheezed in agonized paroxysms until she cleared her air passages, and then it was almost as though the sweet sea air was too strong and rich for her, it burned like fire and she gasped and laboured like an asthmatic.

Slowly she managed to control her breathing, but the waves came at her unexpectedly out of the darkness, breaking over her head, smothering her again so she had to train herself to regulate each breath to the rhythm of the ocean. Between the breaking swells, she tried to assess her own condition and found herself undamaged. No bones seemed broken or cracked, despite that terrible gut-swooping drop from the ship's rail and the stunning impact on water as hard as a cobbled street. She still had full control of her limbs and her senses, but then she felt the first stealthy invasion of the cold through her clothing, into her body and her blood.

'I have to get out of the water,' she realized. 'One of the lifeboats.'

Now for the first time she listened for sounds and at first there was only the wind and the rushing break of white caps. Then she heard faintly, very faintly, a gabble of human voices, a magpie chorus of croaks and cries, and she opened her mouth and called for help, but a wave broke in her face and she took more water and gasped and choked.

It took her minutes to recover, but as soon as her lungs were clear, she struck out grimly towards where she thought the voices were, no longer wasting strength on vainly beseeching the aid of others. The heavy lifejacket dragged and the crests broke over her, she was lifted on the swells and dropped into the troughs, but she kept swimming.

'I have to get out of the water,' she kept telling herself. 'The cold is the killer – I have to reach one of the boats.'

She reached out for the next stroke and hit something solid with a force that broke the skin of her knuckles, but instantly she grasped for it. It was something large that floated higher than her head, but she could find no secure handholds upon it and in panic realized that already she was too far gone to drag herself up by main strength. She began to grope her way around the piece of floating wreckage, searching for a handhold.

'Not big—' In the darkness she judged it to be not more than twelve feet long, and half as broad, made of timber but coated with smooth oil paint, one edge of it torn and splintered so that she scratched her hand on it. She felt the sting of the tearing skin, but the cold numbed the pain.

One end of the wreckage floated high, the other end dipped below the surface, and she pulled herself on to it, belly down.

Immediately she felt how precariously balanced the structure was. Although she had only dragged her upper body on to it, and her legs from the waist down were still hanging in the water, the wreckage tipped dangerously towards her, and there was a hoarse cry of protest.

'Be careful, you bloody fool – you'll have us over.'

Somebody else had found the raft before her.

'I'm sorry,' she gasped, 'I didn't realize—'

'All right, lad. Just be careful.' The man on the raft had mistaken her voice for that of one of the ship's boys. 'Here, give me a hand.'

Centaine groped frantically and touched outstretched fingers. She seized the offered hand.

'Easy does it.' She kicked as the man pulled her up the

sloping angle of slippery painted wreckage, and then with her free hand she found a hold. She lay belly down on the tossing, unstable deck, and felt suddenly too weak and trembling to lift her head.

She was out of the deadly water.

'Are you all right, son?' Her rescuer was lying beside her, his head close to hers.

'I'm all right.' She felt the touch of his hand on her back.

'You've got a lifejacket, good boy. Use the tapes to tie yourself to this strut – here, let me show you.'

He lashed Centaine to the strut in front of her.

'I've tied a slippery knot. If we capsize, just pull this end, savvy?'

'Yes – thank you. Thank you very much.'

'Save it for later, lad.' The man beside her lowered his head on to his arms and they lay shivering and sodden and rode the headlong rush of waves out of the night on their frail, unstable vessel.

Without speaking again, without even being able to see more than each other's vague shapes in the darkness, they quickly learned to balance the raft between them with co-ordinated, subtle movements of their bodies. The wind increased in viciousness, but although the sea rose with it, they managed to keep the higher side of the raft headed into it, and only an occasional burst of spray splattered over them.

After a while, Centaine lapsed into an exhausted sleep, so deep that it was almost comatose. She awoke in daylight, a muted grey and dreary light in a world of wild grey waters and low sagging grey clouds. Her companion on the raft was squatting on the canted insecure deck beside her, and he was watching her steadfastly.

'Miss Sunshine,' he said, as soon as she stirred and opened her eyes. 'Never guessed it was you when you came aboard last night.'

She sat up quickly and the tiny raft dipped and rocked dangerously under them.

'Steady on, luv, that's the ticket.' He put out a gnarled hand to restrain her. There was a tattoo of a mermaid on his forearm.

'My name's Ernie, miss. Leading Seaman Ernie Simpson. Of course, I knew you right away. Everybody on board knows Miss Sunshine.' He was skinny and old, thin grey hair plastered with salt to his forehead, and his face wrinkled as a prune, but though his teeth were yellow and crooked, his smile was kindly.

'What has happened to the others, Ernie?' Frantically, Centaine looked around her, the true horror of their situation coming over her again.

'Gone to Davy Jones – most of them.'

'Davy Jones, who is he?'

'Drowned, I mean. Rot the bloody Hun who did it.'

The night had hidden the true extremity of their situation from Centaine. The reality that was revealed now was infinitely more frightening than her imaginings. As they dropped into the swells, they were dwarfed by the cold opaque canyons of the sea, and as they rode up and over the crests, the vista of loneliness was such as to force Centaine to cringe down on the tiny deck. There was nothing but the water and the sky, no lifeboat nor swimmer, not even a seabird.

'We are all alone,' she whispered. '*Tous seuls*.'

'Cheer up, luv. We are still kicking, that's what counts.'

Ernie had been busy while she still slept. She saw that he had managed to glean a few fragments of debris and floating wreckage from the sea around them. There was a sheet of heavy-gauge canvas dragging behind the raft, around its edge short lengths of hemp rope had been spliced into eye holes. It floated like some monstrous octopus with limp tentacles.

'Lifeboat cover,' Ernie saw her interest. 'And those are

ship's spars and some other odds and sods – begging your pardon, miss – never know what will come in useful.'

He had lashed this collection of wreckage together with the lengths of rope from the lifeboat cover, and even while he explained to Centaine, he was working with scarred but nimble fingers splicing short pieces of rope into a single length.

'I'm thirsty,' Centaine whispered. The salt had scalded her mouth and her lips felt hot and bloated.

'Think about something else,' Ernie advised. 'Here, give us a hand with this. Can you splice?'

Centaine shook her head. Ernie dropped all his aitches and as a French woman, she sympathized with him, and found it easy to like him.

'It's easy, come on, luv. I'll learn you how. Watch!'

Ernie had a clasp knife attached by a lanyard to his belt, and he used the spike on the back of it to open the weave of the hemp.

'One over one, like a snake into its hole! See!'

Quickly Centaine got the hang of it. The work helped to take her mind off their awful predicament.

'Do you know where we are, Ernie?'

'I'm no navigator, Miss Sunshine, but we are west of the coast of Africa – how far off, I haven't a clue, but somewhere out there is Africa.'

'Yesterday at noonsight, we were 110 miles offshore.'

'I'm sure you're right,' Ernie nodded. 'All I know is we've got the current helping us, and the wind also—' He turned his face up to the sky. 'If only we can use the wind.'

'Have you got a plan, Ernie?'

'Always got a plan, miss – not always a good one, I admit.' He grinned at her. 'Just get this rope finished first.'

As soon as they had a single length of rope, twenty feet long, Ernie handed her the clasp knife.

'Tie it around your middle, luv. That's the ticket. We don't want to drop it now, do we?'

He slid over the side of the raft and paddled like a dog to the dragging wreckage. With Centaine heaving and shoving under his direction, they worked two of the salvaged spars into position and lashed them securely with the hemp rope.

'Outriggers,' Ernie spluttered with seawater. 'A trick I learned from the darkies in Hawaii.'

The raft was dramatically stabilized, and Ernie crawled back on board. 'Now we can think about putting up some kind of sail.'

It took four abortive attempts before the two of them were able to rig a jury mast, and hoist a sail hacked from the canvas of the boat cover.

'We aren't going to win the America's Cup, luv, but we are moving. Look at the wake, Miss Sunshine.'

They were spreading a sluggish oily wake behind their cumbersome craft, and Ernie trimmed their tiny sail carefully.

'Two knots at least,' he estimated. 'Well done, Miss Sunshine, you're a game one, and no mistake. Couldn't have done that alone.' He was perched on the stern of the raft, steering with a salvaged length of timber as a tiller. 'Now you settle down and take a rest, luv, you and I will have to stand watches, back to back.'

All the rest of that day the wind came at them in gusts and squalls, and twice their clumsy mast was thrown overboard. Each time Ernie had to go into the water to retrieve it, and the effort required to lift the heavy spar and the wet canvas, then to restep and lash it back in place, left Centaine trembling and exhausted.

At nightfall the wind moderated and held steady and gentle out of the south-west. The clouds broke up so they had glimpses of the stars.

'I'm tuckered out. You'll have to take a turn at the tiller, Miss Sunshine.' Ernie showed her how to steer, and the raft responded sullenly to the push of the tiller. 'That red star there, that's Antares, with the small white star on each side of him, just like a sailor on shore leave with a girlfriend on each arm, begging your pardon, Miss Sunshine, but you just keep heading towards Antares and we'll be all right.'

The old seaman curled up at her feet like a friendly dog, and Centaine crouched on the stern of the raft and held the crude tiller under one arm. The swells dropped with the wind and it seemed to her that their passage through the water was faster. Looking back, she could see the green phosphorescence of their wake spreading out behind them. She watched the red giant Antares with his two consorts climb up the black velvet curtain of the sky. Because she was lonely and still afraid, she thought of Anna.

'My darling Anna, where are you? Are you still alive? Did you reach one of the lifeboats, or are you, too, clinging to some scrap of wreckage, waiting on the judgement of the sea?'

Her longing for the solid bulky assurance of her old nurse was so intense that it threatened to turn her into a child once more, and she felt the childlike tears scalding her eyelids, and Antares' glaring red light blurred and multiplied before her. She wanted to crawl into Anna's lap and bury her face in the warm, soapy smell of her vast bosom, and she felt all the resolve and purpose of the day's struggle melt in her, and she thought how easy it would be to lie down beside Ernie and not have to try any more.

She sobbed aloud.

The sound of her own sob startled her, and suddenly she was angry with herself and her own weakness. She wiped the tears away with her thumbs and felt the gritty crunch of dried salt crystals on her eyelashes. Her anger grew stronger, and deliberately she turned it away from herself to the fates which so afflicted her.

'Why?' she demanded of the great red star. 'What have I ever done that you single me out? Are you punishing me? Michel, and my father, Nuage and Anna – everything I have ever loved. Why do you do this to me?' She broke off the thought, appalled at how close she had come to blasphemy. She hunched over, placed her free hand on her own belly and shivered with the cold. She tried to feel some sign of the life in her body, some swelling, some lump, some movement, but she was disappointed and her anger returned full strength, and with it a kind of wild defiance.

'I make a vow. As mercilessly as I have been afflicted, so hard will I fight to survive. You, whether you are God or Devil, have thrust this upon me. So I give you my oath. I will endure, and my son will endure through me.'

She was raving. She realized it but did not care, she had risen to her knees and was shaking her fist at the red star in defiance and anger.

'Come!' she challenged. 'Do your worst, and let's have done!'

If she had expected a blast of thunder and a lightning bolt, there was none – only the sound of the wind in the rude mast and the scrap of sail, and the bubble of the wake under the stern of the raft. Centaine sagged back on to her haunches and gripped the tiller and grimly pointed the raft up into the east.

In the first light of the day, a bird came and hovered above Centaine's head. It was a small seabird, the dark blue-grey of a rifle barrel with soft white chalky marks over its beady black eyes, and its wings were beautifully shaped and delicate, and its cry was lonely and soft.

'Wake up, Ernie,' Centaine cried, and her swollen lips split at the effort and a bubble of blood ran down her chin. The inside of her mouth was furry and dry as an old rabbit skin, and her thirst was a bright, burning thing.

Ernie struggled up and looked about him dazedly. He seemed to have shrunk and withered during the night, and his lips were flaky and white and encrusted with salt crystals.

'Look, Ernie, a bird!' Centaine mumbled through her bleeding lips.

'A bird,' Ernie echoed, staring up at it. 'Land close.'

The bird turned and darted away, low over the water, and was lost to sight, steel-grey against the dark grey sea.

In the middle of the morning Centaine pointed ahead, her mouth and her lips so desiccated that she could not speak. There was a dark tangled object floating on the surface just ahead of the raft. It wallowed and waved its tentacles like a monster from the depths.

'Sea kelp!' Ernie whispered, and when they were close enough, he gaffed it with the tiller arm and drew the heavy mat of vegetation alongside the raft.

The stalk of the kelp was thick as a man's arm and five metres long, with a bushy head of leaves at the end. It had obviously been torn from the rocks by the storm.

Moaning softly with thirst, Ernie cut a length of the thick stalk. Under the rubbery skin there was a pulpy section of stem, and a hollow air chamber within. Ernie shaved the pulp with the clasp knife and thrust a handful of the shavings into Centaine's mouth. It was running with sap. The taste was strong and unpleasant, iodine and peppery, but Centaine let the liquid trickle down her throat and whispered with delight. They gorged themselves on the juice of the kelp and spat out the pith. Then they rested a while and felt the strength flowing back into their bodies.

Ernie took the tiller again and headed the raft down the path of the wind. The storm clouds had blown away, and the sun warmed them and dried their clothing. At first they held their faces up to its caress, but soon it became oppressive, and they tried to huddle away from it in the tiny patch of shade from the sail.

When the sun reached its zenith, they were exposed to the scourge of its full strength and it sucked the moisture from their bodies. They squeezed a little more of the kelp juice, but now the unpleasant chemical taste nauseated Centaine and she realized that if she vomited, she would lose so much of her precious fluids. They could drink the kelp juice only sparingly.

With her back against the jury mast, Centaine stared out at the horizon, the great ring of threatening water that surrounded them unbroken except in the east where a line of sombre cloud lay low on the sea. It took her almost an hour to realize that despite the wind, the cloud had not changed shape. If anything, it had firmed and grown a hairline taller along the horizon. She could make out tiny irregularities, low peaks and valleys that did not alter shape as ordinary clouds would.

'Ernie,' she whispered, 'Ernie, look at those clouds.'

The old man blinked his eyes and then rose slowly into a crouch. He started to make a soft moaning sound in his throat, and Centaine realized it was a sound of joy.

She rose beside him, and for the first time looked upon the continent of Africa.

Africa rose from the sea with tantalizing deliberation, and then almost shyly swathed herself in the velvet robes of night and retreated once more from their gaze.

The raft trundled on gently through the hours of darkness, and neither of them slept. Then the eastern sky began to soften and glow with the dawn, the stars paled out and there close before them rose the great purple dunes of the Namibian Desert.

'How beautiful it is!' Centaine breathed.

'It's a hard fierce land, miss,' Ernie cautioned her.

'But so beautiful.'

The dunes were sculptured in mauve and violet, and

when the first rays of the sun touched the crests, they burned red gold and bronze.

'Beauty is as beauty does,' mumbled Ernie. 'Give me the green fields of old blighty and bugger the rest, begging your pardon, Miss Sunshine.'

The yellow-throated gannets came out in long formations from the land, flying high enough to be gilded by the sunlight, and the surf upon the beaches sighed and rumbled like the breathing of the sleeping continent. The wind that had stood steadily behind them for so long now felt the land and eddied and twisted. It caught their tiny sail aback, and the mast collapsed and fell overboard in a tangle of canvas and ropes.

They stared at each other in dismay. The land was so very close, it seemed that they might reach out and touch it – and yet they were forced to go through the whole weary business of restepping the mast. Neither of them had the energy for this new endeavour.

Ernie roused himself at last, wordlessly untied the lanyard of the clasp knife and handed it to Centaine. She fastened it around her own waist as the old man slid over the side of the raft once again and paddled to the peak of the stubby mast. On her knees, Centaine began to untangle the sheets and lines. The knots had all swollen with moisture and she had to use the spike of the clasp knife to break them open.

She coiled the ropes, and looked up as Ernie called, 'Are you ready, luv?'

'Ready.' She stood and balanced uncertainly on the tossing raft with the guide rope from the top of the mast in her hands taking up the slack, ready to assist Ernie to raise it back into position.

Then something moved beyond the old man's bobbing head, and she froze and lifted her hand to shade her eyes. She puzzled over the strangely shaped object. It rode high on the green current, as high as a man's waist, and the early morning sun glinted upon it like metal. No, not metal, but like a lustrous dark velvet. It was shaped like the sail of a child's yacht – and with a nostalgic pang she remembered the little boys around the village pond on a Sunday afternoon, dressed in their sailor suits, sailing their boats.

'What is it, luv?' Ernie had seen her expectant pose and her puzzled expression.

'I don't know,' she pointed. 'Something strange, coming towards us – fast, very fast!'

Ernie swivelled his head.

'Where? I don't see—' At that moment a swell lifted the raft high.

'God help us!' screamed Ernie, and flailed the water with his arms, tearing at it in an ungainly frenzy as he tried to reach the raft.

'What is it?'

'Help me out!' Ernie gulped, smothering in his own wild spray. 'It's a bloody great shark.'

The word paralysed Centaine. She stared in stony horror at the beast, as another swell lifted it high, and the angle of the sunlight changed to pierce the surface and spotlight it.

The shark was a lovely slaty-blue colour, dappled by the rippling surface shadows, and it was immense, much longer than their tiny raft, wider across the back than one of the hogsheads of cognac from the estate at Mort Homme. The double-bladed tail slashed as it drove forward, irresistibly attracted by the wild struggles of the man in the water, and it surged down the face of the swell.

Centaine screamed and recoiled.

The shark's eyes were a catlike golden colour with black, spade-shaped pupils. She saw the nostril slits in its massive, pointed snout.

'Help me!' screamed Ernie. He had reached the edge of

the raft and was trying to drag himself on board. He was kicking up a froth of water and the raft rocked wildly and listed towards him.

Centaine dropped to her knees and grabbed his wrist. She leaned back and pulled with all the strength of her terror, and Ernie slid halfway up on to the raft, but his legs still dangled over the side.

The shark seemed to hump out of the water, its back rose glistening blue, streaming with sea water, and the tall fin stood up like an executioner's blade. Centaine had read somewhere that a shark rolled on its back to attack, so she was unprepared for what happened now.

The great shark reared back and the grinning slit of its mouth seemed to bulge open. The lines of porcelain-white fangs, rank upon rank of them, came erect like the quills of a porcupine as the jaws projected outwards, and then they closed over Ernie's kicking legs. She clearly heard the grating rasp of the serrated edges of its fangs on bone, then the shark slid back, and Ernie was jerked backwards with it.

Centaine kept her grip on his wrist, although she was pulled down on to her knees and started to slide across the wet deck. The raft listed over steeply under their combined weight and the heavy drag of the shark on Ernie's legs.

Centaine could see its head under the surface for an instant. Its eye stared back at her with a fathomless savagery, and then the inner nictitating membrane slid across it in a sardonic wink, and quite slowly the shark rolled in the water with the irresistible weight of a teak log, exerting a shearing strain on to the jaws still clamped over Ernie's legs.

Centaine heard the bones part with a sound like breaking green sticks. The drag on the old man's body was released so suddenly that the raft bobbed up and swung like a crazy pendulum in the opposite direction.

Centaine, still with her grip on Ernie's arm, fell back-

307

wards, dragging him up on to the raft after her. He was still kicking, but both his legs were grotesquely foreshortened, taken off a few inches below the knee, the stumps protruding from the torn cuffs of his duck trousers. The cuts were not clean, dangling ribbons of torn meat and skin flapped from the stumps as Ernie kicked, and the blood was a bright fountain in the sunlight.

He rolled over and sat up on the pitching raft, and stared at his stumps. 'Oh merciful mother, help me!' he moaned. 'I'm a dead man.'

Blood spurted from the open arteries, dribbled and ran in rivulets across the white deck, cascaded to the surface of the sea and stained it cloudy brown. The blood looked like smoke in the water.

'My legs!' Ernie clutched at his wounds, and the blood fountained up between his fingers. 'My legs are gone. The devil has taken my legs.'

There was a huge swirl almost under the raft, and the dark triangular fin came up and knifed the surface, cutting through the discoloured water.

'He smells the blood,' Ernie cried. 'He won't give up, the devil. We are all dead men.'

The shark turned, rolling on his side, so they saw his snowy belly and the wide grinning jaws, and he came back, sliding through the bright clear water with majestic sweeps of his tail. He thrust his head into the blood clouds, and the wide jaws opened as he gulped at the taste. The scent and the taste infuriated him and he turned again; the waters roiled and churned at the massive movement below the surface, and this time he drove straight under the raft.

There was a crash as the shark struck the underside of the raft with his back, and Centaine was thrown flat with the force of the impact. She clung to the raft with clawed fingers.

'He is trying to capsize us,' shouted Ernie. Centaine had never seen so much blood. She could not believe that the thin ancient body held so much, and still it spurted from Ernie's severed stumps.

The shark turned and came back. Again the heavy crash of rubbery flesh into the timbers of the raft and they were lifted up high. The raft hovered on the edge of capsizing and then fell back on to an even keel and bobbed like a cork.

'He won't give up,' Ernie was sobbing weakly. 'Here he comes again.'

The shark's great blue head rose out of the water, the jaws opened and then closed on the side of the raft. Long white fangs locked into the timber, and it crunched and splintered as the shark hung on.

It seemed to be staring directly at Centaine as she lay on her belly clinging to the struts of the raft with both hands. It looked like a monstrous blue hog, snuffling and rooting at the frail timbers of the little raft. Once again it blinked its eyes – the pale translucent membrane slipping over inscrutable black pupils was the most obscene and terrifying thing Centaine had ever seen – and then it began to shake its head, still gripping the side of the raft in its jaws. They were thrown about roughly, as the raft was lifted out of the water and swung from side to side.

'Good Christ, he'll have us yet!' Ernie dragged himself away from the grinning head. 'He'll never stop till he gets us!'

Centaine leapt to her feet, balancing like an acrobat, and she seized the thick wooden tiller and swung it high overhead. With all her strength she brought it down on the tip of the shark's hoglike snout. The blow jarred her arms to the shoulders, and she swung again and then again. The tiller landed with a rubbery thump, then bounced off the great head without even marking the sandpapery blue hide, and the shark seemed not to feel it.

He went on worrying the side of the raft; rocking it wildly, and Centaine lost her balance and fell half overboard, but instantly she dragged herself back and on her knees kept beating the huge invulnerable head, sobbing with the effort of each stroke. A section of the woodwork tore away in the shark's jaws, and the blue head slipped below the surface again, giving Centaine a moment's respite.

'He's coming back!' Ernie cried weakly. 'He will keep coming back – he won't give up!' And as he said it, Centaine knew what she had to do. She couldn't allow herself to think about it. She had to do it for the baby's sake. That was all that counted, Michel's son.

Ernie was sitting flat on the edge of the raft, those fearfully mutilated limbs thrust out in front of him, turned half away from Centaine, leaning forward to peer down into the green waters below the raft.

'Here he comes again!' he shrieked. His sparse grey hairs were slicked down over his pate by seawater and diluted blood. His scalp gleamed palely through this thin covering. Beneath them the waters roiled, as the shark turned to attack once more, and Centaine saw the dark bulk of him coming up from the depths, driving back at the raft.

Centaine came to her feet again. Her expression was stricken, her eyes filled with horror, and she tightened her grip on the heavy wooden tiller. The shark crashed into the bottom of the raft, and Centaine reeled, almost fell, then caught her balance.

'He said himself he was a dead man.' She steeled herself.

She lifted the tiller high and fixed her gaze on the naked pink patch at the back of Ernie's head and then with all her strength she swung the tiller down in an axe-stroke.

She saw Ernie's skull collapse under the blow.

'Forgive me, Ernie,' she sobbed, as the old man fell forward and rolled to the edge of the raft. 'You were dead already, and there was no other way to save my baby.'

The back of his skull was crushed in, but he rolled his

head and looked at her. His eyes were afire with some turbulent emotion and he tried to speak. His mouth opened, then the fire in his eyes died and his limbs stretched and relaxed.

Centaine was weeping as she knelt beside him.

'God forgive me,' she whispered, 'but my baby must live.'

The shark turned and came back, its dorsal fin standing higher than the deck of the raft, and gently, almost tenderly, Centaine rolled Ernie's body over the side.

The shark whirled. It picked up the body in its jaws and began to worry it like a mastiff with a bone, and as it did so the raft drifted away. The shark and its victim sank gradually out of sight into the green waters and Centaine found she still had the tiller in her hands.

She began to paddle with it, pushing the raft towards the beach. She sobbed with each stroke, and her vision was blurred. Through her tears she saw the kelp beds swaying and dancing at the edge of the ocean, and beyond them the surf humping and then hissing over a beach of brassy yellow sands. She paddled in a dedicated frenzy, and an eddy of the current caught the raft, assisting her efforts, and bore it in towards the beach. Now she could see the bottom, the corrugated patterns of sea-washed sands, through the limpid green water.

'Thank you, God – oh thank you, thank you!' she sobbed in time to her strokes, and then again there came that shattering impact of a huge body into the underside of the raft.

Centaine clung desperately to the strut again, her spirits plunging with despair. 'It's come back again.'

She saw the massive dappled shape pass beneath the raft, starkly outlined against the gleaming sandy bottom.

'It never gives up.' She had won only temporary respite. The shark had devoured the sacrifice she had offered it within minutes, then drawn by the odour of the blood that was still splattered over the raft, it had followed her into water barely as deep as a man's shoulder.

It came around in a wide circle and then raced in from the sea side to attack the raft again, and this time the impact was so shattering that the raft began to break up. The planks had been worked loose by the heavy flogging of the storm, and they opened now under Centaine, so her legs dropped through and she touched the horrid beast beneath the raft. She felt the rasping of its coarse hide across the soft skin of her calf, and screamed as she jack-knifed her lower body up away from it.

Inexorably the shark circled and came back, but the slope of the beach forced it to come from the sea side and its next attack, murderous as it was, drove the raft in closer to the beach, and for a moment or two the colossal beast was stranded on the shelving sand. Then, with a swirl and a high splash, it pulled free and circled out into deeper water, but with its fin and broad blue back exposed.

A wave hit the raft, completing the demolition that the shark had begun, and the raft shattered into a welter of planks and canvas and dangling ropes. Centaine was tumbled into the surging waters, and spluttering and coughing came to her feet.

She was breast-deep in the cold green surf, and through eyes streaming with salt water, she saw the shark come boring full at her. She screamed and tried to back up the shelving beach, brandishing the tiller she still had in her hands.

'Get away!' she screamed. 'Get away! Leave me!'

The shark hit her with his snout and threw her high in the air. She fell back on top of the huge black back, and it reared under her like a wild horse. The feel of it was cold and rough and unspeakably loathsome. She was thrown clear of it and then was struck a heavy blow by the flailing tail. She knew it had been a glancing blow – a full sweep of that tail would have crushed in her ribcage.

The shark's own wild thrashing had churned up the sandy bottom, blinding it so that it could not see its prey, but it sought her with its mouth in the turbid water. The jaws champed like an iron gate slamming in a hurricane, and Centaine was beaten and hammered by the swinging tail and the massive contortions of the blue body.

Slowly she fought her way up the sloping beach. Every time she was knocked down, she struggled up, gasping and blinded and striking out with the tiller. The gnashing fangs closed on the thick folds of her skirt and ripped them away, and immediately her legs were freed. As she stumbled back a last few paces, the level of the water fell below her waist.

At the same moment, the surf drew back, sucking away from the beach, and the shark was stranded, suddenly powerless as it was deprived of its natural element. It wriggled and writhed on the sand, helpless as a bull elephant in a pitfall, and Centaine backed away from it, knee-deep in the dragging surf, too exhausted to turn and run – until miraculously she realized that she was standing on hard-packed sand above the waterline.

She threw the tiller aside and staggered up the beach towards the high dunes. She did not have the strength to go that far. She collapsed just above the high-water line and lay face down in the sand. The sand coated her face and body like sugar, and she lay in the sunlight and wept with the fierce gales of fear and sorrow and remorse and relief that racked her entire body.

She had no idea how long she lay in the sand, but after a while she became aware of the sting of the harsh sunlight on the backs of her bare legs, and she sat up slowly. Fearfully she looked back to the edge of the surf, expecting still to see the great blue beast stranded there, but the flooding tide must have lifted it and it had escaped out into deep water. There was no sign of it at all. She let out her breath in an involuntary gasp of relief and stood up uncertainly.

Her body felt battered and crushed and very weak, and looking down at it she saw how contact with the rough abrasive hide of the shark had grazed her skin raw, and that already there were dark blue bruises spreading across her thighs. Her skirts had been torn off her by the shark, and she had discarded her shoes before she jumped from the deck of the hospital ship, so except for her sodden uniform blouse and a pair of silk cami-knickers, she was naked. She felt a rush of shame, and looked around her quickly. She had never been further from other human presence in her life.

'No one to peek at me here.' She had instinctively covered her pudenda with her hands, and she let them fall to her sides again, and touched something hanging from her waist. It was Ernie's clasp knife, dangling on its lanyard.

She took it in her hand and stared out over the ocean. All her guilt and remorse returned to her with a rush.

'I owe you my life,' she whispered, 'and the life of my son. Oh, Ernie, how I wish you were still with us.'

The loneliness came upon her with such an overpowering rush that she sagged down on to the sand again and covered her face with her hands. The sun roused her once again. She felt her skin beginning to prickle and burn again under its baleful rays, and immediately her thirst returned to nag at her.

'Must protect myself from the sun.' She dragged herself upright and looked around her with more attention.

She was on a wide yellow beach backed by mountainous dunes. The beach was totally deserted. It stretched away in sweeping curves on each side of her to the very limit of her vision, twenty or thirty kilometres, she estimated, before it shaded into the sea fret. It seemed to Centaine to be the picture of desolation; there was no rock or leaf of vegetation, no bird or animal, and no cover from the sun.

Then she looked at the edge of the beach where she had struggled ashore, and she saw the remnants of her raft swirling and tumbling in the surf. Fighting down her terror of the shark, she waded in knee-deep and dragged the tangled sail and sheets of the raft high above the tideline.

For a skirt, she cut a strip of canvas and belted it around her waist with a length of hemp rope. Then she cut another piece of canvas to cover her head and shoulders from the sun.

'Oh! I'm so thirsty!' She stood at the edge of the beach and longingly peered out to where the kelp beds danced in the current. Her thirst was more powerful than her distaste for the kelp juice, but her terror of the shark was greater than both, and she turned away.

Though her body ached and the bruises were purple and black across her arms and legs, she knew her best chance was to start walking, and there was only one direction to take. Cape Town lay to the south. However, nearer than that were the German towns with strange names – she recalled them with an effort, Swakopmund and Lüderitzbucht. The nearest of these was probably five hundred kilometres away.

Five hundred kilometres – the enormity of that distance came over her, and her legs turned to water under her and she sat down heavily on the sand.

'I won't think about how far it is,' she roused herself at last. 'I will think only one step ahead at a time.'

She pushed herself to her feet and her whole body ached with bruises. She began to limp along the edge of the sea, where the sand was wet and firm, and after a while her muscles warmed and the stiffness eased so she could extend her stride.

'Just one step at a time!' she told herself. The loneliness

was a burden that would weigh her down if she let it. She lifted her chin and looked ahead.

The beach was endless, and there was a frightening sameness to the vista that stretched before her. The hours that she trudged on seemed to have no effect upon it and she began to believe that she was on a treadmill with always the unbroken sands ahead of her, the changeless sea on her right hand, the tall wall of the dunes on her left, and over it all the vast milky blue bowl of the sky.

'I am walking from nothingness on to nothing,' she whispered, and she longed with all her soul for the glimpse of another human form.

The soles of her bare feet began to hurt and when she sat down to examine them, she found that seawater had softened her skin and the coarse yellow sand had abraded it almost down to the flesh. She bound up her feet with strips of canvas and went on. The sun and the exertion dampened her blouse with sweat, and thirst became her constant spectral companion.

The sun was halfway down the western sky when in the distance ahead of her a rocky headland appeared, and merely because it altered the dreary vista, she quickened her pace. But her step soon faltered again and she realized how the single day's trek had already weakened her.

'I haven't eaten for three days, and I haven't drunk since yesterday—'

The rocky headland seemed to come no nearer, and at last she had to sit down to rest, and almost immediately her thirst began to rage.

'If I don't drink very soon, I won't be able to go on,' she whispered, and she peered ahead at the low rampart of black rock and straightened up incredulously; her eyes were tricking her. She blinked them rapidly and stared again.

'People!' she whispered and pulled herself to her feet. 'People!' She began to stagger forward.

They were sitting on the rocks, she could see the

movement of their heads silhouetted against the pale sky, and she laughed aloud and waved to them.

'There are so many – am I going mad?' She tried to shout, but it came out as a reedy little whine.

Disappointment, when it struck, was so intense that she reeled as though from a physical blow.

'Seals,' she whispered, and their mournful honking cries carried to her on the soft sea breeze.

For a while she did not think that she had the strength to go on. And then she forced one foot in front of the other, and plodded on towards the headland.

Several hundred seals were draped over the rocks, and there were many more bobbing about in the waves that broke over the rocky point, and the stench of them came to Centaine on the wind. As she approached, they began to retreat towards the sea, flopping over the rocks in their ludicrously clownish way, and she saw that there were dozens of calves amongst them.

'If I could only catch one of those.' She gripped the clasp knife in her right hand and opened the blade. 'I have to eat soon—' But already alarmed by her approach, the leaders were sliding from the rocks into the surging green water, their ungainly lumberings transformed instantly into miraculous grace.

She started to run, and the movement precipitated a rush of dark bodies over the rocks; she was still a hundred yards from the nearest of them. She gave up and stood panting weakly, watching the colony escape into the sea.

Then suddenly there was a wild commotion amongst them, a chorus of squeals and terrified cries, and she saw two dark agile wolf-like shapes dart from amongst the rocks and drive into the densely packed troop of seals. She realized that her approach had distracted the colony, and given these other predators a chance to launch their own attack. She did not recognize them as brown hyena for she had only seen illustrations of the bigger and more ferocious

317

spotted hyena which almost every book on African exploration contained.

These animals were the 'beach wolf' of the Dutch settlers, the size of a mastiff, but with sharp pointed ears and a shaggy mane of long ashy yellow fur that was now erect in excitement as they dashed into the colony of seals; unerringly they picked out the smallest and most defenceless of the infants, seizing them from the flanks of their cumbersome dams, and dragged them away, easily avoiding the grotesque efforts that the mothers made to defend their young.

Centaine began running again, and at her approach the female seals gave up and flopped down the black rocks into the surf. She snatched up a club of driftwood from the pile of rubbish on the high-tide mark and raced across the end of the headland to cut off the nearest of the brown hyena.

The hyena was hampered by the squealing baby seal that it was dragging, and Centaine managed to get ahead of it. The animal stopped and lowered its head in a threatening stance, and watched Centaine approaching. The young seal was bleeding copiously from where the hyena's fangs were locked into its glossy pelt, and it was crying like an human infant.

The hyena growled fiercely and Centaine stopped, facing the beast, and swung the club and shrieked at it.

'Drop it! Get away, you brute! Leave it!'

She sensed that the hyena was perplexed by her aggressive attitude, and though it growled again, it backed up a few steps and crouched protectively over its wriggling prey.

Centaine tried to stare it down, holding the gaze of the formidable yellow eyes as she shouted and brandished the club. Abruptly the hyena dropped the badly injured seal cub and rushed directly at Centaine, baring long yellow fangs and making a roaring bellow in its throat. Instinctively Centaine knew that this was the crucial moment. If she ran the hyena would follow her and savage her.

She rushed forward to meet the animal's charge, redoubling her yells and swinging the club with all her strength. Evidently the hyena had not expected this reaction. Its courage failed. It turned and ran back to its floundering prey, and burying its fangs in the silky skin of its neck, began to drag it away again.

At Centaine's feet was a crevice in the rocks and it was filled with water-worn round stones. She grabbed one of these, the size of a ripe orange, and hurled it at the hyena. She aimed for the head, but the heavy stone fell short and it hit the creature's paw, crushing it against the rocky ground. The hyena squealed, dropped the seal cub and limped swiftly away on three legs.

Centaine ran forward and opened the clasp knife. She was a country girl and had helped Anna and her father slaughter and dress animals before. With a single, swift, merciful stroke, she cut the seal's throat and let it bleed. The hyena circled back, growling and whining, limping heavily, undecided and confused by the attack.

Centaine snatched up stones from the crevice in both hands and threw them. One of them struck the hyena on the side of its bushy-maned head and it yelped and fled fifty paces before stopping and staring back at her over its shoulder with hatred.

She worked swiftly. As she had watched Anna do so often with a sheep's carcass, she slit open the belly cavity, angling the point of the blade so as not to nick the stomach sac or the entrails, sawing through the cartilage that closed the front of the ribcage.

With bloodied hands she hurled another stone at the circling hyena, and then carefully lifted out the infant seal's stomach. The need for moisture was a raging fever within her; already she sensed that lack of it was threatening

319

the existence of the embryo in her own womb, and yet her gorge rose at the thought of what she must do.

'When I was a girl,' Anna had told her, 'the shepherds used to do it whenever a suckling lamb died.'

Centaine held the seal cub's little stomach bag in her cupped and bloodied hands. The stomach lining was yellowish and translucent so that she fancied that she could see the contents through the walls. The cub must obviously have been lying with its mother up to the moment of the hyena attack, and it must have been suckling greedily. The small stomach was drum-tight with milk.

Centaine gulped with revulsion and then told herself, 'If you don't drink, you'll be dead by morning – you and Michel's son, both.'

She made a tiny incision in the stomach wall, and immediately the thick white curds of milk oozed from it. Centaine closed her eyes and placed her mouth over the slit. She forced herself to suck the hot curdled milk. Her empty stomach heaved and she choked with an involuntary retching reflex, but she fought and at last controlled it.

The curds had a slightly fishy taste but were not altogether repulsive. After she had forced down the first mouthful, she thought it tasted a little of the goat's-milk cheese that Anna made, strong with rennet.

She rested after a while, and wiped the blood and mucus from her mouth with the back of her hand. She could almost feel the fluid soaking back to replace that lost by her body tissues, and new strength seemed to radiate through her exhausted body.

She hurled another rock at the hyena, and then drank the rest of the thick curdled milk. Carefully she slit open the tiny empty stomach sac, and licked up the last drops. Then she threw the empty membrane to the hyena.

'I will share it with you,' she told the snarling beast.

She skinned the carcass, cutting off the head and the rudimentary limbs, and threw those to the hyena also. The big doglike carnivore seemed to have resigned itself. It sat on its haunches twenty paces from Centaine, with its pointed ears pricked up and a comically expectant expression, waiting for the scraps she threw it.

Centaine cut as many long narrow strips of the bright red seal meat as she could get off the skeleton, and wrapped them in the canvas of her headdress. Then she retreated and the hyena rushed forward to lick up the spilled blood from the rocks and to crush the small skeleton in its ugly, over-developed jaws.

At the top of the headland the wind and wave action had cut a shallow overhang from the compacted sandstone, and it had provided a shelter for others before Centaine. She found the scattered ashes of a long-dead cooking fire on the sandy floor of the cave, and when she scratched in the dirt, she turned up a small triangular flint scraper or cutting tool, similar to those for which she and Anna had hunted on the hillock behind the château at Mort Homme. It gave her a peculiarly nostalgic pang to hold the scrap of flint in the grubby palm of her hand, and when she felt self-pity overcoming her, she placed the sliver of stone in the pocket of her blouse, and forced herself to face harsh reality rather than mope over bygone days in a far-off land.

'Fire,' she said, as she examined the dead sticks of charcoal, and she laid out the precious scraps of seal meat on a rock at the mouth of the cave to dry in the wind and went back to gather an armful of driftwood.

She piled this beside the ancient hearth and tried to remember everything she had ever read about making fire.

'Two sticks – rub them together,' she muttered.

It was a human need so basic, so taken for granted in her life until then, that now the lack of fire with its warmth and comfort was an appalling deprivation.

The driftwood was impregnated with salt and damp. She selected two pieces, not having the vaguest notion of the qualities of the wood she required, and she set about experimenting. She worked until her fingers were raw and hurting, but she could not induce a single spark or even a wisp of smoke from her scraps of wood shavings.

Depressed and despondent, she lay back against the rear wall of the rock shelter and watched the sun set into the darkening sea. She shivered with the chill of the evening breeze and wrapped the canvas shawl more securely around her shoulders; she felt the small lump of flint press into her breast.

She noticed how tender her nipples had become recently, and how her breasts had begun to swell and harden, and she massaged them now. Somehow the thought of her pregnancy gave her renewed strength, and when she looked southwards, she saw Michael's special star hanging low on the horizon where a sombre ocean was blending into the night sky.

'Achernar,' she whispered. 'Michel—' and as she said his name her fingers touched the flint in her pocket again. It was almost as though it was Michael's gift to her, and her hands shook with excitement as she struck the flint against the steel blade of the clasp knife, and the white sparks flared in the darkness of the rocky shelter.

She worried the threads of canvas into a loose ball, mixed with fine wood shavings, and struck flint and steel over it. Although each attempt produced a shower of bright white sparks, it took all her care and persistence before at last a wisp of smoke rose from the ball of kindling and she blew it into a tiny yellow flame.

She grilled the strips of seal meat over the coals. They tasted like both veal and rabbit. She savoured each bite and after she had eaten, she anointed the painful red blisters that the sun had raised on her skin with seal fat.

She set aside the remaining strips of cooked meat for the days ahead, built up the fire, wrapped the canvas around her shoulders and settled herself against the near wall of the shelter with the club beside her.

'I should pray—' and as she began, Anna seemed very close, watching over her as she had so often before when Centaine, the child, knelt beside her bed with hands clasped before her.

'Thank you, Almighty God, for saving me from the sea and thank you for the food and drink you have provided, but—' The prayer petered out, and Centaine felt recriminations rather than gratitude pressing to her lips.

'Blasphemy.' She almost heard Anna's voice and she ended the prayer hastily.

'And, oh Lord, please give me the strength to face whatever further trials you have in store for me in the days ahead, and if it please you, give me also the wisdom to see your design and purpose in heaping these tribulations upon me.' That was as much of a protest as she would risk, and while she was still trying to decide on a suitable ending for the prayer, she fell asleep.

When she awoke, the fire had died down to embers, and she did not at first know where she was or what had woken her. Then her circumstances came back to her with a sickening rush, and she heard some large animal out in the darkness just beyond the opening of the shelter. It sounded as though it was feeding.

Quickly she piled driftwood on the fire and blew up a flame. At the edge of the firelight she saw the lurking shape of the hyena and she realized that the package of cooked seal meat that she had so carefully wrapped in a strip of canvas the previous evening was gone from the rock beside the fire.

Sobbing with rage and frustration, she picked up a flaming brand and hurled it at the hyena.

'You horrible thieving brute!' she screamed, and it yelped and galloped away into the darkness.

The seal colony lay basking on the rocks below her shelter in the early morning sunlight, and already Centaine felt the first stirrings of the hunger and the thirst that the day would bring.

She armed herself with two stones, each the size of her fist, and the driftwood club, and with elaborate stealth crawled down one of the gulleys in the rocks, attempting to get within range of the nearest members of the colony. However, the seals fled honking before she had covered half the distance and they would not emerge from the surf again while she was in sight.

Frustrated and hungry, she went back to the shelter. There were spots of congealed white seal fat on the rock beside the hearth. She crushed a knob of charcoal from the dead fire to powder and mixed it with the fat in the palm of her hand, then she carefully blacked the tip of her nose and her cheeks, the exposed areas which had been burned by the sun the previous day.

Then she looked around the shelter. She had the knife and the scrap of flint, the club and canvas hood, all her worldly possessions, and yet she felt a dragging reluctance to leave the shelter. For a few hours it had been her home. She had to force herself to turn and go down to the beach, and to set out southwards into that ominously monotonous seascape once again.

That night there was no cave shelter and no pile of driftwood trapped against a rocky headland. There was no food and nothing to drink and she rolled herself in the strip of canvas and lay on the hard sand under the dunes. All night a chill little wind blew the fine sands over her so that at dawn she was coated with sparkling sugary particles. Sand had encrusted her eyelashes, and salt and sand were thick in her hair. She was so stiff with cold and bruises and over-taxed muscles that at first she hobbled like an old woman, using the club as a staff. As her muscles warmed, the stiffness abated, but she knew she was getting weaker and as the sun rose higher, so her thirst became a silent scream in the depths of her body. Her lips swelled and cracked, her tongue bloated and furred over with thickening gluey saliva that she could not swallow.

She knelt in the edge of the surf and bathed her face, soaked the canvas shawl and her skimpy clothing, and resisted somehow the temptation to swallow a mouthful of the cool, clear sea water.

The relief was only temporary. When the sea water dried on her skin, the salt crystals stung the sun-tender spots and burned her cracked, dry lips, her skin seemed to stretch to the point of tearing like parchment, and her thirst was an obsession.

In the middle of the afternoon, far ahead of her on the smooth wet sand, she saw a cluster of black moving shapes, and she shaded her eyes hopefully. However, the specks resolved into four large seagulls, with pure white chests and black backs, squabbling and threatening each other with open yellow bills as they competed for a piece of flotsam washed ashore by the tide.

They rose on outsretched wings as Centaine staggered towards them, leaving their disputed prize, too heavy for them to carry, lying on the sand. It was a large dead fish, already badly mutilated by the gulls, and with new strength Centaine ran the last few paces and dropped on her knees. She lifted the fish with both hands and then gagged and dropped it again, wiping her hands on her canvas skirt. The fish was stinking rotten, her fingers had sunk into the soft putrefying flesh as though into cold suet.

She crawled away and sat with her arms wrapped around her knees, hugging them to her breast, staring at the lump of stinking carrion and trying to subdue her thirst.

It took all her courage, but at last she crawled back to it, and with her face turned away from the stench, hacked off a fillet of the maggot-white flesh. She cut a small square of it and placed it cautiously in her mouth. Her stomach heaved at the taste of sickly sweet corruption, but she chewed it carefully, sucked out the reeking juices, spat out the pulpy flesh and then cut another lump from the fillet.

Sickened as much by her own degradation as by the rotten flesh, she kept sucking out the juices and when she reckoned that she had forced a large cupful down her throat, she rested a while.

Gradually the fluids fortified her. She felt much stronger, strong enough to go on again. She waded into the sea and tried to wash the stench of rotten fish from her hands and lips. The taste lingered in her mouth as she started once more plodding along the edge of the beach.

Just before sunset a new, crippling wave of weakness came over her and she sank down on to the sand. Suddenly an icy sweat broke across her forehead and cramp, like a sword thrust through her belly, doubled her over. She belched, and the taste of rotten fish filled her mouth and nostrils.

She heaved, and hot reeking vomit shot up her throat. She felt despair as she saw so much of her vital fluids splash on to the sand, but she heaved again, and at the contraction she felt a spluttery explosive release of diarrhoea.

'I'm poisoned.' She fell and writhed on the sand as spasm after spasm gripped her and her body involuntarily purged itself of the toxic juices. It was dark by the time the attack passed, and she dragged off her soiled camiknickers and threw them aside. She crawled painfully into the sea and washed her body, splashed her face and rinsed the taste of rotten fish and vomit from her mouth, prepared to pay for the momentary relief of a clean mouth with later thirst.

Then still on her hands and knees, she crawled up above the high-water mark, and in the darkness, shaking with cold, she lay down to die.

At first Garry Courtney was so involved in the excitement of planning the rescue expedition into the Namib desert, across that dreaded littoral that was named the Skeleton Coast for very good reason, that he did not have the leisure to weigh the chances of success.

It was enough for Garry to be playing the man of action. Like all romantics, he had daydreamed of himself in this role on so many occasions, and now that the opportunity was thrust upon him, he seized it with a frenzy of dedicated effort.

In the long months after the war department cable had arrived – that coarse buff envelope with its laconic message, 'His Majesty regrets to inform you that your son Captain Michael Courtney has been reported killed in action' – Garry's existence had been a dark void, without purpose or direction. Then had come the miracle of the second cable from his twin brother: 'Michael's widow expecting your grandson has been rendered homeless and destitute by tides of war stop I am arranging priority passage on first sailing for Cape Town stop will you meet and take into your care stop reply urgently stop letter follows Sean.'

A new sun had risen in his life. When that in its turn had been cruelly extinguished, plunged into the cruel green waters of the Benguela current. Garry had realized instinctively that he could not afford to let reason and reality beat him down once again into the dark night of despair. He had to believe, he had to push aside any calculation of the probabilities and cling mindlessly to the remote possibility that Michael's wife and her unborn child had somehow survived sea and desert, and were waiting only for him to find and rescue them. The only way to do this was to replace reasoned thought with feverish activity, however meaningless and futile, and when that failed, to draw upon the limitless reserve of Anna Stok's rock-solid and unwavering faith.

The two of them arrived at Windhoek, the old capital

of German South West Africa which had been captured two years before, and were met at the railway station by Colonel John Wickenham, who was acting military governor of the territory.

'How do you do, sir.'

Wickenham's salute was diffident. He had received a string of cables in the last few days, amongst them one from General Jannie Smuts and another from the ailing prime minister, General Louis Botha – all of them instructing him to extend to his visitor full assistance and co-operation.

This alone did not account for the measure of his respect towards his guest. Colonel Garrick Courtney was the holder of the highest award for gallantry, and his book on the Anglo-Boer War, *The Elusive Enemy*, was required reading at the Staff College that Wickenham had attended, while the political and financial influence of the brothers Courtney was legend. 'I should like to offer you my condolences on your loss, Colonel Courtney,' Wickenham told him as they shook hands.

'That is very decent of you.' Garry felt like an imposter when addressed by his rank. He always felt the need to explain that it had been a temporary appointment with an irregular regiment in a war almost twenty years past; to cover his uneasiness he turned to Anna, standing four-square beside him in her solar topee and long calico skirts.

'I would like to introduce Mevrou Stok,' Garry switched to Afrikaans for her benefit, and Wickenham followed him quickly.

'*Aangename kennis* – a pleasant meeting, Mevrou.'

'Mevrou Stok was a passenger on the *Protea Castle*, and one of the survivors picked up by the *Inflexible*.'

Wickenham gave a little whistle of sympathy. 'A most unpleasant experience.' He turned back to Garry. 'Let me assure you, Colonel Courtney, that it will be my pleasure to offer you any possible assistance.'

Anna replied for him. 'We will need motor-cars, many motor-cars, and men to help us. We will need them quick, very quickly!'

For the command car they had a new 'T' model Ford, repainted from factory black to a pale sand colour. Despite its frail appearance, it was to prove a formidable vehicle in the desert conditions. The light vanadium steel body and slow-revving engine carried it over soft sand that would have sucked down heavier machines. Its only weakness was a tendency to over-heat and send a jet of precious water streaming high in the air to scald driver and passengers in the open body.

As supply vehicles, Wickenham provided them with four Austin lorries, each capable of carrying half a ton of cargo, and a fifth vehicle which had been modified in the railway workshops by army engineers and fitted with a cylindrical steel tank with a capacity of five hundred gallons of water. Each of the vehicles was assigned a corporal driver with an assistant.

With Anna firmly crushing any tendency of Garry's to procrastinate, and riding roughly over the practical objections of engineers and mechanics and military experts, the convoy was ready to leave from the capital thirty-six hours after her arrival. It was fourteen days since the German torpedoes had struck the *Protea Castle*.

They clattered out of the sleeping town at four in the morning, the trucks piled high with equipment and fuel stores and the passengers bundled against the cold highland night airs. They took the wagon road that ran beside the narrow-gauge railway line down to the coastal town at Swakopmund, over two hundred miles away.

Steel-shod wagon wheels had cut ruts so deep that the rubber tyres of the vehicles were trapped in them and could not be steered out except at the rocky sections where the double ruts became boulder-strewn gulleys more like the bed of a dry mountain stream than a road. Laboriously they climbed down those rugged passes, crashing and jolting over the heavy going, forced to stop unexpectedly to repair a punctured tyre or replace a broken spring leaf, descending four thousand feet in fourteen hours of bone-cracking, neck-wrenching travel.

They came out on the flat, scrub-covered coastal plains at last, and raced across them at an exhilarating twenty-five miles per hour, dragging behind them a long rolling pall of dun-coloured dust like the smoke from a runaway bush fire.

The town of Swakopmund was a startling touch of Bavaria transported to the southern African desert, complete with quaint Black Forest architecture and a long pier stretching out into the green sea.

It was Sunday noon when their dusty cavalcade trundled down the paved main street. There was a German oom-pa-pa band playing in the gardens of the residency, the band members dressed in green lederhosen and alpine hats. They lost the beat and trailed into silence as Garry's convoy pulled up outside the hotel across the road. Their trepidation was understandable, for the walls of the building were still pitted with shrapnel from the last British invasion.

After the dust and heat of the desert crossing, the local Pilsner, product of a master brewer from Munich, tasted like resurrection in Valhalla.

'Set them up again, barman,' Garry ordered, revelling in the masculine camaraderie, in the afterglow of the achievement of having brought his command safely down from the mountains. His men bellied up to the long teak bar with a will, and when they raised their tankards and grinned at him, their masks of packed dust cracked and powdered into their beer.

'Mijnheer!' Anna had performed her perfunctory ablutions and appeared in the doorway of the saloon. She stood with her thickly muscled arms akimbo, and her face, already inflamed by sun and wind, was slowly becoming truly fiery with outrage.

'Mijnheer, you are wasting time!'

Garry rounded on his men swiftly. 'Come on, you fellows, there is work to do. Let's get on with it.'

By this time none of them had any doubts as to who was in ultimate command of the expedition, and they gulped their beers and trooped out into the sunlight, shamefacedly wiping the froth from their lips and unable to meet Anna's eye as they sidled past her.

While his men refuelled, filled the water tanks, repacked the loads that had come loose on the journey, and carried out maintenance and running repairs on the vehicles, Garry went off to make inquiries at the police station.

The police sergeant had been warned of Garry's arrival. 'I'm very sorry, Colonel, we weren't expecting you for three or four days. If only I had known—' He was eager to be of assistance. 'Nobody knows much about that country up there,' as he glanced from the window of the charge office towards the north, the sergeant shivered involuntarily, 'but I have a man who can act as a guide for you.' He took down his key-ring from the hook on the wall behind the desk and led Garry through to the cells.

'Hey, you *swart donder* – you black thunder!' he growled as he unlocked one of the cells, and Garry blinked as his chosen guide shuffled out sullenly and glowered about him.

He was a villainous-looking Bondelswart Hottentot with a single malevolent eye; the other was covered by a leather eye-patch, and he smelled like a wild goat.

'He knows that land out there, he should do,' the sergeant grinned. 'That's where he poached the rhinoceros horn and ivory that is going to send him to the clanger for five years, isn't that right, Kali Piet?'

Kali Piet opened his leather jerkin and searched his chest hair reflectively.

'If he works well for you, and you are pleased with him,

he might get off with only two or three years' breaking stones,' the sergeant explained, and Kali Piet found something amongst his body hair and cracked it between his fingernails.

'And if I am not pleased with him?' Garry asked uncertainly. *Kali* was the Swahili word for 'bad' or 'wicked', and it inspired no great confidence.

'Oh,' the sergeant said airily, 'then don't bother to bring him back. Just bury him where nobody will find him.' Kali Piet's attitude changed miraculously.

'Good master,' he whined in Afrikaans, 'I know every tree, every rock, every grain of sand. I will be your dog.'

Anna was waiting for Garry, already seated in the rear seat of the 'T' model.

'What took you so long?' she demanded. 'My baby has been out there in the wilderness alone for sixteen days now!'

'Corporal,' Garry handed Kali Piet into the care and keeping of the senior NCO. 'If he tries to escape,' Garry tried unconvincingly to look leeringly sadistic, 'shoot him!'

As the last whitewashed red-tiled buildings fell away behind them, Garry's driver belched softly and retasted the beer with a dreamy smile.

'Enjoy it,' Garry warned him, 'it will be a long trek to the next tankard.'

The track ran along the edge of the beach, while at their left hand the green surf tipped with ostrich feathers of spume pounded the smooth yellow sands, and before them stretched that dismal featureless littoral, shrouded in a haze of sea fret.

The track was used by kelp gatherers who collected the cast-up seaweed for fertilizer, but as they followed it northwards, so it became progressively less defined until it petered out altogether.

'What is ahead?' Garry demanded of Kali Piet, who had been led forward from the rear vehicle.

'Nothing,' said Kali Piet, and never had Garry sensed in a common-place word such menace.

'We will make our own road from here on,' Garry told them with a confidence he did not feel, and the next forty miles took four days to cover.

There were ancient water courses, dry for a hundred years perhaps, but with steep sides and their bottoms strewn with boulders like cannon-balls. There were treacherous flats on which the vehicles sank unexpectedly to their axles in soft sand and had to be manhandled through. There was broken ground where one of the lorries toppled over on its side and another broke a rear axle and had to be abandoned, together with a pile of luggage which they had discovered was superfluous, tents and camp chairs, tables and an enamel bath, boxes of trade goods to bribe savage chieftains, cases of tea and tinned butter and all the other equipment which had seemed essential when they were shopping in Windhoek.

The abbreviated and lightened convoy struggled northwards.

In the noonday heat the water boiled in the radiators, and they drove with plumes of white steam spurting from the safety valves, and they were forced to halt every half hour to allow the engines to cool. In other places there were fields of black stone, sharp as obsidian knives, which slashed through the thin casing of their tyres. In one day Garry counted fifteen halts to change wheels, and at night the stink of rubber solution hung over the bivouac as exhausted men sat up until midnight repairing the ruined inner tubes by the light of hurricane lanterns.

On the fifth day they camped with the seared bare peak of the Brandberg, the Burned Mountain, rising out of the purple evening mist ahead of them, and in the morning Kali Piet was gone.

He had taken a rifle and fifty rounds of ammunition, a blanket and five water-bottles, and as a final touch, the gold hunter watch and the coin case with twenty gold sovereigns in it that Garry had placed carefully beside his blanket roll the previous evening.

Furiously, threatening to shoot him on sight, Garry led a punitive expedition after him in the 'T' model. However, Kali Piet had chosen his moment, and less than a mile beyond the camp he had entered an area of broken hills and sheer valleys where no vehicle could follow him.

'Let him go,' Anna ordered. 'We are safer without him, and it's twenty days since my darling—' she broke off. 'We must go forward, Mijnheer, nothing must stand in our way. Nothing.'

Each day now the going became more difficult, and their progress slower, more frustrating.

At last, facing another barrier of rock that rose out of the sea like the crest on the back of a dinosaur and ran inland, jagged and glittering in the sunlight, Garry felt suddenly physically exhausted.

'This is madness,' he muttered to himself as he stood on the cab of one of the trucks, shading his eyes against the flat blinding glare and trying to spy out a way through this high impenetrable wall. 'The men have had enough.' They were standing in dispirited little groups beside the dusty, battered trucks. 'It's almost a month – and nobody could have survived out here that long, even if they had been able to get ashore.' The stump of Garry's missing leg ached and every muscle in his back was bruised, every vertebra in his spine felt crushed by the vicious jolting over rough ground. 'We'll have to turn back!'

He clambered down off the cab, moving stiffly as an old man, and limped forward to where Anna stood beside the Ford at the head of the column.

'Mevrou,' he began, and she turned to him and laid a big red hand on his arm.

'Mijnheer—' Her voice was low, and when she smiled at him Garry's protests stilled, and he thought for the first time that except for the redness of her face and the forbidding frown lines, she was a handsome woman. The line of her jaw was powerful and determined, her teeth were white and even, and there was a gentleness in her eyes that he had never noticed before.

'Mijnheer, I have been standing here thinking that there are few men who would have brought us this far. Without you we would have failed.' She squeezed his arm. 'Of course I knew that you were wise, that you had written many books, but now I know also that you are strong and determined, and that you are a man who allows nothing to stand in your way.' She squeezed his arm again. Her hand was warm and strong. Garry found that he was enjoying her touch. He straightened his shoulders, and tipped his slouch hat forward at a debonair angle. His back was not quite so painful. Anna smiled again.

'I will take a party over the rocks on foot – we must search the sea front, every foot of it, while you lead the convoy inland and find another way around.'

They had to slog four miles inland before they found a narrow precarious route over the rocks and could turn back towards the ocean.

When Garry saw Anna's distant figure striding manfully through the heavy beach sands far ahead, with her party straggling along behind her, he felt an unexpected relief, and realized how painfully he had missed her for even those few brief hours.

That evening as the two of them sat side by side, with their backs against the side of the 'T' model Ford, eating bully beef and hard biscuit and washing it down with strong coffee heavily sweetened with condensed milk, Garry told her shyly:

'My wife's name was Anna also. She died a long time ago.'

'Yes,' Anna agreed, chewing steadily. 'I know.'

'How do you know?' Garry was startled.

'Michel told Centaine.' The variation of Michael's name still disconcerted Garry.

'I always forget that you know so much about Michael.' He took a spoonful of bully, and stared out into the darkness. As usual, the men had bivouacked a short distance away to give them privacy, and their fire of driftwood cast a yellow nimbus and their voices were a murmur in the night.

'On the other hand, I don't know anything about Centaine. Tell me more about her, please, Mevrou.'

This was a subject that never palled for either of them. 'She's a good girl,' Anna always began with this statement, 'but spirited and headstrong. Did I ever tell you about the time – ?'

Garry sat close to her with his head cocked towards her attentively, but this evening he wasn't really listening.

The light of the camp fire played on Anna's homely lined face, and he watched it with a feeling of comfort and familiarity. Women usually made Garry feel inadequate and afraid, and the more beautiful or sophisticated they were, the greater his fear of them. He had long ago come to terms with the fact that he was impotent, he had found that out on his honeymoon, and the mocking laughter of his bride still rang in his ears over thirty years later. He had never given another woman the opportunity to laugh at him again – his son had not truly been his son, his twin brother had done that work for him – and at well over fifty years of age Garry was still a virgin. Occasionally, as now, when he thought about it, that fact made him feel mildly guilty.

With an effort he put the thought aside and tried to recapture the feeling of content and calm, but now he was aware of the smell of the body of the woman beside him. There had been no water to spare for bathing since they had left Swakopmund, and her odour was strong. She smelled of earth and sweat and other secret feminine musks, and Garry leaned a little closer to her to savour it. The few other women he had known smelled of cologne and rosewater, insipid and artifical, but this one smelled like an animal, a strong warm, healthy animal.

He watched her with fascination, and still talking in her low thick voice she lifted her hand and pushed back a few strands of grey hair from her temple. There was a thick dark bush of curls in her armpit, still damp with the day's heat, and staring at it Garry's arousal was sudden and savage as a heavy blow in his groin. It grew out of him like the branch of a tree, rigid and aching with sensations that he had never dreamed of, thick with yearning and loneliness, tense with a wanting that came from the very depths of his soul.

He stared at her, unable to move or speak, and when he did not reply to one of her questions, Anna glanced up from the fire and saw his face. Gently, almost tenderly, she reached out and touched his cheek.

'I think, Mijnheer, it is time for my bed. I wish you good sleep and pleasant dreams.' She stood up and moved heavily behind the tarpaulin that screened her sleeping place.

Garry lay on his own blankets, his hands clenched at his sides, and listened to the rustle of her clothing from behind the tarpaulin screen, and his body hurt like a fresh bruise. From behind the screen came a long-drawn-out rumble that startled him; for a moment he could not place it. Then he realized that Anna was snoring. It was the most reassuring sound he had ever heard, for it was impossible to be afraid of a woman who snored; he wanted to shout his joy into the desert night.

'I'm in love,' he exulted. 'For the first time in over thirty years, I'm in love.'

However, in the dawn all the transient courage he had gathered in the night had evaporated, only his love was still intact. Anna's eyes were swollen and red with sleep, her grey-streaked hair was powdered with crystals of sand that the night wind had blown over her, but Garry watched her with adoration until she ordered him brusquely, 'Eat quickly – we must go forward at first light. I have a feeling that today will be good. Eat up, Mijnheer!'

'What a woman!' Garry told himself admiringly. 'If only I could inspire a little of such devotion, such loyalty!'

Anna's premonition seemed at first to be well founded, for there were no more rocky barriers in their path, instead an open undulating plain ran right down to where the beach began, and the surface was firm gravel studded with knee-high salt bush. They could motor over it as though it were an open highway, forced only to swerve and weave in column to avoid the lumpy scrub, keeping just above the coppery beach so that they could spot any wreckage, or the signs left by a castaway on the soft sand.

Garry sat beside Anna on the back seat of the Ford and when they bumped over uneven ground, they were thrown together. Garry murmured an apology but left his good leg pressed against her thigh, and she made no effort to withdraw from his touch.

Suddenly, in the middle of an afternoon that trembled with heat, the watery curtains of mirage opened ahead of them for a few moments and they saw the beginning of the dunelands rise sheer out of the plain. The little convoy stopped before them, and everybody climbed out and stared up at them with awe and disbelief.

'Mountains,' Garry said softly, 'a mountain range of sand. Nobody ever warned us of this.'

'There must be a way through!'

Garry shook his head dubiously. 'They must be five hundred feet high.'

'Come,' Anna said firmly. 'We will go to the top.'

'Good Lord!' Garry exclaimed. 'The sand is so soft – it's so high, it might be dangerous—'

'Let's go! The others will wait here.'

338

They toiled upwards with Anna leading, following the sloping razorback spine of one of the sand ridges. Far below them the cluster of vehicles was toylike, the waiting men tiny as ants. Beneath their feet the orange-coloured sand squeaked as their feet sank in to the ankles. When they stepped too close to the edge of the razorback, the lip collapsed and an avalanche of sand went hissing down the slip-face.

'This is dangerous!' Garry murmured. 'If you went over the edge, you'd be smothered.'

Anna hoisted her thick calico skirts and tucked them into her bloomers, then she plodded on upwards, and Garry stared after her, his mouth dry and his heart banging against his ribs, driven with exertion and shock at the sight of her bared legs. They were massive and as solid as tree trunks, but the skin at the backs of her knees was creamy and velvety, dimpled like that of a little girl, the most exciting thing he had ever seen.

Incredibly, Garry felt his body react again, as though a giant's hand had seized his crotch, and his fatigue fell away. Sliding and stumbling in the soft footing, he scrambled upwards after her, and Anna's haunches, wide as those of a brood mare under the thick skirts, swayed and rolled at the level of his staring eyes.

He came out on the crest of the dune before he realized it, and Anna put out a hand to steady him.

'My God,' he whispered, 'it's a world of sand, an entire universe of sand.'

They stood upon the foothills of the great dunes and even Anna's faith wilted.

'Nobody – nothing could get through them.'

Anna was still holding his arm, and now she shook him.

'She is out there. I can almost hear her voice calling to me. We cannot fail her, we must get through to her. She can't last much longer.'

'To attempt to go in on foot would be certain death. A man wouldn't last a day in there.'

'We *must* find a way round.' Anna shook herself like a huge St Bernard dog, throwing off her doubts and momentary weakness. 'Come.' She led him back from the crest. 'We must find the way round.'

The convoy with the Ford leading turned inland, skirting the edge of the high dunes while the day wasted away and the sun fell down the sky and bled to death upon their soaring crests. That night as they camped below them, the dunes were black and remote, implacable and hostile against the moonlit silver of the sky.

'There is no way round.' Garry stared into the fire, unable to meet Anna's eyes. 'They go on for ever.'

'In the morning we will go back towards the coast,' she told him placidly, and rose to go to her sleeping place, leaving him aching with his want of her.

The next day they retraced their tracks, riding in their own tyre-prints, and it was evening again before they had returned to the point where the dunes met the ocean.

'There is no way,' Garry repeated hopelessly, for the surf ran right up under the sand mountains and even Anna sagged miserably, staring silently into the flames of their camp fire.

'If we wait here,' she whispered huskily, 'perhaps Centaine is making her way down towards us. Surely she knows that her only hope is to head southwards. If we cannot go to her, we must wait for her to come to us.'

'We are running out of water,' Garry told her, quietly. 'We can't—'

'How long can we last?'

'Three days, no more.'

'Four days,' Anna implored, and there was such a desolation in her voice and her expression that Garry acted without thought. He reached for her with both arms. He felt a kind of delicious terror as she came to meet him, and they clung to each other, she in despair and he in a fearful frenzy of lust. For a few moments Garry worried that the men at the other fire would see them – then he no longer cared.

'Come.' She raised him to his feet and led him behind the canvas screen. His hands were shaking so that he could not unfasten the buttons of his shirt. Anna chuckled fondly.

'Here,' she undressed him, 'my silly baby.'

The desert wind was cool on his back and flanks, but he was burning internally with fires of long-suppressed passion. He was no longer ashamed of his hairy belly that bulged out in a little pot, nor of his thighs that were thin as those of a stork and too long for the rest of his body. He scrambled on top of her with frantic haste, desperate to bury himself in her, to lose himself in that great white softness, to hide there from the world that had been so cruel to him for so long.

Then suddenly it happened again, and he felt the heat and strength drain from his groin, he felt himself wilt and shrivel just as he had on that other dreadful night over thirty years before. And he lay on the white mattress of her belly, cradled between her thick, powerful thighs, and he wished to die of shame and futility. He waited for her taunting laughter and her scorn. He knew it would destroy him utterly this time. He could not escape, for her powerful arms were wrapped around him and her thighs held his hips in a fleshy vice.

'Mevrou,' he blurted. 'I am sorry, I'm no good – I've never been any good.'

She chuckled again, and it was a fond and compassionate sound.

'There's my baby,' she whispered huskily in his ear. 'Let me help you a little.' And he felt her hand go down, pressing between their naked bellies.

'Where's my puppy?' she said, and he felt her fingers fold

341

about him and he panicked. He began to struggle to be free, but she held him easily and he could not escape her fingers. They were rough as sandpaper from hard manual work, but cunning and insistent, tugging and plucking at him, and her voice was purring and happy.

'There's a big boy, then. What a big boy.'

He couldn't struggle any more, but every nerve and muscle in his body was tensed to the point of pain, and her fingers kneaded and coaxed and her voice became deeper, almost drowsy, without urgency, calming him so he felt his body unclenching.

'Ah!' she gloated. 'What's happening to our big puppy, then?'

Suddenly there was a stiffening resistance to her touch, and she chuckled again, and he felt the great thighs that held him fall slowly apart. 'Gently, gently,' she cautioned him, for he was beginning to struggle again, bucking against her. 'Like that! Yes, there, that's it.' She was guiding him, trying to control him, but he was desperate with haste.

Suddenly there was a hot gust of her body smell in his nostrils, rich and strong, the marvellous aroma of her own arousal, and he felt the new surge of strength into the core of his being. He was a hero, an eagle, the very hammer of the gods. He was strong as a bull, long as a sword, hard as granite.

'Oh yes!' she gasped. 'There, like that!' and resistance to him was not to be brooked, he drove forward and broke through and went sliding into the depths of her and the exquisite heat which was far beyond any place he had been in his entire existence. With increasing urgency and violence, she rose and fell beneath him as though he were a ship in an ocean gale and she made little crooning sounds, and urged him on in a ragged throaty voice, until the sky crashed down upon him and he was crushed between it and the earth.

He came back slowly from far away, and she was holding

him and caressing him and talking to him like a child again.

'There, my baby. It's all right. It's all right now.'

And he knew that it was so. It was all right now. He had never felt so safe and secure. He had never known such deep pervading peace. He pressed his face between her breasts, and smothered himself in her abundant motherly flesh and wanted to rest there for ever.

She stroked the sparse silky hairs back from off his ears, looking down on him fondly, and the bald pink patch at the crown of his scalp gleamed in the firelight and made her breasts ache with the need to comfort him. All her pent-up love and concern for the missing girl found new directions, for she was born to give succour and loyalty and duty to others. She began to rock him, cradling him and crooning to him.

Then, in the dawn, Garry found that there had been another miracle. For when he crept out of the camp and went down to the head of the beach, he found the way was open for them. Under the influence of a waxing moon, the ocean was building up to full spring tides, and the waters had drawn back, leaving a wide strip of hard smooth wet sand below the dunes.

Garry rushed back to the bivouac and hauled his senior NCO out of his blankets.

'Get your men looking alive, Corporal!' he shouted. 'I want the Ford refuelled, loaded with rations including water-cans for four people for three days, and I want it ready to leave in fifteen minutes, is that clear? Well then, get on with it, man, don't stand there gaping at me!'

He turned and ran back to meet Anna as she emerged from behind the tarpaulin.

'Mevrou, the tide! We can get through.'

'I knew you would find a way, Mijnheer!'

'We'll go in with the Ford, you and I and two men. We will drive hard until the tide turns, then push the Ford up

343

above the high-water mark, and when it's out again we'll press on. Can you be ready to leave in ten minutes? We have to take full advantage of the tide.' He wheeled away from her. 'Come on, Corporal, get these men moving!'

And as he turned away, the Corporal rolled his eyes and grumbled just loudly enough for the others to hear him. 'What's come over our old sparrow – damned if all of a sudden he isn't acting like a turkey cock!'

They had two hours of hard driving, pushing the Ford to her top speed of forty miles an hour when the sand was firm and hard. When it turned soft, the three passengers, including Anna, leaped over the side and kept her rolling, throwing their full combined weight behind her, and then, as the sand firmed again, they scrambled on board, and hooting with excitement, sped northwards again.

At last the tide came surging back at them, and Garry picked out a gap in the dunes into which they backed the Ford, manhandling her through the dry, floury sand until she was well above the high-water mark.

They built a fire of driftwood, brewed coffee, and ate a picnic meal, and then settled down to wait for the next low tide to open the beach for them. The three men stretched out in the shade of the vehicle, but Anna left them and began picking her way along the high-water mark, pausing every once in a while to shade her eyes against the glare of sea and sand and peer restlessly into the north again.

Propped on one elbow, Garry watched her with such overwhelming affection and gratitude, that he found difficulty in breathing.

'In the autumn of my life she has given me the youth that I never knew. She has brought me the love that passed me by,' he thought, and when she reached the corner of the next sandy bay and disappeared behind the guardian dune, he could not bear to let her out of his sight.

He sprang up and hurried after her. As he reached the

corner, he saw her a quarter of a mile ahead. She was stooped over something at the head of the beach, but now she straightened and saw him, and waved both hands over her head, shouting at him. The boom of the surf drowned out her voice, but her excitement and agitation was so obvious that he began to run.

'Mijnheer,' she ran to meet him, 'I have found—' She could not finish, but seized his arm and dragged him after her.

'Look!' She fell on her knees next to the object. It was almost completely buried in the beach sand, and already the incoming tide was washing and swirling around it.

'It's part of a boat!' Garry dropped beside her, and together they attacked the sand with their bare hands, frantic to expose the fragment of white-painted woodwork.

'Clinker-built,' Garry grunted. 'Looks like part of an Admiralty-type lifeboat.'

The next wave rushed up the beach and wetted them to the waist, but as it drew back it washed away the sand that they had loosened and exposed the name that was painted in black letters on the shattered hull.

'*Protea C*—' The rest of it was missing; the timbers were raw and splintered where they had broken up in the hammering surf.

'The *Protea Castle*,' whispered Anna, and wiped the sand away from the lettering with her sodden skirts.

'Proof!' She turned her face to Garry, and tears were running freely down her red cheeks. 'Proof, Mijnheer, it's proof that my darling has reached the shore and is safe.'

Even Garry, who was as eager as a bridegroom to please her, who wanted desperately to believe that he would have a grandson to replace Michael, even he gawked at her.

'It's proof that she is alive – you do believe that now, don't you, Mijnheer?'

'Mevrou,' Garry fluttered his hands in an agony of embarrassment, 'there is an excellent chance, I do agree.'

'She is alive. I know it. How can you doubt it? Unless you believe—' Her red face folded into a ferocious scowl, and Garry capitulated nervously.

'I do – oh yes! I certainly believe it! No question she's alive, absolutely no question.'

Having carried the field, Anna faced the incoming tide, and turned the full force of her displeasure upon the ocean.

'How long must we wait here, Mijnheer?'

'Well, Mevrou, the tide flows for six hours and then ebbs for six,' he explained apologetically. 'It will be another three hours before we can go on.'

'Every minute we waste now could make all the difference,' she told him fiercely.

'Well, I'm frightfully sorry, Mevrou.' Humbly Garry took full responsibility for the rhythm of the universe upon himself, and Anna's expression softened. She glanced around her to make certain they were unobserved and then slipped her hand into the crook of his elbow.

'Well, at least we know she is still alive. We will go forward again the very minute we are able. In the meantime, Mijnheer, we have three hours.' She looked at him speculatively, and Garry's knees began to shake so that she could barely support him.

Neither of them spoke again while she led him back off the beach into a secluded gully between two tall dunes.

A s the tide turned and began its ebb, they drove the Ford down on to the sand. The rear wheels threw fish-tails of glistening seawater and wet sand high into the air behind them as they sped northwards.

Twice within five miles they found flotsam cast up on the beach, a canvas lifejacket and a broken oar. They had obviously been exposed to the elements for a considerable time, and although neither of these were marked with

346

identifying numbers or lettering, they confirmed Anna's faith. She sat in the back seat of the Ford with a scarf knotted under her chin, holding her solar topee on her head, and every few minutes Garry darted a loving glance at her like an amorous fox terrier paying court to a bulldog.

It was the slack of low tide, and the Ford was travelling thirty miles per hour when they hit the quicksand. There was little warning. The beach appeared as hard and smooth as it had been for the last mile. There was only a slight change in its contour. It was dished and the surface trembled like a jelly as seawater welled up beneath the sand, but they had been moving too fast to notice the warning signs, and they went in at speed.

The front wheels dropped into the soft porridge, and stopped dead. It was like running into the side of a mountain. The driver was hurled against the steering column. With a harsh crackle the spokes of the steering wheel collapsed, but the steel shaft tore through his sternum, pinning him like a mullet on a fish spear, and the jagged point ripped out of his back below his shoulder blade.

Anna was thrown high out of the back seat, and landed in the soft mire of quicksand. Garry's forehead thudded into the dashboard, a flap of skin was torn from the bone and dangled over his eyebrow, while blood poured down his face. The corporal was caught in a tangle of loose equipment, and his arm broke with a crack like a dry stick.

Anna was first to recover and she waded knee-deep through the soft sand, and with an arm around Garry's shoulder, helped him out of the front seat and dragged him to where the beach sand hardened.

Garry fell on his knees. 'I'm blind,' he whispered.

'Just a little blood!' Anna wiped his face with her skirt. She ripped a strip of calico from the hem of her skirt and hastily bound the flap of skin back in place, then left him and waded back to the Ford.

It was sinking slowly, tipping forward as it went down. Already the engine bonnet was covered by soft yellow mush, and it was pouring gluttonously over the doors and filling the interior. She seized the driver by the shoulders and tried to drag him clear, but he was firmly impaled on the steering shaft, and bone grated on steel as she tugged at him. His head rolled lifelessly from side to side, and she left him and turned to the corporal.

He was mumbling and twitching spasmodically as he regained consciousness. Anna pulled him free and dragged him back to the hard sand, grunting red-faced with the effort. He screamed weakly with pain and his left arm dangled and twisted as she lowered him to the sand.

'Mijnheer,' Anna shook Garry roughly, 'we must save the water before it sinks also.'

Garry staggered to his feet. His face was painted with his own blood, and his shirt was streaked and splattered, but the flow had quenched. He followed her back to the doomed Ford and between them they dragged the water-cans to the beach.

'There is nothing we can do for the driver,' Anna grunted, as they watched the Ford and the dead man gradually settle below the treacherous surface. Within minutes there was no trace of them. She turned her attention to the corporal.

'The bone is broken.' His forearm was swelling alarmingly, and he was pale and haggard with agony. 'Help me!' While Garry held him, Anna straightened the damaged limb and using a piece of driftwood as a splint, strapped it. Then she fashioned a sling from another strip of her skirt, and while she settled the arm into it, Garry said hoarsely, 'I calculate it's forty miles back—' but he could not finish, for Anna glared at him.

'You are talking of turning back!'

'Mevrou,' he made a little fluttery, conciliatory gesture,

'we have to turn back. Two gallons of water and an injured man – we will be extremely fortunate to save ourselves.'

She continued to glare at him for a few seconds longer, then gradually her shoulders slumped.

'We are close to finding her, so near to Centaine. I can sense it – she may be around the next headland. How can we give her up?' Anna whispered. It was the first time that he had ever seen her defeated, and he thought his heart might burst with love and pity.

'We will never give her up!' he declared. 'We will never give up the search, this is only a setback. We will go on until we find her.'

'Promise me that, Mijnheer.' Anna looked up at him with pathetic eagerness. 'Swear to me that you will never give up, that you will never doubt that Centaine and her baby are alive. Swear to me here and now in the sight of God that you will never give up the search for your grandson. Give me your hand and swear to it!'

Kneeling together on the beach, with the incoming tide swirling around their knees, facing each other and holding hands, he made the oath.

'Now we can go back,' Anna climbed heavily to her feet. 'But we will return, and go on until we find her.'

'Yes,' Garry agreed. 'We will return.'

C entaine must indeed have died a small death, because when she regained consciousness, she was aware of the morning light through her closed lids. The prospect of another day of torment and suffering made her clench her eyelids tightly and try to retreat again into black oblivion.

Then she became aware of a small sound like the morning breeze in a pile of dry twigs, or the noise of an insect moving with clicking armoured limbs over a rocky surface. The sound troubled her, until she made the enormous effort required to roll her head towards it and open her eyes.

A small humanoid gnome squatted ten feet from where she lay, and she knew that she must be hallucinating. She blinked her eyes rapidly and the congealed mucus that gummed her lids smeared across her eyeballs and blurred her vision, but she could just make out a second small figure squatting behind the first. She rubbed her eyes and tried to sit up, and her movements provoked a fresh outburst of the strange soft crepitating and clicking sounds, but still it took her a few seconds to realize that the two little gnomes were talking to each other in suppressed excitement, and that they were real, not merely the figments of her weakness and illness.

The one nearest to Centaine was a woman, for a pair of floppy dugs hung from her chest to well below her belly-button. They looked like empty pigskin tobacco pouches. She was an old woman – no, Centaine realized that old was not the word to describe her antiquity. She was as wrinkled as a sun-dried raisin. There was not an inch of her skin that did not hang in loose folds and tucks, that was not crinkled and riven. The wrinkles were not aligned in one direction only, but crossed each other in deep patterns like stars or puckered rosettes. Her dangling breasts were wrinkled, as was her fat little belly, and baggy wrinkled skin hung from her knees and elbows. In a dreamlike way, Centaine was utterly enchanted. She had never seen another human being that vaguely resembled this one, not even in the travelling circus that had visited Mort Homme every summer before the war. She struggled up on one elbow and stared at her.

The little old woman was an extraordinary colour, she seemed to glow like amber in the sunlight, and Centaine thought of the polished bowl of her father's meerschaum pipe which he had cured with such care. But this colour was even brighter than that, bright as a ripe apricot on the tree, and despite her weakness, a little smile flickered over Centaine's lips.

Instantly the old woman, who had been studying Centaine with equal attention, smiled back. The network of wrinkles constricted about her eyes, reducing them to slanted Chinese slits. Yet there was such a merry sparkle in those black shiny pupils that Centaine wanted to reach out and embrace her, as she would have embraced Anna. The old woman's teeth were worn down almost to the gums and were stained tobacco brown, but there were no gaps in them, and they appeared even and strong.

'Who are you?' Centaine whispered through her dark swollen dry lips, and the woman clicked and hissed softly back at her.

Under the loose wrinkled skin she had a small, finely shaped skull, and her face was sweetly heart-shaped. Her scalp was dotted with faded grey woolly hair that was twisted into small tight kernels, each the size of a green pea, and there was bare scalp between them. She had small pointed ears lying close to the skull like the pixies in Centaine's nursery books, but there were no lobes to the ears, and the effect of sparkling eyes and pricked ears was to give her an alert, quizzical expression.

'Do you have water?' Centaine whispered. 'Water. Please.'

The old woman turned her head and spoke in that sibilant clicking tongue to the figure behind her. He was almost her twin, the same impossibly wrinkled, apricot, glowing skin, the same tight wisps of hair dotting the scalp, bright eyes and pointed lobeless ears, but he was male. This was more than evident, for the leather loincloth had pulled aside as he squatted and a penis out of all proportion to his size hung free, the uncircumcised tip brushing the sand. It had the peculiar arrogance and half-erect tension of the member of a man in full prime. Centaine found herself staring at it, and swiftly averted her eyes.

'Water,' she repeated, and this time Centaine made the motion of drinking. Immediately a spirited discussion flickered back and forth between the two little old people.

'O'wa, this child is dying from lack of water,' the old Bushwoman told her husband of thirty years. She pronounced the first syllable of his name with the popping sound of a kiss. 'Kiss-wa.'

'She is already dead,' the Bushman replied quickly. 'It is too late, H'ani.' His wife's name began with a sharp, explosive aspirate and ended with a soft click made with the tongue against the back of the top teeth, the sound that in Western speech usually signifies mild annoyance.

'Water belongs to all, the living and the dying, that is the first law of the desert. You know it well, old grandfather.' H'ani was being particularly persuasive, so she used the enormously respectful term 'old grandfather'.

'Water belongs to all the people,' he agreed, nodding and blinking. 'But this one is not San, she is not a person. She belongs to the others.' With that short pronouncement O'wa had succinctly stated the Bushman's view of himself in relation to the world about him.

The Bushman was the first man. His tribal memories went back beyond the veils of the ages to the time when his ancestors had been alone in the land. From the far northern lakes to the dragon mountains in the south, their hunting grounds had encompassed the entire continent. They were the aboriginals. They were the men, the San.

The others were creatures apart. The first of these others had come down the corridors of migration from the north, huge black men driving their herds before them. Much later, the others with skins the colour of fish's belly that redden in the sun, and pale, blind-looking eyes had come out of the sea from the south. This female was one of those. They had grazed sheep and cattle on the ancient hunting grounds, and slaughtered the game which were the Bushman's kine.

With his own means of sustenance wiped out, the Bushman had looked upon the domesticated herds that had replaced wild game on the veld. He had no sense of property, no tradition of ownership nor of private possession. He had taken of the herds of the others as he would have taken of wild game, and in so doing had given the owners deadly offence. Black and white, they had made war upon the Bushmen with pitiless ferocity, ferocity heightened by their dread of his tiny childlike arrows that were tipped with a venom that inflicted certain, excruciating death.

In impis armed with double-edged stabbing assegais, and in mounted commandos carrying firearms, they had hunted down the Bushmen as though they were noxious animals. They had shot them and stabbed them and sealed them in their caves and burned them alive, they had poisoned and tortured them, sparing only the youngest children from the massacre. These they chained in bunches, for those that did not pine and die of broken hearts could be 'tamed'. They made gentle, loyal and rather lovable little slaves.

The Bushmen bands that survived this deliberate genocide retreated into the bad and waterless lands where they alone, with their marvellous knowledge and understanding of the land and its creatures, could survive.

'She is one of the others,' O'wa repeated, 'and she is already dead. The water is only sufficient for our journey.'

H'ani had not taken her eyes off Centaine's face, but she reproached herself silently. 'Old woman, it was not necessary to discuss the water. If you had given without question, then you would not have been forced to endure this male foolishness.' Now she turned and smiled at her husband.

'Wise old grandfather, look at the child's eyes,' she wheedled. 'There is life there yet, and courage also. This one will not die until she empties her body of its last breath.' Deliberately, H'ani unslung the rawhide carrying bag from her shoulder, and ignored the little hissing sound of disapproval that her husband made. 'In the desert the water belongs to everybody, the San and the others, there is no distinction, such as you have argued.'

From the bag she took out an ostrich egg, an almost perfect orb the colour of polished ivory. The shell had been lovingly engraved with a decorative circlet of bird and animal silhouettes and the end was stoppered with a wooden plug. The contents sloshed as H'ani weighed the egg in her cupped hands and Centaine whimpered like a puppy denied the teat.

'You are a wilful old woman,' said O'wa disgustedly. It was the strongest protest the Bushman tradition allowed him. He could not command her, he could not forbid her. A Bushman could only advise another, he had no rights over his fellows; amongst them there were no chiefs nor captains, and all were equal, man and woman, old and young.

Carefully H'ani unplugged the egg and shuffled closer to Centaine. She put her arm round the back of Centaine's neck to steady her and lifted the egg to her lips. Centaine gulped greedily and choked, and water dribbled down her chin. This time H'ani and O'wa hissed with dismay, each drop was as precious as life blood. H'ani withdrew the egg, and Centaine sobbed and tried to reach for it.

'You are impolite,' H'ani admonished her. She lifted the egg to her own lips and filled her mouth until her cheeks bulged. Then she placed her hand under Centaine's chin, bent forward and covered Centaine's mouth with her own lips. Carefully she injected a few drops into Centaine's mouth and waited while she swallowed before giving her more. When she had passed the last drop into Centaine's mouth, she sat back and watched her until she deemed that she was ready for more. Then she gave her a second mouthful, and later a third.

'This female drinks like a cow elephant at a waterhole,' O'wa said sourly. 'Already she has taken enough water to flood the dry riverbed of the Kuiseb.'

He was right, of course, H'ani conceded reluctantly. The girl had already used up a full day's adult ration. She replugged the ostrich egg, and though Centaine pleaded and stretched out both hands appealingly, she replaced it firmly in the leather carrying satchel.

'Just a little more, please,' Centaine whispered, but the old woman ignored her and turned to her companion. They argued, using their hands, graceful birdlike gestures, fluttering and flicking their fingers.

The old woman wore a headband of flat white beads round her neck and upper arms. Around her waist was a short leather skirt and over one shoulder a cape of spotted fur. Both garments were made from a single skin, unshaped and unstitched. The skirt was held in place by a rawhide girdle from which were suspended a collection of tiny gourds and antelope-horn containers, and she carried a long stave, the sharp end of which was weighted by a pierced stone.

Centaine lay and watched her avidly. She recognized intuitively that her life was under discussion, and that the old woman was her advocate.

'All that you say, revered old grandfather, is undoubtedly true. We are on a journey, and those who cannot keep up and endanger the rest, must be left. That is the tradition. Yet, if we should wait that long,' H'ani pointed to a segment of the sun's transit across the sky which was approximately an hour, 'then this child might find enough strength and such a short wait would put us in no danger.'

O'wa kept making a deep glottal sound and flicking both hands from the wrist. It was an expressive gesture that alarmed Centaine.

'Our journey is an arduous one, and we still have great distances to travel. The next water is many days; to loiter here is folly.'

O'wa wore a crown on his head, and despite her plight Centaine found herself intrigued by it, until suddenly she realized what it was. In a beaded rawhide headband the old man had placed fourteen tiny arrows. The arrows were made of river reeds, the flights were eagles' feathers, and the heads, which were pointed sykwards, were carved from white bone. Each barb was discoloured by a dried paste, like freshly made toffee, and this it was that recalled to Centaine the description from Levaillant's book of African travels.

'Poison!' Centaine whispered. 'Poisoned arrows.' She shuddered, and then remembered the hand-drawn illustration from the book. 'They are Bushmen. These are real live Bushmen!'

She managed to push herself upright, and both the little people looked back at her.

'Already she is stronger,' H'ani pointed out, but O'wa began to rise.

'We are on a journey, the most important journey, and the days are wasting.'

Suddenly H'ani's expression altered. She was staring at Centaine's body. When Centaine sat up, the cotton blouse, already ragged, had caught and exposed one of her breasts. Seeing the old woman's interest, Centaine realized her nudity and hastily covered herself, but now the old woman hopped close to her and leaned over her. Impatiently she pushed Centaine's hands aside and with the surprisingly powerful fingers of her narrow, delicate-looking hands, she pressed and squeezed Centaine's breasts.

Centaine winced and protested and tried to pull away, but the old woman was as determined and authoritative as Anna had been. She opened the torn blouse and took one of Centaine's nipples between forefinger and thumb and milked it gently. A clear droplet appeared on the tip and H'ani hummed to herself and pushed Centaine backwards on to the sand. She put her hand up under the canvas skirt, and her little fingers prodded and probed skilfully into Centaine's lower belly.

At last H'ani sat back on her heels and grinned at her mate triumphantly.

'Now you cannot leave her,' she gloated. 'It is the strongest tradition of the people that you cannot desert a woman, any woman, San or other, who carries new life within her.'

And O'wa made a weary gesture of capitualtion and sank down to his haunches again. He affected an aloof air, sitting a little detached as his wife trotted down to the edge of the sea with the weighted digging stick in her hands. She inspected the wet sand carefully as the wavelets swirled around her ankles and then she thrust the point of the stick into the sand and walked backwards, ploughing a shallow furrow. The point of the stick struck a solid object beneath the sand and H'ani darted forward, digging with her fingers, picked out something and dropped it into her carrying bag. Then she repeated the process.

Within a short time she returned to where Centaine lay and emptied a pile of shellfish from her bag on to the sand. They were double-shelled sand clams, Centaine saw at once, and she was bitterly angry at her own stupidity. For days she had starved and thirsted as she had hobbled over a beach alive with these luscious shellfish.

The old woman used a bone-cutting tool to open one of the clams, holding it carefully so as not to spill the juices from the mother-of-pearl-lined shell, and she passed it to Centaine. Ecstatically, Centaine slurped the juices from the half-shell and then dug out the meat with her grubby fingers and popped it into her mouth.

'*Bon!*' she told H'ani, her whole face screwed up with exquisite pleasure as she chewed, '*Très bon!*'

H'ani grinned and bobbed her head, working on the next clam with the bone knife. It was an inefficient tool that made the opening of each shell a laborious business and broke chips of the shell on to the body of the clam that gritted under Centaine's teeth. After three more clams, Centaine groped for her clasp knife and opened the blade.

O'wa had been demonstrating his disapproval by squatting a little apart and staring out to sea, but at the click of the knife blade his eyes swivelled to Centaine and then widened with intense interest.

The San were men of the Stone Age, but although the quarrying and smelting of working iron were beyond their culture, O'wa had seen iron implements before. He had seen those picked up by his people from the battlefields of the black giants, others that had been taken secretly from camps and bivouacs of strangers and travellers, and once he had known a man of the San who had possessed an implement such as this girl now held in her hand.

The man's name had been Xja, the clicking sound at the back of his teeth that a horseman makes to urge on his steed, and Xja had taken O'wa's eldest sister to wife thirty-five years before. As a young man, Xja had found the skeleton of a white man at a dry water-hole at the edge of the Kalahari. The body of the old elephant hunter had lain beside the skeleton of his horse, with his long four-to-the-pound elephant gun at his side.

Xja had not touched the gun, because he knew from legend and bitter experience that thunder lived in this strange magical stick, but gingerly he had examined the contents of the rotting leather saddle-bags and discovered such treasures as Bushmen before him had only dreamed of.

Firstly there was a leather pouch of tobacco, a month's supply of it, and Xja had tucked a pinch under his lip and happily examined the rest of the hoard. Quickly he discarded a book and a roll of cardboard, which contained small balls of heavy grey metal – they were ugly and of no possible use. Then he discovered a beautiful flask of yellow metal on a leather strap. The flask was filled with useless grey powder which he spilled into the sand, but the flask itself was so marvellously shiny that he knew no woman would be able to resist it. Xja, who was not a mighty hunter nor a great dancer or singer, had long pined after the sister of O'wa who had a laugh that sounded like running water. He had despaired of ever catching her attention, had not even dared to shoot a miniature feather-tipped arrow from his ceremonial love bow in her direction, but with his shiny flask in his hand he knew that at last she would be his woman.

Then Xja found the knife, and he knew that with it he would win the respect of the men of his tribe for which he longed almost as much as he longed for the lovely sister of O'wa. It was almost thirty years since O'wa had last seen Xja and his sister. They had disappeared into the lonely wastes of the dry land to the east, driven from the clan by the strange emotions of envy and hatred that the knife had evoked in the other men of the tribe.

Now O'wa stared at a similar knife in this female's hands as she split open the clam shells and wolfed raw the sweet yellow meat, and drank the running juices.

To this moment he had been merely repelled by the female's huge ungainly body, bigger than any man of the San, and her enormous hands and feet, by her thick wild bush of hair and her skin which the sun had parboiled, but when he looked at the knife, all the confusing feelings of long ago flooded back and he knew he would lie awake at night thinking about the knife.

O'wa stood up. 'Enough,' he said to H'ani. 'It is time to go on.'

'A little longer.'

'Whether carrying a child or not, no one can endanger

the lives of all. We must go on,' and again H'ani knew he was right. They had already waited much longer than was wise. She stood up with him and adjusted the carrying bag on her shoulder.

She saw panic flare in Centaine's eyes as she realized their intention. 'Wait for me! *Attendez!*' Centaine scrambled to her feet, terrified at the thought of being deserted.

Now O'wa shifted the small bow into his left hand, tucked his dangling penis back into the leather loincloth and tightened the waistband. Then, without glancing back at the women, he started off along the edge of the beach.

H'ani fell in behind him. The two of them moved with a swaying jogtrot and for the first time Centaine noticed their pronounced buttocks, enormous protuberances that jutted out so sharply behind that Centaine was sure that she could sit astride H'ani's backside and ride on it as though on a pony's back, and the idea made her want to giggle. H'ani glanced back at her and flashed an encouraging smile, and then looked ahead. Her backside bobbed and joggled and her ancient breasts flapped .against her belly.

Centaine took a step after them and then came up short, stricken by dismay.

'Wrong way!' she cried. 'You're going the wrong way!'

The two little pygmies were heading back into the north, away from Cape Town and Walvis Bay and Lüderitzbucht and all of civilization.

'You can't—' Centaine was frantic, the loneliness of the desert lay in wait for her and like a ravening beast it would consume her if she were left alone again. But if she followed the two little people she was turning her back on her own kind and the succour that they might hold out for her.

She took a few uncertain paces after H'ani. 'Please don't go!'

The old woman understood the appeal, but she knew

there was only one way to get the child moving. She did not look back.

'Please! Please!'

That rhythmic jogtrot carried the two little people away disturbingly quickly.

For a few moments longer Centaine hesitated, turning to look away southwards, torn and desperate. H'ani was almost quarter of a mile down the beach and showing no sign of slackening.

'Wait for me!' Centaine cried and snatched up her driftwood club. She tried to run but after a hundred paces settled down to a short, hampered but determined walk.

By noon the two figures she followed had dwindled to specks and finally disappeared into the sea fret far ahead up the beach. However, their footprints were left upon the brassy sands, tiny childlike footprints, and Centaine fastened her whole attention upon them and never really knew how or where she found the strength to stay on her feet and live out that day.

Then in the evening when her resolve was almost gone, she lifted her eyes from the footprints and far ahead she saw a drift of pale blue smoke wafting out to sea. It emanated from an outcrop of yellow sandstone boulders above the high-water mark and it took the last of her strength to carry her to the encampment of the San.

She sank down, utterly exhausted, beside the fire of driftwood, and H'ani came to her, chittering and clucking, and like a bird with its chick fed her water from mouth to mouth. The water was warm and slimy with the old woman's saliva, but Centaine had never tasted anything so delicious. As before, there was not enough of it and the old woman stoppered the ostrich-egg shell before Centaine's thirst was nearly slaked.

Centaine tore her gaze away from the leather carrying bag full of eggs and looked for the old man.

She saw him at last. Only his head was visible as he ferreted amongst the kelp beds out in the green waters. He had stripped naked, except for the beads around his neck and waist, and had armed himself with H'ani's pointed digging stick. Centaine watched him stiffen to point like a gundog and then launch a cunning thrust with the stick, and the water exploded as O'wa wrestled with some large and active prey. H'ani clapped her hands and ululated encouragement, and finally the old man dragged a kicking struggling creature on to the beach.

Despite her weariness and weakness, Centaine rose up on her knees and exclaimed with amazement. She knew what the quarry was, indeed lobster was one of her favourite dishes, but still she thought that her senses must have at last deserted her for this creature was too big for O'wa to lift. Its great armoured tail dragged in the sand, clattering as it flapped, and its long thick whiskers reached above O'wa's head as he gripped one in each of his little fists. H'ani rushed down to the water's edge armed with a rock the size of her own head and between them they beat the huge crustacean to death.

Before it was dark O'wa killed two more, each almost as large as the first, and then he and H'ani scraped a shallow hole in the sand and lined it with kelp leaves.

While they prepared the cooking hole, Centaine examined the three huge crustaceans. She saw immediately that they were not armed with claws like a lobster, and so must be the same species as the Mediterranean *langouste* that she had eaten at her uncle's table in the château at Lyon. But these were a mammoth variety. Their whiskers were as long as Centaine's arm and at the root were as thick as her thumb. They were so old that barnacles and seaweed adhered to their spiny carapaces as if they were rocks.

O'wa and H'ani buried them in a kelp-lined pit under a thin layer of sand and then heaped a bonfire of driftwood over them. The flames lit their glowing apricot-coloured bodies as they chatted exuberantly. When their work was finished O'wa sprang up and began a shuffling little dance, singing in a cracked falsetto voice as he circled the fire. H'ani clapped a rhythm for him and hummed in her throat, swaying where she sat, and O'wa danced on and on while Centaine lay exhausted and marvelled at the little man's energy, and wondered vaguely at the purpose of the dance and the meaning of the words of the song.

'I greet you, Spirit of red spider from the sea, And I dedicate this dance to you,' sang O'wa, jerking his legs so that his naked buttocks that protruded from under the leather loincloth bounced like jellies.

'I offer you my dance and my respect, for you have died that we may live—'

And H'ani punctuated the song with shrill piping cries.

O'wa, the skilled and cunning hunter, had never killed without giving thanks to the game that had fallen to his arrows or his snares, and no creature was too small and mean to be so honoured. For being himself a small creature, he recognized the excellence of many small things, and he knew that the scaly anteater, the pangolin, was to be honoured even more than the lion, and the praying mantis, an insect, was more worthy than the elephant or the gemsbok, for in each of them reposed a special part of the godhead of nature which he worshipped.

He saw himself as no more worthy than any other of these creatures, with no rights over them other than those dictated by the survival of himself and his clan, and so he thanked the spirits of his quarry for giving him life, and when the dance ended he had beaten a pathway in the sand around the fire.

He and H'ani scraped away the ashes and sand and exposed the carcasses of the giant crayfish, now turned deep vermilion in colour and steaming on the bed of kelp.

They burned their fingers and squealed with laughter as they broke open the scaly red tails and dug out the rich white meat.

H'ani beckoned to Centaine and she squatted beside them. The legs of the crayfish contained sticks of flesh the size of her finger, the thorax was filled with the yellow livers which had been broken down in the cooking to a custard. The San used this as sauce for the flesh.

Centaine could not remember ever having so much enjoyed eating. She used the knife to slice bite-sized chunks off the tail of the crayfish. H'ani smiled at her in the firelight, her cheeks bulging with food, and she said, 'Nam!' and then again, 'Nam!'

Centaine listened carefully, then repeated it, with the same inflexion as the old woman had used.

'Nam!'

And H'ani squealed gleefully. 'Did you hear, O'wa, the child said "Good!"'

O'wa grunted and watched the knife in the female's hand. He found he could not take his eyes off it. The blade sliced through the meat so cleanly that it left a sheen on it. How sharp it must be, thought O'wa, and the sharpness of the blade spoiled his appetite.

With her stomach so full that it was almost painful, Centaine lay down beside the fire, and H'ani came to her and scraped out a hollow for her hip in the sand beneath her. It was immediately more comfortable and she settled down again, but H'ani was trying to show her something else.

'You must not lay your head on the ground, Nam Child,' she explained. 'You must keep it up, like this.' H'ani propped herself on one elbow and then laid her head on her own shoulder. It looked awkward and uncomfortable, and Centaine smiled her thanks but lay flat.

'Leave her,' grunted O'wa. 'When a scorpion crawls into her ear during the night, she will understand.'

'She has learned enough for one day,' H'ani agreed. 'Did you hear her say "Nam"? That is her first word and that is the name I will give her, "Nam",' she repeated it, 'Nam Child.'

O'wa grunted and went off into the darkness to relieve himself. He understood his wife's unnatural interest in the stranger and the child she carried in her womb, but there was a fearful journey ahead and the woman would be a dangerous nuisance. Then, of course, there was the knife – thinking about the knife made him angry.

Centaine awoke screaming. It had been a terrible dream, confused but deeply distressing – she had seen Michael again, not in the flaming body of the aeroplane, but riding Nuage. Michael's body was still blackened by the flames and his hair was burning like a torch, and beneath him Nuage was torn and mutilated by the shells and his blood was bright on the snowy hide and his entrails dangled from the torn belly as he ran.

'There is my star, Centaine,' Michael pointed ahead with a hand like a black claw. 'Why don't you follow it?'

'I cannot, Michel,' Centaine cried, 'oh, I cannot.'

And Michael galloped away across the dunes into the south without looking back and Centaine screamed after him, 'Wait, Michel, wait for me!'

She was still screaming when gentle hands shook her awake.

'Peace, Nam Child,' H'ani whispered to her. 'Your head is full of the sleep demons – but see, they are gone now.'

Centaine was still sobbing and shivering and the old woman lay down beside her and spread her fur cape over them both and held her and stroked her hair. After a while Centaine quietened down. The old woman's body smelled of woodsmoke and animal fat and wild herbs, but it was not offensive and her warmth comforted Centaine, and after a while she slept again, this time without the nightmares.

H'ani did not sleep. Old people do not need the sleep that the young do. But she felt at peace. The bodily contact with another human being was something she had missed all these long months. She had known from childhood how important it was. The infant San was strapped close to its mother's body, and lived the rest of its life in intimate physical contact with the rest of the clan. There was a saying of the clan, 'The zebra on his own falls easy prey to the hunting lion,' and the clan was a close-knit entity.

Thinking thus, the old woman became sad again, and the loss of her people became a great stone in her chest too heavy to carry. There had been nineteen of them in the clan of O'wa and H'ani – their three sons and their wives and the eleven children of their sons. The youngest of H'ani's grandchildren was still unweaned and the eldest, a girl whom she loved most dearly, had just menstruated for the first time when the sickness came on the clan.

It had been a plague beyond anything in the annals of the clan and of the San; something so swift and savage that H'ani still could not comprehend it or come to terms with it. It had started first as a sore throat which changed to raging fever, a skin so hot that it was almost searing to the touch and a thirst beyond anything the Kalahari itself, which the San called 'the Great Dry', could generate.

At this stage the little ones had died, just a day or two after the first symptoms, and the elders had been so debilitated by the sickness that they did not have the strength to bury them and their tiny bodies decomposed swiftly in the heat.

Then the fever passed and they believed that they had been spared. They buried the babies, but they were too weak even to dance for the spirits of the infants or to sing them away on their journey into the other world.

They had not been spared, however, for the sickness had only changed its form, and now there came a new fever, but at the same time their lungs filled with water and they rattled and choked as they died.

They all died, all of them except O'wa and H'ani – but even they were so close to death that it was many days and many nights before they were strong enough to appreciate the full extent of the disaster that had overtaken them. When the two old people were sufficiently recovered, they danced for their doomed clan, and H'ani cried for her babies that she would never again carry on her hip nor enchant with her fairy-tales.

Then they had discussed the cause and the meaning of the tragedy, they discussed it endlessly around their camp-fire in the night, grieving still to the depths of their beings, until one night O'wa had said, 'When we are strong enough for the journey – and you know, H'ani, what a fearsome journey it is – then we must go back to the Place of All Life, for only there will we find the meaning of this thing, and learn how we can make recompense to the angry spirits who have smitten us so.'

H'ani became once more aware of the young and fruitful body in her arms and her sadness lifted a little and she felt the resurgence of the mother instinct in her milkless and withered bosom, which had been snuffed out by the great sickness.

'It may be,' she thought, 'that already the spirits are mollified because we have begun the pilgrimage, and that they will grant this old woman the boon of hearing once more the birth cry of a new infant before she dies.'

In the dawn H'ani unstoppered one of the little buck-horns that hung from her girdle and with an aromatic paste dressed the sun blisters on Centaine's cheeks and nose and lips, and the grazes and bruises on her legs and arms, chattering away to her as she worked. Then she allowed Centaine a carefully measured ration of water. Centaine was still savouring it, holding it in her mouth as though it were a rare Bordeaux, when without further ceremony the two San stood up, turned their faces northwards and set off along the beach in that rhythmic jogtrot.

Centaine sprang up in consternation and without wasting breath on entreaties, she snatched up her club, adjusted the canvas hood over her head and started after them.

Within the first mile she realized how the food and rest had strengthened her. She was at first able to hold the pair of tiny figures in sight. She saw H'ani prod the sand with her digging stick, scoop up a sand clam almost without breaking stride and hand it to O'wa, then pluck another for herself and eat it on the run.

Centaine sharpened one end of the club to a point and imitated her, at first unsuccessfully, until she realized that the clams were in pockets in the beach – and H'ani had some means of locating them. It was useless to scrape at random. From then on she dug only where H'ani had marked the sand and drank the juice from the shells thankfully as she trotted along.

Despite her best efforts, Centaine's pace soon flagged and gradually the two San drew away from her and once again disappeared from her view. By midday Centaine was down to a dragging walk and knew that she had to rest. As she accepted it, she lifted her eyes and recognized far ahead of her the headland of the seal colony.

It was almost as though H'ani had divined the exact limit of her endurance, for she and O'wa were waiting for her in the rock shelter, and she smiled and chittered with pleasure as Centaine dragged herself up the slope into the cave and fell exhausted on to the floor beside the fire.

H'ani gave her a ration of water, and while she did so, there was another lively argument between the old people which Centaine watched with interest, noticing that every time H'ani pointed at her she used the word 'nam'. The gestures that the old people made were so expressive that

Centaine was sure she understood the old woman wanted to stay for her sake, while O'wa wanted to go on.

Every time H'ani pointed at her mate, she made that kissing pop of her lips. Suddenly Centaine interrupted the discussion by also pointing at the little Bushman and saying, 'O'wa!'

They both stared at her in stupefied amazement, and then with delighted squeals of glee acknowledged her accomplishment.

'O'wa!' H'ani prodded her husband in the ribs, and hooted.

'O'wa!' The old man slapped his own chest, and bobbed up and down with gratification.

For the moment the argument was forgotten, as Centaine had intended, and as soon as the first excitement had passed, she pointed at the old woman, who was quick to understand her query.

'H'ani?' she enunciated clearly.

On the third attempt, Centaine sounded the final click to H'ani's satisfaction and high delight.

'Centaine.' She touched her own chest, but this precipitated shrill denials and a fluttering of hands.

'Nam Child!' H'ani slapped her gently on the shoulder, and Centaine resigned herself to another christening. 'Nam Child!' she agreed.

'So, revered old grandfather,' H'ani rounded on her husband, 'Nam Child may be ugly, but she learns fast and she is with child. We will rest here and go on tomorrow. The matter is at an end!' And grumbling under his breath O'wa shuffled out of the shelter, but when he came back at dusk, he carried the fresh carcass of a half-grown seal over one shoulder, and Centaine felt so rested that she joined in the ceremony of thanksgiving, clapping with H'ani and imitating her piping cries while O'wa danced around them and the seal meat grilled over the embers.

The ointment which H'ani had used on her injuries

brought rapid results. The raw burns and blisters on her face dried up, and her skin with its Celtic pigmentation darkened to the colour of teak as it became conditioned to the sun, though she used her fingers to brush out her thick dark hair to shade as much of her face as possible.

Each day she grew stronger as her body responded to hard work and the protein-rich diet of seafood. Soon she could really reach out with her long legs and match the pace that O'wa set, and there was no more lagging behind, or argument about early halts. For Centaine it became a matter of pride to keep up with the old couple from dawn until dusk.

'I'll show you, you old devil,' she muttered to herself, fully aware of the strange antagonism which O'wa felt towards her but believing that it was her weakness and helplessness and her drag on the party that was the cause.

One day as they were about to begin, and despite the old woman's protests, she took half the water-filled ostrich eggs from H'ani's load and slung them in her canvas shawl. Once H'ani realized her intention, she acquiesced willingly and ribbed the old man mercilessly as they set out on the day's trek.

'Nam Child carries her share, just like a woman of the San,' she said, and when she had exhausted her gibes she turned all her attention to Centaine and began her instruction in earnest, pointing with her digging stick and not satisfied until Centaine had the word right or showed that she understood the lesson.

At first Centaine was merely humouring the old woman, but soon she was delighting in each fresh discovery and the day's journey seemed lighter and swifter as her body strengthened and her understanding grew.

What she had at first believed was a barren wasteland was instead a world teeming with strange and wonderfully adapted life. The kelp beds and underwater reefs were treasure houses of crustaceans and shellfish and seaworms, and occasionally the low tide left a shoal of fish trapped in a shallow rock pool. They were deep, full-bodied fish with gunmetal gleaming scales and a slightly greenish tinge to the flesh, but when split and grilled on the coals, were better than turbot.

Once they came across a nesting colony of jackass penguins. The penguins were on a rocky island, connected to the mainland by a reef across which they waded at low tide, although Centaine had shark horrors all the way over. The thousands of black and white jackass penguins nested on the bare ground, and hissed and brayed with outrage as the Bushmen harvested the big green eggs and filled the canvas carrying bag with them. Roasted in the sand under the fire they were delicious, with transparent, jelly-like whites and bright yellow yolks, but so rich that they could only be eaten one at a time and the supply lasted many days.

Even the shifting dunes with precipitous slip-faces of loosely running sand were the homes of sand-burrowing lizards and the venomous side-winding adders that preyed upon them. They clubbed both lizards and adders and cooked them in their scaly skins, and after Centaine had mastered her initial aversion, she found that they tasted like chicken.

As they trekked northwards, the dunes became intermittent, no longer presenting an unbroken rampart, and between them were valleys whose bottoms were of firm earth, albeit as bare and as blasted as the dunes or the beaches. H'ani led Centaine over the rocky ground and showed her succulent plants which exactly resembled stones. They dug beneath the tiny inconspicuous leaves and found a bloated root the size of a football.

Centaine watched while H'ani grated the pulp of the root with her stone scraper, then took a handful of the shavings, held them high with her thumb pointed downwards like a teat on a cow's udder and squeezed. Milky liquid ran down her thumb and dribbled into her open mouth, and when she had squeezed out the last drop, she used all the remaining damp pulp to scrub her face and arms, grinning all the while with pleasure.

Quickly Centaine followed her example. The juice was quinine-bitter, but after the first shock of the taste, Centaine found that it slaked her thirst more effectively than water alone, and when she had scrubbed her body with the pulp, the dryness caused by wind and sun and salt was alleviated and her skin felt and looked cleaner and smoother. The effect was to make her aware of herself for the first time since the shipwreck.

That evening as they sat around the fire waiting for the kebabs of limpets threaded on a piece of driftwood to broil, Centaine whittled a stick and with the point cleansed between her teeth, and then used her forefinger dipped in evaporated crystals of seasalt that she had scraped from the rocks to scrub them again. H'ani watched her knowingly, and after they had eaten, she came and squatted behind Centaine and crooned softly to her as she used a twig to pick the knots and tangles out of her hair, and then dressed it into tight new braids.

C entaine woke when it was still dark to the realization that a change had taken place while she slept. Although the fire had been built up, the light was weirdly diffused, and the excited voices of H'ani and O'wa were muted as though they came from a distance. The air was cold and heavy with moisture and it took Centaine a while to realize that they were enveloped in dense fog that had rolled in from the sea during the night.

H'ani was hopping with excitement and impatience.

'Come, Nam Child, hurry.' Centaine's vocabulary

already contained a hundred or so of the most important words of San, and she scrambled up.

'Carry. Bring.' H'ani pointed at the canvas container of ostrich eggs and then picking up her own leather bag scampered away into the fog. Centaine ran after her to keep her in sight, for the world had been obliterated by the pearly fog banks.

In the valley between the dunes H'ani dropped to her knees.

'Look, Nam Child.' She seized Centaine's wrists and drew her down beside her, and pointed to the desert plant that was spread out flat against the ground. The thick smooth skin that covered the stone-like leaves chameleoned to the exact colour of the surrounding earth.

'Water, H'ani!' Centaine exclaimed delightedly.

'Water, Nam Child.' H'ani cackled with laughter.

The fog had condensed on the smooth leaves and had run down the slanted surface to gather in the trough-like depressions of the point where the foreshortened stems disappeared into the earth. The plant was a marvellously designed gatherer of moisture, and Centaine understood now how that bloated subterranean root was replenished at each coming of the fog.

'Quick!' H'ani ordered. 'Sun come soon.' She stood one of the empty ostrich shells upright in the soft earth and unplugged it. With a ball of animal fur she mopped up the glistening pool of dew and then squeezed it carefully into the egg-bottle. With that demonstration, she handed Centaine a wad of fur.

'Work!' she ordered.

Centaine worked as quickly as the old woman, listening to her chattering happily and understanding only an occasional word as they hurried from plant to plant.

'This is a blessing indeed, the spirits are kind to send the water-smoke from the sea. Now the crossing to the

Place of All Life will be less arduous. Without the water-smoke we might have perished. They have made the road smooth for us, Nam Child – perhaps your baby will be born at the Place of All Life. What a prodigious benevolence that would be. For then your child would have the special mark of the spirits upon him for all his life, he would be the greatest of hunters, the sweetest of singers, the nimblest of dancers and the most fortunate of all his clan.'

Centaine did not understand, but she laughed at the old woman, feeling lighthearted and happy, and the sound of her own laughter startled her, it had been so long – and she replied to the old woman's chatter in French.

'I had begun truly to hate this harsh land of yours, H'ani. After all the anticipation I had to see it, after all the wonderful things that Michel told me and all the things I had read about it, how different it all was, how cruel and how malicious.'

Hearing the tone of her voice, H'ani paused with the wet wad of fur poised over the egg-bottle and looked at her quizzically.

'Just now was the first time I have laughed since I have been in Africa.' Centaine laughed again, and H'ani giggled with relief and returned her attention to the bottle. 'This day Africa has shown me its first kindness.' Centaine lifted the sodden fur to her lips and sucked the cold sweet dew from it. 'This is a special day, H'ani, this is a special day for me and my baby.'

When all the egg-bottles were brimming full and carefully replugged, they indulged themselves, drinking the dew until they were satiated, and only then did Centaine look around her and begin to appreciate what the fog meant to the plants and creatures of the desert.

Bright red ants had come up from their deep nests to take advantage of it. The worker-ants scurried from plant to plant, sucking up the droplets so that their abdomens swelled and became translucent, on the point of bursting before they disappeared back into the burrows. At the entrance to each burrow a cluster of other ants were assembled, the wedding party to see off the breeding queens and their consorts as they lifted into the foggy air on paper-white wings, fluttering off, most of them to die in the desert, but a very few of them to survive and found new colonies.

The sand lizards had come down from the dunes to feast on the flights of ants, and there were small rodents, gingery-red in colour, that hopped down the valley floor on overdeveloped hindlegs like miniature kangaroos.

'Look, H'ani, what is this?' Centaine had discovered a strange insect the size of a locust which was standing on its head in an exposed position. The dew condensed in silver droplets on its shiny iridescent armour plating, then trickled slowly down the grooves in the carapace and were channelled into the creature's hooked beak.

'Good eat,' H'ani told her and popped the insect into her mouth, crunched it up and swallowed it down with relish.

Centaine laughed at her, 'You dear, funny old thing.' Then she looked around at the small secret life of the desert. 'What an enchanted land Africa is! At last I can understand a little of what Michel tried to explain to me.'

With an African abruptness that no longer surprised Centaine, the mood changed. The curtains of fog peeled away, the sun struck through and within minutes the gem-like droplets of dew had vanished from the stone-plants. The ants disappeared into their burrows, sealing the entrances behind them, and the sand lizards scurried back into the slippery dunes, leaving the dismembered paper wings of the flying ants they had devoured to blow idly on the small offshore wind.

At first the lizards, still chilled by the fog, basked on the sunny front of the dunes, but within minutes the heat was oppressive and they ran across the ridges of the slip-face to shelter on the shady side. Later, when the noon sun dispelled all the shadows, they would dive below the surface and swim down through it to the cooler sands beneath.

H'ani and Centaine shouldered their carrying bags and, bowed under the weight of the egg-bottles, went down to the beach. O'wa was already at the camp and he had a dozen fat lizards impaled on a stick of driftwood, and a goodly bag of the gingery desert rats laid out on the flat stone beside the fire.

'Oh, husband, what an intrepid provider you are.' H'ani laid down her carrying bag the better to praise the old man's efforts. 'Surely there has never been a hunter of all the San to match your skills!'

O'wa preened quite unashamedly at the old woman's blatant flattery, and H'ani averted her face for a moment and her eyes flashed a message to Centaine in the secret language of womankind.

'They are little boys,' her smile said clearly. 'From eight to eighty, they remain children.' And Centaine laughed again and clapped her hands and joined in H'ani's little pantomime of approbation.

'O'wa good! O'wa clever!' And the old man bobbed his head and looked solemn and important.

The moon was only four or five days from full, so that after they had eaten, it was bright enough to throw purple dark shadows below the dunes. They were all still too excited by the fog visitation to sleep, and Centaine was trying to follow and even join in the chatter of the two old San.

Centaine had by now learned the four click sounds of the San language, as well as that glottal choke which sounded as though the speaker was being strangulated. However, she was still struggling to understand the tonal variations. The different tones were almost undetectable to the Western ear, and it was only in the last few days that Centaine had even become aware of their existence. She had puzzled over the way H'ani seemed to repeat the same word and showed exasperation when Centaine had obviously not been able to detect any difference in the pronunciations. Then, quite suddenly, as though wax plugs had been removed from her ears, Centaine had heard five distinct inflexions, high, middle, low, rising and falling, that changed not only the sense of a word but the relationship of the word to the rest of the sentence.

It was difficult and challenging and she was sitting close to H'ani so she could watch her lips, when suddenly she let out a surprised gasp and clutched her stomach with both hands.

'It moved!' Centaine's voice was filled with wonder. 'He moved – the baby moved!'

H'ani understood immediately and she reached out swiftly and lifted Centaine's brief tattered skirt and clasped her stomach. Deep in her body there was another spasm of life.

'Ai! Ai!' shrilled H'ani. 'Feel him! Feel him kick like a zebra stallion!' Fat little tears of joy squeezed out of her slanted Chinese eyes and as they ran down the deep corrugated wrinkles on her cheeks, they sparkled in the light of the fire and the moon. 'So strong – so brave and strong! Feel him, old grandfather.'

O'wa could not refuse such an invitation, and Centaine, kneeling in the firelight with her skirts lifted high over her naked lower body, felt no embarrassment at the old man's touch.

'This,' announced O'wa solemnly, 'is a most propitious thing. It is fitting that I should dance to celebrate it.' And O'wa stood up and danced in the moonlight for Centaine's unborn infant.

The moon dipped into the dark, slumbrous sea, but already the sky over the land was turning to the colour of ripe orange at the approach of day and Centaine lay for only a few seconds after she awoke. She was surprised that the two old people still lay beside the dead ash of last night's fire, but she left the camp hurriedly, knowing that that day's trek would begin before sunrise.

At a discreet distance from the camp she squatted to relieve herself, then stripped off her rags and ran into the sea, gasping at the cold invigorating water as she scrubbed her body with handfuls of sand. She pulled her clothing over her wet body and ran back to the camp. The old people were still wrapped in their leather cloaks and lying so still that Centaine felt a moment of panic, but then H'ani coughed throatily and stirred.

'They are still alive, anyway,' Centaine smiled and assembled her few possessions, feeling virtuous for usually H'ani had to chivvy her, but now the old woman stirred again and mumbled sleepily.

Centaine understood only the words 'Wait, rest, sleep.' Then H'ani subsided and pulled her cloak over her head again.

Centaine was puzzled. She fed a few sticks to the fire and blew up a flame, then sat to wait.

Venus, the morning star, lay on the backs of the dunes, but paled and faded at the approach of the sun, and still the two San slept on, and Centaine began to feel irritated by the inactivity. She was so strong and healthy already that she had actually been looking forward to the day's journey.

Only when the sun cleared the tops of the dunes did H'ani sit up and yawn and belch and scratch herself.

'Go?' Centaine used the rising tone that changed the word into a question.

'No, no,' H'ani made the negative waving sign. 'Wait –

378

night – moon – go there.' And she pointed with a quick stabbing thumb at the dunes.

'Go land?' Centaine asked, not sure that she understood.

'Go land,' H'ani agreed, and Centaine felt a quick thrill. They were going to leave the seashore at last.

'Go now?' Centaine demanded impatiently.

Twice during the last few days when they had stopped to make camp, Centaine had climbed to the top of the nearest dune and stared inland. Once she had imagined the distant outline of blue mountains against the evening sky, and she had felt her spirit summoned away from this monotonous seascape towards that mysterious interior.

'Go now?' she repeated eagerly, and O'wa laughed derisively as he came to squat at the fire.

'The monkey is eager to meet the leopard,' he said, 'but listen to it squeal when it does!'

H'ani clucked at him in disapproval and then turned to Centaine. 'Today we will rest. Tonight we will begin the hardest part of our journey. Tonight, Nam Child, do you understand that? Tonight, with the moon to light us. Tonight, while the sun sleeps, for no man nor woman can walk hand in hand with the sun through the land of the singing sands. Tonight. Rest now.'

'Tonight,' Centaine repeated. 'Rest now.' But she left the camp and once again climbed up through the sliding slippery sands to the top of the first line of dunes.

On the beach four hundred feet below her, the two tiny figures sitting at the campfire were insignificant specks. Then she turned to look inland and she saw that the dune on which she stood was a mere foothill to the great mountains of sand that rose before her.

The colours of the dunes shaded from pale daffodil yellow, through gold and orange, to purplish-brown and dark *sang de boeuf*, but beyond them she imagined she saw ghost mountains with rocky crenellated peaks. Even as she stared, however, the horizon turned milky-blue and began to waver and dissolve, and she felt the heat come out of the desert, a whiff of it only, but she recoiled from its scalding breath, and before her eyes the land was veiled by the glassy shimmering veils of heat mirage.

She turned and went down to the camp again. Neither O'wa nor H'ani was ever completely idle. Now the old man was shaping arrowheads of white bone, while his wife was putting together another necklace, fashioning the beads from pieces of broken ostrich shell, chipping them into coins between two small stones and then drilling a hole through each with a bone sliver, and finally stringing the finished beads on a length of gut.

Watching her work Centaine was reminded vividly of Anna. She stood up quickly and left the camp again, and H'ani looked up from the string of beads.

'Nam Child is unhappy,' she said.

'There is water in the egg-bottles and food in her belly,' O'wa grunted as he sharpened his arrowhead. 'She has no reason to be unhappy.'

'She pines for her own clan,' H'ani whispered, and the old man did not reply. Both of them understood vividly and were silent as they remembered those they had left in shallow graves in the wilderness.

'I am strong enough now,' Centaine spoke aloud, 'and I have learned how to keep alive. I don't have to follow them any more. I could turn back to the south again – alone.' She stood uncertainly, imagining what it would be like, and it was that single word that decided her. 'Alone,' she repeated. 'If only Anna were still alive, if only there was somewhere out there for me to go to, then I might attempt it.' And she slumped down on the beach and hugged her knees despondently. 'There is no way back. I just have to go on. Living each day like an animal, living like a savage, living with savages.' And she looked down at the rags which barely covered her body. 'I just have to go on, and I don't even know where,' and her despair threatened to overwhelm her completely. She had to fight it off as though it were a living adversary. 'I won't give in,' she muttered, 'I just won't give in, and when this is over I will never want again. I'll never thirst and starve nor wear rags and stinking skins again.' She looked down at her hands. The nails were ragged and black with dirt and broken off down to the quick. She made a fist to cover them. 'Never again. My son and I will never want again, I swear it.'

It was late afternoon when she wandered back into the primitive camp site under the dunes. H'ani looked up at her and grinned like a wizened little ape, and Centaine felt a sudden rush of affection for her.

'Dear H'ani,' she whispered. 'You're all I have got left.' And the old woman scrambled to her feet and came towards her, carrying the finished necklace of ostrich shell in both hands.

She stood on tiptoe and placed the necklace carefully over Centaine's head and arranged it fussily down her bosom, cooing with self-satisfaction at her handiwork.

'It's beautiful, H'ani,' Centaine's voice husked. 'Thank you, thank you so very much,' and suddenly she burst into tears. 'And I called you a savage. Oh, forgive me. With Anna you are the sweetest, dearest person I've ever known.' She knelt so that their faces were level and she hugged the old woman with a desperate strength, pressing her temple against H'ani's withered wrinkled cheek.

'Why is she weeping?' O'wa demanded from beside the fire.

'Because she is happy.'

'That,' O'wa opined, 'is a most stupid reason. I think this female is a little moon-touched.'

He stood up, and still shaking his head, began the final preparations for the night's journey.

The little old people were unusually solemn, Centaine noticed, as they adjusted their cloaks and carrying satchels, and H'ani came to her and checked the sling of her bag, then knelt to adjust the canvas booties bound around Centaine's feet.

'What is it?' Their serious mien made Centaine uneasy.

H'ani understood the question, but did not try to explain. Instead she called Centaine and the two of them fell in behind O'wa.

O'wa raised his voice. 'Spirit of Moon, make a light for us in this night to show us the path.' He used the cracked falsetto tone which all the spirits particularly enjoyed, and he performed a few shuffling dance steps in the sand. 'Spirit of Great Sun, sleep well, and when you rise tomorrow be not angry, that your anger burn us up in the singing sands. Then when we have passed safely through and have reached the sip-wells, we will dance for you and sing our thanks.'

He finished the short dance with a leap and a stamp of his small childlike feet. That was enough for now, a small down-payment, with the balance promised when the spirits had honoured their part of the contract.

'Come, old grandmother,' he said. 'Make sure that Nam Child stays close and does not fall behind. You know that we cannot turn back to search for her if she does.' And in that quick, swaying jog, he started up the slope of the beach into the mouth of the valley, just as the moon broke clear of the darkening horizon and started its journey across the starry heavens.

It was strange to travel in the night, for the desert seemed to take on new and mysterious dimensions, the dunes seemed taller and closer, decked in silver moonlight and dark purple shadows, and the valleys between them were canyons of silence, while above it all the vast panoply of the stars and the milky way and the moon were closer and brighter than Centaine had ever believed possible. She had the illusion that by simply reaching up she could pluck them down like ripe fruit from the bough.

The memory of the ocean stayed with them long after it was out of sight, the soft hiss of their footsteps in the sand semed to echo its gentle kissing surf on the yellow beaches, and the air was still cooled by its vast green waters.

They had been following the valley for almost a half of the moon's rise to its zenith when suddenly Centaine trotted into an eddy of heat. After the ocean-cooled airs it was like running into a solid barrier. Centaine gasped with surprise and H'ani murmured without breaking the rhythm of her gait, 'Now it begins.' But they passed swiftly through it, and beyond the air was so cold by contrast that Centaine shivered and drew her cloak closer about her shoulders.

The valley twisted and as they came around the corner of a towering dune on which the moon shadows lay like bruises, the desert breathed upon them again.

'Stay close, Nam Child.' But the heat had a viscosity and weight so that Centaine felt that she was wading into a lava flow. At midnight it was hotter than in the boiler room at Mort Homme with the furnace stoked with oak logs, and as she breathed it into her lungs, she felt the heat entering her body like an invader, and with each breath expelled, she could feel it taking her moisture like a thief.

They paused once, only briefly, and drank from an egg-bottle. Both H'ani and O'wa watched carefully as Centaine lifted it to her lips, but neither of them had to caution her now.

When the sky began to lighten, O'wa slackened his pace a little, and once or twice paused to survey the valley with a critical eye. It was obvious that he was choosing a place to wait out the day, and when at last they halted, it was close under the lee of a steep dune wall.

There was no material for a fire, and H'ani offered Centaine a piece of sun-dried fish wrapped in seaweed, but she was too tired and hot to eat and afraid also that food would increase her thirst during the day ahead. She drank her ration of water from the egg-bottle, and then wearily stood up and moved a short distance from the others. But as soon as she squatted, H'ani let out a shrill reprimand and hurried to her.

'No!' she repeated, and Centaine was embarrassed and confused, until the old woman fished in her satchel and brought out the dried wild gourd that she used as a bowl and ladle.

'Here, this one—' She proffered it to Centaine, who still did not understand. Exasperated, the old woman snatched back the gourd and holding it between her own legs urinated into it.

'Here – do.' She offered the bowl to Centaine again.

'I can't, H'ani, not in front of everybody,' Centaine protested modestly.

'O'wa, come here,' H'ani called. 'Show the child.' The old man came across and noisily reinforced H'ani's demonstration.

Despite her embarrassment, Centaine could not help feeling a touch of envy. 'How much more convenient!'

'Now, do!' H'ani offered her the gourd once again, and Centaine capitulated. She turned away modestly and with both the old people encouraging her loudly, she added her own tinkling stream to the communal gourd. H'ani bore it away triumphantly.

'Hurry, Nam Child,' she beckoned. 'The sun will come soon.' And she showed Centaine how to scoop a shallow trench in the sand in which to lie.

The sun struck the face of the dune on the opposite side of the valley, and it flung reflected heat at them like a mirror of polished bronze. They lay in the strip of shade and cringed into their trenches.

The sun rose higher and the dune shadow shrank. The heat rose and filled the valley with silvery mirage so that the dunes began to dance, and then the sands began to sing. It was a low but pervading vibration as though the desert was the sounding box of a gigantic string instrument. It rose and fell and died away and then started again.

'The sands are singing,' H'ani told her quietly, and Centaine understood. She lay with her ear to the ground and listened to the strange and wonderful music of the desert.

Still the heat increased, and following the example of the San, Centaine covered her head with the canvas shawl and lay quietly. It was too hot to sleep, but she fell into a sort of stupefied coma, and rode the long swelling waves of heat as though they were the sound of the sea.

Still it became hotter, and the shade shrivelled away as the sun nooned, and there was no relief or asylum from its merciless lash. Centaine lay and panted like a maimed animal, and each quick and shallow breath seemed to abrade her throat and burn the strength from her body.

'It can't get worse,' she told herself. 'This is the end of it, soon it will begin to cool.'

She was wrong. The heat grew stronger yet and the desert hissed and vibrated like a tortured beast, and Centaine was almost afraid to open her eyes lest it sear her eyeballs.

Then she heard the old woman moving and she lifted the corner of her head cover and watched her carefully mixing sand into the gourdful of urine. She brought the bowl to where Centaine lay and plastered the wet sand over her baking skin.

Centaine gasped with relief of the cool touch of it, and before it could dry in the fierce heat, H'ani filled in the shallow trench with loose sand, burying Centaine under a thin layer and then arranging the shawl over her head.

'Thank you, H'ani,' Centaine whispered, and the old woman went to cover her husband.

With the damp sand next to her skin and the protective layer over that, Centaine lasted out those hottest hours of the desert day, and then with that African suddenness she felt the temperature on her cheeks change, and the sunlight was no longer stark dazzling white, but shaded with a mellow, buttery tone.

At nightfall they rose out of their beds and shook themselves, throwing off the sand. They drank in a transport that was almost religious, but again Centaine could not force herself to eat, and then O'wa led them off.

Now there was no novelty or fascination for Centaine in the night's trek, and the heavenly bodies were no longer marvels to gaze upon with awe but merely instruments to mark the long tortuous passage of the hours.

The earth beneath her changed its character from loose sand that gave under each step and ragged at her feet, to hard, compacted mica flats where the flowerlike crystals called 'desert roses' had edges to them like knives; they cut through her canvas sandals, and she had to pause to rebind them. Then they left the flats and crossed the low spine of a sub-dune, and from its crest saw another vast valley yawn before them.

O'wa never wavered or showed the least hesitation. Although Centaine realized that these mountains of sand would walk before the prevailing winds, endlessly changing shape, trackless and unknowable, yet the little man moved through them the way a master mariner rides upon the shifting currents of the ocean.

The silence of the desert seemed to enter Centaine's head like molten wax, deadening her sense of hearing, filling her eardrums with the sussurations of nothingness as though she held a seashell to her ear.

'Will the sand never end?' she asked herself. 'Is this a continent of dunes?'

In the dawn they halted and prepared their defences to resist the siege of the sun, and in the hottest hour of the day as Centaine lay in her shallow grave-like bed, coated with urine-damp sand, she felt her baby move within her more strongly this time, as though he too were fighting the heat and the thirst.

'Patience, my darling,' she whispered to him. 'Save your strength. We must learn the lessons and the ways of this land, so that we will never have to suffer like this again. Never again.'

That evening, when she rose from the sand, she ate a little of the dried fish for the baby's sake, but as she had feared, the food made her thirst almost insupportable. However, the strength it gave her bore her up through the night's journey.

She did not waste strength by speaking aloud. All three of them were conserving energy and moisture, no unnecessary words or actions, but Centaine looked up at the sky as it made its grand and ponderous revolution, and she could still see Michael's star standing across the black void of the South Pole from her own.

'Please let it end,' she prayed silently to his star. 'Let it end soon, for I don't know how much longer I can go on.'

But it did not end, and it seemed that the nights grew longer, the sand deeper and more cloying around her feet, while each day seemed fiercer than the last and the heat beat down upon them like a blacksmith's hammerstrokes on the iron of the anvil.

Centaine found that she had lost track of the days and nights, they had blended in her mind into a single endless torment of heat and thirst.

'Five days, or six or even seven?' she wondered vaguely, and then she counted the empty egg-bottles. 'It must be six,' she decided. 'Only two full bottles left.'

Centaine and H'ani each placed one of the full bottles in their pack, sharing the load exactly, then they ate the last shreds of dried fish and stood up to face the night's journey, but this time it did not begin immediately.

O'wa stared for a while into the east, turning his head

387

slightly from side to side as though he were listening, and for the first time Centaine detected a fine shade of uncertainty in the way he held his small head with its crownlike nimbus of arrow shafts. Then O'wa began to sing softly in what Centaine had come to recognize as his ghost-voice.

'Spirit of great Lion Star,' he looked up to Sirius shining in the constellation of Canis Major, 'you are the only one who can see us here, for all the other spirits avoid the land of singing sand. We are alone, and the journey is harder than I remember it when I passed here as a young man. The path has become obscure, great Lion Star, but you have the bright eye of a vulture and can see it all. Lead us, I beg of you. Make the path clear for us.'

Then he took the egg-bottle from H'ani's satchel and drew the stopper and spilled a little of the water on to the sand. It formed small round balls, and Centaine made a little moaning sound in her throat and sank on to her knees.

'See, spirit of great Lion Star, we share water with you,' O'wa sang and replugged the bottle, but Centaine stared at the little wet balls of sand and moaned again.

'Peace, Nam Child,' H'ani whispered to her. 'To receive a special boon, it is sometimes necessary to give up what is precious.'

She took Centaine's wrist and pulled her gently to her feet, and then turned to follow O'wa over the endless dunes.

With the silences deafening her, and weariness a crushing burden to carry, and thirst a raging torment, Centaine struggled on, once again losing all sense of time or distance or direction, seeing nothing but the two dancing figures ahead of her, transformed by the rays of the waning moon into tiny hobgoblins.

They stopped so suddenly that Centaine ran into H'ani and would have fallen had not the old woman steadied her, and then quietly drawn her down until they lay side by side.

'What—' Centaine began, but H'ani placed a hand over her mouth to quieten her.

O'wa lay beside them, and when Centaine was quiet he pointed over the lip of the dune on which they were lying.

Two hundred feet below at the dune's foot began a level plain, awash with soft silver moonlight. It reached to the very limit of Centaine's night vision, flat, without end, and it gave her hope that at last the dunes were behind them. Upon this plain stood a scattered forest of long-dead trees. Léprous-grey in the moonlight, they lifted the blighted and twisted limbs of arthritic beggars of an uncaring sky. The weird scene invoked in Centaine a superstitious chill, and when something large but shapeless moved amongst the ancient trees like a monster from mythology, she shivered and wriggled closer to H'ani.

Both the San were trembling with eagerness like hunting dogs on the leash, and H'ani shook Centaine's hand and pointed silently. As Centaine's eyes adjusted, she saw that there were more living shapes than the one she had first spotted, but they were as still as great grey boulders. She counted five of them altogether.

Lying on his side, O'wa was restringing his little hunting bow, and when he had tested the tension of its string, he selected a pair of arrows from the leather band around his forehead, made a sign to H'ani and then slithered back from the crest of the dune. Once he was off the skyline, he leaped to his feet and slipped away into the shadows and folds of windblown sands.

The two women lay behind the ridge, still and silent as the shadows. Centaine was learning the animal patience that this ancient wilderness demanded of all its creatures. The sky began to bloom with the first promise of day, and now she could see more clearly the creatures on the plain below them.

They were huge antelopes. Four of them lying quietly, while one of them, larger and more thickset in shoulders and neck, stood a little apart. Centaine judged that he was the herd bull, for at his shoulder he stood as tall as Nuage, her beloved stallion, but he carried a magnificent pair of horns, long and straight and vicious, and Centaine was reminded vividly of the tapestry *La Dame à la Licorne* at the Musée de Cluny, which her father had taken her to see on her twelfth birthday.

The light strengthened and the bull gleamed a lovely soft mulberry-fawn colour. His face was marked with darker lines in a diamond pattern, that looked as though he were wearing a head halter, but there was that wild dignity about him that immediately dispelled any suggestion of captivity.

He swung his noble head towards where Centaine lay, extended his trumpet-like ears and swished his dark bushy horse-like tail uneasily. H'ani laid her hand on Centaine's arm and they shrank down. The bull stared in their direction for many minutes, rigid and still as a marble carving, but neither of the women moved, and at last the bull lowered his head and began to dig in the loose earth of the plain with his sharp black forehooves.

'Ah, yes! Dig for the sweet root of the bi plant, great and splendid bull,' O'wa exhorted him silently. 'Do not lift your head, you marvellous chieftain of all gemsbok, feed well, and I will dance you such a dance that all the spirits of the gemsbok will envy you for ever!'

O'wa lay one hundred and fifty feet from where the gemsbok bull was standing, still far beyond the range of his puny bow. He had left the shadow of the dune valley almost an hour before, and in that time had covered less than five hundred paces.

There was a slight depression in the surface of the plain, a mere indentation less than a hand's span deep, but even

in the vague light of the moon O'wa had picked it out
unerringly with his hunter's eye and he had slid into it like
a small amber-coloured serpent, and like a serpent moved
on his belly with slow, sinuous undulations and silent
prayers to the spirits of Lion Star who had guided him to
this quarry.

Suddenly the gemsbok flung up his head and stared
about him suspiciously, ears flared wide.

'Don't be alarmed, sweet bull,' O'wa urged him. 'Smell
the bi tuber and let peace enter your heart again.'

The minutes stretched out, and then the bull blew a
small fluttery sound through his nostrils, and lowered his
head. His harem of fawn-coloured cows who had been
watching him warily relaxed, and their jaws began working
again as they chewed on the cud.

O'wa slithered forward, moving under the flattened lip
of the depression, his cheek touching the earth so as not to
show a head silhouette, pushing himself over the soft earth
with his hips and his knees and his toes.

The gemsbok had rooted out the tuber and was chewing
on it with noisy gusto, holding it down with a forehoof to
break off a mouthful, and O'wa closed the gap between
them with elaborate, patient stealth.

'Feast well, sweet bull, without you three persons and an
unborn child will be dead by tomorrow's sun. Do not go,
great gemsbok, stay a while, just a little while longer.'

He was as close as he dared approach now, but it was
still too far. The gemsbok's hide was tough and his fur
thick. The arrow was a light reed, and the point was bone
that could not take the same keen edge as iron.

'Spirit of Lion Star, do not turn your face away now,'
O'wa beseeched, and raised his left hand so that the tiny
pale-coloured palm was turned towards the bull.

For almost a minute nothing happened, and then the
bull noticed the disembodied hand that seemed to rise out

391

of the earth, and he lifted his head and stared at it. It seemed too small to be dangerous.

After a minute of utter stillness, O'wa wriggled his fingers seductively and the bull blew through his nostrils and stretched out his muzzle, sucking in air, trying to get the scent, but O'wa was working into the small, fitful morning breeze, with the deceptive dawn light behind him.

He held his hand still again and then slowly lowered it to his side. The bull took a few paces towards him and then froze – another few paces, craning inquisitively, ears pricked forward, he peered at the shallow indentation where O'wa lay pressed to the earth without breathing. Then the bull's curiosity took him forward again into range of O'wa's bow.

In a flash of movement, like the strike of the adder, O'wa rolled on to his side, drew the eagle feather flights to his cheek and let the arrow fly. It darted like a bee across the space between them and alighted with a slapping sound on the patterned cheek of the bull, fixing its barbs in the soft skin below his trumpet-like ear.

The bull reared back at the sting of it, and whirled away. Instantly his harem cows sprang from their sandy couches into full gallop and the whole herd went away after the running bull, switching their long dark tails and dragging a pale train of dust behind them.

The bull was shaking his head, trying to rid himself of the arrow that dangled from his cheek, and he swerved in his run and deliberately brushed his head against the trunk of one of the ancient dead trees.

'Stick deep!' O'wa was on his feet, capering and yelling. 'Hold fast, arrow, carry the poison of O'wa to his heart. Carry it swiftly, little arrow.'

The women came running down from the dune to join him.

'Oh, what a cunning hunter,' H'ani lauded her husband, and Centaine was breathless but disappointed for the herd was already out of sight across the dark plain, lost in the grey of pre-dawn.

'Gone?' she asked H'ani.

'Wait,' the old woman answered. 'Follow soon. Watch now. O'wa make magic.'

The old man had laid aside his weapons, except for two arrows which he arranged in his headband to prick up at the same angle as the horns of a gemsbok. Then he cupped his hands on each side of his head into trumpet-shaped ears, and subtly altered his entire stance and the way he carried his head. He snorted through his nostrils and pawed at the ground, and before Centaine's eyes was transformed into a gemsbok. The mimicry was so faithful that Centaine clapped her hands delightedly.

O'wa went through the pantomime of seeing the beckoning hand, approaching it warily, and then being struck by the arrow. Centaine had a sense of *déjà vu*, so accurately was the incident portrayed.

O'wa galloped away with the same stride and carriage as the gemsbok, but then he began to weaken and stagger. He was panting, his head drooping, and Centaine felt a pang of sympathy for the stricken beast. She thought of Nuage and tears sprang into her eyes, but H'ani was clapping and uttering little shrieks of encouragement.

'Die, oh bull that we revere, die that we may live!'

O'wa blundered in a wide circle, his horned head too heavy to carry, and he sagged to the earth and went into the final convulsions as the poison coursed through his blood.

It was all so convincing that Centaine was no longer seeing the little San, but rather the bull that he was portraying. She did not for a moment doubt the efficacy for the sympathetic spell that O'wa was weaving over his quarry.

'Ah!' H'ani cried. 'He is down. The great bull is finished,' and Centaine believed without question.

They drank from the egg-bottles, and then O'wa broke a straight branch from one of the dead trees and shaped one end to fit the spearhead made from the thighbone of a buffalo which he carried in his pouch. He bound the spearhead in place and weighed the heavy weapon in his hand.

'It is time to go after the bull,' he announced, and led off across the plain.

Centaine's first impression was correct. They had passed beyond the dune country, but the plain that lay ahead of them was every bit as forbidding, and the strange shapes of the dead forest gave it a surreal and other-worldly feeling. Centaine wondered how long ago the forest had died, and shivered as she realized that these trees might have stood like this for a thousand years, preserved by the desiccated air as the mummies of the pharaohs had been.

O'wa was following the tracks of the gemsbok herd, and even over the hard pebbled expanses of the plain where Centaine could see no sign of their passing, the little San led them at a confident unwavering trot. He paused only once to pick up the shaft of his arrow, lying at the base of the dead tree upon which the bull had brushed itself. He held it up and showed it to the women.

'See. The barb has struck.'

The head of the arrow was missing. O'wa had deliberately designed it in two pieces with a weak section just at the back of the poisoned barb so that it would break away.

The light improved swiftly, and H'ani, trotting ahead of Centaine, pointed with her digging stick. At first Centaine could not see what she was indicating, then she noticed a small dried vine with a few parched brown leaves lying close to the earth, and the first sign of living plant life since they had left the coast.

Because she now knew where and how to look, Centaine

noticed other plants, brown and blasted and insignificant, but she had learned enough of this desert to guess what lay beneath the surface. It gave her spirits a small lift when she noticed the first scattered clumps of fine silver dry desert grass. The dunes were behind them, and the land about them was coming alive again.

The morning breeze that had aided O'wa in his stalk persisted after the sun had cleared the horizon, so the heat was not as oppressive as it had been in the dune country. The whole temper of the San was lighter and more carefree, and even without H'ani's assurances – 'Good now, eat, drink soon' – Centaine was sure that they had passed through the worst stage of the journey. She had to screw up her eyes and shade them, for already the low sun sparkled in dazzling points of white light from the mica chips and bright pebbles and the sky was aglow with a hot soapy radiance that dissolved the horizon and washed out all colour and altered shape and substance.

Far ahead of them Centaine saw the humped shape lying, and beyond it the four gemsbok cows lingering loyally but fearfully by their fallen liege bull. They abandoned him at last only when the little file of human shapes was within a mile, and they galloped away into the shimmering heat haze.

The bull lay as O'wa had mimed him, panting and so weakened by the poison of the arrowhead that his head rolled and his long straight annulated horns waggled from side to side. His eyes glistened with tears and his eyelashes were as long and curved as those of a beautiful woman, yet he tried to rise to defend himself as O'wa faced him, and hooked with those rapier horns that could impale a full-grown lion, swinging them in a vicious flashing arc, before sagging back.

O'wa circled him cautiously, seeming so frail against the animal's bulk, waiting for his opening, the clumsy spear poised, but the bull dragged its semi-paralysed body around to face him. The arrowhead still dangled from the wound beneath his ear, and the lovely black and white pattern of his face mask was smeared with dark coagulated blood from the poisoned wound.

Centaine thought of Nuage again, and she wanted the suffering to end quickly. She laid down her satchel, loosened her skirt and held it like a matador's cape and sidled up to the stricken bull on the far side from O'wa.

'Be ready, O'wa, be ready!' The bull turned to her voice. She caped the bull and he lunged at her, his horns hissed in the air like a swinging cutlass, and he dragged himself towards her, kicking up dust with his giant hooves, and Centaine leaped nimbly aside.

As he was distracted, O'wa rushed forward and lanced the bull in the throat, driving the bone spearhead deep, twisting and worrying it, seeking the cartoid artery. Bright arterial blood sprayed like a flamingo feather in the sunlight, and O'wa leapt back and watched him die.

'Thank you, great bull. Thank you for letting us live.'

B etween them they rolled the carcass on to its back, but when O'wa prepared to make the first cut with his flint knife, Centaine opened the blade of her clasp knife and handed it to him.

O'wa hesitated. He had never touched that beautiful weapon. He believed that if he did it might cleave to his fingers and he would never be able to give it up again.

'Take, O'wa,' Centaine urged him, and when he still hesitated, staring at the knife with a timid reverence, Centaine with a sudden intuitive flash realized the true reason for O'wa's antagonism towards her.

'He wants the knife, he is lusting after it.'

She almost laughed but controlled it. 'Take, O'wa,' and

the little man reached out slowly and took it from her hand.

He turned it lovingly between his fingers. He stroked the steel, caressing the blade, and then tested the edge with his thumb.

'Ai! Ai!' he exclaimed as the steel sliced through his skin and raised a beaded chain of blood drops across the ball of his thumb. 'What a weapon. Look, H'ani!' He displayed his injured thumb proudly. 'See how sharp it is!'

'My stupid husband, it is usual to cut the game and not the hunter!'

O'wa cackled happily at the joke, and bent to the task. He took the bull's scrotum in his left hand and drew it out, then with a single stroke lopped it free.

'Ai! How sharp!' He laid the scrotum aside – the testicles grilled on the coals were a delicacy and the sac of soft skin would make a fine pouch for arrowheads and other small valuables.

Starting from the wound between the bull's hindlegs, he made a shallow cut through the skin, angling the blade forward so as not to pierce the belly cavity. He led the cut with his forefinger hooked under the skin, up between the bull's forelegs under its throat to the point of the chin. He made ring cuts around the bull's neck, and around the hocks of all four limbs, then sliced down the inside of the legs until he intercepted the first long lateral incision. With the women pulling on the white underside of the skin and the blue marbled muscles sheathed in their transparent capsules, they flayed the hide off the carcass in a single sheet. It made a soft, tearing crackling sound as it came away; they spread it out, fur-side down on the ground.

Then O'wa opened the stomach cavity with the precision of a surgeon, lifted out the heavy wet viscera and laid them on the sheet of skin.

H'ani scurried away and collected a bunch of the fine

pale desert grass. She had to range widely, for the clumps of grass were scattered and sparse. She hurried back and arranged the grass over the gourd bowl, while O'wa slit open the slippery white bag of the bull's rumen and lifted out a double handful of the contents. Water dribbled from the undigested vegetation even before O'wa began to squeeze it out.

Using the bunch of grass as a sieve, O'wa filled the gourd with fluid and then lifted it with both hands to his lips. He drank deeply, closing his eyes with ecstasy, and when he lowered the bowl, he belched thunderously and grinned hugely as he passed the gourd to H'ani. She drank noisily and finished with a belch and a hoot of appreciation, wiping her mouth on the back of her hand as she passed the gourd to Centaine.

Centaine examined the pale greenish-brown liquid. 'It's only vegetable juice,' she consoled herself. 'It hasn't even been chewed or mixed with gastric juices yet—' and she lifted the gourd.

It was much easier than she had anticipated, and it tasted like a broth of herbs and grass, with the bitter aftertaste of the bi tuber. She handed the empty gourd back to O'wa, and while he squeezed and strained the rest of the contents of the rumen, she imagined the long table at Mort Homme set with silver and crystal and Sèvres porcelain, and the way Anna fussed over the flowers, the freshness of the turbot, the temperature of the wine and the exact shade of pink of the slices of freshly carved *filet*, and she laughed aloud. She had come a long, long way from Mort Homme.

The two little San laughed with her in complete misunderstanding, and they all drank again and then again.

'Look at the child,' H'ani invited her husband. 'In this land of the singing sand I feared for her, but already she blooms like the desert flowers after the rain. She is a strong one, with the liver of a lion — did you see how she helped at the moment of the kill, by drawing the eye of the bull to herself?' H'ani nodded and cackled and belched. 'She will breed a fine son – you hear the word of old H'ani – a fine son indeed.'

O'wa, his belly ballooning with good water, grinned and was about to concede, when his eye dropped to the knife that lay between his feet, and the grin faded.

'Silly old woman, you chatter like the brainless spotted guinea fowl, while the meat spoils.' He snatched up the knife. Envy was an emotion so alien to his nature that O'wa was deeply unhappy and not really certain of the reason why, but the thought of handing the knife back to the girl filled him with a corrosive anger that he had never known before. He frowned and muttered as he dressed out the viscera of the bull, cutting thin slices of the rubbery white tripes and chewing them raw as he worked.

It was mid-morning before they had festooned the branches of one of the dead trees with long ribbons of bright scarlet gemsbok meat, and the heat built up so swiftly that the meat darkened and dried out almost immediately.

It was too hot to eat. Between them H'ani and Centaine spread the wet gemsbok skin over a framework of dead branches and they huddled under this tent-like structure, taking refuge from the sun, cooling their bodies with the evaporating fluids of the gemsbok's secondary stomach.

At sundown O'wa took out his fire sticks and began the laborious process of coaxing a spark from them, but impatiently Centaine took the ball of dry kindling from him. Up to that time she had always been too intimidated by the little San and her own feeling of total inadequacy to make any show of initiative. Now, somehow, the crossing of the dunes and her part in the gemsbok hunt emboldened her, and she laid out the kindling and the knife and flint with the San looking on curiously.

She struck a shower of sparks into the kindling and

stooped quickly to blow it into the flame. The San shrieked in amazement and consternation, and backed away in superstitious awe. Only once the fire was burning steadily could Centaine reassure them, and they crept back and marvelled over the steel and the flint. Under Centaine's tutelage, O'wa at last succeeded in striking sparks, and his joy was spontaneous and childlike.

As soon as the night brought relief from the heat of the sun, they prepared a feast of broiled liver and tripes and kidneys wrapped in the lacework of white fat that had enclosed the intestines. While the women worked at the fire, O'wa danced for the spirit of the gemsbok, and as he had promised, he leaped as high as he had done when he was a young man, and he sang until his voice cracked and failed. Then he squatted down at the fire and began to eat.

The two San ate with the fat greasing their chins and running down on to their cheeks; they ate until their stomachs were distended and bulged out like balloons, hanging down on their laps; they went on eating long after Centaine was gorged and satiated.

Every once in a while Centaine was sure they were faltering, as their jaws slowed and they blinked at each other like sleepy owls in the firelight. Then O'wa would place both hands on his bulging stomach and roll on to one buttock, his wrinkled face contorted, and he would grunt and strain until he was able to clap off a resounding fart. Across the fire, H'ani would answer him with a squealing blast every bit as ear-splitting, and they both hooted with laughter and crammed more meat into their mouths.

As Centaine drifted off into sleep with her own stomach stuffed with meat, she realized this orgy was a natural reaction of a people accustomed to privation faced suddenly with a mountain of food and no means of preserving it. When she woke at dawn they were still feasting.

With the sun the two San lay under the tent of gemsbok

hide, their bellies distended, and snored through the heat, but at sunset they blew up the fire and began feasting again. By this time what remained of the gemsbok was smelling high and strong, but this seemed if anything to stimulate their appetite.

When O'wa rose to stagger out of the firelight on private business, Centaine saw that his buttocks, which had been slack and sagging and wrinkled when they came down from the dunes, were now tight and round and polished.

'Just like a camel's hump,' Centaine giggled, and H'ani giggled with her and offered her a slice of the belly fat, cooked brown and crisp.

Once again they slept through the day like a nest of pythons digesting the gargantuan banquet, but at sunset with the carrying bags packed with the hard black strips of dried gemsbok meat, O'wa led them eastwards across the moonlit plain. He carried the folded gemsbok skin balanced on his head.

G radually the plain over which they travelled altered in character. Amongst the fine desert grasses there appeared scraggy little scrubs, not as high as Centaine's knee, and once O'wa stopped and pointed ahead at a tall ghostly shape that crossed with a high-stepping trot ahead of them in the night, a dark body fringed with fluffy white, and only as it disappeared into the shadows did Centaine realize that it was a wild ostrich.

At dawn O'wa spread the gemsbok hide as a sun shelter and they waited out the day. At sunset they drank the last drops of water from the egg-bottles, and the San were quiet and serious as they set out again. Without water, death was only hours away.

At dawn, instead of going into camp immediately, O'wa stood for a long time examining the sky, and then he ranged in a half-circle ahead of their track, like a gundog quartering for the bird, lifting his head, turning it slowly from side to side, his nostrils sucking at the air.

'What is O'wa doing?' Centaine asked.

'Smell.' H'ani snuffled to show her. 'Smell water.'

Centaine was incredulous. 'No smell water, H'ani.'

'Yes! Yes! Wait, you see.'

O'wa reached a decision. 'Come!' he beckoned, and the women snatched up their satchels and hurried after him. Within an hour Centaine realized that if O'wa was mistaken, then she was dead. The egg-bottles were empty, the heat and the sun were sucking the moisture out of her, and she would be finished before the real burning heat of noon fell upon them.

O'wa broke into a full run, the gait that the San called 'the horns', the run of the hunter when he sees the horns of his quarry on the skyline ahead, and the women under their burdens could not try to match him.

An hour later they made out his tiny form far ahead, and when they at last came up with him, he smiled a broad welcome and with a sweep of his arm announced grandly, 'O'wa has led you unerringly to the sip-wells of the elephant with one tusk.' The origins of the name were lost far back in the oral history of the San. O'wa swaggered shamelessly as he led them down the gentle slope of the river bed.

It was a wide water-course, but Centaine saw immediately that it was completely dry, filled with sand as loose and friable as that of the dune country, and she felt her spirits drop sharply as she looked about her.

The winding serpentine water-course was about a hundred paces wide, cutting through the gravel beds of the plain, and although there was no water, both banks were dark with much denser plant growth than the arid flats beyond. The scrub was almost waist-high, with an occasional dull green bush rising above the rest. The San were chattering brightly, and H'ani followed closely behind

402

her husband as he strutted about importantly in the sand of the river bed.

Centaine sank down, picked up a handful of the bright orange-coloured sand and let it trickle through her fingers disconsolately. Then for the first time she noticed that the river bed was widely trampled by the hooves of the gemsbok, and that in places the sand had been heaped as though children had been digging sandcastles. O'wa was now examining one of these piles critically, and Centaine dragged herself up and went to see what he had found. The gemsbok must have been digging in the river bed, but sand had trickled into the hole, almost filling it. O'wa nodded sagely, and he turned to H'ani.

'This is a good place. Here we will make our sip-well. Take the child and show her how to build a shelter.'

Centaine was so thirsty and heat-lashed that she felt dizzy and sick, but she slipped off the strap of her bag and wearily climbed the river bank after H'ani to help her cut whippy saplings and thorny branches from the scrub.

In the river bed they quickly erected two rudimentary shelters, sticking the saplings into the sand in a circle, bending them over to meet on top and roofing one of them with branches and the other with the stiff, stinking gemsbok skin. They were the most primitive shelters, without sides and floored with river sand, but Centaine flopped gratefully into the shade and watched O'wa.

Firstly he removed the poisoned heads from his arrows, handling them with elaborate care, for a single scratch would be fatal. He wrapped each arrowhead in a scrap of rawhide and packed them into one of the pouches on his belt.

Then he began to fit the reed arrows together, sealing the joints with a ball of acacia gum, until he had a single length of hollow reeds longer than he was tall.

'Help me, little flower of my life,' he sweetened H'ani blatantly, and with their hands they began to dig together in the sand. To prevent the sand running back into the hole, they made it funnel-shaped – wide at the top and gradually narrowing until O'wa's head and shoulders disappeared into it, and at last he started throwing up handfuls of darker, damp sand. Deeper still he dug, until H'ani had to hold him by the ankles while his entire body was jammed in the hole. At last, in response to muffled cries from the depths, she passed the long hollow reed down to him.

Upside down in the well, O'wa placed the open end of the reed carefully and then fitted a filter of twigs and leaves around the open end of it to prevent it becoming clogged. With both the women hauling on his ankles, they drew him out of the narrow well, and he emerged coated with orange sand. H'ani had to clean out his ears and brush it from the corms of his grey hair, and from his eyelashes.

Carefully, a handful at a time, O'wa refilled the well, leaving the filter and reed undisturbed, and when he was finished, he patted the sand down firmly, leaving a short length of the end of the reed pipe sticking out above the surface.

While O'wa put the finishing touches to his well, H'ani chose a green twig, stripped off the thorns and peeled it. Then she helped Centaine unplug the egg-bottles and set them out in a neat row beside the well.

O'wa stretched himself out, belly down on the sand, and placed his lips over the end of the reed tube. H'ani squatted beside him attentively, the row of egg-bottles within reach and the peeled green twig in her hand.

'I am ready, hunter of my heart!' she told him, and O'wa began to suck.

From under her shelter Centaine watched as O'wa turned himself into a human bellows; his chest swelled and subsided, seeming to double in size with each hissing intake of air, and then Centaine could sense the impediment of a heavy load in the tube. O'wa's eyes closed tightly, disappearing behind a network of baggy wrinkles, and his face darkened with effort to the colour of toffee. His body pumped and pulsated, he swelled like a bull frog and shrank and swelled again, straining to draw a heavy weight up the long thin reed tube.

Suddenly he made a mewing sound in his throat without breaking the rhythm of his powerful suctions, and H'ani leaned forward and gently fitted the peeled twig into the corner of his mouth. A diamond-bright drop of water bubbled out between O'wa's lips and slid down the twig; it quivered on the tip for an instant and then dropped into the egg-bottles that H'ani held below it.

'Good water, singer of my soul,' H'ani encouraged him. 'Good sweet water!' And the flow from the old man's mouth became a steady silver dribble, as he sucked it in and let it run on the exhale.

The effort required was enormous, for O'wa was lifting the water over six feet, and Centaine watched in awe as he filled one egg-bottle, then another, and still a third without pause.

H'ani squatted over him, tending him, encouraging him, adjusting the twig and the bottles, cooing to him softly, and suddenly Centaine was struck with a strange feeling of empathy for this pair of little old people. She realized how they had been forged by joy and tragedy and unremitting hardship into a union so fast and strong that they were almost a single entity. She saw how the hard years had gifted them with humour and sensitivity and simple wisdom and fortitude, but most of all with love, and she envied them without rancour.

'If only,' she thought, 'if only I could be bound to another human being as these two are bound to each other!' And in that moment she realized that she had come to love them.

At last O'wa rolled away from the tube and lay gasping and panting and shaking like a marathon runner when the race is run, and H'ani brought one of the egg-bottles to Centaine.

'Drink, Nam Child,' she offered it to Centaine.

Almost reluctantly, achingly aware of the effort that had gone into reaping each priceless drop, Centaine drank.

She drank sparingly, piously, and then handed the bottle back.

'Good water, H'ani,' she said. Though it was brackish and mingled with the old man's saliva, Centaine now understood completely that the San definition of 'good water' was any fluid which would sustain life in the desert.

She rose and went to where O'wa lay in the sand.

'Good water, O'wa.' She knelt beside him, and she saw how the effort had drained him, but he grinned up at her and bobbed his head, still too tired to rise.

'Good water, Nam Child,' he agreed.

Centaine unfastened the lanyard from around her waist and held the knife in both hands. It had saved her life already. It might do so again in the hard days ahead, if she kept it.

'Take, O'wa,' she offered it to him. 'Knife for O'wa.'

He stared at the knife, and the dark, blood-suffused tones of his wrinkled face paled, and a great devastation seemed to empty all expression from his eyes.

'Take, O'wa,' Centaine urged him.

'It is too much,' he whispered, staring at the knife with stricken eyes. It was a gift without price.

Centaine reached out, took his wrist and turned his hand upwards. She placed the knife in his hand and folded his fingers over it. Sitting in the harsh sunlight with the knife in his hand, O'wa's chest heaved as powerfully as it had as he drew water from the sip-well, and a tear welled out of the corner of one eye and ran down the deep groove alongside his nose.

'Why are you weeping, you silly old man?' H'ani demanded.

'I weep for joy of this gift.' O'wa tried to maintain dignity, but his voice choked.

'That is a stupid reason to weep,' H'ani told him, and twinkled mischievously as she covered her laughter with one slim, graceful old hand.

They followed the dry river bed into the east, but now the urgency that had accompanied their night marches through the dune country was left behind them, for there was good water under the sand.

They travelled from before sunrise until the heat drove them into shelter, and then from late afternoon until after dark; the pace was leisurely for they foraged and hunted on the march.

H'ani cut a special digging stick for Centaine, peeled it and hardened the point in the fire, and showed her how to use it. Within a few short days Centaine was recognizing the surface indications of many of the edible and useful tubers and plants. It soon became evident that though O'wa was so adept in the bushcraft and lore of the desert and that although his hunting and tracking skills were almost supernatural, it was the foraging and gathering of the women that provided their little clan with the staples of life. In the days and weeks when game was scarce or simply non-existent, they lived on the plants which the two of them brought into camp.

Although Centaine learned swiftly and her young eyes were hawk-sharp, she knew that she would never be able to match the innate knowledge and gifts of perception of the old woman. H'ani could find the plants and insects that gave no sign on the surface of their hiding-place deep down in the earth, and when she dug the hard dirt flew in all directions.

'How do you do it?' Centaine could at last demand, for

407

her command of the San language increased every day she spent listening and responding to the old woman's chatter.

'Like O'wa found the sip-wells from afar,' H'ani explained. 'I smell it, Nam Child. Smell! Use your nose!'

'You tease me, revered old grandmother!' Centaine protested, but she watched H'ani carefully after that, and she saw that she indeed gave every indication of smelling out the deep nests of termites to raid them of the crumbling white ant 'bread' which she made into a foul-tasting but nutritious porridge.

'Just like Kaiser Wilhelm,' Centaine marvelled, and she called to H'ani *'Cherche!'* the way that she and Anna had called to the gross boar when they had hunted truffles in the forest at Mort Homme.

'Cherche, H'ani!' and the old woman laughed and hugged herself with glee at the joke she did not understand, and then quite casually produced a miracle.

She and Centaine had fallen behind O'wa on the evening stage of the journey, for the old man had gone ahead to search for an ostrich nesting ground that he remembered from his last visit many years before.

The two of them were arguing amiably.

'No, no! Nam Child, you must not dig two roots from the same place. You must always walk past one before you dig again – I have told you that before!' H'ani scolded.

'Why?' Centaine straightened up and pushed the thick bushy curls off her forehead, leaving a sweaty smear of mud on her face.

'You must leave one for the children.'

'Silly old woman, there are no children.'

'There will be—' H'ani pointed at Centaine's belly significantly. 'There will be. And if we leave nothing for them, what will they say of us when they are starving?'

'But there are so many plants!' Centaine was exasperated.

'When O'wa finds the nest of the ostrich, he will leave

some of the eggs. When you find two tubers, you will leave one of them, and your son will grow strong and smile when he repeats your name to his children.'

H'ani broke off from her lecture and scurried forward to a bare, stony patch on the bank of the dry river bed, her nose twitching as she stooped to examine the earth.

'*Cherche*, H'ani!' Centaine laughed at her, and H'ani laughed back as she started to dig, and then she dropped to her knees and lifted something from the shallow excavation.

'This is the first one you have seen, Nam Child. Smell it. It tastes very good.'

She handed the lumpy, dirt-crusted, potato-like tuber to Centaine, and Centaine sniffed it gingerly, and her eyes flew wide open at the well-remembered aroma. Quickly she wiped the clinging dirt from the lumpy surface and bit into it.

'H'ani, you old darling,' she cried. 'It's a truffle! A real truffle. It's not the same shape or colour, but it smells and tastes just like the truffles from our own land!'

O'wa had found his ostrich nests and Centaine whipped one of the eggs in its own half-shell and mixed in the chopped truffles and cooked an enormous *omelette aux truffes* on a flat stone heated in the camp fire.

Despite the dirt from Centaine's fingers, which gave it a faintly greyish colour, and the grains of sand and egg-shell chips that crunched under their teeth, they ate it with relish.

It was only afterwards as she lay under the primitive roof of twigs and leaves, that Centaine gave in to the homesickness which the taste of truffles had invoked, and she buried her face in the crook of her arm to muffle her sobs.

'Oh, Anna – I would give anything, anything at all just to see your lovely ugly old face again.'

As they followed the dry river bed, and the weeks turned into months, so Centaine's unborn child grew strongly.

With her sparse but healthy diet and the daily exercise of walking and digging and carrying and reaching, the child never grew big and she carried it high, but her breasts filled out and sometimes when she was alone, scrubbing her body with the juicy pith of the bi tuber, she looked down at them proudly and admired the jaunty upward tilt of the rosy tips.

'I wish you could see them now, Anna,' she murmured. 'You couldn't tell me I still look like a boy. But as always you'd complain about my legs, too long and thin and with hard muscles – oh, Anna, I wonder where you are.'

One morning at sunrise when they had already been travelling for many hours, Centaine stopped on the top of a low rise and looked around her slowly.

The air was still cool from the night and so clear that she could see to the horizon. Later, with the heat, it would thicken to an opaline translucence and the sun would drain all colour from the landscape. The heat mirage would close in around her, and shapes would be weirdly deformed, the most mundane groups of rocks or clump of vegetation transformed into quivering monsters.

Now they were sharp-edged and rich with their true colours. The undulating plains were hazed with pale silver grasses, and there were trees, real, living trees, not those heat-struck ancient mummies that had stood upon the plains below the dunes.

These stately camel-thorn acacias grew well separated. Their massive trunks, clad in rough crocodile-skin bark, were at odds with the wide umbrella-shaped crown of airy and delicate silvery-green foliage. In the nearest of them a colony of sociable weavers had built a communal nest the size of a haystack, each generation of these insignificant, dun-coloured little birds adding to it, until one day the weight would be too much and would split the great tree. Centaine had seen others lying on the earth beneath the shattered acacia, still attached to the supporting branches and stinking with carcasses of hundreds of fledglings and broken eggs.

Beyond this open forest there were steep hills rising abruptly out of the plain, the kopjes of Africa, riven by wind and split by the sun's heat into geometrical shapes as hard-edged as dragons' teeth. The soft light of the early sun struck hues of sepia and red and bronze from their rocky walls, and the antediluvian kokerboom trees with their fleshy trunks and palm-like heads crowned their summits.

Centaine paused and leaned upon her digging stick, awed by the harsh grandeur of the scene. Upon the dust-coloured plain grazed herds of dainty antelope. They were pale as smoke and as insubstantial, graceful little animals with lyre-shaped horns, the lovely bright cinnamon brown of their backs divided from the snow white lower parts by a lateral band of chocolate red.

As Centaine watched, the nearest antelopes took fright at the human presence, and began stotting, the characteristic alarm behaviour that gave them their name of springbok. They lowered their heads until their muzzles almost touched their four bunched hooves and shot stiff-legged straight into the air, at the same time opening the long folded pouch of skin that ran down their backs and flashing the feather mane of white hair that it concealed.

'Oh, look at them, H'ani!' Centaine cried. 'They are so beautiful.'

The alarm stotting was wildly infectious, and across the plain hundreds of springbok bounced on high, with white manes flashing.

O'wa dropped his burden, lowered his head and imitated

411

them perfectly, prancing stiff-legged, flicking his fingers over his back, so that he seemed transformed into one of the fleet little antelope, and the two women were so overcome with laughter that they had to sit down and hug each other. The joy of it lasted long after the mountains had receded into the heat mists, and it alleviated the crushing misery of the noonday sun.

During those long halts in the middle of the day, O'wa took to separating himself from the women, and Centaine became accustomed to seeing his tiny figure sitting crosslegged in the shade of an adjacent camel-thorn tree, scraping with the clasp knife at the gemsbok skin that was spread across his lap. He carried the skin carefully folded and rolled into a bundle on his head during the day's march, and once when Centaine had begun to examine it casually, O'wa had become so agitated that she quickly placated him.

'I meant no harm, old grandfather.'

But her curiosity had been piqued. The old man was a craftsman, and usually he was delighted to show off his handiwork. He had not protested when Centaine watched as he split the pliable yellow bark off the trunk of a kokerboom tree, rolled it into a quiver to hold his spare arrows and decorated it with designs of birds and animals burned into the bark with a coal from the campfire.

He showed her how to shape arrowheads from hard white bone by patiently grinding them against a flat stone, and Centaine was surprised at the keenness of the cutting edges and the points. He even took Centaine with him when he went out to hunt for the grubs from which he made the arrow poisons which had brought down the great gemsbok bull, and which could kill a man within hours. She helped him dig beneath a particular type of scrub and pick out of the dirt the brown pellet-like capsules which were the chrysalis in which the fat white grubs of the embryo *diamphidia* beetle were enclosed.

Handling the insects with elaborate caution, for the minutest quantity of their body juice entering through a scratch would mean lingering but certain death, O'wa pounded them to paste which he thickened with the juice of the wild sansevieria plant before dressing his arrowheads with the sticky mixture. From the sansevieria he separated the fibres from which he braided the twine to bind the arrowhead to the shaft.

He even allowed Centaine to watch while he whittled a primitive pen-like flute on which he accompanied himself with piercing blasts when he danced, or while he carved the decorations into the heavy throwing stick which he used to knock the rocketing coqui francolin out of the air in a puff of pretty feathers or the blue-headed lizards from the uppermost branches of the camel-thorn trees – but when he worked on the gemsbok skin he went off to a discreet distance and he worked alone.

The river of sand which they had followed for so long finally contorted into a series of tight bends, like the convulsions of a dying adder, and then abruptly ended in a dry pan, so wide that the trees on the far side were merely a dark wavering line on the horizon. The surface of the pan was white with crystals of evaporated salts. The reflection of the noon sun from this surface was painful to look at directly, and it turned the sky above it to pale silver. The Bushmen's name for it was 'the big white place'.

On the steep bank of the pan they built shelters sturdier and better thatched than any of the others had been, giving an air of permanence to the camp, and the two little San settled down to an undemanding routine, albeit with an underlying air of expectancy which Centaine detected and queried.

'Why do we stop here, H'ani?' Each uneventful day made her more impatient and restless.

'We wait to make the crossing,' was all that the old woman would tell her.

'Crossing to where? Where are we going?' Centaine insisted, but H'ani became vague and pointed in a wide arc into the east, and answered with a name that Centaine could only translate as 'a place were nothing must die'.

Centaine's child grew strongly within her pouting belly. Sometimes it was difficult to breathe, and almost impossible to be comfortable on the bare ground. She made herself a nest of soft desert grass in her little sun shelter, which amused the two old people. For them the bare earth was bed enough, and they used their own shoulders as pillows.

Centaine lay in her nest and tried to count the days and months since she and Michael had been together, but time was blurred and telescoped so that all she could be sure of was that her time would be upon her soon. H'ani confirmed her estimate, probing her belly with gentle, knowing fingers.

'The baby rides high and fights to be free. It will be a boy, Nam Child,' she promised, and took Centaine off into the desert to gather special herbs that they would need for the birthing.

Unlike many Stone Age peoples, the San were fully aware of the processes of procreation and saw sexual intercourse not as an isolated and random act, but as the first step in the long voyage to birth.

'Where is the father of your growing infant, Nam Child?'

H'ani asked, and when she saw the tears in Centaine's eyes she answered herself softly. 'He is dead in the north lands at the ends of the earth. Is that not so?'

'How did you know that I came from the north?' Centaine asked, glad to turn away from the pain of Michael's memory.

'You are big – bigger than any of the San of the desert,' H'ani explained. 'Therefore you must come from a rich land where living is easy, a land of good rains and plentiful food.' To the old woman water was all of life. 'The rain winds come from the north, so you also must come from the north.'

Intrigued by her logic, Centaine smiled. 'And how did you know I was from far away?'

'Your skin is pale, not darkened like the skin of the San. Here in the centre of the world the sun stands overhead, but it never goes north or south, and in the east and west it is low and wasting, so you must come from far away where the sun lacks the warmth and strength to darken your skin.'

'Do you know of other people like me, H'ani, big people with pale skins? Have you ever before seen people like me?' Centaine asked eagerly, and when she saw the shift in the old woman's gaze, she seized her arm. 'Tell me, wise old grandmother, where have you seen my people? In what direction, and how far away? Would I be able to reach them? Please tell me.'

H'ani's eyes clouded with a film of incomprehension and she picked a grain of dried mucus from her nostril and examined it with minute attention.

'Tell me, H'ani.' Centaine shook her arm gently.

'I have heard the old people talk of such things,' H'ani grudgingly admitted, 'but I have never seen these people, and I do not know where they could be found.' And Centaine knew she was lying. Then, in a sudden vehement gabble, H'ani went on. 'They are fierce as lions and poisonous as the scorpion, the San hide from them—' She jumped up in agitation, seized her satchel and digging stick and hurried from the camp and did not return until sunset.

That night after Centaine had curled in her grass bed, H'ani whispered to O'wa. 'The child yearns for her own people.'

'I have seen her look southwards with sadness in her eyes,' O'wa admitted.

'How many days' travel to reach the land of the pale giants?' H'ani asked reluctantly. 'How far to travel to her own clan?'

'Less than a moon,' O'wa grunted, and they were both silent for a long time, staring into the hot bluish flames of the camel-thorn log fire.

'I want to hear a baby cry once more before I die,' H'ani said at last and O'wa nodded. And both their little heart-shaped faces turned towards the east. They stared out into the darkness, towards the Place of All Life.

Once when H'ani found Centaine kneeling alone and praying in the wilderness, she asked, 'Who are you speaking to, Nam Child?' and Centaine was at a loss, for though the San language was rich and complex in its descriptive powers of the material aspects of the desert world, it was extremely difficult to use it to convey abstract ideas.

However, after long discussion spread over many days while they foraged in the desert or worked over the cooking fire, Centaine managed to describe her concept of the Godhead, and H'ani nodded dubiously and mumbled and frowned as she considered it.

'You are talking to the spirits?' she asked. 'But most of the spirits live in the stars, and if you speak so softly, how will they hear you? It is necessary to dance and sing and whistle loudly to attract their attention.' She lowered her voice. 'And it is even then not certain they will listen to you, for I have found the star spirits to be fickle and forgetful.' H'ani glanced around her like a conspirator. 'It is my experience, Nam Child, that Mantis and Eland are much more reliable.'

'Mantis and Eland?' Centaine tried not to show her amusement.

'Mantis is an insect with huge eyes that see all and with arms like a little man. Eland is an animal – oh, yes, much larger than the gemsbok, with a dewlap so full of rich fat that it sweeps the earth.' The San's love of fat was almost equal to their love of wild honey. 'And twisted horns that sweep the sky. If we are fortunate we will find both Mantis and Eland at the place to which we are going. In the meantime, talk to the stars, Nam Child, for they are beautiful, but put your trust in Mantis and Eland.'

Thus simply H'ani explained the religion of the San, and that night she and Centaine sat under a brilliant sky and she pointed out Orion's glittering train.

'That is the herd of celestial zebras, Nam Child – and there is the inept huntsman,' she picked out the star Aldebaran, 'sent by his seven wives,' she stabbed a gnarled finger at the Pleiades, 'to find meat. See how he has shot his arrow, and it has flown high and wide to fall at the feet of Lion Star.' Sirius, the brightest of all the fixed stars, seemed truly lionlike. 'And now the huntsman is afraid to retrieve his arrow and afraid to return to his seven wives, and he sits there for ever twinkling with fear, which is just like a man, Nam Child.' H'ani hooted with laughter, and dug her bony thumb into her husband's scrawny ribs.

Because the San were also star-lovers, Centaine's bond of affection for them was so strengthened that she pointed out Michael's star and her own in the far south.

'But, Nam Child,' O'wa protested, 'how can that star belong to you? It belongs to no one and to everybody, like

417

the shade of the camel-thorn, and the water in the desert pool, or the land on which we tread – to nobody and yet to everybody. Nobody owns the eland, but we may take of his fat if we have need. Nobody owns the big plants but we may gather them on condition that we leave some for the children. How can you say that a star belongs to you alone?' It was an expression of the philosophy which was the tragedy of his people, a denial of the existence of property which had doomed them to merciless persecution, to massacre and slavery or to exile in the far reaches of the desert where no other people could exist.

So the monotonous days of waiting were passed in discussion and the leisurely routine of hunting and foraging, and then one evening both the San were galvanized by excitement and they faced into the north with their little amber faces turned up to a sky that was the flawless blue of a heron's egg.

It took Centaine a few minutes to discover what had excited them, and then she saw the cloud. It groped up over the rim of the northern horizon like the finger of a gargantuan hand, and it grew as she watched it, the top of it flattened into an anvil shape, and the distant thunder growled like a hunting lion. Soon the cloud stood tall and heaven-high, burning with the colours of the sunset and lit with its own wondrous internal lightnings.

That night O'wa danced and whistled and sang the praises of the cloud spirits until at last he collapsed with exhaustion, but in the morning the thunderhead had dispersed.

However, the sky had changed from unsullied blue, and there were streaks of high mare's-tails cirrus smeared across it. The air itself seemed also to have changed. It was charged with static that made Centaine's skin prickle, and the heat was heavy and languorous, even harder to bear than the dry harsh noons had been, and the thunderheads climbed above the northern horizon and tossed their monstrous billowing heads to the sky.

Each day they grew taller and more numerous, and they massed in the north like a legion of giants and marched southward, while an enervating blanket of humid air lay upon the earth and smothered it and everything upon it.

'Please let it rain,' Centaine whispered each day, while the sweat snaked down her cheeks and the child weighted her womb like an ironstone boulder.

In the night O'wa danced and sang.

'Spirit of Cloud, see how the earth waits for you the way that a great cow eland in heat trembles for the bull. Come down from on high, Spirit of Cloud whom we venerate, and spill your generative fluids upon your earth wife. Mount your lover and from your seed she will bring forth new life in abundance.' And when H'ani trilled and piped the chorus, Centaine cried out just as fervently.

One morning there was no sun, the clouds stretched in a solid grey mass from horizon to horizon. Low to begin with, they sank lower still, and a stupendous bolt of lightning tore from their great grey sowlike belly and clanged upon the earth so that it seemed to jump beneath their feet. A single raindrop struck Centaine in the centre of her forehead, and it was as heavy as a stone, so that she reeled back at the shock of it and cried out in astonishment.

Then the hanging clouds burst open and the rain fell from them thick as locusts. Each drop as it struck the surface of the pan rolled into a globule of mud, or made the wiry scrub branches around the edge jump and quiver as though flocks of invisible birds had alighted upon them.

The rain stung Centaine's skin, and one drop struck her in the eye and blinded her for a second. She blinked it clear and laughed to see O'wa and H'ani capering across the pan. They had thrown aside their meagre clothing and they danced naked in the rain. Each drop burst in a silver puff upon their wrinkled amber skin and they howled delightedly at the pricks of it.

Centaine ripped off her own canvas skirt, threw aside the shawl, and mother-naked stood with her arms thrown open and her face turned to the clouds. The rain thrashed her, and melted her long dark hair down across her face and shoulders. She pushed it aside with both hands and opened her mouth wide.

It was as though she stood under a waterfall. The rain poured into her mouth as fast as she could swallow. The far edge of the pan disappeared behind the blue veils of falling rain, and the surface turned to yellow mud.

The rain was so cold that a rash of goose bumps ran down Centaine's forearms and her nipples darkened and hardened, but she laughed with joy and ran out to the pan to dance with the San, and the thunder sounded as though massive boulders were rolling across the roof of the sky.

The earth seemed to dissolve under the solid sheets of silver water. The pan was ankle-deep and the silky mud squelched up between Centaine's toes. The rain gave them new life and strength and they danced and sang until O'wa stopped abruptly and cocked his head to listen.

Centaine could hear nothing above the thunder and the lash of the rain, but O'wa shouted a warning. They floundered to the steep bank of the pan, slipping in the glutinous mud and the yellow waters which by now reached to their knees. From the bank Centaine heard the sound which had alarmed O'wa, a low rushing like a high wind in tall trees.

'The river,' O'wa pointed through the thick palisade of silver rain, 'the river is alive again.'

It came like a living thing, a monstrous frothing yellow python down the sandy river bed, and it hissed from bank to bank, carrying the bodies of drowned animals and the branches of trees in its flood. It burst into the flooded pan and raced in serried waves across the surface, breaking on the bank beneath their feet, swirling on to catch them around the legs and threatening to drag them under.

They snatched up their few possessions and waded to higher ground, clinging to each other for support. The rain clouds brought on premature night, and it was cold. There was no chance of a fire and they huddled together for warmth and shivered miserably.

The rain fell without slackening all that night.

In the dull leaden dawn they looked across a drowned landscape, a vast shimmering lake with islands of higher ground from which the water streamed, and stranded acacia trees like the backs of whales.

'Will it never stop?' Centaine whispered. Her teeth chattered uncontrollably, and the chill seemed to have to reached into her womb, for the infant writhed and kicked in protest.

'Please let it stop now.' The San suffered the cold with the fortitude they showed for all hardship. Rather than slackening, the rain seemed to increase in tempo, and hid the sorry drowned land from them behind a glassy curtain.

Then the rain stopped. There was no warning, no faltering or tapering off; one second it was falling in a solid cascade and the next it was over. The ceiling of low bruised cloud split open and peeled away like the skin from a ripe fruit, revealing the clean washed blue of the sky, and the sun burst upon them with blinding brilliance, once more stunning Centaine with the sudden contrasts of this wild continent.

Before noon, the thirsty earth had drunk down the waters that had fallen upon it. The floods sank away without trace. Only in the pan itself surface water still lay glittering sulphurous-yellow from bank to far bank. However, the land was cleansed and vivid with colour. The dust that had coated each bush and tree was washed away and Centaine saw greens that she had never dreamed this tan, lion-coloured land could contain. The earth, still damp, was rich with ochres and oranges and reds and the songs of the little desert larks were joyous.

They laid out their scant possessions in the sun and they steamed as they dried. O'wa could not contain himself and he danced ecstatically.

'The cloud spirits have opened the road for us. They have replenished the water-holes to the east. Make ready, H'ani, my little flower of the desert: before the dawn tomorrow we will march.'

Within the first day's march they entered a new country, so different that Centaine could scarcely believe it was on the same continent. Here the ancient dunes had compacted and consolidated into gentle undulations, and they now supported abundant plant life.

Stands of mopani and tall kiaat, alternating with almost impenetrable thickets of paper-bark, stood tall along the ridges of high ground where the dunes' crests had weathered and flattened. Occasionally a giant silver terminalia or a monumental baobab soared seventy feet above the rest of the forest.

In the valleys, fields of sweet golden grasses and scattered giraffe acacias with flat tops gave the scene a park-like and cultivated aspect. Here also, in the lowest depressions, the recent rains had been trapped in the shallow water-holes, and the land seemed to hum and seethe with life.

Through the yellow grasses fresh tender shoots of delicate green appeared. Gardens of wild flowers, daisies and arum lilies and gladioli and fifty other varieties which Centaine did not recognize, sprang up as though at a magician's flourish, delighting her with their colours and delicate beauty, and causing her to wonder anew at Africa's prolificness. She picked the blooms and plaited them into necklaces for herself and H'ani, and the old woman preened like a bride.

'Oh, I wish I had a mirror to show you how adorable you look.' Centaine embraced her.

Even from the sky Africa gave of her abundance. There were flocks of quelea thick as hiving bees as they wheeled overhead, shrikes in the undergrowth with chests of purest glowing ruby, sandgrouse and francolin fat as domestic chickens, and water fowl on the brimming water-holes, wild duck and long-legged stilts and gaunt blue heron.

'It's all so beautiful,' Centaine exulted. Each day's journey was light and carefree after the hardships of the arid western plains, and when they camped, there was the untold luxury of unlimited water and a feast of wild fruits and nuts and game from O'wa's snares and arrows.

One evening O'wa climbed high into the swollen fleshy branches of a monstrous baobab and smoked the hive that had inhabited its hollow trunk since his great-grandfather's time and beyond. He came down with a gourd full of thick waxen combs running with dark honey redolent of the perfume of the yellow acacia blossoms.

Each day they met new species of wild animals: sable antelope, black as night with long scimitar horns that swept back almost to their hind quarters, and Cape buffalo with mournful drooping heads of massively bossed horn stinking like herds of domestic cattle.

'They have come down from the big river and the swamps,' O'wa explained. 'They follow the water, and when it dries again they will go back into the north.'

In the night Centaine woke to a new sound infinitely more fearsome than the yelping of the black-backed jackal or the maniacal screams and sobs of the hyena packs. It was a storm of sound that filled the darkness, rising to an impossible crescendo and then dying away in a series of deep grunts. Centaine scrambled out of her little hut and ran to H'ani.

'What was that, old grandmother? It is a sound to turn the belly to water!' Centaine found she was trembling and the old woman hugged her.

'Even the bravest of men trembles the first time he hears the roar of the lion,' she placated her. 'But do not fear, Nam Child, O'wa has made a charm to protect us. The lion will find other game tonight.'

But they crowded close to the fire all the rest of the night, feeding it with fresh logs, and it was obvious that H'ani had as little faith in her husband's magical charms as Centaine did.

The lion pride circled their camp site, keeping at the very limit of the firelight so that Centaine caught only an occasional pale flicker of movement amongst the dark, encroaching bushes, but with the dawn their dreadful chorus receded as they moved away into the east, and when O'wa showed her the huge catlike pawmarks in the soft earth, he was garrulous with relief.

Then on the ninth morning after they had left the pan of 'the big white place', they were approaching another water-hole through the open mopani forests when ahead of them there was a crack like a shot of cannon and they all froze.

'What is it, H'ani?' But she waved Centaine to silence, and now she heard the crackle of breaking undergrowth and then suddenly a ringing blast of sound clear as a trumpet call.

Quickly O'wa tested the wind as Centaine had seen him do at the beginning of every hunt, and then he led them in a wide stealthy circuit through the forest until he stopped again beneath the spreading glossy green foliage of a tall mopani tree where he laid aside his weapons and his pack.

'Come!' he signalled to Centaine and, swiftly as a

424

monkey, shinned up the trunk. Hardly hampered at all by her fruitful belly, Centaine followed him into the tree and from a fork in the top branches looked down into the valley of grassland beyond and the water-hole that it contained in its shallow bottom.

'Elephant!' She recognized the huge grey beasts instantly. They were streaming down the far slope of the valley towards the water, striding out with their ponderous rolling gait, heads swinging so that their enormous ears flapped, and their trunks rolling and reaching reflexively as they anticipated the sweet taste of water.

There were rangy old queens with tattered earlobes and the knuckles of their spines sticking out of their gaunt backs, young bulls with yellow ivories, tuskless youngsters, boisterous unweaned calves running to keep up with their dams and, at their head, the herd bull strode majestically.

He stood over ten feet tall at the shoulder and he was scarred and grey, thick baggy skin hanging from his knees and bunched between his back legs. His ears were spread like the mainsail of a tall ship, and his tusks were twice as long and thick as any of his lesser bulls.

He seemed aged and yet ageless, huge and rugged, possessed of a grandeur and mystery which seemed to Centaine to contain the very essence of this land.

Lothar De La Rey cut the spoor of the elephant herd three days after they had left the Cunene river, and he and his Ovambo trackers studied it carefully, spreading out and circling over the trodden earth like gundogs. When they assembled again, Lothar nodded at his headman.

'Speak, Hendrick.' The Ovambo was as tall as Lothar, but heavier in the shoulders. His skin was dark and smooth as molten chocolate.

'A good herd,' Hendrick gave his opinion, 'forty cows, many with calf, eight young bulls.' The dark turban of the warrior was wound around his proud head, and garlands of necklaces strung with trade beads hung down on to his muscular chest, but he wore riding breeches and a bandolier of ammunition over one shoulder.

'And the herd bull is so old that his pads are smooth, so old that he can no longer chew his food and his dung is coarse with bark and twigs. He walks heavily on his forelegs, his ivory weighs him down, he is a bull to follow,' Hendrick said, and shifted the Mauser rifle into his right hand and hefted it in anticipation.

'The spoor is windblown,' Lothar pointed out quietly, 'and scratched over by insect and quail. Three days old.'

'They are feeding,' Hendrick opened his arms, 'spread out, moving slowly, the calves slow them down.'

'We will have to send the horses back,' Lothar persisted. 'We cannot risk them in the tsetse fly. Can we catch them on foot?'

Lothar unknotted his scarf and wiped his face thoughtfully. He needed that ivory. He had ridden north to the Cunene as soon as his scouts had sent him word that good rains had fallen. He knew that the new growth and surface water would lure the herds across the river out of Portuguese territory.

'On foot we can make them in two days,' Hendrick promised, but he was a notorious optimist and Lothar teased him.

'And at each night's camp we will find ten pretty Herero girls each carrying a beerpot on her head waiting for us.'

Hendrick threw back his head and laughed his deep growling laugh. 'Three days then,' he conceded with a chuckle, 'and perhaps only one Herero girl, but very beautiful and obliging.'

Lothar pondered the chances a moment longer. It was a good bull, and the younger bulls would all carry mature

426

ivory; even the cows would yield twenty pounds each, and ivory was commanding 22s 6d a pound.

He had twelve of his best men with him, though two would have to be sent back with the horses, but there were still enough riflemen to do the job. If they could come up with the herd they had a good chance of killing every animal that showed ivory.

Lothar De La Rey was flat broke. He had lost his family fortune, he had been declared a traitor and an outlaw for continuing the fight after the surrender of Colonel Franke, and there was a price on his head. Perhaps this would be his very last chance to repair his fortune. He knew the British well enough to realize that when the war was over, they would turn their attention to administering the new territories that they had won. Soon there would be district commissioners and officers in even the remotest areas, enforcing every detail of the law and paying special attention to the illegal hunting of ivory. The old free-booting days were probably numbered. This could be his last hunt.

'Send back the horses!' he ordered. 'Take the spoor!'

Lothar wore light hunting veldskoen. His men were all tempered and hardened by long years of war, and they ran on the spoor, taking it in turns to come to the front and take the point, then dropping back to rest as another man hit the front.

They entered the fly-belt in the late afternoon, and the vicious little tsetse swarmed out of the shade of the forest to plague them, settling light-footed on their backs to drive their blood-sucking probosces deep into the flesh. The men cut switches of green leaves and brushed the tsetse off each other's backs as they ran. By nightfall they had gained two days on the herd, and the spoor was so fresh that the ant-lions had not yet built their tiny funnel-shaped traps in the crisply trodden pad marks.

Darkness stopped them. They lay on the hard earth and

slept like a pack of hounds, but when the moon climbed over the tops of the mopani trees, Lothar kicked them to their feet. The slant of moonlight was in their favour, outlining the spoor with a rim of shadow, and the raw trunks of the mopani trees, from which the feeding elephant had stripped the bark, shone like mirrors to guide them through the night, and when the sun rose they lengthened their stride.

An hour after sunrise they suddenly ran out of the tsetse-fly belt. The territory of these little winged killers was sharply demarcated; the border could be crossed in a hundred paces, from swarming multitudes to complete relief. The swollen itching lumps on the back of their necks were the only souvenirs of their onslaught.

Two hours before noon, they reached a good water-hole in one of the valleys of the mopani forest. They were only hours behind the herd.

'Drink quickly,' Lothar ordered, and waded knee-deep into the filthy water which the bathing elephant had churned to the colour of *café au lait*. He filled his hat and poured the water over his own head. His thick, red-gold locks streamed down over his face, and he snorted with pleasure. The water was acrid and bitter with the salt of the elephant urine – the beasts always emptied their bladders at the shock of cold water – but the hunters drank and refilled the water-bottles.

'Quickly,' Lothar chivvied them, keeping his voice low, for sound carries in the bush and the herd was very close.

'Baas!' Hendrick signalled him urgently, and Lothar waded to the edge of the pool, and skirted it quickly.

'What is it?'

Wordlessly the big Ovambo pointed at the ground. The spoor was perfectly imprinted in the stiff yellow clay, and it was so fresh that it overlaid that of the elephant herd; water was still seeping into the indentations.

'Men!' Lothar exclaimed. 'Men have been here since the herd left.'

Hendrick corrected him harshly. 'San, not men. The little yellow cattle-killers.' The Ovambo were herdsmen, their cattle were their treasure and their deep love. 'The desert dogs who cut the teats off the udders of our finest cows,' the traditional revenge of the San for the atrocities committed upon them, 'they are only minutes ahead of us. We could catch them within the hour.'

'The sound of gunfire would carry to the herd.' Lothar shared his headman's hatred of the Bushmen. They were dangerous vermin, cattle-thieves and killers. His own great-uncle had been killed during one of the great Bushmen hunts of fifty years before; a tiny bone-tipped arrow had found the chink in his rawhide armour, and family history had recorded his death in every excruciating detail.

Even the English with their sickly sentimentality towards the black races had realized that there was no place in this twentieth-century world for the San. The standing orders of Cecil Rhodes' famous British South Africa Police contained instructions that all San and wild dogs encountered on patrol were to be shot out of hand. The two species were considered as one.

Lothar was tempted, torn between the pleasure of performing the public service of following and destroying the pack of San, and of mending his own fortune by following the elephant.

'The ivory,' he decided. 'No, the ivory is more important than culling a few yellow baboons.'

'Baas – here!' Hendrick had moved around the edge of the pool and stopped abruptly. His tone and the alert set of his head made Lothar hurry to him, and then sit quickly on his heels, the better to examine this new set of prints.

'Not San!' Hendrick whispered. 'Too big.'

'But a woman,' Lothar replied. The narrow foot and

small shapely toe marks were unmistakable. 'A young woman.' The toe marks were deeper than the heel, a springy step, a young step.

'It is not possible!' Hendrick sank down beside him and without touching the print traced the arched portion between ball and heel. Lothar sat back and shook his wet dangling locks again.

The black people of Africa who go barefooted from their very first step leave a distinctive flat imprint.

'A wearer of shoes,' Hendrick said softly.

'A white woman? No, it's impossible!' Lothar repeated. 'Not here, not travelling in the company of wild San! For the love of God, we are hundreds of miles from civilization!'

'It is so, a young white girl, a captive of the San,' Hendrick confirmed, and Lothar frowned.

The tradition of chivalry towards women of his own race was an integral part of Lothar's upbringing, one of the pillars of his Protestant religion. Because he was a soldier and hunter, because it was part of the art of his trade, Lothar could read the sign left upon the earth as though he were actually seeing the beast or the man, or woman, who had made it. Now as he squatted over these dainty prints, an image formed in his mind. He saw a girl, fine-boned, long-legged, gracefully proportioned, but strong and proud, with a raking stride that drove her forward on the balls of her feet. She would be brave also, and determined. There was no place in this wilderness for weaklings, and clearly this girl was flourishing. As the image formed, Lothar became aware of an emptiness deep in his soul.

'We must go after this woman,' he said softly, 'to rescue her from the San.'

Hendrick rolled his eyes towards the sky and reached for his snuff gourd, and poured a little of the red powder into his pink palm.

'The wind is against us,' he waved one hand along the

run of the spoor, 'they are travelling downwind. We will never come up with them.'

'There are always one hundred good reasons why we should not do what you don't want to do.' Lothar raked his wet hair back with his fingers and retied it with the leather thong at the nape of his neck. 'We will be following San, not animals. The wind is of no consequence.'

'The San are animals.' Hendrick blocked one of his wide flat nostrils with his thumb and sucked red snuff up the other before going on. 'With this wind they will smell you from two miles and hear you long before you sight them.' He dusted his hands and flicked the residual grains from his upper lip.

'A beautiful story!' Lothar scoffed. 'Even for you, the greatest liar in all of Ovamboland.' And then, brusquely, 'Enough chatter, we are going after the white girl. Take the spoor.'

From the high fork of the mopani tree, Centaine watched the elephant herd at the water-hole with mounting delight. Once she had got over the trepidation caused by their size and monumental ugliness, she swiftly became aware of the endearing bond that seemed to unite all the members of the herd. They began to seem almost human to her.

The patriarch bull was crotchety and his arthritic joints obviously ached. They all treated him with respect, and left one side of the pool for him alone. He drank noisily, squirting the water down his throat. Then he lowered himself, groaning with pleasure, into the mud, and scooped it up in his trunk to slap it on to his dusty grey head. It ran down his cheeks, and he closed his eyes ecstatically.

On the opposite side of the pool the young bulls and

431

cows drank and bathed, blowing mud and water out of their trunks like fire hoses, squirting themselves between the forelegs and down the flanks, lifting their heads and thrusting their trunks deep down their throats to send gallons of water hissing into their bellies. Satiated, they stood happily, trunks entwined in a loving embrace, and seemed to beam indulgently at the calves cavorting around their legs and under their bellies.

One of the smallest calves, not much bigger than a pig and just as fat, tried to wriggle under the trunk of a dead tree that had fallen into the pool and stuck fast in the mud. In comical panic it let out a squeal of alarm and terror. Every elephant in the herd reacted instantly, changing from contented indolence into raging behemoths of vengeance. They rushed back into the pool, beating the water and kicking it in a froth with their great hooves.

'They think a crocodile has caught the calf,' O'wa whispered.

'Poor crocodile!' Centaine whispered back.

The mother yanked the calf out from under the dead tree, hindfeet first, and it shot between her front legs and fastened on to one of her teats where it suckled with almost hysterical relief. The enraged herd quietened down, but with every evidence of disappointment that they had been denied the pleasure of tearing the hated crocodile into small pieces.

When the old bull finally heaved himself upright and, glistening with mud, strode away into the forest, the cows hastily rounded up their offspring, chasing them from their muddy pleasures with swinging trunks, and obediently they all trooped after the patriarch. Long after they had disappeared into the forest, Centaine could hear the crack of breaking branches and the rumble of their water-filled bellies as they fed away southwards.

She and O'wa climbed down from the mopani grinning with pleasure.

432

'The little ones were so naughty,' Centaine told H'ani, 'just like human babies.'

'We call them the big people,' H'ani agreed, 'for they are wise and loving as the San.'

They went down to the edge of the water-hole and Centaine marvelled at the mountainous piles of yellow dung that the elephants had dropped. Already the clucking francolin were scratching in the steaming mounds for undigested nuts and seeds.

'Anna would love that for the vegetable garden—' she caught herself. 'I mustn't think so much of the past.'

She stooped to bathe her face, for even the muddy water offered relief from the rising heat, but suddenly O'wa stiffened and cocked his head, turning it towards the north, in the direction from which the elephant herd had come.

'What is it, old grandfather?' H'ani was instantly sensitive to his mood.

O'wa did not answer for a second, but his eyes were troubled and his lips twitched nervously.

'There is something, something on the wind – a sound, a scent, I am not sure,' he whispered. Then, with sudden decision, 'There is danger – close. We must go.'

H'ani jumped up instantly and snatched up the satchel of egg-bottles. She would never argue with her husband's intuition, it had saved them often during their lifetime together.

'Nam Child,' she said softly but urgently, 'hurry.'

'H'ani—' Centaine turned to her with dismay. She was already knee-deep in the muddy pool. 'It is so hot, I want to—'

'There is danger, great danger.' The two San whirled together like startled birds and flew back towards the forest refuge. Centaine knew that in seconds she would be left alone, and loneliness was still her greatest terror. She ran from the pool, kicking spray before her, grabbed her carrying bag and stick and dressed as she ran.

433

O'wa circled quickly through the mopani forest, moving across the wind until it blew upon the back of his neck. The San, like the buffalo and the elephant, always fled downwind when alarmed, so that the scent of the pursuer would be carried down to them.

O'wa paused for Centaine to catch up with them.

'What is it, O'wa?' she gasped.

'Danger. Deadly danger.' The agitation of both the old people was obvious, and infectious. Centaine had learned not to ask questions in a situation such as this.

'What must I do?'

'Cover sign, the way I showed you,' O'wa ordered her, and she remembered the patient instruction that he had given her in the art of anti-tracking, of confusing and hiding the spoor so that a pursuer would find it difficult if not impossible to follow them. It was one of the skills on which San survival depended.

'H'ani first, then you.' O'wa was in complete command now. 'Follow her. Do as she does. I will come at the back and cover your mistakes.'

The old woman was as quick and agile as a little brown francolin. She flitted through the forest, avoiding the game paths and open ground on which their tracks would stand out clearly, picking the difficult line, ducking under thorn thickets where a pursuer would not expect them to pass, stepping on grass clumps or running along the trunks of fallen trees, changing her length of stride, hopping sideways over harder ground, employing every ruse she had learned in a long hard lifetime.

Centaine followed her, not as nimble, leaving an occasional blurred footprint, knocking a green leaf from a bush as she passed, disturbing the grass slightly. O'wa came close behind her, a broom of grass stalks in his hand to brush over the sign that Centaine left, stooping to pick up the tell-tale green leaf, delicately rearranging the bent grass stems that signposted the direction of their flight.

He guided H'ani with small chirping bird calls and whistles, and she responded instantly, turning left or right, speeding up or freezing for a few seconds so that O'wa could listen and sniff the breeze for the scent of the pursuit, then plunging forward again at his signal.

Suddenly another open glade spread before them, half a mile wide, studded with a few tall flat-topped giraffe acacia; beyond it rose the low ridge, heavily forested with paper-bark trees and dense wild ebony thickets for which O'wa was heading.

He knew that the ridge was composed of rock-hard calcrete, lumpy and broken, and he knew also that no human being could follow him over that ground. Once they reached it, they were safe, but the glade lay before them, and if they were caught there in the open, they would be easy prey, especially if their pursuers were armed with the smoke that kills from far off.

He wasted a few precious seconds to sniff at the air. It was hard to judge the distance of that faint offensive taint upon the light breeze, the stink of carbolic soap and snuff, of unwashed woollen clothing and socks, of the rancid cattle fat with which the Ovambo anointed their bodies, but he knew that he had to risk the open ground.

His most skilful anti-tracking could not cover all the signs that Nam Child had left over the soft sandy earth. His efforts to do so would merely impede the pursuit, but he knew that the bushcraft of the Ovambo was almost equal to his own. Only on the hard calcrete ridge could he be certain of losing them. He whistled, the call of a crimson-breasted shrike, and obediently H'ani started out into the open glade, scuttling through the short yellow grass.

'Run, little bird,' O'wa called softly. 'If they catch us in the open, we are dead.'

'They have smelled us,' Hendrick looked back at Lothar. 'See how they are covering sign.'

At the forest edge it seemed as though their quarry had turned into birds and taken to the air. All trace of them seemed to disappear. Brusquely Hendrick signalled to the other Ovambo hunters, and they spread out swiftly. Throwing a wide net, they moved forward in line. A man on the right flank whistled softly and then waved underhanded, indicating a new direction.

'They have turned down the wind,' Hendrick murmured to Lothar, who was ten paces out on his flank. 'I should have guessed it.'

The net of trackers wheeled on to the line, and moved forward. A man whistled on the left, and confirmed the line with that graceful underhand wave; they speeded up, breaking into a trot.

Just ahead Lothar noticed a faint colour difference on the seemingly undisturbed earth, a tiny patch of lighter sand no bigger than a man's foot, and he stooped to examine it. A footprint had been carefully brushed over and obliterated. Lothar whistled softly, and waved them forward on the line.

'Now do you believe the San can smell like an elephant?' Hendrick asked him as they jogged on.

'I believe only what I see,' Lothar grinned. 'When I see a Bushman sniffing the ground, then I will believe.'

Hendrick chuckled, but his eyes were cold and humourless.

'They will have arrows,' he said.

'Do not let them get close,' Lothar replied. 'Shoot them down the moment you see them, but be careful of the white woman. I will kill the man who harms her. Pass it on to the others.'

Lothar's order was called softly down the line. 'Shoot the San, but take great care of the white woman.'

Twice they lost the spoor. They had to back up to the

last marked sign, cast around it, and then move off again on the new line. The San were winning time and distance with every check, and Lothar fretted.

'They are getting away from us,' he called to Hendrick. 'I am going to run ahead on this line – you follow on the spoor, in case they jink again.'

'Be careful!' Hendrick shouted after him. 'They may lie in ambush. Watch out for the arrows.'

Lothar ignored the warning and raced through the forest, no longer tracking the sign, but taking the chance that it was straight ahead, hoping to startle the Bushmen and force them to show themselves, or to push them so hard that they would abandon their captive. He took no notice of the hooked thorns that ripped at his clothing. He ducked under the low mopani branches and hurdled fallen logs, running at the very peak of his speed.

Suddenly he burst from the forest into an open glade and he pulled up, his chest heaving for breath, sweat running into his eyes and soaking the back of his shirt between the shoulder-blades.

On the far side of the glade below the low forested ridge he saw movement, small black specks above the tops of the swaying yellow grass, and he turned back to the nearest tree and scrambled into the first fork for a better view.

Gasping wildly for breath, he fumbled the small brass telescope out of his hunting bag and pulled it to full extension. His hands were shaking, so it was difficult to focus the telescope, but he swept the far edge of the open glade.

Three human shapes appeared in the round field of the lens. They were in Indian file, heading directly away from him, almost at the palisade formed by the trunks of the paper-bark trees. Only their heads and shoulders showed above the grass, bobbing up and down as they ran. One was taller than the other two.

He watched them for seconds only before they reached

the tree line, and two of them disappeared instantly, but the tallest figure paused, stepped up on to a fallen log and looked back across the glade towards Lothar.

It was a girl. Her long dark hair was divided into two thick braids that hung on to her shoulders. Through the telescope Lothar could see her expression, fearful, yet defiant. The lines of her chin and brow were aristocractic, and her mouth was full and firm, dark eyes proud and bright, her skin stained to deep honey-gold, so for an instant he thought she might be a mulatto. As he watched she shifted the bag she carried from one shoulder to the other, and the coarse material that clothed her upper body fell open for an instant.

Lothar saw a flash of pale smooth skin, untouched by the sun, the form of a full young breast, rosy tipped and delicately shaped, and he felt a weakness in his legs that was not from hard running. His breath stopped for an instant, and then roared in his own ears as he panted to fill his lungs.

The girl turned her head away from him, offering him a profile, and in that instant Lothar knew that he had never seen a woman more appealing. Everything in him yearned towards her. She turned her back to him and sprang lithely out of the field of the lens, and disappeared. The branches of the edge of the forest trembled for a few seconds after she was gone.

Lothar felt like a man blind from birth, who for a fleeting instant had been shown the miracle of sight, only to be plunged back into darkness again. He stared after the girl, his feeling of deprivation so appalling that he could not move for many seconds, and then he leapt from the tree, rolling to his knees, breaking his fall, and sprang to his feet again.

He whistled sharply and heard his call answered by Hendrick far behind him in the mopani, but he did not wait for his men to come up. He crossed the glade at a full run, but his feet seemed weighted with lead. He reached the spot where the girl had stopped to look back towards him, and found the tree stump on to which she had climbed. The marks of her bare feet that she had left in the soft earth as she jumped down from the stump were deep and clear, but a few paces farther she had reached the calcrete of the ridge. It was hard as marble, rough and broken, and Lothar knew that it would hold no sign. He did not waste a moment searching for it, but forced his way up through the thick bush to the crest of the ridge, hoping for another sighting from there.

The forest hemmed him in, and even when he climbed into the top branches of a solitary boabab, he looked down on the unbroken roof of the forest that spread away, grey and forbidding, to the horizon.

He climbed down and wearily retraced his steps to the edge of the glade. His Ovambos were waiting for him there.

'We have lost them on the hard ground,' Hendrick greeted him.

'Cast ahead, we must find them,' Lothar ordered.

'I have tried already, the spoor is closed.'

'We cannot give up. We will work at it – I will not let them go.'

'You saw them,' Hendrick said softly, watching his master's face.

'Yes.'

'It was a white girl,' Hendrick insisted. 'You saw the girl, did you not?'

'We cannot leave her here in the desert.' Lothar looked away. He did not want Hendrick to see into the empty place in his soul. 'We must find her.'

'We will try again,' Hendrick agreed, and then with a sly telling grin, 'She was beautiful, this girl?'

'Yes,' Lothar whispered softly, still not looking at him. 'She was beautiful.' He shook himself, as though waking from a dream, and the line of his jaw hardened.

'Get your men on to the ridge,' he ordered.

They worked over it like a pack of hunting dogs, quartering every inch of the adamant yellow rock, stooping over it and moving in a slow painstaking line, but they found only one further mark of the passage of the San and the girl.

In one of the overhanging branches of a paper-bark tree, near the crest of the ridge, just at the level of Lothar's shoulder, a lock of human hair was caught, torn from the girl's scalp as she ducked beneath the branch. It was curly and springy, as long as his forearm, and it glistened in the sunlight like black silk. Lothar wound it carefully around his finger, and then when none of his men was watching, he opened the locket that hung around his neck on a golden chain. In the recess was a miniature of his mother. He placed the curl of hair over it and snapped the lid of the locket closed.

Lothar kept them hunting for signs until it was dark, and in the morning he started them again as soon as they could see the ground at their feet. He split them into two teams. Hendrick took one team along the eastern side of the ridge, and Lothar worked the western extremity where the calcrete merged into the Kalahari sands, trying to discover the spot at which their quarry had left the ridge again.

Four days later they had still not intersected the spoor, and two of the Ovambo had deserted. They slipped away during the night, taking their rifles with them.

'We will lose the rest of them,' Hendrick warned him quietly. 'They are saying that this is a madness. They cannot understand it. Already we have lost the elephant herd, and there is no profit in this business any longer. The spoor is dead. The San and the woman have slipped away. You will not find them now.'

Hendrick was right – it had become an obsession. A single glimpse of a woman's face had driven him mad.

Lothar sighed, and slowly turned away from the ridge on which the pursuit had foundered.

'Very well.' He raised his voice so that the rest of his men, who had been trailing disconsolately, could hear him. 'Drop the spoor. It is dead. We are going back.' The effect upon them was miraculous. Their step quickened and their expressions sparkled to life again.

Lothar remained on the ridge as the gang started back down the slope. He stared out over the forest towards the east, towards the mysterious interior where few white men had ventured, and he fingered the locket at his throat.

'Where did you go? Was it that way, deeper into the Kalahari? Why didn't you wait for me – why did you run?' There were no answers, and he dropped the locket back into the front of his shirt. 'If I ever cut your spoor again, you won't lose me so easily, my pretty. Next time I'll follow you to the ends of the earth,' he whispered, and turned back down the slope.

O'wa jinked back and followed the ridge towards the south, keeping just below the crest, driving the women as hard as they could run heavily laden over the rough footing. He would not allow them to rest, although Centaine was beginning to tire badly, and pleaded with him over her shoulder.

In the middle of the afternoon he allowed them to drop their satchels and sprawl on the rocky slope while he scurried on down to reconnoitre the contact line of the sands and the calcrete intrusion for a point at which to make the crossover. Halfway down he paused and sniffed; picking up the faint stench of carrion, he turned aside and found the carcass of an old zebra stallion. Reading the sign, O'wa saw that hunting lions had caught him as he crossed the ridge and dragged him down. The kill was weeks old, the tatters of skin and flesh had dried hard and the bones were scattered amongst the rocks.

O'wa searched quickly and found all four of the zebra's feet intact. The hyena had not yet crunched them to splinters. With the clasp knife he prised the horny sheath of the actual hooves from the bony mass of the metatarsals, and hurried back to fetch the women. He led them down to the edge of the soft ground, and knelt in front of Centaine.

'I will take Nam Child off, and then come back for you,' he told H'ani as he bound the hoof sheaths to Centaine's feet with sansevieria twine.

'We must hurry, old grandfather, they could be close behind us.' H'ani sniffed the light breeze anxiously, and cocked her head towards each small forest sound.

'Who are they?' Centaine had recovered not only her breath, but her curiosity and reason. 'Who is chasing us? I haven't seen or heard a thing. Are they people like me, O'wa, are they my people?'

Swiftly H'ani cut in before O'wa could reply. 'They are black men. Big black men from the north, not your people.' Although she and O'wa had both seen the white man at the edge of the glade when they looked back from the ridge, they had reached agreement in a few words that they would keep Nam Child with them.

'Are you sure, H'ani?' Centaine teetered on the zebra hooves, like a little girl in her first high-heeled shoes. 'They were not pale-skinned like me?' The dreadful possibility that she was fleeing from her rescuers had suddenly occurred to her.

'No! No!' H'ani fluttered her hands in extreme agitation. The child was so close to birth – to witness that moment was the last thing in her life that she still cared about. 'Not pale-skinned like you.' She thought of the most horrific being in San mythology. 'They are big black giants who eat human flesh.'

442

'Cannibals!' Centaine was shocked.

'Yes! Yes! That is why they pursue us. They will cut the child from your womb and—'

'Let's go, O'wa!' Centaine gasped. 'Hurry! Hurry!'

O'wa, with the other pair of hooves strapped to his own feet, guided Centaine away from the ridge, walking behind her and creating the illusion of a zebra having left the rocky ground and wandered away into the forest.

A mile from the ridge he hid Centaine in a clump of thorny scrub, removed the hooves from her feet, reversed the pair upon his own feet and set off back to fetch H'ani. The two San, each of them wearing hoof sandals, tracked back along the same trail and when they reached Centaine's hiding-place, discarded the hooves and all three of them fled into the east.

O'wa kept them going all that night, and in the dawn while the women slept exhausted, he circled back on their trail and guarded it against the possibility that the pursuers had not been deceived by his ruse with the zebra hooves. Although he could discover no evidence of pursuit, for three more days and nights he force-marched, allowing no cooking fires, and used every natural feature to anti-track and hide their trail.

On the third night, he was confident enough to tell the women, 'We can make fire.' And by its ruddy wavering light he danced with dedicated frenzy and sang the praise of the spirits in turn, including Mantis and Eland, for, as he explained seriously to Centaine, it was uncertain who had aided their escape, who had directed the wind to carry the warning scent to them in the first place, and who had subsequently placed the zebra carcass so conveniently to hand. 'It is necessary, therefore, to thank them all.' He danced until moonset, and the next morning slept until sunrise. Then they resumed the familiar leisurely pattern of march, and even halted early that first day when O'wa discovered a colony of spring-hare.

'This is the last time we can hunt, the spirits are most insistent. No man of the San may kill any living thing within five days' march of "the Place of All Life",' he explained to Centaine, as he selected long whippy saplings of the grewia bush, peeled them and lashed them together until he had a strong flexible rod almost thirty feet long. On the final section, he left a side branch that grew back at an acute angle to the main stem, like a crude fish-hook, and he sharpened the point of this hook and hardened it in the fire. Then he spent a long time carefully examining the burrows of the spring-hare colony, before selecting one which suited his design.

While the women knelt beside him, he introduced the hooked end of the rod into the opening of the burrow, and like a chimney-sweep worked it gently down the shaft, deftly guiding it around the subterranean curves and bends until almost the entire length was down in the earth.

Suddenly the rod pulsed strongly in his hands, and immediately O'wa struck, jerking back like a hardline fisherman who feels the pull of the fish.

'He is kicking at the rod now, trying to hit it with his back legs,' O'wa grunted, pushing the rod deeper into the hole, tempting the trapped spring-hare to kick out at it again.

This time, as he struck, the rod came alive in his hands, kicking and twitching and jerking.

'I have hooked him!' He threw his weight back on the rod, driving the sharpened wooden point deeper into the animal's flesh. 'Dig, H'ani. Dig, Nam Child!'

The two women flew at the soft friable earth with their staves, digging down swiftly. The muffled shrieks of the hooked spring-hare grew louder as they came nearer to the end of the long gaff, until finally O'wa heaved the furry creature clear of its earth. It was the size of a large yellow cat, and it leaped about wildly on the end of the pliant rod on its powerful kangaroo back legs, until H'ani despatched it with a swinging blow of her stave.

By nightfall they had killed two more spring-hare, and after they had thanked them, they feasted on the sweet tender roasted flesh, the last they would eat for a long time.

In the morning when they set out again on the final leg of the journey, a sharp hot wind blew into their faces.

Although it was taboo for O'wa to hunt, the Kalahari bloomed in a rich and rare abundance both below and above the ground. There were flowers and green leafy plants to be eaten as salads, roots and tubers, fruits and protein-rich nuts, and the water-holes, all of them brimming, were easy marches apart. Only the wind hampered them, standing steadily into their faces, hot and abrasive with blown sand, forcing them to cover their faces with their leather shawls and lean into it.

The mixed herds of fat handsome zebra and ungainly blue wildebeest with their scraggy manes and skinny legs standing out on the wide pans or on the grassy glades turned their rumps into the sultry blast. The wind ripped the talcum-fine dust off the surface of the pans and whirled it into the sky, turning the air misty, so the sun itself was a hazy orange globe and the horizons shrank in upon them.

The dust floated on the surface of the water-holes in a thin scum, and it turned to mud in their nostrils and grated between their teeth. It formed little wet beads in the corners of their eyes and dried and cracked their skins so that H'ani and Centaine had to roast and crush the seeds of the sour plum tree to extract the oil to dress their skins and the soles of their feet.

However, with each day's march the old people became stronger, more active and excited. They seemed less and

445

less affected by the scouring wind. There was a new jauntiness in their step and they chattered animatedly to each other on the march, while Centaine faltered and dropped far behind, almost as she had done at the beginning.

On the fifth evening after crossing the ridge, Centaine staggered into the camp that the San had already set up on the edge of yet another open pan. Centaine lay on the bare earth, too hot and exhausted to gather grass for her bed.

When H'ani came to her with food, she pushed it away petulantly. 'I don't want it. I don't want anything. I hate this land – I hate the heat and the dust.'

'Soon,' H'ani soothed her, 'very soon we will reach the Place of All Life, and your baby will be born.'

But Centaine rolled away from her. 'Leave me – just leave me alone.'

She woke to the cries of the old people, and she dragged herself up, feeling fat and dirty and unrested, even though she had slept so late that the sun was already tipping the tops of the trees on the far side of the pan. Immediately she saw that the wind had dropped during the night and most of the dust had settled out of the air. The residue transformed the dawn to a kaleidoscope of flamboyant colour.

'Nam Child, do you see it!' H'ani called to her, and then trilled like a Christmas beetle, inarticulate with excitement. Centaine straightened up slowly and stared at the scene that the dust clouds had obscured the previous evening.

Across the pan a great whale-backed mountain rose abruptly out of the desert, steep-sided and with a symmetrically rounded summit. Aglow with all the rich reds and golds of the dawn, it looked like a headless monster. Parts of the mountain were bald and bare, glowing red rock and smooth cliffs, while in other places it was heavily forested;

trees much taller and more robust than those of the plain crowned the summit or grew up the steep sides. The strange reddish light suffused with dust and the silences of the African dawn cloaked the entire mountain in majestic serenity.

Centaine felt all her miseries and her woes fall away as she stared at it.

'"The Place of All Life"!' As H'ani said the name, her agitation passed and her voice sank to a whisper. 'This is the sight we have travelled so far and so hard to look upon for the last time.'

O'wa had fallen silent as well, but now he bobbed his head in agreement. 'This is where we will make our peace at last with all the spirits of our people.'

Centaine felt the same sense of deep religious awe that had overcome her when first she had entered the cathedral of Arras, holding her father's hand, and looked up at the gemlike stained glass in the high gloomy recesses of the towering nave. She knew that she stood on the threshold of a holy place, and she sank slowly to her knees and clasped her hands over the swell of her stomach.

The mountain was further off than it had seemed in the red light of the dawn. As they marched towards it, it seemed to recede rather than draw closer. As the light changed, so the mountain changed its mood. It became remote and austere, and the stone cliffs glittered in the sunlight like a crocodile's scales.

O'wa sang as he trotted at the head of the file:

> See, spirits of the San
> We come to your secret place
> With clean hands, unstained by blood.

See, spirit of Eland and Mantis,
We come to visit you with
Joyous hearts, and songs for your amusement—

The mountain changed again, began to quiver and tremble in the rising heat. It was no longer massive stone, but rippled like water and wavered like smoke.

It broke free of the earth and floated in the air on a shimmering silver mirage.

O, bird mountain
That flies in the sky
We bring you praises.
O, Elephant Mountain, greater than
Any beast of earth or sky, we hail you,

O'wa sang, and as the sun swung through its zenith and the air cooled, so the Mountain of All Life settled to earth again and loomed high above them.

They reached the scree slopes, loose stone and debris that lay piled against the cliffs, and paused to look up at the high summit. The rocks were painted with lichen growth, sulphur-yellow and acid-green, and the little hyrax rock rabbits had stained the cliffs with seepage from their middens, like tears from an elephant's eyes.

On a ledge three hundred feet above them stood a tiny antelope. It took fright and with a bleat like a child's penny whistle, shot straight up the cliff, leaping from ledge to unseen ledge with all the nimbleness of a chamois, until it disappeared over the crest.

They scrambled up the steep scree slope until they touched the base of the cliff. The rock was smooth and cool and overhung them, leaning out at a gentle angle like a vast cathedral roof.

'Be not angry, ye spirits, that we come into your secret place,' H'ani whispered, and tears were coursing down her ancient yellow cheeks. 'We come in humble peace, kind spirits, we come to learn what our offence has been, and how we can make amends.'

O'wa reached out and took his wife's hand and they stood like two tiny naked children before the smooth rock.

'We come to sing for you and to dance,' O'wa whispered. 'We come to make peace, and then with your favour to be reunited with the children of our clan who died of the great fever in a far place.'

There was such vulnerability in this intimate moment that Centaine felt embarrassed to watch them. She drew away from the two old people, and wandered alone along the narrow gallery before the cliff. Suddenly she stopped, and stared up in wonder at the high rock wall that hung out over her head.

'Animals,' she whispered.

She felt the goose-flesh of superstitious fear rise along her forearms, for the walls were decorated with paintings, frescoes of weirdly wrought animals, the childlike simplicity of form giving them a beauty that was dreamlike, and yet a touching resemblance to the beasts that they depicted. She recognized the darkly massive outlines of tusked elephants and horned rhinoceros, the wildebeest and sassaby with horns like crescent moons marching in closely packed phalanxes across the rock walls.

'And people,' Centaine whispered, as she picked out the sticklike human shapes that ran in pursuit of the herds of wild game. Fairy beings, the San's view of himself, armed with bows and crowned with wreaths of arrows, the men adorned with proudly erect penises, disproportionately large, and the women with prominent breasts and buttocks, the badges of feminine beauty.

The paintings climbed so high up the sheer walls that the artists must have built platforms, in the fashion of Michelangelo, to work from. The perspectives were naive, one human figure larger than the rhinoceros he was hunting, but this seemed to deepen the enchantment, and Centaine lost herself in wonder, sinking down at last to examine and admire a lovely flowing waterfall of overlapping eland, ochre and red, with dewlaps and humped shoulders, so lovingly depicted that their special place in San mythology could not be overlooked.

H'ani found her there, and squatted beside her.

'Who painted these things?' Centaine asked her.

'The spirits of the San, long, long ago.'

'Were they not painted by men?'

'No! No! Men do not have the art, these are spirit drawings.'

So the artists' skills were lost. Centaine was disappointed. She had hoped that the old woman was one of the artists and that she would have an opportunity to watch her work.

'Long ago,' H'ani repeated, 'before the memory of my father or my grandfather.'

Centaine swallowed her disappointment and gave herself up to enjoyment of the marvellous display.

There was little left of the daylight, but while it lasted, they picked their way slowly around the base of the cliff, walking with heads thrown back to marvel at the gallery of ancient art. At places the rock had broken away, or the storms and winds of the ages had destroyed the frescoes, but in the protected gulleys and beneath the sheltering overhangs the paint seemed so fresh, and the colours so vivid, that they might have been painted that very day.

In the last minutes of daylight they reached a shelter where others had camped before them, for the hearth was thick with wood ash and the cliff was blackened with soot, and there was a pile of dead wood left beside it, ready for use.

'Tomorrow we will learn if the spirits are hostile still, or if we will be allowed to proceed,' H'ani warned Centaine. 'We will start very early, for we must reach the hidden place before the sun rises, while it is still cool. The guardians become restless and dangerous in the heat.'

'What is this place?' Centaine insisted, but once again the old woman became vague and deliberately absent-minded. She repeated the San word which had the various meanings 'hidden place' or 'safe shelter' or 'vagina', and would say no more.

As H'ani had warned, they started out long before sunrise the next morning and the old people were quiet and anxious and, Centaine suspected, fearful.

The sky was barely lighting with the dawn when abruptly the path turned a sharp corner in the cliff and entered a narrow wedge-shaped valley; the floor was thickly covered with such luxuriant growth that Centaine realized there must be good water below the surface. The path was ill-defined, overgrown and clearly had not been trodden for many months or years. They had to duck under the interlocking branches and step over fallen boughs and new growth. In the cliffs high above them Centaine made out the huge shaggy nests of vultures, and the grossly ugly birds with their bare pink heads crouched on the rim of their nests.

'The Place of All Life.' H'ani saw her interest in the nesting birds. 'Any creature born here is special, blessed by the spirits. Even the birds seem to know this.'

The high cliffs closed in upon them as the valley narrowed, and at last the path ended against the rock in the angled corner where the valley finally pinched out, and the sky was hidden from them.

O'wa stood before the wall and sang in his hoarse ghost-chant, 'We wish to enter your most secret place, Spirits of all Creatures, Spirits of our clan. Open the way for us.' He spread his arms in entreaty. 'May the guardians of this passage let us pass through.'

O'wa lowered his arms, and stepped into the black rock of the cliff and disappeared from Centaine's sight. She

451

gasped with alarm, and started forward, but H'ani touched her arm to restrain her.

'There is great danger now, Nam Child. If the guardians reject us, we will die. Do not run, do not wave your arms. Walk slowly, but with purpose, and ask the blessing of the spirits as you pass through.' H'ani released her arm, and stepped into the rock, following her husband.

Centaine hesitated. For a moment she almost turned back, but at last curiosity and fear of loneliness spurred her and she went slowly to the wall where H'ani had disappeared. Now she saw the opening in the rock, a narrow vertical crack, just wide enough for her to pass through if she turned her shoulders.

She drew a deep breath and slipped through.

Beyond the narrow portals she paused to allow her eyes to become accustomed to the gloom, and she found herself in a long dark tunnel. It was a natural opening, she saw at once, for the walls had not been worked by tools, and there were side branches and openings high overhead. She heard the rustle of the old people's bare feet on the rocky floor ahead of her, and then another sound. A low, murmurous hum, like the sea surf heard from afar.

'Follow, Nam Child. Stay close,' H'ani's voice floated back to her, and Centaine went forward slowly, staring into the shadows, trying to find the source of that deep vibrating murmur.

In the gloom above her she saw strange shapes, plate-like projections from the walls, like the leaves of fungus growing on the trunk of a dead tree, or the multiple wings of roosting butterflies. They drooped so low that she had to duck beneath them – and with a sudden chill she realized where she was.

The cavern was an enormous beehive. These deep wing-like structures were the honeycombs, so massive that each would contain hundreds of gallons of honey. Now she could see the insects swarming over the combs, glittering dully in the poor light, and she remembered the stories that Michael had told her of the African bees.

'Bigger and blacker than your bees,' he had boasted, 'and so vicious that I have seen them sting a bull buffalo to death.'

Barely allowing herself to breathe, her skin crawling in anticipation of the first burning dart, forcing herself not to run, she followed the diminutive figures ahead of her. The swarming masses of venomous insects were only inches above her, and the humming chorus seemed to rise angrily until it threatened to deafen her.

'This way, Nam Child. Do not fear, for the little winged people will smell your fear,' H'ani called softly, and a bee alighted on Centaine's cheek.

She raised her hand instinctively to strike it off her, and then with an effort checked the movement. The bee tickled across her face on to her upper lip – then another settled on her upraised forearm.

She peered at it in horror. It was enormous, black as coal, with dark golden rings around its abdomen. The filmy wings were closed like scissor-blades and its multiple eyes twinkled in the poor light.

'Please, little bee, please—' Centaine whispered, and the insect arched its back, and from its banded abdomen the point of its sting protruded, a dark red needle-point.

'Please, let me and my baby pass!'

The bee curved its body and the sting touched the soft tanned skin of her inner elbow. Centaine tensed herself; she knew that the stabbing pain would be followed by the sickly sweet odour of the venom that would madden and infuriate the vast swarm above her. She imagined herself smothered under a living carpet of bees, writhing on the floor of the cavern, dying the most hideous of deaths.

'Please,' she whispered. 'Let my baby be born in your secret place, and we will honour you all the days of our lives.'

The bee retracted the throbbing sting and performed an intricate weaving dance upon her arm, turning and curtseying and reversing, and then with a quicksilver flicker of its wings darted away.

Centaine walked on slowly, and ahead of her she saw a golden nimbus of reflected light. The insect on her face crawled down over her lips, so she could not speak again, but she prayed silently.

'"Though I walk through the valley of the shadow of death" please, little bee, let me go for my baby's sake.'

A sharp buzz and the bee flashed before her eyes, a golden mote as it left her, and though her skin tingled and itched from the memory of its horny feet, she kept her hands at her sides and walked on with a measured step. It seemed for ever, then she reached the tunnel's end and stooped through it into the early dawn light, and her legs began to fold in reaction to her terror. She might have fallen if O'wa had not steadied her.

'You are safe now. The guardians have allowed us to enter the sacred place.'

The words roused her, and though she still trembled and her breathing was rough, Centaine looked around her.

They had passed through into a hidden basin in the heart of the mountain, a perfectly round amphitheatre in the rock. The walls were sheer, hundreds of feet high and with a dark satanic sheen to them, as though scorched in the flames of a blast furnace, but above that it was open to the sky.

The deep bowl of rock was perhaps a mile across at its widest point. At this time of day the sunlight had not penetrated down to the floor, and the groves of graceful trees that covered it were cool and dewy. They reminded Centaine of olives, with fine pale leaves and bunches of reddish-yellow fruit on the wide-spread boughs. The floor of the valley was gently dished, and as Centaine followed

H'ani down through the trees, the ground beneath them was carpeted with fallen fruit.

H'ani picked up one of them and offered it to Centaine.

'Mongongo – very good.'

Centaine bit into it and exclaimed as her tooth struck painfully on the large kernel in its centre. There was only a thin layer of flesh around it, but it was tart and tasty as a palm date, though not as sweet.

From the branches above them a flight of plump green pigeons exploded into noisy flight, and Centaine realized that the valley was alive with birds and small animals come in the dawn to feast on the fruits of the mongongo groves.

'The Place of All Life,' she whispered, entranced by the weird beauty, by the stark contrast of bare blasted rock cliffs against this gently wooded bottom land.

O'wa hurried along the rough path that led down into the centre of the bowl, and as Centaine followed she glimpsed a small hillock of black volcanic rock through the trees ahead. Centaine saw that the hill was symmetrical and cone-shaped, and set in the exact centre of the amphitheatre like the boss in the centre of a shield.

Like the valley floor, the hill itself was heavily forested. Tall elephant grass and mongongo trees grew profusely among the black volcanic boulders. A troop of black-faced vervet monkeys chattered at them from the trees and ducked their heads threateningly, grimacing with alarm, as they approached the hillock.

When Centaine and H'ani caught up with O'wa, he was standing facing a dark opening in the side of the hill. It looked like the mouth of a mine-shaft, but as she peered into it Centaine realized that the floor of the shaft sloped down at a gentle angle. She pushed past O'wa the better to examine it, but the old man seized her arm.

'Be not hasty, Nam Child, we must make preparation in

the correct manner.' And he drew her back and led her gently away.

A little further on, there was an ancient San campsite amongst the sheltering rocks. The thatched roofs of the shelters had collapsed with age. O'wa burned them to the ground, for disused huts harbour snakes and vermin, and the two women rebuilt them with saplings and freshly cut grass.

'I am hungry.' Centaine realized that she had not eaten since the previous evening.

'Come.' H'ani led her into the grove, and they filled their satchels with the fallen fruit of the mongongo trees. Back in the camp, H'ani showed Centaine how to strip off the outer layer of flesh and then to crack the hard central nut between two flat stones. The kernel looked like a dried almond. They ate a few of these, to take the edge off their hunger. They tasted like walnuts.

'We will eat them in many ways,' H'ani promised. 'And each way they taste different, roasted, pounded with leaves, boiled like maize bread – they will be our only food in this place where all killing is forbidden.'

While they prepared the meal, O'wa returned to camp with a bundle of freshly dug roots, and went aside to prepare them in private, scraping and chopping with his beloved clasp knife.

They ate before dark, and Centaine found the meal of nuts unexpectedly satisfying. As soon as her stomach was filled, the effect of the day's excitements and exertions caught up with her, and she could barely drag herself to her shelter.

She awoke refreshed and with a sense of unexplained excitement. The San were already busy around the camp fire and as soon as she joined them and squatted in the circle, O'wa, puffed up with nervous anticipation and self-importance, told them, 'We must now prepare to go down

456

into the most secret of places. Do you agree to the purification, old grandmother?' It was obviously a formal question.

'I agree, old grandfather.' H'ani clapped softly in
acquiescence.

'Do you agree to the purification, Nam Child?'

'I agree, old grandfather.' Centaine clapped in imitation
and O'wa bobbed his head and from the pouch on his belt
brought out a buck-horn. The top had been pierced, and
O'wa had stuffed the horn with the chopped roots and
herbs that he had gathered the previous afternoon.

Now he picked a live coal out of the fire with his fingers,
and juggling it to prevent it burning his skin, he dropped it
into the trumpet-shaped opening of the buckhorn. He blew
upon it and a tendril of blue smoke rose in the still air as
the herbs smouldered.

Once the pipe was burning evenly, O'wa rose and stood
behind the two squatting women. He placed his mouth
over the pierced tip of the horn and sucked on it strongly,
then blew the smoke over them. It was acrid and sharply
unpleasant, and left a bitter taste in Centaine's throat. She
murmured a protest and began to rise, but H'ani pulled her
down again. O'wa kept puffing and exhaling, and after a
while Centaine found the smoke less offensive. She relaxed
and leaned against H'ani. The old woman placed an arm
around her shoulders. Slowly Centaine became aware of a
marvellous sense of well-being. Her body felt as light as
that of a bird, she felt she could float up with the spirals of
blue smoke.

'Oh, H'ani, I feel so good,' she whispered.

The air around her seemed sparkling clear, her vision
sharp and magnified so she could see every crack and
crevice in the surrounding cliffs, and the groves of trees
seemed to be made of green crystals. They reflected the
sunlight with an ethereal radiance.

She became aware that O'wa was kneeling in front of

her, and she smiled at him dreamily. He was offering something, holding it out towards her with both hands.

'It is for the child,' he told her, and his voice seemed to come from far away and echo strangely in her ears. 'It is the birthing mat. His father should have made it for him, but that could not be. Here, Nam Child, take it and bear a brave son upon it.'

O'wa leaned forward and placed the gift upon her lap. It took long seconds before she realized that it was the gemsbok skin over which O'wa had worked so long and so intently. She unfolded it with exaggerated care. The skin had been scraped and tanned to the pliability and softness of the fine cloth. She stroked it and the fur felt like satin.

'Thank you, old grandfather,' her voice came from far away, and reverberated strangely in her own ears.

'It is for the child,' he repeated, and sucked on the buckhorn pipe.

'For the child, yes,' Centaine nodded and her head seemed to float free of her body. O'wa gently exhaled a stream of blue smoke into her face and she made no effort to avoid it, rather she leaned forward to stare into his eyes. O'wa's pupils had shrunk to glittering black pinpricks, the irises were the colour of dark amber with a fanlike pattern of black lines surrounding the pupils. They mesmerized her.

'For the child's sake, let the peace of this place enter your soul.' O'wa spoke through the smoke, and Centaine felt it happen.

'Peace,' she murmured, and at the centre of her being was a wondrous stillness, a monumental calm.

Time and space and white sunlight mingled and became one. She sat at the centre of the universe and smiled serenely. She heard O'wa singing far away, and she swayed gently to the rhythm and felt each beat of her heart and the slow pump of her blood through her veins. She felt the child lying deep within her, curled in an attitude of prayer, then, unbelievably, she felt the tiny heart beating like that of a trapped bird, and the wonder of it engulfed her whole being.

'We have come to be cleansed,' O'wa sang. 'We have come to wash away all offence, we have come to make atonement—'

Centaine felt H'ani's hand creep into hers like a fragile-boned animal, and she turned her head slowly and smiled into the beloved old face.

'It is time, Nam Child.'

Centaine drew the gemsbok skin over her shoulder. It required no effort to rise. She floated above the earth, with H'ani's little hand clutched in hers.

They came to the opening in the hillside, and though it was dark and steep, Centaine went forward smiling, and she did not feel the coarse volcanic rock beneath her feet. The passageway descended for a short distance, and then levelled out and opened into a natural cavern. They followed O'wa down.

Light filtered from the stairway behind them and from a number of small openings in the domed roof. The air was warm and moist and steamy. The clouds of steam rose gently from the surface of a circular pool that filled the cavern from side to side. The surface of the pool seethed and bubbled softly, and the steam smelled strongly of sulphur. The waters were cloudy green.

O'wa let his loincloth fall to the rocky floor and stepped into the pool. It reached to his knees but as he waded forward it deepened, until only his head was above the surface. H'ani followed him naked into the pool, and Centaine laid the gemsbok skin aside, and let her skirt fall.

The water was hot, almost scalding, a thermal spring welling up out of the matrix, but Centaine felt no discomfort. She moved deeper and then sank down slowly on to her knees until the water came to her chin. The floor of the pool was coarse pebble and gravel. The fierce heat of the waters soaked into her body. It swirled and eddied about her, kneading her flesh, as it bubbled up out of the depths of the earth.

She heard O'wa singing softly, but the steam clouds closed in around her and blinded her.

'We wish to make atonement,' O'wa sang. 'We wish to be forgiven our offences to the Spirits—'

Centaine saw a shape forming in the steam, clouds, a dark, insubstantial phantom.

'Who are you?' she murmured, and the shape firmed, and she recognized the eyes – the other features were obscure – as those of the old seaman she had sacrificed to the shark.

'Please,' she whispered, 'forgive me. It was for my baby. Please forgive my offence.' It seemed that for a moment there was understanding in those sad old eyes, and then the image faded and vanished in the steam banks, to be replaced by others, a host of memories and dream creatures, and she spoke to them.

'Oh, Papa, if I had only been strong enough, if only I could have filled Mama's place—'

She heard the voices of the San in the steam, crying out in greeting to their own ghosts and memories. O'wa hunted again with his sons, and H'ani saw her babies and her grandchildren and crooned her love and mourning.

'Oh, Michel,' his eyes were a marvellous blue, 'I will love you for ever. Yes, oh yes, I will name your son for you. I promise you that, my love, he will carry your name.'

How long she remained in the pool she did not know, but gradually the fantasies and the phantoms faded, and then she felt H'ani's hands leading her to the rocky lip. The scalding waters seemed to have drained all the strength from her. Her body glowed a bright brick colour, and the ingrained dirt of the desert was scoured from the pores of her skin. Her knees were weak and rubbery.

H'ani draped the gemsbok skin over her wet body and helped her up the rocky passage to the surface. Night had fallen already, and the moon shone bright enough to cast shadows at their feet. H'ani led her to the rude shelter and wrapped her in the gemsbok skin.

'The Spirits have forgiven,' she whispered. 'They are pleased that we have made the journey. They sent my babies to greet me and tell me so. You can sleep well, Nam Child, there is no more offence. We are welcome in this place.'

C entaine woke in confusion, not sure what was happening to her, not even certain where she was, imagining for the first few seconds that she was back in her chamber at Mort Homme and that Anna was standing beside her bed. Then she became aware of the coarse grass and hard earth beneath her and the smell of the rawhide that covered her, and immediately following that the pain came again. It was as though a claw had closed on her lower body, a cruel taloned claw, cramping and crushing her, and she cried out involuntarily and doubled over, clutching her stomach.

With the pain, reality rushed back upon her. Her mind was clear and sharp after the hallucinations of the previous day. She knew what was happening, she knew instinctively that the immersion in the heated waters of the pool and the drugged smoke she had breathed must have precipitated it.

'H'ani!' she called, and the old woman materialized out of the grey half-light. 'It has begun!'

H'ani helped her to her feet, then gathered up the gemsbok skin.

'Come,' she whispered. 'We must go where we can be alone.'

H'ani must have already chosen the place, for she led Centaine directly to a hollow a short way beyond the

461

camp, but screened from it by the mongongo grove. She spread the gemsbok skin at the base of a large mongongo tree and settled Centaine upon it. She knelt over her and removed her ragged canvas skirt, then with quick, strong fingers, she made a brief but thorough examination and then rocked back on her heels.

'Soon, Nam Child – very soon now,' she smiled happily, but Centaine's reply choked off as another spasm caught her.

'Ah, the child is impatient!' H'ani nodded.

The spasm passed and Centaine lay and panted, but she had barely caught her breath before she stiffened again.

'Oh, H'ani, hold my hand – please! Please!'

Something burst deep within Centaine's body and hot liquid poured from her, and sprayed down her legs.

'Close – very close now,' H'ani assured her, and Centaine gave a little hunted cry.

'Now—' H'ani pulled her into a sitting position, but she slumped back.

'It's coming, H'ani.'

'Get up!' H'ani snapped at her. 'You must help it now. Get up. You cannot help the baby if you lie on your back!' She forced Centaine into a squatting position, with her feet and knees splayed apart, the natural position for voiding.

'Hold the tree to steady yourself,' she instructed her urgently. 'There!' She guided Centaine's hands on to the rough bark and Centaine moaned and pressed her forehead hard against the trunk.

'Now!' H'ani knelt behind her, and encircled Centaine's body with her thin wiry arms.

'Oh, H'ani—' Centaine's cry rose sharply.

'Yes! I will help you push him out.' And she tightened her grip as Centaine bore down instinctively. 'Push, Nam Child – hard! Hard! Push!' H'ani entreated her as she felt the girl's stomach muscles bunch up and harden into bands of iron.

There was a great blockade within her and Centaine clung to the tree and strained and moaned – and then she felt the obstruction move a little, then jam hard again.

'H'ani!' she cried, and the thin arms locked around her and the old woman moaned with her as they strained together. H'ani's naked body was pressed to Centaine's arched back, and she felt strength flowing out of the old wizened flesh like an electrical current.

'Again, Nam Child,' H'ani grunted in her ear. 'He is close – so close. Now! Nam Child, push hard.'

Centaine bore down with all her strength and will. Her jaws were clenched so that she thought her teeth would crack, and her eyes swelled in their sockets. Then she felt something tear, a stinging burning pain, but despite the pain she found strength for another rigorous convulsion. It moved again, then there was a rush, a release and something enormous and impossibly heavy slid out of her at the same moment H'ani's hand reached under her buttocks to guide and welcome and protect.

Like a benediction, the pain wilted away, and left her shaking as though in high fever and running with her own sweat – but empty, blessedly empty, as though her viscera had been drawn out of her.

H'ani released her grip, and Centaine clutched at the tree trunk for support, and drew long ragged breaths.

Then she felt something hot and wet and slippery squirming between her feet, and she pushed herself wearily away from the tree trunk and looked down. A tangle of fleshy glistening tubes still dangled out of her, and joined to them, enmeshed in their coils, the infant lay in a pool of blood-speckled fluid on the gemsbok-skin mat.

It was small, she was surprised at how small, but its limbs were stretching in spasmodic clutching and kicking gestures. The face was turned away from her but the small neat head was covered with a dense cap of sodden black curls, plastered to the skull.

H'ani's hands reached down between her legs from behind and lifted the baby out of her sight. Instantly Centaine felt a devastating sense of deprivation – but she was too weak to protest. She felt a gentle twitching and tugging on the umbilical cord as H'ani handled the child, and then suddenly there was a furious squalling howl. It struck Centaine to the heart.

Then H'ani's laughter joined in chorus with the angry bawls. Centaine had never heard a sound of such unequivocal joy.

'Oh, listen to him, Nam Child. He roars like a lion cub!'

Centaine waddled around awkwardly, hampered by the fleshy ropes dangling from her own body and still linking her to the infant. He was struggling in H'ani's hands, all wet and defiant, his face red with anger and his bee-stung eyes tight closed, but his toothless pink mouth wide as he howled his outrage.

'A boy, H'ani?' Centaine panted wildly.

'Oh yes,' H'ani laughed, 'by all means, a boy,' and with the tip of her forefinger she tickled his tiny penis. It stuck out stiffly as though to endorse his anger, and at H'ani's touch released a powerful arcing jet of urine.

'Look! Look!' H'ani choked with laughter. 'He pisses on the world. Bear witness, all the Spirits of this place, a veritable lion cub has been birthed this day.'

She offered the squirming red-faced infant to Centaine.

'Clean his eyes and nose,' she ordered, and, like a mother cat, Centaine did not need further instruction. She licked the mucus from the tiny swollen eyelids, from his nostrils and mouth.

Then H'ani took the child, handling him with familiar expertise, and she tied off the umbilical cord with the soft white inner bark threads of the mongongo tree, before severing it with a quick slash of her bone knife. Then she rolled the end of the tube in the medicinal leaves of the wild quince and bound it in place with a rawhide strip around his middle.

Sitting on the soiled gemsbok skin, in a puddle of her own blood and amniotic fluids, Centaine watched her work with shining eyes.

'Now!' H'ani nodded with vast self-satisfaction. 'He is ready for the breast.' And she placed him in Centaine's lap.

He and Centaine needed only the barest introduction. H'ani squeezed Centaine's nipple and touched the milk-wet tip to the infant's lips, and he fastened on it like a leech, with a noisy rhythmic suction. For a few moments Centaine was startled by the sudden sharp sympathetic contractions of her womb as the child suckled, but this was lost and forgotten in the wonder and mystery of examining her incredible accomplishment.

Gently she unfolded his fist and marvelled at the perfection of each tiny pink finger, at the pearly nails, each no bigger than a grain of rice, and when he suddenly seized her finger in the surprisingly powerful grip, he squeezed her heart as well. She stroked his damp dark hair, and as it dried it sprang up into ringlets. It awed her to see the pulsing movement under the thin membrane that covered the opening of his skull.

He stopped suckling and lay quiescent in her arms, so she could take him from her breast and examine his face. He was smiling. Apart from the puffy eyelids, his features were well formed, not squashed and rubbery like those of the other newborn infants she had seen. His brow was broad and deep and his nose was large. She thought of Michael – no, it was more arrogant than Michael's nose – and then she remembered General Sean Courtney.

'That's it!' she chuckled aloud. 'The true Courtney nose.'

The infant stiffened and broke wind simultaneously both fore and aft, a trickle of her milk dribbled from the corner of his mouth, and instantly he began to hunt for the nipple again, mouthing demandingly, rolling his head from side to side. Centaine changed him to her other arm, and guided her nipple into his open mouth.

Kneeling in front of her, H'ani was working between Centaine's knees. Centaine winced and bit her lip as the afterbirth came free, and H'ani wrapped it in the leaves of the elephant-ear plant, tied it with bark and scampered away into the grove with the bundle.

When she returned, the child was asleep in Centaine's lap, with his legs splayed and his belly tight as a balloon.

'If you permit, I will fetch O'wa,' H'ani suggested. 'He will have heard the birth cries.'

'Oh, yes, fetch him quickly.' Centaine had forgotten the old man, and now was delighted at the opportunity to exhibit her marvellous acquisition.

O'wa came shyly and squatted a little way off, showing the usual masculine lack of temerity when faced with the feminine mystery of birth.

'Approach, old grandfather,' Centaine encouraged him, and he shuffled closer on his haunches and peered solemnly at the sleeping child.

'What do you think?' Centaine asked. 'Will he be a hunter? As skilful and brave a hunter as O'wa?'

O'wa made the little clicking sound reserved for those rare occasions when he was at a loss for words, and his face was a web of convoluted wrinkles like that of a worried Pekinese lap dog. Suddenly the child kicked out strongly and yelped in his sleep, and the old man dissolved into uncontrolled giggles.

'I never thought I would see it again,' he wheezed, and gingerly reached out and took a tiny pink foot in his hand.

The child kicked again and it was too much for O'wa.

He sprang up and began to dance. Shuffling and stamping, circling the mother and child on the gemsbok skin, around and around he went, and H'ani controlled herself for three circuits, then she too leaped to her feet and danced with her husband. She followed him, with her hands on his hips, leaping when he leaped, twitching her protruding backside, performing the intricate stamp and double shuffle, and singing the chorus to O'wa's praise song:

> His arrows will fly to the stars
> and when men speak his name
> it will be heard as far—

and H'ani came in with the chorus.

> —And he will find good water,
> wherever he travels, he will find good water.

O'wa squeaked and jerked his legs and made his shoulders shake.

> His bright eye will pick out the game
> when other men are blind.
> Effortlessly he will follow the spoor over rocky ground—
> —And he will find good water,
> at every camp site he will find good water—
> —prettiest maidens will smile and
> tiptoe to his camp fire in the night—

And H'ani reiterated in her reedy singsong:

> —And he will find good water,
> wherever he goes, he will find good water.

They were blessing the child, wishing upon him all the treasure of the San people, and Centaine felt that her heart would break with love for them and for the small pink bundle in her lap.

When at last the old people could dance and sing no more, they knelt in front of Centaine.

'As the great-grandparents of the child, we would like to give him a name,' H'ani explained shyly. 'Is it permitted?'

'Speak, old grandmother. Speak, old grandfather.'

H'ani looked at her husband and he nodded encouragement.

'We would name the child Shasa.'

Tears prickled Centaine's eyelids as she realized the great honour. They were naming him after the most precious, life-sustaining element in the San universe.

'Shasa – Good Water.'

Centaine blinked back the tears and smiled at them.

'I name this child Michel Shasa de Thiry Courtney,' she said softly, and each of the old people reached out in turn and touched his eyes and mouth in blessing.

The sulphurous, mineralized waters of the subterranean pool were possessed of extraordinary qualities. Every noon and evening Centaine soaked in their heat, and the manner in which her birth injuries healed was almost miraculous. Of course, she was in superb physical health, without an ounce of superfluous fat or flesh upon her, and Shasa's neat lean body and the ease of his delivery was a consequence of this. Furthermore the San looked upon parturition as such a routine process that H'ani neither pampered her, nor encouraged her to treat herself as an invalid.

Young muscles, elastic and well exercised, swiftly regained their resilience and strength. Her skin, not over-stretched, was free of stria, and her belly swiftly shrank back into its greyhound profile. Only her breasts were swollen hard with copious milk, and Shasa gorged and grew like one of the desert plants after rain.

Then again there was the pool and its waters.

'It is strange,' H'ani told her, 'the nursing mothers who drink this water always grow children with bones as hard as rock and teeth that shine like polished ivory. It is one of the blessings of the spirits that guard this place.'

At noon the sun struck through one of the apertures in the domed roof of the cavern, a solid white shaft of light through the steam-laden air, and Centaine loved to bask in it, moving across the pool as the beam swung, to keep in its charmed circle of light.

She lay chin-deep in the seething green water, and listened to Shasa snuffling and mewing in his sleep. She had wrapped him in the gemsbok skin and laid him on the ledge beside the pool where she could see him merely by turning her head.

The bottom of the pool was lined with gravel and pebbles. She scooped up handfuls of them and held them up in the sunlight, and they gave her a special kind of pleasure for they were strange and beautiful. There were veined agates, waterworn and smooth as swallows' eggs, stones of soft blue with lines of red through them, or pink or yellow, and jaspers and carnelians in a hundred shades of burgundy, shiny black onyx and tiger's eyes of gold barred with iridescent waves of shifting colour.

'I will make a necklace, for H'ani. A gift to thank her, from Shasa!'

She began to collect the prettiest stones with the most interesting and unusual shapes.

'I need a centrepiece for the necklace,' she decided, and she dredged handfuls of gravel and washed them in the hot green waters, then examined them in the sunlight until at last she found exactly what she was searching for.

It was a colourless stone, clear as water, but when it

caught the sunlight it contained a captive rainbow, an internal fire that burned with all the colours of the spectrum. Centaine spent a long lazy hour in the pool, turning this stone slowly in the beam of sunlight to make it flash and sparkle, staring into its depths with delight, watching it explode into wondrous cascades of light. The stone was not large – only the size of one of the ripe mongongo fruit – but it was a symmetrical many-sided crystal, perfect for the centrepiece of the necklace.

She designed H'ani's necklace with infinite care, spending many hours while Shasa nursed at her breast, arranging and rearranging her collection of pebbles until at last she had them in the order which most pleased her. Yet still she was not entirely satisfied, for the colourless central stone, so sparkling and regular in shape, made all the other coloured stones seem somehow drab and uninteresting.

Nevertheless, she began to experiment in stringing the pebbles in a necklace and here she immediately encountered problems. One or two of the pebbles were so soft that by dint of persistent effort and many worn-out bone augers she was finally able to drill a stringing hole through them. Others were brittle and shattered, and others again were too hard. In particular, the sparkling crystal resisted her best efforts, and remained absolutely unblemished after she had broken a dozen bone tools upon it.

She appealed to O'wa for assistance, and once he understood what she was working on, he was boyishly enthusiastic. They experimented and met with failure a dozen times before they finally worked out a means of cementing the harder stones on to the plaited sansevieria twine with acacia gum. Centaine began to assemble the necklace, and almost drove O'wa to distraction in the process, for she discarded fifty lengths of twine.

'This is too thick,' she would say. 'This is not strong enough.' And O'wa, who, when working on his own

470

weapons and tools, was also a perfectionist, took the problem very seriously.

Finally Centaine unravelled the hem of her canvas skirt and by plaiting the threads with the sansevieria fibres, they had a string for the necklace that was fine and strong enough to satisfy both of them.

When the necklace was at last finished, O'wa's self-satisfaction could not have been more overbearing had he conceived, planned and executed the project entirely on his own. It was a more of a pectoral than a necklace, with a single string around the back of the neck and the stones woven together in a plate-like decoration which hung on the breast with the big crystal in the centre, and a mosaic of coloured agates and jaspers and beryls surrounding it.

Even Centaine was delighted with her handiwork.

'It's turning out better than I had hoped,' she told O'wa, speaking in French and holding it up and turning it to catch the sunlight. 'Not as good as Monsieur Cartier,' she remembered her father's wedding gift to her mother which he had allowed her to wear on her birthdays ' – but not too bad for a wild girl's first effort in a wild place!'

They made a little ceremony of the presentation, and H'ani sat beaming like a little amber-coloured hobgoblin while Centaine thanked her for being such a paragon of a grandmother and the best midwife of the San, but when she placed the gift around the old woman's neck it seemed too big and weighty for the frail wrinkled body.

'Ha, old man, you are so proud of that knife of yours, but it is as nothing to this,' H'ani told O'wa as she stroked the necklace lovingly. 'This is a true gift. Look you! Now I wear the moon and the stars around my throat!'

She refused to remove it. It thumped against her breastbone as she wielded her digging stick or stooped to gather the mongongo nuts. When she crouched over the cooking fires, it dangled between the empty pouches of her swinging dugs. Even in the night as she slept with her head cradled on her own bare shoulder, Centaine looked across from her own shelter and saw the necklace shining on her chest, and it seemed to weigh the little old body down to the earth.

Once Centaine's preoccupation with the necklace was over, and her strength and vitality fully recovered after childbirth, she began to find the days too long and the rock cliffs of the valley as restrictive as the high walls of a prison.

The daily routine of life was undemanding, and Shasa slept on her hip or strapped to her back while she gathered the fallen nuts in the grove or helped H'ani bring in the firewood. Her menses resumed their course, and she itched with unexpected energy.

She had sudden moods of black depression, when even H'ani's innocent chatter irritated her, and she went off alone with the baby. Though he slept soundly through it all, she held him on her lap and spoke to him in French or English. She told him about his father and the château, about Nuage and Anna and General Courtney, and the names and the memories instilled in her a deep and undirected melancholy. Sometimes in the night, when she could not sleep, she lay and listened to the music in her head, the strains of Aïda or the songs the peasants sang in the fields at Mort Homme during the vendange.

So the months passed and the seasons of the desert rotated. The mongongo tree flowered and fruited again, and one day Shasa lifted himself on to hands and knees and to the delight of all set off on his first explorations of the valley. Yet Centaine's mood swung more violently than the seasons, her joy in Shasa and her contentment in the old people's company alternating with blacker moods when she felt like a life prisoner in the valley.

'They have come here to die,' she realized as she saw how the old San had settled into an established routine, 'but I don't want to die – I want to live, to live!'

H'ani watched her shrewdly until she realized it was time, and then told O'wa, 'Tomorrow Nam Child and I are going out of the valley.'

'Why, old woman?' O'wa looked startled. He was entirely contented and had not yet thought about leaving.

'We need medicines, and a change of food.'

'That is no reason to risk passing the guardians of the tunnel.'

'We will go out in the cool of the dawn, when the bees are sleepy, and return in the late evening – besides, the guardians have accepted us.'

O'wa started to protest further, but she cut him short. 'It is necessary, old grandfather, there are things that a man does not understand.'

As H'ani had intended, Centaine was excited and happy with the promised outing, and she shook H'ani awake long before the agreed hour. They slipped quietly through the tunnel of the bees, and with Shasa bound tightly to her back and her carrying satchel slung over one shoulder, Centaine ran down the narrow valley and out into the endless spaces of the desert like a schoolchild released from the classroom. Her mood lasted through the morning and she and H'ani chattered happily as they moved through the forest, searching and digging for the roots that H'ani said she needed.

In the heat of the noonday they found shelter under an acacia, and while Centaine nursed the baby, H'ani curled up in the shade and slept like an old yellow cat. Once Shasa had drunk his fill, Centaine leaned back against the trunk of the acacia and dozed off as well.

The stamp of hooves and horsey snorts disturbed her, and she opened her eyes, but remained absolutely still. With the breeze behind them, a herd of zebra had grazed down upon the sleeping group, not noticing them in the waist-high grass.

There were at least a hundred animals in the herd – newly born foals with legs too long for their fluffy bodies and with smudged chocolate-coloured stripes not yet set into definite patterns, staying close to their dams and staring around at the world with huge dark apprehensive eyes, older foals quick and surefooted as they chased each other in circles through the trees, the breeding mares, sleek and glossy, with stiff upstanding manes and pricked ears, some of them huge with foal, milk already swelling in their black udders. Then there were the stallions with powerful bulging quarters, necks arched proudly as they challenged each other or snuffled one of the mares, reminding Centaine vividly of Nuage in his prime. Barely daring to breathe, she lay against the acacia trunk and watched them with deep pleasure. They moved down still closer; she could have reached out and touched one of the foals as it gambolled past her. They passed so close that she could see that each animal was different from the others, the intricate patterns of their hides as distinct as fingerprints, and the dark stripes were shadowed by a paler orangey-cream duplicate, so that every animal was a separate work of art.

As she watched, one of the stallions, a magnificent animal standing twelve hands and with a bushy tail sweeping below his hocks, cut a young mare out of the main pack of the herd, nipping at her flanks and her neck with square yellow teeth, heading her off when she tried to circle back, pushing her well away from the other mares, but closer to the acacia tree, before he started to gentle her by nuzzling her neck.

The mare bridled flirtatiously, well aware of her highly

desirable condition, and she rolled her eyes and bit him viciously on his muscled glossy shoulder so that he snorted and reared away, but then circled back and tried to push his nose up under her tail where she was swollen tensely with her season. She squealed with a modest outrage and lashed out with both back legs, her shiny black hooves flying high past his head, and she spun around to face him, baring her teeth.

Centaine found herself unaccountably moved. She shared the mare's mounting excitement, empathized with her charade of reluctance that was spurring the circling stallion to greater ardour. At last the mare submitted and stood stock-still, her tail lifted as the stallion nosed her gently. Centaine felt her own body stiffen in anticipation – then when the stallion reared over her and buried his long pulsing black root deeply in her, Centaine gasped and pressed her own knees together sharply.

That night in her rude thatched shelter beside the steaming thermal pool, she dreamed of Michael and the old barn near North Field, and woke to a deep corroding loneliness and an undirected discontent that did not subside even when she held Shasa to her breast and felt him tugging demandingly at her.

Her dark mood persisted, and the high rocky walls of the valley closed in around her so she felt she could not breathe. However, four more days passed before she could wheedle H'ani into another expedition out into the open forests.

Centaine looked for the zebra herd again as they meandered amongst the mopani trees, but this time the forests seemed strangely deserted and what wild game they did see was mistrusting and skittish, taking instant alarm at the first distant sign of the upright human figures.

'There is something,' H'ani muttered as they rested in the noon heat, 'I do not know what it is, but the wild things sense it also. It makes me uneasy, we should return to the valley that I might talk with O'wa. He understands these things better than I do.'

'Oh H'ani, not yet,' Centaine pleaded. 'Let us stay here a little longer. I feel so free.'

'I do not like whatever is happening here,' H'ani insisted.

'The bees—' Centaine found inspiration ' – we cannot pass through the tunnel until nightfall,' and though H'ani grumped and frowned, she at last agreed.

'But listen to this old woman, there is something unusual, something bad—' and she sniffed at the air and neither of them could sleep when they rested at noon.

H'ani took Shasa from her as soon as he had fed.

'He grows so,' she whispered, and there was a shadow of regret in her bright black eyes. 'I wish I could see him in his full growth, straight and tall as the mopani tree.'

'You will, old grandmother,' Centaine smiled, 'you will live to see him as a man.'

H'ani did not look up at her. 'You will go, both of you, one day soon. I sense it, you will go back to your own people.' Her voice was hoarse with regret. 'You will go, and when you do there will be nothing left in life for this old woman.'

'No, old grandmother,' Centaine reached out and took her hand. 'Perhaps we will have to go one day. But we will come back to you. I give you my word on that.'

Gently H'ani disentangled her grip, and still without looking at Centaine, stood up. 'The heat is past.'

They worked back towards the mountain, moving widely separated through the forest, keeping each other just in sight, except when denser bush intervened. As was her habit, Centaine chatted to the sleeping infant on her hip, speaking French to train his ear to the sound of the language, and to keep her own tongue exercised.

They had almost reached the scree slope below the cliffs when Centaine saw the fresh tracks of a pair of zebra stallions imprinted deeply in the soft earth ahead of her. Under H'ani's instruction, she had developed acute powers of observation, and O'wa had taught her to read the signs of the wild with fluent ease. There was something about these tracks that puzzled her. They ran side by side, as though the animals that made them had been harnessed to each other. She hefted Shasa on to her other hip and turned aside to examine them more closely.

She stopped with a jerk that alarmed the child, and he squawked in protest. Centaine stood paralysed with shock, staring at the hoof prints, not yet able to comprehend what she was seeing. Then suddenly a rush of emotions and understanding made her reel back. She understood the agitated behaviour of the wild creatures, and H'ani's undirected premonition of evil. She began to tremble, at the same moment filled with fear and joy, with confusion and shaking excitement.

'Shasa,' she whispered, 'they are not zebra prints.' The hooves that had made these chains of tracks were shod with crescents of steel. 'Horsemen, Shasa, civilized men riding horses shod with steel!' It seemed impossible. Not here, not in this desert fastness.

Instinctively her hands flew to the opening of the canvas shawl she wore about her shoulders, and from which her breasts thrust out unashamedly. She covered them and glanced around her fearfully. With the San she had come to accept nudity as completely natural. Now she was aware that her skirts rode high on her long slim thighs, and she was ashamed.

She backed away from the prints as though from an accuser's finger.

'Man – a civilized man,' she repeated, and immediately the image of Michael formed in her mind, and her longing

477

overcame her shame. She crept forward again and knelt beside the spoor, staring at it avidly, not able to bring herself to touch it in case it proved to be hallucination.

It was fresh, so very fresh that even as she watched the crisply outlined edge of one hoofprint, it collapsed and slid in upon itself in a trickle of loose sand.

'An hour ago, Shasa, they passed only an hour ago, not longer.'

The riders had been walking their horses, moving at less than five miles an hour.

'There is a civilized man within five miles of us at this very moment, Shasa.'

She jumped up and ran along the line, fifty paces, before she stopped again and dropped to her knees. She would not have seen it before – without O'wa's instruction she had been blind – but now she picked out the alien texture of metal, even though it was only the size of a thumbnail and had fallen into a clump of dry grass.

She picked it out and laid it in her palm. It was a tarnished brass button, a military button with an embossed crest, and the broken thread still knotted in the tang.

She stared at it as though it were a priceless jewel. The design upon it depicted a unicorn and an antelope guarding a shield and below there was a motto in a ribbon.

'*Ex Unitate Vires*,' she read aloud. She had seen the same buttons on General Sean Courtney's tunic, but his were brightly polished. 'From Unity Strength.' The coat of arms of the Union of South Africa.

'A soldier, Shasa! One of General Courtney's men!'

At that moment there was a distant whistle, H'ani's summons, and Centaine sprang to her feet and hovered undecidedly. All her instinct was to race desperately after the horsemen, and to plead to be allowed to travel with them back to civilization, but then H'ani whistled again and she turned to look back.

She knew how terrified the San were of all foreigners,

478

for the old people had told her all the stories of brutal persecution. 'H'ani must not see these tracks.'

She shaded her eyes and stared longingly in the direction in which the spoor pointed, but nothing moved amongst the mopani trees. 'She will try to stop us following them, Shasa, she and O'wa will do anything to stop us. How can we leave the old people, and yet they can't come with us, they will be in great danger—' she was torn and undecided ' – but we can't let this chance go. It might be our only—'

H'ani whistled again, this time much closer, and Centaine saw her small figure amongst the trees coming towards her. Centaine's hand closed guiltily on the brass button and she thrust it into the bottom of her satchel.

'H'ani mustn't see the tracks,' she repeated, and glanced quickly up at the cliffs, orientating herself so that she could return and find them herself, and then whirled and ran to meet the old woman and led her away, back towards the hidden valley.

That evening, as they performed the routine camp chores, Centaine had difficulty disguising the nervous excitement that gripped her, and she replied distractedly to H'ani's questions. As soon as they had eaten and the short African dusk ended, she went to her shelter and settled down as though to sleep, pulling the gemsbok skin over both the infant and herself. Although she lay quietly, and regulated her breathing, she was fretting and worrying, as she tried to reach her decision.

She had no means of guessing who the horsemen were, and she was determined not to lead the San into mortal danger, yet she was equally determined to take her own chances and to follow up those tantalizing tracks for the promise they held of salvation and return to her own world – of escape from this harsh existence which would at last turn her and her infant into savages.

'We must give ourselves a start, so that we can catch up

with the horsemen before H'ani and O'wa even realize we have gone. That way they will not follow us, will not be exposed to danger. We will go as soon as the moon rises, my baby.'

She lay tense and still, feigning sleep, until the gibbous moon showed over the rim of the valley. Then she rose quietly and Shasa murmured and grunted sleepily as she gathered up her satchel and stave and crept quietly out on to the path.

She paused at the corner of the hill and looked back. The fire had died to embers, but the moonlight played into the old people's shelter. O'wa was in the shadows, just a small dark shape, but the moonlight washed H'ani.

Her amber skin seemed to glow in the soft light, and her head, propped on her own shoulder, was turned towards Centaine. Her expression seemed forlorn and hopeless, a harbinger of the terrible sorrow and loss that Centaine knew she would suffer when she woke, and the necklace of pebbles gleamed dully on her bony old chest.

'Goodbye, old grandmother,' Centaine whispered. 'Thank you for your great humanity and kindness to us. I will always love you. Forgive us, little H'ani, but we have to go.'

Centaine had to steel herself before she could turn the rocky corner that cut her off from the camp. As she hurried up the rough pathway to the tunnel of the bees, her own tears blurred the moonlight and tasted of seawater as they ran into the corners of her mouth.

She groped her way through the utter darkness and the warm honey smell of the tunnel and out into the moonlight in the narrow valley beyond. She paused to listen for the sound of bare feet on the rocks behind her, but the only sound was the yelp of the jackal packs out on the plains below, and she started forward again.

As she reached the plain Shasa mewed and wriggled on her hip, and without stopping she adjusted his sling so that he could reach her breast. He fastened on it greedily, and she whispered to him as she hurried through the forest, 'Don't be afraid, baby, even though this is the first time we have been alone at night. The horsemen will be camped just a short way ahead. We will catch up with them before sunrise, before H'ani and O'wa are even awake. Don't look at the shadows, don't imagine things, Shasa—' She kept talking softly, trying to shore up her own courage, for the night was full of mystery and menace, and she had never realized until that moment how she had come to rely on the two old people.

'We should have found the spoor by now, Shasa.' Centaine stopped uncertainly and peered about her. Everything looked different in the moonlight. 'We must have missed it.'

She turned back, breaking into an anxious trot. 'I'm sure it was at the head of this glade.' And then, with a rush of relief, 'There it is, the moon was against us before.' Now the hoofprints were rimmed clearly with shadow and the steel shoes had bitten deeply into the sandy earth. How much O'wa had taught her! She saw the tracks so clearly that she could break into a trot.

The horsemen had made no effort to hide their spoor, and there was no wind to wipe it out. They had ridden the easy line, keeping out in the open, following well-beaten game paths, not pushing their mounts above an easy ambling walk, and once Centaine found where one of them had dismounted and led his horse for a short distance.

She was elated when she saw that this man wore boots. Riding-boots with medium high heels, and well-worn soles. Even in the uncertain moonlight, Centaine could tell by the length of his stride and the slight toe-out gait that he was a tall man with long narrow feet and an easy, yet confident stride. It seemed to confirm all her hopes.

'Wait for us,' she whispered. 'Please, sir, wait for Shasa and me to catch up.'

She was gaining rapidly. 'We must look for their camp fire, Shasa, they will be camped not far from—' she broke off. 'There! What's that, Shasa? Did you see it?'

She stared into the forest.

'I'm sure I saw something.' She stared about her. 'But it's gone now.' She changed Shasa to her other hip.

'What a big lump you are becoming! But never mind, we'll be there soon.' She started forward again, and the trees thinned out and Centaine found herself at the head of another long open glade. The moonlight laid a pale metallic sheen on the short grass.

Eagerly she surveyed the open ground, focusing her attention on each dark irregularity, hoping to see hobbled horses near a smouldering fire and human shapes rolled into their blankets, but the shapes were only tree stumps or anthills, and at the far side of the glade a small herd of wildebeest grazing heads down.

'Don't worry, Shasa,' she spoke louder to cover her own intense disappointment, 'I'm sure they'll be camped in the trees.'

The wildebeest threw up their heads and erupted into a rumbling snorting stampede, streaming away into the trees, fine dust hanging behind them like mist.

'What frightened them, Shasa? The wind is with us, they could not have taken our scent.' The sound of the running herd dwindled. 'Something chased them!'

She looked around her carefully. 'I'm imagining things. I'm seeing things that aren't there. We mustn't start panicking at shadows.' Centaine started forward firmly, but within a short distance she stopped again fearfully.

'Did you hear that, Shasa? There is something following us. I heard the footfalls, but it's stopped now. It's watching us, I can feel it.'

At that moment a small cloud passed over the moon and the world turned dark.

'The moon will come out again soon.' Centaine hugged

the infant so hard that Shasa gave a little bleat of protest. 'I'm sorry, baby.' She relaxed her grip and then stumbled as she started forward.

'I wish we hadn't come – no, that's not true. We had to come. We must be brave, Shasa. We can't follow the spoor without the moon.'

She sank down to rest, looking up into the sky. The moon was a pale nimbus through the thin gunmetal cloud, and then it broke out into a hole in the cloud layer and for a moment flooded the glade with soft platinum light.

'Shasa!' Centaine's voice rose into a high thin scream.

There was something out there, a huge pale shape, as big as a horse, but with sinister, stealthy, unhorselike carriage. At her cry, it sank out of sight below the tops of the grass.

Centaine leapt to her feet and raced towards the trees, but before she reached them the moon was snuffed out again, and in the darkness Centaine fell full length. Shasa wailed fretfully against her chest.

'Please be quiet, baby.' Centaine hugged him, but the child sensed her terror and screamed. 'Don't, Shasa. You'll bring it after us.'

Centaine was trembling wildly. That big pale thing out there in the darkness was possessed of an unearthly menace, a palpable aura of evil, and she knew what it was. She had seen it before.

She pressed herself flat to the earth, trying to cover Shasa with her own body. Then there was a sound, a hurricane of sound that filled the night, filled her head – seemed to fill her very soul. She had heard that sound before, but never so close, never so soul-shattering.

'Oh, sweet mother of God,' she whispered. It was the full-blooded roar of a lion. The most terrifying sound of the African wilds.

At that moment, the moon broke out of the cloud again, and she saw the lion clearly. It stood facing her, fifty paces away, and it was immense, with its mane fully extended, a peacock's tail of ruddy hair around the massive flat head. Its tail swung from side to side, flicking the black tuft like a metronome, and then it extended its neck and humped its shoulders, lowering and opening its jaws so that the long ivory fangs gleamed in the moonlight like daggers – and it roared again.

All the ferocity and cruelty of Africa seemed to be distilled into that dreadful blast. Though she had read the descriptions of the travellers and hunters, they could not prepare her for the actuality. The blast seemed to crush her chest, so that her heart checked and her lungs seized. It loosened her bowels and her bladder so she had to clench fiercely to keep control of herself. In her arms Shasa screeched and wriggled, and that was enough to jar Centaine out of her paroxysm of terror.

The lion was an old red tom, an outcast from the pride. His teeth and claws were worn, his skin scarred and almost bald across the shoulders. In the succession battle with the young prime male who had driven him from the pride, he had lost one eye, a hooked claw had ripped it from the socket.

He was sick and starving, his ribs racked out under his scraggy hide, and in his hunger he had attacked a porcupine three days before. A dozen long poisonous barbed quills had driven deeply into his neck and cheeks and were already suppurating and festering. He was old and weak and uncertain, his confidence shattered, and he was wary of man and the man odour. His ancestral memories, his own long experience had warned him to stay clear of these strange frail upright creatures. His roarings were symptoms of his nervousness and uncertainty. There was a time when, as hungry as he was now, he would have gone in swiftly and silently. Even now his jaws had the strength to crunch through a skull or thighbone and a single blow of one massive forepaw could shatter a man's spine. However, he hung back, circling the prey. Perhaps, if there had been no moon, he would have been bolder, or if he had ever eaten human flesh before, or if the agony of the buried quills had been less crippling, but now he roared indecisively. Centaine leaped to her feet. It was instinctive. She had watched the old black stable tom cat at Mort Homme with a mouse, and his reflex action to his victim's attempted flight. Somehow she knew that to run would be to bring the great cat down on her immediately.

She screamed, and holding the pointed stave high, she rushed straight at the lion. He whirled and galloped off through the grass, fifty paces, and then stopped and looked back at her, lashing his tail from side to side, and he growled with frustration.

Still facing him, clutching Shasa under one arm and the stave in the other hand, Centaine backed away. She glanced over her shoulder – the nearest mopani tree stood isolated from the rest of the forest. It was straight and sturdy with a fork high above the ground, but it seemed to be at the other end of the earth from where she stood.

'We mustn't run, Shasa,' she whispered, and her voice shook. 'Slowly. Slowly, now.' Her sweat was running into her eyes though she shivered wildly with cold and terror.

The lion circled around towards the forest, swinging its head low, ears pricked, and she saw the gleam of his single eye like the flash of a knife-blade.

'We must get to the tree, Shasa,' and the infant whined and kicked on her hip. The lion stopped and she could hear it sniffing.

'Oh God, it's so big.' Her foot caught and she almost fell. The lion rushed forward, grunting terrible exhalations of sound, like the pistons of a locomotive, and she screamed and waved the stave.

The lion stopped, but this time stood its ground, facing her, lowering its great shaggy head threateningly and lashing the long, black-tipped tail, and when Centaine began to back away, it moved forward, slinking low to the earth.

'The tree, Shasa, we must reach the tree!'

The lion started to circle again, and Centaine glanced up at the moon. There was another dark blot of cloud trundling down from the north.

'Please don't cover the moon!' she whispered brokenly. She realized how their lives depended on that soft uncertain light, she instinctively knew how bold the great cat would become in darkness. Even now its circles were becoming narrower, it was working in, still cautious and wary, but watching her and perhaps beginning to realize how utterly helpless she was. The final killing charge was only seconds away.

Something hit her from behind and she shrieked and almost fell, before she realized that she had walked backwards into the base of the mopani tree. She clung to it for support, for her legs could not hold her, so intense was her relief.

Shaking so much that she almost dropped it, she unslung the leather satchel from her shoulder and tipped the ostrich-egg bottles out of it. Then she pushed Shasa feet first into the bag, so only his head protruded, and slung him over her back. Shasa was redfaced and yelling angrily.

'Be quiet, please be quiet—' She snatched up her stave again, and stuck it into her rope belt like a sword. She jumped to catch the first branch above her head and she got a hold and scrambled with her bare feet for a grip on the rough bark. She would never have believed it possible, but in desperation she found untapped reserves and she hauled herself and her load upwards by the main strength of arms and legs, and crawled on to the branch.

Still, she was only five feet above the ground, and the lion grunted fearsomely and made a short rush forward. She teetered on the branch and reached up for another hold, and then another. The bark was rough and abrasive as crocodile skin and her fingers and shins were bleeding by the time she scrambled into the fork of the mopani thirty feet above the ground.

The lion smelled the blood from her grazed skin and it drove him frantic with hunger. He roared and prowled around the base of the mopani, stopping to sniff at the ostrich eggs that Centaine had dropped, and then roaring again.

'We are safe, Shasa,' Centaine was sobbing with relief, crouched in the high fork, holding the child on her lap and peering down through the leaves and branches on to the broad muscled back of the old lion. She realized that she could see more clearly, the light of dawn was flushing the eastern sky. She could clearly make out that the great cat was a gingery reddish colour, and unlike the drawings she had seen, his mane was not black but the same ruddy colour.

'O'wa called them red devils,' she remembered, hugging Shasa and trying to still his outraged yells. 'How long until it's light?' She looked anxiously to the east and saw the dawn coming in a splendour of molten copper and furnace reds.

'It will be day soon, Shasa,' she told him. 'Then the beast will go away—'

Below her the lion reared up on its hindlegs and stood against the trunk, looking up at her.

'One eye – he's only got one eye.' The black scarred socket somehow made the other glowing yellow eye more murderous, and Centaine shuddered wildly.

The lion ripped at the trunk of the tree with the claws of both front feet, erupting into those terrible crackling roars once more. It ripped slabs and long shreds of bark from the trunk, leaving wet wounds weeping with sap.

'Go away!' Centaine screamed at it, and the lion gathered itself on its hindquarters and launched itself upwards, hooking with all four feet.

'No! Go away!'

Michael had told her and she had read in Levaillant that lions did not climb trees, but this great red cat came swarming up the trunk and then pulled itself on to the main branch ten feet above the ground and balanced there staring up at her.

'Shasa!' She realized then that the lion was going to get her, her climb had merely delayed the moment. 'We've got to save you, Shasa.'

She dragged herself upward, standing in the fork, and clutching the side branch.

'There!' Above her head there was a broken branch that stuck out like a hatpeg, and using all that remained of her strength, she lifted the rawhide bag with Shasa in it and hooked the strap over the peg.

'Goodbye, my darling,' she panted. 'Perhaps H'ani will find you.'

Shasa was struggling and kicking, the bag swung and twisted, and Centaine sank back on to the fork and drew the sharpened stave from her belt.

'Be still, baby, please be still.' She did not look up at him. She was watching the lion below her. 'If you are quiet it might not see you, it might be satisfied.'

The lion stretched up with its forelegs, balancing on the branch, and roared again. She smelt it now, the stink of its festering wounds and the dead carrion reek of its breath, and then the beast hurled itself upwards.

With claws ripping the bark, clinging with all four paws, it came up in a series of convulsive leaps. Its head was thrown back, its single yellow eye fastened on Centaine, and with those monstrous explosions of sound bursting up out of its gaping pink jaws, it came straight at her.

Centaine screamed and drove the point of her stave down into the jaws with all her strength. She felt the sharpened end bite into the soft pink mucus membrane in the back of its throat, saw the spurt of scarlet blood, and then the lion locked its jaws on the stave and with a toss of its flying mane ripped it out of her hands and sent it windmilling out and down to hit the earth below.

Then with bright blood streaming from its jaws, blowing a pink cloud every time it roared, the lion reached up with one huge paw.

Centaine jack-knifed her legs upwards, trying to avoid it, but she was not quick enough; one of the curled yellow claws, as long and thick as a man's forefinger, sank into her flesh above her bare ankle, and she was jerked savagely downwards.

As she was pulled out of the fork, she flung both her arms around the side branch and with all her remaining strength she held on. She felt her whole body racked, drawn out, the unbearable weight of the lion stretching her leg until she felt her knee and hip joint crack, and pain shot up her spine and filled her skull like a bursting sky rocket.

She felt the lion's claw curling in her flesh, and her arms started to give way. Inch by inch she was drawn out of the tree.

'Look after my baby,' she screamed. 'Please God, protect my baby.'

It was another wild-goose chase, Garry was absolutely convinced of it, though of course he would never be fool-hardy enough to say so. Even the thought made him feel guilty, and he glanced sideways at the woman he loved.

Anna had learned English and lost a little weight in the eighteen short sweet months since he had met her, and the latter was the only circumstance in his life he would have altered if it had been in his power; indeed he was always urging food upon her. There was a German pâtisserie and confectioner's opposite the Kaiserhof Hotel in Windhoek where Garry had taken a permanent suite. He never passed the shop without going in to buy a box of the marvellous black chocolates or a creamy cake – Black Forest cherry cake was a favourite – which he took back to Anna. When he carved, he always reserved the fattest, juiciest cuts for her, and replenished the plate without allowing her time to protest. However, she had still lost weight.

They didn't spend enough time in the hotel suite, he brooded. They spent too much of their time chasing about the bush, as they were doing now. No sooner had he put a few pounds on her than they were off again, banging and jolting over remote tracks in the open Fiat tourer that had replaced the 'T' model Ford, or when the tracks faded, resorting to horses and mules to carry them over rugged ranges of mountains or through the yawning canyons and rock deserts of the interior, chasing the will-o'-the-wisp of rumour and chance and often of deliberately misleading information.

'The crazy old people', *'Die twee ou onbeskofters'* – that was the title which they had gained themselves from one end of the territory to the other, and Garry took a perverse and defiant pleasure in the fact that he had earned it the hard way. When he had totted up the actual cost in hard cash of the continuing search, he had been utterly appalled, until suddenly he had thought, 'What else have I got to spend it on anyway, except Anna?' And then, after a little further reflection, 'What else is there except Anna?' And with that discovery he had thrown himself headlong into the madness.

Of course, sometimes when he woke in the night and thought about it clearly and sensibly, he knew that his grandson did not exist, he knew that the daughter-in-law that he had never seen had drowned eighteen months ago, out there in the cold green waters of the Atlantic, taking with her the last contact he could ever have with Michael. Then that terrible sorrow came upon him once again, threatening to crush him, until he groped for Anna in the bed beside him and crept to her, and even in her sleep she seemed to sense his need and she would roll towards him and take him to her.

Then in the morning he awoke refreshed and revitalized, logic banished and blind faith restored, ready to set out on the next fantastic adventure that awaited them.

Garry had arranged for five thousand posters to be printed in Cape Town, and distributed to every police station, magistrate's court, post office and railway station in South West Africa. Wherever he and Anna travelled, there was always a bundle of posters on the back seat of the Fiat or in one of the saddle-bags, and they stuck them on every blank wall of every general dealer's or bar-room they passed, they nailed them to tree trunks at desolate cross-roads in the deep bush, and with a bribe of a handful of sweets dished them out to black and white and brown urchins they met on the roadside, with instructions to take them to their homestead or kraal or camp and hand them to their elders.

£5000 *REWARD* £5000

For information leading to the rescue of CENTAINE DE THIRY COURTNEY A SURVIVOR OF THE HOSPITAL SHIP PROTEA CASTLE most barbarously torpedoed by a GERMAN SUBMARINE on the 28th Aug. 1917 off the coast of SWAKOPMUND.

MRS COURTNEY would have been cast ashore and may be in the care of wild TRIBESMEN or alone in the WILDERNESS.

Any information concerning her whereabouts should be conveyed to the undersigned at the KAISERHOF HOTEL WINDHOEK.

LT. COL. G. C. COURTNEY

Five thousand pounds was a fortune, twenty years' salary for the average working man, enough to buy a ranch and stock it with cattle and sheep, enough to provide a man with a secure living for his entire life, and there were dozens eager to try for the reward, or for any lesser amount that they could wheedle out of Garry by vague promises and fanciful stories and outright lies.

In the Kaiserhof suite he and Anna interviewed hopefuls who had never ventured beyond the line of rail but were willing to lead expeditions into the desert, others who knew exactly where the lost girl could be found, still others who had actually seen Centaine and only needed a grub-stake of £1,000 to go and fetch her in. There were spiritualists and clairvoyants who were in constant contact with her, on a higher plane, and even one gentleman who offered to sell his own daughter, at a bargain rate, to replace the missing girl.

Garry met them all cheerfully. He listened to their stories and chased their theories and instructions, or sat around an ouija board with the spiritualists, even followed one of them who was using one of Centaine's rings suspended on a piece of string as a lodestone, on a five hundred-mile pilgrimage through the desert. He was presented with a number of young ladies, varying in texture and colour from blonde to *café au lait*, all claiming to be Centaine de Thiry Courtney, or willing to do for him anything that she could do. Some of them became loudly abusive when they were refused and had to be evicted from the suite by Anna in person.

'No wonder she is losing weight,' Garry told himself, and leaned over to pat Anna's thigh as she sat beside him in the open Fiat tourer. The words of the blasphemous old grace came into his mind:

'We thank the Lord for what we have,
But for a little more we would be glad.'

He grinned at her fondly, and aloud he told her, 'We

should be there soon.' She nodded and replied, 'This time I know we will find her. I have a sure feeling!'

'Yes,' Garry agreed dutifully. 'This time will be different.'

He was quite safe in that assertion. No other of their many expeditions had begun in such a mysterious manner.

One of their own reward posters had arrived folded upon itself and sealed with wax, bearing a postmark dated four days previously at Usakos, a way station on the narrow-gauge railway line halfway between Windhoek and the coast. The package was unstamped – Garry had been obliged to pay the postage – and it was addressed in a bold but educated hand, the script unmistakably German. When Garry split the wax seal and unfolded it he found a laconic invitation to a rendezvous written on the foot of the sheet, and a hand-drawn map to guide him. The sheet was unsigned.

Garry immediately telegraphed the postmaster at Usakos, confident that the volume of business at such a remote station would be so low that the postmaster would remember every package handed in for postage. The post-master did indeed recall the package and the circumstances of its delivery. It had been left on the threshold of the post office during the night and nobody had even glimpsed the correspondent.

As the writer probably intended, all this intrigued both Garry and Anna, and they were eager to keep the rendez-vous. It was set for a site in the barren Kamas Hochtland a hundred and fifty miles from Windhoek.

It had taken them all of three days to negotiate the atrocious roads, but after losing themselves at least a dozen times, changing approximately the same number of punc-tured tyres, and sleeping rough on the hard ground beside the Fiat, they had now almost reached the appointed meeting place.

The sun blazed down from a cloudless sky and the breeze from behind blew eddies of red dust over them as they rattled and rumbled over the stony ruts. Anna seemed impervious to all the heat and dust and hardship of the desert and Garry, gazing at her in unstinted admiration, almost missed the next tight bend in the track. His off-wheels skidded over the verge, and the Fiat teetered and rocked over the yawning void that opened abruptly before them. He hauled the steering over, and as they bumped back into the wheel ruts he pulled on the handbrake.

They were on the rim of a deep canyon that cut the plateau like an axe stroke. The track descended into the depths in a series of hairpin twists like the contortions of a maimed serpent, and hundreds of feet below them the river was a narrow ribbon that threw dazzling reflections of the noon sun up the orange-coloured cliffs.

'This is the place,' Garry told her, 'and I don't like it. Down there we will be at the mercy of any bandit or murderer.'

'Mijnheer, we are already late for the meeting—'

'I don't know if we'll ever get out of there again, and God knows, nobody is likely to find us here. Probably just our bare bones.'

'Come, Mijnheer, we can talk later.'

Garry drew a deep breath. Sometimes there were distinct drawbacks to being paired with a strong-willed woman. He let off the handbrake and the Fiat rolled over the rim of the canyon, and once they were committed, there was no turning back.

It was a nightmare descent, the gradient so steep that the brake shoes smoked, and the hairpin bends so tight that he had to back and fill to coax the Fiat through them.

'Now I know why our friend chose this place. He has us at his mercy down here.'

Forty minutes later they came out in the gut of the canyon. The walls above them were so sheer that they blotted out the sun. They were in shadow, but it was stiflingly hot. No breeze reached down here, and the air had a flinty bite on the back of the throat.

There was a narrow strip of level land on each bank of the river, covered with coarse thorn growth, and Garry backed the Fiat off the track and they climbed down stiffly and beat the red dust from their clothing. The stream bubbled sullenly over a low causeway of rock, and the water was opaque and a poisonous yellow colour like the effluent from a chemical factory.

'Well,' Garry surveyed both banks and the cliffs above them, 'we seem to have the place to ourselves. Our friend is nowhere to be seen.'

'We will wait.' Anna forestalled the suggestion she knew was coming.

'Of course, Mevrou.' Garry lifted his hat and mopped his face with the cotton bandanna from around his neck. 'May I suggest a cup of tea?'

Anna took the kettle and went down the bank. She tasted the river water suspiciously, and then filled it. When she climbed back, Garry had a fire of thornwood crackling between two hearthstones. While the kettle boiled, Garry fetched a blanket from the back of the Fiat, and the bottle of schnapps from the cubbyhole. He poured a liberal dram into each of the mugs, added a heaped spoon of sugar, then topped them up with strong hot tea. He had found that schnapps, like chocolate, had a most tempering effect on Anna, and he was never without a bottle. Perhaps the journey would not be entirely wasted, he thought, as he added another judicious splash of spirits into Anna's mug and carried it to where she sat in the middle of the rug.

Before he reached her, Garry let out a startled cry and dropped the mug, splashing his boots with hot tea. He stood staring into the bush behind her, and raised both hands high above his head. Anna glanced round and then bounded to her feet and seized a brand of firewood which she brandished before her. Garry edged swiftly to her side and stood close to her protective bulk.

'Keep away!' Anna bellowed. 'I warn you, I'll break the first skull—'

They were surrounded. The gang had crept up on them through the dense scrub.

'Oh Lord, I knew it was a trap!' Garry muttered. They were almost certainly the most dangerous-looking band of cut-throats he had ever seen.

'We have no money, nothing worth stealing—' How many of them? he wondered desperately. Three – no, there was another behind that tree – four murderous ruffians. The obvious leader was a purple-black giant with bandoliers of ammunition criss-crossing his chest, and a Mauser rifle in the crook of his arm. A ruff of thick woolly beard framed his broad African features like the mane of a man-eating lion.

The others were all armed, a mixed band of Khoisan Hottentots and Ovambo tribesmen, wearing odd items of military uniform and civilian clothing, all of it heavily worn and faded, patched and tattered, some of them barefooted and others with scuffed boots, shapeless and battered from hard marches. Only their weapons were well cared for, glistening with oil and borne lovingly, almost the way a father might carry his firstborn son.

Garry thought fleetingly of the service revolver he kept holstered under the dashboard of the Fiat, and then swiftly abandoned such a reckless notion.

'Don't harm us,' he pleaded, crowding up behind Anna, and then with a feeling of utter disbelief, Garry found himself abandoned as Anna launched her attack.

Swinging the burning log like a Viking's axe, she charged straight at the huge black leader.

'Back, you swine!' she roared in Flemish. 'Get out of here, you bitch-born son of Hades!'

Taken by surprise, the gang scattered in pandemonium,

496

trying to duck the smoking log as it hissed about their heads.

'How dare you, you stinking bastard spawn of diseased whores—'

Still shaking with shock, Garry stared after her, torn between terror and admiration for this new revelation of his lover's accomplishments. He had heard some great cursers in his life – there had been the legendary sergeant-major whom he had known during the Zulu rebellion; men travelled miles to listen to him addressing a parade ground. The man was a Sunday School preacher in comparison. Garry could have charged admission fees to Anna's performance. Her eloquence was matched only by her dexterity with the log.

She caught one of the Hottentots a crashing blow between the shoulders and he was hurled into a thorn bush, his jacket smoking with live coals, shrieking like a wounded warthog. Two others, reluctant to face Anna's wrath, leaped over the river bank and disappeared with high splashes beneath the yellow waters. That left only the big black Ovambo to bear the full brunt of Anna's onslaught. He was quick and agile for such a big man, and he avoided the wild swings of the log and danced behind the nearest camel-thorn tree. With nimble footwork he kept the trunk between Anna and himself, until at last she stopped, gasping and redfaced, and panted at him, 'Come out, you yellow-bellied black-faced apology for a blue-testicled baboon!' Garry noticed with awe how she managed to cram the metaphor with colour. 'Come out where I can kill you!'

Warily the Ovambo declined, backing off out of reach. 'No! No! We did not come to fight you, we came to fetch you—' he answered in Afrikaans. She lowered the log slowly.

'Did you write the letter?' and the Ovambo shook his head. 'I have come to take you to the man who did.'

The Ovambo ordered two of his men to remain and

497

guard the Fiat. Then he led them away along the floor of the canyon. Although there were stretches of open easy-going on the river bank, there were also narrow gorges through which the river roared and swirled, and the path was steep and so narrow that only one man could pass at a time.

These gaps were guarded by other guerrillas. Garry saw only the tops of their heads and the glint of their rifle barrels amongst the rocks, and he noticed how cunningly the site for the rendezvous had been chosen. Nobody could follow them undetected. An army would not be able to rescue them. They were totally vulnerable, completely at the mercy of these rough hard men. Garry shivered in the sweltering gut of the canyon.

'We'll be damned lucky to get out of this,' he muttered to himself, and then aloud, 'My leg is hurting. Can't we rest?' But no one even looked back at him, and he stumbled forward to keep as close to Anna as he was able.

Quite unexpectedly, long after Garry had relapsed into resigned misery, the Ovambo guide stepped around the corner of a yellow sandstone monolith and into a temporary camp site under an overhanging cliff on the river bank. Even in his exhaustion and unhappiness, Garry saw that there was a steep pathway up the canyon wall behind the camp, an escape route against surprise attack.

'They have thought of everything.' He touched Anna's arm and pointed out the path, but all her attention was on the man who sauntered out from the deep shadow of the cavern.

He was a young man, half Garry's age, but in the first seconds of their meeting he made Garry feel inadequate and foolish. He didn't have to say a word. He merely stood in the sunlight and stared at Garry with a catlike stillness about his tall elegant frame, and Garry was reminded of all the things he was not.

His hair was golden, hanging to his bare shoulders,

streaked white by the sun, yet as lustrous as raw silk, offering a startling contrast to his deeply tanned features. These might once have been as beautiful as those of a comely girl, but all softness had been burned by the flames of life's furnace, and like forged iron, the marks of the anvil had been left upon them.

He was tall but not gawky or round-shouldered, and he was lean, with hard, flat muscle. He wore only riding-breeches and boots, and the hair on his chest sparkled like fine copper wire. Around his neck on a gold chain he had hung a small gold locket, something that no English gentleman would ever do. Garry tried to feel superior, but under that flat level gaze it was difficult.

'Colonel Courtney,' he said, and again Garry was taken off balance. Though accented, it was the voice of an educated and cultivated man, and his mouth altered shape, losing its hard stern line as he smiled.

'Please do not be alarmed. You *are* Colonel Courtney, are you not?'

'Yes.' It took an effort for Garry to speak. 'I am Colonel Courtney – did you write the letter?'

He took the poster from his breast pocket, and tried to unfold it, but his hands were shaking so that it fluttered and tore in his fingers. The man's smile gently mocked him as he nodded, 'Yes, I sent for you.'

'You know where the lost girl can be found?' Anna demanded, stepping closer to him in her eagerness.

'Perhaps,' he shrugged.

'You have seen her?' Anna insisted.

'First things come first.'

'You want money—' Garry's voice was unnecessarily loud. 'Well, I have not brought a single sovereign with me. You can be sure of that. If your intention is to rob us, I have nothing of value on me.'

'Ah, Colonel,' the golden man smiled at him, and it was so charming, so unexpectedly exuberant and boyish that he could feel Anna's stiff and antagonistic stance melt beneath that smile, 'my nose tells me that is not true.' He sniffed theatrically. 'You have something of immense value – Havana!' he said and sniffed again. 'No doubt about it, Havana! Colonel, I must warn you that I would kill for a Havana cigar.'

Garry took a hurried step backwards involuntarily before he realized it was a jest. Then he grinned weakly and reached for the cigar case in his hip pocket.

The golden man inspected the long black cigar. 'Romeo y Julieta!' he murmured reverently and then sniffed it lovingly. 'A whiff of Paradise.' He bit off the tip and struck a match off the sole of his boot. He sucked the flame into the cigar and closed his eyes with ecstasy. When he opened them again, he bowed slightly to Anna.

'I beg your pardon, madam, but it has been a long time, over two years, since I tasted a good cigar.'

'All right,' Garry was bolder now. 'You know my name and you are smoking my cigar – the least you can do is introduce yourself.'

'Forgive me.' He drew himself up and snapped his heels together in the teutonic manner. 'I am Lothar De La Rey, at your service.'

'Oh my God.' All Garry's new-found courage deserted him. 'I know all about you. There is a price on your head – they'll hang you when they catch you. You are a wanted criminal and a notorious outlaw, sir.'

'My dear Colonel, I prefer to think of myself as a soldier and patriot.'

'Soldiers do not go on fighting and destroying property after a formal surrender. Colonel Franke capitulated nearly four years ago—'

'I did not recognize Colonel Franke's right to surrender,' Lothar interjected contemptuously. 'I was a soldier of the Kaiser and Imperial Germany.'

'Even Germany surrendered three months ago.'

'Yes,' Lothar agreed. 'And I have not perpetrated an act of war since then.'

'But you are still in the field,' Garry pointed out indignantly. 'You are still under arms, and—'

'I have not gone in to give myself up yet for the very good reason that you have so succinctly stated: if I do, your people will hang me.'

As if under Garry's scrutiny he had suddenly become aware that he was bare to the waist, Lothar reached for his tunic. Freshly laundered, it hung from a thorn bush beside the entrance to the cave. As he shrugged into it, the brass buttons sparkled and Garry's eyes narrowed.

'Damn you, sir, your insolence is insupportable. That's a British military tunic – you are wearing one of our uniforms. That in itself is cause enough to shoot you out of hand!'

'Would you prefer I went naked, Colonel? It must be obvious even to you that we are reduced in circumstances. It gives me no pleasure to wear a British jacket. Unfortunately there is no choice.'

'You insult the uniform in which my son died.'

'I take no pleasure in your son's death, just as I take no pleasure in these rags.'

'By God, man, you have the effrontery—' Garry puffed himself up to deliver a devastating broadside, but Anna cut across him impatiently.

'Mijnheer De La Rey, have you seen my little girl?' And Garry subsided as Lothar turned back to her, his features taking on a strangely compassionate cast.

'I saw a girl – yes, I saw a young girl in the wilderness, but I do not know if she was the one you seek.'

'Could you lead us to her?' Garry demanded, and Lothar glanced at him, his expression hardening again.

'I would try to find her again on certain conditions.'

'Money,' said Garry flatly.

'Why are rich men always obsessed with their money?' Lothar drew on the cigar, and let the fragrant smoke trickle over his tongue. 'Yes, Colonel, I would need some money,' he nodded. 'But not £5,000. I would need £1,000 to equip an expedition to go into the desert fastness where I first saw her. We would need good horses – ours are almost worn out – and wagons to carry water, and I would need to pay my men. £1,000 would cover those expenses.'

'What else?' Garry demanded. 'There must be some other price.'

'Yes,' Lothar nodded. 'There is. I am tired of living in the shadow of the gallows.'

'You want a pardon for your crimes!' Garry stared incredulously. 'What makes you think that is in my power!'

'You are a powerful man, Colonel. A personal friend of both Smuts and Botha, your brother is a general, a cabinet minister in the Botha Government—'

'I would not thwart the course of justice.'

'I fought an honourable war, Colonel. I fought it to the bitter end, like your friends Smuts and Botha once fought their war. I am no criminal, I am no murderer. I lost a father, a mother, a wife and a son – I paid the price of defeat in a heavy coin. Now, I want the right to live the life of an ordinary man – and you want this girl.'

'I couldn't agree to that. You are an enemy,' Garry blustered.

'You find the girl,' said Anna softly, 'and you will be a free man. Colonel Courtney will arrange it. I give you my word on it.'

Lothar glanced at her and then back at Garry, and he smiled again as he divined the true chain of authority here.

'Well, Colonel, do we have an agreement?'

'How do I know who this girl is? How do I know she is my daughter-in-law?' Garry hedged uncomfortably. 'Will you agree to a test?'

Lothar shrugged. 'As you wish.' And Garry turned to Anna.

'Show him,' he said. 'Let him choose.'

Between them, Garry and Anna had designed this test to thwart the rogues and chancers that the reward posters had attracted. Anna snapped open the clasp of the voluminous carpet bag she carried on a strap over one shoulder and took out a thick buff envelope. It contained a pack of postcard-sized photographs, and she handed these to Lothar.

He studied the top photograph. It was a studio portrait of a young girl, a pretty girl in a velvet dress and feathered hat; dark ringlets hung to her shoulders. Lothar shook his head and placed the photograph at the bottom of the pack. Swiftly he flicked through the rest of them, all of young women, and then handed them back to Anna.

'No,' he said. 'I'm sorry to have brought you so far for nothing. The girl I saw is not amongst those,' he looked over his shoulder at the big Ovambo. 'Very well, Hendrick, take them back to the drift.'

'Wait, Mijnheer.' Anna dropped the pile of photographs into the bag and took out another smaller stack. 'There are more.'

'You are careful,' Lothar smiled in acknowledgement.

'We have had many try to cheat us – £5,000 is a great deal of money,' Garry told him, but Lothar did not even look up from the photographs.

He turned over two of the paste boards, then stopped at the third.

'That's her.'

Centaine de Thiry, in her white confirmation dress, smiled self-consciously up at him.

'She is older now, and her hair—' Lothar made a gesture describing a thick wild bush. 'But those eyes. Yes, that's her.'

Neither Garry nor Anna could speak. For a year and a half they had worked for this moment, and now that it had come they could not truly believe it.

'I have to sit down!' Anna said faintly, and Garry helped

her to the log beside the entrance to the cave. While he tended her, Lothar pulled the gold locket from his shirt front, and snapped open the lid. He took out a lock of dark hair and offered it to Anna. She accepted it from him almost fearfully, and then with a fiercely protective gesture she pressed the lock to her lips. She closed her eyes, but from the corners of her clenched lids two fat oily tears squeezed out and began to trickle slowly down her red cheeks.

'It's just a hank of hair. It could be anyone's hair. How do you know?' Garry asked uncomfortably.

'Oh, you silly man,' Anna whispered hoarsely. 'On a thousand nights I brushed her hair. Do you think I would not know it again – anywhere?'

'How long will you need?' Garry asked again, and Lothar frowned with irritation.

'In the name of all that's merciful, how many times must I tell you I don't know?'

The three of them were seated around the fire at the entrance to the overhanging cave. They had been talking for hours, already the stars showed along the narrow strip of sky that the canyon walls framed.

'I have explained where I saw the girl, and the circumstances. Didn't you understand, must I go over it all again?'

Anna lifted a hand to placate him. 'We are very anxious. We ask stupid questions. Forgive us.'

'Very well.' Lothar relit the butt of the cigar with a burning twig from the fire. 'The girl was the captive of the wild San. They are cunning and cruel as animals. They knew I was following them and they threw me off the spoor with ease. They could do it again, if I ever find their spoor. The area I will have to search is enormous, almost the size of Belgium. It's over a year since I last saw the girl, she could be dead of disease or wild animals or those murderous little yellow apes.'

'Do not even say it, Mijnheer,' Anna pleaded, and Lothar threw up both hands.

'I do not know,' he said. 'Months, a year? How can I tell how long I will need?'

'We should come with you,' Garry muttered. 'We should be allowed to take part in the search, at least be told in what area of the territory you first saw her.'

'Colonel, you did not trust me. Very good. Now I don't trust you. As soon as the girl is in your hands, my usefulness to you is at an end.' Lothar took the cigar butt from his mouth and inspected it ruefully. There was not another puff left in it; sadly he dropped it into the fire.

'No, Colonel, when I find the girl we will make a formal exchange – amnesty for me, and your daughter for you.'

'We accept, Mijnheer.' Anna touched Garry's elbow. 'We will deliver the sum of £1,000 to you as soon as possible. When you have Centaine safely with you, you will send us the name of her white stallion. Only she can tell you that, so that way we will know you are not cheating us. We will have your pardon signed and ready.'

Lothar held out his hand across the fire.

'Colonel, is it agreed?'

Garry hesitated a moment, but Anna prodded him so heavily in the ribs that he grunted and reached to take the proffered hand.

'It's agreed.'

'One last favour, Mijnheer De La Rey. I will prepare a package for Centaine. She will need good clothes, women's things. I will deliver it to you with the money. Will you give it to her when you find her?' Anna asked.

'If I find her,' Lothar nodded.

'When you find her,' Anna told him firmly.

It took almost five weeks for Lothar to make his preparations and then trek back to that remote water-hole below the Cunene river where he had cut the spoor of his quarry.

There was still water in the pan – it was amazing how long those shallow unshaded basins retained water even in the sweltering desert conditions, and Lothar wondered, as he had before, if there wasn't some subterranean seepage from the rivers in the north that found its way into them. In any event, the fact that there was still surface water boded well for their chances of being able to penetrate deeper eastwards, the direction which the long-dead spoor had taken.

While his men were refilling the water barrels from the water-hole, Lothar strolled around the periphery of the circular pan and there, incredibly, was the girl's footprint still preserved in the clay, just as he had last seen it.

He knelt beside it, and with his finger traced out the shape of the small, graceful foot. The cast was baked by the sun as hard as a brick. Though all around it the mud had been trampled by buffalo and rhinoceros and elephant, this single print remained.

'It's an omen,' he told himself, and then chuckled cynically. 'I've never believed in omens – why should I begin now?' Yet his mood was buoyant and optimistic when he assembled his men around the camp fire that evening.

Apart from the camp servants and the wagoners, he had four mounted riflemen to help him conduct the actual search. All four of them had been with him since the days of the rebellion. They had fought and bled together, shared a looted bottle of Cape smoke, or a woollen blanket on a frosty desert night, or the last shreds of tobacco in the pouch, and he loved them a little, though he trusted them not at all.

There was 'Swart Hendrick' or 'Black Henry', the tall, purplish-black Ovambo and 'Klein Boy' or 'Little Boy', his bastard son by a Herero woman. There was 'Vark Jan' or 'Pig John', the wrinkled yellow Khoisan. Mixed blood of Nama and Bergdama and even of the true San ran in his veins, for his grandmother had been a Bushman slave, captured as a child on one of the great commando raids of the last century that the Boers had ridden against the San people. Lastly there was 'Vuil Lippe', the Bondelswart Hottentot with lips like fresh-cut liver and a vocabulary that gave him his name 'Dirty Lips'.

'My hunting pack,' Lothar smiled, half-affectionately and half in revulsion as he looked them over. Truly the term 'outlaw' had meaning when applied to them, they were beyond the rules of tribe or tradition. He studied their faces in the firelight. 'Like half-tamed wolves, they would turn and savage me at the first sign of weakness,' he thought.

'All right, you sons of the great hyena, listen to me. We are looking for San, the little yellow killers.' Their eyes sparkled. 'We are looking for the white girl they had as their captive, and there are a hundred gold sovereigns for the man who cuts her spoor. This is how we will conduct the hunt—' Lothar smoothed the sand between his feet and then traced out the plan for them with a twig.

'The wagons will follow the line of the water-holes, here and here, and we will fan out, like this and like this. Between us we can sweep fifty miles of country.'

So they rode into the east, as he had planned it, and within the first ten days they cut the spoor of a small party of wild San. Lothar called in his outriders and they followed up the trail of tiny childlike footprints.

They moved with extreme caution, carefully spying out the terrain ahead through Lothar's telescope, and skirting each stand where an ambush could be laid. The idea of a poisoned bone arrowhead burying itself in his flesh made Lothar shudder every time he let himself think about it. Bullets and bayonets were the tools of his trade, but the filthy poisons that these little pygmies brewed unmanned him, and he hated them more each hot tortuous nerve-racking mile that they followed the spoor.

Reading the sign, Lothar learned that there were eight San in the party they were following: two adult males and two women, probably their wives. There were also four small children, two still at the breast and two just old enough to walk on their own.

'The children will slow them down,' Vark Jan gloated, 'they will not be able to stand the pace.'

'I want one of them alive,' Lothar warned them. 'I want to know about the girl.'

Vark Jan's slave grandmother had taught him enough of the San language to interrogate a captive and he grinned. 'Catch one of them and I will make him talk, be sure of that.'

The San were hunting and foraging and Lothar's band gained on them rapidly. They were only an hour behind when the San, with their animal perceptions, sensed their presence.

Lothar found the spot where they had become aware, the spot where the trail seemed to vanish.

'They are anti-tracking,' he growled. 'Get down and search,' he ordered.

'They are carrying the children,' Vark Jan squatted to examine the earth, 'the babies are too young to cover their own spoor. The women are carrying them, but they will tire quickly under the load.'

Though the trail seemed to end and the ground beyond seemed unmarked even to Lothar's experienced eye, yet even the San had left sign that Vark Jan and Swart Hendrick could follow. The pace was slower, for they had to dismount to be closer to the earth, but still they followed, and within four hours Swart Hendrick nodded and grinned.

'The women are tiring quickly. They are leaving better sign and moving slower. We are gaining on them now.'

Far ahead the San women, toiling under the weight of the children, looked back and wailed softly. The following horses showed across the plain, magnified by the mirage until they loomed like monsters, but even the sight of their pursuers could not drive the women on at a better speed.

'So I must play the plover,' said the oldest of the San hunters. He was referring to the way the plover feigns injury to lead a predator away from its nest. 'If I can make them follow me, I may be able to burn up their horses with thirst,' he told his clan. 'Then when you reach the next water-hole and after you have drunk and filled the water-eggs—' He proffered a sealed buckhorn container to his wife and he did not have to say the fateful words. Poisoning a water-hole was such a desperate deed that none of them wanted to talk of it. 'If you can kill the horses, you will be safe,' the hunter told them. 'I will try to give you time to do it.'

The old San hunter went quickly to each of the children and touched their eyelids and lips in blessing and farewell, and they stared at him solemnly. When he went to his woman who had borne him two sons, she gave a short keening wail. He admonished her with a glance which told her clearly, 'Show no fear in front of the little ones.'

Then as he shed his clothing and his leather satchel, the old San whispered to the younger man, his companion in a thousand hunts, 'Be a father to my sons.' He handed his satchel to him, and stepped back. 'Now, go!'

While he watched his clan trot away, the old man restrung his little bow and then carefully unwound the strips of leather that protected the heads of his arrows. His family disappeared across the plain, and he turned his back upon them and went to meet his pursuers.

Lothar was fretting at the pace. Though he knew that

the quarry was only an hour ahead, they had lost the spoor again and were held up while his flanks cast forward to pick it up. They were in open country, a flat plain that stretched away to an indeterminate meeting with the sky. The plain was dotted with dark clumps of low scrub, and the mirage made them dance and squirm in the field of the telescope. It would be impossible to pick out a human figure amongst them at more than a mile distance.

The horses were almost knocked up, they had to have water soon. Within the next hour he would have to call off the pursuit and turn back to the water wagon. He lifted the telescope again, but a wild shout made him start and glance around. Swart Hendrick was pointing out to the left. The man on the extreme left flank, 'Vuil Lippe', the Bondelswart, was trying to control his mount. It was rearing and walking on its hindlegs, dragging him with it in a sheet of flying dust.

Lothar had heard that a horse would react to the hot scent of a wild Bushman as though to that of a lion, but he had doubted it. Vuil Lippe was helpless, both hands on the reins, his rifle in the boot on the saddle, and as Lothar watched he was dragged over one of the salt bushes and sprawled in the dirt.

Then quite miraculously another human shape seemed to appear out of the very earth. The tiny naked pixie-like shape stood up only twenty paces beyond the dragging rider. Unlikely as it seemed, he must have been completely concealed behind a clump of scrub that should not have hidden a hare.

As Lothar watched with helpless horror, the little mannikin drew his bow and let fly. Lothar saw the flight of the arrow, like a dust mote in the sunlight, and then the naked Bushman whirled and trotted directly away from the line of horsemen.

Lothar's men were all shouting and struggling to remount, but terror seemed to have infected the horses, and they pranced and circled. Lothar was the first up. He did not touch the stirrups, but with a hand on his horse's withers, sprang into the saddle, turned its head and galloped down the line.

Already the running Bushman was disappearing amongst the low mirage-shrouded scrub, in a swinging trot that carried him away at an incredible rate. The man he had fired at had let his horse run free and had pulled himself to his feet. He stood with his legs braced apart, swaying slightly from side to side.

'Are you all right?' Lothar shouted as he rode up, and then he saw the arrow.

It dangled down Vuil Lippe's chest, but the arrowhead was buried in his cheek, and he stared up at Lothar with a bewildered expression. Lothar jumped down and caught him by the shoulders.

'I'm a dead man,' Lippe said softly, his hands hanging by his sides, and Lothar seized the dangling arrow and tried to pull it free. The flesh of Lippe's cheek was drawn out in a peak and he screamed and staggered. Gritting his teeth, Lothar heaved again, but this time the frail reed shaft snapped, leaving the bone arrowhead embedded in the man's flesh, and he began to struggle.

Lothar seized a handful of his greasy black hair and twisted his head over to examine the wound. 'Keep still, damn you.' A short length of bone protruded from the wound. It was caked with a black rubbery coating.

'Euphorbia latex.' Lothar had examined San weapons before; his father had once possessed an important collection of tribal artefacts. Now Lothar recognized the poison, the distilled latex from the roots of one of the rare desert euphorbia plants. Even as he studied it, he could see the poison spreading beneath the skin, discolouring it a deep lavender-purple, blooming like crystals of permanganate of potash dropped into water, following the course of the shallow blood vessels as it was absorbed.

'How long?' Lippe's tortured eyes held Lothar's, beseeching comfort.

The latex looked freshly distilled, none of its virulence dissipated, but Vuil Lippe was big and strong and healthy, his body would fight the toxin. It would take time, a few dreadful hours that would seem like eternity.

'Can't you cut it out?' Lippe pleaded.

'It's gone deep, you'd bleed to death.'

'Burn it out!'

'The pain would kill you.'

Lothar helped him down into a sitting position, just as Hendrick rode up with the bunch.

'Two men stay to look after him,' Lothar ordered. 'Hendrick, you and I will go after the little yellow swine.'

They pushed the tired horses, and within twenty minutes they saw the Bushman ahead of them. He seemed to dissolve and dance in the heat mirage, and Lothar felt a dark rage seize him; the kind of hatred a man can only feel towards something he fears in the deep places of his soul.

'Go right!' Lothar waved Hendrick over. 'Head him off if he turns.' And they spurred forward, riding down swiftly on the fleeing figure.

'I'll give you a death to wipe out the other,' Lothar promised grimly, and he loosened his blanket roll from the pommel in front of him.

The sheepskin that he used as a mattress would shield him from the frail bone-tipped arrows. He wrapped it around his torso, and tucked the end over his mouth and nose. He pulled his wide-brimmed hat low, leaving only a slit for his eyes.

The running Bushman was two hundred yards ahead. He was naked, except for the bow in one hand and the halo of tiny arrows in the leather thong around his head. His body shone with a coating of sweat, and it was the colour of bright amber, almost translucent in the sunlight.

512

He ran lightly as a gazelle, his small neat feet seemed to skim the earth.

There was the crack of a Mauser and a bullet kicked a fountain of pale dust just beyond the running Bushman like the spout of a sperm whale, and the Bushman jerked and then, unbelievably, increased the speed of his flight, drawing away from the two galloping horsemen. Lothar glanced across at Hendrick; he was riding with a loose rein, using both hands to reload the Mauser.

'Don't shoot!' Lothar yelled angrily. 'I want him alive!' and Hendrick lowered the Mauser.

For another mile the Bushman kept up that last wild spring, then gradually he faltered. Once again they began to overhaul him.

Lothar saw his legs begin to wobble under him, his feet flopping from the ankles with exhaustion, but Lothar's mount was almost blown. It was lathering heavily, and froth splattered his boots as he drove it forward.

Fifty yards ahead the exhausted Bushman spun round to face him, standing at bay, his chest pumping like a bellows, and sweat dripping from his small spade-shaped beard. His eyes were wild and fierce and defiant as he fitted an arrow to the bow.

'Come on, you little monster!' Lothar yelled, to draw the Bushman's aim from the horse to himself, and the ruse succeeded.

The Bushman threw up the bow, and drew and loosed in a single movement, and the arrow flew like a beam of light. It struck Lothar at the level of the throat, but the thick wool of the sheepskin smothered it, and it fell away, tapping against his riding boot and falling to the dry earth.

The Bushman was trying desperately to notch another arrow as Lothar leaned out of the saddle like a polo player reaching for a forehand drive, and swung the Mauser. The rifle barrel crunched into the side of the Bushman's skull above the ear and he collapsed.

Lothar reined down his horse and sprang from the saddle, but Hendrick was there before him, swinging wildly with his Mauser butt at the Bushman's head as he lay against the earth. Lothar grabbed his shoulder and pushed him away with such force that he staggered and almost fell.

'Alive, I told you!' Lothar snarled, and went down on his knees beside the sprawling body.

There was a sluggish trickle of blood out of the Bushman's earhole, and Lothar felt a prickle of concern as he felt for the pulse of the carotid artery in the throat, and then grunted with relief. He picked up the tiny bow and snapped it in his hands and threw the pieces aside, then with his hunting knife he cut the leather thong around the Bushman's forehead and one at a time broke the poisoned arrowheads from their shafts, and handling them with extreme care threw them as far from him as he could.

As he rolled the Bushman on to his belly, he shouted at Hendrick to bring the leather thongs from his saddle-bag. He trussed the captive securely, surprised at his perfect muscular development and at the graceful little feet and hands. He knotted the leather thongs at wrist and elbow, and at knee and ankle, and pulled the knots so tight that they bit deeply into the bright amber skin.

Then he picked up the Bushman in one hand, as though he were a doll, and slung him over the saddle. The movement revived the Bushman and he lifted his head and opened his eyes. They were the colour of new honey, and the whites were smoky yellow. It was like looking into the eyes of a trapped leopard – so ferocious that Lothar stepped back involuntarily.

'They are animals,' he said, and Hendrick nodded.

'Worse than animals, for they have the cunning of a man without being human.'

Lothar took the reins and led his exhausted steed back to where they had left the wounded Vuil Lippe.

The others had rolled him in a grey woollen blanket

and laid him on a sheepskin. Clearly they were waiting on Lothar to attend to him, but Lothar was reluctant to involve himself. He knew that Vuil Lippe was beyond any help he could give, and he put off the moment by dragging the bound Bushman out of the saddle and dropping him on the sandy earth. The little body curled up defensively, and Lothar hobbled his horse and went slowly to join the circle around the blanket-wrapped form.

He could see immediately that the poison was acting swiftly. One side of Lippe's face was grotesquely swollen and laced with furious purple lines. One eye was closed by the swelling, and the lid looked like an over-ripe grape, shining and black. The other eye was wide open but the pupil was shrunken to a pinprick. He made no sign of recognition as Lothar stooped over him and had probably already lost his sight. He was breathing with extreme difficulty, fighting wildly for each breath as the poison paralysed his lungs.

Lothar touched his forehead and the skin was cold and clammy as that of a reptile. Lothar knew that Hendrick and the others were watching him. On many occasions they had seen him dress a bullet wound, set a broken leg, draw a rotten aching tooth, and perform all manner of minor surgery. They were waiting for him to do something for the dying man, and their expectations and his own helplessness infuriated Lothar.

Suddenly Lippe uttered a strangled cry and began to shake like an epileptic, his single open eye rolled back into his skull, showing the yellow blood-shot white, and his body arched under the blanket.

'Convulsions,' said Lothar, 'like a mamba bite. It won't be long now.'

The dying man bit down, grinding his teeth together, and his swollen protruding tongue was caught between them. He chewed on his tongue, mincing it to ribbons while Lothar tried desperately and futilely to prise his jaws

515

open, and the blood poured down the Hottentot's own throat into his semi-paralysed lungs and he choked and moaned through his locked jaws.

His body arched in another rigid convulsion, and there was a spluttering explosion beneath the blanket as his racked body voided itself. The sweet faecal stench was nauseating in the heat. It was a long-drawn-out and messy death, and when it was over at last, it left those hardened men shaken and morose.

They scraped a shallow grave and rolled Vuil Lippe's corpse, still in the soiled grey blanket, into it. Then they hastily covered it, as though to be rid of their own loathing and horror.

One of them built a small fire of brush twigs, and brewed a canteen of coffee. Lothar fetched the half-bottle of Cape brandy from his saddle-bag. As they passed it from hand to hand, they avoided looking at where the Bushman lay curled naked in the sand.

They drank the coffee in silence, squatting in a circle, and then Vark Jan, the Khoisan Hottentot who spoke the San language, flicked his coffee grounds on to the fire and stood up.

He crossed to where the San lay and picked him up by his bound wrists, forcing his arms high behind him as they bore his full weight. He carried him back to the fire and picked out a burning twig. Still holding the San dangling from one hand, he touched the naked glans of his penis with the glowing tip of the twig. The San gasped and wriggled wildly and a blister formed miraculously on the skin of his genitals. It looked like a soft silver slug.

The men around the fire laughed, and in their laughter was the sound of their loathing and their terror of the death by poison, and their sorrow for their companion, of their craving for vengeance and the sadistic need to inflict pain and humiliation, the worst that they could devise.

Lothar felt himself shaken by the quality of that laugh-

516

ter, felt the insecure foundations of his humanity totter, and the same animal passions arise in him. With a supreme effort he forced them back. He rose to his feet. He knew he could not prevent what was about to happen, just as you cannot drive hungry lions from their fresh kill. They would turn on him if he tried.

He averted his eyes from the Bushman's face, from those wild haunted eyes. It was clear that he knew that death awaited him, but even he could not guess at the manner of it. Instead Lothar looked at the faces of his own men, and he felt sickened and soiled by what he saw. Their features seemed distorted as though seen through a poorly glazed window, thickened and smeared with lust.

He thought that after the Bushman had been mounted by each of them in turn, ravished as though he were a woman, he would probably welcome what awaited him at the very end.

'So.' Lothar tried to keep his expression neutral, but his voice was hoarse with disgust. 'I am returning to the wagons now. The San is yours, but I must know if he has seen or has heard of the white girl. He must answer that one question. That is all.'

Lothar went to his horse and mounted. He rode away towards the wagons without looking back. Just once, far behind, he heard a cry of such outrage and agony that it made his skin prickle, but then it was muted and lost on the moan of the desert wind.

Much later when his men rode up to the wagons, Lothar was lying under the side awning of his living wagon, reading his faithful old copy of Goethe by the light of a hurricane lantern – stained and battered, it had sustained him a hundred times before when the substance of his being had been drawn thin.

The laughter of his men as they dismounted and unsaddled had a fat, satisfied sound, like that of men who had well feasted and drunk, and were replete. Swart

Hendrick came to where he lay, swaggering as though he had taken wine, and the front of his breeches was speckled with black drops of dried blood.

'The San had not seen a white woman, but there was something strange and unexplained that he had heard whispered at the fire when they met other San in the desert; a tale of a woman and a child from a strange land where the sun never shines, who lived with two old people of the San.'

Lothar came up on his elbow. He remembered the two little Bushmen he had seen with the girl.

'Where? Did he say where?' he demanded eagerly.

'There is a place, deep in the Kalahari, that is sacred to all the San. He gave us the direction—'

'Where, Hendrick, damn you. Where?'

'A long journey, fifteen days of their travel.'

'What is this place? How will we know it?'

'That,' Hendrick admitted sadly, 'he did not say. His will to stay alive was not as great as we thought it might be. He died before he could tell us.'

'Tomorrow we will turn in that direction,' Lothar ordered.

'There are the other San that we lost today. With fresh horses we might catch them before sundown tomorrow. They have women with them—'

'No!' Lothar snarled at him. 'We go on towards this sacred place in the wilderness.'

When the great bald mountain rose abruptly out of the plain, Lothar believed at first that it must be some trick of the desert light.

He knew of no description in the folklore or verbal history of the desert tribes to warn that the existence of such a place was possible. The only white men who had travelled this country – Livingstone and Oswell on their route to the discovery of Lake Ngami, and Anderson and Galton on their hunting forays – had made no mention of such a mountain in their writing.

Thus Lothar doubted what he was seeing in the uncertain evening light, and the sunset was so laden with dust, so garish and theatrical as to heighten the effect of a stage illusion.

However, in the first light of the next day when he looked for it eagerly, the silhouette was still there, dark and clearly incised against a sky that was turned to mother-of-pearl by the coming of the dawn. As he rode towards it, so it rose higher and still higher from the plain, and finally detached itself from the earth and floated in the sky on its own shimmering mirage.

When at last Lothar stood beneath the tall cliffs, he did not doubt that this was the sacred place of which the San had spoken as he died, and his conviction was made complete when he scrambled up the scree slopes and discovered the wondrous paintings upon the sheltered cliff face.

'This is the place, but it's so extensive,' Lothar realized. 'If the girl is here, we might never find her. So many caves and valleys and hidden places – we could search for ever.'

He divided his men again and sent them on foot to explore and search the nearest slopes of the mountain. Then he left the wagons in a shaded grove in the charge of Swart Hendrick, whom he mistrusted least, and taking only a spare horse set out to circumnavigate the mountain's bulk.

After two days of travel, during which he kept notes and sketched a rough map with the aid of his pocket compass, he could estimate with some certainty that the mountain was probably about thirty miles long and four or five miles wide, a long extended ridge of gneiss and intruding sandstone strata.

He rounded the eastern extremity of the mountain and deduced from his compass readings that he was heading back along the opposite side from where he had left the wagons. Whenever some feature of the cliffs caught his attention, a fissure or a complex of caves, for instance, he hobbled the horses and climbed up to explore.

Once he discovered a small spring of clear sweet water welling up from the base of the cliff and trickling into a natural rock basin. He filled his water canteens, then he stripped and washed his clothes. At last he bathed, gasping with delight at the cold, and went on refreshed.

At other places he found more of the San paintings covering the rock face, and he marvelled at the accuracy of the artist's eye and hand that depicted the shape of eland and buffalo so that even his hunter's eye could find no fault. However, these were all ancient signs and he found nothing of recent human presence.

The forest and plain below the cliffs teemed with game, and he had no difficulty in shooting a plump young gazelle or antelope each day and keeping himself in fresh meat. On the third evening, he killed an impala ewe and made a kebab of the tripes and kidneys and liver, impaling them on a green twig and grilling them over the coals.

However, the scent of fresh meat attracted unwelcome attention to his camp, and he had to spend the rest of the night standing by the horses with his rifle in his hand while a hungry lion grunted and moaned in the darkness just outside the circle of firelight. He examined the beast's tracks in the morning and found that it was an adult male, past its prime and with a damaged limb that forced it to limp heavily.

'A dangerous brute,' he muttered, and hoped that it had moved away. But this was a vain hope, he discovered that evening when the horses began to fidget and whicker as the sun set. The lion must have followed him at a distance during the day, and emboldened by the gathering dusk, it again closed in and began to prowl around his camp fire.

'Another sleepless night.' He resigned himself and heaped wood on the fire. Preparing to stand guard, he pulled on his overcoat, and suffered another minor irritation. One of the brass buttons was missing, which would let in the cold of the desert night.

It was a long, unpleasant night, but a little after midnight the lion seemed at last to tire of its fruitless vigil and it moved away. He heard it utter one last string of moaning grunts at the head of the grassy vlei half a mile away, then there was silence.

Wearily Lothar checked the head halters on the horses and then went to the fire and rolled himself in his blankets, still fully dressed, and keeping his boots on. Within minutes he had fallen into a deep dreamless sleep.

He came awake with bewildering suddenness and found himself sitting up with the rifle in his hands, and the din of an angry lion's thunderous roars echoing in his ears.

T he fire had died down to white ash but the tree-tops were black against the paling morning sky. Lothar threw off his blankets and scrambled to his feet. The horses were stiff with alarm, their ears pricked forward, staring towards the open glade whose silver grasses just showed through the screen of mopani forest.

The lion roared again, and he judged it as a half-mile distant, in the direction in which the horses were staring. So clearly does the roar of a lion carry in the night, that an inexperienced ear would have reckoned it much closer and been unable to pinpoint the direction, for it played ventriloquist tricks upon the ear.

Once more the awful cacophony filled the forest. Lothar

had never heard one of these beasts behaving like this, such sustained anger and frustration in those great blasts of sound, and then his head jerked with shock. In the lull between this roar and the next, he heard another unmistakable sound, a human scream of utmost terror.

Lothar reacted without thought. He seized the head halter of his favourite hunting horse and leaped to its bare back. He socked his heels into its ribs, urging it into a gallop, and guided it with his knees, turning it towards the head of the glade. He lay forward on the horse's neck as the low branches lashed past his head, but as he broke into the open glade, he straightened and looked about him frantically.

In the few minutes since he had woken, the light had strengthened, and the eastern sky was a throbbing orange glow. There was a single tall mopani tree standing detached from the rest of the forest, surrounded by the low dry grass of the glade. High in its branches was a huge dark mass, and indistinct but violent movement made the branches of the mopani wave and thrash against the sky.

Lothar turned his horse towards it, and the thunderous growls of a lion were punctuated by yet another high-pitched shriek. Only then could Lothar distinguish what was happening in the top of the mopani, and he found it hard to believe.

'Great God!' he swore with surprise, for he had never heard of a lion climbing a tree. There was the great tawny cat high in the waving branches, clinging with its hindlegs to the trunk and reaching up with vicious swipes of its forepaws towards the human shape just beyond its reach.

'Ya! Ya!' Lothar worked his horse with elbows and heels, urging it to its top speed, and as he reached the mopani he flung himself from its back, and rode the shock of landing with his legs and back. Then he danced out to one side, head thrown back, rifle at high port across his chest, trying for a clear shot at the animal high above him.

The lion and its victim made an indistinguishably confused silhouette against the sky; a shot from below could hit one as easily as the other, and there were thick intervening branches of the mopani to deflect his bullet.

Lothar dodged sideways until he found a hole in the branches, and he flung the rifle up to his shoulder, braced himself over backwards, aiming straight up, but still reluctant to chance the shot. Then the lion snatched the human shape half off its precarious perch, dragging it down – and the screams were so piteous, so agonized, that Lothar could not wait longer.

He aimed for the lion's spine, at the root of the tail, a point as far as possible from the twisting body of its victim who was still clinging with desperate strength to one of the mopani branches. He fired and the heavy Mauser bullet smashed into the base of the lion's spine, between its bunched and straining haunches, and tore upwards, following the line of the vertebrae for the span of a hand, shattering and crushing the bony knuckles, destroying the great nerves of the legs at their roots, before ripping out again from the centre of the lion's back.

The lion's hindlegs spasmed, the long yellow claws retracted involuntarily into their sheaths in the leathery pads, loosening their grip on the mopani bark, and the paralysed legs could hold no longer. The great tawny cat came sliding and twisting and roaring down out of the tree, crashing against the lower branches as it fell, arching back on itself, snapping at the pain in its shattered spine with gaping pink jaws.

It brought its human victim down with it, its foreclaws still hooked deeply into tender flesh, shaking and throwing the frail body about with its convulsions. They hit the earth in a tangle, with an impact that jarred up through the soles of Lothar's boots. He had jumped clear as they came down through the branches, but now he ran forward.

The lion's back legs were splayed behind it like those of

a toad, and it lay half over the human body. Now it reared up on its forelegs, pinned by its paralysed hindquarters, and as it dragged itself towards Lothar, it opened its jaws and bellowed. The stench of its breath was carrion and corruption, and hot stinking froth splattered his face and bare arms.

Lothar thrust the muzzle of the Mauser almost into that dreadful mouth and without aiming, he fired. The bullet entered the soft palate at the back of the lion's throat, tore through the back of its skull, and erupted in a fountain of pink blood and brains. For a second longer, it stood braced on its stiff forelegs, then with a gusty sigh its lungs emptied and it rolled slowly over on to its side.

Lothar dropped the Mauser and fell on his knees beside the huge twitching yellow carcass, and tried to reach the body beneath it, but only the bottom half protruded, a pair of slim brown naked legs, the narrow, boyish loins bound up in a tattered canvas kilt.

Lothar sprang up and seized the lion's tail; he flung all his weight upon it, and sluggishly the furry carcass rolled over on to its back, freeing the body beneath it. A woman, he saw at once, and he stooped and lifted her. Her head with its thick mop of dark curling hair flopped lifelessly, and he cupped his hand at the back of her neck, as though he were holding a newborn infant, and he looked into her face.

It was the face of the photograph, the face he had glimpsed so long ago in the field of his telescope, the face that had haunted and driven him, but there was no life in it.

The long dark eyelashes were closed and meshed together, the smooth, darkly tanned features were without expression, and the strong wide mouth was slack; the soft lips drooped open to reveal the small white even teeth and a little string of saliva dribbled from one corner of her mouth.

'No!' Lothar shook his head vehemently. 'You can't be dead – no, it's not possible, after all this. I won't—' He broke off. Out of the thick dark mane of her hair a serpent crawled down across the broad forehead towards her eye, a slow dark red serpent of new blood.

Lothar snatched the cotton bandanna from around his neck and wiped away the blood, but it flooded down her face as fast as he could clear it. He parted her crown of curls and found the wound in her shiny white scalp, a short but deep cut where she had hit one of the mopani branches. He could see the gleam of bone in the bottom of the wound. He pressed the lips of the cut together and wadded his kerchief over it, then bound it in place with the bandanna.

He cradled the injured head against his shoulder and lifted the limp body into a sitting position. One of her breasts flopped out of her skimpy fur cloak, and he felt an almost blasphemous shock, it was so pale and tender and vulnerable. He covered it swiftly and guiltily, then turned his attention to her injured leg.

The wounds were frightening: parallel slashes that had ripped deep into the flesh of her calf, cutting down to the heel of her left foot. He laid her back gently and knelt at her feet, lifting the leg and dreading the sudden spurting rush of arterial blood. It did not come, there was only the dark seepage of venous blood, and he sighed.

'Thank you, God.' He dragged off his heavy military greatcoat, and placed the wounded leg upon it to keep it out of the dirt, then he pulled his shirt over his head. It had not been washed since the rock spring two days before and it stank of his stale sweat.

'Nothing else for it.' He ripped the shirt into strips and bound up the leg.

He knew that this was the real danger; the infections that a carrion eater, such as a lion, carried on its fangs and its claws were almost as deadly as the poisons of a

Bushman's arrowhead. The claws of a lion particularly were sheathed in deep scabbards in the pads. Old blood and putrefied meat lodged in the cavities, an almost certain source of virulent mortification and gas-gangrene.

'We have to get you to the camp, Centaine.' He used her name for the first time, and it gave him a tiny flicker of pleasure, quickly smothered by fear as he touched her skin again and felt the cold, the mortuary chill upon it.

Quickly he checked her pulse and was shocked at its weak, irregular flutter. He lifted her shoulders and wrapped her in the thick greatcoat, then looked about him for his horse. It was down at the far end of the glade, grazing head down. Bare to the waist and shivering in the cold, he ran after it and led it back to the mopani.

As he stooped to lift the girl's unconscious body, he froze with shock.

From above his head came a sound that ripped along his nerves and triggered his deepest instincts. It was the loud cry of an infant in distress, and he straightened swiftly and stared up the tall trunk. There was a bundle hanging in the top branches, and it twitched and swung agitatedly from side to side.

'A woman and a child.' The words of the dying Bushman came back to Lothar.

He pillowed the unconscious girl's head against the warm carcass of the lion, then jumped to catch the lowest mopani branch. He drew himself bodily upwards and swung one leg over the branch. He climbed swiftly up to the suspended bundle, and found it was a rawhide satchel. He unhooked the straps and lowered it until he could peer into the opening.

A small, indignant face scowled up at him, and as it saw him, it flushed and yelled with fright.

The memory of Lothar's own son assailed him so suddenly and bitterly that he winced and swayed on the high branch, and then drew the kicking, yelling child more securely against his own body and smiled, a painful, lopsided smile.

'That is a big voice for a small man,' he whispered huskily. It never occurred to him that it might be a girl – that arrogant anger could only be male.

It was easier to shift his camp to the mopani tree under which Centaine lay, than move her to the camp. He had to carry the child with him, but he managed it in less than twenty minutes. He was fearful every minute that he left the helpless mother alone, and vastly relieved when he led the pack horse back to where she lay. Centaine was still unconscious, and the child he carried had soiled itself and was ravenous with hunger.

He wiped off the boy's small pink bottom with a handful of dry grass, remembering how he had performed the same service for his own son, and then placed him under the greatcoat where he could reach his unconscious mother's breast.

Then he set a canteen of water on a small fire and dropped the curved sacking needle and a hank of white cotton thread from his canvas housewife into the boiling water to sterilize. He washed his own hands in a mug of hot water and carbolic soap, emptied the mug, refilled it and began to scrub out the deep tears in the girl's calf. The water was painfully hot, and he lathered carbolic soap and forced his finger to the bottom of each wound, poured hot water into it, and then washed it out again and again.

Centaine moaned and thrashed about weakly, but he held her down and scrubbed grimly at the fearful lacerations. At last, not truly satisfied, but certain that if he persisted in his rough cleansing he would do irreparable damage to delicate tissue, he went to his saddle-bag and fetched a whisky bottle which he had carried with him for four years. It had been given to him by the German Lutheran missionary doctor who had nursed him through the wounds he had received during the campaign against Smuts' and Botha's invasion. 'It may save your life one day,' the doctor had told him. The handwritten label was illegible now, 'Acriflavin' – with an effort he remembered the name, and the dark yellow-brown liquid had evaporated to half its volume.

He poured it into the open wounds and worked it in with his forefinger, making certain that it reached the bottom of each deep cut. He used the last drops from the bottle on the rent in Centaine's scalp.

He fished the needle and cotton from the boiling canteen. With the girl's leg in his lap, he took a deep breath. 'Thank the Lord she's unconscious,' and he held the lips of raw flesh together and worked the point of the needle through them.

It took him nearly two hours to sew the meat of her tattered calf together again, and his stitches were crude but effective, the work of a sailmaker rather than a surgeon. He used strips from one of his clean shirts to bind up the leg, but as he worked he knew that despite his best efforts, infection was almost certain. He transferred his attention to her scalp. Three stitches were sufficient to close that wound, and afterwards the nervous strain of the last hours swamped him, and he felt shaken and exhausted.

It took an effort of will to begin work on the litter. He skinned out the carcass of the lion, and strung the wet hide between two long limber mopani saplings with the fur side uppermost. The horses shied and fidgeted at the rank smell of lion, but he gentled them and fitted the straight poles of the drag litter on to the pack horse, then tenderly lifted Centaine's limp body, wrapped in the greatcoat, into the litter and strapped her securely with strips of mopani bark.

Carrying the now sleeping child in the satchel and leading the pack horse with the litter sliding along behind it, he set off at a walk towards the wagons. He calculated that it was a full day's march, and it was now long past noon, but he could not force the pace without risk of injuring the girl in the litter.

A little before sundown, Shasa woke and howled like a hungry wolf. Lothar hobbled the horses and took him to his mother. Within minutes Shasa was howling with frustration and kicking under the flap of the greatcoat, presenting Lothar with a difficult decision.

'It's for the child, and she will never know,' he decided.

He lifted the flap of the greatcoat, and hesitated again before touching her so intimately.

'Forgive me, please,' he apologized to the unconscious girl, and took her barest breast in his hand. The weight and the heat and velvet feel of it was a shock in his loins, but he tried to ignore it. He pressed and kneaded, with Shasa blustering and mouthing furiously at his hand, and then rocked back on his heels and covered Centaine with the coat.

'Now, what the hell do we do, boy? Your mother's lost her milk.' He picked Shasa up. 'No, don't try me, my friend, this is another dry house, I'm afraid. We'll have to camp here while I go shopping.'

He cut thorn branches and dragged them into a circular laager to keep out hyena or other predators and built a large fire in the centre.

'You'll have to come with me,' he said to the querulous infant, and strapping the canvas bag across his shoulder, he rode out on his hunting horse.

He found a herd of zebra around the next bluff of the mountain. Using his horse as a screen, he worked to within easy rifle-shot of the herd and picked out a mare with a young foal at her side. He hit her cleanly in the head and she dropped instantly. When he walked up to the dead zebra, the foal ran only a few yards, and then circled back.

'Sorry, old fellow,' Lothar said to it. The orphan would

have no chance of survival and the bullet he gave it in the head was swift mercy.

Lothar knelt beside the dead mare and pulled back her top leg to expose the swollen black udders. He was able to draw half a canteen of warm milk from her. It was rich and topped with thick yellow cream. He diluted it with an equal quantity of warm water and soaked a folded square of cotton torn from his shirt into the mixture.

Shasa spluttered and kicked and turned his head away, but Lothar persisted. 'This is the only item on the menu.'

Suddenly Shasa learned the trick of it. Milk dribbled down his chin, but some of it went down his throat, and he yelled impatiently every time Lothar pulled the wad of shirt out of his mouth to resoak it.

Lothar slept that night with Shasa against his chest, and woke before dawn when the child demanded his breakfast. There was zebra milk remaining from the previous evening. By the time he had fed the boy, and then washed him in a mug of water warmed on the fire, it was after sunrise. When Lothar set him down, Shasa set off at a gallop on his hands and knees towards the horses, giving breathless cries of excitement.

Lothar felt that swollen feeling in his chest that he had not known since the death of his own son, and lifted him on to the horse's back. Shasa kicked and gurgled with laughter, and the hunting pony reached back and snuffled at him with ears pricked.

'We'll make a horseman of you before you walk,' Lothar laughed.

However, when he went to Centaine's litter and tried gently to rouse her, his concern was intense. She was still unconscious, though she moaned and rolled her head from side to side when he touched the leg. It was swollen and bruised, and clotted blood had dried on the stitches.

'My God, what a mess,' he whispered, but when he

searched for the livid lines of gangrene up her thigh, he found none.

There was another unpleasant discovery, however: Centaine needed the same attention as her son.

He undressed her quickly. The canvas skirt and mantle were her only clothing, and he tried to remain unmoved and clinical when he looked at her.

He could not do so. Up to this time Lothar had based his concept of feminine beauty on the placid round blonde Rubenesque charms of his mother, and after her, his wife Amelia. Now he found his standards abruptly overturned. This woman was lean as a greyhound, with a tucked-in belly in which he could see the separate muscles clearly defined beneath the skin. That skin, even where it was untouched by the sun, was cream rather than pure milk. Her body hair, instead of being pale and wispy, was thick and dark and curly. Her limbs were long and willowy, not round and dimpled at elbow and knee. She was firm to the touch, his fingers did not sink into her flesh as they had into other flesh he had known, and where the sun had reached her legs and arms and face, she was the colour of lightly oiled teak.

He tried not to dwell upon these things, as he rolled her deftly but gently on to her face, but when he saw that her buttocks were round and hard and white as a perfect pair of ostrich eggs, something flopped in his stomach, and his hands shook uncontrollably as he finished cleaning her.

He experienced no revulsion at the task, it was as natural as his attention to the child had been, and afterwards he wrapped her in the greatcoat again and squatted on his heels beside her to examine her face minutely.

Again he found her features differed from his previous conception of feminine beauty. That halo of thick, kinky dark hair was almost African, those black eyebrows were

531

too stark, her chin too thrusting and stubborn, the whole cast and set of her features was far too assertive to bear comparison with the gentle compliance of those other women. Even though she was totally relaxed, Lothar could still read on her face the marks of great suffering and hardship, perhaps as great as his own, and as he touched the smooth brown cheek, he felt almost fatalistically drawn to her, as though it had been ordained from that first glimpse of her so many months before. Abruptly he shook his head with annoyance and a quick sense of his own ridiculous sentimentality.

'I know nothing of you, or you of me.' He looked up quickly, and with a guilty start realized that the child had crawled away under the horses' hooves. With chuckles of glee, he was snatching at their inquisitive puffing nostrils, as they stretched down to him, sniffing at him.

Leading the pack horse and carrying the child, Lothar reached his wagons late that same afternoon.

S wart Hendrick and the camp servants ran out to meet him, agog with curiosity, and Lothar gave his orders.

'I want a separate shelter for the woman, alongside mine. Thatch the roof to keep it cool, and hang canvas sides we can raise to let in the breeze – and I want it ready by nightfall.'

He carried Centaine to his own cot and bathed her again before dressing her in one of the long nightgowns that Anna Stok had provided.

She was still not conscious, though once she opened her eyes. They were unfocused and dreamy, and she muttered in French so he could not understand.

He told her, 'You are safe. You are with friends.'

The pupils of her eyes reacted to light, which he knew was an encouraging sign, but the lids fluttered closed and she relapsed into unconsciousness, or sleep from which he was careful not to rouse her.

With access to his medicine chest again, Lothar was able to redress her wounds, spreading them liberally with an ointment which was his favourite cure-all inherited from his mother. He bound them up in fresh bandages.

By this time the child was once again hungry and letting it be widely known. Lothar had a milch-goat amongst his stock, and he held Shasa on his lap while he fed him the diluted goat's milk. Afterwards he tried to make Centaine drink a little warm soup, but she struggled weakly and almost choked. So he carried her to the shelter which his servants had completed, and laid her on a cot of laced rawhide thongs with a sheepskin mattress and fresh blankets. He placed the child beside her and during the night he woke more than once from a light sleep to go to them.

Just before dawn he at last fell into deep sleep, only to be shaken awake almost immediately.

'What is it?' He reached instinctively for the rifle at his head.

'Come quickly!' Swart Hendrick's hoarse whisper at his ear. 'The cattle were restless. I thought it might be a lion.'

'What is it, man?' Lothar demanded irritably. 'Get on with it, spit it out.'

'It was not a lion – much worse! There are wild San out there. They have been creeping around the camp all night. I think they are after the cattle.'

Lothar swung his legs over the cot and groped for his boots.

'Have Vark Jan and Klein Boy returned yet?' It would be easier with a large party.

'Not yet,' Hendrick shook his head.

'Very well, we'll hunt alone. Saddle the horses. We must not let the little yellow devils get too much of a start on us.'

As he stood up, he checked the load of the Mauser,

then pulled the sheepskin off his cot and stooped out of the shelter. He hurried to where Swart Hendrick was holding the horses.

O'wa had not been able to force himself to approach closer than two hundred paces to the camp of the strangers. Even at that distance the strange sounds and odours that carried to him confused him. The ring of axe on wood, the clatter of a bucket, the bleat of a goat made him start; the smell of paraffin and soap, of coffee and woollen clothing troubled him, while the sounds of men speaking in unfamiliar cadence and harsh sibilance were as terrifying to him as the hissing of serpents.

He lay against the earth, his heart hammering painfully, and whispered to H'ani, 'Nam Child is with her own kind at last. She is lost to us, old grandmother. This is a sickness of the head, this crazy following after her. We both knew well that the *others* will murder us if they discover that we are here.'

'Nam Child is hurt. You read the sign beneath the mopani tree where the naked carcass of the lion lay,' H'ani whispered back. 'You saw her blood on the earth.'

'She is with her own kind,' O'wa repeated stubbornly. 'They will care for her. She does not need us any more. She went in the night and left us without a word of farewell.'

'Old grandfather, I know that what you say is true, but how will I ever smile again if I never know how badly she has been hurt? How will I ever sleep again if I never see little Shasa safe at her breast?'

'You risk both our lives for a glimpse of someone who has departed. They are dead to us now, leave them be.'

'I risk my own life, my husband, for to me it has no further value if I do not know that Nam Child, the

534

daughter of my heart if not of my own womb, is alive and will stay alive. I risk my own life for the touch of Shasa once more. I do not ask you to come with me.'

H'ani rose, and before he could protest, scuttled away into the shadows, heading towards the faint glow where the watch-fire showed through the trees. O'wa came up on his knees, but his courage failed him again, and he lay and covered his head with an arm.

'Oh, stupid old woman,' he lamented. 'Do you not know that without you my heart is a desert? When they kill you, I will die a hundred deaths to your one.'

H'ani crept towards the camp, circling downwind, watching the drift of smoke from the fire, for she knew that if the cattle or the horses scented her, they would stamp and mill and alert the camp. Every few paces she sank to the ground and listened with all her soul, staring into the shadows around the wagons and the crude huts of the encampment, watching for those tall, very black men, dressed in outlandish apparel and hung with glittering metal weapons.

They were all asleep, she could make out the shapes around the fire and the stink of their bodies in her nostrils made her shake with fear. She forced herself to rise and go forward, keeping one of the wagons between her and the sleeping men, until she could crouch beside the tall rear wheel of the wagon.

She was certain that Nam Child was in one of the thatched shelters, but to choose the wrong one would bring disaster upon her. She decided on the nearest of the shelters and crawled on her hands and knees to the entrance. Her eyes were good in the gloom, almost like those of a cat, but all she could see was a dark indefinite bundle on a raised structure at the far end of the shelter, a human shape, perhaps, but there was no way of being certain.

The shape stirred, and then coughed and grunted.

'A man!' Her heart thudded so loudly, she was certain it would wake him. She drew back, and crawled to the second shelter.

Here there was another sleeping form. H'ani crept towards it timidly, and when she was within arm's length, her nostrils flared. She recognized the milky smell of Shasa, and the odour of Nam Child's skin which to the old woman was as sweet as the wild melon.

She knelt beside the cot, and Shasa sensed her presence and whimpered. H'ani touched his forehead, and then slipped the tip of her little finger into his mouth. She had taught him well; all Bushmen children learned to be still under this special restraint, for the safety of the clan could depend on their silence. Sasha relaxed under the familiar touch and smell of the old woman.

H'ani felt for Nam Child's face. The heat of her cheeks told her that Nam Child was in light fever, and she leaned forward and smelled her breath. It was soured with pain and sickness, but lacked the rank feral stench of virulent infection. H'ani longed for the opportunity to examine and dress her wounds, but knew it was vain.

Instead she placed her lips against the girl's ear and whispered, 'My heart, my little bird, I call all the spirits of the clan to protect you. Your old grandfather and I will dance for you, to strengthen and cure you.'

The old woman's voice reached something deep in the unconscious girl's being. Images formed in her mind.

'Old grandmother,' she muttered, and smiled at the dream images. 'Old grandmother—'

'I am with you,' H'ani replied. 'I will be with you always and always—' That was all she could say, for she could not risk the sob that crouched in her throat ready to burst through her lips. She touched them each once more, the child and the mother, on their lips and their closed eyes, then she rose and scuttled from the shelter. Her tears blinded her, her grief swamped her senses, she passed close to the thorn laager where the horses stood.

One of the horses snorted and stamped and tossed its head at the sharp unfamiliar scent. As H'ani disappeared into the night, one of the men lying beside the fire sat up and threw aside his blanket to go to the restless horses. Halfway there, he paused and then stooped over the tiny footprint in the dust.

It was strange how weary H'ani felt now, as she and O'wa made their way back around the base of the mountain towards the secret valley.

While they had followed the trail of Nam Child and Shasa, she had felt as though she could run for ever, as though she were a young woman again, imbued with boundless energy and strength in her concern for the safety of the two she loved as dearly as she loved her ancient husband. Now, however, when she had turned her back upon them for ever, she felt the full weight of her age, and it pressed her down so that her usual alert swinging trot was reduced to a heavy plod, and the weariness ached in her legs and up her spine.

In front of her O'wa moved as slowly, and she sensed the effort that each pace cost him. In the time that it had taken the sun to rise a handspan above the horizon, both of them had been deprived of the force and purpose that made survival in their harsh world possible. Once more they had suffered terrible bereavement, but this time they did not have the will to rise above it.

Ahead of her O'wa halted and sank down on his haunches. She had never in all the long years seen him so beaten, and when she squatted beside him, he turned his head slowly to her. 'Old grandmother, I am tired,' he whispered. 'I would like to sleep for a long time. The sun hurts my eyes.' He held up his hand to shield them.

'It has been a long hard road, old grandfather, but we are at peace with the spirits of our clan, and Nam Child is safe with her own kind. We can rest a while now.' Suddenly she felt the grief come up her throat and she choked upon it, but there were no tears. It seemed that all the moisture had dried from her wizened old frame. There were no tears, but the need to weep was like an arrow in her chest, and she rocked on her heels and made a little humming sound in her throat to try to alleviate the pain, so she did not hear the horses coming.

It was O'wa who dropped his hand from his eyes and cocked his head to the tremor on the still morning air, and when H'ani saw the fright in his eyes, she listened and heard it also.

'We are discovered,' said O'wa, and for a moment H'ani felt drained of even the will to run and hide.

'They are close already.' The same resignation was in his eyes, and it spurred the old woman.

She pulled him to his feet. 'On the open ground they will run us down with the ease of a cheetah taking a lame gazelle.' She turned and looked to the mountain.

They were at the foot of the scree slope, with scattered brush and loose rock ramping gently up to the mountain's bulk.

'If,' H'ani whispered, 'if we could reach the top, no horse could follow us.'

'It is too high, too steep,' O'wa protested.

'There is a way.' With a bony finger, H'ani pointed out the faint track that zigzagged up the vast bare rocky flank of the mountain.

'Look, old grandfather, see, the spirits of the mountain are showing us the way.'

'Those are klipspringer,' O'wa muttered. The two tiny chamois-like antelope, alarmed by the approach of horsemen in the forest below, went prancing lightly up the barely discernible track. 'They are not mountain spirits,' O'wa repeated, watching the nimble brown animals fly almost straight up the tall rock-face.

'I say they *are* spirits in the guise of antelope.' H'ani dragged him towards the scree slope. 'I say they *are* showing us the way to escape our enemies. Hurry, you stupid and argumentative old man, there is no other way open to us.'

She took his hand in hers, and together they hopped and skipped from boulder to boulder, climbing with the awkward agility of a pair of ancient baboons up the tumbled rock of the scree slope.

However, before they reached the base of the cliff, O'wa was dragging back on her hand, and gasping with pain, reeling weakly as she urged him on.

'My chest,' he cried and staggered. 'In my chest an animal is eating my flesh, I can feel its teeth—' and he fell heavily between two boulders.

'We cannot stop,' H'ani pleaded as she stood over him. 'We must go on.' She tried to drag him up.

'There is such pain,' he wheezed. 'I can feel its teeth ripping out my heart.'

With all her strength she heaved him into a sitting position, and at that moment there was a faint shout from the foot of the scree slope below them.

'They have seen us,' H'ani said, looking down at the two horsemen as they rode out of the forest. 'They are coming up after us.'

She watched them jump down from their horses, tether them and then come at the slope. One was a black man and the other had a head that shone like sunlight off a sheet of still water, and as they came on to the slope they shouted again, a fierce and jubilant sound, like the clamour of hunting hounds when they first take the scent.

That sound roused O'wa and with H'ani's help he came unsteadily to his feet, clutching at his chest. His lips had

539

blanched and his eyes were like those of a mortally wounded gazelle; they terrified her as much as the shouts of the men below.

'We must go on.' Half-carrying, half-dragging him, she led him to the base of the cliff.

'I cannot do it.' His voice was so faint she had to put her ear to his lips. 'I cannot go up there.'

'You can,' she told him stoutly. 'I will lead you, place your feet where I place mine.' And she went on to the rock, on to the steep pathway that the klipspringer had marked with their sharp pointed hooves, and behind her the old man came on unsteadily.

One hundred feet up they found a ledge, and it shielded them from the men below. They toiled upwards, clinging to the harsh abrasive surface with their fingertips, and the open drop below them seemed to steady O'wa. He climbed more determinedly. Once when he hesitated and swayed outwards from the wall, she reached back and caught his arm and held him until the fit of vertigo passed.

'Follow me,' she told him. 'Do not look down, old grandfather. Watch my feet and follow me.'

They went upwards, higher and still higher, and although the plain opened below them, yet the hunters were hidden beneath the sheer of the cliff.

'Only a little further,' she told him. 'See, there is the crest, just a little further and we will be safe. Here, give me your hand.' And she reached out to help him over a bad place where the drop opened below them and they had to step across the void.

H'ani looked down between her feet and she saw them again, dwarfed by distance and foreshortened and misshapened by the overhead perspective. The two hunters were still at the base of the cliff, directly below her, looking up at her. The white man's face shone like a cloud, so strangely pale and yet so malignant, she thought. He lifted his arms and pointed at her with the long staff he carried. H'ani had never seen a rifle before, and made no effort to hide herself as she stared down at him. She knew she was far out of range of an arrow from even the most powerful bow, and, unafraid, she leaned out from the narrow ledge for a better view of her enemy. She saw the white man's extended arms jerk, and a little feather of white smoke flew from the tip of his staff.

She never heard the rifle shot, for the bullet arrived before the sound. It was a soft lead-nosed Mauser bullet and it entered low down in the front of her stomach and passed obliquely upwards, traversing her body, tearing through her bowels and her stomach, up through one lung and out through her back a few inches to one side of the spinal column. The force of the impact flung her backwards against the rock wall, and then her lifeless body bounced loosely forward and spun out over the edge.

O'wa cried out and reached for her as she went over. He touched her with his fingertips, before she fell away from him and he teetered on the brink of the precipice.

'My life!' he called after her. 'My little heart!' And the pain and the grief were too intense to be borne. He let his body sway outwards, and as it passed its centre of gravity, he cried softly, 'I am coming with you, old grandmother, to the very end of the journey.' And he let himself plunge unresisting into the void, and the wind ripped at him as he fell, but he made not another sound, not ever.

Lothar De La Rey had to climb twenty feet to where the body of one Bushman had wedged in a crack in the cliff face.

He saw it was the corpse of an old man, wrinkled and skeletal-thin, crushed by the fall and with the skin and flesh ripped away to expose the bone of his skull. There was very little blood, almost as though the sun and the wind had desiccated the tiny body while it was still alive.

About the narrow, childlike waist there was a brief loin-cover of tanned rawhide and then, remarkably, a lanyard from which dangled a clasp knife. It was an Admiralty-type knife with a horn handle such as British sailors carried, and Lothar had not expected to find a tool like this one on a Bushman's corpse in the wastes of the Kalahari. He unlooped the lanyard and dropped the knife into his pocket. There was nothing else of value or interest on the body, and he certainly would not bother to bury it. He left the old man jammed into the rocky crevice and climbed back down to where Swart Hendrick waited for him.

'What did you find?' Hendrick demanded.

'Just an old man, but he had this.' Lothar showed him the knife, and Swart Hendrick nodded without particular interest.

'Ja. They are terrible thieves, like monkeys. That's why they were creeping around our camp.'

'Into the kloof there, amongst that horn bush. It will be dangerous to climb down. I would leave it.'

'Stay here, then,' Lothar told him and went to the edge of the deep ravine and looked down. The bottom was choked with dense thorn growth, and the climb would indeed be dangerous, but Lothar felt a perverse whim to go against Swart Hendrick's advice.

It look him twenty minutes to reach the bottom of the ravine, and as long again to find the corpse of the Bushman he had shot. It was like trying to find a dead pheasant in thick scrub without a good gundog to sniff it out, and in the end it was only the buzz of big metallic-blue flies that led him to the hand protruding from a clump of scrub, with the pink palm uppermost. He dragged the body out of the thorn scrub by the wrist and realized that it was a female,

542

an ancient hag with impossibly wrinkled skin and dangling breasts like a pair of empty tobacco pouches.

He grunted with satisfaction when he saw the bullet hole exactly where he had aimed. It had been an extremely difficult shot, at that range and deflected. He transferred his attention immediately from the bullet wound to the extraordinary decoration that the old woman wore around her neck.

Lothar had never seen anything like it in southern Africa, although in his father's collection there had been a Masai necklace from east Africa, which was vaguely similar. However, the Masai jewellery had been made with trade beads, while for this collar the old woman had collected coloured pebbles and had graded and arranged them with remarkable aesthetic appreciation. Then she had most cunningly fastened them into a breast plate that was at once strong and decorative.

Lothar realized that it would have considerable value for its rarity, and he rolled the old woman on to her face to unknot the string that held it at the back of her neck. Blood from the massive exit wound had soaked the string, run down it and clotted on some of the coloured stones, but he wiped it off carefully.

Many of the stones were in their original crystalline form, and others were water-worn and polished. The old woman had probably picked them out of the gravel banks in the dry river beds. He turned them to catch the light and smiled with pleasure at the lovely sparkle of reflected sunlight. He wrapped the necklace in his bandanna and placed it carefully in his breast pocket.

One last glance at the dead Bushwoman convinced him that there was nothing else of interest about her, and Lothar left her lying on her face and turned to the difficult climb up the ravine wall to where Swart Hendrick waited above him.

Centaine became aware of the feeling of woven cloth upon her body, and it was so unfamiliar that it brought her to the very threshold of consciousness. She thought that she lay upon something soft, but she knew that was impossible, as was the filtered light through green canvas. She was too tired to ponder these things, and when she tried to keep her eyelids open, they drooped against her best efforts and she became aware of her weakness. Her insides had been scooped out of her as though she were a soft-boiled egg, and only her brittle outer shell remained. The thought made her want to smile, but even that effort was too great and she drifted away into that lulling darkness again.

When next she became aware, it was to the sound of someone singing softly. She lay with her eyes closed and realized that she could understand the words. It was a love song, a lament for a girl that the singer had known before the war began.

It was a man's voice, and she thought it was one of the most thrilling voices she had ever heard. She did not want the song to end, but suddenly it broke off, and the man laughed.

'So, you like that do you?' he said in Afrikaans, and a child said, 'Da! Da!' so loudly and so clearly that Centaine's eyelids flew open. It was Shasa's voice and every memory of that night with the lion in the mopani came rushing back at her, and she wanted to scream again.

'My baby, save my baby!' and she rolled her head from side to side, and found she was alone in a hut with thatched roof and canvas sides. She lay on a camp cot, and she was dressed in a long cool cotton nightgown.

'Shasa!' she called out, and tried to sit up. She managed only a spasmodic jerk, and her voice was a dull, hoarse whisper.

'Shasa!' This time she summoned all her strength. 'Shasa!' and it came out as a croak.

There was a startled exclamation, and she heard a stool clatter as it was overturned. The hut darkened as someone stepped into the doorway, and she rolled her head towards the opening.

A man stood there. He was holding Shasa on his hip.

He was tall, with wide shoulders, but the light was behind him so she could not see his face.

'So, the sleeping princess awakes—' that deep, thrilling voice ' – at last, at long last.'

Still carrying her son, he stepped to the side of her cot and bent over her.

'We have been worried,' he said gently, and she looked up into the face of the most beautiful man she had ever seen, a golden man, with golden hair and yellow leopard's eyes in his tanned golden face.

On his hip Shasa bounced up and down and reached towards her.

'Mama!'

'My baby!' She lifted one hand, and the stranger swung Shasa off his hip and placed him beside her on the cot.

Then he lifted Centaine's shoulders and propped her into a sitting position with a bolster behind her. His hands were brown and strong, yet the fingers were as elegant as those of a pianist.

'Who are you?' Her voice was a husky whisper, and there were dark smears below her eyes, the colour of fresh bruises.

'My name is Lothar De La Rey,' he answered, and Shasa clenched his fists and pounded his mother's shoulder in a gesture of overwhelming affection.

'Gently!' Lothar caught his wrist to restrain him. 'Your mama is not up to so much love, not yet.' She saw how Lothar's expression softened as he looked at the child.

'What happened to me?' Centaine asked. 'Where am I?'

'You were attacked and mauled by a lion. When I shot the beast, you fell out of the tree.'

She nodded. 'Yes, I remember that, but afterwards—'

'You suffered concussion and then the wounds from the lion claws mortified.'

'How long?' she breathed.

'Six days, but the worst is past. Your leg is still very swollen and inflamed, Mevrou Courtney.'

She started. 'You use that name. Where did you learn that name?'

'I know that your name is Mevrou Centaine Courtney and that you were a survivor from the hospital ship *Protea Castle*.'

'How? How do you know these things?'

'I was sent by your father-in-law to search for you.'

'My father-in-law?'

'Colonel Courtney, and that woman, Anna Stok.'

'Anna? Anna is alive?' Centaine reached out and seized his wrist.

'There is no doubt about that at all!' Lothar laughed. 'She is very much alive.'

'That is the most wonderful news! I thought she was drowned—'

Centaine broke off as she realized that she was still holding his wrist. She let her hand fall to her side and sank back against the bolster.

'Tell me,' she whispered, 'tell me everything. How is she? How did you know where to find me? Where is Anna now? When will I see her?'

Lothar laughed again. His teeth were very white. 'So many questions!' He drew the stool to her cot. 'Where shall I begin?'

'Begin with Anna, tell me all about her.'

He talked and she listened avidly, watching his face, asking another question as soon as one was answered, fighting off the weakness of her body to revel in the sound of his voice, in the intense pleasure of hearing glad tidings of the real world from which she had been so long excluded, of communicating with one of her own kind and looking on a white and civilized face again.

The day was almost gone, the evening gloom filling her little shelter when Shasa let out a demanding shout and Lothar broke off.

'He is hungry.'

'I will feed him if you will leave us a while, Mijnheer.'

'No,' Lothar shook his head. 'You have lost your milk.'

Centaine's head jerked as though the words were a blow in her face, and she stared at him while thoughts tumbled and crowded in her mind. Up to that moment she had been so wrapped up in listening and questioning that she had not considered that there was no other woman in the camp, that for six days she had been entirely helpless, and that somebody had tended her, washed her and changed her, fed her and dressed her wounds. But his words, such an intimate subject spoken of in direct fashion, brought all this home to her, and as she stared at him, she felt herself begin to blush with shame. Her cheeks flamed – those long brown fingers of his must have touched her where only one other man had touched before. She felt her eyes smart, as she realized what those yellow eyes of his must have looked upon.

She felt herself burning up with embarrassment, and then incredibly with a hot and shameful excitement, so that she had difficulty breathing, and she lowered her eyes and turned her head away so that he could not see her scarlet cheeks.

Lothar seemed to be entirely unaware of her predicament. 'Come on, soldier, let's show mama our new trick.' He lifted Shasa and fed him with a spoon, and Shasa bounced on his lip and said, 'Hum! Hum!' as he saw each spoonful coming, and then launched himself at it with mouth wide open.

'He likes you,' Centaine said.

'We are friends,' Lothar admitted, as he removed the

heavy coating of gruel from Shasa's forehead and chin and ears with a damp cloth.

'You are good with children,' Centaine whispered and saw the sudden biting pain reflected in the darkening gold of his eyes.

'Once I had a son,' he said, and placed Shasa at her side, then picked up the spoon and empty bowl and went to the doorway.

'Where is your son?' she called softly after him, and he paused in the opening, then turned slowly back to her.

'My son is dead,' he said softly.

She was ripe and over-ripe for love. Her loneliness was a hunger so intense that it seemed it could not be assuaged, not even by those long languid conversations under the awning of the wagon tent when, with Shasa between them, they talked away the hottest hours of those lazy African days.

Mostly they discussed the things she held dearest, music and books. Although he preferred Goethe to Victor Hugo and Wagner to Verdi, these differences gave them grounds for amusing and satisfying dispute. In those arguments she discovered that his learning and scholarship far exceeded her own, but she strangely did not resent it. It merely made her more attentive to his voice. It was a marvellous voice; after the clicking and grunting of the San language, she could listen to it for the lilt and cadence as though it were music in itself.

'Sing for me!' she ordered, when they had for the moment exhausted a particular topic. 'Both Shasa and I command it.'

'Your servant, of course!' he smiled and gave them a mocking little bow, then he sang without any self-consciousness.

'Take the chick and the hen will follow you.' Centaine had often heard Anna repeat the old proverb, and when she watched Shasa riding around the camp on Lothar's shoulder, she realized the wisdom behind it, for her eyes and her heart followed both of them.

At first she felt quick resentment whenever Shasa greeted Lothar with cries of 'Da! Da!'. That name should have been reserved for Michael alone. Then with a painful stab she remembered that Michael was lying in the cemetery at Mort Homme.

After that it was easy to smile when Shasa's first attempts at walking unaided on his own two legs ended with a precipitous and headlong return to earth and he bawled for Lothar and crawled to him, seeking comfort. It was Lothar's tenderness and gentleness with her son that nudged her affections and her need for him forward, for she recognized that beneath that handsome exterior he was a hard man and fierce. She saw the awe and respect in which his own men held him, and they were tough men themselves.

Just once she witnessed him in a cold, killing rage that terrified her as much as it did the man against whom it was directed. Vark Jan, the wrinkled yellow Khoisan, in indolence and ignorance had ridden Lothar's hunting horse with an ill-fitting saddle and galled the creature's back almost to the bone. Lothar had knocked Vark Jan down with a fist to the head, and then cut the jacket and shirt off his back with razor strokes from his sjambok, a five-foot whip of cured hippo-hide, and left him unconscious in a puddle of his own blood.

The violence had appalled and frightened Centaine, for she had witnessed every brutal detail from where she lay on her cot beneath the awning. Later, however, when she was alone in her shelter, her revulsion faded and in its place was a trembly feeling of exhilaration and a heat in the pit of her stomach.

'He's so dangerous,' she thought, 'so dangerous and cruel,' and she shivered again and could not sleep. She lay and listened to his breathing in the shelter beside hers, and thought about how he must have undressed her and touched her while she was unconscious, and her flesh tingled at the memory and she blushed in the darkness.

In startling contrast the next day he was gentle and tender, holding her injured leg in his lap while he snipped the threads of cotton and plucked them from her swollen, inflamed flesh. They left dark punctures in her skin, and he bent over her leg and sniffed the wound.

'It's clean now. That redness is only your body attempting to rid itself of the stitches. It will heal swiftly now they are gone.'

Lothar was right. Within two days she was able, with the help of the crutch he had whittled for her, to make her first foray out of the canvas shelter.

'My legs feel wobbly,' she protested, 'and I am as weak as Shasa.'

'You'll soon be strong again.' He placed his arm around her shoulders to steady her, and she trembled at his touch and hoped he would not notice and withdraw his arm.

They paused by the horse lines and Centaine petted the animals, stroking their silky muzzles and revelling in that nostalgic horse odour.

'I want to ride again,' she told him.

'Anna Stok told me you were a skilled horsewoman – she told me you had a stallion, a white stallion.'

'Nuage.' Tears prickled her eyes as she remembered, and she pressed her face against the neck of Lothar's hunting horse to hide them. 'My white cloud, he was so beautiful, so strong and swift.'

'Nuage,' Lothar took her arm, 'a lovely name.' Then he went on, 'Yes, you will ride again soon. We have a long journey ahead of us, back to where your father-in-law and Anna Stok will be waiting for you.'

It was the first time she had considered an end to this magical interlude, and she pulled away from the horse and stared at him over its back. She didn't want it to end, she didn't want him to leave her, as she knew he soon would.

'I'm tired,' she said. 'I don't think I am ready to start riding just yet.'

That evening as she sat under the awning with a book in her lap, pretending to read, while watching him from under her lowered lids, he looked up suddenly and smiled with such a knowing glint in his eye that she blushed and looked away in confusion.

'I'm writing to Colonel Courtney,' he told her, sitting at the collapsible travelling bureau with the pen in his hand smiling across at her, 'I will send a rider back to Windhoek tomorrow, but it will take him two weeks or more to get there and back. I am letting Colonel Courtney know when and where we can meet, and I have suggested a rendezvous for the 19th day of next month.'

She wanted to say, 'So soon?' but instead, she nodded silently.

'I am sure you are most anxious to be reunited with your family, but I don't think we will be able to reach the rendezvous before that date.'

'I understand.'

'However, I would be delighted to send any letter that you might care to write, with the messenger.'

'Oh, that would be wonderful – Anna, dear Anna, she will be fussing like an old hen.'

Lothar stood up from the bureau. 'Please seat yourself here and use the pen and what paper you need, Mrs Courtney. While you are busy, master Shasa and I will see to his dinner.'

Surprisingly, once she penned the opening salutation, 'My dearest dear Anna,' she could think of nothing to follow it, mere words seemed so paltry.

'I give thanks to God that you survived that terrible night, and I have thought of you every day since then—' The dam holding back the words burst, and they flooded out on to the paper.

'We will need a packhorse to carry that epistle.' Lothar stood behind her shoulder, and she started as she realized that she had covered a dozen sheets with close script.

'There is so much still to tell her, but the rest will have to wait.' Centaine folded the sheets and sealed them with a wax wafer from the silver box fitted into the top of the bureau, while Lothar held the candle for her.

'It was strange,' she whispered. 'I had almost forgotten how to hold a pen. It has been so long.'

'You have never told me what happened to you, how you escaped from the sinking ship, how you survived so long, how you came to be so many hundreds of miles from the coast where you must have come ashore—'

'I don't want to talk about it.' She cut him off quickly. She saw for a moment in her mind's eye the little heart-shaped, wrinkled, amber-coloured faces, and suppressed her nagging guilt at having deserted them so cruelly.

'I don't even want to think about that. Kindly never address the subject again, sir.' Her tone was stingingly severe.

'Of course, Mrs Courtney.' He picked up the two sealed letters. 'If you will excuse me, I will give these to Vark Jan now. He can leave before dawn tomorrow.' He was stiff-faced and resentful of the rebuff.

She watched him cross to the servants' fire and heard the murmur of voices as he gave Vark Jan his orders.

When he returned to the shelter, she made a pretence of being engrossed with her book, hoping that he would interrupt her, but he seated himself at the bureau and opened his journal. It was his nightly ritual, his entry in the leather-bound journal. She listened to his pen scratch-

552

ing on the paper, and she resented his attention being focused anywhere but on herself.

'There is so little time left to us,' she thought, 'and he squanders it so.' She closed her book loudly but he did not look up.

'What are you writing?' she demanded.

'You know what I am writing, since we have discussed it before, Mrs Courtney.'

'Do you write everything in your journal?'

'Almost everything.'

'Do you write about me?'

He laid down the pen and stared at her, and she was flustered by the direct gaze of those serene yellow eyes, but could not bring herself to apologize.

'You were prying into things that did not concern you,' she told him.

'Yes,' he agreed with her, and to cover her discomfort, she demanded, 'What have you written about me in your famous journal?'

'And now, madam, it is you who are inquisitive,' he told her as he closed his diary, placed it in the drawer of the bureau and stood up. 'If you will excuse me, I must make my rounds of the camp.'

So she learned that she could not treat him the way she had treated her father, or even the way she had treated Michael Courtney. Lothar was a proud man and would not allow her to trespass on his dignity, a man who had fought his whole life for the right to be his own master. He would not permit her to take advantage of his strong sense of chivalry to her and to little Shasa. She learned that she could not bully him.

The next morning she found herself dismayed by his

formal aloof bearing, but as the day wore on she became angry. 'Such a small tiff, and he sulks like a spoiled child,' she told herself. 'Well, we'll see who sulks longest and hardest.'

By the second day her anger had given way to loneliness and unhappiness. She found herself longing for his smile, for the pleasure of one of their long convoluted discussions, for the sound of his laughter and his voice when he sang to her.

She watched Shasa tottering around the camp, hanging on to one of Lothar's hands and engaging him in loquacious conversation that only the two of them could understand, and was appalled to find that she was jealous of her own child.

'I will give Shasa his food,' she told him coldly. 'It is time I resumed my duties. You need no longer discommode yourself, sir.'

'Of course, Mrs Courtney.'

And she wanted to cry, 'Please, I am truly sorry,' But their pride was a mountain range between them.

She listened all that afternoon for the sound of his horse returning. She heard only the sound of distant rifle fire, but it was after dark when Lothar rode in, and she and Shasa were already in their cots. She lay in the darkness and listened to the voices and the sounds as the carcasses of the springbok that Lothar had shot were offloaded from his hunting horse and hung upon the butchering rack. Lothar sat late at the fire with his men, and bursts of their laughter carried to her as she tried to compose herself to sleep.

At last she heard him come to the shelter beside hers, and she listened to the splash of water as he washed in the bucket at the entrance, the rustle of his clothing and finally the creak of the lacings of his cot as he settled upon it.

Shasa's cries awoke her, and she knew instantly that he

was in pain, and she swung her legs off the cot and still half-asleep groped for him. A match flared and lantern light bloomed in Lothar's shelter.

'Shh! Quiet, my little one.' She cradled Shasa against her chest, and his hot little body alarmed her.

'May I enter?' Lothar asked from the entrance.

'Oh, yes.'

He stooped into the tent and set down the lantern.

'Shasa, he's sick.'

Lothar took the child from her. He wore only a pair of breeches, his chest and feet were bare. His hair was tangled from the pillow.

He touched Shasa's flushed cheek and then slipped a finger into his squalling mouth. Shasa choked off his next howl and bit down on the finger like a shark.

'Another tooth,' Lothar smiled, 'I felt it this morning.' He handed Shasa back to her and he let out a howl of rejection.

'I'll be back, soldier,' and she heard him rummaging in the medicine chest he kept bolted to the floor of his wagon.

He had a small bottle in his hand when he returned, and she wrinkled her nose at the pungent odour of oil of cloves as he pulled the cork.

'We'll fix that bad old tooth, won't we just.' Lothar massaged the child's gums as Shasa sucked on his finger. 'That's a brave soldier.'

He laid Shasa back in his cot and within minutes he had fallen asleep again.

Lothar picked up the lantern. 'Good night, Mrs Courtney,' he said quietly, and went to the entrance.

'Lothar!' His name on her lips startled her as it did him.

'Please,' she whispered, 'I've been alone for so long. Please, don't be cruel to me any more.'

She held out both arms towards him and he crossed to her and sank down on to the edge of the cot beside her.

'Oh, Lothar—' Her voice was choked and gusty, and she

wrapped her arms around his neck. 'Love me,' she pleaded, 'oh, please love me,' and his mouth was hot as fever on hers, his arms about her so fierce that she gasped as the breath was driven from her lungs.

'Yes, I was cruel to you,' he told her softly, his voice trembling in his throat, 'but only because I wanted so desperately to hold you, because I ached and burned with my love for you—'

'Oh, Lothar, hold me and love me – and never ever let me go.'

The days that followed were full recompense for all the hardships and loneliness of the months and years. It was as though the fates had conspired to heap upon Centaine all the delights that she had been denied for so long.

She woke each dawn in the narrow cot and before her eyes were open, she was groping for him with a tantalizing terror that he might no longer be there – but he always was. Sometimes he was feigning sleep and she had to try and open one of his eyelids with her fingertips, and when she succeeded, he rolled his eyeball upwards until only the white showed, and she giggled and thrust her tongue deeply into his ear, having discovered that that was the one torture he could not endure, and the gooseflesh sprang up on his bare arms and he came awake like a lion and seized her and turned her giggles to gasps and then to moans.

In the cool of the morning they rode out together with Shasa on the saddle in front of Lothar. For the first few days they kept the horses to a walk and stayed close by the camp. However, as Centaine's strength returned, they ventured further and on the return they covered the last mile at a mad flying gallop, racing each other, and Shasa, secure in Lothar's arms, shrieked with excitement as they tore into the camp, all of them flushed and ravenous for their breakfasts.

The long sultry desert noondays they spent under the thatched shelter, sitting apart, touching only fleetingly when he handed her a book or when passing Shasa between them, but caressing each other with their eyes and their voices until the suspense was a kind of exquisite torment.

As the heat passed and the sun mellowed, Lothar again called for the horses and they rode to the foot of the scree slope below the mountain. They hobbled the horses and with Shasa riding on Lothar's shoulder climbed up into one of the narrow sheer-sided valleys. Here, below a fresco of ancient Bushman paintings, screened by dense foliage, Lothar had discovered another of the thermal springs. It spurted from out of the cliff face and drained into a small circular rock pool.

On their first visit, it was Lothar who had to be coaxed out of his clothes, while Centaine, happy to be rid of long skirts and petticoats which still irked her, delighting in the freedom of nakedness to which the desert had accustomed her, splashed him with water and teased and challenged him until at last, almost defiantly, he dropped his breeches and plunged hurriedly into the pool.

'You are shameless,' he told her, only half-jokingly.

Shasa's presence placed a restraint upon them, and they touched lightly and furtively under the concealment of the green waters, driving each other to trembling distraction, until Lothar could bear it no longer, and reached for her with that determined set to his jaw that she had come to know so well. Then she would evade his clutches with a maidenly squeal, and leap from the pool, slipping on her skirts over her long wet gleaming legs and her bottom that glowed pink from the heat of the water.

'Last one home misses his dinner!'

It was only after she had laid Shasa in his cot, and blown out the lantern, that she crept breathlessly through to Lothar's shelter. He was waiting for her, strung out by all the touching and teasing and artful withdrawals of the day. Then they went at each other in a desperate frenzy, almost as though they were antagonists locked in mortal combat.

Much later, lying in the darkness in each other's arms, talking very softly so as not to disturb Shasa, they made their plans and their promises for a future that stretched before them as though they stood on the threshold of paradise itself.

I t seemed he had been gone only a few days, when in the middle of a baking afternoon, on a lathered horse, Vark Jan rode back into camp.

He carried a package of letters, sewed up in canvas wrapping and sealed with tar. One letter was for Lothar, a single sheet, and he read it at a glance.

I have the honour to inform you that I have in my possession a document of amnesty in your favour, signed by both the Attorney-General of the Cape of Good Hope and the Minister of Justice of the Union of South Africa.

I congratulate you on the success of your endeavours and I look forward to our meeting at the time and place nominated when I shall take pleasure in handing the document to you.

Yours truly,
Garrick Courtney (Col.)

The other letters were both for Centaine. One was also from Garry Courtney, welcoming her and Shasa to the family and assuring them both of all the love and consideration and privilege that that entailed.

558

From the most miserable creature, immersed in unbearable grief, you have transformed me at a stroke into the happiest and most joyful of all fathers and grandfathers.

I long to embrace you both.

Speed that day,

Your affectionate and dutiful father-in-law,
Garrick Courtney

The third letter, many times thicker than the other two combined, was in Anna Stok's clumsy, semi-literate scrawl. Her face flushed with excitement, alternately laughing aloud with joy or her eyes sparkling with tears, Centaine read snatches aloud for Lothar's benefit, and when she had reached the end, she folded both letters carefully.

'I long to see them, and yet I am reluctant to let the world intrude upon our happiness together. I want to go, and yet I want to stay here for ever with you. Is that silly?'

'Yes,' he laughed. 'It certainly is. We leave at sunset.'

They travelled at night to avoid the heat of the desert day.

With Shasa sound asleep in the wagon cot, lulled by the motion of rolling wheels, Centaine rode stirrup to stirrup with Lothar. His hair shone in the moonlight, and the shadows softened the marks of hardship and suffering on his features, so she found it difficult to take her eyes from his face.

Each morning before the dawn, they went into laager. If they were between water-holes, they watered the cattle and the horses from the bucket before they sought the shade of the wagon awnings to wait out the heat of the day.

In the late afternoon while the servants packed up the

camp and inspanned for the night's trek, Lothar would ride out to hunt. At first Centaine rode with him, for she could not bear to be parted from him for even an hour. Then one evening in failing light Lothar made a poor shot and the Mauser bullet ripped through the belly of a beautiful little springbok.

It ran before the horses with amazing stamina, a tangle of entrails swinging from the gaping wound. Even when at last it went down, it lifted its head to watch Lothar as he dismounted and unsheathed his hunting knife. After that Centaine stayed in camp when Lothar went out for fresh meat.

So Centaine was alone this evening when the wind came suddenly out of the north, niggling and chill. Centaine climbed up into the living wagon to fetch a warm jacket for Shasa.

The interior of the wagon was crammed with gear, packed and ready for the night's trek. The carpet bag which contained all the clothing that Anna had provided was stowed at the rear and she had to scramble over a yellow wood chest to reach it. Her long skirts hampered her, and she teetered on the top of the chest and put out her hand to steady herself.

Her nearest handhold was the brass handle on the front of Lothar's travelling bureau which was lashed to the wagon bed. As she put her weight on it the handle gave slightly, and the drawer slid open an inch.

'He has forgotten to lock it,' she thought, 'I must warn him.' She pushed the drawer closed and crawled over the chest, reached the stowed carpet bag, pulled out Shasa's jacket, and was crawling back when her eye fell again on the drawer of the bureau – and she checked herself sharply and stared at it.

Temptation was like the prickle of a burr. Lothar's journal was in that drawer.

'What an awful thing to do,' she told herself primly, and yet her hand went out and touched the brass handle again.

'What has he written about me?' She pulled the drawer open slowly and stared at the thick, leather-covered volume. 'Do I really want to know?' She began to close the drawer again, and then capitulated to that overwhelming temptation. 'I'll only read about me;' she promised herself.

She crawled quickly to the wagon flap and peered out guiltily. Swart Hendrick was bringing up the draught oxen preparatory to inspanning.

'Has the master returned yet?' she called to him.

'No, missus, and we have heard no shots. He will be late tonight.'

'Call me if you see him coming,' she ordered, and crept back to the bureau.

She squatted beside it with the heavy journal in her lap, and she was relieved to find it was written almost entirely in Afrikaans with only occasional passages in German. She riffled through the pages until she found the date on which he had rescued her. The entry was four pages long, the longest single entry in the entire journal.

Lothar had given a full account of the lion attack and the rescue, of their return to the wagons while she was unconscious, and a description of Shasa. She smiled as she read:

'A sturdy lad, of the same age as Manfred when last I saw him, and I find myself much affected.'

Still smiling, she scanned the page for a description of herself, and her eyes stopped at the paragraph:

'I have no doubt that this is indeed the woman, though she is changed from the photograph and from

561

my brief memory of her. Her hair is thick and fuzzy as that of a Nama girl, her face thin and brown as a monkey—' Centaine gasped with affront '—yet when she opened her eyes for a moment, I thought my heart might crack, they were so big and soft.'

She was slightly mollified and skimmed forward, turning the pages quickly, listening like a thief for the sound of Lothar's horse. A word caught her eye in the neat blocks of teutonic script: '*Boesmanne.*' Her attention flicked to it. 'Bushmen' – and her heart tripped, her interest entirely captivated.

'Bushmen harassing the camp during the night. Hendrick discovered their spoor near the horse lines and the cattle. We followed at first light. A difficult hunt—'

The word '*jag*' stopped Centaine's eye. 'Hunt?' she puzzled. This was a word only applied to the chase, to the killing of animals, and she raced on.

'We came up with the two Bushmen, but they almost gave us the slip by climbing the cliff with the agility of baboons. We could not follow and would have lost them, but their curiosity was too strong – again, just like baboons. One of them paused at the top of the cliff and looked down at us. It was a difficult shot, at extreme upward deflection and long range—'

The blood drained from Centaine's face. She could not believe what she was reading, each word reverberated in her skull as though it were an empty place, cavernous and echoing.

'However, I held true and brought the Bushman down. Then I witnessed a remarkable incident. I had no need

562

of a second shot, for the remaining Bushman fell from the cliff top. From below it seemed almost as though he threw himself over the edge. However, I do not believe that this was the case, an animal is not capable of suicide. It is more likely that in terror and panic, he lost his footing. Both bodies fell in difficult positions. However, I was determined to examine them. The climb was awkward and dangerous, but I was in fact, well rewarded for my endeavours. The first body, that of a very old man, the one that had slipped from the cliff, was unremarkable except that he carried a clasp knife made by "Joseph Rodgers" of Sheffield on a lanyard about his waist.'

Centaine began to shake her head from side to side. 'No!' she whispered. 'No!'

'This, I believe, must have been stolen from some other traveller. The old rogue probably entered our camp in the hope of similar booty.'

Centaine saw again little O'wa squatting naked in the sunlight with the knife in his hands and the tears of pleasure running down his withered cheeks.

'Oh, in the name of mercy, no!' she whimpered, but her eye was drawn remorselessly on by the orderly ranks of brutal words.

'The second body, however, yielded the greater trophy. It was that of a woman. If anything she was more aged than the man, but around her neck she wore a most unusual decoration—'

The book slid from Centaine's lap and she covered her face with both hands.

'H'ani!' she cried out in the San tongue. 'My old

563

grandmother, my old and revered grandmother, you came to us. And he shot you down!'

She was rocking from side to side, humming in her throat, the San attitude of grief.

Suddenly she hurled herself at the bureau. She pulled the drawer from its runners, scattering loose pages of writing-paper and pens and sticks of wax on the floor of the wagon.

'The necklace,' she sobbed. 'The necklace. I have to be certain!'

She seized the handle of one of the small lower compartments and tugged at it. It was locked. She snatched the handle of the wagon jack from its slot in the frame, and with the steel point shattered the lock and jerked the compartment open. It contained a silver framed photograph of a plump blonde woman with a child in her lap and a wad of letters tied up with a silk ribbon.

She spilled them on to the floor and smashed open the next compartment. There was a Luger pistol in a wooden holster, and packet of ammunition. She threw them on top of the letters, and at the bottom of the compartment she found a cigar box.

She lifted the lid. It contained a bundle wrapped in a patterned bandanna and as she picked it out with shaking hands, H'ani's necklace tumbled from the roll of cloth. She stared at it as though it was a deadly mamba, holding her hands behind her back and blubbering softly, 'H'ani – oh, my old grandmother.'

She brought her hands to her mouth, and pressed her lips to stop them quivering. Then she reached out slowly for the necklace and held it up, but at the full stretch of her arms.

'He murdered you,' she whispered, and then gagged as she saw the black stains of blood still upon the gaudy stones. 'He shot you down like an animal.'

She hugged the necklace to her breast, and began to

564

hum and rock herself again, her eyes tightly closed to dam back her tears. She was still sitting like that when she heard the drum of hooves and the shouts of the servants welcoming Lothar back to the wagons.

She stood up and swayed on her feet as an attack of giddiness seized her. Her grief was like an affliction, but then when she heard his voice, 'Here, Hendrick, take my horse! Where is the missus?' her grief changed shape, and though her hands still shook, her chin lifted and her eyes burned not with tears but with a consuming rage.

She snatched up the Luger pistol and drew it from its curved wooden holster. She snapped back the slide and watched a shiny brass cartridge feed up into the chamber. Then she dropped it into the pocket of her skirt and turned to the wagon flap.

As she jumped down, Lothar was coming towards her, and his face brightened with pleasure at the sight of her.

'Centaine—' he paused as he saw her expression. 'Centaine, something is wrong!'

She held out the necklace towards him, and it glittered and twinkled between her shaking fingers. She could not speak.

His face darkened and his eyes were hard and furious.

'You have opened my bureau!'

'You killed her!'

'Who?' He was truly puzzled, and then, 'Oh, the Bushwoman—'

'H'ani!'

'I don't understand.'

'My little grandmother.'

He was alarmed now. 'Something is very wrong, let me—'

He stepped towards her, but she backed away and screamed, 'Keep away – don't touch me! Don't ever touch me again!' She reached for the pistol in her skirt.

'Centaine, calm yourself.' And then he stopped as he saw the Luger in her hands.

'Are you mad?' He gazed at her in amazement. 'Here, give that to me.' Again he stepped forward.

'You murderer, you cold-blooded monster – you killed her.' And she held the pistol double-handed, the necklace entangled with the weapon, the barrel waving in erratic circles. 'You killed my little H'ani. I hate you for it!'

'Centaine!' He put out his hand to take the pistol from her.

There was a flash of gunsmoke and the Luger kicked upwards, flinging Centaine's hands above her head. The shot cracked like a trek whip, numbing her eardrums.

Lothar's body jerked backwards and he spun on his heels. His long golden locks flickered like ripe wheat in a high wind as he collapsed on to his knees, and then toppled on to his face.

Centaine dropped the Luger and fell back against the side of the wagon, as Hendrick rushed forward and snatched the Luger out of her hand.

'I hate you,' she panted at Lothar. 'Die, damn you. Die and go to hell!'

C entaine rode with a slack rein, letting her mount choose its own pace and path. She had Shasa on her hip with a sling under him to support his weight. She held his head in the crook of her arm, and he slept quietly against her.

The wind had scourged the desert for five days now without cease, and the driven sands hissed and slithered across the earth's surface like sea spume across a beach, and the round seed pods of tumbleweed trundled across the plain like footballs. The small herds of springbok turned their backs to its chilling blast and tucked their tails up between their legs.

Centaine had wound a scarf around her head like a turban, and thrown a blanket over her shoulders to cover Shasa and herself. She hunched down in the saddle and the cold wind tugged at the corners of the blanket and tangled her horse's long mane. She slitted her eyes against the gritty wind, and saw the Finger of God.

It was still far ahead, indistinct through the dun dust-laden air, but it spiked the low sky, even in this haze visible from five miles off. This was the reason that Lothar De La Rey had chosen it. It was unique, there could be no confusion with any other natural feature.

Centaine pulled up the pony's head and urged him into a trot. Shasa whimpered a protest in his sleep at the change of gait, but Centaine straightened in the saddle, trying to throw off the sorrow and rage that lay upon her with a weight that threatened to crush her soul.

Slowly the silhouette of the Finger of God hardened against the dusty yellow sky, a slim pillar of rock, thrusting towards the heavens and then thickening into a flaring cobra's head, two hundred feet above the plain. Staring at it, Centaine was aware of the same superstitious awe that must have gripped the old Hottentots who named it 'Mukurob'.

Then from the base of the great stone monument a dart of light, reflected off metal, pricked her eyes and she shaded them with the blanket and peered intently.

'Shasa,' she whispered. 'They are there! They are waiting for us.'

She urged the weary pony into a canter, and rose in the stirrups.

In the shadow of the stone pillar was parked a motor vehicle, and beside it a small green cottage tent had been erected. There was a campfire burning in front of the tent, and a plume of smoke, blue as a heron's feather, smeared by the wind across the plain.

Centaine whipped the turban from her head and waved it like a banner.

'Here!' she screamed. 'Hullo! Here I am!'

The two indistinct human figures rose from beside the fire, staring towards her.

She waved and hulloed, still at full gallop, and one of the figures broke into a run. It was a woman, a big woman in long skirts. She held them up over her knees, ploughing with desperate haste through the soft footing. Her face was bright scarlet with effort and emotion.

'Anna!' Centaine screamed. 'Oh, Anna!'

There were tears streaming down that broad red face, and Anna dropped her skirts and stood with her arms spread wide.

'My baby!' she cried, and Centaine flung herself from the saddle and, clutching Shasa to her breast, ran into her embrace.

They were both weeping, holding hard to each other, trying to talk at once, but incoherently, laughing between the sobs, when Shasa, crushed between them, let out a protesting howl.

Anna snatched him from her and hugged him.

'A boy – he's a boy.'

'Michel.' Centaine sobbed happily. 'I named him Michel Shasa.' And Shasa let out a hoot and grabbed with both hands at that marvellous face, so big and red as a fruit ripe for eating.

'Michel!' Anna wept as she kissed him. Shasa, who knew all about kissing, opened his mouth wide and smeared warm saliva down her chin.

Still carrying Shasa, Anna dragged Centaine by one arm towards the tent and the camp fire.

A tall, round-shouldered figure came towards them diffidently. His thinning sandy-grey hair was swept back from a high scholarly forehead, and his mild, vaguely myopic eyes were a muddier shade of the Courtney blue than Michael's had been; his nose, while every bit as large as General Sean Courtney's, seemed somehow to be ashamed of the fact.

'I am Michael's father,' he said shyly, and it was like looking at a faded and smudged photograph of her Michael. Centaine felt a rush of guilt, for she had been false to her vows and to Michael's memory. It was as though Michael confronted her now. For an instant she remembered his twisted body in the cockpit of the burning aircraft, and in grief and guilt she ran to Garry and threw her arms around his neck.

'Papa!' she said, and at that word Garry's reserve collapsed and he choked and clung to her.

'I had given up hope—' Garry could not go on, and the sight of his tears set Anna off again, which was too much for Shasa. He let out a doleful wail, and all four of them stood together beneath the Finger of God and wept.

The wagons seemed to swim towards them through the streaming dust, rolling and pitching over the uneven ground, and as they waited for them to come up, Anna murmured, 'We must be eternally grateful to this man—' She sat in the back seat of the Fiat tourer with Shasa on her lap and Centaine beside her.

'He will be well paid.' Garry stood with one booted foot on the running-board of the Fiat. In his hand he held a rolled document, secured with a red ribbon. He tapped the roll against his artificial leg.

'Whatever you pay him will not be enough,' Anna affirmed, and hugged Shasa.

'He is an outlaw and a renegade,' Garry scowled. 'It goes very much against the grain—'

'Please give him what we owe him, Papa,' Centaine said softly, 'then let him go. I don't want ever to see him again.'

The small, half-naked Nama boy leading the ox-team whistled them to a halt, and Lothar De La Rey climbed down slowly from the wagon seat, wincing at the effort.

When he reached the ground, he paused for a moment, steadying himself with his free hand against the wagon body. His other arm was in a sling across his chest. His face was a yellowish putty colour beneath the smoothly tanned skin. His eyes were darkly underscored, the lines of suffering at the corners of his mouth accentuated, and a dense stubble of pale beard covered his jaws and sparkled even in the poor light.

'He has been hurt,' Anna murmured. 'What happened to him?' And beside her Centaine silently turned her head away.

Lothar braced himself and went to meet Garry. Halfway between the Fiat and the wagon they shook hands briefly, Lothar awkwardly offering his uninjured left hand.

They spoke in low tones that did not reach to where Centaine sat. Garry offered him the roll of parchment, and Lothar loosened the ribbon with his teeth and spread the sheet against his thigh, holding it with his one good hand as he stooped to read it.

After a minute he straightened and let the parchment spring back into a roll. He nodded at Garry and said something. His face was expressionless, and Garry shuffled selfconsciously and made an uncertain gesture, half-offering another handshake and then thinking better of it, for Lothar was not looking at him.

He was staring at Centaine, and now he pushed past Garry and started slowly towards her. Immediately Centaine snatched Shasa off Anna's lap and crouched in the furthest corner of the seat, glaring at him, holding Shasa away from him protectively. Lothar stopped, lifted his good hand towards her in a small gesture of appeal, but let it drop to his side when her expression did not change.

Puzzled, Garry glanced from one to the other of them.

'Can we go, Papa?' Centaine spoke in a clear sharp voice.

'Of course, my dear.' Garry hurried to the front of the Fiat and stooped to the crank handle. As the engine fired, he ran round to the driver's seat and adjusted the ignition lever.

'Is there nothing you wish to say to the man?' he asked, and when she shook her head, he clambered up behind the wheel and the Fiat jerked forward.

Centaine looked back only once, after they had bumped over a mile of the sandy track. Lothar De La Rey still stood below the towering monument of rock, a tiny lonely figure in the desert, and he stared after them.

The green hills of Zululand were so utterly different from the desolation of the Kalahari or the monstrous dunes of the Namib that Centaine had difficulty believing that she was on the same continent. But then, she remembered, they were on the opposite side of Africa, a thousand miles and more from the Finger of God.

Garry Courtney stopped the Fiat on the crest of the steep escarpment high above the Baboonstroom river and switched off the engine and helped both women down.

He took Shasa from Centaine and led them to the edge.

'There,' he pointed. 'That's Theuniskraal where both Sean and I – and then Michael – were all born.'

It stood at the foot of the slope, surrounded by rambling gardens. Even from this distance Centaine could see that the gardens were unkempt and overgrown as tropical jungle. Tall palms and flowering spathodea trees were hung with untrammelled mantles of purple bougainvillaea creepers, and the ornamental fishponds were poisonous green with algae growth.

'Of course the house was rebuilt after the fire,' Garry hesitated, and a shadow passed behind his muddy blue eyes, for in that fire Michael's mother had died, then he hurried on. 'I've added to it over the years.'

Centaine smiled, for the house reminded her of a haphazard old woman who had thrown on garments of a dozen different fashions, none of which suited her. Grecian columns and Georgian red brick glared sullenly at the white painted curlicue gables in the Cape Dutch style. The twisted barley sugar chimney-pots huddled in uneasy alliance with crenellated buttresses and towers of stonework. Beyond it, stretching to the horizon, were waving fields of green sugar cane that moved in the light wind like the surface of a summer sea.

'And over there is Lion Kop.' Garry turned to point to the west, where the escarpment made a stately sweep, forming a heavily forested amphitheatre around the town of Ladyburg. 'That's Sean's land – all of it from my boundary. There! Right as far as you can see. Between us, we own the whole escarpment. That's the homestead of Lion Kop, you can just make out the roof through the trees.'

'It's so beautiful,' Centaine breathed. 'Oh look, there are mountains beyond, with snow on the peaks!'

'The Drakensberg Mountains, a hundred miles away.'

'And that?' Centaine pointed over the roofs of the town, over the complex of sugar refinery and lumber mills, to an elegant white mansion on the slope of the valley. 'Is that Courtney land also?'

'Yes.' Garry's expression changed. 'Dirk Courtney, Sean's son.'

'I didn't know that General Courtney had a son.'

'Sometimes he wishes he did not,' Garry murmured, and then briskly, before she could pursue it, 'Come along everybody, it's almost lunchtime, and if we are in luck and the postman has delivered my cable, the servants will be expecting us.'

'How many gardeners do you keep, Mijnheer?' Anna asked, as the Fiat puttered up Theuniskraal's long twisting driveway, and Anna surveyed the confusion of vegetation with a disapproving frown.

'Four, I think – or maybe five.'

'Well, Mijnheer, you are not getting your money's worth,' Anna told him severely, and Centaine smiled at the certainty that from now on the unsuspecting bevy of gardeners would be earning every sou of their wages. Then her attention was diverted.

'Oh, look!' She stood up impulsively and gripped the front seat, holding on to her hat with the other hand. On the far side of the white-painted fence that ran beside the driveway, a troop of yearlings took mock alarm at the clattering Fiat and fled across the lush green kikuyu grass paddock, manes streaming, hooves flying and glossy hides flashing in the sunlight.

'One of your duties, my dear, will be to see that the horses are kept in exercise.' Garry twisted round in the driver's seat to smile at her. 'And we will have to pick out a pony for young Michel here.'

'He is not yet two years old,' Anna intervened.

'Never too young, Mevrou.' Garry transferred the smile to her, and it changed to a lascivious leer. 'Or too old!'

Although her frown stayed firmly in place, Anna could not prevent the softening of her eyes before she turned her face away from him.

'Ah, good! The servants are expecting us after all!' Garry exclaimed, and braked the Fiat to a halt before the double teak front doors. The servants stepped forward in order of seniority to be introduced, beginning with the

Zulu chef in his tall white hat and ending with the grooms and the gardeners and stable boys, all of them clapping their hands respectfully and beaming with white teeth so that Shasa leapt in Centaine's arms and let out an excited shout.

'Ah, Bayete,' the chef laughed, as he gave Shasa the royal salute, 'all hail, little chieftain, and may you grow as strong and straight as your father!'

They went into Theuniskraal, and Garry led them proudly through the cavernous rooms in their genteel disarray. Though Anna ran her finger over every object that came in range and scowled at the dust that came off on it, yet from the long baronial dining-room with hunting trophies decorating the walls to the library with more expensive but dusty volumes stacked on the desk and the floor than on the shelves, the homestead of Theuniskraal possessed a benign and friendly atmosphere.

Centaine felt at home almost immediately.

'Oh, it will be so good to have young people here again, and pretty girls, and a small boy.' Garry put it into words, 'The old place so needs livening up.'

'And a little cleaning up won't hurt it either,' growled Anna, but Garry was dashing up the central staircase, sprightly as a lad with excitement.

'Come along, let me show you your rooms.'

The room Garry had selected for Anna was beside his own suite, and although the significance of this was lost on Centaine, Anna lowered her eyes and looked like a demure bulldog as she noticed that a discreet door connected with Garry's dressing-room.

'This will be your room, my dear.' Garry led Centaine along the upper gallery and ushered her into a huge sunny room with french doors opening on to a wide terrace that overlooked the gardens.

'It's lovely.' Centaine clapped her hands with delight and ran out on to the terrace.

'Of course it needs redecorating, but you must choose your own colours and carpets and curtains – now, come along, let's look at young Michel's room.'

As Garry opened the door across the gallery facing Centaine's room, his mood changed dramatically, and as she stepped into the room, Centaine realized the reason.

Michael's presence was everywhere. From the framed photographs on the walls he smiled down at her; Michael in rugby football togs standing arms folded across his chest with fourteen other grinning young men, Michael in white cricket flannels with bat in hand, Michael with a shotgun and a brace of pheasant, and the shock drained the blood from Centaine's face.

'I thought it would be appropriate for Michel to have his father's room,' Garry murmured apologetically. 'Of course, my dear, if you don't agree, there are fifteen other rooms to choose from.'

Slowly Centaine looked around her at the shotguns in their racks, and the fishing-rods and cricket-bats standing in the corner, at the books on the shelves above the writing-desk, at the oilskins and tweed jackets hanging from their pegs.

'Yes,' she nodded. 'This will be Shasa's room, and we'll keep it just as it is.'

'Oh, good!' Garry nodded happily. 'I'm so glad you agree.' And he bustled out into the gallery, shouting orders at the servants in Zulu.

Centaine moved slowly around the room, touching the bed on which Michael had slept, stopping to press a fold of the rough tweed jacket against her cheek and imagining she could smell that special clean odour of his body upon the cloth, moving on to his desk and tracing with her fingertips his initials 'MC' carved in the oaken top, lifting down a copy of *Jock of the Bushveld* from the shelf and opening it at the flyleaf: 'This book was stolen from

Michael Courtney.' She closed the book and turned back to the door.

There was a mild commotion in the passageway, and Garry bustled back, directing two of the Zulu servants who were staggering under the weight of a child's cot. Its high sliding sides and massive mahogany construction would have caged a full-grown lion.

'This was Michael's – I think it should hold his son, what do you think, my dear?' Before Centaine could answer, the telephone rang demandingly in the hall downstairs.

'Show them where to put it, my dear,' Garry called as he dashed out again. He was gone for almost half an hour, and Centaine heard the telephone jangling at irregular intervals. When Garry came rushing in again, he was bubbling over.

'Damned telephone just won't stop. Everybody wants to meet you, my dear. You are a very famous lady. Another ruddy journalist wants to interview you—'

'I hope you told them "no", Papa.' It seemed that in the last two months every journalist in the Union had requested an interview. The story of the lost girl rescued from the African wilds with her infant had, for the moment, captivated the fickle interest of every newspaper editor from Johannesburg and Sydney to London and New York.

'I sent him packing,' Garry assured her. 'But there is someone else very eager to see you again.'

'Who is it?'

'My brother, General Courtney – he and his wife have come up from their home in Durban to their other home in Lion Kop. They want us to go across to have luncheon and spend the day with them tomorrow. I accepted on your behalf. I hope I did the right thing?'

'Oh, yes – oh, indeed yes!'

A nna refused to accompany them to the luncheon at
Lion Kop.

'There is too much that needs doing here!' she
declared. The servants of Theuniskraal had already given
her the name 'Checha' – 'Hurry up!' the first word of the
Zulu language Anna had learned, and all of them had
conceived for her a wary and growing respect.

So Garry and Centaine drove up the escarpment with
Shasa on the seat between them and as they pulled up
before the sprawling homestead of Lion Kop with its lovely
thatched roof, the familiar burly, bearded figure came
limping swiftly down the front stairs to take both of
Centaine's hands in his.

'It's like having you back from the dead,' Sean Courtney
said softly. 'Words cannot express what I feel.' Then he
turned to take Shasa from Garry's arms. 'So this is Michael's
son!' Shasa crowed with delight, grabbed a double handful
of the general's beard and attempted to pull it out by the
roots.

Ruth Courtney, Sean's wife, in that period of her life
beyond forty years of age and below fifty when a magnificent woman reaches the zenith of her beauty and elegance,
kissed Centaine's cheek and told her gently, 'Michael was
a very special person to us, and you will take his place in
our hearts.'

Waiting behind her was a young woman, and Centaine
recognized her immediately from the framed photograph
that the general had kept with him in France. Storm
Courtney was even more beautiful than her photograph,
with a skin like a rose petal and her mother's glowing
Jewish eyes, but there was a pout to her lovely mouth and
the petulant expression of a child indulged to the highest
degree of discontent. She greeted Centaine in French.

'Comment vas-tu, chérie?' Her accent was atrocious.
They looked into each other's eyes and their dislike was
strong, mutual and clearly acknowledged by both of them.

577

Beside Storm was a tall, slim young man with a serious mien and gentle eyes. Mark Anders was the general's private secretary, and Centaine liked him as instinctively as she had disliked the girl.

General Sean Courtney took Centaine on one arm and his wife on the other and led them into the homestead of Lion Kop.

Though the two houses were separated by only a few miles, they could have been worlds apart. The yellow wood floor of Lion Kop gleamed with wax, the paintings were in light cheerful colours – Centaine recognized a whimsical Tahitian scene by Paul Gauguin – and everywhere there were great bowls of fresh flowers.

'If you'll excuse Garry and myself for a few minutes, ladies, we'll leave young Mark here to entertain you.'

Sean led his brother away to his study while his secretary poured each of the ladies a cordial.

'I was in France with the general,' Mark told Centaine, as he brought her glass to her, 'and I know your village of Mort Homme quite well. We were billeted there while waiting to go up the line.'

'Oh, how wonderful to have a memory of my home!' Centaine cried, and impulsively touched his arm, and from across the drawing-room Storm Courtney, who was curled with an elaborately languid air on the silk-covered sofa, shot Centaine a look of such undiluted venom as to make her exult silently.

'Alors, chérie! So that is the way it is!' And she turned back to Mark Anders and looked up into his eyes and exaggerated her throaty French accent.

'Do you perhaps recall the château, beyond the church to the north of the village?' she asked, making the question sound like an invitation to forbidden delights, but Ruth Courtney intuitively caught the whiff of gunpowder in the air and intervened smoothly.

578

'Now, Centaine, come and sit by me,' she ordered. 'I want to hear all about your incredible adventures.'

So Centaine repeated, for the fiftieth time since her rescue, her carefully edited version of the torpedoing and her subsequent wanderings in the desert.

'Extraordinary!' Mark Anders interjected at one stage. 'I have often admired the Bushman paintings in the caves of the Drakensberg Mountains, some of them are really quite beautiful, but I did not realize that there were still wild Bushmen in existence. They were hunted out of these mountains sixty years ago – dangerous and treacherous little blighters by all accounts – and I understood that they had all been exterminated.'

On the silk sofa Storm Courtney shuddered theatrically. 'I just can't think how you could bear to let one of those little yellow monsters touch you, *chérie*. I know I would have simply expired!'

'*Bien sûr, chérie*, and you would not have enjoyed eating live lizards and locusts either?' Centaine asked sweetly, and Storm paled.

Sean Courtney stumped back into the drawing-room and interrupted them. 'Well, now, it's good to see how already you are one of the family, Centaine. I know that you and Storm are going to be great chums, what?'

'Indubitably, Pater,' Storm murmured and Centaine laughed.

'She is so sweet, your Storm, I love her already.' Centaine chose unerringly the one adjective 'sweet' that brought forth a blooming of furious roses in Storm's perfect cheeks.

'Good! Good! Is the lunch ready, my love?' and Ruth rose to take Sean's arm and lead them all out on to the patio where the table was set under a canopy of jacaranda. The very air seemed coloured purple and green by the sunlight through the blossom-laden boughs, and they might have been in an underwater grotto.

The Zulu servants, who had been hovering expectantly, at a nod from Sean bore Shasa away like a prince to the kitchens. His pleasure in their smiling black faces was as obvious as their delight in him.

'They'll spoil him, if you let them,' Ruth warned Centaine. 'Only one thing a Zulu loves better than his cattle, and that's a boy child. Now, will you sit next to the general, my dear?'

During the luncheon Sean made Centaine the complete centre of attention, while Storm tried to look aloof and bored at the end of the table.

'Now, my dear, I want to hear all about it.'

'Oh God, Pater, we've just been over it all.' Storm rolled her eyes.

'Language, girl,' Sean warned her, and then to Centaine, 'Begin on the last day I saw you, and don't leave anything out, do you hear? Not a single thing!'

Throughout the meal Garry was withdrawn and silent, in contrast to his ebullient mood of the last weeks, and after the coffee he stood up quickly when Sean said, 'Well, everybody, you must excuse us for a few minutes. Garry and I are taking Centaine off for a little chat.'

The general's study was panelled in mahogany, the books on the shelves were bound in maroon calf, while the chairs were upholstered in buttoned brown leather.

There were oriental carpets on the floor and an exquisite little bronze by Anton Van Wouw on the corner of his desk, ironically a sculpture of a Bushman hunter with his bow in his hand, peering out across the desert plains from under his other hand. It reminded Centaine so vividly of O'wa that she drew breath sharply.

With his cigar Sean waved her into the wingback chair facing his desk, and it seemed to dwarf her. Garry took another chair to the side.

'I've spoken to Garry,' Sean opened, without prelimi-

580

naries. 'I've told him the circumstances of Michael's death, before the wedding.'

He sat down behind his desk and turned his own gold wedding ring on his finger thoughtfully.

'We all of us here know that in every sense but the legal one, Michael was your husband, and the natural father of Michel. However, technically Michel is,' he hesitated, 'Michel is illegitimate. In the eyes of the law, he is a bastard.'

The word shocked Centaine. She stared at Sean through the rising wreaths of cigar smoke while the silence drew out.

'We can't have that,' Garry broke it. 'He's my grandson. We can't have that.'

'No,' Sean agreed. 'We can't have that.'

'With your consent, my dear,' Garry's voice was almost a whisper, 'I should like to adopt the lad.' Centaine turned her head towards him slowly, and he hurried on, 'It would only be a formality, a legal device to ensure his status in the world. It could be done most discreetly, and it would in no way affect the relationship between you. You would still be his mother and have custody of him, while I would be honoured to become his guardian and do for him all the things that his father cannot.' Centaine winced, and Garry blurted, 'Forgive me, my dear, but we have to talk about it. As Sean has said, we all accept that you are Michael's widow, we would want you to use the family name and we would all treat you as though the ceremony had taken place that day,' he broke off, and coughed throatily. 'Nobody would ever know, except the three of us in this room, and Anna. Would you give your consent, for the child's sake?'

Centaine stood up and crossed to where Garry sat. She sank on to her knees before him and placed her head in his lap.

'Thank you,' she whispered. 'You are the kindest man I know. You have truly taken the place of my own father now.'

The months that followed were the most contented that Centaine had ever known, secure and sunny and rewarding, filled with the sound of Shasa's laughter, and with the benign if diffident presence of Garry Courtney always in the background and the more substantial figure of Anna in the foreground.

Centaine rode every morning before breakfast and again in the cool of the evening, and often Garry accompanied her, regaling her with tales of Michael's childhood or relating the family history as they climbed the forested tracks along the escarpment or paused to water the horses at the pool below the falls of the river where the spray and white water fell a hundred feet over wet black rock.

The rest of the day was spent in choosing curtaining and wallpaper, and supervising the artisans who were redecorating the house, consulting with Anna on the restructuring of Theuniskraal's domestic arrangements, romping with Shasa and trying to prevent the Zulu servants from spoiling him utterly, taking instruction from Garry Courtney in the subtle art of steering and driving the big Fiat tourer, in pondering the printed invitations that arrived with every day's mail, and generally taking over the management and running of Theuniskraal as she had that of the château at Mort Homme.

Every afternoon she and Shasa took tea with Garry in the library where he had been ensconced for most of the day, and with his gold-rimmed spectacles on the end of his nose he would read aloud to her his day's writings.

'Oh, it must be wonderful to have such a gift!' she exclaimed, and he lowered the sheaf of manuscript.

'You admire those of us that write?' he asked.

'You are a breed apart.'

'Nonsense, my dear, we are very ordinary people except that we are vain enough to believe that other people might want to read what we have to say.'

'I wish I could write.'

'You can, your penmanship is excellent.'

'I mean really *write*.'

'You can. Help yourself to paper and get on with it. If that's what you want.'

'But,' she stared at him aghast, 'what could I write about?'

'Write about what happened to you out there in the desert. That would do very well for a beginning, I should say.'

It took three days for her to accustom herself to the idea, and brace herself to the effort. Then she had the servants move a table into the gazebo at the end of the lawns and sat down at it with a pencil in her hand, a pile of Garry's blank paper in front of her and terror in her heart. She experienced that same terror each day thereafter when she drew the first blank sheet of paper towards her, but it passed swiftly as the ranks of words began to march down across the emptiness.

She moved pleasant and familiar things into the gazebo to alleviate the loneliness of creative endeavour, a pretty rug for the tiled floor, a Delft vase on the table-top which Anna filled with fresh flowers each day, and in front of her she placed O'wa's clasp knife. She used it to resharpen her pencils.

At her right hand she placed a velvet-lined jewelbox and in it she laid H'ani's necklace. Whenever she lacked inspiration, she threw down her pencil and took up the necklace. She rubbed the bright stones between her fingers like Greek worry beads and their cool smooth touch seemed to calm her and recharge her determination.

583

Every afternoon from the end of lunch until it was time to take tea with Garry in the library, she wrote at the table in the gazebo, and Shasa slept in the cot beside her or climbed over her feet.

It did not take many days for Centaine to realize that she could never show what she was putting on to the paper to another living soul. She found that she could hold nothing back, that she was writing with a brutal candour that admitted no reserve or equivocation. Whether it was the details of her lovemaking with Michael, or the description of the taste of rotten fish in her mouth as she lay dying beside the Atlantic, she knew that nobody could read them without being shocked and horrified.

'It's for myself alone,' she decided. At the end of each session when she laid the handwritten sheets on the jewelbox on top of H'ani's necklace, she was suffused with a sense of satisfaction and worthwhile achievement.

There were, however, a few jarring notes in this symphony of contentment.

Sometimes in the night she would rise to the surface of consciousness and reach instinctively for the lithe golden body that should have been beside hers, longing for the feel of hard smooth muscle and the touch of long silky hair that smelled like the sweet grasses of the desert. Then she would come fully awake and lie in the darkness hating herself for her treacherous longings and burning with shame that she had so debased the memory of Michael and O'wa and little H'ani.

On another morning Garry Courtney sent for her and, when she was seated, handed her a package.

'This came with a covering note to me. It's from a lawyer in Paris.'

'What does it say, Papa?'

'My French is awful, I'm afraid, but the gist of the matter is that your father's estates at Mort Homme have been sold to defray his debts.'

'Oh, poor Papa.'

'They had presumed that you were dead, my dear, and the sale was ordered by a French court.'

'I understand.'

'The lawyer read of your rescue in a Parisian paper, and has written to me explaining the situation. Unfortunately the Comte de Thirty's debts were considerable, and as you are too well aware, the château and its contents were destroyed in the fire. The lawyer has set out an accounting, and after all the debts were paid and the legal expenses including this fellow's not inconsiderable fees, were deducted, there is very little that remains to you.'

Centaine's healthy acquisitive instincts were aroused. 'How much, Papa?' she asked sharply.

'A little less than £2,000 sterling, I'm afraid. He will send a bank draft when we return the acknowledgement to him duly signed and attested. Fortunately I am a commissioner of oaths, so we can do the business privately.'

When the draft finally arrived, Centaine deposited the most part with the Ladyburg Bank at 3½ per cent interest, indulging only her new passion for speed. She used £120 to buy herself a 'T' model Ford, resplendent in brass and glistening black paintwork, and when for the first time she tore up the driveway of Theuniskraal at thirty miles per hour, the entire household turned out to admire the machine. Even Garry Courtney hurried from the library, his gold-rimmed spectacles pushed up on top of his head, and it was the first time he ever chided her.

'You must consult me, my dear, before you do these things – I will not have you squandering your own savings. I am your provider, and besides which—' he looked lugubrious ' – I was looking forward to buying you a motorcar for your next birthday. You have gone and spoiled my plans.'

'Oh, Papa, do forgive me. You have given us so much already, and we love you for it.'

It was true. She had come to love this gentle person in many ways as she had loved her own father, but in some ways even more strongly, for her feelings towards him were bolstered by growing respect for and awareness of his unvaunted talents and his hidden qualities, his deep humanity and his fortitude in the face of a fate that had deprived him of a limb, a wife and a son, and had withheld from him until this late hour a loving family.

He treated her like the mistress of his household, and this evening he was discussing the guest-list for the dinner-party they were planning.

'I must warn you about this fellow Robinson. I gave myself pause before inviting him, I'll tell you!'

Her mind had been on these other things, however, not on the invitation list, and she started.

'I am so sorry, Papa,' she apologized, 'I did not hear what you were saying. I am afraid I was dreaming.'

'Dear me,' Garry smiled at her. 'I thought I was the only dreamer in the family. I was warning you about our guest of honour.'

Garry liked to entertain twice a month, not more often, and there were always ten dinner guests, never more.

'I like to hear what everybody has to say,' he explained. 'Hate to miss a good story at the end of the table.'

He had a discerning palate and had accumulated one of the finest cellars in the country. He had stolen his Zulu chef from the Country Club in Durban, so his invitations were sought after even though acceptance usually involved a train journey and an overnight stay at Theuniskraal.

'This fellow Joseph Robinson may have a baronetcy, which in many cases is the mark of an unprincipled scoundrel too cunning to have been caught out, he may have more money than even old Cecil John ever accumulated – the Robinson Deep and Robinson Goldmine belong to him, as does the Robinson Bank – but he is as mean as any man I've ever met. He'll spend £10,000 on a painting and grudge a starving man a penny. He is also a bully and the greediest, most heartless man I've ever met. When the prime minister first tried to get a peerage for him, there was such an outcry that he had to drop the idea.'

'If he is so awful, why do we invite him, Papa?'

Garry sighed theatrically. 'A price I have to pay for my art, my dear. I am going to try to prise from the fellow a few facts that I need for my new book. He is the only living person who can give them to me.'

'Do you want me to charm him for you?'

'Oh no, no! We don't have to go that far, but you could wear a pretty dress, I suppose.'

Centaine chose the yellow taffeta with the embroidered seed-pearl bodice that exposed her shoulders, still lightly tanned by the desert sun. As always, Anna was there to prepare her hair and help her dress for the dinner.

Centaine came through from her private bathroom, which was one of the great luxuries of her new life, with a bathrobe wrapped around her still-damp body and a hand towel around her head. She left wet footprints on the yellow wood floor as she crossed to her dressing-table.

Anna, who was seated on the bed restitching the hook and eye on the back of the yellow dress, bit off the thread, spat it out and mumbled, 'I have let it out three full centimetres. Too many of these fancy dinner-parties, young lady.' She laid out the dress with care and came to stand behind Centaine.

'I do wish you would sit down to dinner with us,' Centaine grumbled. 'You aren't a servant here.' Centaine would have had to be blind not to have realized the relationship that was flourishing between Garry and Anna. So far, however, she had not found an opportunity of discussing it, though she longed to share Anna's joy, if only vicariously.

Anna seized the silver-backed brush and attacked

Centaine's hair with long powerful strokes which jerked her head backwards.

'You want me to waste my time listening to a lot of fancy folk hissing away like a gaggle of geese?' She imitated the sibilance of the English tongue so cleverly that Centaine giggled delightedly. 'No, thank you, I can't understand a word of that clever chatter and old Anna is a lot happier and more useful in the kitchen keeping an eye on those grinning black rogues.'

'Papa Garry so wants you to join the company, he's spoken to me ever so often. I think he is becoming so fond of you.'

Anna pursed her lips and sniffed. 'That's enough of that nonsense, young lady,' she said firmly, as she set down the brush and arranged the fine yellow net over Centaine's hair, capturing its springing curls in the spangled mesh set with yellow sequins. '*Pas mal!*' She stood back and nodded critical approval. 'Now for the dress.'

She went to fetch it from the bed, while Centaine stood up and slipped the bathrobe from her shoulders. She let it fall to the floor and stood naked before the mirror.

'The scar on your leg is healing well, but you are still so brown,' Anna lamented, and then broke off and stood with the yellow dress half-extended, frowning thoughtfully, staring at Centaine.

'Centaine!' Her voice was sharp. 'When did you last see your moon?' she demanded, and Centaine stooped and snatched up the fallen robe, covering herself with it defensively.

'I was sick, Anna. The blow on my head – and the infection.'

'How long since your last moon?' Anna was remorseless.

'You don't understand, I was sick. Don't you remember when I had pneumonia I also missed—'

'Not since the desert!' Anna answered her own question. 'Not since you came out of the desert with that German,

588

that cross-breed German Afrikaner.' She threw the dress on to the bed and pulled the covering robe away from Centaine's body.

'No, Anna, I was sick.' Centaine was trembling. Up to that minute she had truly closed her mind against the awful possibility that Anna now presented.

Anna placed her big calloused hand on Centaine's belly, and she cringed from the touch.

'I never trusted him, with his cat's eyes and yellow hair and that great bulge in his breeches,' Anna muttered furiously. 'Now I understand why you would not speak to him when we left, why you treated him like an enemy, not a saviour.'

'Anna, I have missed before. It could be—'

'He raped you, my poor child! He violated you! You could not help it. That is how it happened?'

Centaine recognized the escape that Anna was offering her, and she yearned to take it.

'He forced you, my baby, didn't he? Tell Anna.'

'No, Anna. He did not force me.'

'You allowed him – you let him?' Anna's expression was formidable.

'I was so lonely.' Centaine sank down on to the stool and covered her face with her hands. 'I had not seen another white person for almost two years, and he was so kind and beautiful, and I owed him my life. Don't you understand, Anna? Please say you understand!'

Anna enfolded her in those thick powerful arms, and Centaine pressed her face into her soft warm bosom. Both of them were silent, shaken and afraid.

'You cannot have it,' Anna said at last. 'We will have to get rid of it.'

The shock of her words racked Centaine, so she trembled afresh and tried to hide from the dreadful thought.

'We cannot bring another bastard to Theuniskraal, they would not stand for it. The shame would be too much.

They have taken one, but Mijnheer and the general could not take another. For the sake of all of us, Michael's family and Shasa, for yourself, for all those whom I love, there is no choice in the matter. You must get rid of it.'

'Anna, I can't do that.'

'Do you love this man who put it in your belly?'

'Not now. Not any more. I hate him,' she whispered. 'Oh God, how I hate him!'

'Then get rid of his brat before it destroys you and Shasa and all of us.'

The dinner was a nightmare. Centaine sat at the bottom of the long table and smiled briefly, though her eyes burned with shame and the bastard in her belly felt like an adder, coiled and ready to strike.

The tall elderly man beside her droned on in a particularly rasping and irritating tone, directing his monologue almost exclusively at Centaine. His bald head had been turned by the sun to the colour of a plover's egg, but his eyes were strangely lifeless, like those of a marble statue. Centaine could not concentrate on what he was saying, and it became unintelligible as though he were speaking an unknown language. Her mind wandered off to pluck and worry at this new threat that had loomed up suddenly, a threat to her entire existence and that of her son.

She knew that Anna was right. Neither the general nor Garry Courtney could allow another bastard into Theuniskraal. Even if they were able to condone what she had done, and it was beyond reason or hope that they could, even then they could not allow her to bring disgrace and scandal not only upon Michael's memory, but upon the entire family. It was not possible – Anna's way was the only escape open to her.

She jumped in her seat and almost screamed aloud.

Below the level of the dinner-table, the man beside her had placed his hand upon her thigh.

'Excuse me, Papa.' She pushed back her chair hurriedly, and Garry looked down the length of the table with concern. 'I must go through for a moment,' and she fled into the kitchen.

Anna saw her distress and ran to meet her, then led her into the pantry. She locked the door behind them.

'Hold me, please Anna, I am so confused and afraid – and that awful man—' she shuddered.

Anna's arms quieted her, and after a while she whispered, 'You are right, Anna. We must get rid of it.'

'We will talk about it tomorrow,' Anna told her gently. 'Now bathe your eyes with cold water and go back to the dining-room before you make a scene.'

Centaine's rebuff had served its purpose, and the tall, bald-headed mining magnate did not even glance at her when she came back to her seat beside him. He was addressing the woman on his other hand, but the rest of the company was listening to him with the attention due to one of the richest men in the world.

'Those were the days,' he was saying. 'The country was wide open, a fortune under every stone, by gad. Barnato started with a box of cigars to trade, bloody awful cigars too, and when Rhodes bought him out he gave him a cheque for £3,000,000, the largest cheque ever issued up to that time, though I can tell you I myself have written a few bigger since then—'

'And how did you start, Sir Joseph?'

'Five pounds in my pocket and a nose to sniff out a real diamond from a *schlenter* – that's how I got my start.'

'And how do you do that, Sir Joseph? How do you tell a real diamond?'

'The quickest way is to dip it into a glass of water, my dear. If it comes out wet, it's a *schlenter*. If it comes out dry, it's a diamond.'

The words passed Centaine without seeming to leave any impression, for she was so preoccupied, and Garry was signalling her from the head of the table that it was time to take the ladies through.

However, Robinson's words must have made a mark deep in her subconscious, for the next afternoon as she sat in the gazebo staring unseeingly out across the sundrenched lawns, fiddling miserably with H'ani's necklace, rubbing the stones between her fingers, almost without conscious thought she suddenly leaned over the table and from the crystal carafe poured a tumbler full of spring water.

Then she lifted the necklace over the tumbler and slowly lowered it into the water. After a few seconds she lifted it out and studied it distractedly. The coloured stones glistened with water, and then suddenly her heart began to race. The white stone, the huge crystal in the centre of the necklace, was dry.

She dropped the necklace back into the water and pulled it out again. Her hand began to shake. Like the breast of a swan, shining white, the stone had shed even the tiniest droplets, although it glistened more luminously than the wet stones that surrounded it.

Guiltily she looked around her, but Shasa slept on his back with a thumb deep in his mouth and the lawns were deserted in the noonday heat. For the third time she lowered the necklace into the glass and when the white stone came out dry once again, she whispered softly, 'H'ani, my beloved old grandmother, will you save us again? Is it possible that you are still watching over me?'

Centaine could not consult the Courtney family doctor in Ladyburg, so she and Anna planned a journey to the capital town of the province of Natal, the sea port of Durban. The pretext for the journey was the perennial feminine favourite, shopping to be done.

They had hoped to get away from Theuniskraal on their own, but Garry would not hear of it.

'Leave me behind, forsooth! You've been on at me, both of you, about a new suit. Well, it's a fine excuse for me to visit my tailor, and while I'm about it I might even pick up a pair of bonnets or some other little gewgaws for two ladies of my acquaintance.'

So it was a full-scale family expedition, with Shasa and his two Zulu nannies, with both the Fiat and the Ford needed to convey them all down the winding dusty hundred and fifty miles of road to the coast. They descended on the Majestic Hotel on the beach front of the Indian Ocean, and Garry took the two front suites.

It needed all the ingenuity of both Anna and Centaine to evade him for a few hours, but they managed it. Anna had made discreet enquiries and had the name of a doctor with consulting-rooms in Point Road. They visited him under assumed names, and he confirmed what they had both known to be true.

'My niece has been a widow for two years,' Anna explained delicately. 'She cannot afford scandal.'

'I'm sorry, madam. There is nothing I can do to help you,' the doctor replied primly, but when Centaine paid him his guinea, he murmured, 'I will give you a receipt.' And he scribbled on the slip of paper a name and an address.

In the street Anna took her arm. 'We have an hour before Mijnheer expects us back at the hotel. We will go – to make the arrangements.'

'No, Anna,' Centaine stopped. 'I have to think about this. I want to be alone for a while.'

'There is nothing to think about,' said Anna gruffly.

'Leave me, Anna, I will be back long before dinner. We will go tomorrow.' Anna knew that tone and that expression. She threw up her hands and climbed into the waiting rickshaw.

As the Zulu runner bore her off in the high two-wheeled carriage, she called, 'Think all you like, child, but tomorrow we do it my way.'

Centaine waved and smiled until the rickshaw turned into West Street, then she spun round and hurried back towards the harbour.

She had noticed a shop when they passed it earlier: M. NAIDOO. JEWELLER.

The interior was small, but clean and neat, with inexpensive jewellery set out in glass-topped display cabinets. The moment she entered, a plump, dark-skinned Hindu in a tropical suit came through the bead screen from the rear of the building.

'Good afternoon, honoured madam, I am Mr Moonsamy Naidoo at madam's service.' He had a bland face and thick wavy hair dressed with coconut oil until it glowed like coal fresh from the face.

'I would like to look at your wares.' Centaine leaned over the glass-topped counter and studied the display of silver filigree bracelets.

'A gift for a loved one, of course, good madam, these are truly 100 per cent pure silver hand-manufactured by learned craftsmen of the highest calibre.'

Centaine did not reply. She knew the risks that she was about to take, and she was trying to form some estimate of the man. He was doing the same to her. He looked at her gloves and shoes, infallible gauges of a lady's quality.

'Of course, these trinkets are mere bagatelle. If esteemed madam would care to see something more princely, or more princessly?'

'Do you deal in – diamonds?'

'Diamonds, most reverend madam?' His bland plump face creased into a smile. 'I can show you a diamond fit for a king – or a queen.'

'And I will do the same for you,' Centaine said quietly, and placed the huge white crystal on the glass counter-top between them.

The Hindu jeweller choked with shock, and flapped his hands like a penguin. 'Sweet madam!' he gasped. 'Cover it, I beseech you. Hide it from my gaze!'

Centaine dropped the crystal back into her purse and turned towards the door, but the jeweller was there before her.

'An instant more of your time, devout madam.'

He drew down the blinds over the windows and the glass door, then turned the key in the lock, before he came back to her.

'There are extreme penalties,' his voice was unsteady, 'ten years of durance of the vilest sort – and I am not a well man. The gaolers are most ugly and unkind, good madam, the risks are infinite—'

'I will trouble you no further. Unlock the door.'

'Please, dear madam, if you will follow me.' He backed towards the bead screen, bowing from the waist and making wide flourishing gestures of invitation.

His office was tiny, and the glass-topped desk filled it so there was barely room for both of them. There was one small high window. The air was stifling and redolent with the aroma of curry powder.

'May I see the object again, good madam?'

Centaine placed it on the centre of the desk, and the Hindu screwed a jeweller's loupe into his eye before he picked up the stone and held it towards the light from the window.

'Is it permitted to ask where this was obtained, kind madam?'

'No.'

He turned it slowly under the magnifying lens, and then placed in on the small brass tray of the jeweller's balance that stood on the side of the desk. As he weighed it he murmured, 'IDB, madam, Illicit Diamond Buying – oh, the police are most strict and severe.'

Satisfied with the weight, he opened the drawer of the desk and brought out a cheap glass-cutter, shaped like a pen, but with a sharp chip of boart, the black industrial-grade diamond, set in the tip.

'What are you going to do?' Centaine asked suspiciously.

'The only real test, madam,' the jeweller explained. 'A diamond will scratch any other substance on earth except another diamond.' To illustrate the point he drew the stylus of boart across the glass top of the desk. It screeched so that Centaine's skin prickled and her teeth were set on edge, but the point left a deep white scratch across the glass surface. He looked up at her for permission and then Centaine nodded; he braced the white stone firmly against the desk-top, and drew the point of the stylus across it.

It slipped smoothly over one plane of the crystal as though it had been lubricated, and it left no mark on the surface.

A droplet of sweat fell from the Hindu's chin and splashed loudly on the glass. He ignored it, and made another stroke across the stone, putting more strength behind the stylus. There was no sound, no mark.

His hand began to tremble, and this time he leaned the full weight of his arm and shoulder as he attempted to make the cut. The wooden shaft of the stylus snapped in half, but the white crystal was unmarked. They both stared at it, until Centaine said softly, 'How much?'

'The risks are terrible, good madam, and I am an excessively honest man.'

'How much?'

'One thousand pounds,' he whispered.

'Five,' said Centaine.

'Madam, dear sweet madam, I am a man of impeccably high reputation. If I were apprehended in the act of IDB—'

'Five,' she repeated.

'Two,' he croaked, and Centaine reached for the stone.

'Three,' he said hurriedly, and Centaine held back.

'Four,' she said firmly.

'Three and a half, dear madam, my very last and most earnest offer. Three and a half thousand pounds.'

'Done,' she said. 'Where is the money?'

'I do not keep such vast sums of lucre on my person, good madam.'

'I will return tomorrow at the same time, with the diamond. Have the money ready.'

'I don't understand,' Garry Courtney wrung his hands miserably. 'Surely all of us could accompany you?'

'No, Papa. It is something I have to do alone.'

'One of us, then, Anna or myself? I just can't let you go off again.'

'Anna must stay and look after Shasa.'

'I will come with you, then. You need a man—'

'No, Papa. I beg your indulgence and understanding. I have to do this alone. Entirely on my own.'

'Centaine, you know how much I have come to love you. Surely I have some rights – the right to know where it is you are going, what you intend doing?'

'I am desolated, for much as I love you in return, I cannot tell you. To do so would destroy the whole point of my going. Think of it as a pilgrimage which I am obliged to make. That is all I can tell you.'

Garry rose from his desk, crossed to the tall library windows and stood looking out into the sunlight with his hands clasped behind his back.

'How long will you be gone?'

'I am not sure,' she told him quietly. 'I do not know how long it will take – some months at least, perhaps much longer,' and he lowered his head and sighed.

When he returned to the desk he was sad but resigned.

'What can I do to help?' he asked.

'Nothing, Papa, except look after Shasa while I am gone and forgive me for not being able to confide in you fully.'

'Money?'

'You know I have money, my inheritance.'

'Letters of introduction? You will at least let me do that for you?'

'They will be invaluable, thank you.'

With Anna it was not so easy. She suspected part of what Centaine planned and she was angry and stubborn.

'I cannot let you go. You will bring disaster on yourself and on all of us. Enough of this madness. Get rid of it the way I have arranged, it will be swift and final.'

'No, Anna, I cannot murder my own baby, you can't make me do that—'

'I forbid you to leave.'

'No.' Centaine went to her and kissed her. 'You know you can't do that either. Just hold me a while – and look after Shasa once I am gone.'

'At least tell Anna where you are going.'

'No more questions, dearest Anna. Just promise me that you will not try to follow me, and that you will prevent Papa Garry from doing so, for you know what he will find if he does.'

'Oh, you wicked stubborn girl!' Anna seized her in a bear-hug. 'If you don't come back, you will break old Anna's heart.'

'Don't even talk like that, you silly old woman.'

598

The smell of the desert was like the smell of flint struck off steel, a burnt dry odour that Centaine could detect underlying the harsher odour of coal smoke from the locomotive. The bogey clattered to the rhythm of the cross-ties and the carriage kept the beat, lurching and swaying in time.

Centaine sat in the corner of the small coupé compartment upon the green leather seat and stared through the window. A flat yellow plain stretched to the long far horizon, while the sky above it was traced the faint promise of blue mountains. There were clusters of springbok grazing on the plain, and when the steam whistle of the locomotive shrilled abruptly, they dissolved into pale cinnamon-coloured smoke and blew away towards the horizon. The animals closest to her carriage pranced high in the air, and painfully Centaine remembered little O'wa miming that arched-back and head-down stotting gait. Then the pain passed and only the joy of his memory remained to her, and she smiled as she stared out into the desert.

The great spaces, seared by the sun, seemed to draw out her soul, like iron to the magnet, and slowly she became aware of a sense of building anticipation, that peculiar excitement that a traveller feels on the last homeward mile of a long journey.

When later the evening shadows turned the plains soft mauve, they gave definition to the land so that the undulations and low hillocks emerged from the glare of the midday and the glassy curtains of heat mirage, and she looked upon this austere and majestic landscape and felt a deep sense of joy.

At sunset she put a coat around her shoulders and went out on to the open balcony at the rear of the coach. In fuming dusty reds and orange the sun went under, and the stars pricked out through the purple night. She looked up and there were two particular stars, Michael's star and hers with only the ghostly Magellanic clouds shining between them.

'I haven't looked up at the sky, not since I left this wild land,' she thought, and suddenly the green fields of her native France and the lush rolling hills of Zululand were only an effete and insipid memory. 'This is where I belong – the desert is my home now.'

Garry Courtney's lawyer met her at the Windhoek railway station. She had telegraphed him before the train left from Cape Town. His name was Abraham Abrahams, and he was a dapper little man with large pricked-up ears and sharp alert eyes, very much like one of the tiny battered desert foxes. He waved away the letter of introduction from Garry that Centaine offered him.

'My dear Mrs Courtney, everybody in the territory knows who you are. The story of your incredible adventure has captured all our imaginations. I can truthfully say that you are a living legend, and that I am honoured to be in a position to render you assistance.'

He drove her to the Kaiserhof Hotel and after he had made sure she was settled and well cared for, he left her for a few hours to bath and rest.

'The coal dust gets into everything, even the pores of the skin,' he sympathized.

When he returned and they were seated in the lounge with a tray of tea between them, he asked, 'Now, Mrs Courtney, what can I do for you?'

'I have a list, a long list.' She handed it to him. 'And as you see, the first thing I want you to do is to find a man for me.'

'That won't be too difficult.' He studied the list. 'The man is well known, almost as well known as you are.'

The road was rough, the surface freshly blasted rock, sharp as knife-blades. Long ranks of black labourers, stripped to the waist and glistening with sweat, were pounding the rock with sledgehammers, breaking up the lumps and levelling the roadway. They stood aside, resting on their hammers, as Centaine drove up the pass in Abraham Abrahams' dusty Ford, bumping slowly over the jagged stone, and when she shouted a question, they grinned and pointed on upwards.

The road became steeper as it wound into the mountains and the gradients became so severe that at one place Centaine had to turn the Ford and reverse up the slope. At last she could go no further. A Hottentot foreman ran down the rough track to meet her, waving a red flag over his head.

'*Pasop*, missus! Look out, madam! They are going to fire the charges.'

Centaine parked on the verge of the half-built road under a sign-board that read:

De La Rey Construction Company
Road-building and Civil-Engineering

And she climbed down, and stretched her long legs. She was wearing breeches and boots and a man's shirt. The Hottentot foreman stared at her legs until she told him sharply, 'That will be all. Go about your duties, man, or your boss will know of it.'

She unwound the scarf from around her head and fluffed out her hair. Then she dampened a cloth from the canvas water-cooler that hung on the side of the Ford and wiped the dust from her face. It was fifty miles from Windhoek, and she had been driving since before dawn. She lifted the wicker basket off the back seat and set it beside her as she settled on the running-board of the Ford. The hotel chef had provided ham and egg sandwiches and a bottle of cold sweetened tea, and she was suddenly hungry.

As she ate she gazed out across the open plains far below her. She had forgotten how the grass shone in the sunlight like woven silver cloth – then suddenly she thought of long blond hair that shone the same way, and against her will she felt a rising heat in the pit of her belly and her nipples tightened and started out.

Instantly she was ashamed of that momentary weakness, and she told herself fiercely, 'I hate him – and I hate this thing he has placed inside me.'

Almost as though the thought might have triggered it, it squirmed with her, a deep and secret movement, and her hatred wavered like a candle flame in the draught.

'I must be strong,' she told herself. 'I must be constant, for Shasa's sake.'

From behind her, up at the head of the pass, there came the distant shrilling of a warning whistle, followed by a brittle waiting silence. Centaine stood up and shaded her eyes, involuntarily tensing in expectation.

Then the earth leaped beneath her and the shock wave of the explosion beat upon her eardrums. A dust column shot high into the blue desert air, and the mountain was cleaved as though by a gargantuan axe-stroke. Sheets of grey-blue shale peeled away from the slope and slid in a liquid avalanche down into the valley below. The echoes of the explosion leapt from kloof to kloof, dwindling gradually, and the dust column blew softly away.

Centaine remained standing, staring up the slope, and after a while the figure of a horseman was outlined on the high crest. Slowly he rode down the raw track, the horse picking its way gingerly over the broken treacherous footing, and he was tall in the saddle, graceful and limber as a sapling in the wind.

'If only he were not so beautiful,' she whispered.

He lifted the wide-brimmed hat with its ostrich feathers from his head and slapped the dust from his breeches. His golden hair burned like a beacon fire, and she swayed slightly on her feet. At the foot of the slope, a hundred paces from Centaine, he threw his leg over the horse's neck, slipped to the ground, and threw the reins to the Hottentot foreman.

The foreman spoke urgently and pointed to where Centaine waited. Lothar nodded and came striding down towards her. Halfway, he stopped abruptly and stared at her. Even at that distance she saw his eyes turn bright as yellow sapphires and he launched into a run.

Centaine did not move. She stood stiffly, staring up at him, and ten paces from her he saw her expression and halted again.

'Centaine. I never thought to see you again, my darling.' He started forward.

'Don't touch me,' she said coldly, fighting down the panic rising within her. 'I warned you once – don't ever touch me again.'

'Why do you come here then?' he asked harshly. 'Isn't it enough that your memory has plagued me these long lonely months since I last you? Must you come in the flesh to torment me?'

'I have come to make a bargain with you.' Her voice was icy, for she had control over herself now. 'I come to offer you a trade.'

'What is your bargain? If you are a part of it, then I accept before you state your terms.'

'No,' she shook her head. 'I would kill myself first.'

His chin came up angrily, though his eyes were wretched and hurting. 'You are without mercy.'

'That I must have learned from you!'

'State your terms.'

'You will take me back to the place in the desert where

you found me. You will provide transport and servants and all that is necessary for me to reach the mountain, and to exist there for a year.'

'Why do you want to go there?'

'That does not concern you.'

'That is not true, it does concern me. Why do you need me?'

'I could search for years, and die without finding it.'

He nodded. 'You are right, of course, but what you are asking will cost a great deal. Everything I have is in this company, I don't have a shilling in my pocket.'

'I want your services only,' she told him. 'I will pay for the vehicles, the equipment and the wages of the servants.'

'Then it is possible – but what about my side of the bargain?'

'In exchange,' she placed her right hand over her stomach, 'I will give you the bastard you left in me.'

He gaped at her. 'Centaine—' Slow, deep joy spread over his face. 'A child! You are to have our child!' Instinctively, he came towards her again.

'Stay back,' she warned him, 'not our child. It's yours alone. I want nothing to do with it after it is born. I don't even want to see it. You will take it from the childbed, and do whatever you want with it. I don't want it. I hate it – and I hate the man who put it in me.'

With Lothar's wagons the journey from the Place of All Life to their rendezvous with Garry Courtney at the Finger of God had taken weeks. Their return to the mountain range took only eight days, and would have been quicker, except that they had to build the road for the motor vehicles through several rocky valleys and numerous dry river beds. Twice Lothar had to resort to dynamite to break a way through obdurate rock.

The convoy consisted of the Ford and two lorries, which Centaine had purchased in Windhoek. Lothar had chosen six camp servants, two black drivers for the lorries, and as a bodyguard for Centaine and camp overseer, he selected Swart Hendrick, his Ovambo henchman.

'I cannot trust him,' Centaine had protested. 'He's like a man-eating lion.'

'You can trust him,' Lothar assured her, 'because he knows that if he fails you in even the smallest degree, I will kill him very, very slowly.' He said it in front of Swart Hendrick, who grinned cheerfully.

'It is true, missus, he has done it to others.'

Lothar travelled in the lead truck with Swart Hendrick and the construction gang. In forest country the black gang ran ahead of the slow-moving convoy, hacking out the road, and when the forest opened, they swarmed on to the back of the truck and the convoy bowled forward at a good speed. The second lorry, heavily laden with stores and equipment, followed the first, and Centaine brought up the rear at the wheel of the Ford.

Each night she ordered her tent to be set up well separated from the rest of the camp. She ate her meals there and slept with a loaded shotgun beside the bed. Lothar seemed to have accepted her terms of contract; his bearing was proud, but he became increasingly silent and he spoke to her only when the conduct of the expedition demanded it.

Once in the middle of the morning when they halted unexpectedly, Centaine climbed down from the Ford and impatiently hurried up to the head of the convoy. The lead truck had hit a spring-hare burrow and broken a half-shaft. Lothar and the driver were working on it, and Lothar had stripped off his shirt. He had his back to her and did not hear her come up.

She stopped abruptly when she saw the pale muscles of his back bulging as he pumped on the jack-handle, and she stared fascinated at the ugly purple scar where the Luger bullet had torn out of his back.

'How close it must have come to his lung!'

She felt quick sharp remorse and turned away, the angry words that had been on her lips left unspoken, and she went softly back to her place at the end of the column.

When at last on the eighth day the mountain appeared ahead of them, floating on its glistening lake of mirage like some great ark of orange stone, Centaine stopped and climbed up on the bonnet of the Ford, and as she stared at it, she relived a hundred memories and found herself swayed by many conflicting emotions, borne up on the joy of homecoming and at the same time crushed down by the leaden burden of grief and doubt.

Lothar roused her from her reverie; he had come back from the head of the column without her even seeing him.

'You have not told me exactly where you wish me to take you.'

'To the lion tree,' she told him. 'To the place where you found me.'

The marks of the beast's claws were still slashed into the trunk of the mopani, and its bones were scattered in the grass beneath it, white as stars and shining in the sun.

Lothar worked with his construction gang for two days to establish a permanent camp for her. He built a private stockade of mopani poles around the solitary tree and piled thorn branches against the exterior wall of the stockade to reinforce it and make it proof against predators. He dug a screened latrine pit connected to the stockade by a tunnel of poles and woven thorn branches, and then he set up Centaine's tent in the centre of the stockade, shaded by the mopani, and built an open hearth for her camp fire in front of it. At the entrance to her stockade he constructed a heavy timber gate and a guard house.

'Swart Hendrick will sleep here, always within call,' he told Centaine.

At the edge of the forest, two hundred paces from her camp, he built another larger stockade for the servants and labourers, and when it was all finished, he came to Centaine again.

'I have done all that is necessary.'

She nodded. 'Yes, you have completed your side of the bargain,' she agreed. 'Come back in three months' time, and I will complete my side.'

He left within the hour in the second truck, taking only the black driver with him and sufficient water and gasoline for the return journey to Windhoek.

As they watched the truck disappear into the mopani, Centaine said to Swart Hendrick, 'I will wake you at three o'clock tomorrow morning. I want four of the construction men to come with us. They must bring their blankets and cooking pots, and rations for ten days.'

The moon lit their way as Centaine led them up the narrow valley to the cavern of the bees. At the dark entrance, she explained where she was going to take them, and Swart Hendrick translated for those who could not understand Afrikaans.

'There is no danger if you remain calm and do not run.' But when they heard the deep hum resound through the cavern, the labourers backed out hurriedly, threw down their loads and gathered into a mutinous, sullen bunch.

'Swart Hendrick, tell them they have a choice,'

Centaine ordered. 'They can either follow me through or you will shoot them, one at a time.'

Hendrick repeated this with such relish, and unslung his Mauser in such workmanlike fashion, that they hurriedly gathered up their loads again and crowded up behind Centaine. As always, the transit of the cavern was nerve-racking but swift, and as they filed out into the secret valley, the moon was silvering the mongongo grove and polishing the high surrounding cliffs.

'There is much work to do, and we will live here, in this valley, until it is finished. That way you will only have to pass through the place of the bees one more time. That is when we leave.'

Abraham Abrahams had instructed Centaine in every aspect of pegging a mining claim. He had written out a sample notice for her and showed her how to set it up. With a steel measuring tape he had demonstrated the trick of squaring a claim across the diagonals, and how to overlap each claim slightly so that there were no holes to give a claim-jumper a toehold.

Still it was hot, exhausting and monotonous work. Even with the four labourers and Swart Hendrick to help her, Centaine had to make every measurement herself and write out each claim notice and attach it to the claim posts of Mongongo timber that they set up ahead of her.

At dusk every evening, Centaine dragged herself wearily down to the thermal pool in the subterranean grotto and soaked away her sweat and the aches of her body in the steaming waters. She was already starting to feel the drag of her advancing pregnancy. She was bigger this time and it seemed harder and more wearying than Shasa's pregnancy had been, almost as though the foetus sensed her feeling towards it, and was responding vindictively. Her back ached particularly viciously, and by the end of the ninth day she knew that she could not continue much longer without a rest.

However, the bottom land of the valley was crisscrossed with neat lines of claim pegs, each standing on its little cairn of stones. The gang had by now become accustomed to the work and it was going more quickly.

'One more day,' she promised herself, 'and then you can rest.'

On the evening of the tenth day it was done. She had pegged out every square foot of the valley bottom.

'Pack up,' she told Swart Hendrick. 'We are going out tonight.' And as he turned away, 'Well done, Hendrick, you are a lion and you can be sure I will remember that on pay day.'

Hard work shared had made them companions.

He grinned at her. 'If I had ten wives as strong as you, and who worked like you, missus, I could sit in the shade and drink beer all day long.'

'That is the nicest compliment anyone ever paid me,' she replied in French, and found just enough strength left for a short, breathless laugh.

Back in Lion Tree Camp Centaine rested for a day and then the next morning settled down at her camp table in the mopani shade and filled in the claim forms. This was also monotonous and demanding work, for there were 416 claims to process, and every number had to be transposed from her notebook and then fitted into her sketchmap of the valley. Abraham Abrahams had explained to her just how important this was, for each claim would be scrutinized by the government mining inspector and his surveyor and a careless error could invalidate the entire property.

It was another five days before she placed the last completed form on the pile and then bundled them into a brown paper package and sealed them with wax.

'Dear Mr Abrahams,' she wrote, 'please file the accompanying claims with the mining office in my name and deposit the claim deeds with the Standard Bank in Windhoek to the account over which you hold my power of attorney.

'I would be grateful if you could then make enquiries for the most eminent independent mining consultant available. Make a contract with him to survey and evaluate the property which is the subject of these claims and send him to me here by return of the vehicle which brings you this letter.

'When the vehicle returns to me, please see that it is loaded with the stores I have listed below and pay for these from my account.

'One final favour. I would be most grateful if, without disclosing my whereabouts, you would be good enough to telegraph Colonel Garrick Courtney at Theuniskraal to make enquiry of my son, Michel, and my companion, Anna Stok. Convey to all three of them my affection and duty, assure them of my good health and my longing to see them again.

'To you my sincere thanks and good wishes.
'Centaine de Thiry Courtney'

She gave the package and letter to the driver of the lorry and set him on the track back to Windhoek. Because the track was now well blazed and all the difficult places had been made good, the truck was back within eight days. There was a tall elderly gentleman sitting up beside the driver in the cab.

'May I introduce myself, Mrs Courtney? My name is Rupert Twentyman-Jones.'

He looked more like an undertaker than a mining engineer. He even affected a black alpaca jacket with high collar and black string tie. His hair was dead black and sleeked down, but his sideburns were fluffy and white as cotton wool. His nose and the tips of his ears were eroded by rodent ulcers from the tropical sun so that they looked as though mice had been nibbling at them. There were bags under his eyes like those of a basset, and he wore the same lugubrious expression.

'How do you do, Mr Jones.'

'Dr Twentyman-Jones,' he corrected her mournfully. 'Double barrel, as in shotgun. I have a letter for you from Mr Abrahams.' He handed it over like an eviction notice.

'Thank you, Dr Twentyman-Jones. Won't you take a cup of tea while I read it?'

'Please do not be misled by the man's sad mien,' Abraham Abrahams assured her in the letter. 'He was assistant to Doctor Merensky who discovered the elevated diamond terraces of the Spieregebied, and is now regularly consulted by the directors of the De Beers Consolidated Mines. If further evidence of his standing is required, consider the fact that his fee for this contract is 1,200 guineas.

'I am assured by Colonel Courtney that both Mevrou Anna Stok and your son Michel are in astonishingly good health and all of them send their loving wishes and hopes for your swift return.

'I am sending the stores you require, and after paying for these and settling Dr Twentyman-Jones' fee in advance, the balance standing to the credit of your account at the Standard Bank is £6. 11s. 6d. The deeds to your claims are safely deposited in the bank's strong room.'

Centaine folded the letter carefully. Of her inheritance and the proceeds of the sale of H'ani's diamond, there was little over £6 remaining – she did not even have the price of a fare back to Theuniskraal, unless she sold the vehicles.

However, Twentyman-Jones had been paid and she

could survive for three months longer on the stores she had in camp.

She looked up at him, sitting on her camp chair sipping hot tea.

'Twelve hundred guineas, sir – you must be good!'

'No, madam,' he shook his head mournfully. 'I am quite simply the best.'

She led Twentyman-Jones through the cavern of the bees in the night, and when they emerged into the secret valley, he sat down on a rock and mopped his face with a handkerchief.

'This really isn't good enough, madam. Something must be done about those revolting insects. We will have to get rid of them, I'm afraid.'

'No.' Centaine's reply was swift and decisive. 'I want as little damage done to this place and its creatures as possible, until—'

'Until, madam?'

'Until we discover if it is necessary.'

'I do not like bees. I swell most horribly from their stings. I will return the balance of the fees to you, and you can find another consultant.' He began to stand up.

'Wait!' Centaine restrained him. 'I have explored the cliffs over there. There is a way to get into this valley over the crest. It will, unfortunately, mean rigging a bucket and pulley system from the top of the cliffs.'

'That will greatly complicate my endeavours.'

'Please, Dr Twentyman-Jones, without your help—' and he made grumpy little noncommittal noises and stumped off into the darkness, holding his lantern high.

As the dawn light strengthened, he began his preliminary survey. All that day as Centaine sat in the shade of the mongongo, she caught glimpses of his lanky figure striding here and there, chin against his chest, pausing every few minutes to pick up a chip of rock or a handful of soil, and then disappearing again amongst the trees and the rocks.

It was late afternoon before he returned to where she waited.

'Well?' she asked.

'If you are asking for my opinion, madam, then you are a little premature. It will take me some months before—'

'Months?' Centaine cried out in alarm.

'Certainly—' and then he saw her face, and his voice dropped. 'You didn't pay me all that money for a guess. I have to open it up and see what's down there. That will take time and hard work. I will need all the labourers you have available, as well as those I have with me.'

'I hadn't thought of that.'

'Tell me, Mrs Courtney,' he asked gently, 'just what is it you are hoping to find here?'

She drew a deep breath and behind her back she made the sign of the horns, which Anna had taught her averted the evil eye.

'Diamonds,' she said, and was immediately terrified that saying it out aloud would bring the worst possible luck upon her.

'Diamonds!' Twentyman-Jones repeated, as though it was news of his father's death. 'We'll see.' His expression was lugubrious. 'We'll see!'

'When do we start?'

'We, Mrs Courtney? You will remain out of this place. I do not allow anyone else around me when I am working.'

'But,' she protested, 'am I not allowed even to watch?'

'That, Mrs Courtney, is a rule I never vary – you will have to contain yourself, I'm afraid.'

613

So Centaine was banished from her valley, and the days in Lion Tree Camp passed slowly. From her stockade she could see Twentyman-Jones' labour gangs toiling up the cliff path under their loads of equipment to the summit and then disappearing over the crest.

After almost a month of waiting she made the ascent herself. It was an onerous and taxing climb, and she was aware of the load in her womb every step of the way. However, from the top she had an exhilarating eagle's view of the plains that seemed to stretch to the ends of the earth, and when she looked down into the secret valley, it was as though she were looking into the very core of the earth.

The pulley and rope system from the lip of the cliff looked as insubstantial as a spider's thread, and she shuddered at the thought of stepping into the canvas bucket and being lowered down into the depths of the amphitheatre. Far below she could make out the antlike specks of the prospect teams and the mounds of earth they had thrown up from their potholes. She could even distinguish Twentyman-Jones' lank storklike gait as he passed from one to another of the prospects.

She sent down a note to him in the bucket. 'Sir, have you found anything?'

And the reply came back an hour later. 'Patience, madam, is one of the great virtues.'

That was the last time she went up the cliff, for the child seemed to be growing like a malignant tumour. She had borne Shasa with joy, but this pregnancy brought pain and discomfort and unhappiness. She found no surcease even in the books she had brought with her, for she found it difficult to concentrate to the end of a page. Always her eyes would go up from the printed word to the cliff path, as though for sight of that lanky figure coming down to her.

The heat became every day more oppressive as the summer advanced into the suicide days of late November, and she could not sleep. She lay in her cot and sweated away the nights, then dragged herself out again in the dawn, feeling drained and depressed and lonely. She was eating too much, her only opiate against the boredom of those long sultry days. She had developed a craving for devilled kidneys, and Swart Hendrick hunted every day to bring them fresh to her.

Her belly swelled and the child grew huge, so that it forced her knees apart when she sat, and it buffeted her mercilessly, thumping and kicking and rolling inside her like a great fish struggling on the end of a line until she moaned, 'Be still, you little monster – oh God, how I long to be rid of you.'

Then one afternoon, when she had almost despaired, Twentyman-Jones came down the mountain. Swart Hendrick saw him on the cliff path and came hurrying to her tent to warn her, so that she had time to rise from her cot, bathe her face and change her sweat-damp clothes.

When he strode into the stockade, she was seated at her camp table, concealing her great belly behind it, and she did not rise to greet him.

'Well, madam, there is your report.' He laid a thick folder on the table before her.

She untied the tapes and opened it. There, in his neat pedantic handwriting, was page after page of figures and numbers, and words she had never seen before. She turned the pages slowly while Twentyman-Jones watched her sadly. Once he shook his head and looked as though he were about to speak, instead he pulled the handkerchief from his top pocket and noisily blew his nose.

Finally, she looked up at him.

'I'm sorry,' she whispered, 'I don't understand any of this. Explain it to me.'

'I'll be brief, madam. I sank forty-six prospect holes, each to a depth of fifty feet and sampled at six-foot intervals.'

'Yes,' she nodded. 'But what did you find?'

'I found that there is a layer of yellow ground overlaying the entire property to an average depth of thirty-five feet.'

Centaine felt dizzy and sick. 'Yellow ground' sounded so ominous. Twentyman-Jones broke off and blew his nose again. It was quite obvious to Centaine that he did not want to say the final words that would kill for ever her hopes and dreams.

'Please, go on,' she whispered.

'Below this stratum we ran into—' his voice fell and he looked as though his heart was aching for her ' – we ran into blue ground.'

Centaine lifted her hand to her mouth, and she thought she would faint.

'Blue ground.' It sounded even worse than yellow ground, and the child heaved and struggled in her, and despair came down upon her like a flow of poisonous lava.

'All for nothing,' she thought, and she was no longer listening as he went on.

'It's the classic pipe formation, of course, the decomposing breccia composite above with the harder impermeable slaty-blue formation below.'

'So there were no diamonds after all,' she said softly, and he stared at her.

'Diamonds! Well, madam, I've worked out an average value of twenty-six carats to a hundred loads.'

'I still don't understand,' she shook her head stupidly. 'What does that mean, sir? What is a hundred loads?'

'A hundred loads is approximately eighty tons of earth.'

'And what does twenty-six carats mean?'

'Madam, the Jagersfontein assays at eleven carats to a hundred loads, even the Wesselton goes only sixteen carats to a hundred loads – and they are the two richest diamond mines in the world. This property is almost twice as rich.'

'So there are diamonds after all?' She stared at him, and from the side pocket of his alpaca jacket he took a bundle of small buff-coloured envelopes, tied together with string, and placed these on top of the report folder.

'Please do not mix them up, Mrs Courtney, the stones from each prospect hole are in separate envelopes, all carefully notated.'

With fingers that felt numb and swollen, she untied the string and fumbled open the top envelope. She poured the contents into her hand. Some of the stones were chips not much bigger than sugar grains, one was the size of a large ripe pea.

'Diamonds?' she asked again, wanting his assurance.

'Yes, madam, and of peculiarly good quality on the average.'

She stared dumbly at the little pile of stones in her hand; they looked murky and small and mundane.

'You will excuse the liberty, madam, but may I ask you a question? You might of course, choose not to answer.'

She nodded.

'Are you a member of a syndicate – do you have partners in this venture?'

She shook her head.

'You mean, you are the sole holder and owner of this property? That you discovered this pipe and pegged the claims entirely on your own account?'

She nodded again.

'Then,' he shook his head mournfully, 'at this moment, Mrs Courtney, you are probably one of the wealthiest women in the world.'

T wentyman-Jones remained at Lion Tree Camp for three days longer.

He went over every line of his report with her, explaining any item of which her understanding was unclear. He opened each of the packages of sample stones, and picked out unusual or typical diamonds with a pair of jeweller's forceps, laid them on the palm of her hand and pointed out their special features to her.

'Some of these are so small – do they have any worth at all?' She rolled the sugar-grain chips under the forefinger.

'Those industrials, madam, will be your bread and butter. They will pay your costs. And the big jewellery-grade stones, like this one, will be the jam on top of it all. Strawberry jam, madam, of the very best quality – Crosse and Blackwell, if you like!' It was as close as she ever heard him come to a witticism, and even then his expression was morose.

The last section of his report was twenty-one pages of recommendations for the exploitation of the property.

'You are extremely fortunate, madam, to be able to open this pipe systematically. All the other great diamond pipes, from Kimberley to Wesselton, were pegged by hundreds of individual miners, and each started working independently of his neighbour's efforts. The result was utter chaos.' He shook his head and tugged at his fluffy white sideburns mournfully. 'Hundreds of plots each thirty feet square all going down at different speeds, with roadway in between them, a tangle of wires and pulleys and buckets connecting each to the lip. Chaos, madam, pandemonium! Costs inflated, men killed in cave-ins, thousands of extra labourers required – madness!' He looked up at her. 'While you, madam, have here the opportunity of constructing a model working, and this report,' he laid his hand upon it, 'explains exactly how you should do it. I have even surveyed the ground and put in numbered pegs to guide you. I have calculated your volumes of earth at each stage. I have laid

618

out your first incline shaft for you, and explained how you should plan each level of excavation.'

Centaine broke in on his dissertation. 'Dr Twentyman-Jones, you keep saying "*you*". You don't expect me personally to perform all these complicated tasks, do you?'

'Good Lord, no! You will have to have an engineer, a good man, with experience of earth-moving. Ultimately I envisage that you will be employing several engineers and many hundreds, possibly thousands, of men at the—' he hesitated ' – do you have a name for the property? The Courtney Mine, perhaps?'

She shook her head. 'The H'ani Mine,' she told him.

'Unusual. What does it mean?'

'It is the name of the San woman who guided me here.'

'Very appropriate, then. Now, as I was saying, you will require a good engineer to put in hand the initial developments that I have outlined.'

'Do you have a man in mind, sir?'

'Difficult,' he mused. 'Most of the best men are employed permanently by De Beers, and of the others the one that comes to mind first was recently crippled in a blasting accident.' He thought for a moment. 'Now then, I have heard good reports of a young Afrikaner chappie. Never worked with him myself – damn me, what was his name again. Oh, yes, that's it. De La Rey!'

'No!' Centaine exclaimed violently.

'I'm sorry, madam. Do you know him?'

'Yes. I don't want him.'

'As you wish – I'll try and think of someone else.'

In her cot that night Centaine tossed from side to side, trying to get comfortable, trying to adjust the suffocating weight of the child so that she could sleep, and she thought of Twentyman-Jones's suggestion and sat up slowly.

'Why not?' she said aloud in the darkness. 'He must return here, anyway. A stranger coming here at this time might see more than I would wish him to.' And she cupped both hands under her belly. 'It need only be for the initial development stages. I'll write Abraham Abrahams right now and tell him to send Lothar!'

And she lit the lantern and waddled across the tent to her camp table.

I n the morning Twentyman-Jones was ready to leave. All his gear was packed into the back of the lorry and his black labourers were sitting on top of it.

Centaine handed him back the report.

'Would you be so good as to give your report to my lawyer in Windhoek, sir, together with this letter?'

'Of course, madam.'

'He will want to go over the report with you, and then, as I have instructed Mr Abrahams to solicit a loan from my bank, the bank-manager will probably want to speak to you as well, to have your views on the value of the property.'

'I expected that,' he nodded. 'You can rest assured that I will inform him of the enormous value of your discovery.'

'Thank you. In this letter I have instructed Mr Abrahams to pay you from the loan an amount equal again to your original fee.'

'That is unnecessary, madam, but very generous.'

'You see, Dr Twentyman-Jones, at some future date I might wish to retain your services as a permanent consultant to the H'ani Mine – I wish you to have a good opinion of me.'

'It does not require a fee for that, Mrs Courtney, I find you an extraordinarily plucky, intelligent and comely young lady. I would consider it an honour to work with you again.'

'Then I will ask one final service of you.'

'Anything, madam.'

'Please do not repeat anything of my personal circumstances that you may have observed here.'

His eyes dropped for just a fleeting instant to the front of her dress.

'Discretion, madam, is not the least prerequisite of my profession. Besides which I would never do anything to injure a friend.'

'A good friend, Dr Twentyman-Jones,' she assured him, as she held out her right hand.

'A very good friend, Mrs Courtney,' he agreed, as he took her hand, and for one incredible moment she thought he was going to smile. But he controlled himself and turned from her to the waiting lorry.

Once again the journey and the return from Lion Tree Camp to Windhoek took her truck-driver eight days, and Centaine wondered more than once during that time if she had not left it too late. The child in her was big and urgent. Impatiently it demanded release, so that when she at last heard the distant beat of the motors of the returning vehicles, her relief was intense.

From the canvas flap she watched the arrival. In the lead truck rode Lothar De La Rey, and though she tried to ignore it, she felt her pulse quicken when she watched him climb down from the cab, tall and elegant and graceful, despite the dust and heat of the long journey.

The next traveller whom Lothar handed down from the truck took Centaine by surprise. A nun in habit and hood of the Benedictine order.

'I told him a nurse, I didn't expect a sister,' she muttered angrily. In the back of the truck were two young Nama girls. Golden-brown skins and pretty little cheerful pug faces, each of them with an infant on her hip, their breasts heavy with milk beneath the cotton print trade dresses they wore, so much alike that they must be sisters.

'The wet nurses,' she realized, and now that they were here, these brown strangers of another race that would give suck to her child, Centaine felt the first truly bitter pang of regret at what she must do.

Lothar came to her tent, his bearing still aloof and reserved, and handed her a packet of letters before introducing the nun to her.

'This is Sister Ameliana of the hospital of St Anne,' he told her. 'She is of my mother's family, a cousin. She is a trained midwife, but she speaks only German. We can rely upon her completely.'

A gaunt, white-faced woman, Sister Ameliana had the smell of dried rose petals about her, and her eyes were frosty and disapproving as she looked at Centaine and said something to Lothar.

'She wishes to examine you,' Lothar translated. 'I will return later to discuss the work you have for my company.'

'She does not like me.' Centaine returned Sister Ameliana's flat hostile stare, and Lothar hesitated before he explained.

'She does not approve of our bargain. Her whole life is devoted to the birth and care of babies. She does not understand how you can give up your own infant – as is apparent, neither do I.'

'Tell her that I do not like her either, but she is to perform the task she came for and not place herself in judgement over me.'

'Centaine—' he protested.

'Tell her,' Centaine insisted, and they spoke rapidly in German before he turned back to Centaine.

'She says that you understand each other. That is good. She has come only for the child. As to judgement, she leaves that to our Heavenly Father.'

'Tell her to get on with the examination then.'

622

After Sister Ameliana had finished and left, Centaine read her letters. There was one from Garry Courtney, full of all of Theuniskraal's news, and at the end he had affixed Shasa's inky thumbprint below his own signature with the notation: 'Michel Courtney, his mark.'

Anna's voluminous wad of notepaper, covered with her large ill-formed scrawl, though difficult to decipher, left Centaine with a warm after-glow of pleasure.

Then she broke the seal of Abraham Abraham's letter, the last in the package.

My dear Mrs Courtney,

Your letter and Dr Twentyman-Jones's intelligence have thrown me into a fever of incredulous amazement. I cannot find the words to express my admiration for your achievement nor the pleasure I feel for your great good fortune. However, I will not weary you with my felicitations and will come directly to business.

Dr Twentyman-Jones and I have conducted extensive negotiations with the directors and managers of the Standard Bank, who have studied and evaluated the samples and report. The bank has agreed to make available to you a loan at 5½ per cent interest per annum in the sum of £100,000. You may draw upon this as you require it, and it is further agreed that this is merely a preliminary figure, and that additional amounts will be forthcoming to you in future. The loan is secured by the claim deeds of the H'ani Mine.

Dr Twentyman-Jones has also met with Mr Lothar De La Rey, and set out for him in detail the requirements of 'phase one' of the development of the property.

Mr De La Rey has tendered a contract price of £5,000 for the commission of this work. By virtue of your authority, I have accepted this tender and delivered to him the initial payment of £1,000, for which I hold his receipt—'

623

Centaine skimmed through the rest of the letter, smiling at Abrahams' comment:

> 'I have sent you the stores you required. However, I am much intrigued by the two dozen mosquito nets you have asked for. Perhaps one day you will explain what you intend to do with these, and thereby allay my burning curiosity.'

Then she set the letter aside for later rereading and sent for Lothar.

He came immediately. 'Sister Ameliana assures me that all is well, that the pregnancy proceeds naturally without any complication, and that it is very nearly over.'

Centaine nodded and indicated the camp chair facing her.

'I have not yet congratulated you on your discovery,' he said as he sat down. 'Doctor Twentyman-Jones puts a conservative value on your mining property of £3,000,000 sterling. It almost surpasses belief, Centaine.'

She inclined her head slightly and told him in a straight and level voice, 'As you are working for me and because of the circumstances of our personal relationship, I believe the correct address in future will be Mrs Courtney. The use of my given name suggests a familiarity that no longer exists between us.'

His smile shrivelled and died. He remained silent.

'You wish me to begin at once, not after the birth?'

'At once, sir,' she said sharply, 'and I will personally oversee the clearing of the tunnel that leads into the valley, which is the first step. We will begin tomorrow night.'

By dusk they were ready. The pathway leading up the valley to the entrance of the cavern of the bees had been cleared and widened, and Lothar's labour gangs had carried up the cords of mopani wood and stacked them at hand.

It was as though the bees of the great hive were aware of the threat, for as the sun set, its rays were shot through with the darting golden motes of the swift little insects, and the heated air trapped between the cliffs vibrated with the hum of their wings as they swirled about the heads of the sweating labourers. If it had not been for the protective mosquito nets, it was certain that all of them would have been stung repeatedly.

As the darkness fell, however, the flights of disturbed insects vanished back into the depths of the cavern. Centaine allowed an hour to pass, for the hive to quieten and settle for the night, then she told Lothar quietly, 'You can light the smoke-pots.'

Four men, Lothar's most reliable, bent over their pots. These were five-pound bully-beef cans, the sides perforated, the insides packed with charcoal and the herbs which Centaine had pointed out to them for gathering. The secret of the herbs was a legacy to her from O'wa, and she thought of the old Bushman now as they lit the smoke-pots and the acrid odour of burning herbs prickled her nostrils. Lothar's men were swinging the smoke-pots on short lengths of wire, to fan the charcoal. They reminded Centaine of the incense-bearers in the Easter procession to the cathedral of Arras on Good Friday.

When all four smoke-pots were burning evenly, Lothar gave a quiet order to his men and they moved towards the entrance of the cavern. In the lantern light, they looked like wraiths. Their lower bodies were protected by heavy calf boots and leather breeches, while over their heads and torsos were draped the ghostly white mosquito nets. One by one they stooped into the entrance of the cavern, thick blue smoke boiling up from the swinging smoke-pots.

Centaine let another hour pass before she and Lothar followed them into the cavern.

The acrid smoke had fogged the interior so that she could only see a few paces ahead, and the eddying blue clouds made her giddy and nauseated. However, the dynamo hum of the great hive had been lulled by the smoke. The multitudes of glittering insects hung in drugged clusters from the ceiling and the honeycombs. There was only a sleepy whisper of sound.

Centaine hurried out of the cavern and lifted the net from her sweating face, drinking down draughts of the cool sweet night air to still her nausea, and when she could speak again, she told Lothar, 'They can begin stacking the cordwood now, but warn them not to disturb the combs. They hang low from the roof.'

She did not enter the dark cavern again, but sat aside while Lothar's men carried in the cords of mopani.

It was after midnight when he came out to report to her.

'It is ready.'

'I want you to take your men and go down to the bottom of the valley. Stay there for two hours, and then return.'

'I don't understand.'

'I want to be alone here for a while.'

She sat alone and listened to their voices recede down into the dark gut of the valley. When it was silent, she looked up and there was O'wa's star above the valley.

'Spirit of great Lion Star,' she whispered, 'will you forgive this thing?'

She stood up, and moved heavily to the cliff face.

Standing below it she raised the lantern high over her head and stared up at the gallery of Bushman painting that glowed in the yellow light. The shadows wavered so that the giant paintings of Eland and Mantis seemed to pulse with life.

'Spirit of Eland and of Mantis, forgive me. All you guardians of the "Place where nothing must die" forgive me for this slaughter. I do it not for myself but to provide good water for the child who was born in your secret place.'

She went back to the entrance of the cavern, moving heavily with child and remorse and guilt.

'Spirits of O'wa and of H'ani, are you watching? Will you withdraw your protection once this is done? Will you still love and protect us, Nam Child and Shasa, after this terrible betrayal?'

She sank down on her knees and prayed in silence to all the spirits of all the San gods and she did not realize that two hours had passed until she heard the voices of the men coming back up the valley.

Lothar De La Rey held a can of gasoline in each hand as he stood before her at the entrance to the cavern.

'Do it!' she said, and he went into the cavern of the bees.

She heard the clank of a knife-blade piercing the thin metal of the cans, and then the gurgle of running liquid. The pungent stench of raw gasoline flooded from the dark narrow entrance in the rock, and in her ears was the sound of a million bees roused from their smoke-drugged stupor by the reek.

Lothar came out of the cavern, running backwards, spilling the last of the gasoline on the rocky floor, leaving a wet trail behind him, then dropped the empty can and ran back past her.

'Quickly!' he panted. 'Before the bees come out!'

Already bees were darting about in the lantern light, settling on the netting that screened her face, and more and still more boiled from the apertures in the cliff face above her.

627

Centaine backed away, and then swung the lantern over her head and hurled it into the entrance of the cavern. The lantern bounced off the rock, the glass shattered and it rolled over the uneven floor. The little yellow flame flickered and was almost snuffed from the wick and then suddenly the spilled gasoline caught. In a whooshing implosion that seemed to rock the earth beneath Centaine's feet and which hurled her backwards, a great breath of flame shot down the mountain's throat and its gaping mouth filled with fire. The cavern was shaped like a blast furnace, a gale of wind was sucked into it and red flames shot from the openings high up in the cliff face, burning like fifty torches, illuminating the valley with noon light. The rushing wind swiftly drowned out the agonized din of a million burning bees, and within seconds there remained only the steady roar of the flames.

As the stacked mopani timbers caught and burned, she could feel the heat leap out at her like a savage thing, and Centaine backed away from it and gazed with a horrid fascination at the destruction. From the fiery cavern she heard a new sound that puzzled her, the sound of soft heavy weights thudding to the stone floor, almost as though many living bodies were dropping from the roof of the cavern. She did not understand what it was until she saw a snake of dark liquid, slow and viscous as oil, creep out of the cavern's entrance.

'Honey!' she whispered. 'The honeycombs are melting!'

Those huge combs, the product of a century of labour by a myriad bees, were softening in the heat and falling, a hundredweight at a time, from the high roof into the flames below. The trickle of molten honey and wax turned into a running rivulet, then into a flood of boiling steaming liquid that seethed in the ruddy furnace glow. The hot sweet stench of boiling honey seemed to thicken the air, and the flood of molten gold drove Centaine back before it.

'Oh God,' she whispered, 'oh God, forgive me for what I have done.'

Centaine stood by as the flames burned through the rest of that night, and in the dawn light the cliffs were blackened with soot, the cavern was a ruined black maw and the floor of the valley was coated thickly with a caramelized layer of black sticky sugar.

When Centaine staggered wearily into the stockade of Lion Tree Camp, Sister Ameliana was waiting to help her to her cot, and to bathe the sugar-reeking soot from her face and body.

An hour after noon, Centaine went into labour.

It was more like mortal combat than giving birth. Centaine and the child fought each other through the rest of that burning afternoon and on into the night.

'I will not cry out,' Centaine muttered through clenched teeth, 'you will not make me cry, damn you.'

And the pain came in waves that made her think of the high surf of the Atlantic breaking on the barren beaches of the Skeleton Coast. She rode them, from their crests into the depths of each sickening trough.

Each time, at the pinnacle of pain, she tried to struggle up into the squatting birthing stance that H'ani had taught her, but Sister Ameliana pushed her down on to her back, and the child was locked within her.

'I hate you,' she snarled at the nun, and the sweat burned her eyes and blinded her. 'I hate you – and I hate this thing inside me.' And the child felt her hatred and ripped at her, twisting its limbs to block her.

'Out!' she hissed. 'Get out of me!' and she longed to feel H'ani's thin strong arms around her, sharing the strain as she bore down.

Once Lothar asked at the tent, 'How does it go, Sister?'

The nun replied, 'It's a terrible thing – she fights like a warrior, not a mother.'

Two hours before dawn in one last spasm that seemed to cleave through her spine and separate the joints of her thighs from her pelvis, Centaine forced out the child's head, big and round as a cannon-ball, and a minute later the birth cry rang out into the night.

'You cried,' she whispered triumphantly, 'not me!'

As she subsided on to the cot the strength and resolve and hatred flowed out of her, so she was left an empty, aching husk.

When Centaine awoke, Lothar was standing at the foot of her cot. The dawn was lighting the canvas of the tent behind him, so he was in dark silhouette only.

'It's a boy,' he told her. 'You have a son.'

'No,' she croaked. 'Not mine. He's yours.'

A son, she thought, a boy – part of me, part of my body, blood of my blood.

'His hair will be gold,' Lothar said.

'I didn't want to know – that was our bargain.'

So his hair will burn in the sunlight, she thought, and will he be as beautiful as his father?

'His name is Manfred, after my firstborn.'

'Call him what you will,' she whispered, 'and take him far away from me.'

Manfred, my son, and she felt her heart breaking, tearing like silk in her chest.

'He is at the nurse's breast now – she can bring him to you if you wish to see him.'

'Never. I never want to see him. That was our bargain.

Take him away.' And her swollen untapped breasts ached to give suck to her golden-headed son.

'Very well.' He waited for a minute for her to speak again, but she turned her face away from him. 'Sister Ameliana will take him with her. They are ready to leave for Windhoek immediately.'

'Tell her to go, and let her take your bastard with her.'

The light was behind him, so she could not see his face. He turned and left the tent and minutes later she heard the motor of the truck, as it started and then dwindled away across the plain.

She lay in the quiet tent watching the sunrise through the green canvas of the wall. She breathed the flinty desert air that she loved, but it was tainted by the sweet odour of blood, the birth blood of her son, or was it the blood of a little old San woman clotting and congealing in the hot Kalahari sun? The image of H'ani's blood on the rocks changed in her mind's eye, and became dark seething puddles of boiling honey running like water from the sacred places of the San, and the choking sugary smoke blotted out the smell of blood.

Through the smoke she thought she saw H'ani's little heart-shaped face peering sadly out at her.

'Shasa, my baby, may you always find good water.' But his image smudged also and his dark hair turned to gold. 'You, too, my little one, I wish you good water also.'

But it was Lothar's face now, or was it Michael's face – she was no longer certain.

'I'm so alone!' she cried into the silent spaces of her soul. 'And I don't want to be alone.'

Then she remembered the words: 'At this moment, Mrs Courtney, you are probably one of the wealthiest women in the world.'

She thought, 'I would give it all, every single diamond in the H'ani Mine, for the right to love a man, and have him love me – for the chance to have both my babies, both my sons, for ever at my side.'

She crushed down the thought angrily. 'Those are the woolly sentimental notions of a weak and cowardly woman. You are sick and weary. You will sleep now,' she told herself harshly. 'And tomorrow—' she closed her eyes ' – you will be brave again, tomorrow.'